TALE OF THE SOULOUS
ROAD TO THE EVERGREEN
By Alastair R. Johns

Author's Notes~

Firstly, thank you for the support in my story 'Tale of the Soulous'. I had conceived this story many years ago back when I was in high school. For years I thought about the tale, fantasised about the characters and wondered if I would ever put this creation to paper. Years after my education came to an end, I continued to add to my idea and jot down notes but never truly found inspiration to flesh out the story. Eventually after working in retail for almost 6 years I finally decided to take a leap of faith and focus all my time and energy into writing. The finished product is the novel 'Tale of the Soulous: Road to the Evergreen' which is part one of a planned four part book series. I'm excited to continue to adventure into the world I have created and write stories for people to read and enjoy, as well as expand on the vast lore I have considered and formed for said series.

Hope you enjoy the first of the new series,

Alastair R. Johns

Part 1: Tale of the Soulous– Road to the Evergreen

Part 2: Tale of the Soulous – The Crusade of the Fallen

Part 3: Tale of the Soulous – The Third Coming

Part 4: Tale of the Soulous – Tears from the Above

Written by Alastair .R. Johns
Editing – Denise Everett
Illustration – Sharon Fielding and Ian Cocklin

Email – alastairjohns@live.co.uk
Twitter – @AR_Johns

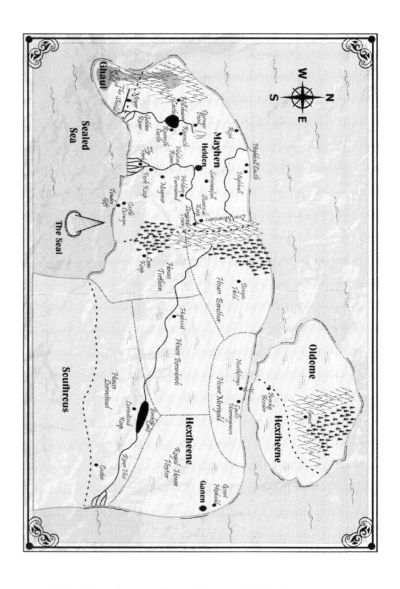

The Kingdoms of Mayhen and Hextheene

Prologue

~Rayar~

"Hurry up Rayar!" The young Ayla called out as she skipped through the bustling tournament grounds. She had always been reckless and adventurous, not like him. Rayar would have preferred to have stayed in the Heldon castle gardens and avoided the entire tournament. Rayar found it crazy that they were the same age and brought up in the same home yet they were so wildly different. Of course, he was not a true Granlia; he was taken into the royal family as a baby. He had asked many times about his true parentage, but his father Rumeo always closed such discussions, claiming he would learn when he was older. Rayar was impatient, he wanted to know now. Why should he have to wait? However, such intense thoughts could not be on the forefront of his mind at the moment, trying to keep up with his sister felt much more pressing. The young girl darted between noblemen, onlookers and guardsmen without even breaking into a sweat, whilst he struggled to keep up with her unnatural pace. They had lost their Royal Blades in the crowd; the soldiers designated to protect them from all harm, which was of course Ayla's idea.

"Slow down Ayla!" Rayar called out as he tried to catch his breath. His golden hair stuck to his forehead as the sweat trickled down his face. It was hot, horribly hot, and too hot for running in any case. How these men and women strode around in armour was beyond him, even the idea of wearing such crude attire was something he never wished upon himself. His long coat and regal clothes would suit him just fine. Ayla skidded to a halt as she reached the edge of the jousting grounds. Being young children, it was easy for them to slip through the crowd unseen. Eventually Rayar caught up with his sister and craned forward to catch his breath.

"Look Rayar, look!" She called out, her small hand thrusting forward towards the lords upon their steeds, galloping

5

on either side of a long fence. She had always enjoyed the jousting; she loved the idea of lords and ladies. Heroic noble lords and gracefully beautiful ladies, she called them. It is almost like she forgot her own station, concerning herself with simple lords and ladies. Rayar on the other hand had no interest in fancy people doing fancy things; it all seemed like too much hassle. Across the jousting field, a large stand draped in numerous banners stood above the rest of the spectators. Upon it the King sat, beside his Queen and various other Noble Lords and Ladies. The King wore that warm smile that forever graced his lips, laughing and joking with those around him. He was a good man.

"We should not be here, Ayla. What if father finds out we ran away?" Rayar pleaded to her. As he should have expected, she shrugged off his concerns and gave him a shove. The poor golden haired boy stumbled and fell against a man close by, enjoying the entertainment.

"Hey, watch it boy!" The man snapped. Rayar gulped in fear as he gazed up, up, and up finally reaching the man's face. The adult shook his head at the boy's antics and returned his attention to the jousting in front of them. As always, when he was nervous, Rayar fidgeted with the pearl upon a chain draped around his neck. A trinket of his old family, at least this is what his father had told him. He was torn from his fear by Ayla ruffling his golden hair.

"Do not be silly. We can get a better view from here. I want to see the horses!" she said reassuringly with a wide smile from ear to ear. How was she so brave? A loud clash of wood upon wood exploded from the jousting; splinters of wood flew all over the dirt ground ahead of them. Ayla squealed in delight and clapped her hands, while the crowd around them cheered for their chosen victor. Both the lords remained upon their steeds however, as they readied their next charge.

'We should not be here…' Rayar thought as he gripped his pearl as tightly as his fingers would allow. Suddenly Ayla darted forwards. Why? Where was she going? The young girl sprinted towards the barrier between both jousters. Rayar

couldn't breathe, he could only move forward. He sprinted after her as quickly as he could. The horses charged forward, they did not see the small children run into their path. Some of the crowd gasped in horror as they could foresee what would happen. Ayla remained just out of his reach. He stretched his hand out to grab her arm yet his fingers only scraped the cloth of her dress.

'Help,' in a flash they were both snatched up, quicker than he had time to register what was happening. The horse, moments from colliding with the pair of children, suddenly reared back and the lord upon it collapsed backwards and dropped to the floor in a heap. Rayar had clamped his eyes shut as he awaited the galloping steed to stampede over them, yet that moment had not come. Instead he found himself wrapped tightly in the arms of a man. Slowly, cautiously, his emerald eyes reopened to gaze upon their saviour, Hinsani, his Royal Blade. The dark haired swordsman had grabbed both him and Ayla, while crouched in front of the horse, prepared to take the full force of the charge himself.

"Master Hinsani…," Rayar whimpered out. The stone faced warrior eyed him; his cold gaze could freeze a raging fire. Rayar could feel what was coming, he would be yelled at, scolded, eaten alive by anger. Ayla was still in shock, though her hands were grasped together, gently holding something. A small baby bird chirping quietly, afraid, protected by the young girl.

"Are you two alright?" Hinsani asked. Unable to speak, Rayar nodded and it appeared Ayla was in the same boat, as she shyly nodded as well. The Royal Blade rose to his feet, with both children still under each arm, and turned to return to the stands across the jousting field. He ignored the lord who had tumbled to the ground, he ignored the crowd behind them, he ignored everything that did not involve returning them to their father. Rayar felt his heart pounding against his chest, they were in trouble. They had to be. Ayla always did this. None of this would have happened if he had just stayed in the castle gardens like he wanted to. As many times as he told

7

himself this, he knew deep down, if Ayla asked him to do something, he would do it. Hinsani set both children down upon the stands, in front of their father, King Rumeo Granlia. The young boy slowly ran his eyes up to meet his father's. The large, chunky King stood tall with his hands balled into fists pressed into his hips and his brow heavy on his aging features.

"What do you think you were doing!?" Rumeo snapped. Both the children shuddered in fear and shot their eyes back down to the floor. Behind the King, Queen Julian stood. Her face had shown more concern than anger. Rayar's hand had instinctively found itself back around the pearl, as if holding it kept him from floating off into the sky.

"I am sorry father," he mumbled. Ayla however, was not so timid in her apology. The young girl held open her hands and revealed the baby bird to her mother and father.

"But father, I needed to help the baby. It was in trouble," she stated plainly. Her kind natured logic was something to admire, at least. Rumeo sighed heavily and lowered himself down on one knee. It was impossible for this man to ever remain angry, even more so when Ayla was involved.

"I love you both dearly, you know that. Do you have any idea what could happen to you when you are so reckless? What would your mother and I do if anything happened to you?" The King asked as he placed a hand on each of their shoulders. Rayar felt his father's large hand squeeze his shoulder. "You are our children. You are a prince and a princess. You cannot go running around putting yourselves in danger? Do you understand me?" He asked, though it was more of a demand. They both nodded together. It was not only fear Rayar felt now, it was guilt too.

"It will not happen again, father," Rayar exclaimed while Ayla nodded in agreement. Knowing her, however, she would always do what she wanted. Rumeo wrapped his arms around them both and pulled them into a warm embrace.

"Good! You silly things, come, you will join us on the stands. I will ensure you get the best view. And Ayla, for your bravery in saving the poor helpless bird, you can have any new dress come tomorrow," once again their father was as joyous as he always seemed to be.

"Rumeo," Julian warned with a lopsided smile. "You are going to treat her after that?" the Queen asked. Rumeo chuckled and returned to his seat while placing both children on his knees.

"Of course. I want my children safe, but they should always help those in need," he exclaimed joyfully. The Queen shook her head and chuckled lightly under her breath. No wonder Ayla was the way she was, she got it from their father. Rayar loved his father, more than anything. He loved all his family, the Granlias. He would always be a Granlia. Rumeo ruffled his golden hair and pointed towards the jousting, which had only just reorganised itself to continue the performance.

"One day you will be riding horses and making women swoon, you know son," the King teased. Rayar shook his head quickly and gripped the pearl around his neck.

"I just want to be like you, father," the young boy replied. Rumeo smiled softly and gave him a tight hug.

"Just be you, Rayar. That is all I ask for."

* * *

'The Earth will crack and the fires of the World Beneath shall erupt upon us. There is no escaping it, no fighting it, no avoiding it. As humans we shall struggle, naturally, but it shall be in vain. All will be lost. I shall watch from the World Above and pray for those left behind to face such a tragedy. This is my nightmare that I have seen. No matter what time is granted for preparation, Hell shall swallow us all.'

-Severan Hextor, King of Hextheene; 455 AS to 488 AS

Chapter I
Hawk of Mayhen
~Rayar~

The city of Heldon, Capital of the Mayhen nation was known as a place of rich culture and richer men of political power. At the heart of the city stood a heaven piercing castle with high proud walls in gleaming white stone. It was a magnificent sight of the greatest human craftsmanship. Whether it had been constructed by man and brawn or had the assistance of magical energy was unknown, but regardless, it was a grand spectacle. Those were the thoughts of the young Prince Rayar Granlia in any case as he perched himself on the vine covered wall of the castle's royal garden. As always he was dressed in regal attire, as such things were expected of royalty in the nation of Mayhen. He stood taller than most in Mayhen, who were generally short in stature. His hair was thick and golden blonde, the colour also a rare trait in Mayhen, which he kept slicked backwards. All in all, it made him stand out among the crowd rather significantly, whether he was a prince or not. He was generally the kind of man to easily get lost in thought and even more so, after a lesson with the court librarian. He tended to find himself curious about the world outside the walls of Heldon. Would he be perceived as a prince outside the city? He had never felt in place within the castle itself, in fact inside in general, yet outside in the natural world, he felt at home. Rayar gazed off to the large woods to the north-west, with a feeling of longing. This complacency was torn apart by a sudden hard tug on the trim of his cloak. He gasped in surprise as his arms clung quickly to the wall, his heart pounding against his chest. He quickly turned his gaze around to see the culprit and without much surprise, he found it was his youngest sister, Nymin.

"Above and Below, Nymin, must you always pull such pranks on me?" He asked in a courteous yet frustrated tone. The young girl grinned from ear to ear with large dimples pressed into her cheeks. She wore the usual attire for one of royalty much like her brother. A long green dress frilled at the collar and base with long sleeves covering her hands with thin lace. Rayar noted spots of dirt across the hemline and some even over her sleeves, indicating she had been sneaking along the flower beds to find the best opportunity to launch her attack upon him. A light sigh escaped his lips as he slid down the wall and landed beside her.

"Did you forget what mother told you?" His hand ruffled the top of her head as a smile touched his lips. "If you trample the flowers one more time, you shall be in the courtyard serving the gardens until your hands are swollen. You know how she loves her flowers," Rayar teased. The young princess sniffed arrogantly and rolled her eyes. She clearly called her mother on her bluffs.

"Off in your own world again Rayar, I swear you are as bad as Hyar. The old man never does anything but day dream, even when he is supposed to be protecting me," she spoke of her Blade; all the royal children had one. He had never really gotten along too well with his own due to his sense of duty being insufferable. On the other hand the man was a swordsman without equal, or so the rumours said.

"Old? He is just over thirty. Do not let father catch you saying such things, you will upset him. He misses the days of being young and thirty," Nymin laughed at the small joke much to the enjoyment to Rayar. He did not think he was that funny but the rare attempt here and there to make jests could hurt only his pride.

"Now, should you not also be in a lesson with Master Vayers? I am fairly certain your classes are after mine." There was only a look of reluctance on the girls face. He sighed again, unable to hold his ground. "But if you would prefer, you can stay with me in the garden. I will not hide you if he comes looking though, that is your own job." Nymin quickly launched herself towards her older brother and wrapped her arms around his waist in a tight squeeze.

"Thank you Rayar!" She cheered. He knew it was a way for her to get on his good side, she would have done whatever she pleased whether he offered his support or not. The pair strode down a gravelled path between radiant plants and colourful beds. The entire garden stretched almost completely around the huge keep of Heldon like a buffer shielding the castle from the town. It was somewhat raised allowing those in the gardens to look down upon the buildings as well as the scenery surrounding the city. Perhaps one day he would visit the land between him and the edge of the world. His father always said that time would come but it was hard to teach patience to an adventurous man. The sweet smell of the freshly trimmed grass tickled his nostrils as he strolled along with his sister. Dotted about the garden were the Heldoran Guard. All fitted with silver armour and long spears that could pierce a horse without issue. The black bear of Mayhen sat on their chest plate, the banner of Mayhen. Another face further down the path stole his attention. The graceful dancing melody of words on a finely tuned voice filled his ears and caused a rather bashful smile to grow over his face. Her gentle song that filled the courtyard seemed no more than a hum, yet it still filled his heart with joy.

"Ayla," he mumbled to himself. The sharp ears of Nymin caught his shy whisper and gave him a firm flick across his ear lobe, though it was a bit of a stretch to reach that high.

"Above and Below!" he cursed as he moved to defensively cover his ear and tend to his wound. The princess gave him only a 'tut' in reply before she gleefully skipped over to her older sister. Princess Ayla, one of the most beautiful women he had ever laid his eyes upon. Her long black hair shone in the light of the sun and reached all the way down her spine to her hip. Her dress was patterned along the trim with golden threads, the primary tone a deep sea blue. He had never been too skilled with girls. Addressing them was manageable but showing any sort of charm was beyond him. When it came to Nymin, he had grown attached to her and knew her really well, which allowed him to feel comfortable in her presence. He had also been around for her birth though fortunately for him, had not witnessed it in person. Ayla on the other hand was a different breed. A fair maiden with all the qualities a man looked for. As he had got older, his dealings with the opposite sex had become more commonplace, yet whenever he spent time with her, he always seemed to regress to a pubescent teenager with an innocent crush.

"Rayar, come join us!" She called out with a wave of her hand. The youngest Granlia had already plopped herself on the ground with her dress squashed into the mud.

'Well, seems like my time alone is completely out of the window then. Though, I cannot complain.' Like a deer in the woodsman's sights, he stalked forward, eyes everywhere seeking the non-existent hunter.

"Ah, thank you. You look well, Ayla. What is it you are doing out here, you are not the type to be on your own in the garden?" She smiled affectionately and patted the seat next to her to encourage him to sit. With a small flush of red over his cheeks, he took the invitation with his hands tightly pressed together in his lap.

"Enjoying it while I can, brother, I shall be leaving soon to meet my husband to be," Rayar raised a brow in question but in fact he had known full well it would come to this.

"Only one man I can think of, Kerrin Hextor, no?" The man whose beauty outshone that of a woman, the gossips said. He always wondered how a man looking like a woman would cause women to swoon but such thoughts were not meant for the idle consideration of a man. A soppy grin sat on her gentle features at the very mention of his name. Nymin snorted at her love-struck sister who received a light kick for her mockery.

"I cannot wait to see the Kingdom of Hextheene. Father says it is twice the size of Mayhen with towns that match the grand sight of Heldon, while the cities simply blow you into awe. Father has been planning this marriage for some time. I overheard him saying that this marriage would mend the relations between our two nations but I do not care for something like that. I would become the future queen of Hextheene. How exciting is that Rayar!" Her joy was overwhelming. In fact he even felt somewhat excited by simply listening to her. He would be lying if he said he was not slightly jealous but they were brother and sister even if not by blood. Seeing her happy filled his heart with more joy than anything.

"I have known you all your life, Ayla, but in all that time a smile so broad and full never graced your lips. I am sure it shall be a lifetime of wonderment and loving moments. How long is it until you are meant to leave?" He asked furtively. The fair princess bit her lip in thought as her fingers drummed on her leg through the cloth of her skirt.

"It should be no more than a month I believe. We are awaiting a reply from Hextheene and then, well, I shall be thrown into a world I do not know. I am excited, yet nervous. Rayar, you know of what I speak. How did you handle it being thrown into the Royal House of Granlia after what happened?" This was very rare of her. In all her beauty and grace she rarely thought of more than what she shall wear and how she was presented. To bring up his past meant she was clearly preparing her mind for a shift in her lifestyle. She was right though, he could relate to these things and the fact that she mentioned his past, only showed her obliviousness to the details of it. Rayar slumped slightly on the bench and turned his gaze elsewhere; he had no memories of it, he had only been a baby.

"I still know nothing from seventeen years ago. I was only a baby when I came here. I have heard rumours though that my parents did not often come to court or have guests. I do sometimes wonder about my parents, who they were and how they were... you know." His brow dipped slightly in thought and frustration. However before he could be swallowed up by the grief of loss, Nymin appeared in front of his face with an intense expression. The prince blinked a few times in horror at the shock of seeing his little sister's face so close to his.

"You are an idiot," she stated plainly.

"Excuse me?" He replied still somewhat alarmed by her peculiar behaviour.

"You are a Granlia. Rayar Granlia, Prince of Mayhen. It makes you one of the Four Children of the Royal House. It does not matter how you came to be; it only matters who you are now. I do not wish for my brother to become a soppy mess. It will be even worse after Ayla leaves!" Rayar's cheeks flushed which was swiftly followed by a merciless tickling session in retaliation. Ayla only chuckled into her hand at her sibling's antics. It was clear from her face that she would miss these moments. Suddenly from down the courtyard path, a loud booming voice filled the air.

"Lady Nymin!" The three Granlias halted like frightened mice and froze. "You cannot avoid lessons, your father commands it. Come to the library now!" The man bellowed out. Rayar looked over to see none other than master librarian, Vayers, stomping down the garden towards them. He was a leathery faced elderly man with a look of wisdom in his eyes and stress on his skin. The years of sitting down and reading had given him time to gain considerable weight. Nonetheless, he charged down the garden like a stallion in a race, prepared to stop at nothing to fulfil the King's command. Nymin on the other hand did not care for such things. She stuck out her tongue towards Vayers and like an arrow she bolted down the path towards freedom. Vayers was close behind. Rayar watched and laughed with Ayla at the midday entertainment. He too would miss times like this.

"Master Rayar, Lady Ayla!" Another sudden voice called out from behind the pair. Both looked back to see the head maid, Alessia, motioning them towards her. She was a plump woman with a motherly face and warm heart. "Dinner is being prepared for you. The King has summoned you both to join him and the Queen. Wash up dears," Alessia disappeared back into the doorway of the keep behind them.

"I suppose Nymin has her class to attend, do you think Nyer will be there?" Ayla asked the blonde prince, with a glint in her eye. Nyer was the oldest of the children and the one who would eventually succeed the throne. Laws of succession in Mayhen were considerably different from those in the surrounding nations. Rayar shrugged his shoulders.

"Who knows? She is probably attending official business. Above and Below, that woman never stops." As he began to stand to head to the keep, he felt a firm grip on his cheek, the flesh being pinched. Ayla had him gripped tightly with a teasing look on her face.

"You curse so often. A prince should be more refined. See to it you cease your foul tongue or I shall cease it for you." While it was a commanding statement, the jest was obvious in her voice. Rayar had imagined a moment like this and how he had planned a witty remark or a smooth retort, yet now he was actually in the situation his reply came only as a bundle of mumbles that were unknown to the common language. "Oh my, seems like you may need more lessons with Master Vayers on basic vocabulary. Come, we will be late if we dawdle." His cheek was released from her slender grip and like a subtle leaf on a light breeze she glided from the bench towards the castle's door. It took a few moments for the prince to regain his composure, before he rose to follow suit. A flicker of movement in the corner of his eye halted him in his tracks. He looked over to see what had drawn his attention, to find a hawk on the far garden wall. The bird flapped its wings a few times then locked its gaze firmly onto him.

"Ayla look at this…," He muttered but to no avail; she had already departed. In the brief moment he flicked his eyes from the hawk to the door and back again, the bird had already taken off and was flying off into the sky. He watched it silently from the ground, never moving from his spot. It was odd to find such a bird in these parts; he had been taught that hawks were birds of the southern land of Southrous. Finding a hawk in Mayhen

17

was as far as he knew, completely unheard of. Rayar put the thought aside leaving it only as something to reveal to Vayers at a later date and retired inside the castle. The smell of Alessia's glorious cooking already leading his nose.

*

~Rumeo~

"Being nosey again, dear?" A soft voice sounded from behind a large, plump man. Rumeo Granlia, King of Mayhen, leant on the banister of the balcony outside his own and his ladies chambers. His curly grey hair hung loosely over his crown that wrapped around his forehead and his clothes were as regal as ever. He wore a long heavy cloak that graced the ground with each step he took and a thick, warm tunic underneath. He was widely known as a friendly and jolly man but at the moment there was a look of concern upon his face. His wife, Julian Granlia, joined him on the balcony and placed her head on his arm. At the feel of her cheek, he redirected his attention to her with his usual loving smile. He still could not believe his luck in acquiring such a woman as his queen. The marriage may have been arranged, as most royal marriages were in Mayhen, but to find the woman he believed to be the love of his life at such odds, was something for which he was forever thankful. Whilst he was an older gentleman, cursed with wrinkles on his face and greying hair, her vibrant and smoother skin betrayed her much younger age than his own. This too was a royal custom.

"You know me Julian; I like to keep an eye on my children. Ayla looks more and more like you every day that passes. She is truly a beautiful daughter to be blessed with." The queen of Mayhen chuckled into her hand and gave her husband a pat on the cheek.

"You think so? How flattering. Nymin is taking after you, I think," Rumeo gave his head a brisk shake.

18

"I hope not. If she gets my belly and beard she will never forgive me," another lullaby of laughter escaped his wife. Julian turned Rumeo to face her with a small and warm smile on her lips.

"That is not what I mean. She has your passion in her eyes and your gentleness on her face. All our children have your resolve and morals dear. You have raised them all well. Even Rayar," at the mention of the boy's name, Rumeo cast his eyes elsewhere and moved back from his complimenting wife. She did not appear surprised at his reaction and only saw to comfort him further.

"He is your son. He is a Granlia, like Nyer and Ayla and Nymin, like your brother and his family. You love him, do you not?" Rumeo, like a stubborn child, nodded sombrely.

"Of course I do. I know he is my son. That is the problem. He is a prince and will one day play a major part in the running of this kingdom. You would not guess who has their eye on him as well." The queen raised a brow before grinning as if she knew everything.

"Melayne Hextor?" Rumeo gave her a flat look before he continued.

"Melayne Hextor. The preparations to wed Ayla and that fancy boy Kerrin are already underway and now the Hextor family are pushing for a second marriage?" Julian nodded as she listened to her husband's woes and did her best to calm his frustration with a gentle smoothing of his curly locks.

"Is this truly about the Hextor family or about Rayar becoming his own man?" The all wise and powerful King of Mayhen pouted like a teenager before he turned back towards the banister for its support.

"Can I stop him from becoming his own man, to follow his own path? No. Can I assist him on finding the right one? I bloody hope so," Rayar was his son regardless of blood. Such ties were by family and trust, not just blood. The risk of letting him spread forth into the world too quickly constantly weighed heavily on his mind. He had hoped to keep Rayar in the city and castle forever, well out of harms way, much like his other children, but part of being a good parent was being able to let go.

"Come dear," Julian said from inside the chambers, tearing the King from his train of thought. "The dinner will be ready in a minute or two, we should head downstairs." He nodded in agreement and turned from the balcony.

*

~*The Figure*~

On the outskirts of the city, the elegant hawk swooped through the sky. It soared over the lush landscape of the Mayhen farms and finally reached the northern forest of Summerfall. The creature majestically shot through and passed trees and branches in its path, until it reached a hooded figure sitting on a large thick branch deep within the forest and landed on their outstretched arm. The hooded figure and the bird of prey looked at each other in what seemed to be silence for a good few moments, until the figure finally spoke.

"We can't be certain but it's enough to keep watching. Return to the castle for the moment," the hawk squawked out loudly before it released its grip from the figure's arm and zoomed off into the sky as quickly as it had arrived. The person covered by the shadow of the trees as well as the darkness of their hood, placed a hand on the pommel of a sword hidden under their cloak.

"Not long now," a sudden burst of wind brushed through the thicket of trees and in an instant, the figure disappeared.

* * *

Chapter II
The Royal Children
~Rayar~

The grand hall of the castle stretched for what seemed like forever. It was one of the only rooms in the keep that Rayar felt comfortable in. Windows were placed along the length of one wall allowing the light of the sun to fill the dark hall and nature to creep inside. The room itself had a roof that reached the heavens giving the illusion of a ceiling not being present at all and was full of decorations. Thick red curtains hung beside each window, a carpet that reached from one end of the giant table to the other. Candles flickered beside the wall opposite the windows, though their assistance to the granting of light was rather insignificant. At the head of the long table, which had been placed in the centre of the grand hall, was the household throne for the nation's King. It too was embellished with magnificent markings along the arm rests and the high back of the chair. Behind the throne, nailed to the stone wall, was the flag of Mayhen, a black bear on a field of silver. The young prince had never been too fond of his country's banner. It seemed too rough and ferocious for the sophisticated people of Mayhen. He would have chosen something much more elegant but then again as his father had told him; the country was founded in war and the old king was compared to the ruthless snow bear of the northern lands.

"You are playing with your food Rayar," Rayar was snapped from his day dream by the voice of his mother. He lowered his eyes from the banner that hung above his father's head and down to the glorious meal that had been produced for the royal family. Servants dotted the wall behind the royal family whilst a pair of musicians filled the hall with background music, which was supposed to be calming and soothing. At the head of the table the plump King Rumeo wasted no time in happily munching down his meal, enjoying it more than anyone. Next to him Julian chewed on her own with much more serenity than her enthusiastic husband. Opposite her, Rayar and Ayla sat next to each other, both quietly eating so as not to disturb Nyer; it was rare to witness her at the dinner table. As usual she was engrossed in her own affair as Head Lady of the court even while eating. Rumeo was a good King and a good man but the duty of handling the finer details had been given to his oldest daughter. The façade was that it helped prepare her for a future of ruling the country but in secret the old King simply preferred the time off. As cheeky as it was Nyer did not complain, she saw the opportunity as the former. The oldest sibling of the Granlia children was not as decorated as the other three, in fact she portrayed herself as the plainest and the most no nonsense. Physical appearance was not high on her list of importance compared to running a country.

"Put the work down Nyer and enjoy the meal!" Rumeo called out from across the table, waving a drumstick in the air to emphasize his point. The eldest princess passed her father a stern look that caused him to slump in this throne. The fair haired prince felt like taking a stab at a conversation as well.

"The food is quite pleasant. It is a shame Nymin has to attend her class or we would be together as a family. It has not happened for a while if I recall," the King laughed cheerfully and patted the table.

"We think alike," Rumeo agreed. Just then Nymin came bursting through the doors of the grand hall with an irritated looking Vayers at her heel. Still in her mud speckled dress, she slid into a chair next to Nyer and peered over her shoulder at her work.

22

"Boring as usual, hmm?" She teased. Her older sister sighed and pushed the young teenager away. The youngest princess was about to erupt into a fit of anger but before she could, Julian clonked the table with her fork.

"Settle down children," the duo muttered under their breaths before replying in concession.

"Yes, Mother." Rayar did his best not to get involved and quietly focused on his meal as did Ayla. The silence was quickly broken.

"So father you brought us all together," Nyer said, half looking towards him and half managing various scrolls on the table. "Is there something you wish to share with us all? If so I am all ears. The sooner we are done here the sooner I can take my leave." The Granlia family all shuffled uncomfortably at her sheer rudeness towards the King. Father or not, he was the king of the nation. Rayar knew he would never act so boorish towards that man; he owed him way too much.

"Do not forget I am not only your father but King. The duties I have granted you can be taken if you believe yourself above me already, my sweet daughter. Lineage is one thing but leadership is another. You do not wish to be nicknamed the Grumpy Old Queen do you?" Even though he spoke with command and was steadfast in his choice of words, he still allowed an inkling of fatherly love to come through in his reprimanding. Rayar looked between his father and his sister as if he was caught between a raging wave in the sea and a falling landslide. Facing either side would not end pleasantly. Eventually Nyer bowed her head apologetically and gave into her father's dominance. He had noticed she sometimes got ahead of herself but at the end of the day, she loved and respected the King.

"Of course father, I forgot my place," she finally abandoned her documents and focused all her attention upon her parents.

"You are not wrong though. I made sure you were all here for there is something I must address to you all. As I hope you are aware, the friction between Hextheene and Southrous has put a strain on all the nation's relations yet our sweet Ayla will soon mend the bond with a marriage to their eldest, Kerrin Hextor. Naturally this is not a political move; I would not even consider such a play unless my daughter was not head over heels for the … boy," he offered his middle daughter a side long glance, only to see her face brighten up at the mere mention of his name. Rayar was also in his sights. The two made eye contact and spoke without words. He thought his father was thinking something along the lines of 'Women'. That is what he was thinking anyway. "This will place a strong union between our countries and may cause us to be dragged into this skirmish they call a war. As my children and the next generation of this kingdom, I wish to hear your views on this. I have heard the words of my advisors and from my commanders but the world from the eye of the new worlds' leaders is something one should always take into account," the Granlia children looked between each other. Rayar ran his eyes over Nymin first and as expected she did not seem to take in what her father had said and instead was continuing to enjoy the meal put before her. She only looked up to throw her brother a cheery smile before returning to her food. Nyer on the other hand seemed to be seriously contemplating the situation. The weight of the country would be on her shoulders one day, whatever the outcome; her choices would have to be intensely thought out. Ayla was still day dreaming about the ever fascinating Kerrin. As a woman who would follow her heart, her view was clear.

"Father I think it is wonderful. Hextheene is the oldest country there is and their King is descended from the first Hextor, the woman who led the armies that united the world under The First Coming. I would gladly be the one to help bind our countries together." Who would expect anything else from Ayla? A woman's heart, when filled with love was unswayable. Rumeo nodded. Rayar wondered if he did so just to pretend he took her advice seriously. He knew the only ones he really to wanted hear from on a serious note were himself and Nyer. The prince fidgeted with his pearl necklace, as he normally did when nervous, and awaited the wisdom of his older sister to prevail.

"I do not like it."

'I cannot help but think it is a way to disagree with father rather than an actual honest opinion,' he thought as he watched Nyer voicing her views.

"Ever since the old war between Mayhen and Hextheene, our countries have always been on shaky terms, but intertwining our family is not means to mend that. Not to mention the consequences of being pulled into their fray with Southrous," Nyer stated, as stubborn as always. Rumeo simply nodded once more until he finally settled his eyes onto his son.

"What about you Rayar, what do you think?" He returned the look with one of reluctance. While his mind believed one view his heart spoke another and the smiling princess beside him, swayed his decision too dramatically.

'If she will be happy...,'

"I think it is a good idea. Ayla would make a wonderful queen and the times of peace would be fruitful," Nyer stared daggers at him. They pierced so deeply he had to keep his eyes ahead on Ayla and Rumeo, just to avoid being pinned to the ground by the mere glare of the woman. Much to his surprise, Rumeo too had figured out the reasoning behind his choice and seemed rather disappointed.

"I see. Well soon we shall receive a response from King Braska and begin our planning. I doubt he will want to waste any time. The man I know is not one to sit and wait. I want you all there to show we are united as a family. If we are united as a family we can be united as a country, no matter your feelings on the matter. Family always stick together. That is all for now, Nymin ready yourself for bed. The rest of you have matters to attend to I assume, so complete them before you also head up for your slumber," Rumeo smiled to each of his children in a fatherly manner before departing the table and then the grand hall. Julian moved over to the youngest Granlia and began to ferry her towards her chambers.

"Come dear you heard your father, to bed with you." As all children her age she was not thrilled about the idea but gave in and stalked up towards the bedrooms. Rayar avoided Nyer as he left the hall. He could still feel her cold gaze staring into his soul.

The day had grown darker as the evening had fallen upon the city. The many servants of the castle had begun to settle in for the night as had the Granlia family. Rayar was not allowed the luxury of sleep just yet. At the request of the King he had one other responsibility to attend before he was able to retire to his chambers. He strode down the hallway from the royal quarters towards what was known in the keep as The Royal Blades Sanctuary, wearing rather thicker attire than before; a red tunic of padded leather to give him a little bit of defence against a whack to the torso. One important role of being a prince of Mayhen was being able to take up arms should the situation call for it. His uncle had followed the same road and it had led him to the famous Shield of Mayhen, the barricade on the border of Ghaul to the South.

'Uncle Vesir is said to be one of the greatest swordsmen there is, though I wonder if he could beat Hinsani. I would love to visit the Shield one day. I would at least be outside the walls of Heldon in any case.'

"Rayar," a woman's voice echoed from behind. He turned to see Ayla, leaning on the wall behind him in her night gown with an oil lamp in her hand. The dim flicker of the flame was pretty much all that kept the hallway lit aside from the sparsely appointed torches throughout the corridor. This caused all light to be on her and being in a white silk gown did nothing but elaborate her beauty. The cloth hung loosely on her shoulders and reached all the way to the floor.

'If father found her out like this, there would be the World Below to pay. Yet I had to be the unlucky one,' he forced a smile on his lips and prayed the darkness hid his flushed cheeks.

26

"What are you doing here so late?" He asked simply enough. The princess smoothly glided forwards until she reached him. He felt his heart pounding as if it were about to break free from his chest and flee. She placed herself directly in front of him, her large eyes wide and alluring, with one nimble movement she placed a kiss on the side of his cheek.

"Thank you," she whispered. It took Rayar a few moments to come to terms with what had just occurred but once he had regained his senses, he forced out a few words.

"For what…?" The princess let out a light laugh and floated past him only to circle around as she spoke.

"For your support, of course. I know father is dubious about this arrangement but mother seems to think if I really love him then I shall have nothing to worry over. I believe it Rayar. I believe it with all my heart," even now he was happy to see such joy in her face and to hear such happiness in her voice. Regardless of what Nyer thought, perhaps this really was the right course of action for Mayhen to take. One side of his lips turned into a smile as he did his best to accept the coming future. They were all growing up.

"As long as you are happy Ayla then I do not see why you should not follow what you think is right. I will always support you." The pair hugged each other which once again caused Rayar to tense up in awkwardness. Once the moment had past, she shifted the subject to his purpose in heading to the Royal Blades quarters.

"Heading to training with your Blade are you, I simply must indulge. You would not find issue with me joining you would you?" He could not help but frown. For one, he doubted it would be allowed but even worse he was afraid of making a complete fool of himself. Unfortunately his weakness was staring him directly into the eyes knowing full well he could not refuse.

"Fine, fine," he muttered while he took off his cloak and placed it over her shoulders. He would not be the gentleman he was if he let her wander about in nothing but a night gown. It was actually somewhat surprising to see her in only that attire;

27

she was usually much more refined. Over the years, they had drifted apart as their paths led to different destinations. When they were young, they had been inseparable. Now she was seeking a closer relationship while he still stumbled about his words. Together they reached the doorway that led to the Royal Blades training hall. The sound of metal clashing and vibrant exercise could be heard from outside. It seemed like they never found any time to rest. Well, one of them in particular. Slowly Rayar pushed open the broad wooden door, the feel of the wood showing its age. As the pair entered they saw a muscular individual across the room wielding a one sided sword in a stern and powerful stance. He raised his sword above his head and in one slash; he smoothly cut straight through a large wooden stand shaped like a man. As the two halves began to topple he quickly shifted his stance and slashed horizontally to cut the defenceless wooden man into four pieces. Clonks sounded throughout the room as each piece hit the ground and bounced numerous times.

'My instructor and protector, as terrifying as ever,' Rayar gave his head a small shake at the performance while Ayla seemed awe struck. Hinsani Tannaroth, a man whose swordsmanship and prowess was renown throughout Mayhen and even the far reaches of Southrous. The man was not much shorter than he but surpassed him in muscular tone and broadness. His raven black hair, like many others of Mayhen, was slicked back and smooth. It reached down his spine just above the small of his back and was braided over the ears. His face was hard like stone; in fact he rarely ever smiled. Rayar could not recall a single time the rock like man had ever cracked a grin. There was a shadow of facial hair as if he had trimmed it in the morning and it had grown again over the length of the day. He wore a dark leather sleeveless top with a single shoulder pad on his left arm and black slacks tucked into a pair of dark leather boots. Hinsani was a masculine figure to say the least. Once he realised the prince had arrived, he swiftly sheathed his blade in a smooth arc and slid it back into its scabbard at his hip.

"My Lord, My Lady," he stated proudly as he bowed respectfully to the pair.

"Before you say anything, she nagged me to come but I am fine to get on with the lesson," Rayar could read his mind. The look Hinsani gave the princess was one of caution. The Blade rose back to full height with a hand resting on the pommel of his sword and frowned with deepness only he could master.

"Forgive me my Prince Rayar, but are you sure that is wise. I recommend she returns to her chambers at once. I have not been instructed to watch after her as well," a loyal man but not much of a thinker is something Rayar always thought to himself.

"Let the princess stay. What harm can it do?" A man who had previously kept his presence hidden spoke up from the back of the training room. His sudden inception startled both the royal children but they quickly regained composure for appearances sake. The man was none other than Nymin's Royal Blade, Hyar Dedred. Like Hinsani he wore the dark clothes with a single metal shoulder pad, the difference being a long thick cloak covering most of his form. He had sat himself in a nonchalant manner with a book in his hand and feet on a desk. The most striking characteristic of this man was he shared something only Rayar had in Mayhen. Golden hair, though his was combed forward and connected to a trimmed but full beard covering most of his face and his eyes were a deep brown unlike his own. "If you are cautious for trouble even this deep into our territory, I'll watch Lady Ayla myself." Though the offer was there his eyes did not lift from the book in his hand.

"Excellent, then it is settled. I shall watch from the safety of Hyar's position." The long haired teen hastily skipped to Hyar's side and settled onto a spare seat. The sterner Royal Blade could only grumble in his defeat as he reached for two practice swords and tossed one over towards his pupil. Prince or not the training was tough and no quarter would be given. Rayar caught it rather clumsily yet due to the training he had been receiving for the past few months, he was able to regain his balance and grasp the wooden weapon, just in time to deflect a side-way swipe from Hinsani.

"Watch the movements. This Blade Dance is named The Wolf Gnarls. You strike at their lower abdomen to relieve them of their insides. Focus," the swordsman snapped as he flung himself forward and thrust the wooden sword towards the prince's side. He was able to block it barely, even though he knew it was coming, but the pressure from the sheer power caused him to stumble back. Rayar cursed under his breath as he struggled to return to balance. He was being firmer on him than usual today without a doubt. This was even more obvious when Hinsani denied him time to recover and pressed on him again with a double strike. The wooden blades clashed and intertwined which resulted in a quick disarming of the golden haired prince and to make matters worse the impact forced him to fall onto his back. Like a swooping bird, the tip of the wooden sword narrowed its aim on his throat. If it were not an exercise with blunt weapons, the blade would have pierced his flesh but luckily he was not on the true field and the weapon halted right above his jugular.

"Swooping of the Hawk, disarm and swoop in for the kill," the word hawk caused a twinge in his brow. It reminded him of the irregular bird he witnessed not hours before. Such coincidences however, meant nothing. Ayla clapped her hands together from the side lines. She had been watching intently, analysing every movement they both made and was completely mesmerized.

"Chin up Rayar. Show him what a Granlia is made of!" He was pulled to his feet by his instructor before being thrown the wooden sword.

"Again!"

* * *

Chapter III
The Shield of Mayhen
~Wedyar and Briyar~

The sun hung high over the land of Mayhen. It stretched from the capital in the centre of the nation to the far south where the wall known as the Shield of Mayhen had made its home. The warm weather was a nice change for the men of the southern wall, as they were used to the unpredictability of scorching heat or heavy rain in most the country. Perhaps they were being praised by Above for all their years of faithful service to a cause only few could still recall. The wall itself was a masterpiece of construction. Tall and broad, put together with sweat and stone and wood from the most skilled craftsman and builders from before the current inhabitants' time. The only entrance through the wall lay in a massive gate at the centre of the great length. The door was gigantic and thick; as strong as the wall itself which meant it took a considerable amount of time to even open. This of course was put in place for increased defence. The Shield of Mayhen was not allowed any sort of weakness from the terror that lay beyond. From the condition of the outer sides of the walls, it was clear that in its time it had witnessed abuse. It held cuts in the wooden structure and claw marks along the stone barriers. Though one would assume a beast had made those claw marks, the eldest of the walls defenders said that those marks were made by men. Many tales of old relished in the idea that men had gone insane on the other side of the wall and now were nothing but

31

mindless husks. All the possible causes varied from sorcery to a woman's scorn for the men's laziness, to the most favoured; the Red Mist. In the far distance, almost out of view, the edge of the mist coloured as blood could be seen covering the land. It was impossible to see through it and every century it was not uncommon for someone to claim it was advancing. No man who had ventured into its grasp had ever returned and the last time anything came out of it, was supposedly when the current King's grandfather was still in his mother's womb. The men here had a duty however that they had all sworn to uphold, 'To protect the land of Mayhen from the shadow beyond the mist' and to this day they had succeeded in their task. A small town known as Meyer, sat upon the wall's northern side which homed many of the soldier's families and houses nearby allowing them to live their lives in servitude to their King and country while also seeing those they cared for on a daily basis. Such an arrangement had been wisely constructed by the current commander of the Shield of Mayhen. The man was known as Vesir Granlia, brother to the king, one of the finest commanders in the known lands. He was a man who was considered as kind and just as his brother yet lacked the maturity the King had acquired in his position. A warrior with a strong blade and warm heart, a true vision of what the Granlia House wished to bestow upon the rest of the noble families. Two guards stood on the wall doing their best to withstand the unnatural heat that bore down from above. They wore the attire of the Mayhen military with the Shields emblem upon their chest to signify their rank and position in the army, a large golden shield with the black bear of Mayhen in the centre. They both grasped spears which were being used as standing supports; weariness could be seen in their gaze.

"How long until our shift is over?" one soldier questioned his companion. He seemed to be the youngest of the pair with a bit more weight on his person with evidence of hair only barely poking through the skin of his chin. Like most men of Mayhen he had darkened hair which had been tied into a small ball down the back of his neck. The man he addressed was much taller with a gaunt face and a stubbly beard from one ear to the other. His hair was cut short and neatly kept.

"Not long, Wedyar," the taller man replied after he blew out a puff of smoke. After a light tap upon his pipe he let out a tired sigh. "I would be glad to head back to town yet I know the wife has some more complaints. Can you believe she attempted to scold me for walking through our house with muddy boots? I'm a soldier! I swear, the woman thinks I am a bloody child. Above and Below," the rounder man could not help but chuckle at his companion's problem.

"Well at least you have a wife Briyar. I'm still sleeping in the barracks. The only affection I'm at risk of getting is if a rabid dog wanders in at night," the man named Briyar let out a snort.

"Let me know if one does so I can trade with you," Wedyar's laughter became even more boisterous while the other soldier kept a rather stern and controlled expression. The pair stood for a few moments of silence that allowed another cloud of smoke to escape the lips of the taller man.

"We're on the edge of a changing era, you know," Briyar said as he shifted most of his weight onto his spear with both hands around the shaft. He got a strange look from the shorter man that only edged him to continue his point. "Princess Ayla is soon to marry Kerrin Hextor of Hextheene which would unite both nations in an alliance. Some of the men seem to think it's a ploy from the Hextheene King, Braska Hextor, to gain support for his war with Southrous. If the two countries did unite, then the entire balance of the world as we know it will shift. Nations like Southrous or even the smaller ones even further south, will feel threatened. Perhaps then they would all unite under one banner to counter the united Mayhen and Hextheene. We could be on the doorstep of one of the largest wars since The First Coming pushed the beasts of the World Beneath back down below." There was once again a long silence after the speech as a stunned soldier tried to understand the ridiculousness of his companion.

"You over think things, you know," is all he could care to reply to the rambling. For a man who seemed to be calm and collected most of the time, he certainly had an extensive imagination. The pair had known each other for a good few years now and whenever these sorts of conversations came up, Wedyar could not help but find them surprising. His friend truly did have the mind of philosopher more so than a simple soldier like himself. Then it truly hit him what had actually been said and he blinked in surprise.

"Hang on a moment, Princess Ayla is marryin' Prince Kerrin of Hextheene?" This was news to him. The slender guard rubbed his gloved hand over his chin and muttered in annoyance at how he spilled the beans so easily. It was something even he was not supposed to be aware of.

"I heard the Captain Commander discussing it with his wife a few days ago when I was patrolling at night," Wedyar shook his head. These sorts of antics always got his friend into trouble. Once again he had been listening in where simple men like themselves should steer clear. There was no helping it now.

"You should be cautious. If the Captain Commander caught you eaves droppin', he'd hang you from the wall by your loin cloth for a day and have the children throw eggs at ya. He has a knack for pranks and punishments coincidin'," Briyar finally cracked a slim smirk as he simply replied.

"Well, that wasn't the only sound that escapes their room during the night. For a man who has seen forty-seven or so years he certainly hasn't lost his touch. Well, his wife certainly thinks so anyway," The pair laughed raucously, while even bending over from the strain in their stomachs. Just then the sound of wood being clashed together began to echo over the wall along with the voices of men perhaps in battle. Being assigned to the wall for so long and seeing no sign of danger for the many years of the service, the pair were well accustomed to what the noise arose from. Briyar rubbed his nose with his sleeve before he let out a drained sigh.

"They're at it again, eh?"

~Vesir~

The skill of his opponent had truly grown over the many years of sparring. The Commander Vesir Granlia smoothly glided in every motion across the length of the wall as the wooden blade in his grasp flowed gracefully in continuation with another. The soldier wore a black tunic with silver trimming and a royal black cloak pinned around his neck with the Shield of Mayhen's emblem. His skin showed obvious signs of wrinkles between the brow and laugh lines across his face, whilst his hair had been plaited into a long single tail tied into balls all the way to his lower back. It coloured a dark brown with streaks of grey blending into it which connected into his tamed beard that covered the lower half of his face. The young man being trained was his second eldest son Jonnas, a strong built man who stood taller and broader than his father, with short raven black hair and unattended stubble. Jonnas was becoming known throughout Mayhen as a man to be wary of, who was not a member of the Royal Blades of Heldon. With such a reputation he had yet to ever best his father who in his prime was perhaps the greatest warrior in the west. Those days were long behind him. Now he enjoyed the somewhat calmer duty of the commanding of the Shield. Not that it was supposed to be considered a relaxing position yet due to the lack of activity on the other side of the wall, it generally was a peaceful charge for him to undergo. Naturally he did his best to keep the soldiers well prepared for any situation that may have befallen them, but also made sure to keep them in good standing.

"Is this all you can do, son?" Vesir teased as he deflected every strike from his son and remained on the defensive. Both were sweating from the exercise, however on the lips of the father sat a smile and on the son an expression that appeared to be much more focused and strained. "I thought I was sparring with my grandmother then, she could certainly strike with a cane harder than you with a blade. Perhaps you need to lie down, get a massage, a tea if you need the energy to keep going?" The taunting caused Jonnas to snort in annoyance and increase the ferocity of his attack. The pair fluidly crossed practice swords along the path of the wall, weaving in and out of guards who shifted to avoid being knocked over by the Granlia swordsmen. Their spar continued for some time to the point where the guardsmen around them began to cheer for their Commander or for his defeat at the hands of the second son. Suddenly they were halted in their antics as a loud voice bellowed across the wall. The pair turned to see where the noise originated. There stood another Granlia, this time the same height as Vesir with short but well kept black hair and a long dark green coat covering his form. He was narrow faced and his nose resembled a hook. He looked nothing like his father. The man who had shouted across the wall was Vesir's oldest son Zanmir. Unlike his father, he did not hold any of his fighting prowess or desire to do so, though his intelligence and tactical mind was something Vesir always found fascinating. He always wondered why his eldest son remained at the wall with such a gift which could be of much more use in the capital yet whenever the subject was breached, the answer had always remained the same.

'I have no interest in waging wars with petty people,' Zanmir always had a way with words that Vesir could not truly grasp. He pushed these thoughts aside as he strode to meet his son with Jonnas in toe.

"Rare to see you upon the stands Zanmir and yelling as well, did you knock your head too hard on a book or something?" Jonnas chuckled at his poke towards his brother which only produced a roll of his brother's eyes.

"Amusing. Even with a knock to the head I would still be able to out-wit an oaf like you, little brother," the broad Granlia snorted in annoyance but before the squabble could continue, Vesir ruffled the younger brother's hair and focused his attention on the slender son in front of him.

"As 'witty' as he was, he has a point; what is going on son?" Zanmir turned his attention to him, his expression as cold as ever. His two sons were like fire and water. He had teased his wife from time to time that he would not be surprised to find a hook nosed stable boy some day and realise who Zanmir's true father was. While she found this amusing, she also usually gave him a smack across the back of the head for those types of comments.

"Father, nothing of great note, I simply came to remind you of a simple matter that you had requested a few weeks prior, mother's birthday tomorrow. I have made the arrangements on the wall for that... hm, romantic meal you had planned on the tower, of course. Though with your memory I felt the need to ensure you will be present unlike last year when you instead took yourself to The Sullen Crone and ended up being carried home by your son here. I hope we will not have a repeat of last year," Vesir blinked and scratched his nose in an awkward manner. His eldest certainly had a way of prolonging that particular flaw. Perhaps he had stretched it out so long because he enjoyed any moment he could, to chastise his rather laid back father. He knew he was very lenient with his children and their behaviours and this was not about to change now. The Commander flicked his eyes to Jonnas who only replied with a shrug which implied he had also forgotten what tomorrow was.

"Ah of course! You think I would forget my own Flowers birthday... again! Hahaha trust me Zanny, I will definitely be there," Zanmir cocked a brow in response.

"Zanny?" Vesir quickly continued.

"And of course, you prove to be on top of your game as always son, I know I can always rely on you for these important occasions. What would I do without you?" He joked with a joyous grin upon his face. Vesir imagined Jonnas being unable to hold back a smirk as he watched this exchange. He may not have been able to see it, but he could sense it.

"Naturally you would be looking for a new wife, father," with that quick comment Zanmir turned on his heel and strode down the wall towards the keep. While Zanmir was an ice cold boy, he loved his mother deeply and cared for her more than any of his sons. While Vesir was very grateful he could never quite read the boy. What he wanted or what he was after had never been disclosed. He always seemed so distant except when it came to Kaylen, Vesir's loving wife and the boy's mother. With a swift motion, Vesir turned and jabbed Jonnas on the shoulder with the edge of the practice blade.

"Alright then, enough for today, take two guards to the eastern wall and see to their duties. I have some things to attend to," Jonnas nodded while he rubbed his non-existent wound.

"Things?"

"Stuff and things, I am the Commander after all, if you can barely remember," He grinned at his son and followed his eldest towards the keep. Jonnas saluted his father, by taking his sword hand and pressing it against his opposite shoulder.

*

~Wedyar and Briyar~

Briyar and Wedyar had watched the small exchange in silence and knew exactly what was coming. Jonnas turned to them, there was no escape now.

"You two, with me," the pair saluted the Captain, with the slender of the duo doing his best to avoid a sigh of annoyance. As Jonnas walked past them along the stone and wooden wall towards the eastern side, the pair traded looks that betrayed their desire to continue their inactive shift where they were, but sadly they knew they had no choice and began to follow the Granlia with small jog to catch up with his long stride.

* * *

Chapter IV
Unwelcome Guests

~Nyer~

It was a rare occurrence to meet a member of the famous Order. Mages they were called with a home no one could ever dare to uncover, and with the power to bend the abnormal to their will. However, none she had ever met had claimed to see such power in person. Claims that this power had been truly obtained by these fanatics lay only in whispers and rumours. Nyer did not lay much faith in whispers and rumours, only on what her own eyes could see. She was a practical woman. Not as romantic as Ayla, not as carefree as Nymin and not as much of a day dreamer as Rayar. She was a woman who focused on logic and her own perception. While some saw this as cold, they were simply too involved in their own fantasies to understand the real world. Now, she had a chance to see something not many in Heldon, no, in Mayhen had witnessed - a man of the Order. She sat in the Chamber of Relations, a name the advisor of Heldon had proclaimed it be called. Lanni Ni'Tella, an old deteriorating woman. Nyer thought she was as weak as her father when it came to serious delegation and correspondence. This old hag confused age with wisdom; well that was Nyer's feelings on the old bag in any case. When she became Queen there would be no place for people like her in such positions of high regard. Though, that time would still be some years ahead. Lanni had the look of age in everything about her, wrinkled features, hair the colour of iron, a cane always in hand. She wore dark robes the colour of a dying forest that covered her entire body.

"Who does she think she is? A mythical druidae? Please!" Nyer whispered under her breath to another woman beside her. This woman was known as Titania, Only Titania. By her attire she was clearly a Royal Blade, the only female one at that. Nyer had chosen her at a young age a couple of years ago after witnessing her strength in a tournament, though they had also been friends since they were children. Rumeo had always commented that she chose this warrior because she was a woman but Nyer was not so finicky. This woman was chosen because she was skilled and she was no nonsense like herself. Unlike the other Royal Blades, Titania was nearly always by her side. Loyal, honest, brave, she would stand beside Nyer, in any situation. That is what a Royal Blade should be. Not like that fool Hyar. Above and Below, she detested that man with his inability to treat her and those in the royal family with the respect they were due.

"My Lady, as you say," Titania whispered back. She was a lean woman with dark red hair tied into a Mayhen knot. At her hip, an arming sword hung. The leather grip was brown and strapped around metal; the guard golden like the pommel. On the pommel a fawn's head was crafted. The only Noble Family in Mayhen whose banner branded a fawn was the family closest to Hellsbane castle to the east. Nyer never pried into such affairs, this woman was loyal and skilled and that is all she cared for. Across the table sat her father and next to him, Heldon's Commander Brayton Gallina, a broad bull of a man. His chin held a dark raven beard and his long black hair was tied into a ball at his nape. This man held slightly more respect in her eyes but his evident love of her father made him ignorantly loyal to the King's arbitrary nature. Nyer's examination of those invited to this conference was disrupted by a soldier entering the chamber. The soldier graciously bowed to his King and princess and saluted the commander.

"Your Grace. The envoy from the Order has arrived," Rumeo nodded to the man as a signal to allow the man to enter.

A few paces behind the soldier this famous man arrived. Nyer's frown was ever present as she sized him up. He was tall, very tall and aged between perhaps thirty and forty. He had long chestnut hair slicked back which reached his shoulders and connected with a well groomed beard all over the lower half of his face. His clothes were both simple yet regal with a dark brown cloak covering his body and strange symbols laced on the sleeves and collar. She did not recognise them, though they were so small it was hard to decipher them from across the room. The man she was examining seemed to be doing the same to her and the others in the chamber. His dark grey eyes were flickering between each person there, though she could have sworn his eyes lingered on her slightly longer than the rest. After the few seconds of staring and gauging, the tall man bowed to the King. His voice was husky and direct.

"Your Grace. Allow me to introduce myself. I am Ler'Del of the Order. My Lord was greatly humbled by your final acceptance to allow an audience with us, though he is unwaveringly apologetic that he could not attend this meeting. He has business far south in Brexxia," Nyer cocked a brow. Brexxia was as south as south could be. What business could anyone have in that wasteland? Though that is simply what she had been taught it was. Relations between Mayhen and Brexxia were practically non-existent. They never troubled each other as the journey between here and there would take one through not only Southrous, but also the Lost Desert.

"I see, Lord Ler'Del. Do not be concerned, you are here in his place and I am sure you will serve your Lord as if I was speaking to him. Now, I am King Rumeo Granlia as you are already aware, haha," The King patted his large stomach as he chuckled. "This is my commander, Brayton Gallina; he has served this country since he was an officer in the Battle of the Pass, my first advisor Lanni Ni'Tella, and of course my beautiful daughter and heir, Princess Nyer Granlia. We welcome you here and we are excited to hear what needs the Order has with my little corner of the Freeland," Ler'Del acknowledged each as they were introduced, this time Nyer

41

was sure his eyes lingered on her again too long for her patience. She would not return his smile; she would only reward him with a scowl. The man of the Order politely requested a seat and sat at the opposite end of the long table. Servants scurried around filling glasses of wine which Ler'Del politely refused and took only the water.

"Your keep is stunning Your Grace, you know rumours of the years forgotten, claim that it was mastered with the use of magic. The detail in every stone is exquisite. Though, much mastery of those skills is long forgotten, even by my Order. Magic is not what it used to be Your Grace," Rumeo nodded as he listened to the compliments of his home. Nyer tapped her finger on the table impatiently.

'I hate people who beat around the bush. Get to the point,' she withheld her thoughts flowing to her tongue. Though, it seemed Rumeo caught her dissatisfaction in the corner of his eye and gave her a stern look. She rolled her eyes and did her best to sit through this three course meal of pandering.

"Why thank you Lord Ler'Del. It is true my father and his father and World Above, his father before him spoke of magic in the stones but I like to think craftsmen and builders showed their true quality in designing our home." Ler'Del smiled a smile that you could not read. It was simply blank, emotionless.

"Of course Your Grace. I suppose you are wondering why My Lord wished an audience with you. Well I will not beat around the bush."

'Are you serious?' The young princess struggled to hold back a dark chuckle as if her thoughts had been read.

"Our influence stretches far, Your Grace. Every nation in this land has a member of the Order as an advisor, supporting that country in its growth and preparations for the future. All lands excluding two. The great Kingdom of Mayhen and, of course, Hextheene. I am sure you are aware of their feelings on those who have magical abilities in their blood," Rumeo nodded. Nyer was aware too. She had heard of King Braska and his crusade to find any who had such power and wipe them from the Freeland. Such hate for something that she believed to be nothing but illusion was a farce. As far as she could tell, this King simply chased nightmares of his own doing, with twisted men around him fuelling that fire for their own gain. It was an unfunny joke. "Not only this but also... I hope you are not offended Your Grace, but word has reached us of a certain marriage between one of your beautiful children, to the Hextor family. I was sent to advise against...," Ler'Del cut his words short as Rumeo raised his hand. Nyer shot a glance to her father; his brow was furrowed as was his commander's and advisor's. The pair whispered to the King, yet she could not catch the words.

"How are you aware of this, I must ask? Only the Granlia family and those closest to me are privy to this. This concerns me," Nyer followed her father's concern. Spies? Unlikely, this man would not reveal this information if they had spies in their keep. Big mouthed people were the more likely option. She could hold her tongue no longer.

"And what do you have to gain from telling us this? If you are watching our family you put yourself here in questionable situation. No, perhaps you intended to put us in the questioning position with those we hold close?" This oh so wise man from the Order looked between the King and princess, yet showed no sign of worry on his face. He remained calm and respectful throughout this meeting.

"Do not be alarmed. The Order does what it must to keep order. That is our saying. We would not dare insult your great noble family with ears where they should not be. No nothing like that. I am sorry to say, that word of this has already begun to spread to the common people. Perhaps someone with you slipped on their words, or perhaps someone with the Hextor family did so. Either way this knowledge is not silent."

Nyer was not buying this.

"Why would you come all this way from... wherever you come from on the word of a rumour yet speak of it as a fact? I do not need to ask why you are against this marriage in a month. Any support Hextheene has is support against your Order, no?" Ler'Del now focused on her. She could feel his

43

eyes burning into her cold shell. She would not flinch from his gaze. She was stronger, she knew it. Before this so called mage could speak, the King took the reins.

"Forgive my daughter, she can be a tad too suspecting of others." This surprised her. She shot her cold glare towards her father. The man did not return this look. He only spoke to the robed man at the other end of the table. "Regardless of how you came to know this, it does not matter. I must apologise for your journey here but I also must decline your requests. I have my advisers and any marriages, true or not, are simply between me and my family. Not you. If there is anything else you need, please ask. Otherwise I do not believe there is much else to discuss on this matter. You are welcome to stay in court for the night before your return to your home." While Rumeo spoke with authority, his politeness was ever apparent. It was something Nyer doubted she could ever master. Her anger was beginning to boil over. Ler'Del rattled his fingers on the table as he seemed to ponder his next move.

"I see, Your Grace, this is most upsetting but you need not apologise. You are a King and I am a humble servant of My Lord, Your Grace and the realm. I will return now with your answer and wish you all good health and prosperity in the coming tides." The bearded man slowly pulled back his chair and stood. He gave another look around the table at those present. He was not quite finished. "Yet I must give caution. Order is beginning to crumble and many changes are coming. If you would reconsider, which I plead you do, Your Grace." His tone became harsher, much to the annoyance of the commander Brayton as he began to stand as if to defend the King, even against words. "Even a country that has lasted a thousand years can come to ruin with the poor decision of a single ruler." Before Nyer could interject the commander broke his silence.

"Is that a threat to our King!?" He bellowed. The soldiers at the door suddenly placed hands on their swords and moved into a position to act if called upon quickly. The air was tense; the glares between the men were boiling. The princess did not even realise that Titania had already stepped closer to her side with a hand upon her fawn pommel sword. Ler'Del did not flinch, he was as confident as he had been upon entering the hall though he still offered a bow to those present.

"The Order would never threaten. We simply see what is to come. If Mayhen does not wish to prepare with us, then you prepare alone. Well, with Hextheene and the blood thirsty King. Now, I humbly ask am I allowed to be on my way, Your Grace? I regret any offense I may have caused." Brayton looked to his King; the man was prepared at any moment to apprehend this cretin. Rumeo on the other hand leaned back in his chair with a pondering look.

"You may go. Thank you for your visit, it has been eye opening, my Lord," with that the dark robed man turned and began his way to the exit. His stride was quick as it seemed he wished to hastily leave the situation. There were a few minutes as the tension died down in the chamber. There was silence until Nyer broke it, she could hold her tongue no longer.

"Father I do not understand. Why are you not concerned about the fact he has that kind of information?" Rumeo rubbed his grey beard and sighed. It was Lanni who spoke; the old woman had remained silent apart from quiet whispers, until now.

"Nyer, you are a very smart girl. He may have come on the word of a rumour yet he also was seeing if we would admit it was fact, or just a rumour. You gave him the former," Nyer blinked in shock. How could she have been so careless?

"My dear," Rumeo smiled a loving smile, he wasn't angry. For some reason this annoyed Nyer even more. Princess or not she had made a terrible mistake and her father was still as forgiving as always. "Whether he knew it was true or not, and even if you did give it away, it does not matter. Do not let it get you down, we all are human, we all make mistakes. Move past it and focus on what we do next. Planning a wedding, yes?" Nyer could feel the anger once more. She sat there silently gritting her teeth. She was angry at herself but angry at her father for not reprimanding her as he should. He was the bloody King.

"Titania!" She snapped as she stood from her seat. The Royal Blade was already at attention and at her back, prepared to move. "I apologise Your Grace, it will not happen again," Nyer said with strain before she turned to leave the chamber.

'Embarrassing,' echoed in her head.

Nyer and Titania made their way along the battlements around the castle courtyard. The sun was burning in the sky, the heat seemed like it would never free the rain again. Nyer's long dark blue dress did little to keep her cool with sleeves that reached down to her wrists and lace pattern gloves that covered her hands. Though they were thin, any extra clothing seemed needless in this heat. She would go and change into something somewhat more appropriate if her mind was not so clouded with the events that had just transpired.

"Titania," She began. "What do you think my father is thinking?" It was quite an open question. Perhaps she just needed some clarification from her Royal Blade and friend. Anything to help her contemplate what she should do. Titania was generally quite good at giving advice in her matters of court, though she never openly spoke them in the presence of any but Nyer.

"If I may, My Lady, what I find most curious is that after so long of not accepting an audience with someone from the Order, he does so now, just before this wedding goes ahead. His majesty is not as simple minded as he seems to portray, as you know," the red headed woman spoke as a matter of fact. She was not wrong. As much as her father's laid back persona got on her nerves, he did show from time to time his strength in his position, the few times she had looked up to him.

"Perhaps my father sees something we do not. My father also knows the result of marrying into the Hextor family. He is not a man of war or battle, he never has been, yet I am sure he will be expected to provide support against Southrous. Until I learn more, I will not be able to make sense of it all. I can assume all I like; sooner or later I will need to hear it from him. What is his plan?" Nyer stopped in her stride and leant on the battlement that looked over into the courtyard. Below she could see her adopted brother Rayar speaking with the old crone Lanni. They must have left the chamber not long after she had. She stared at the pair for a time.

'Rayar. You remind me of father and you do not even share the same blood as him, nor me. You were but a baby when you came here. Now you are in line for the throne after me until I have a child. How ludicrous. Granlia blood or not, I wonder what you would have said in that meeting. Anything? Or sat there and been as much use as a rotting beam of wood supporting a castle. Though... you have potential, I think.' Her Royal Blade leant on the wall beside her and followed her eyes.

"What are you thinking about, My Lady?" The red headed woman asked. Nyer did not look over and continued to watch the boy below.

"Hmm... What that fool from the Order said. Prepare for what? I must know. I will not sit in the audience, I will lead this performance," Titania nodded slowly and remained silent. The pair of them could sit in silence for hours and still have a stronger bond than most. Nyer bit her bottom lip and frowned as thoughts of the coming storm spiralled in her mind. What could it be? She needed answers.

* * *

Chapter V
Whispers of the Past
~Rayar~

"You truly are growing into quite the man Rayar," The elderly advisor Lanni said to him in that croaky voice of hers. Even though they both had residence in the castle of Mayhen, he rarely had much chance to converse with the woman known as Lanni Ni'Tella. She had always been so busy and concerned with realm affairs they would rarely cross paths. Being a prince had its duties as much as its freedom. Still he respected this woman with a wealth of wisdom and knowledge and always enjoyed the brief moments they had to talk. The pair strode through the castle courtyard. Unlike the garden it was littered with guards throughout, with many craftsmen working within. The blacksmith tempered blades off to his left under his small shelter and the servants cared for those passing through, who were part of court. Lords and peasants alike from throughout Mayhen, came for an audience with the King and passed through the courtyard towards the inner keep. Wagons were inspected by guardsmen at the gate into the courtyard. For a brief moment he wondered what was contained within those wagons, though his attention soon turned to that of the gate itself. Through that large white stone doorway, covered in vines and flowers upon the foundation, was the world outside he longed to see. The sea, the desert, the mountains, villages and cities; many people all of a different way of life.

"Prince Rayar?" He was stolen back to reality. Even as he respected this woman greatly and loved a chance to speak with her, he still found himself falling into one of his day dreams. He hoped he had not appeared rude.

"I apologise Mistress Ni'Tella. I was-," She smiled a wrinkly smile.

"Another day dream, my boy?" He laughed softly and nodded to her.

"Indeed. I feel as if I am kept within these walls. Not like a cage, no, but I do not feel as if I have the freedom to wander out as I please. Nyer has seen much of the land, yet I have not been afforded such an opportunity. Every time I have brought it up with the King, he claims my time will come. I have seen eighteen springs now. I think he intends to keep me safe as a newborn until I am his age." They both chuckled at his jest though Rayar could not help but feel a pinch of truth to it. Lanni shook her head slowly and placed a leathery hand on his shoulder. She scanned the area briefly around them, to check no one was within ear shot of their conversation.

"Your time is coming, I assure you. He cares for you. The past perhaps keeps him wary of your safety," the golden haired boy halted in his step. He too made sure no one else was nearby before he lowered his tone.

"I know I have asked many times, to you, the King, the Queen, Above and Below even Nyer whom always chastises me for being petty. What sort of people were my parents? All the answers I have gotten these past years, that I can remember, have been hazy recollections or that they died in the great fire in Highhall Castle. I do not mean to pester." The elderly woman shook her head again and linked arms with Rayar and led him further across the courtyard.

"It is no trouble, dear Rayar. Your family were very reclusive. They did not interact with others often. I only ever met your father once or twice and never your mother. I could not even describe what they looked like to you, my memory is sadly not as precise as it used to be you see. Though I must admit I did not know much of their passing, very few did and they have passed themselves, or do not wish to speak of it. You really wish to speak of such things or perhaps something that will lighten the heart instead?" She gave him a cracked grin and he could not help but smile in return. With his free hand he ran it over his golden blonde hair and slicked it back before fiddling with the pearl around his neck.

"You are right. I have heard it so many times, hearing it again would not change a thing. Well, I have been told as much as anyone knows. Outside our family and yourself, I believe, I am just the son of King Rumeo," Rayar said. Lanni cackled in response.

"Indeed, Indeed. A fact he revealed to you at a young age. King Rumeo is an honest man. He could have kept that from you as well. Maybe it would have been easier on you? Though from what I vaguely remember, Princess Nyer was not as warming to you as he would have liked. He always had trouble controlling that one. She has a great future before her, but I think her temper sometimes gets the better of her." He could agree with that. As calm and composed as she showed herself to be on the outside, he could feel her temper at breaking point more often than not. The pair continued to walk through the courtyard until they entered the keep. Inside was the main hall which was as glorious as the throne room. Banners hung from the ceiling; shields and swords plastered on the walls and white stone held the structure together. Flowers and greenery ran down the sides of the main hall towards the large wooden doors that led into the throne room.

The pair stepped away from the guards along the hall and into a small room located on the left. The doorway led to a circular stone staircase towards the advisor's office. The main hall was large which caused sound to travel quite well within it, so any conversation that Lanni wished to have with him concerning delicate affairs of his heritage, could only be discussed in private. The pair entered the office; it was just as he remembered from his few times seeing it. Scrolls littering the tables and floors, a large bookcase that held countless volumes of knowledge and a small window that looked out upon the gardens outside. By the window a cage hung, with the advisor's personal messenger pigeon which she had trained for years to only return to her. Some would assume it would be used for secret plots and schemes but since the advisor knew so many people in her lifetime, it was primarily used for idle talk between friends over long distances. Lanni offered him a drink of water before she made her way to window. Her eyes trailed over the scenery in a moment of contemplation. This caused Rayar to shuffle awkwardly where he stood, unsure whether to speak or sit. Luckily for his sake, this moment did not last long.

"Your father, Lord Rendal Vienne, I do not remember much of him. As I said, he was not a man to converse with others. He did not attend court; I only vaguely remember seeing this man twice. He attended a festival here in Heldon and I saw him in the war with Hextheene. A young strapping man he was." She let out a small sigh, as if she briefly recalled his looks. Perhaps even a longing sigh. Rayar creased his nose but let it go. "He was one of your grandfathers... sorry, King Wiliam Granlias' Royal Guard. At a young age I believe he led men into battle. From the report of the Battle of the Pass, he performed well. King Rumeo spoke of that being the day they became friends. Good friends at that. I am sure King Rumeo has filled you in about that day?" She asked as she finally turned away from the window and focused on the young prince. Rayar fiddled with his pearl and nodded ever so slightly.

"Somewhat. You know what he is like. He does not like to speak of battle or my father whatsoever. Whenever I had asked, he always had this sullen look upon his face. I stopped asking eventually. I would not want to pry information from him, should it cause him pain," Lanni took a sip of her own cup of water, her expression showing she understood.

"Yes. Old wounds and all. King Rumeo is an honest man. He has witnessed many terrible things in his youth. Yes, it is better not to pry. You have a family who love and care for you. Many do not have that luxury. You are a lucky boy Rayar, very lucky," was she trying to make him feel guilty? If she was, it

51

worked. This was not news to him though. Knowing this had been one of the reasons he stopped poking around to find out more. Rumeo was his father, Julian was his mother, and Nyer, Ayla and Nymin were his sisters. As he had gotten older, he had asked less and less, until he just accepted it was how it was, yet recently the desire to know more had been creeping back into his mind. Perhaps it was something to do with this desire to see the outside world that had pricked his interest.

"You spoke of a festival, I've heard a few have taken place here in Heldon, but not since I was a child have I seen any. I remember because Hinsani had been requested numerous times to enter the combat and he kept refusing. What was it he said? 'I do not fight with those I do not intend to kill' though he spars with me every other day, perhaps I am on his kill list?" Rayar joked. Lanni cracked a grin.

"Oh Hinsani, what a man he has become as well. You are fortunate to have that man watching your back. Duty is everything to him after all. He would follow you all the way to the World Below. Yes, a festival. It was while King Rumeo was still a prince like you, after the war with Hextheene had reached its end. All the great Noble Lords and Ladies from the nearby lands celebrated. Feasts, dances, music, melee and jousting if I recall correctly. The faces all seem rather hazy to me yet I remember your real father came second in the melee. He took a rather harsh smack upon his helmet and lost to Noble Lord Jachin Leodri. Oh dear he was a beast of a man. His son rules in Castle Crewyn now I believe. Up to that point he was a very skilled swordsman. I remember this, because I tried to come to his aid and tend to him, yet a young girl got to him first. A maid I believe, but other than that memories escape me," Rayar listened intently. It was not much but it was something. As her story came to a close she watched him inquisitively.

"Did that help you, hearing this story?" He blinked in surprise.

'Did it help? Well I learnt something but...,' He let out a soft sigh. His fingers fiddled with the pearl around his neck

while his other hand placed down the small cup of water. He could learn all he wanted but it would not change anything. He was not a Vienne. He was a Granlia. She continued before he could answer. "I am sure there are more tales some could tell you, I am sure you have heard others. Yet you focus too much on what has happened Rayar, not on what is to come. Serve your country, serve your family and lead as a prince. There will be a time when you will be looked to for leadership, as a leader of an army or a House, or even follow in Vesir's footsteps. Whatever course the current takes you, you must look to where you are going and not always from where you have come." Even through her leathery face, her smile was soft and kind. Rayar took a few moments to take in her words, before he bowed his head respectfully.

"I will take my leave Mistress Ni'Tella... Thank you," another laugh escaped her lips.

"A handsome young prince bowing to me, please, you make me feel like a young woman again. Get out of here." He returned the smile and made his way towards the exit. If only he could talk to girls his own age with the same confidence, he would not have such a problem choking on his own courage. He reminded himself that he was not known as the brooder, he was known as the day dreamer and her words had rung true. It was the future he looked to, not what could have been.

* * *

Chapter VI
Ganon
~Braska~

The great city of Ganon. Huge in stature and cursed in poverty. It sat on the Eastern border of Hextheene by the coast with vast and undisputed access to the eastern sea. It had held its place here for centuries being the home of the rulers of Hextheene. This overpopulated city was less than an hour ride from the castle. The inhabitants ranged from those living in the muddy and crowded streets to those who lived in great halls closer to the castle itself. Many sought to join the Hextheene army as a way to make ends meet. The king was always in need of fresh meat to join his wars. The city itself was dark and noisy with people performing their trades in the streets and guard patrols making their way through unwelcoming gatherings throughout the city. They spoke of a time where Ganon had been a place of ambition and opportunity, yet now from years of people moving to the city, its resources had grown fewer. Those at the bottom of the food chain struggled daily to survive and those with name and position flourished on their misery. The castle itself was known as The Great Hexhold, named hundreds of years ago when the first of the Hextor family rescued the Northern part of the Freeland from death, though this was only considered to be myth and legend these days. The Great Hexhold showed its banner all over the walls; a white soldier holding a great sword in front of him on a field of black. Being King of such a nation was a taxing position. There was never any rest for those who fought for the good of all by vanquishing those who would oppose the great nation of Hextheene and wield the magic of the World Below.

He sat on his large grey throne, crafted from iron and steel. It was not as glamorous as the Mayhen throne but Braska Hextor had no desire for glamour or anything that did not have a necessity. The King of Hextheene was a giant of a man, standing almost 8 feet in height and with the power to crush a man with one hand. Some whispered he was the true second coming of the first Hextor, back in the Firsts Age, with the height and strength of a mammoth, creatures long lost in the tides of time. His hair was a dark brown shade with signs of greying over his ears and hung just above his shoulders, constantly pushed back close to his skull. He generally wore an expression of scorn; his brow wrinkled to always show a frown and his eyes dark from the terrible things he had witnessed, which had set him on his path towards the destruction of magic. Even in court he wore his armour with pride; so heavy no man could wear such metal without their body crumbling in defeat. Unlike his men, the Knights of Hextheene with their banners and colours, his armour was simply steel and grey. Braska did not even wear his crown. The only outward sign of his identity beside his legendary giant stature was a golden ring on his finger with the seal of Hextor.

"You stand before the Great King Braska Hextor the Second, Protector of the Land, Lord of the Hextheene Knights, and Watcher of the North. Speak your business and pray to Above for your audience," a snake like man announced in the throne room of Hexhold. Braska sat upon his throne, surrounded by men and women of the court receiving those in the land who wished to plea or make business with him. This was a daily occurrence and to him it had gotten old long, long ago. Down a large flight of stairs much lower than where the throne was sat, an old man, wrinkled and weathered, nervously grasping a small red hat. He bowed awkwardly, fear slithered through his body.

"Y-your grace!" The whimpering man exclaimed.

55

"Speak," he replied. Another farmer he thought. Perhaps this man would surprise him with something more interesting than lack of grain. The army needed to be fed; it was how it had to be.

"Yes, yes of course Your Grace. I've come from my village south from the great and... and... magnificent capital to beg, humbly beg for the crown's support. Our...," he gulped, trying to force the words out. Braska's facial expression did not change, making his reactions unreadable. This seemed to make the man even more nervous. "We've... we've been havin' raids from bandits of the sea, killin' our fisherman that supply my village with food and stealin' our women, when they went too close to the coast. We can't keep our children fed... we... we...," this was clearly an emotional moment for the elderly man. Braska raised his hand for silence and the court fell so.

"You did not tell me your name or your village," the King simply asked. There was a moment longer with nothing but silence, as the elderly man realised he had been so nervous of the meeting, he had not even performed the basic introduction to the King. From what Braska could tell, this only stirred the old man's nerves even more. The snake like man beside him leaned down to speak.

"Your Grace, he is Wayne Hadden, Mayor of the village of Meer. Right near the Southrous border at that," like a shadow, this advisor slipped back into nothingness, as if he had never been present.

'Bandits he says? No. Southrous raiders,' those cowards never engaged in field battle they only sent their spies and raiding parties to cripple whatever part of Hextheene they could. For years and years, it had been this way. The last field battle that he could remember there was magic. The giant of a man leaned back in his throne and rattled his fingers on the arm rest.

"You will increase your trade of fishery to the army, and support the camps west of your village that currently are defending your lives even as we have this conversation. There are many soldiers there who could benefit from increased rations. In return to allow this service to go unhindered, I will send two galleys to the coastline near your village to apprehend and execute any raiders that dare attempt to interfere with your people. Soldiers will also be stationed within the village, an encampment will be formed. Will this suffice, Mayor Hadden?" He spoke with an air of authority and power. Even though that statement ended in a question, everyone in the court knew that he only expected one answer. Wayne bowed his head, falling to his old crooked knees and praised the King for his wisdom and mercy.

"Your business is done. Be on your way," the snake man commanded the mayor. As fast as a crossbow bolt, the mayor bowed shuffling backwards and bumbled out of the throne room door. The next person to speak with the King would soon be on his way. The advisor took his opportunity to speak with his King. "Your Grace. Southrous you assumed?" Braska made a deep noise but no words that a man could understand. "Your wisdom is unmatched Your Grace. We should not spread our fleet too thin, Your Grace. Should that bile of a foe, Raiva of Southrous, see an opening by sea, he would surely take it," the hook nose man advised cautiously. Braska turned his gaze ever so slightly to have the man in sight, his eyes as dark as a pitch black night. This man, Sli Moran, advised his father and his brother and now him. His hate for magic almost matched his own. Though as grotesque as his appearance was, he was loyal and supported the crown through many hardships. Sometimes he overstepped his place.

"Good," he wanted this. He had grown weary of waiting and skirmishing. If Southrous would launch an attack by sea, he would destroy them without mercy. Soon with the support of Mayhen through marriage, he would take the fight to their land, their castles and their homes. None would be left alive.

"You stand before the Great King Braska Hextor the Second, Protector of the Land, Lord of the Hextheene Knights, and Watcher of the North. Speak your business and pray to Above for your audience." The giant of a man turned his attention to the next who wished to speak with him. Many more followed suit. It would be a long day today but much was to be done before night came.

As night fell upon the city of Ganon, the cut throats and brigands of the city crawled from their holes in the shadows to begin making their living. Braska did not have time for the antics of the city; the guards were placed to deal with such matters. He was a King of war who did not have the patience for the crying of babes in the city depths. No, his mind and direction were focused on much larger goals than that. War brought these antics to the surface and once the war was won, then the quelling of filth in the streets could be attended to. He stood alone in his throne room. No members of the court and not even a single guardsman were stationed in the hall. He was Braska Hextor; he did not require guards to protect him. He was the greatest protector he could think of. His attention sat upon the Hextheene throne, as he silently contemplated his next moves. The door of the throne room creaked open, stealing his attention.

"Your Grace, father," a soft voice spoke. The voice of the weakness in his bloodline. His son. The giant man turned to see why his moments of reflection had been interrupted. There stood his son, Kerrin Hextor, a fair haired, slim and weakly boy. While many said his beauty far out shone that of a woman's, Braska only saw this as weak and pathetic. To be measured like a woman was embarrassing for his family. Beside him strode the prince's friend and bodyguard. A dark skinned man with a shaven head and lean build; a man from the south but much further south than Southrous. Zackary Rengecko. A slim fencing blade hung at his hip and his leather attire was used for court and for battle. They had been friends since they were children and luckily for Zackary, due to his achievements in the field, Braska had accepted him into court to be by his son's side.

"Speak," Braska commanded. The beautiful young prince flicked his eyes between his father and his friend before he held out a scroll to his father. The giant man snatched it from the boys grasp and ran his eyes down the page.

'King Braska Hextor II

I, King Rumeo, am very grateful at your interest to wed my second daughter, Princess Ayla Granlia to your first son, Prince Kerrin Hextor. We request the wedding itself take place within the nation of Mayhen in Heldon before my daughter takes her leave to your capital and joins your court. I wish for your attendance in the ceremony as there are matters which I must discuss with you in person, King Braska Hextor. I hope this letter finds you well and the fouls of war are not too strenuous in your reign.

My sincerest regards,

King Rumeo of Mayhen.'

This was interesting. Very interesting. Though of course the letter sparked concerns and intrigue to Rumeo's intentions. Braska did not intend to attend any sort of wedding even of his son in these times, and Rumeo knew him well enough to know he would not have been present. Yet to personally ask for his attendance meant something was in dire need of discussion. The Kings did not entirely see eye to eye, they never had since their fathers had the Northern War. He read through the letter several more times for any more hints that may have given him more information about the matter but it seemed Rumeo had only given enough to pique his interest. That gluttonous old jester, what was he up to?

"Your Grace, father, this is good news, no? I have heard her beauty is of a fallen star and that her kindness causes all those around her to fall in love. I think-," Kerrin was cut off with a strike around his pale cheek. Braska continued to study the letter with one hand free to slap his son back handed across the face.

"Stop with your nonsensical blabbering, boy. Beauty like a fallen star?" Braska sniffed and passed the letter back to his son who stood there stunned as he held his now reddened cheek. "King Rumeo is an honest man, yet in this letter he hides something. Something he could not let any other lay eyes upon,

59

which means he only desires me to hear these words. Your marriage is to support the family and the realm, not for your foolish whimsical ideologies of love. You think I married your mother for love? Hmph. Gold and family strength, the only downside to this marriage was you coming into this world," Braska strode up to his throne and placed himself down upon the metal seat. His son had regained his composure while his friend, Zachary remained completely motionless as he waited for the pair to be dismissed.

"Shall I prepare a reply, Your Grace?" Kerrin choked out. He could see his eyes glistening with tears, as he tried so hard to hold them back. It was pathetic.

"Yes. Send for the scholar, stir him from his sleep. One month from now we will hold the marriage in Mayhen and I shall personally attend this farce. Send word to Commander-at-Arms Caskin Camaron, to return to the capital, for he shall run the Castle in my absence. Prince Kerrin Hextor, I will not let this marriage make you weaker than you already are. After this, we will begin the march that will change the world and begin our assault upon that monstrous Order. One day you will take the throne from me, in my death, and I will not let you allow this great country to fall to ruin," the fear that ever clouded his mind. Hextheene was not a land of kindness and mercy, it was a land of strength and iron and power. He would have his son become such before his last breath. If any man could turn someone into a great and merciless leader, it was Caskin.

*

~Kerrin~

'I hate him,' it was the only feeling he could grasp when thinking about his father. That man was nothing but hate with a twisted desire for revenge for something that happened years and years ago. Kerrin recalled a day long ago when he loved his father, before he truly knew what his father was like. His biggest fear was turning out to be the same as his father. Kerrin

sat in his chambers, drinking wine cup after cup. Zachary sat across the table from him enjoying the wine yet not at the pace of his friend. The bedroom shone with reflected light as mirrors hung throughout the room, every wall brandishing one. The bed itself was trimmed with a golden finish as did most of the furniture in the room. It looked as delicate as the man who inhabited the chamber.

"From the delightful vineyard of the Wishful Hills, soft and smooth like a maidens kiss, do you not agree, Zachary?" Kerrin asked his friend as he twirled the cup of wine in his grasp. His eyes were icy blue much like his mothers. His beauty was also taken from her. In fact many traits about him did not resemble his father whatsoever. He would even suggest that Braska was not his father at all; that he was a bastard, if it was not for the holy blood that ran through his veins. As much of an abyss of darkness his father was, he was of holy blood through the line of Hextor.

"You know me. I do not care much for wine Kerrin. By the looks of it you care for it a bit too much," the shaven haired fencer commented as he placed down his cup, a small smile sat upon his lips. The prince chuckled and took another swig.

"When you have such a hard life as mine, wine is somewhat a necessity. Did you hear the words he spouted at me? Above and Below, what a beast," Kerrin snorted as once again wine met his lips.

"He does not mince words your father, does he," Zachary responded. While it was true, his father was a man who spoke his mind and without remorse on those he harms with his words, even he was not usually that abrupt. He had been used to the abuse of his father for many years now, but that was something else entirely. Perhaps it was the strain of his duties taking a toll on his old war mongering mind.

"He is a plague. He has been since the day my uncle was... brutally torn from this world. I get it, Zachary. I get the hatred he has. I would be angry as well but his intent on forcing everyone under his boot will be his downfall. As long as he is king, I will forever be chastised for not being him. How could anyone wish to be him?" Braska was a man who ruled with fear and distress, not love nor kindness. A ruler should be loved not feared. This is what he thought anyway. "When I become King, my friend, this land will change. I will call for peace with Southrous and together with the nation of Mayhen. We will bring prosperity back to the realm. Hextheene, I was told as a child, used to be so beautiful and stunning and now because of my father, his father, and Above and Below, his father too, it has become a nation of war," Another sip of wine came.

"As long as your father is King, that dream will have to wait and that is if he does not bring this land to ruin before then," Zachary retorted though he did not look upon Kerrin, only the large glassed window across the room. The prince waited a moment in silence as he hashed out the words in his increasingly intoxicated mind.

"As long... as he is King?"

"As long as he is King." Outside the window messenger pigeons took flight. One soared west towards Mayhen while the other south towards the forward encampment of the Commander-At-Arms, Caskin Camaron.

* * *

Chapter VII
Soldiers
~Caskin~

Truly a place he could feel alive. They were no more than a rabble to him and his sword. Any opportunity to wield his blade in battle, he would surely take. In the southern part of the realm, in the border between Hextheene and Southrous, was where those who sought to spill blood could spill it. The battlefield of choice this day was a small village deep within the vast countryside. The houses used to be quaint and appealing to those who sought a quiet life. They could farm on the fertile dirt or pick the apples in the right season. They could care for livestock and dance in the festival of The First come the New Year. Honest village people, honest workers of Hextheene. This had not saved them however. In fact they were lucky that the soldier's encampment was so close, that a scout caught wind of the smoke and reported back to the camp with haste. Otherwise they would have all been slaughtered like the cattle they herd without their plight ever being known to the realm. The once serene village was now aflame. Smoke filled the sky and bodies the ground. Men were nailed to doors with swords and women had their throats slit after being used as toys. Children were thrown into fires and burnt to a crisp. To any normal man, this sight was a horror. The village reeked of death and fear. Those who had committed these atrocities had been arrogant; they had lingered too long to continue their games with the surviving villagers. They had not expected the might of the Hextheene soldiers to come crashing down upon them. The attackers were dressed in fur and leather with no banner of where they hailed from. Their helmets curved around into masks with faces of horror painted devilishly on them usually in blood. Their weapons were that of the south; curved swords, axes as sharp as a con man's tongue and small but quick bows. Be soldiers of Southrous or merely raiders from that toxic land, there was one order they all followed. Mayhem in Hextheene.

"Stop! Please!" A man roared as he was held down by these attackers. A woman also screamed though her gurgles and cries for help were incoherent. Another man held her down and was slowly slicing away her skin from her leg with a small sharp blade. His laughter of joy could be heard from beneath his mask, smeared with the woman's blood. Every cut into her flesh caused the man, who must have been her husband, to shriek and cry, trying to do anything to be free and get to his beloved. After what they had already done to the woman, no man could withhold his rage. Scenes like this were occurring throughout the village. Good Hextheene people crying for help and the Southrous dogs taking pleasure in their acts of violence.

A loud horn blew in the village, the horn that sounded the arrival of the soldiers of Hextheene led by Caskin, the Commander-At-Arms and Hextheene Knight. As the dagger wielding attacker looked up towards the sound, a bastard sword struck him across the gullet and ripped his head from his shoulders. The savages began to scatter into their formations as they prepared for the charge of cavalry. Caskin sat upon his large mount, bastard sword in his left hand. He was adorned with a full set of heavy armour, his white tabard stained with the splattered blood of his first victim. From the smoke, the Hextheene cavalry charged down the paths of the village and across its fields, smashing into the raider's infantry. There were over fifty men on horseback and another hundred pouring into the village on foot.

'Put up a challenge!' Caskin thought, encased entirely in armour. As he rode through the men like an avalanche, he reached his way to the town centre. With his men at his back he swiftly dismounted and began his advance towards the horde that lay before him. All these enemies in leather and fur were not prepared for the wrath of a knight. The first came at him, curved sword used for slicing but not something to underestimate. This man was to be made an example for the other savages to see what he was capable of. Caskin brought up his sword and parried the first attack forcing the attacker to stumble. He did not give the man a chance to correct his footing and with a second motion he thrust down his sword across the chest of his attacker. Blood spewed from his wound and like a rag doll; he dropped to the floor, choking on his last gasp for air.

"Next," Caskin taunted from behind his full faced helmet. They obliged even if his words could not reach them. The horde charged with their screams they called their war cry. The Hextheene soldiers moved into a shield formation and began their advance in retaliation. Caskin on the other hand marched towards his enemy, bastard sword in his left hand. The two sides collided. The Knight tore through his enemies in the chaos of battle. The first he grabbed by the throat, his hand protected by a gauntlet and rammed his head into the mask. That being leather did little to protect the savage's face. Next he threw the unconscious body into the foes and pierced his second enemy through the chest as if like butter. Blood mists covered the men who were already dirtied from the mud and muck surrounding them. The savages rattled on the shields unable to break the formation. Many attempted to strike the commander who had left himself open from the ranks. Arrogance or skill, this position made him vulnerable. Each attacker found themselves being struck down, sword in his left hand and occasionally using both to cut down his foes. Whenever he became overwhelmed, spears struck forth from the shields to pierce those around Caskin. He planned this from the beginning of course, even this was part of his tactic. Those mindless beasts of men would undoubtedly try and take down their enemies' commander, which lured them straight to him. The skill he held however was enough to make him confident he could handle any of these whelps and with his men supporting his flanks, they were slowly pushed back into a tight mess of bodies. This gave the cavalry an opening to make an impression.

"Cavalry incoming, advance!" Caskin roared back to his men. As intended from the flanks, the remaining soldiers on horseback came swooping down the sides, slaughtering the savages in a continual stampede. They tore apart the flank horseman after horseman, making the enemy cluster even tighter. The footmen pushed and thrust their blades, piercing the confused trapped mice. There was no chance of escape now. They had been driven into the centre of the village surrounded by fire, smoke and now footmen and cavalry. Any who tried to flee were struck down by a horseman as they continued to ride in and out of the smoke. When they tried to push the formation, their lack of organisation had them butchered. With every man Caskin cut down in his path, the mist of blood filled his nostrils and sullied his white colours. He did not care. This is what he lived for. Battle was where he felt alive, felt like a man. The enemy were obliterated.

"Water, sir?" Caskin sat in the encampment. His armour still stained with the signs of battle. The full faced helmet sat beside him. His fair hair was cut short, almost shaven at the sides with the top stuck to his head with sweat. On his other side, his sword was thrust into the ground, covered in dried blood and dirt. Most of his armour remained on his form, with only his head and hands freed from the entrapment. For someone like himself, he tried to be prepared for fighting at any moment. Out here at the border to Southrous, every other day he found himself drawing blood. Skirmishes were all well and good, however...

'This is no war....,' He pondered to himself. The young boy who had offered him water stood their awkwardly as he waited

for a reply, water in hand. After a few moments Caskin reached out and took the calfskin canteen with a nod gesture of thanks to the boy and emptied the water over his head. Another battle over and more dead to bury and dead to burn. Another young lad approached him, older than the last and still in his armour of Hextheene, grey and bland. It was mainly chainmail with sections of steel and the banner of Hextheene on the chest. Not all had the luxury of being knights like himself and be able to wear such protective armour.

"Report on the battle. What of the village and the dead?" The knight asked as he tried to take a sip from his canteen before he realised he had emptied it all already.

"Sir. All enemies slain, one captured and given to Captain Rivers for questioning. Ten soldiers of ours fallen, Sir. Thanks to your tactic the number is low. The village Caster is burnt to a crisp. Most of the inhabitants have been killed. The survivors are being tended to before we move them north. Anything else, Sir?" Caskin shook his head and the young lad saluted by clenching his fist, patting it in the centre of his chest before extending it outwards. The salute was returned which allowed the boy to be dismissed.

'I suppose I better see what fun Rivers is having,' With that thought, the knight pulled himself to his feet, slid his sword home and began to make his way through the camp. The camp itself was pretty basic. Tents lined a pathway that led to his quarters at the far end of the stretch. Men sat around cleaning their weapons and drinking, after their intense conflict. Some were cheering at yet another victory, whilst others sombrely sat around fires with little or no words between them. In the distance the bodies of the enemy were being burned. He could tell by the smoke rising in the sky nearby. The smell would reach them soon with the direction of the wind. What a rookie mistake someone had made. Around the tents were wooden barricades with patrols always on watch; pikes and crossbows in hand. Around them were open fields to allow them to see if any of these Southrous dogs wished to try their luck. Caskin almost hoped they would. To have those hounds rally against

him and march on his camp, the fight would be magnificent and his glory for victory would be unquestionable. Just at the edge of the camp tents, was a small brown tent with no guards, no men relaxing outside, only the cries and whimpers of someone within. Caskin pushed open the entrance to reveal its contents. Inside, a rather unremarkable man stood with dark messy hair and an apron covering his form, in his hands were various tools covered in blood. Next to this man sat a chained savage, it seemed as if Rivers had already begun his game. The poor fellow's fingernails had been removed and places upon his naked body had been cut and sewn back up.

"Captain Rivers," Caskin greeted as he entered the tent. Rivers turned quickly towards him and cracked a wide smile.

"Ah! Commander Camaron! What brings you to my little abode?" He asked in an overly enthusiastic manner considering the scene in this tent.

'This man, many underestimate him. Even I wouldn't want to be caught in his clutches,' he thought as he took a seat across the tent. On a table next to him sat a small knife and an apple. He jabbed the knife through the flesh of the juicy fruit and began to munch away in a nonchalant manner.

"You know me, Rivers. I'm always dying to hear what news you have for me." The torturer cackled loudly and turned back to his victim, the man in the chair could only squeal and wriggle as he begged for mercy.

"You know these southerners, not big talkers. I've tried to get something of use out of him. He is a brigand I can tell you that, not a soldier I am sorry to say. From what this lovely dove has honoured me with, it is clear he only does as he is told. His leader told him and his fellows to ransack, rape and pillage the poor little village of Caster and he did just that. Nothing more just yet I am afraid," as Rivers spoke he was slowly peeling back the last finger nail of the crying man. Caskin took another bite from his apple and leant back in the creaking chair.

"Shame. I was hoping we could nab ourselves an orchestrator or a soldier at least. Every battle we have seems to be with these whelps. Bloody frustrating I tell you," another scream echoed through the tent.

"I know what you mean Commander. It would be nice to work my art upon someone with a bigger story to tell. My babies have only touched basic savage men for so long. They miss the taste of those with history. Oh dear, he's passed out." The tortured man slumped in the chair, his face red from screaming and sweat covered his entire body, alongside blood of course. "One moment," Rivers shuffled across the room and began plundering through his keepsakes.

"Well I'll leave you to it. If you get lucky and find out anything let me know, otherwise write a report as usual and have it sent to my tent," Rivers nodded vigorously as he tore apart his desk, mumbling 'yes' and 'where is it' over and over. Caskin chuckled quietly to himself as he made his way to the exit.

"Commander," the knight turned to see the man still going through his numerous apparatuses searching for, one could only assume, something to wake the sleeping prisoner. "Before I forget, a messenger pigeon arrived for you during the battle, from the capital. It's in your tent. Good day, my friend!" Caskin thanked him and swiftly left the tent. While this kind of work did not bother him anymore, he still had no desire for the smell that lingered in that man's tent. After what these so called people had been found doing, not only in this village but throughout the border of Hextheene, he had no sympathy for their treatment at the hands of Rivers.

It was only a short walk back to his place of rest. It was similar to the other tents except that it was considerably larger with enough room for a queen size bed, a table littered with reports and a map of Hextheene and notably more luxuries than the rest of the troops. Inside, stands to hold his armour and weapons sat in one corner and in the other a metal bath for tending to his hygiene. Caskin made sure the entrance to the tent was closed as tightly as it could be and began to remove the rest of his equipment.

"You're back," a soft voice spoke from within the silk sheets of his bed. Her naked form was only hidden by the thin cloth that wrapped around her body. Long red hair hung loosely over the pillow. She was stunning and serene.

"And you're still in my bed. Spent the entire time enjoying my pleasures Fifonia. As expected of a whore," he stated bluntly. A gentle laugh was her response as she sat up in his bed and held the sheets up to keep her body covered.

"You paid me much more than my fee, I thought you wished for me to remain to tend to you upon your return?" she joked. Caskin rolled his eyes as he attached his armour to the stands. As a man who had never married even at his age and as a knight, it was not hard for him to find women in the places he visited yet this woman continually found her way into his bed. Gift or a curse he found that her company was one of the few moments where he could relax. Once his armour had been successfully removed and he stood in nothing but slacks, his eyes ran over the table of documents in the centre of the tent.

"There's supposed to be a letter from the capital. Have you seen it?" he asked as he searched through the paperwork.

"I may have," she said teasingly. He knew what that meant. Ever so slowly he turned to the red headed woman to see her on her knees covered by the silk sheet still perched on his bed. The knight let a small smile escape him. "You'll have to find it, my valiant knight." Caskin sauntered to the bed and climbed on the edge, his hand slipping under the sheets. His hand gently caressed her thigh, his rough fingers stroked up her smooth skin; it felt softer than his sheets. "You're close," she teased again as she bit down on her lip. Ever so effortlessly, Caskin slipped his hand free with his fingers clutching the letter. Fifonia let out a small sigh and winked seductively. "Oh my, you found it, that's a shame," the fair haired commander laughed coyly, though he was not as seductive as her. He sat on the edge of the bed and tore open the letter. His blue eyes ran down the length of the paper as he studied it carefully. Fifonia's soft hands found their way over his back, tracing the many scars over his body. "What does it say, my valiant knight?"

'So I am to return to the capital without my men? It does not say why, just that I must return immediately. Has something happened?' Many thoughts passed through his mind, all the terrible things that could need his urgent attention or maybe something that is in his favour. Regardless of what it was, there was only one option and that was to return to the capital with haste.

"Caskin?" she asked once more.

"I am to return home at once. Leave the camp and defence of the southern border to my men. Doesn't say why though," Fifonia wrinkled her nose behind him; he could feel it on the flesh of his back as her face made contact.

"Are you leaving me here too? You did pay for me for a considerable amount of time. Not going to break a contract are you?" Caskin winced. Leaving her here would mean others would most likely purchase her services but surely taking her back to the capital was out of the question. Fighting it would only prolong the overall outcome of this exchange. It had to happen regardless.

"You know I can't take you with me. We have been over this before, Fifonia."

"We have numerous times and yet here I am, my purse heavy with your coin and you satisfied to your heart is content. The arrangement has worked out well for us, has it not?" Caskin creased his nose in a frown.

"For a whore, you speak as well as a noble. The road home is a long one in itself and my purpose in Ganon is yet to be given to me. For all I know, I could be getting relieved of duty. How would I pay for you then, hm?" The red headed beauty threw her head back in laughter and collapsed onto the bed, her arms outstretched above her head and eyes gleaming at him.

"Then I will find one who can afford me?" Caskin scoffed at her before moving down to lay beside her. Her arms wrapped around his head and gently caressed the fair strands of blonde hair. "I came all this way did I not? I can come back

71

with you now. Not going to leave me to the mercy of your rag tag soldiers are you? I do need to make a living after all. With you gone I suppose I can't be that picky," she whispered. It was calming, a soothing touch of her fingers softly running through his hair. The thought of war and fighting and death always seemed to break free from his mind whenever he was in this woman's arms. She was his poison and she knew it. To think a man of high station such as he being bedded by a whore, day after day. Not that he cared what those at court thought of him, regardless of his rank and title, Caskin Camaron was a soldier and not some prancing courtly noble bottom feeder who only focused on their image. One day he hoped they would enjoy the fulfilment of war and battle once again. That or be destroyed by the terror of it.

"Very well, you can come back with me. Arguing with you is pointless. You know how to sway me too easily. It's a dangerous skill to have, you shouldn't abuse it," the knight joked as he took her hand and placed it on his chest. She gave the man a sly smirk and began to caress his neck with light kisses.

"Shall I tend to your wounds, my valiant knight?" Fifonia teased. She slipped her body above his, her red locks covering his face. His large hand grasped the side of her soft face and pulled her into a kiss.

This is no war.'

* * *

Chapter VIII
Shadows in the Night
~Rayar~

The skies were filled with snowflakes idly dancing in the icy winds in their descent towards the earth. The point of the mountain touched the very boundaries of heaven itself. A searing light filled the landscape, reflecting off the snow covered stone. It was not cold though; there was warmth without a source filling the sky. The clouds were also below the mountain top yet the snowflakes still fell from above, from a pure blue sky. It was an abnormal sight to say the least. Rayar found himself perched on the side of the very tip overlooking the sea of clouds. In the far distance there was another mountain. There was one thing he noticed on the opposite mountain top. A figure sitting in the snow, dressed in black. It was so far away he could not even be sure it was a person but the way it stared directly at him sent a chill down his spine. Behind the second mountain a red mist absorbed the clouds and seemed to be ever so slowly advancing towards him. At the rate it was going, it would probably not reach himself for years but one day he would be consumed. He tried to call out from his sitting position to warn the other figure of the mist which slithered like a snake towards his back but no words came out. Just then the flapping of wings echoed around him. They sounded so heavy the sheer noise could crack the world in two. A hawk swooped from the blue sky and landed on the tip of the mountain beside him. He looked around to study the bird of prey curiously. It stared back at him, the sharp eyes judging him ruthlessly. Rayar's necklace with the pearl amulet reflecting the light of the beaming sun, hung around its neck. A voice whispered in his mind, as the pair continued to stare at each other but the words were so jumbled he could not make heads or tails of it. As if in a fit of anger, the bird shot towards his face screaming at the top of its lungs. In the screech of the creature he heard a single word.

"Wake!"

Rayar awoke abruptly to the sensation of being violently shaken and a voice repeatedly saying 'wake up', over and over. It took him a few moments to realise what was going on but once he had woken up properly he started to make sense of what was happening. Nymin knelt over him with her hands on his shoulders shaking him violently. Her face was one of fear and uncertainty, her eyes screamed as loud as her voice to rouse her brother. It was not only her voice that was loud though, the sounds from outside his room were just as disturbing. It sounded like there was some sort of commotion erupting from the hallway and other rooms.

"Rayar, get up!" Nymin yelped as she thumped his chest. Her eyes were watery now, fear had truly taken her. He may not have been the sharpest blade in the armoury, but even he could figure out there was fighting occurring. He quickly rolled out of his bed knocking his sister aside accidently in the hurry and grabbed his clothes.

"What's happening Nymin!?" He barked in question while pulling some slacks and his long red coat over his sleeping wear. The short princess fumbled back to her feet and ran to his side with her fingers clutched into his coat. She looked up to him.

"I don't know. All these men in black cloaks and armour came out of nowhere and began attacking everyone. I could not get to mother and fathers room with so many around so I ran here," Rayar nodded as he listened. The castle being attacked like this was unbelievable. They were in the royal quarters already which meant they had found a way to sneak inside, or all the guards on the outside were already dead. He was not prepared for this kind of thing, not by a long shot. On the other hand Nymin was here. He would protect her, this was more important than his own nerves. Than is own life.

"It will be alright Nymin. Just stay by my side, we have to find everyone else and make sure they are unharmed." By the sounds of the fighting outside they were getting closer and closer to his chambers. Rayar quickly jogged over to the stand above his stone fire place and drew a long one sided blade from its sheath. He refused to give in. His lessons with Hinsani were precisely for this kind of situation. To protect what is important to you. The screams of men dying filled the chamber. They were close. His little sister trembled at the gruesome noises and clutched the bed sheets between her fingers.

"Let's hide Rayar!" He felt the same but knew it would be futile. "Under the bed and wait for them to go away!" He shook his head quickly in response and grabbed her by the wrist. There was no time to waste.

"They would find us. We have to get you to safety," yet where would safety be? Even though he wanted to crawl under the covers and hide, he had to wear the brave face for Nymin. There was no choice. By his lead, the pair burst through the doorway to find the rest of the family and to get to safety. The smell was horrific and the sounds were even worse. They could hear swords clashing all over the keep. Rayar had never experienced anything like this before, his only experience being the stories told to him by Rumeo and sometimes even Hyar. To think the royal chambers could be raided and everyone killed. The thoughts were quickly slammed aside so he could focus on the current dire situation, hindsight could come later. That is if there was a later to come.

"Found two!" a man yelled from behind them. Rayar glanced back to see the demons his sister spoke of. They were dressed in dark armour with long black cloaks and helmets that covered most of their face. The collar of their cloaks was trimmed with fur. Each carried a long sword that dripped with blood.

"Above and Below, run Nymin!" he yelled. The pair sprinted down the hallway deeper into the royal quarters. The clanging of metal on stone kept him in the knowledge they were being chased. The pair skidded around a corner and began to descend down a flight of stairs towards the great hall. Another curse escaped him as he noticed Nymin beginning to fall behind. It was foolish to think she could run as fast as him or even as fast as the attackers in her current state. He yanked the girl into his arms being careful with the blade in his grasp and continued his escape with the extra weight. Tears rolled down her cheeks in terror, the mens' shouting unnerving them even more. They turned another corner and another and another trying to lose their pursuers but to no avail. Matters only got worse as they turned towards the great hall, only to see another pair of black cloaked soldiers ending the lives of two Heldoran guardsmen.

"Royal children?" one said as he cleaned his blade. The other began to walk towards them.

"Saves us the trouble of looking for them," Rayar leapt back and turned on his heel to escape but was blocked by the previous two coming down the hallway. The only option was the kitchen. He hurried in but misfortune struck at the worst moment. In his sprint he tripped on a loose tile in the floor and flopped forwards. Nymin flew from his arms and rolled along the ground while he slammed face first into the stone floor. The impact caused him to be stunned for a few moments as well as to lose a grip on his blade. His hand stretched out as he sought the blade but the sound of the metal boots closing in on him stole his attention. "Foolish boy," one soldier said standing right above him. Rayar had one chance at this. His fingers touched the handle of his blade and he wasted no time turning onto his back and thrusting it upwards. It worked. The intruder had been swinging down at the same time but his torso had caught the length of the blade and halted his strike mid-air. The pain was too much and he fell to the side in a ball, moaning in agony. Rayar leapt to his feet like a cornered wolf and held his blade in a stance he could recall.

'The Lion Stalks,' he thought to himself as he held the position. The basic Blade Dance Hinsani had taught him. He held the sword with both hands, turned diagonally in front of his chest while slightly pointing it forwards. His legs were spread and knees bent for support. One of the attackers burst into laughter, half at the prince's attempt to resist them and half at his foolish fellow's death.

"If we waste too much time, Vasca will have our heads on spikes. Put the royal brat down." More black cloaked soldiers came in through the kitchen entrance, all with blades stained with their conquests blood. Sweat trickled down his skin; their numbers were too high. It did not make sense. How could this many armoured warriors get into the centre of the keep unheard. Perhaps Heldon really had fallen and he was facing an army. It did not matter how many there were, nor how afraid he was, for he had to protect Nymin. That was his duty now. The young princess was curled up in the corner, watching the events unfold.

'I am sorry Nymin. I am so sorry,' he could not bring himself to say the words. They began their advance on the pair of royalty. The talkative one took the head of the pack with his sword in the air. Once in range he swung it downwards. Rayar did not believe he had the ability to defend against such a horde. He raised his blade as best he could with his eyes accidently yet instinctively closing tightly, to prepare for an oncoming strike. There was indeed the clang of metal but not from his sword with the soldiers.

"Open your eyes Prince Rayar," a familiar voice sounded. The prince slowly opened his eyes and looked over towards its direction. From the great halls entrance to the kitchen, three men stood in a line. In the centre the man who spoke. Hinsani held a stern stance with his blade soaked in blood as well as blood speckled on his leather attire. His expression was as heavy as always, he clearly was not impressed by the turn of events and the attack of the keep. Beside him stood Hyar

Dedred wielding his famous axe in the same state as his companion's sword and his small buckler shield riddled with dents. Lastly Raimon Bren, Ayla's personal Royal Blade and the one who had saved the prince with a thrown knife which now stuck in the wall between them. He was young, the same age as himself with shoulder length brown hair and a narrow face. He also wore the Royal Blade leather attire.

"It's good to see you alive and well Rayar, Nymin. Your sisters have already been taken to safety; we came looking for you," Hyar said as he ran a hand over his golden beard. Relief filled his face at those words. They were alright, there was no better news. Then it hit him. He said sisters, not entire family.

"What about mother and father?" he asked fearing the worst.

"Not yet but…," Raimon began to answer but was cut off by Hinsani.

"Enough. There is a battle. Words can come later. Raimon take them to the others. I and Hyar are more than enough for these whelps." One self-appointed leader of the band of intruders sneered at the insult and turned his sword towards the new arrivals.

"Whelps eh? Bring that arrogance over here and I shall gladly shave it away!" Hinsani slipped into a more complicated Blade Dance, one Rayar had never seen. Before the black cloaked warriors could respond, he was upon them like a whirlwind of sword and death. He cut through the first few like ribbons who had no idea how to react but by then, the others had realised they needed to defend themselves and quickly returned the assault. Hyar strode very calmly towards the fray, giving himself enough time to nod encouragingly towards the prince. Raimon snared up Nymin and grabbed Rayar.

"Then let us make haste," he stated. The group sped out the back door leaving the two expert warriors in battle with the high number of armoured soldiers.

They ran at a steady pace through the stone covered corridor. Rayar could nor help but feel guilty for leaving both

Hinsani and Hyar with the attackers, yet at the same time he had complete faith in their ability to handle themselves. Nymin seemed to have calmed down now that Raimon had appeared. He may have been the newest Royal Blade, but his skills were certainly not lacking. The prince still had concerns about the situation and decided to voice them.

"Do you know what is happening?" the brown haired swordsman gave his head a small shake.

"The keep is under attack from the inside and the gates were barred stopping any reinforcements from coming in. That has recently been remedied. It will not be long before the rest of the Heldon Guard pour into the keep and dispatch everything that poses a threat. That is if Hinsani and Hyar don't kill them all first," Rayar frowned at this. From the inside meant that they had to have snuck in.

"How did they get in?" he reluctantly asked. Raimon sniffed.

"They were let in," his eyes widened in disbelief. Someone on the inside let them in. That was no simple task, which likely meant, that it was someone who lived in the keep. That was a suspicion of his anyway, for there was no proof. By the swordsman's tone, it could very likely be the correct one.

"I'll loot all I want, don't boss me around you filthy crow!" the group stopped in their tracks at the booming sound. From a doorway ahead of them two figures emerged. One was tall and muscular with the same black armour as the intruders, yet with less clothing revealing his toned physique. He wore a horned helmet with a heavy bear fur cloak and had a giant beard that reached down over his chest. The most terrifying aspect of this person was the gigantic axe he had slung over his shoulder. By the looks of bag full of gold in his grasp, they had just exited the treasury. The man beside him was slender and pale skinned. He wore a black coat with a collar that reached up to his ears and the bottom hung down to his knees. His hair was as black as the night, tied into a pony tail. He had a strikingly gaunt face with eyes that could cut with more edge than a sword.

"You are too loud Shan. Simply take what we have come for and we can insert the last seed of destruction into this pathetic country. I grow weary of your greed. The Second Coming will reward you with more than you can imagine. Do not forget that." The barbarian grunted at his counterpart's wisdom before he turned towards the group. Rayar noticed that Raimon had already drawn his sword and was preparing for battle.

"Looks like you were right again. They came right this way. You're always right about this kind of thing Vasca. It's damn queer," retorted Shan. The monster of a man stalked towards the trio without any concern that a Royal Blade stood before him.

"If the soldiers failed, it was simple calculation," the robed man replied to the brute while he calmly watched from the sidelines. He had his hands clasped behind his back in a noble manner of standing. It was even more peculiar than the beast advancing on them.

"I will not let you pass. Stand back Granlias," the pair clashed violently. Sword danced on axe, like a fox testing a bull. His agility was what he had to work with against the overpowering strength of his enemy. Life and death hung in the balance, their lives rested in this man's blade. Rayar held his own one sided sword out in front of him while he defended Nymin.

'If Raimon is defeated then what chance do I possibly have!?' He was struggling to find the light at the end of the tunnel.

"Get out of the way worm!" the man who had been named Shan, roared. His axe pushed clean past the sword and forced Raimon into the wall. Then he hacked mercilessly into the wall once again, crushing the swordsman like jelly. Nymin screeched so loudly it felt as if Rayar's ears would bleed, but it was quickly cut off by her own hands covering her mouth. The man they placed their trust in had been destroyed. Now nothing stood between them and certain death. His mouth felt dry, seeing the shadow of the beast like man looming over him and his sister. He held steadfast with his sword out, prepared to do battle.

"This is the one, right?" the brute asked. The slender character watched emotionlessly.

"He is the one," the bearded man wore a sinister grin and knocked the blade aside with the tip of his axe. With speed Rayar could barely follow, a large hand grasped his neck and slammed him into the wall beside the slumped body of Ayla's former protector. The wind was knocked out of him in an instant, leaving him a helpless limp form at the whim of the barbarian. He could hear Nymin calling out his name in the distance or at least it sounded distant. The barbarians other hand, awkwardly holding the axes grip, began to glow a dark spine tingling shade as it pinched his pearl between its' fingers. The hairy man began to sweat and strain uncontrollably with effort, as if lifting a boulder on his shoulders. Eventually he pried the pearl off the chain and tossed it to Vasca before letting out a long breath of relief. The dark coated man snatched it in midair and gave it an inquisitive investigation.

"All of it is in here then. It makes our job much easier than carrying a person all the way to the Grove. The body is irrelevant then, destroy him just to be safe," Shan's grin only spread in the knowledge he would be causing more loss of life. Rayar stared at him intensely with all his resolve, his sharp green eyes locked in a visual battle with the brute's. The battle inconsequential, as it would not be the glare of his eyes to end the prince's life. The mammoth hand clutched around his throat, gripping so tightly he felt that his face would burst. The feeling was horrible. He could barely think straight to resist and the lack of air was causing his body to react in a pointless struggle that did nothing to halt his attacker's actions. All he heard was the screech of a hawk followed by the other man calling out 'Shan' before air started to return to his lungs. The grip on his throat hand vanished and even the shadow of the man had moved away. Rayar coughed heavily after he collapsed onto his hands and knees.

"Rayar!" Nymin yelped. "Are you alright!?" the obvious answer would have been simply no but he still felt as if he had to put on a brave face for his sister.

"I will be fine…," he was able to croak out. He could only raise his gaze slightly but it seemed they had once again been saved before it was fatal. This time the saviour was unknown to him. In front of him stood a small figure draped in a thick, earthy hooded cloak. The figure held a regular sword in their grasp and a hawk sat upon their shoulder. Why they had been saved by this unknown person could wait, he was simply thankful they had been spared from the same fate was Raimon. Somehow the hooded figure had been able to force back both intruders, giving them some much needed distance from them.

"Didn't see that coming did you?" the brute teased his friend. "Not as all knowing as you would like to think." The taunts did not change the emotionless look on the slender man's face. His glare was only for the disrupter.

"Is that what you think, Shan?" the corridor suddenly felt heavy. An invisible force weighed down on his shoulders, a feeling of dread. It was not immobilizing but simply stomach churning. Rayar was able to push himself back to his feet and move defensively in front of Nymin who was at this point completely beside herself. She had seen death before; Rayar knew that much but to see Raimon die in such a way would easily put a strain on her. A light grabbed his attention back to the one named Vasca as the glow formed in his hand, now aimed towards them. What he witnessed next was unimaginable. A wave of energy burst from his palm towards them, tearing up the walls and ground on either side as it charged through the corridor. The golden haired prince could only stare wide eyed as it came closer and closer. Judging by the damage it was doing to the stone, it was unimaginable what it could do to them.

"Mages…," the hooded figure said, whilst raising a hand towards the oncoming blast. The air around them began to heat up as the flames upon torches along the wall danced like fireflies and finally shot into the figures hand; the flames erupted from their arm and catapulted forward to intercept the magical blast. The impact of the fire and energy shook the foundation of the castle. This kind of immense power was something Rayar had never witnessed in his life. He dropped back onto his behind in a very ungraceful manner befitting a prince and watched in complete awe. He saw through the flickers of the flames, the pair taking their leave from the battlefield.

"They are leaving!" The hooded figure did not respond and only continued to push back the magical power that the black coated man had thrown upon them. A few more moments passed and the flames died down to a gentle flicker. The danger had been avoided. The mysterious men had also escaped but this was something Rayar was not too broken up over. Once again the prince had to push himself back onto his feet. He gave his clothes a quick dusting down before making sure Nymin was as well as she could be. She did not look great, barely standing at all.

"They took the sphere," the hooded figure said, though did not bother to turn and address him. Their arrival out of nowhere was certainly peculiar, yet he was not about to complain after being rescued. Courtesy at least was required.

"Thank you for saving us. I do not know who you are or what power you wield but I am eternally grateful for your assistance. I am Rayar and this is my sister Nymin. We should probably get moving as there will be more of them." The hooded figure finally turned to him and pulled down the mask covering the lower half of their face. Much to his surprise it was a woman and a rather stunning one at that, in her own way. Her eyes were a deep sea blue with the same sharpness he had been complimented for. Strands of her chestnut hair draped from her forehead toning well with her skin that had clearly seen much of the sun. Those thoughtful eyes stared at his own for a brief time before they wandered down to his chest, locked onto where the pearl on his chain once sat. This alerted Rayar to the fact it had actually been stolen by that oaf.

"That ox of a man took it...," the thought filled him with anger. That pearl had been all he had from his old home and from his old family before being adopted into the Granlia House. To have it snatched by some criminal was a hard blow. The woman who had saved them only sniffed at his comment, before she turned on her heel.

"Come. We're leaving. Leave the girl." This certainly turned sour fast. The prince raised a brow in defiance. Being ordered by a stranger was not something he was used to.

"The only place I am going to is safety and I am not leaving my sister. What you say is ludicrous." By her glare back to him, he could tell she was not impressed by his stubbornness. Nymin clung to his hand doing her best to regain some composure.

"Let us get out of the keep and find Ayla and Nyer at least. They will know what to do."

"Do not make this difficult," the cloaked woman interjected. She sheathed her sword into her belt and adjusted her gloves. After she threw fire around like a toy, who knew what else she could do.

"Rayar, Nymin!" those words filled his heart with hope. From dowm the path they had come, their mother was running towards them, her fingers held up her clothing as she did her best to run in a long nightgown. Beside her a court maid did her best to keep up. Nymin rushed towards her and the pair grappled into a tremendous hug. Rayar was not far behind with his arms wrapped around the pair of them

"I was so worried. It gives me light to see you are both alive. What about Ayla and Nyer?" The youngest Granlia buried her face into her mothers shoulder with tears staining the gown.

"They are safe mother, but... but...," she could not bear to say the words nor did she need to. Julian saw the bloody form of the Royal Blade against the wall.

"Oh Above and Below, Raimon." Next she ran her gaze over to the cloaked woman who was simply watching them from afar. Her body tensed in Rayar's arms causing him to lean back, in question.

"You are one of the druidae, are you not?" The woman only nodded in reply. "And did he, Quale, send you?" Once again the woman nodded. By the looks of it she was not much of a talker.

"What is this about mother, do you know her?" he asked. Julian wiped a tear from her eye as she gazed up to her son with a warming look.

"There is much you do not know, my dear. So much, I could not have enough time in my lifetime to reveal it all to you. If she has come to take you as I assume she has, then you must go. These men here today, came for you. The only man who will have answers is Quale." Nervous laughter escaped the prince as he looked between everyone present.

"Quale? Druidae? All this is nonsense. Why would they come for me...?" Julian gave her head a light shake and stroked his cheek once more.

"I am so sorry for everything. No matter what happens you are my son. You are Rumeo's son. We love you with all our hearts. There is something at work here bigger than us all. You cannot stay here any longer. Not just for us but for yourself. Go with her and promise me you will listen to what Quale has to say. Promise me this Rayar!" She seemed to be getting more and more agitated, to the point of pushing him towards the druidae, while her voice was stern and frustrated. Though the pain it was causing her to let him go was devastating for them both.

"No, mother. I cannot simply leave while the keep is in such a state. How could I possibly leave you in danger?" He would not give up without a fight.

"Son, the Royal Blades and our men will have secured the keep in no time, it is their duty. Have a little faith in my own motherly methods of protecting my children too and do as your mother tells you. I shall ask again. Promise me, Rayar." He could not help but sigh as he moved away from his family's arms and towards the woman who would control his fate.

"Very well. I shall go to this man you speak of. Tell father not to worry, and Ayla… and everyone that I shall return shortly. If this will keep the rest of you safe, then I will do what I must." The words were hard to release from his throat. He could not help but wonder if that was something Hinsani would say. Leaving for the greater good of others; it was both a terrifying and exciting thought to be away from the city. He prayed he was not making a grave mistake by throwing his lot in with a woman who he had just met, after such a catastrophic event. From time to time he had been called reckless and impulsive; he could actually see what they were saying after this. Julian smiled weakly with satisfaction at his choice. She had nurtured him since he was a baby, with much love. If she was this adamant for him to fly into the wind, then it was surely of great importance, which only strengthened his resolve and self-belief in his decision.

"Everything will be clear. Niyla here will slip you out of the castle. Take horses from the stables. You must leave unnoticed as being a prince, the guards will stop you to protect you. Hinsani surely will." Rayar trusted his mother. He always had. Even now, when her cryptic words led him down a path of the unknown it felt like the right course of action. For what reason he needed to leave without being detected, was a much larger concern on his mind. For the safety of his family and for his own answers, there was no other option.

"Come, I shall show you the basement and the way out," Niyla, the Queens maid said in a soft and nervous voice. They simply followed her directions but not before the hawk that had calmly been sitting on this druidae's shoulder up to that point, shot off like an arrow and spiralled out of the nearest window. Both the prince and the druidae disappeared into the depths of the keep, to leave unannounced.

*

~*Julian*~

"Please don't cry," Nymin said as she wrapped her arms around Julian once again, even tighter than before. Tears rolled down the queens cheeks as the sadness of pressuring Rayar to go, weighed down on her. There was no choice, if he was to survive. She knew from the bottom of her heart, she had done the right thing.

"I will be alright my dear. Come, let us reach your sisters," she said. Nymin stopped her in her tracks.

"Wait, what about father?" she asked. Julian smiled a nervous, but motherly smile, and patted the girl's hair.

"He is fine. Don't you worry." She shielded her daughter's eyes from Raimon's body and continued towards the door to the keep's courtyard. The princess tightly clutched her mother's gown in her fingers, her eyes too wet with sorrow to lead herself.

"I could not do anything mother. Rayar was in trouble, Raimon was in peril and all I could do was sit and watch. I could not do a single thing to help. I am so weak...," the sudden maturity was a surprise in itself. Julian moved in front of her daughter and knelt before her. She gave Nymin a reassuring look as she spoke.

"You are not weak. You are a Granlia. When we experience fear for the first time, there is little we can do. Courage comes from self belief and there is no believing in yourself, when you think you are weak. No, my dear, you are strong. You will be the strongest woman I can imagine. I know it." Even in these dark times, the motivational lecture placed a light smile on the lips of the young princess. They wasted no more time in their advance towards the keep's exit, but before they could reach it, dozens upon dozens of Heldon guardsman, armoured and armed to the teeth, came pouring in. They instantly moved into a defensive formation around the pair, with the narrow faced Captain, known as Caidarian Kinsani, bowing at the waist.

"Your majesty, your grace. I apologise with all my honour on the delay. We shall secure the keep at once. Please head outside and join your daughters out of harm's way," she smiled warmly and nodded in thanks to the Captain.

"Hold," the king commanded as he strode towards the group. Caidarian bowed again to his king. Julian glanced over her shoulder to catch him in the corner of her eye, her face turned as white as snow. Rumeo held a sword in his hand, stained with the blood of the intruders.

"Captain, take my daughter outside, the rest of you clean up my castle. The bodies cluttering up the keep are an eye sore," Caidarian's mouth dropped and she knew why. Rumeo was known throughout the kingdom as a kind and just king. This sight was extremely irregular for him.

"Y... Yes Your Grace, right away. Your grace," he bowed respectfully to the young princess who seemed as puzzled as the guardsman. Her father had not even passed her a glance. Warily she followed the captain out of the keep, giving her mother an encouraging smile as she departed. The thought of being with her sisters again must have given her strength. The rest of the guardsman jogged in formation, into the keep leaving the king and queen alone in the hallway.

"Where is the boy?" he asked with a sharp tongue. Julian finally built up the strength to face him with her head held high.

"He is gone. You will not be able to do him harm." Rumeo muttered under his breath and shot out a hand to grab her face. His fingers and thumb pressed into her cheeks and held her in place.

"Shame, though things worked out well regardless. Now, you are lucky I do not dismember you where you stand. No, I have a better solution for you." Before she knew it, she could feel her energy being drained from her body. Everything was becoming cold and dark, her blood felt like it had frozen and she felt too weak to even speak. As the shadow began to overtake her she caught one last glimpse of her husband's mad eyes. The sight of him did more damage than anything he could physically do to her.

'*My love I am so sorry. I wish I could have saved you,*' were her last thoughts. Everything went dark.

* * *

Chapter IX
The Path to Summerfall
~*Rayar*~

The city of Heldon grew further and further away as Rayar and the druidae trotted on horseback towards the northern forest of Summerfall. After they had slipped through the keeps basement and under the city to an inn stables, the cloaked woman took the lead. They had barely spoken to one another since leaving Heldon; they rode in silence with the prince looking for the right words to say. He had already figured her to be the rather quiet type, so he would not have been surprised if she was happy to remain in this state for the entire journey. Then it struck him. He knew nothing of where this journey would take them, how far they would go or how long it would take. This truly was a leap of faith. He had not even packed any food or clean clothes; he was still in his sleeping wear covered only by a long red coat. It was cold and eerie on the country road in the middle of the night. He could barely see the scenery around him, but the smells and sounds were present and clear. This was nature outside the castle walls. It was freeing to witness it in person, something he had longed for. After one last glance back towards the shadowy city, he thought about everything he was leaving behind. His family, his home, what he knew. As upsetting as it was, the spark of adventure grew in his soul. This had been what he wanted for a while and now it was actually happening. While the details of why were not yet known to him, half the adventure was discovering them.

"I was surprised," she unexpectedly said. Perhaps he was wrong and she was feeling as awkward as him. Her voice was strong but soothing with a hint of an accent he did not recognise.

"By what?" he naturally asked. The woman looked back to him with a serious expression. It was almost as hard as Hinsani's.

"That you came. You have been living a life of luxury, wealth and safety. You took the risk to go with me on your mother's word. You don't know me; you don't know anything really. Do you think this was the right call?" It was a good question. To leave just after an attack on your home and family did not completely make sense. He was also curious as to why, yet something inside him screamed that this was the right road to take. When he argued before he was simply delaying what he knew he would choose.

"I trust Julian, my mother. She would not have pleaded so profoundly if she had any doubt in me leaving. This is the right choice I have made. It is not only what she said, that has driven me to find this man Quale, but to keep the ones I care about safe. I wish to learn more and prevent such an act occurring again. I would be a selfish fool to go against the wisdom of the Queen as well as the compass of my heart. They will remain safe, I know it. Father will look after them and Ayla will be heading to Hextheene soon anyway. Once I have unburdened my home of this danger, I can return. Who knows? Prince or not, a Granlia must do their duty," he spoke with confidence but the nerves seeped through the cracks. It was a big decision to make, in such a short space of time. In his little speech, he could almost sense her rolling her eyes at his "compass" comment. He felt a little silly after that.

"The greatest choices are made in an instant," she stated, as if she sensed his discomfort. Rayar took a deep breath and agreed. He would continue to follow his instinct.

"I am Prince Rayar Granlia by the way, if you did not already know," he finally introduced himself. They had gone all this way already and had yet to even trade names.

"I know," her reply was quick.

"And... yourself, you have a name?" this was more difficult than a lunch alone with Nyer.

"Shania." That was not so hard was it? He nodded respectfully to her.

"A pleasure Shania, you do not have to call me Prince Rayar if you like, Rayar is fine."

"I would have called you Rayar anyway." The golden blonde boy wrinkled his nose with annoyance before letting out a sigh. This would certainly be a challenge.

The two travelled through the night along the country road that led to a small farming village, half way between the city and the lush forest. Fields of produce stretched out for miles around them, with specs of buildings spotted about the hillsides. They all gradually clustered together, along the dirt road forming the village of Summerfall. This was the main source of food for the nation and even supplied some of Hextheene with trade. The young prince had never ventured from the castle, so this far from the walls was something he was completely unfamiliar with. The darkness had overtaken the sky and the lights of the village were all that guided their way. The pair began to pass through the village and came upon the inn. It was a husky old place; the sound of banter echoed from the hall and the smell of alcohol was ever present. He let out a small sigh at the thought of staying in a place of this standard, as it was foul to say the least. The rest of the village was somewhat more pleasant yet the inn attracted the hard working men of the fields, who needed to release their stress before returning to their families. Drinking seemed to be the biggest method of such. As he began to dismount, the druidae suddenly trotted up against him and her hand held him firmly in place.

"You're not going inside. This is only a brief stop," she commanded. He could only blink in surprise. Once again he had been put back in his place by this woman. Her air of control far exceeded that of most other woman he had met. Perhaps it even matched Nyer and that was saying a lot.

"Oh," he coughed. "Why are we here then?" The prince did not feel like a prince at all, more like a lost puppy. The druidae gracefully dismounted her horse and strode towards the inn doorway. There was no reply, simply an assumption he would do as he was told. Rayar waited patiently from horseback. Due to the time of night, not many villagers were walking around, which made it all the more eerie. In the courtyard of Heldon, there seemed always to be people around, night or day, other members of the court of guardsman. Here seemed desolate; the only reassurance was the noise from the tavern that surprisingly gave him comfort.

'I am just to wait here. Above and Below, I am not some bloody dog,' he complained to himself yet remained sat upon his horse waiting. A few minutes passed by, before Shania returned from the tavern with clothes over her shoulder; a previously white shirt, now with a brownish tint due to continuous wear, dark brown trousers and finally a hooded cloak. Rayar blinked in surprise at what she had gathered up. Was that for him? Shania smoothly returned to her horse that had also waited without issue for her return and she threw the garbs onto his lap.

"Can't have you running around in sleep wear," she stated. Rayar blinked again and inspected his new attire. It was not particularly what he was used to. The clothes he tended to wear were usually a lot more colourful and regal but at least he had brought his long red jacket with him. As he knew it was pointless to argue, he simply nodded and followed her further down the pass, towards the northern exit of the town. As they trotted back into the fields and towards a small area of wilderness close to the village, he rested his hand casually on the hilt of his sword at his hip. Having a hand on his sword somehow made him feel a little less vulnerable in his current situation, almost like a safety blanket. He would never admit it, but the woman slowly riding ahead of him, made him feel somewhat nervous. The more time that passed and the more he regained his composure from the fighting in Heldon, the more he felt uneasy.

'Am I having second thoughts already? What would father say in this situation. Follow your heart? Strap up and man up? No, that is more something Nymin would have said. He would say... You are a Granlia. There is nothing you cannot handle.' A quiet sigh escaped his lips causing Shania to very briefly turn her head, but she remained silent. So the quiet journey would continue.

It was not long before they reached a small wooded area, still within sight of the village Summerfall. It was here Shania stopped and dismounted. Rayar followed suit. He tied the reins to a nearby branch to keep the horses in place and gave the area she had chosen a look over. It was surrounded by trees with a small green stained pond in the centre. It was quite serene, in fact he felt almost at home here, which he found very peculiar. The trees were a lush green, with baby blue flowers dotted throughout the hideaway. His attention turned to his companion, who had removed her long earthy cloak. Under it she wore a long sleeved shirt tucked into brown trousers with knee high brown boots, the stitching along both sides of the legs, up to her hip. Her arming sword was safely in its scabbard but found its way to the ground as she undid her belt setting it aside against a fallen log near the pond. Also under her cloak, that now came to light, was a small pack, a rolled up fur sheet, tied to the base of her spine. That too was removed from her body; she detached the sheet and laid it on the grass. Shania's sharp gaze shot to Rayar, as piercing as ever, giving more commands.

"Sleep here for a couple of hours before we move on." He would not be the gentleman he was, if he did not offer the sheet to the lady, as it was clear she only had one.

"My Lady-," The words were swiftly cut off.

"I am not a lady. I will keep watch with Jac," Rayar cocked a brow. Who was Jac? Just then she motioned up to the trees and perched on a branch, was the hawk that had accompanied her back in Heldon.

"You named it Jac?" He asked.

"His name is Jac," she quickly corrected him. The bird was a majestic animal; its eyes almost seemed the same as Shania's. Perhaps not even almost, they had the same sharpness to them but then that is where the saying came from, the prince supposed; 'eyes of a hawk'.

"Really I do not mind, I can sleep in the grass if I have to," he tried again; he would not give up his gentlemanly ways that easily. Shania sighed in annoyance and sat cross legged on the log beside them, her hand finding its way to the pommel of her sword.

"This is the best bedding I can do. You won't be sleeping in any fancy royal beds for a while. Now sleep, I'm only giving you a couple of hours." She was too stubborn. Bloody stubborn. Rayar shrugged in defeat and removed his long red jacket to use as a pillow. He had taken naps in the royal gardens back in Heldon but this was somewhat wilder than he had ever experienced. His one edged sword found its place next to him on the floor. He would want that nearby, just in case.

"Fine My La... Miss Shania. Tomorrow I want to hear more about who you are and what exactly is going on. Mother called you a druidae but as far as I know and what everyone I have ever met says, that is nothing but a myth. I cannot say I believe it myth after what I saw you do, but... having you lead me somewhere is one thing, but being led there blind, is entirely different." This time he would be stubborn. He was a rather laid back man, he had always been told, but even he had limits to his patience. Shania watched him for a moment; he could tell by her expression she was calculating the risks of telling him anything. After a brief pause she gave him a small piece of satisfaction with a nod.

"Agreed," with that he offered her a smile. It was not returned. Sleep came to him quickly, quicker than he could imagine it would. After the events at home, his body and mind were exhausted.

The world around Rayar was distorted. The ground at his feet swayed like a leaf in the wind. The walls around him curved in and out, unable to remain still. Colours around him did not stay the same for longer than a second. Everything seemed blurry but crystal at the same time. Lanterns periodically ran down the wall, moving in formation but attached to keep the hall he was in well lit, the shadows passing over and over as if in a whirlwind of darkness and light. The young prince however, could easily keep his footing in the maelstrom of illogical events around him. He moved with the ground and the walls, his body stretching and flapping like he was part of the scenery. He felt his stomach heave; he wanted to be sick. The feeling was overwhelming, but every time he tried, he could only cough in pain.

'A nightmare, this has to be a nightmare!' he thought in a panic trying to regain some composure.

"Who are you?" a voice echoed from across the hall. Startled, Rayar gasped and felt he almost had a heart attack as he shot his eyes towards the sound of the voice. Across the room of illusions a man sat in a throne. The throne was high backed with red velvet over the back and arm rests. It stood taller than the one in Heldon and was seemingly made completely of gold. Unlike himself, the man was stable in this room. He was not part of the madness around them and remained calm and composed upon his throne. He had the appearance like no other man the prince had ever seen. His hair was as black as a crow, smoothly pushed back with long strands hanging down over his eyes. Those eyes seemed familiar. They filled the room with a golden glare, the pupils white with dread, as pale as his skin. He wore a black coat, the trims, sleeves and collar all torn and cut from age and use. In fact he was entirely encased in black, from his boots to his gloves. Rayar tried to speak but his words turned to ash.

"I cannot believe I have a visitor and so soon after the last. My, my who was it? A woman, stunning creature, felt like she was only here yesterday. Yet before her, it felt like a century since I last saw another's face. Haha, of course it was longer, maybe less. You lose track of time in this place. So, who are you again?" the man asked with a sniff towards Rayar. "You smell like her." His tongue slithered like a snake, his accent was so strong it was hard to understand him. The words danced and flowed as if he was an expert in the language but it was not his first. One of the most terrifying things about this man before him was the smirk that never seemed to leave his lips. Rayar tried to speak once more, but as he did, ash filled his mouth causing him to cough silently. The figure on the throne ran his long slender fingers over the arm rest, as Rayar could feel himself being sized up. The pressure from the dark robed man caused his body to twist and turn, the life from him being toyed and fondled with, just with his eyes. It was painful, too painful.

"Cannot talk?" this seemed to displease the sitting figure. "Shame. The woman could. She was a lot more interesting. We chatted for what felt like years. Or was it minutes. Who knows anymore? To have two beings visit me in such a small space of time, perhaps means my reunion is getting closer." Rayar watched him speak with a fearful expression on his own face. What in Below was happening? Was this a nightmare or had he been killed and awoken in the World Below. Nothing made any sense. Not the walls, the floor, anything around him; not even his own body. He was a wave in a series of turning tides, never able to remain still but never able to move. It was torture.

"Seems like you are at your limit, boy. I did hope you would focus yourself and give me some of your time but I am not that lucky it seems. It is always nice to hear a bit about the world in my absence. Well, if you are here to make contact with the reunion, keep up the good work. If you are unlucky enough to be here by accident, well, I will be seeing you soon and will not be restricted to my cage. If there are any Hextors left in the world of the living, let them know I will be coming for them soon. Ta-ta!" Suddenly a void surrounded them and began to suck everything into the abyss. The colours were ripped into the black abyss first followed shortly after by the room itself. Rayar screamed a silent scream, ash pouring from his lungs. The last thing he saw before it all went black, was a glowing blue light in the darkness and a giant tree above it, the largest tree he had ever seen, yet the tree was covered in ash.

'Help...'

"ARGH!" Rayar screamed as he shot up from the grass. His entire body shook ferociously while covered in a thick layer of sweat. Breath after breath was more difficult to catch than chasing a rodent. His green eyes faced forward unable to gather the world around him, blank eyed and blank faced. Something pulled him back into reality. A soft hand touched his bare shoulder. The prince looked over to see Shania kneeling beside him with her hand on his flesh and a piercing gaze staring straight into him.

"What happened?" she commanded. Rayar could not answer. He could only pant over and over like an overworked hound. The young woman gave him a shake to try and fully return him back to the world of the living. "Rayar! Calm yourself!" The voice snapped his consciousness back. The breath returned and his body slumped down as his muscles loosened.

"I saw... I do not even know what I saw. I can't... I can't focus. A man... I remember a man in a chair. The world was like a nightmare consuming me entirely. Above and bloody Below... I have never felt anything as... murderous as that," he could barely describe that his mind just unfolded to him. It was more than a dream, more than a nightmare. It was like the very fabric of reality was spiralling out of control in that world.

"The sooner we get to Quale the better. Can't have you going mad before we reach him. He'll give you the answers I can't." Her voice was demanding but he could sense an air of concern in her words. After knowing her for such a short time, it felt strange to sense that from her.

"Right... Quale... I will do my best... Sorry if I startled you... I just. A nightmare like that, I never...," Shania released her grip on him and turned back to her log, to perch upon much like her hawk.

"Don't worry about it. It's over now. Just rest as best you can. We continue on soon, at dawn break." He fell back to the ground with a thud. His body still trembled from the memory of what his mind had just witnessed. The nightmare was not clear, but moments of it he could recall, rather wishing he couldn't.

'Am I going mad?' This was not the first time he had such a dream. Just hours earlier before the attack on his home, his dream then seemed eerily familiar. Was it a coincidence? No it couldn't be. Something had to be going on in his mind that he had no control over. Shania had mentioned the sphere which he suspected meant the pearl. There was something more to the jewel he had carried all his life, which she was not telling him. Answers were needed, reasoning was needed; anything to help him understand and to assure him that he was not going mad. For the remainder of the time given for rest, sleep escaped him, Rayar gazed towards the sky through the leaves of the trees around them. Sleep would not find him again this night. Strands of grass were held tightly between his fingers as if he used them to hold onto the reality of the world. The fear of returning to such a place churned his insides. Why was this happening to him? The time passed slowly. It felt like a lifetime yet without any rest being had. Shania repacked her gear and pulled on her earthy cloak, the hood returning to cover her features and within minutes the druidae was back upon her horse. Rayar followed suit though not as elegantly or as swiftly as his companion. Once they were both back on their steeds, they set off north-east towards a mountainous range in the far distance. Near to those mountains Rayar knew of the keep Stoneside, home of the Loysse Family. They were loyal nobles to the royal family of Granlia. As little as he knew about Shania, she would want to bypass it entirely, but if it was along the way, it seemed like a good place to stop and rest. It would take a couple of days at their speed, to reach the mountains. He would wait until they were closer before making his desire

known to stop there. He did his best to push aside the thoughts of the night for now and focus on going forward as Lanni had once advised him. Julian had told him it was this Quale he must speak to, so he would do just that.

'Stoneside Keep. Built into the mountain side as if part of the mountains itself. Father told me that this castle was the first castle built in Mayhen in the Firsts Age as a stronghold against the creatures from Below. I have always wanted to see it. After days travelling, there will be no harm in stopping by... I hope.'

"What are you thinking?" Shania asked from the head of the pair.

"Nothing," he simply stated. Whether that was a satisfactory answer for her or not there was no reply. The mood was sour. The least he could do was claim on the agreement he was given. "You said you would tell me about you, about the druidae?"

"I did," and at their comfortable pace, the pair continued on, secrets finally escaping from the mysterious woman. The cloth Rayar had used for his rest lay quietly unclaimed in the grass.

* * *

Chapter X
Duty and Honour
~Hinsani~

Things had calmed down in the keep of Heldon after the ambush that occurred in the dead of night. The corpses of the fallen had been removed from the castle halls and ramparts. The patrols had been increased, with many of the guard within the city surrounding the castle, being recalled to ensure the safety of those inside. Many men Hinsani served with, for many years, had died in the night. Butchered by unknown assailants with no known provocation as of yet. The wounded were guided to the barracks infirmary located within the courtyard and tended to by the court physicians and maidens. Hinsani had heard that several of the black armoured intruders had been captured and taken to the cells but other than that, he had heard nothing of their fate. Seemingly he was not privy to all the information concerning the attackers, though he knew some of what fate had befallen the royal family. He knew they all lived. King Rumeo had already made sure he was aware of that, but he also did not seem like himself, yet it was to be expected after his home was attacked from within. Something strange had happened not long after this. After the battle, Hinsani had been commanded to return to the Royal Blade chambers until he was called upon. This was extremely out of the ordinary; Royal Blades always had complete freedom throughout the keep. King Rumeo had ensured this when he created their group of skilled warriors. It was part of the oath in fact. The words he spoke so many years ago rang through his mind once more.

'I swear to protect my charge, the Royal Children, against any and all that threaten them.

I swear to be at their side when beckoned and to give my life to defend theirs.

I swear to see to their safety without guidance of the law of the realm and honourably carry out all duties they require of me.

I swear to be honest and valiant in all my duties as a Royal Blade.'

Those words were spoken so long ago; seventeen years ago it must have been, ever since that day. He could still feel the flames whenever he closed his eyes and focused on his meditation. That feeling helped him serve without hesitation or respite. For the moment he sat crossed legged, alone, in the training hall of the Royal Blade chambers. His one edged blade lay across his lap unsheathed, while his hands clasped onto his knees under the edge. The sharpness of his blade could slice through metal armour and with his speed and skill in the art of killing, he had witnessed this many times. 'Galad', the blade had been named by his former master. The sole survivor of the art Blade Dancing and now he had taken the title of sole survivor. Rayar was his apprentice and with his potential, perhaps one day he would receive this blade. Time would tell and he had a long way to go until that time came. For the moment he would continue to meditate. There was almost silence in the quarters. The gentle sound of the wind against the open window whistling every few moments or so, was not enough to distract Hinsani from his reflection. Only one torch lit the room, which sat on a nearby table amongst the many books Hyar brought to the chamber. His mind grew empty yet sharp, focused and blank. A point of pure instinct yet control. He was aware of everything around him but in a state abstracted from the world. Of course, he shared these chambers with a man, without the same respect for his old ways as himself. At that moment the door creaked open and through it came none other than his companions, Hyar Dedred and Titania. The golden bearded man strode in, drink in hand, undoubtedly something strong, followed by Titania simply carrying herself with her usual grace, hand on the hilt of her sword with an expression of calm composure; that was her way. Hinsani sighed, let the ruckus begin.

"You nap in the strangest ways, Hinsani," Hyar teased as he found his favourite chair and collapsed into it. The red headed woman crossed her arms and leant by the door.

"You say the most ridiculous things, Hyar," she retorted for him. The raven haired warrior pushed himself to his feet, his blade in one fluid motion twirling and sliding into its sheath in his left hand. He attached Galad to his belt and turned to address his fellow Royal Blades.

"So Raimon was killed. Do we know who gave the finishing blow?" Hinsani asked. Titania clucked her tongue but held it. She probably thought that to die in such a way, he probably was not worthy of being a Royal Blade; however Hinsani knew that man was skilled. He may have been the weakest of the four but he was no push over.

"Funny story... Wait not funny, misspoke," Hyar said and chuckled embarrassingly to himself. "Well Nymin was witness to it, as was Rayar, in all the commotion only those two saw what happened. Makes sense we left them in Raimon's care. Yet when I went to speak with Nymin, she has been locked away in her bed chamber. Rayar's bed chamber was full of guards as well but they seemed to be searching it rather than guarding anything. Guards not guarding, eh?" He took a swig from his canteen and rolled his shoulders in confusion. Hinsani creased his brow into a frown.

'Searching?'

*'*If the guards had been guarding in the first place, we would not be in this mess. I haven't had to kill that many men in a good few years," Titania mumbled. Hyar caught the words.

"Truly a man-killer aren't you, just my kind of woman," he teased with a grin. Her eyes only gleamed with distaste.

"Your kind of woman is any woman who has low enough self respect to give you any of their time," Titania snarled. Hyar threw his head back in laughter.

'So Rayar is missing? No, The King would have me sent out in search at once not confined me to these quarters. The King said he was alive. The King would not lie.'

"I wouldn't speak so ill of the women nor men, of Heldon. Upstanding and honourable lovers, all of them. None can resist the Golden Lion of the Royal Blades. One day I'll convince you my red headed beauty, you just wait!" He took a long swig of his drink as he clearly looked for the right buttons to push. Titania growled in annoyance, fingers tapping lightly at the hilt of her sword.

"The only thing you will get from me is my sword through your gut, golden pup." Hinsani had heard enough, there were more important matters to attend.

"Enough! What do you mean being searched? Rayar was not there?"

"Supposedly they were taken to the King's chambers," Titania chipped in. "I spoke with My Lady. She claimed that Rayar was not present when the children were gathered. He, the Queen and Princess Nymin had already been confined." This was peculiar. The King had said they were alive, but he did not say much more on the matter. He did not say if they were harmed or not. Something was not right.

"We should not be sitting here. We should be attending our charge." The idea of waiting in here while he did not know what was going on was beginning to eat away at his temper. The red headed woman pulled herself from the wall and made her way over to a jug of water by the side of the room.

"My Lady Nyer has commanded I come here. From what Hyar has said, he has also been commanded here by Princess Nymin, though not by her words. By the sounds of it, you were not ordered here by Prince Rayar, so pray tell, why are you here?" her words were sharp and judgemental. Her bond with Nyer was the strongest out of the Royal Children. They had been friends as children and now they would remain close for the rest of their lives. Hyar on the other hand was a different story; as laid back as he was, he followed his duty in a more unorthodox manner. Hinsani knew her words rang true. He should not be here. He needed to follow his duty and find Rayar somewhere in the keep.

"What are you planning, Hinsani?" Hyar asked from his seated position. The raven haired man turned to address his companion yet before the words could escape his mouth, there was a knock on the door. There stood a Heldoran Guardsman. He saluted the trio with his fist to his left shoulder.

"Sir Tannaroth, Sir Dedred, Miss Titania. I come with a summons from the King for Sir Tannaroth," the three looked between each other. Well that pretty much collapsed his first idea of simply going to find Rayar but naturally it would lead to the same result. Surely the King could shed some light on the situation. The Royal Blade nodded to the guardsman and began towards the door to follow him.

"Hinsani," Hyar called out as he was leaving. He turned to face his friend, his stone face still locked into a frown. "The King said he lived right? You haven't failed your duty. Don't worry. We would know already if something had happened. The entire attack was such a cluster of madness, he may just be helping the wounded, or with his mother. And well, if you have failed your duty, it was nice knowing you," Hyar cracked him a smile. He knew it was a joke but still the dread was aching on his heart as much as he hid it well. He would never forgive himself if he had failed. They would not need to execute him; he would have done the deed himself. Hinsani nodded back to Hyar and exited the quarters.

It looked like a battle had never taken place. The halls were clear of bodies and weapons, maids hurried around as they wiped down the walls and floors for any sign of blood and other bodily fluids that came with the death of men. Guards were placed through the halls with their weapons and armour cleaned and cloth tidied as if they had never been involved in any fighting whatsoever. It was a quick clean up since only a

105

few hours had passed since the keep was attacked. The litter of fallen was likely too hard for any to bear and returning to normality was the fastest way to settle the minds of those who had lost those close to them. It was not an overly long walk towards the throne room through the winding corridors of Heldon castle, yet as he got closer and closer, the guards began leaving their posts along the hallways and began marching behind him. Another six men had appeared at his back, spears in hand and shields at their sides. Something did not feel right. As he approached the large door to the throne room, a captain by the name of Caidarian Kinsani stood in his path with another twenty guardsmen behind him and along the walls around him. He saluted the Royal Blade respectfully and bowed his head.

"Sir Tannaroth. The King awaits you. Come with me." Hinsani furrowed his brow. Were these guards possibly for him? That couldn't be right. There was the rumour someone had let those attackers in, but they couldn't suspect him could they. Speaking with the King would provide answers. Much needed answers. The captain turned on his heel and professionally strode towards the door, two guardsmen opening each of the large doors at once for the group. Hinsani found himself behind Caidarian and several guardsmen, more on his flank and more at his back, as if he was a prisoner being transported. His hand found its way to the hilt of Galad, as he began to move into a calming state of preparation. Inside the throne room, many people of the court were gathered on either side of the path towards the throne, with guards forming walls on either side so he could not go anywhere but forward. Around the King were more guardsmen, and of course Commander Brayton by the King's side. On the right of Rumeo were four seats, one for Nyer who was present, one for Ayla who was also present yet the seats for Rayar and Nymin were vacant. On the other side, the seat for Queen Julian was also empty. Perhaps Nymin was so distraught from the death of Raimon, Prince Rayar and the Queen was tending to her. That is what he told himself at least, for a bit of clarity of mind. His gaze passed over the two princesses present. The eldest wore a frown so scornful it rivalled his own, while the younger seemed distressed, broken even and her eyes and cheeks wet with former tears.

Once the Royal Blade reached the foot of the small flight of stairs that led to the throne, he lowered to one knee and bowed his head to his King.

"Your Grace," he said in his deep and stern voice. King Rumeo did not respond so Hinsani kept his head down until told otherwise. Instead the King addressed the court.

"People of Mayhen. Today only a few hours ago my home was attacked. My people were killed like dogs in the street. We lost many good soldiers; we lost many good servants of the realm; we lost a Royal Blade. The Queen was wounded in this battle, my wife! We lost much. For what? What was their purpose? Their intention? We do not know just yet, however we will find out. We will not lie in the dirt and be trampled. I will avenge all who have fallen in the name of Granlia this day and any who have threatened us or... betrayed us." His eyes flickered down to Hinsani just as the Royal Blade finally raised his head at the word *betrayed*, to catch each other's glare.

'What is this...?' Rumeo stood from his throne and returned his attention to the crowd gathered in the court. The gasps and murmured whispers filled the room around him. Did they suspect him of such treachery? That could not be possible. Princess Ayla had clenched her eyes shut with tears beginning to reform while Princess Nyer was not so emotional in that respect, her only emotion seemed to be anger.

"As King Rumeo Granlia of Mayhen I swear to you all now. I swear the First Coming and the World Above that we will not rest until all those who have caused Mayhen this harm, are brought to justice. My son, Prince Rayar, betrayed our great country!" Hinsani's eyes widened in shock, perhaps the first time anyone present had seen that kind of shock in his eyes. Within seconds he was on his feet and he could hear the soldiers around him begin to draw their weapons. "My son, my first son! He allowed these men into our home in an attempt to

107

secure the throne for himself with the death of me, my wife and my daughters! Now he flees to the country in an attempt to escape justice. My son or not, none are exempt from the justice of Heldon and the Granlia family. All men and women here will unite their families, seek and find this traitor no matter how far he runs." His attention now rested completely on the Royal Blade. "Sir Hinsani Tannaroth, as Prince Rayar's Royal Blade, you must have known of his ploy and this is not acceptable." Just then Commander Brayton drew his sword at the King's side and pointed it towards Hinsani.

"Arrest him!" Brayton commanded. In a flourish, all the guards in the throne room drew their weapons; spears narrowed their aim on him.

'The Lion Stalks,' as masterful as he was with a sword there was no way he could succeed in this fight.

"Your Grace!" he called out as his eyes briefly flashed between those around him. They did not approach just yet. They all knew what he was capable of and if he chose to fight, the first few to attack him would surely be slain. Still the guardsman as a group began their advance, shuffling forwards slowly. Sweat glistened on their foreheads, even Caidarian seemed hesitant. "There must be some sort of mistake. Your son, the prince, would never betray you. He has been loyal to the family and the country since birth. I beg you reconsider." Even in his pleas to the King, his voice was calm and stone. Hinsani would never break and rather die than fail his duty. King Rumeo snorted at his words.

"Do not question me! I am the King! I will not stand here and be ridiculed by a simple soldier! Enough of this, Brayton, arrest him!" Rumeo roared. His voice carried over the entire throne room like an incoming flood. Commander Brayton moved down from the stairs towards the Royal Blade and closed in to speaking distance.

"Sir Tannaroth, your sword. Surrender now. Do not die here without purpose. Once Prince Rayar is brought back here, he will face justice, and you can die with him if you please, if he is found guilty."

'If?' Hinsani caught that word. *'Then there is still doubt?'* the guardsman around him edged ever closer. His teeth gritted and his fingers clutched his blade so tightly he thought his hands would bleed. What was he to do? There was a brief moment of silence that felt like a lifetime. He had no choice. Galad found its way back to its sheath before anyone had realised what had happened. Very carefully the guards surrounded the man, spears at his neck and his scabbard being removed from the belt. It was painful to be parted from his blade as it was an extension of his very being. For the moment he would have to grit his teeth and see it out.

"You are doing the right thing, Sir Tannaroth," the commander tried to assure him, but it did not help. This was not justice, this was the real treachery.

"He is innocent. I know it. Heldon cells will not be able to hold me forever, I will prove his innocence." The words were heavy. Was this the right call or not? It was this or death. Many guardsmen would have died but his life would have been lost eventually. It had to be the right choice for now.

"I understand, Hinsani. The King... wants any information extracted from you come dawn tomorrow. I am sorry." Hinsani growled at the commander but found his body being grappled by the guards and being dragged away towards the door. One of the last faces he saw was Nyer's beside her father. Her eyes glared with the same anger as his own, though not at him. At King Rumeo. The voices of the people in court were aggravating him, people claiming the guilt of their prince so easily and openly. They were spineless. Once again his oath rang in his head.

'I swear to protect my charge, the Royal Children, against any and all that threaten them.' He had to find a way out of the cells and find the Prince. On his honour, he would follow his duty. No matter what obstacles stood in his way.

'Stay safe, Prince Rayar, I will find you.'

* * *

109

Chapter XI
The Last Druidae
~Rayar~

"Above and Below...," A curse was all Rayar could squeak out at first. Some of the things Shania had told him sounded like fairy tales. To think all those stories that had been told to him as a young child, might actually have been true and not myths as he thought to give him a pleasant night sleep. Like, the tale of 'The Man with the Wooden Face', a story about a man who could control the earth and formed the lands as they were now, after the First's Age. The story said he had been a druidae and used his power so much he became a tree himself and still sat in the Druidae Grove to this day, unable to move or speak, simply watching the world go by. Wasn't that also a myth, the Druidae Grove? The home of all the druidae in the world but hidden from the eyes of regular men and women. Shania was not completely open about everything. She said what she felt he needed to know and that was all. Rayar was sure she had more stories to reveal to him, when she was ready.

'So druidae and mages were enemies for hundreds of years. The druidae hid in a forest so they could not be threatened. That much was another story the wet nurses used to tell, yet to think it may actually be true. That she is the last druidae after the Grove was... burned to the ground. The sphere, no, my pearl from my family, is something someone who has powerful magic is after. The power within it was something of the druidae. Why would my family have such a thing? Bloody

answer my question and give me more to ask. So she can communicate with the hawk through her power as well, but only that one hawk. This is all way too crazy to all be true. Though after what I saw back home, who knows what else is possible.' Rayar rattled in his mind the tale Shania had told him. It took her long enough to really speak however. They travelled for almost a full day with her only occasionally revealing anything, piece by piece. A comment there, a short story here.

'I would have hoped to be given a little bit more, but breaking through this woman's barrier was like trying to carve a turkey with a wooden spoon. No matter how hard I try and prod, she gets defensive. Well at least I know something now instead of wandering in the dark.'

"You've gone quiet. Too much for you?" she asked him over her shoulder as they trotted across a winding dirt road. His mind and body was already exhausted from the lack of sleep and the long journey but now with all this new information, he thought his mind would explode. The young prince considered a moment, what more could she tell him?

"My pearl, King Rumeo told me it had...," he suddenly halted his words. If he was not careful, he would reveal that he was not a true Granlia. "... He told me it was it was a family heirloom. What is so special about it?" Shania stopped her horse and turned on the saddle. Her eyes pierced right through him.

"Quale never told me. All I know is that it has the power to free something evil. I have been with that man for my entire life but he is... not what he used to be. All I do know is that we need to get it back and give it to Quale. He will know what must be done with it. You're not the only one with questions needing answering, Rayar." The prince was a little taken back. Here he thought Shania was the well of all knowledge but by her tone as she spoke and the pain in her face, she too seemed a little lost. She had been sent to find him and the pearl. She had told him that much but it sounded like she was not told why. He could sympathise with her; it would appear they had more in common than he had first thought. Speaking to this man Quale became all that more important.

"I am sorry. I did not mean to pry. I do not mean to be a burden to you," he tried to apologise. She only scoffed at him and reared her head.

"You are. You can't even protect yourself from what I saw. I thought noble boys were supposed to be trained how to fight, you flapped around like a fish out of water with that sword."

"I can fight, and a friend died in that fight. Many I knew died." Anger flashed inside him at her words. He was not as used to battle as she appeared to be and had never seen such events unfold before.

"I'm sorry... It must have been difficult for you," she replied, her tone less sarcastic. Perhaps she was not as cold as he first thought. The apology definitely sounded genuine. Rayar rode his horse next to her; he was tired of talking to the back of a hood.

"I can fight... I just...," she raised her brow to him as if to urge him to continue. "I have never been in a life or death situation before. I froze. I was afraid." Shania nodded to him in response and motioned him to follow. The pair trotted off the pass and she dismounted, he followed her lead, but watched her quizzically. In one smooth motion Shania pulled off her cloak and drew her sword. She gripped it in two hands, defensively in front of her person. Rayar continued to wear a confused expression.

"What are you doing?" he asked. The woman let out a sigh.

"Draw your sword, Rayar. If you can't fight to protect your life, what is the point of fighting at all?" He had always been taught to fight to protect others. That was his father's way and Hinsani's way. Yet he had only ever sparred with practice swords, not with real edged weapons. He could not help but hesitate, shuffling uneasily on his feet.

"Here? Now? Do we not have somewhere to be? And you know, with real weapons. I would not want to hurt you. I was trained by the Royal Blade Sir Hinsani Tannaroth." He spoke the man's name as if she would be aware of who he was, but to his surprise she did not even seem to acknowledge it. The woman scoffed at him again; this was becoming a habit. For the first time he saw a smile briefly grow on her lips, as if she found the situation amusing.

"You hurt me? After what I saw you couldn't beat a baby at her mother's breast in battle, let alone hurt me." Rayar finally gave in and drew his one edged sword. It felt lighter than back in Heldon or was it that he felt stronger. "If you can't fight you'll die, so I'm going to aim to kill you. Don't freeze up!" Rayar barely had the chance to protest her idea of killing him, before she attacked. Her arming sword came from an upwards strike. While he had no chance to speak, his reflexes kicked in and his own sword parried her attack with a swift upwards thrust. She struck again from the side and he parried, and again and again. She struck repeatedly from various angles and points of attack, yet he was able to parry each one. Their swords locked as she pushed against his defence. She was good, very good but nothing compared to Hinsani who he had sparred with night after night for years.

"Why won't you attack!?" she snapped with a growl. Rayar frowned with strain as he kept her in place.

"I told you! I do not wish to risk harming you!" he snapped back at her. Sneakily she lifted her leg and slammed her foot into his side. Now this was something Hinsani would never do, a sneak attack like that. Rayar stumbled back with the wind knocked out of him yet his years of training with a Royal Blade gave him the speed to quickly deflect her next attack, which came from below, towards his thigh.

"That was cheap!" he said through a cough as he gasped back some air. Shania smirked, a second smile on her usually cold features.

"Sometimes being sneaky keeps you alive. You should remember that!" From her back, her hand slipped out a small dagger which she aimed towards his face. Rayar released one hand on the hilt as she did and caught her wrist mid strike. He would not fall for the same stealthy trick twice.

"I am a Prince and a man of honour; I would never resort to tricks like that." With that, the druidae pushed against his defensive pose and jumped backwards to give the pair some distance. With a few smooth motions, the dagger was once again hidden from plain sight and her sword had been tucked back into her belt.

"If you can attack like you can defend, then maybe you're better than I thought. Next time you're attacked and I can promise you, there will be a next time, fight like you just did. If you don't, I may not be there to save you." Rayar wrinkled his nose. He was being battered about verbally and literally by a woman. He knew there were strong women in Heldon like his sister Nyer and Titania but they did not seem to get under his skin like she did. His one sided blade slipped back into its home and he returned to his horse.

"You are pretty good yourself. Who taught you?" She only shrugged at him, another question she was unlikely to give a full answer to.

"Quale is an old fool of a man, but he is wise and skilled in more arts than you and I can even think of." This man they were heading to meet was sounding more and more interesting each time his name came up. Whoever this fellow was he surely had a world of knowledge he could unleash. The prince wondered what sort of man he was. Worldly and wise, tall and broad with a sword at his side and eyes that spoke a thousand words. It was actually rather exciting to meet this man after hearing just a few things about him. He still found it strange that this Quale lived in the mountains between Hextheene and Mayhen. Those rocky spikes were treacherous and dangerous to pass through, let alone live amongst. Many had died trying to explore that mountain range; it wasn't called the Valley of Death for nothing. A very morbid name for the usually rather poetic country of Mayhen. Its true name was the Leon Mountains, but many referred to those perilous mountains as the former.

*

~Hinsani~

The smoke was heavy, filling the courtyard. Flames bellowed all around him. The crackling of wheat and the cries of men and women being burnt throughout the castle. The once proud white tower was in ruin, as the fire swallowed it whole. Faces and people fleeing all around him were nothing but a blur, voices called out as they pleaded or begged for help but the words did not reach him. Hinsani coughed, a hand on the pommel of his sword and the other holding a rag to his face to protect him from the mist of smoke. It was a horror, worse than the battles he had fought. Worse than the death of loved ones. It was total and utter carnage. The flames stole the lives of many, flames were not something he could cut and protect people from. It was a force beyond his capabilities. A hand grasped his shoulder and took his attention, like a cracking whip. The man was wounded, blood covered his face and his leg could barely hold him up. The hair golden and eyes a deep brown. This face, unlike the others, he could see clearly. A man he knew well, now crumbled, in a mess; his body barely able to move as he pleaded.

"She's in the tower... Hinsani, please... she needs you." The man croaked before he dropped to the floor, unable to carry his own weight. Was he dead? As he remembered, he lived. He knew he lived. This had all happened before. As before, like every other time, he darted towards the keep entrance that led to the high tower of the keep. The door was open, luckily, yet flames blazed at every turning. The smoke was blinding. He could feel the heat drying and crisping his skin. It was pain, painful to walk through, painful to keep his eyes open, painful to breathe. He kept low as he moved up through the tower. The steps felt endless, climbing and climbing and climbing. Why was it taking so long? Why was the tower so bloody tall? Why was he even doing this? He was just a soldier. Finally he reached the top of the tower, his armour and leather black from the smoke and face covered in ash. The door felt hot, the fire was up this high as well. He had come this far, he had to go all the way but fear for what he would find on the other side, strangled his heart. After a run up, the young man burst through the door. It splintered and fell to the floor with a loud thud. Blood stained the walls, the floor, the bed, it was everywhere. Fire bloomed over the bed, the furniture, the drapes, everything that could raise a flame, raised one. There on the floor a body lay; a woman's. Blood? Fires don't cause people to bleed. Why was there blood? There was nothing he could do. He had to get out. He had to survive. This is not where he would die. He would not be a pile of ash to be forgotten.

Then he heard it. The cry of a baby. Of course the baby, her son. Across the room wrapped in cloth and covered in water lay, a tiny child stretching, squirming, screaming for his mother. Hinsani darted over and swept the baby into his arms. The fire grew more and more out of control around him.

He needed to get the baby out.

The fire climbed towards them.

He needed to get the baby out.

Hinsani's eyes slowly opened to darkness. The dream had come once again. It had been a long time since he dreamt about that day, the memories of the great fire, but it still tingled his skin as he remembered the feel of the fire against it. The day that everything in his life had changed and led to his position as a Royal Blade; well even more than that, after the event, the Royal Blades were created by King Rumeo. To think that saving that baby would change so much. The King had been away, as had the Lord of that keep and upon the King's return, he was a different man. He did not know the King personally by this point, only the rumours and from afar, but once he had brought that baby to him, the life he knew changed dramatically. Now it had changed again, but this time not for the better. He sat crossed legged in his meditating pose, deep within the cells of Heldon. There was no window for natural light. Chains were attached along the walls to hold prisoners in

116

place and a single torch light high on the wall, which grew dangerously close to going out. Darkness did not bother him as much as others, who feared being unable to see, but for him it was simply a place he could slip into nothingness and focus his mind. On the way down into the dungeon, he expected to see those soldiers, captured in the attack, but none were present. The cells were pretty much deserted apart from the odd guardsman and himself. Most petty criminals were kept in the barrack cells in the city. This place was reserved for those who had plotted or harmed the Royal Family. Hinsani was now counted among this small group of people, without trial or conviction, simply by the King's orders. It did not make sense. The actions of Rayar did not make sense. Why had it all become so confusing? Life had been simple, training Rayar and protecting the keep. Nothing stayed the same forever. He pondered over his next move; breaking free would be difficult and convincing the King they were innocent, seemed to be even more so. Yet luck, or friendship was on his side. The clang of metal keys rang nearby, just outside the large, thick door which was built from wood and iron. Perhaps this was his chance to escape? Slip into the night and make haste towards wherever Rayar had gone. No, he was a man of honour, not a cutthroat in the night. The door slowly opened and there stood a figure, though it was so dark he could not make out who it was.

"Who goes there?" he commanded in his deep voice. There was no answer. The figure draped in a long cloak, with all their features hidden, simply tossed the set of keys to him. Hinsani grabbed them as they landed in his lap and looked back up to the figure.

"You are letting me leave? Has the King ordered it so?" The person did not reply but reached back into their cloak and pulled out something that belonged to Hinsani. The figure tossed it towards him, which this time he caught mid-air, knowing exactly what it was. Galad had returned to him, it should never have left his side. If he had tried to escape, this blade would have been left behind. Galad may have been an extension of himself but the duty he swore to, overruled even this. He ran his fingers across the scabbard that protected his blade. Attached to it was a note wrapped around the leather. Hinsani frowned inquisitively and shot his eyes back up to the doorway.

"What...," before he could finish his sentence, the figure was gone. The Royal Blade pushed himself to his feet and pulled the torch from the wall to read the note that he had been delivered. The flame was weak and would not hold much longer.

'Hinsani.

This is not freedom from justice. This is you following your duty. The King sends men after Prince Rayar, they track him North-East. You must follow them and you will find your charge. I am repaying a debt to you after many years. Do not fail your duty again.

Yours,

A friend.' The Royal Blade scrunched his face as he struggled to read the words in the darkness of the cell. So it was the path of escape he must take. Whoever had freed him, he had supposedly helped in the past. Hinsani was no heroic man who travelled the land, saving people wherever he could but he had helped many in the past few years, in battle. He was thankful to whoever had freed him but he did not have time to seek this person out. That was his way out and he would take it. Without another moment of hesitation the scabbard of his blade returned to his belt and he carefully but quickly darted through the cell doorway and began to make his way across the castle halls. Like a cat stalking in the shadows, he moved from hall to hall, avoiding any and all he could. The stables were his destination and his loyal steed, Dragan, would be waiting for him. Once he had finally slipped back into the light of the dawn breaking over the horizon, across the battlements, he passed a gaze over the courtyard which briefly drew his attention. Below a troop of guardsman sat upon horseback, perhaps a dozen men with a man at the head of the group he did not recognise, draped in black tough leather, a bald head and crane

118

like nose. With him a pack of hounds barked and struggled against their leashes.

'*These must be the men after Prince Rayar, fate is on my side,*' he thought to himself. Just then the crane nosed man whipped his horse and the group shot out of the courtyard gate, taking the east road which by-passed the city of Heldon around them.

'*Dammit, I must hurry,*' Hinsani shot his eyes around for a quicker way to get down to the courtyard. The ravened haired man sprinted across the ramparts towards the stairs on the other side of the courtyard and came across a guardsman on his patrol. Words would not be allowed to escape the poor Heldoran guardsman. Hinsani like a bolt appeared in the man's face and clasped it in his hand followed by roughly slamming him into the wall of the battlement. He did not let the man collapse in his armour and instead caught him as he fell and gently laid him on the ground to avoid any more unneeded attention. The risk of running into more guards along the walls was too great, so he turned back to scanning the ground below and found a spot he might have been able to jump. A full drop could either cause serious injury or death even, yet there was a chance. Taking a leap of faith, he jumped from the wall and landed on a wooden platform that sat above the courtyard smithy. The landing was not as graceful as he would have liked. He completed a smooth roll as his feet hit the wood but the size of the platform was too small and he ended up stumbling over the edge and landing on the dirt below. While he lay on his stomach he coughed into the dirt. Nothing hurt unbearably but the wind had been knocked out of him. Just then the bell of the keep began to ring. Dawn had come and of course he was no longer in his cell. Without wasting any more time, Hinsani shot towards the stable and grasped his personal steed, Dragan, by the reins. Instead of untying the leather, he smoothly sliced through it and jumped upon his horse. Shouts echoed into the courtyard as guardsman started to come from within, to seek the escaping prisoner.

"Fly Dragan, stop for nothing." The horse listened and galloped from the stables and turned harshly towards the courtyard exit that the group of men had just departed from. Guards tried to surround him as he came free, their spears gripped tightly and thrust forward. Each spear that attempted to strike him or his steed was deflected by an expert parry of Galad. They were too slow to block his path or shut the gate and before they could rally themselves to organise and stop him, the Royal Blade was in the wind. Word would not reach the guards further into the city or down the road to the east before his horse could. He was out, but at what cost? Now like Prince Rayar, a wanted man on the run. Those thoughts were meaningless; he had one goal. Find and protect his Prince.

* * *

Chapter XII
Stoneside Keep
~Rayar~

A couple of days had passed, in their ride towards the mountains to the north-east. They had not spoken much in those two days. Rayar had tried several times to start a conversation about druidae, Quale or the pearl he had lost, but she continuously ignored him or shot him down with a sharp remark about focusing on the now. Were women all this bossy? They had kept a steady pace on their journey towards the mountainous region of the country. Mayhen itself was in no way a flat country. Mountains ranged from the north, to the west and the south. It is what had made it quite defensible in the past. Armies could not cross the harsh terrain and were forced into fighting in places the Mayhen soldiers would know they would come; that is how the Battle of the Pass had been fought. The ground around them was hilly and uneven and the horses had grown weary despite the few brief stops for well needed rest. For the most part, they had moved at a canter on horseback towards their destination. Now it was less than an hour away, or so he thought. In honesty, Rayar had no idea where they would enter these treacherous mountains. To the south stood something he had wanted to see for many, many years. It was no more of a ride there as it was to where he assumed Shania was leading him.

'Stoneside Keep....,' the huge structure was as magnificent as he had imagined. The castle was built into the mountain side with one large grey wall around it, in a half-circular fashion,

protected by a moat, and behind that sat another wall that enclosed the castle. The castle itself did not seem all that different from Heldon. It was not as tall or as grand in appearance but appeared stronger. Even further south than the keep, sat a small town, which must have been Stoneside Settle. The names did not seem the most imaginative but he supposed back when this place was first constructed, they simply called it what it looked like and where it was. This could be taken as an opportunity to at least get some good rest before entering the mountains and trying to traverse its dangerous footing.

"Uh, Miss Shania," he began as he trotted quickly behind her, trying to keep up with her speed. She glanced over her shoulder though her features were hidden by her hood. "I do not think we should carry on further without any rest. I am exhausted; my horse is exhausted. You cannot tell me you are not tired. You have slept less than I have." The lack of rest had given them both a rather untidy look. The smell had long since become a regular scent to his nose, but he knew from the first whiff that morning, his current aroma was not a pleasant one.

"What are you suggesting?" she asked him cautiously.

"Over there," he motioned towards the keep. "Stoneside Keep. The Lord and Lady there are loyal nobles of Mayhen and my father. They would put us up for one night before we continue on. I do not know about you, but I would rather make it to this Quale in one piece and not find myself too tired and weak to climb the first rock in the valley." The food they had been eating had quite expertly been caught by Shania and her hawk the past two days. Rabbits mainly, but he did crave a proper cooked and served meal. He was not used to pulling meat apart from a stick.

"We carry on," she stated bluntly. Rayar blinked in surprise and reined his horse to a halt.

"Listen here, Miss Shania!" Shania too abruptly halted her steed and looked back to him with a sharp stare. He could feel a lump in his throat as he suddenly realised now rude his tone had been. Regardless, he soldiered on. "I am Prince Rayar Granlia of Heldon. I am not used to the wild, as you seem to be. I have come far in the past few days with you, with only an hour here or there of rest or meat you have had your hawk catch. If I am to carry on any further, I need a bloody rest. Braving those mountains like this is suicide. If you came from there, you must know." That went well, he thought, he wanted to get his point across after all. The druidae stared at him with daggers for eyes for a few moments, possibly contemplating his words but stubbornly wanting to refuse their truth. Finally a sigh of defeat slipped through.

"Fine. Just for the night to gather *your* strength. To think being cooped up in a castle being waited on hand and foot, could make you so unfit for riding in the country." Her retort was sarcastic but he would let it slide. She seemed somewhat hot and cold with him, sometimes like their spar, she was warming up to him and now she had gone back to treating him like a child. He would never understand women if all outside Heldon were as mad as this one. However he had gained a victory against her this day and his reward would be rest in a proper bed, a prepared meal and the chance to see Stoneside Keep from inside. Rayar was growing more and more excited at the achievement. They both turned their horses towards the keep with now Rayar leading the pair. He did not turn around to her face knowing full well it would project an expression of displeasure. He was better off to ignore that, to avoid any possible feelings of guilt for having his way. He was a gentleman after all.

After what seemed like a short hour, they arrived at the gates of the keep. Up close it looked humongous. The huge sets of doors were layered with steel down the trim. The wood was carved with symbols in the Firsts Tongue, words lost to the folk of this day but still their beauty was admired by many. The wall stretched from one side of the mountain around in an oval shape, to another mountain, protecting the contents within. Currently the gates were left open, as common people passed in-between with carts and trading goods. Along the wall, soldiers patrolled with bows and spears. Their armour was similar to that of the Heldoran guardsman, the only difference being the emblem on their chest; a red bull's face. Only the bull could rule the mountains, the people of Stoneside had been rumoured to say. As they trotted up to the gates, they were halted by a guard while another saw the scene and made his way over.

"Halt, not seen you 'round 'ere before. Speak your business?" The guardsman was short and stocky with a plump face but his armour hid the rest. His companion was a blank looking man who did not seem too concerned about their approach either way.

"Greetings. I am Prince Rayar Granlia of Mayhen and this is my companion Shania. I hail from Heldon on a mission from the Queen. Please may I speak to the Lord or Lady of the House?" The guards clearly seemed taken aback by the announcement, the pair flicking glances between each other, then back to the Prince.

"Prince Rayar, ya' say? From Heldon?" the guard clucked his tongue. "Any proof of that, by your dress you look like a regular boy to me, apart from that fancy red coat. Didn't steal it did ya'?" Now Rayar was the one taken aback. He never thought that people would not recognise him. He was the prince after all. He had just assumed that the country would all know who the Royal Family were and what they looked like. A naive mistake on his part. He could sense the bemused scoff of Shania behind him but she remained silent for the moment.

"My word is my proof. Please find the Lord or Lady, and say Prince Rayar Granlia is here... The golden haired Prince," that was one thing he had, his unnatural hair colour. The only other person he had seen with such colour to their hair was Hyar and he had also been told that his real father shared the same. Though, as his father was no longer among the living it did not seem too relevant at this point.

"Oi, Leynin!" the stocky guard called out to a younger guardsman. This guard looked about the same age as himself, if not younger. The boy came stumbling over awkwardly and saluted.

"Sir!" the talker of the group waved his hand at the salute.

"Run to the keep and tell 'em some kid is sayin' he's Prince Rayar of Granlia, an' that he's got golden hair. Get a bloody move on, then!" The boy almost fell flat on his face as he scrambled towards the inner keep past the first wall.

'Guardsmen are not like this in Heldon... I do not think,' with lack of a better word they seemed like militia, simply peasants. The guardsmen back home always seemed professional and stoic. Perhaps the fact that they were in the capital and in the Royal Keep, meant they did not have a choice but to be the best of the best.

"The famous Prince of Mayhen right?" Shania teased from behind him in a whisper. The more comfortable this woman got around him, the more she seemed to feel the need to tease him. They were not like Ayla's teasing or Nymin's pranks; they were just sugar coated insults. He chose to ignore her, but he could tell she knew it hit the right spot to annoy him. Now came the awkward waiting game. Shania still remained silent; the guards remained silent; the only noise was the bustle of people around them going in and out of the gates. Rayar did his best to lighten the situation.

"Never seen Stoneside Keep before. It is truly a masterpiece of craftsmanship is it not?" He gave the man a warm smile which was returned with a grunt.

"Right."

"My father, the King, told me it was the first defensive point, once the people began to retake the continent back after the First's Age."

"Yup."

"What is it like to live in such a place with all its history and lore? You must feel very proud of your home, Sir...?"

"Uh-huh," this was painful. Shania let out a sigh of disbelief at the prince's attempt at small talk. Rayar wrinkled his nose and gave in to defeat. Awkward wait in silence, it was then. The next ten minutes felt like a lifetime as they now waited silently for the boy to return. The guardsman did not even look at him now; he only picked his nose and leant on the gate and occasionally spoke with his fellow guard who appeared to care even less. Just then came the saving grace, the boy was sprinting back down from the inner keep and skidded to a halt in front of group.

"Finally! What took ya' so long, bloody boy. Well what he say? Send these gits on their way eh?" a boisterous laugh followed his rather unwelcome comment. Was that supposed to be witty? Regardless Rayar sat poised on his saddle.

"The Lord... The lord said...," Leynin raised a finger as he slumped over to catch the ever escaping breath. The anticipation was as painful as the failed conversation. "...To... to..." The guardsman rolled his eyes and snapped at the recruit.

"Spit it out boy!"

"To bring them to the keep immediately and welcome the prince and his companion." Dread dropped on the guardsman like the mountain had lifted itself from the ground and placed itself on his back.

"He... said what? Then he really is...," the formerly rude fellow very quickly changed his song. "Well what are we waitin' for! Escort our prince into the keep then! Get on it boy! It's an honour to 'ave ya' with us Your Grace! I'm eternally regretful of not givin' ya' passage, Your Grace, jus' seein' ya' without any escort threw us is all!" The guardsman bowed his head respectfully; the sweat of his mistake quite obvious. Rayar could not help but let smugness overwhelm him as he trotted past to follow the young Leynin.

"Is it now? I will be sure to let the Lord know how vigil his men are at the gates." The guardsman kept his head low not wanting to make eye contact. Rayar assumed it was due to the shame of refusing entry to a prince. Needless to say it was rather uplifting to have the last laugh.

"Thank ya', Your Grace!" Shania followed him in ensuring her features were still obscured by her hood and the pair made their way forwards, finally, into the keep.

The inside was not as beautiful as he had imagined it would be. The ground was muddy and uneven from constant wagons

126

and horse hoofs as well as the continual population streaming in and around. The walls were mucky and stained from years of neglect, it was as if this place was never cleaned, surely they had courtiers and maids to tend to such things. Guardsman sat around a table drinking and laughing while clearly they should have been performing duties seeing as they were in full attire. The inside of the first wall seemed more like another town with houses and traders everywhere. There were some in the courtyards of Heldon but nothing like this. Nothing so rag tag. Commoners even tried to sell him meat or cloth as he passed them towards the second wall. He did his best to kindly decline each hard sale yet no matter how many traders he refused, more tried their luck, some with the same produce as the seller before them. Luckily for him, not far ahead was the doorway through the second wall. It was not nearly as grand as the one they had just passed through and was half its size. It looked more strategic; the stairs up to the doorway were paved between two walls with arrow slits all along a good fifty meter walk and it got more and more narrow the closer they got. Two guardsmen stood there waiting and this time they opened the door with no interfering pestering about his identity. Word must have spread quickly that a prince was in the keep. That being said, the commoners below treated him just like any other potential customer. The pair led by Leynin, passed through the doorway and on the other side was a very small courtyard that opened out from the narrow pass they had just emerged from. Gaps in the wall on this side, either side of them, led to sections inside the wall that allowed archers to position themselves for the keeps defence and further down the courtyard, stairs led up to the walls to reach the battlements. The journey between the door of the second wall and the actual castle was practically none existent. The inner wall appeared perfect for defence against larger forces. It was congested with many archer slits and a tight bottleneck.

'Do not waste anything on appearances here I suppose,' Rayar pondered as he ran his green eyes over his surroundings.

"Welcome, Your Grace Prince Rayar. It is an honour to have you join us here in Stoneside Keep." In front of him, stood a man dressed in light brown leather, with a shirt underneath that tucked into leather on his sleeves. On one arm, a mantle covered half his body, with the emblem of the Bull, the banner of Stoneside Keep and the family who ruled it; Noble Family Loysse. The man was slender and tall, taller than Rayar was by a forehead, with a slim and long face. His hair was black and tied into the usual Mayhen bun and braid and his eyes were dark, contrasting with his pale skin. Beside him stood a woman who seemed the spitting image of him, but with breasts and in a long navy dress with embroidery dotted over the chest, wrists and hem, in gold. They both wore welcoming smiles yet Shania was first to whisper something into his ear, as they dismounted and allowed their horses to be taken by the stable boy.

"They seem nervous," she stated quietly. Rayar could not sense anything, they seemed fine and welcoming to him.

"You think? Well I am the Prince of Mayhen. Perhaps they are curious to why I am here," he whispered back to her but quickly turned back to their hosts so not to appear rude.

"It is an honour to meet you, Lord and Lady of Stoneside. I hope we are not intruding." Rayar wore his largest smile as he had been taught to do at a young age and summoned all his regal courage to act as royally as possible. Without his parents or his sisters here to take the lead when meeting new people, as they usually did, it was down to him to make the great first impression.

"Not at all," the lady spoke as she curtsied to the Prince.

"As my wife says, not at all Your Grace. I am Lord Tismiar Loysse and this is my wife, Lady Seldine. We did not expect a Prince to come to our home... now... I mean. We heard what occurred in Heldon. Nasty business. Our prayers are with the Royal Family." His words were sincere but his voice seemed to waver. Maybe Shania was right, something did seem a bit off.

"I assure you, my family are well, I left shortly after the attack, on the word of the Queen... to... well, it is hard to explain." He felt a light nudge in his ribs. Shania stood next to him eyeing him with that hawk like glare. "Oh, sorry... I mean... this is my companion, Shania..." It was an embarrassing moment when he realised he did not know her full name.

"Shania Tear," she stated bluntly though her body remained erect and her tone cold. Her behaviour reminded him of how she behaved when they had first met, a few days back.

"Lady Shania Tear. It is an honour to welcome you with the young prince. My, how you have grown," Tismiar said as he looked the young man up and down. "I remember when you were just a child. You were present during your father's tournament in Heldon if I recall. I would remember that golden hair anywhere."

"And into such a handsome young man as well," his wife added. Tismiar chuckled to himself and passed her a teasing but loving glance.

"Not here to steal away my wife, are you, Your Grace?" the slender lord teased. Rayar chuckled awkwardly and shook his head.

"No, no nothing like that. I was actually hoping we could trouble you for a meal and room for the night. We must be continuing on my journey come dawn." His forced regal posturing had dwindled.

"Your journey, Your Grace, where to?" Tismiar asked curiously. Rayar sniffed and flicked his eyes to Shania who merely turned away from him to look around the courtyard. If he did not know any better, she was on guard herself.

"To meet a friend of my mothers... it is... complicated." The lord raised his hands and bobbed his head apologetically.

"I mean no offence Your Grace. I should not presume to question a prince." The lady Seldine then took over.

"Come let us get you out of those rags and into something more befitting your station Your Grace, and perhaps a dress for your companion? I must say I have not heard that accent before." Shania wrinkled her nose and shook her head firmly.

"No dress, thank you. I'm fine as I am." The lady was taken back for a moment before she laughed it off and motioned them to follow.

"Of course, of course, you would not wish to ruin a nice dress riding through the countryside now would you?" The pair followed the lord and lady through the entrance into the keep. As they walked through the main hall and on to the kitchen, Lord Tismiar talked them through the history of his family and how they had ruled in Stoneside Keep for hundreds of years; how his father held off the Hextheene invasion and how he remembered the tournament at Heldon where he first met Rayar.

"You were such a sweet boy if I recall, you gave my wife a flower from the castle garden. I remember you following little Princess Ayla all over the grounds. Your Royal Blade had to keep you two from running into the jousting area." The prince nodded slowly as he began to recall those days. A feeling of sadness fell onto his heart. He did miss home. He missed Ayla and her face when she smiled and the feeling of her hand as she lead him through the gardens.

"I remember. Father scolded us both but Ayla was so sweet and innocent, he ended up treating us instead. I hope they are well in my absence." Once they reached the dining hall, Tismiar nodded to his wife who placed a hand on Shania's shoulder and began to lead her towards the kitchen.

"Come, come my dear. See the kitchens with me. Our chefs will cook you two anything you wish!" the gleeful lady said with a song in her voice. Shania could only look back to Rayar with a pleading look for rescue, but this was only received with a smile and a shrug of his shoulders.

'You are on your own there, druidae.' The lord offered him a seat and had two cups of wine brought over for the pair. The dining hall was much smaller than Heldon's. Simple and quaint, the table looked like it would hold less than a dozen. All the chairs were small and wooden; equal even. This keep looked so much bigger from the outside, the first wall held so much it was like a town and the second wall only held the inner

keep. It was small and basic, yet it was pleasant. Tismiar took a sip of his wine and motioned Rayar to do the same.

"I received a messenger pigeon about the attack on Heldon not long after it occurred. Yet you were there, Prince Rayar. Tell me, if I may pry, what happened?" What was there to say? What could he say? The prince took a deep breath and began his tale of the attack of Heldon. Tismiar sat in silence nodding and listening intently as he told him almost every gruesome detail. How he felt amidst the fighting, how the men came from nowhere, how Hinsani and Hyar saved him and Nymin and how Raimon died at the hands of a beast of a man. He purposely left out that Shania was a druidae and that his mother had sent him out to find a man named Quale, not to mention he left out about the taking of the pearl. He did not want to seem crazy to the lord who had been so welcoming. The slender lord held his chin firmly in thought as he took in everything he was told.

"So, you do not know where these attackers came from at all?" he probed. Rayar shook his head.

"I do not. Raimon did not know but he said some believed they were let in. My mother believes this friend we seek, will have more answers but for the moment I must leave the investigation of it all to my family. My father is a good man and he will see that all are looked after in the castle. I am just... trying to make sure it does not happen again." Tismiar seemed to be studying him and his words very carefully. Strangely but carefully.

"You are being honest...," Of course he was, why would he be lying? Rayar frowned at that comment.

"I... I am. Why do you say this?" The lord sighed heavily and downed the rest of his wine in one long swig. His previous happy demeanour had soured.

"Prince Rayar, there was something else in the letter sent to me, sent to all nobles of the realm. It said-," his words were cut short annoyingly as a guardsman came through the door.

"My Lord! A group of armed men have come to the gate. Heldoran Guards and a man in black. They have demanded your presence." Tismiar looked around to the guard and crooked a brow.

"Demanded?" The guard nodded furiously.

"Yes, My Lord, they claim to be on the King's business!" The lord's face dropped as he seemed to realise something that Rayar did not.

"I see." Attention was once again on the prince. "Prince Rayar, I humbly request to be excused to deal with this. I will have you escorted to your room for the night and your meals shall be brought to you. I apologise for this inconvenience." Rayar felt as confused as ever but he would not turn down the chance for a warm bed and cooked meal. He nodded respectfully to the lord.

"No, no it is no trouble. I thank you for your hospitality." With that Lord Tismiar was on his way to the exit and courtiers began to direct him to their chamber for the night. It only hit him then that he had said room for the night, not rooms.

'Wait, me and Shania are sharing?' he thought as he was guided into the back of the keep.

* * *

Chapter XIII
Choices
~Tismiar~

I do not believe it. The honesty in his eyes, the pain in his voice. The prince could not be guilty of such crimes against the Royal Family. There has to have been some sort of mistake. I want to get to the bottom of this yet... is it my place to do so?' Tismiar thought as he made his way towards the keep doorway. He and all the Noble Lords of Mayhen had received the same message via the messenger pigeon.

'All Loyal Families of Mayhen,

Heldon was attacked during the night and many lost their lives in its protection, aid is not needed at this time but your prayers are welcome for those lost. Prince Rayar, if seen, is to be apprehended without mercy. As a traitor to the Royal Family and orchestrator of the attack, if he resists use any means. Once captured have him escorted to the Royal House of Heldon immediately or body delivered. His female companion is dangerous and must be approached with caution but captured alive,

Serve your Royal Family well,

King Rumeo Granlia of Mayhen.' The slender lord had read the letter so many times he could recite it from memory. While the prince's companion did seem rather odd, she did not appear at all dangerous and he sensed a somewhat protective aura around her towards Rayar. Other Noble Families in the land would have caught them upon sight to win favour with the

King. The man he remembered was not like this, violent and ruthless; he was a man of reason and logic as well as kindness. No, he did not buy this, this was not the King Rumeo he had known and served for his entire life. The lord finally reached the main doorway after stalling in his walk for as long as he could to find his wife waiting there patiently for him. She offered him a warm smile with concern clearly overwhelming the warmth.

"I have had them taken to their room... have these men come to take them, Tismiar?" she asked as she fiddled with the cloth of her dress nervously. The lord rubbed his smooth chin in thought.

"It is likely, dear, it is likely. We will see what they have to say. Watch the conversation and give the Prince and his friend ample time if I am unable to resolve the situation. Who would have thought today was the day I would refuse the King... or whoever sits on that throne." Seldine nodded while her hand rubbed his arm softly.

"Be careful..." now he had to go make her worry even more. Tismiar put on his most confident smile and cupped her chin in his hand.

"I am still Lord of Stoneside Keep, I have guards all around me, and I will be safe. Do not fear." His wife did her best to return the smile. It was true he had many men at his disposal here but it was not as if he could use them to fight men of Heldon. They were King's men, the best he could do was try and convince them the Prince was not here or stall as long as possible. He took a deep breath and pushed his way through the door of his keep. On the other side his men, Stoneside men, were positioned around the unwelcome guests. He had more than twice the "visiting" number of fighting men in the small courtyard but that was irrelevant. There would be no fighting here this day. The group of a dozen or so men stood behind another in black leather. The man looked smug, with a feeling of vileness emitting from his very presence. He was short, very short in fact; Tismiar had to look down to keep eye contact.

However the lord put on his best performance and offered the man and his company a welcoming smile.

"I am Lord Tismiar Loysse of Stoneside keep. My men inform me you come on the King's business. What business brings the King's men to *my* home?" The vile looking man twirled a rolled up scroll in his left hand as smoothly as he would twirl a knife. In the brief pause of its rotation, he caught glimpse of the King's seal, keeping it held with a red ribbon.

"Dear Lord Loysse I come bearing sour news. Sour indeed." The man said with a slithering tongue. Simply vile. "I am Captain Sirus from Heldon, newly appointed. I am sure you have heard of the terrible, terrible business in Heldon as of a few nights prior. Awful business, don't you agree?" The lord nodded to the man wearing a saddened expression. This he did not have to act. What had happened to the Royal Family was truly an awful event.

"I have. Our prays to the Above are with all in Heldon. Yet that does not answer my question. What brings you here?" Sirus, as he called himself, let out a bone chilling cackle under his breath and tossed the letter he had been fiddling with, to the lord before he continued rattling on, while at the same time walking in circular motions around the Lord of Stoneside.

"By order of the King, my band of merry men and I have been charged with the capture of Prince Rayar Granlia and his companion. Now we tracked them out of Heldon, to the north-east through the village of Summerfall. The folk there claimed to have seen nothing; we questioned them thoroughly but to no avail. Then the craziest thing happened. My hounds found this small bedding in the forest, near to the village. We would have thought nothing of it, naturally, but wouldn't you know the scent matched that of Prince Rayar's clothes we had brought with us!" Every word that left this man's lips felt like poison entering his blood. The mask had slipped and now the lord simply watched the spider stalk around him with a deep frown plastered to his face. "I couldn't believe my luck, I guess the traitors just were not quite careful enough. Well my hounds followed that scent all across the countryside and we thought

135

they were heading towards the mountains. Then, as if they changed their minds, they led us straight to this keep. What do you know? They made my life so much easier. To think chasing a couple of criminals in the mountains would have surely been challenging but instead they wandered right into the home of a *loyal* Lord of Mayhen, to hand them over on a plate." Sirus returned to his position in front of the lord and smirked a toothy smirk. "Any questions concerning my authority please look at the scribe." Tismiar clenched his teeth in defeat. This man had made up his mind. By the looks of him he would not give up that easily. All he could do was nod to his wife. In the corner of his eye she scurried off into the keep. She would need to give the prince ample warning, while he dealt with these brigands dressed in Heldoran armour.

"I shall read this letter before anything else occurs. I hope you understand?" He asked, though of course the only answer expected, was compliance. The black leathered man shrugged his shoulders and bowed his head respectfully, giving the lord the time he needed.

"Of course, My Lord." The words never sounded sincere; every word felt as if he insulted anyone he spoke to. Tismiar studied the parchment in his hands. The man spoke truly, it held the seal of the King and the words giving this man the authority to carry out of the King's will and justice by whatever means. This too was an insult. By the looks of it, some jumped up sell-sword had the power to do whatever he pleased in the realm of Mayhen and as Lord of Stoneside Keep; he would have to bow to the demands. He could feel his usual calm demeanour shattering into that of anger.

"Satisfied?" Sirus teased with a vile grin.

"Satisfied? No. You make claims without proof. You insult my home by rolling in here with armed soldiers making a demand from a lord and acting as if the King would make such awful choices. The King Rumeo I know would never denounce his son as a traitor and call for his capture and death. The King Rumeo I know is a good man who uses reason not someone with a bloodlust!" Tismiar snapped at the man whose reaction only angered him further; he stood there with that wide toothy grin unfazed by his outburst.

"Please don't make this difficult. I wouldn't want to embarrass a lord and leave this... beautiful castle without one." Tismiar snarled and his men seemingly in agreement with him drew their swords, followed by the men from Heldon drawing theirs.

"You dare threaten our lord!" One of the men called out as they moved to defend him. Even he knew this was getting out of hand. Sirus raised his hands, unarmed, and motioned for his men to lower their weapons.

"Now now, there is no need for something so brash." A black clad finger tapped the scroll in Tismiar's hand, on the symbol of the King of Mayhen. The comedic man turned darkly serious. "Is this the choice you wish to make, to challenge the King's orders? I'm no lord, I'm a servant of the King, nothing more. Perhaps we get off on the wrong foot. Let me say this a different way. Give me the Prince and his friend or stand aside and let me do my job. There is no third option. I'm not threatening you, Lord Loysse, I'm advising you. The King knows he is surrounded by traitors and whispers of his family's demise. Do we add the Loysse family to this list of suspects or do we serve our King faithfully?" He had no choice and he knew it. He was not a coward nor was he a fool. As much as he wanted to do what was right, as much as he sucked in the courage to stand against injustice, deep down he could not refuse his King. He could not put his family in peril. Yet he would still not make it easy for the man and hoped his wife had moved swiftly.

"Very well." Tismiar stepped to the side in defeat; his men sheathed their weapons and parted the way for the soldiers of Heldon.

"Excellent!" Sirus clapped his hands together and began to stride towards the doorway. "You're doing the right thing, My Lord." The right thing? Nothing had ever felt so wrong.

*

~Rayar~

The room Shania and he had been granted was surprisingly beautiful. Blue drapes hung over the windows blocking out the dusk. Food had been placed on a long engraved table in the middle of the large room. Pork, potatoes, pheasant, carrots and wine, quite a lot of wine in fact. More than he had ever wished to drink at least. The rug below their feet was soft and covered with decorations of Mayhen's banners, with the same writing that was on the gate passed the first wall. Still he had no idea what it said and doubted any did. Rayar had stripped himself down to the commoners' slacks they had picked up in Summerfall, from behind a divider and began to adorn the attire gifted to him by the keep's servants. They had given him black trousers and shiny black leather boots to change into, as well as a white shirt with a golden trim. Since his red jacket had been dirtied so much from using it as a sheet, when they had briefly rested in the countryside, they had offered him a new one, though this time it was green with a golden collar and sleeves. Shania had been given a dress even after her protest, which still sat on the bed, untouched. She stood by the window with her arms crossed, her sharp gaze peering out into the oncoming darkness of night.

"Something is not right." She said with a sniff. Rayar sighed as he was getting changed, awkwardly trying to pull free his slacks.

"After what we have been through, can you not relax for one moment?" he retorted. Once he had finally pulled free his trousers, Shania appeared on his side of the divider with a stern look on her face. Rayar gasped in shock and stumbled back against the wall awkwardly hiding his privates. "What are you bloody doing?!" He said in alarm, his face bright red. Shania scoffed and rolled her eyes.

"After what we have been through, you want to relax? Trust me it's better to keep moving so you don't think about it."

138

She replied. Her eyes flicked up and down his quivering form. "I can still see it." With that she turned back around the divider and towards the window.

'Above and Below! This woman is impossible!' He thought, no longer able to form words as all the air had escaped his lungs. Embarrassed, with his shyness returning he pulled on his new clothes and finally came free from his hiding place walking in an apprehensive manner.

"What do you mean?" The prince asked unable to look her way.

"You have been with me moving forward since the attack in your home. That nightmare you had haunts your sleep. You really want to relax and reflect on those things. Sometimes always having something to do fills' your mind and keeps you distracted from thinking about the horrors that have befallen you." She was not wrong. Since he had that nightmare he had barely had a wink of sleep and the idea of adventuring into the wild had been so impulsive, he had not yet really sat down to think about how things were at home.

'I can be really selfish sometimes...' Rayar chastised himself.

"You keep moving so you do not think of things that have happened to you?" He asked quietly as he stood on the other side of the room. Shania turned to him and forced eye contact, causing his face to brighten once more.

"Yes, but I don't feel sadness anymore." She began as she approached him. The sun kissed druidae walked up to his face and looked up to him with a sharp blade like glare. "It's revenge I want, not to mourn. I don't have time for mourning." The prince frowned at that, briefly forgetting a girl was that close to him.

"Is that all you care about, revenge? Revenge for what happened to your people?" Shania returned the frown as she gazed up to him.

"Of course! Everyone is dead but me and for what? I don't even know. All I know is Quale will help me find out who did it and then I will hunt them down and kill them. You are a piece to finding them. They wanted you, well, they wanted the sphere which you had been holding onto and you can find it again!" In her growing anger she was revealing even more to him. While he was not against a little bit more information into what was going on, seeing her this way was actually painful. What was also painful was the thought he was nothing but a stepping stone for her.

"So, I am a tool for your revenge?" He asked as all his bashfulness was lost. She sighed and shook her head clearly growing agitated by the conversation.

"I didn't say that. That's not what I mean. It's just..." They stared silently at each other for a moment. Rayar could see her anger subsiding as she wanted to say more, but was holding her tongue. He wanted to know more and he wanted to know what she felt.

'This is... strange...' A screech echoed in the bedroom which brought their attention to the open window. There sat perched on the window sill, was Shania's faithful hawk, Jac. The tension broke between them as her attention was redirected to the hawk leaving Rayar standing there with a blank expression. He had felt out of the loop a few times now, when this situation occurred, as much as one could when a woman and a bird somehow conversed without any words. The collar of his new green coat was snagged, as Shania pushed him towards the doorway, before he had any time to question what was happening.

"There's a problem. Some armed people have shown up. They could be after us, we need to leave. Now." How did she get this information? Rayar knocked her hand away with a swift flick of his wrist and reached for his sheathed sword to attach to his belt.

"One of Lords Loysse's soldiers said a group of men on the King's business had come to the keep. You worry for nothing, they are my men as well, as a Prince of Mayhen, but if they have come to take us home, perhaps father has called for my return." Surely it was nothing to panic about. If men from his home had come, then he could explain his mother's wish of

140

him, though the more likely explanation is that the King had requested he abandon this quest; maybe going on alone was too dangerous. Whatever it was, a conversation would clear this up without any need for a commotion but Shania was making it very difficult to resolve. The druidae had thrown on her cloak and attached her sword to her hip and had sent her hawk back out into the sky as quickly as it had come.

"Look, you are worrying for nothing. Let us go speak to them." Shania growled at the prince, followed by a movement too quick for his eyes to track. Before he knew it, he was pinned against the wall with her grip around the neck of his shirt.

"Jac sensed hostile intentions. His senses are never wrong. I can't let you go back now, we have to get to Quale." He grabbed her wrist and gripped it tightly, overpowering the woman and pushing her back.

"You forget I am a Prince!" he growled back at her. Since their relationship started, not once had he felt this angry towards the girl. He could understand that she was from some faraway place and did not understand the rules here. He could forgive that but there was a limit to how far she could push him. Even he, as laid back as he was, had a limit. "Now you will cease treating me like a child or your toy and you will listen to me!" The altercation was interrupted as the Lady of Stoneside Keep burst through the door. They looked to each other with confused faces, each wondering why the other was appearing so dramatic.

"...Prince Rayar, Lady Tear..."

"Lady Loysse..."

"...Hello." There was a moment of silence as they stared at each other. Seldine finally broke it as she shut the door behind her and shot over to the pair to break up their fight.

"There is no time for this, Your Grace. I have not much time to explain but men have come for you and your friend." He nodded to her and waved a hand, once again calm.

"We know, we were just... discussing it between us. They are from Heldon?" The prince asked placing a smile on his lips.

Shania only groaned and moved to the side of the room in exasperation. Lady Loysse spoke through long breaths, clearly exerted from running.

"How do you know this? It does not matter, as I said there is no time. They are from Heldon but they are not your allies. They have come to arrest you both." Rayar frowned at this. Why would men of Heldon come to arrest a prince? That was preposterous. She must have been mistaken.

"I do not understand. What are you talking about?" He asked as he placed a hand on her shoulder to calm her down. The older woman was getting more and more flustered.

"My husband did not tell you the whole story? Above and Below, Your Grace. Things have happened in Heldon, bad things dear. They blame you for the attack in your home, they say you let the enemies in and now you have fled upon your treason failing. You must flee or they will capture you, or worse." Lady Loysse looked between them both and tried to motion them towards the door. Shania nodded and shot towards the doorway, while he could not move a muscle.

'They think I am a traitor at home...? They think... it was me? My family, friends... this cannot be happening.' The prince stood motionless as he stared at the floor, unable to process the information. *'Why... why... why is this happening?'* He had to go home to clear this up. He had to prove he was innocent. No matter what mission the Queen had sent him on or what Shania needed him for or what this Quale could explain to him, he had to go home.

'Father... mother...' Rayar was transfixed in a state of shock. This state was shaken from him as a hand slapped him across his face. He was stunned and even more so by the next action of the druidae, who clasped his face between her hands and pulled him down to her level. She stared into him, those stunning blue eyes locked with his.

"Rayar listen to me. We need to go. We can sort this out together, afterwards. If they think you're a traitor, if they think it was you, then we can prove it wasn't. We can't do anything if you're in chains. Please, I'm begging you, trust me. Just this once." Shania had never spoken to him like this before. She had never shown such compassion to him before. His heart was heavy and his mind weighed with thoughts of his family and what the people at home thought of him. Though he knew she was right, they needed to get away for now and think this over; come up with a plan. He was innocent and he would prove he was innocent.

"... Okay..." The words only just crawled from his mouth like a gentle mew of a kitten. Shania smiled at him, a genuine smile and then yanked him to follow.

"Show us the way." She said to Seldine. The Lady of the keep nodded and motioned them to follow. The trio ran through the rear passages of the keep towards the sally gate on the far northern part of the keep. It was a small tunnel that led through both walls and out into the country as close to the mountain as any would like to be. They would be able to slip into the mountain's passes just minutes after leaving the castle. As they reached the last metal gate, out of the second wall, Seldine stopped in her sprint.

"I can go no further. I must return to my husband. Be safe, understand? My husband has put a lot of faith into you, Your Grace. Please, do not let him down." Rayar, still in shock from the overwhelming information, could only weakly nod back to her and returned to following Shania. Night had finally fallen on the land of Mayhen; it was already dark outside that gate. Very dark. He could not see a thing and he doubted Shania could either but regardless; she pushed open the gate and grabbed his hand to lead him through. It only took a few steps out of the wall to find themselves in peril.

"Found ya'!" A voice rang from the rocky surroundings. Arrows struck the ground around them, herding them into one spot. Rayar followed Shania as she drew her sword but it was to no avail. Faces and figures began to sprout like weeds around them with weapons drawn and bows nocked. The moonlight was strong enough to let him see who approached them, but it was not a face he recognised. Shania snarled like a furtive wolf at the group, her eyes darting between them while

143

he could do nothing but weakly hold his sword at his side. He knew it, his resolve had been shattered.

"Like mice in a trap. I don't normally applaud myself but well done me." A man in black leather clapped his hands together as he stood in front of the pair. "I have to give you some credit though. Out of the sally gate, it's the most obvious trick in the book. You would have been better off putting on some commoners clothes and slipping through the crowds in the town. I only had one man at the front gate. I put all my eggs into this basket and fate allows me to win once again." He threw his head back in laughter, a vile, spine chilling cackle. Realising it was no use; Shania lowered her blade, her eyes briefly flicking to Rayar. He did not want her looking at him, he did not even attempt to put up a fight; he felt weak. These men were Heldon men and they had come to arrest him on his father's word. What was he supposed to do, fight them to the death? No, he only had one choice. Give up. It was not the men around him who had made him weak. It had been merely words that had crumbled him.

* * *

Chapter XIV
Follow to the End
~Rayar~

The night was dark and cold in their corner of the camp. Rayar and Shania sat back to back with their hands and ankles bound. The druidae behind him had been blind-folded as well but his sight had not been obstructed. He partly wished he couldn't see as well to help him forget what was happening. Perhaps being trapped in darkness would be somewhat freeing. Though that was unlikely to be true, it was just how he felt. The Prince of Mayhen being called a traitor and blamed for the deaths of so many at his home and he had not even been there to defend himself. Father would have listened to him if he had just stayed and spoken his piece. Yet no, he had to go off gallivanting on some fantasy adventure right after his home was attacked because his mother had told him to. Not only had he been selfish, he had also been acting like a child. Now he was in this predicament. His emerald eyes gazed around the camp-ground that the group of guards had crafted. There were a dozen men not including the man in black who led this band of kidnappers. They had removed most of their armour now with a couple on watch at the outskirts of the camp, while others were trying to start a fire. They were scattered around the camp, attending their own needs with one rather lazy guard, keeping an eye on them. Well, he would have been keeping an eye if he had stayed awake rather than dozing, slumped against the tree closest to the pair of prisoners. For the most part, the pair were alone, sat in the warm grass with their backs keeping the other from sliding to the ground. Rayar had not spoken much since they had been captured, Above and Below, not much since he found out his father wanted him arrested and returned alive or even dead. His heart felt as if a wild dog had torn it open to feast.

"Are you alright?" He finally asked in a whisper as he turned his head slightly to the side.

"I will be, when we get out of this." Shania stubbornly replied. Even in this situation, she would not give up that easily. Although there was probably a reasonable answer to this he had to ask.

"Why did you not use... fire like you did in Heldon, to fight them off?" He could hear a sigh escape her before she replied.

"It's not that simple. I can't just... create fire. I need something to draw from. I left my cinder stone in the room. However, they are giving me that something as we speak." Rayar blinked and shot his eyes around the camp. Not far from where they were being held, two guardsmen were close to setting their camp fire. So that was her plan, wait until they had given her the weapon to use against them. That was why she was so calm, even though they found themselves in such a tight spot. Above in the trees, her hawk was also watching and waiting. If she did use the fire, she could end up killing these men. They may have captured them but they were still loyal guardsmen of Heldon and he did not want to see them die for following their orders. Not to mention the fact it would make him appear a whole lot more guilty, if he helped kill men who were sworn to his family.

"Wait-"

"What for little Prince?" He was cut off by the slimy voice of the black leather clad cutthroat who called himself Sirus as he bound them. Captain of Heldon he claimed to be, that was some sort of sick joke.

"N-nothing..." The prince mumbled as he looked down to the grass, to avoid eye contact with the stealthy character.

146

Shania did not reply either, she continued her rebelling by sitting up straight, her face forward and a calm composure seeping from her being. Sirus chuckled to himself as he wandered closer to Rayar and perched down in front of the golden haired boy. In one hand, a slim curved dagger twirled and twisted between his fingers so quickly, he could barely follow its movements with his eyes.

"Don't look so glum, Your Grace." The villain began. "This is all in the balance of fate. You tried to kill your family and failed. Now they will try and kill you. Think they will fail too?" Rayar's' anger shot up to the surface quicker than a speeding arrow.

"I did not try to kill my family! It is a lie!" He yelled at the man taunting him. The guards around the camp briefly looked over to the sudden loud distraction before sullenly returning to their jobs and duties. Now their eyes locked, Sirus grew that toothy grin of his and shrugged his shoulders in response.

"Maybe, maybe not. It's not my job to find out if you're innocent or not, it's just my job to find you both and bring you back to Heldon by whatever means." The man reached over and ruffled his golden locks causing him to wince and flick his head to the side to avoid the contact. This only caused more laughter to fill the air. "You're not as timid as I was told you would be. Only been out here a few days and already as wild as a wolf. I like it." Rayar did not know what he was feeling right now. Angry at this man for taunting him and putting him in binds; distraught about his family, confused about his purpose. How was one supposed to feel in this kind of situation? Everything just seemed so uncontrollable and complicated. He felt the need to return home to his bed, wrapped up in his chambers with none of this ever happening to him or his family. The fire for the camp suddenly sparked a light and as it did, he felt a shuffle from Shania behind him. She must have been able to sense the flames without having the need to see them, but she would not know where the enemy were. Sirus pushed himself to his feet just before giving Rayar a cocky wink and smirk.

147

"Well rest as you can, we have a couple of days left until we get you back to your mothers breast. I'll be made a lord after this. Lucky, lucky me." He threw his head back in laughter and turned on his heel. Once the man was definitely out of ear shot this time, Rayar snapped his neck around to speak to his druidae companion.

"What are you going to do? Throw fire around like a mad woman?" He whispered in hushed tones. Shania did not reply as she seemed to be focusing as much as possible, trying to find that blaze and use it.

"We're under attack! The hounds are dead!" A voice roared across the camp. Rayar shot his attention towards the sound of the bellowing voice. A guardsman stood attempting to draw his sword from its sheath but in his panic, he was unable to get it free. From the darkness, a figure shot forward and without mercy carved his blade across the guard's neck and sliced his head clean from his shoulders. The guardsmen scrambled to retrieve their armour and weapons that they had shed for the evening. Helmets, gauntlets, swords, shields – anything they could get their hands on as quickly as possible. Rayar shuffled around to get a better view but due to all the foliage and equipment the men had set up, it was hard to see what was actually happening. Shania from behind her blindfold seemed confused as well, as she wriggled from side to side trying to gain a better idea of what was unfolding.

"Rayar, what do you see!?" She demanded. The Prince stared wide eyed as the attacker flickered in and out of his view. The figure's dance reminded him of just one person. Just one person could move like that; that graceful and that deadly. Guardsman after guardsman found themselves nothing more than lifeless heaps on the ground, or groaning in pain with severed limbs, crying out or for help or death. Sirus stepped back behind the captured pair while three guardsmen made a defensive perimeter around their prize.

"What's going on!?" He heard the man in leather bark from the very back of the group. The fire had been snuffed out by flying dirt and now they only heard screams of dying men in

148

the dark. The three guardsmen around Shania and himself drew their swords in unison and formed a tight defensive line.

"We're under attack sir. Am I going crazy or did that look like one man to you?" one guard asked as he looked into the shadow around them. They all seemed nervous, sweat on their foreheads, even Sirus with daggers in each hand, did not seem prepared for what was about to come.

'It cannot be...' Rayar thought as he leaned back into Shania. The druidae wriggled again as she tried desperately to shake her blindfold off.

"Dammit Rayar, what's going on!?" she yelled again. Rayar slowly turned his attention to Sirus who caught his gaze, the fear of uncertainty clear all over his features. The prince however only returned with a smile, though it was not one of happiness or joy, it was of confidence and sadness.

"I am sorry, Captain, if you do not flee you will be killed along with everyone else," he stated as a matter of fact. Sirus snarled and growled back at him.

"Don't underestimate me boy!" The prince could only nod and return his eyes towards the darkness to await that man. There he was. A symbol of a true warrior. His one edged sword soaked with blood, with specks of red splattered on his leather armour and cheek. He had never been so happy to see this man in his life yet the death that occurred for his rescue was equally as disheartening.

'Hinsani...' He watched the events unfold. Hinsani walked out of the shadows and confronted the four remaining soldiers including the captain, his dark eyes flashing between them as if measuring their capabilities to challenge him. From his stone-like face, one would never be able to tell if he was worried or not, but after his next words Rayar figured he was confident he was currently unmatched.

"Release my Prince at once and flee, that is your only choice to survive. If you do not, I will kill you all." Never a man to mince words. The guards looked between each other; they knew exactly who he was. Not many in Heldon and even Mayhen did not know of the Royal Blade Hinsani Tannaroth, bested by none and rumoured to be the greatest swordsman in the Freeland. The captain however began to run his mouth; the golden haired prince figured this man was the type to poison with his words but he also knew that those kind of tricks did not work on a man like Hinsani.

"Well, well the dog comes running to its master. You certainly made short work of my men then, Royal Blade Sir Tannaroth." Sirus slowly inched closer with his daggers once again in his belt with his hands raised to show he was unarmed. "But I'm surprised, bloody surprised. A Royal Blade of Heldon, an honourable man and here you slay your brothers in arms. These are... we are soldiers of Heldon, of Mayhen and of the King and you killed them. Is that something an honourable, just man would do I ask?" Another inch closer, every few seconds he got closer and closer to the Royal Blade. Hinsani stared at him with his cold stone face not budging nor made no motion to raise his sword.

'What is his trick?' Rayar thought as he watched the scene in anticipation. Sirus was within striking distance now yet his hands still were raised to show he was against any more conflict.

"Can you live with this, I ask? Killing your fellows in such a brutal way... aren't you a good man, Sir Tannaroth?" The vile man forced a smile through his nerves. That grin was soon wiped from his face as Hinsani stared him relentlessly and retorted.

"You arrest my Prince whom I am sworn to protect. I would cut through any man or woman who posed a threat to my duty. No exceptions." Sirus growled and with a flick of his wrist, a small knife slithered from his sleeve. Rayar caught the flash as the moonlight reflected from the blade.

"Hinsani!" He roared out but it was unneeded. As quick as lightening and too fast for Rayar to even grasp in his sight, the Royal Blade swung his sword and returned it to his side. The hand of Sirus wielding the knife lay severed in the dirt and the black leathered captain screeched out in pain and shock while his remaining hand gripped his newly acquired stump.

"Bloody kill him! Kill him!" He screamed as he fell onto his behind and began to push backwards through the grass. The three guardsmen leapt forward in unity to bring down the Royal Blade but as quick as they had struck, they too found themselves in the dirt. The first thrust his blade forward like a spear which Hinsani smoothly avoided. The expert swordsman slid forward and ran his famous blade through the guard's throat before spinning in a circle to deflect the horizontal strike from his right side, the blade ripping free from the flesh of the first victim and parrying the second strike. He was unable to land a counterattack; from his left side the third guardsman tried his luck with a thrust like his unlucky companion. Hinsani shifted to the side and grabbed the guard's wrist which forced him forwards and pierced his friend with the guard's own sword. To finish the dance Hinsani kept hold of the last attacker's sword arm. He twisted his own body and whipped his sword across the guard's face faster than he had a chance to free himself from the grip as tight as a crab. All three bodies lay in the dirt, bloodied and dismantled, with the Royal Blade standing victorious above them. Seeing him fight was truly a performance like no other; he was skilled and swift and strong and everything Rayar wanted to be. Hinsani took a deep breath as he seemed to compose himself, before he cut the bound that held Rayar. The prince rubbed his wrists and ankles, they ached after being tangled for so long, and then gazed around the scene. The man named Sirus had fled in the commotion and was probably scurrying straight back to Heldon at full speed on horseback by now. When the vile man got back to Heldon and told them that the prince's Royal Blade had slaughtered all the guardsmen to free Rayar, what would they think then? There was too much to worry about, too much going on to get his head around.

"Sir Hinsani, what are you doing here? How did you find me?" The Royal Blade pulled Rayar to his feet and dusted off his long green coat. His expression impossible to read as always.

"I followed them and waited for the right time to strike. We have much to discuss but maybe not here. We should move." Hinsani stated as he cleaned his sword known as Galad. The prince nodded in agreement and moved to free Shania who, at this point, had grown very impatient. Once her bindings were removed, she pushed herself to her feet with a cocked brow at the sights around them. Finally her piercing gaze rested on Hinsani, who returned the look with his dark eyes.

"Who are you?" She started.

"None of your concern. Who are you?" He replied.

"Well... none of your concern then. Did you do this?" Rayar blinked as he looked between them.

"I did." Shania wrinkled her nose and went to retrieve both hers and Rayar's weapons from the ground near one of the bodies.

"You killed all of them, at the same time?" A heavy frown grew on Hinsani's face. It felt like a weight Rayar could not even dream to carry.

"I told you, I did. What is so hard to understand?" His tone was growing more stern. Shania tossed Rayar his own one edged sword in its sheath and reattached hers to her belt. The prince caught it yet he was so awestruck by their conversation, that he barely reacted in time to catch it.

"Just, an old man like you able to kill this many men, it's surprising!" Hinsani snorted and placed a hand on the pommel of his blade which now sat in its sheath.

"I am Prince Rayar's Royal Blade. I do what I must to protect him, no matter what the cost or challenge." Shania placed her hand on her hips and rolled her eyes.

"Oh I see, so where have you been so far? I've been the one looking after him until now."

"You dare-" Rayar cut them off as he stood between them, both arms outstretched as an unrealistic blockade.

"Enough! We can argue later. For now Shania, this is Sir Hinsani Tannaroth, he is charged with my protection. Hinsani this is Miss Shania Tear, the last druidae. That is right, a druidae. I did not believe it at first but it is true. Now that is dealt with, let us get out of here. Hinsani, I need to know from someone I can trust, what is happening at home." It was not like him to take charge like that so abruptly and as sad as he felt after hearing about home, it was a good feeling to take control. The pair mumbled to themselves, but gave in to his leadership. Hinsani led them to his steed Dragan and then to two of the horses the guardsmen had vacated. The group headed north from the campsite towards the northern coast. Rayar refused to go to the mountains until he had some answers and heading either to Stoneside Keep once again or even returning home was out of the question. Hinsani made it clear that if they returned to Heldon they would not be treated fairly. The situation was sure to escalate now that his Royal Blade had just slain so many guardsmen, which the prince certainly was not in favour of.

The trio rode for little under an hour with fatigue hitting Rayar like a stampede of horses. He was tired, hungry and mentally exhausted. Just as they achieved some respite, they were once again galloping on horseback without so much as an hour of rest. This travelling thing was truly a tiring experience. Once they had reached a rather remote spot in the woodland, with the coast far off, yet in sight, they dismounted and found a place to sit and collect their thoughts. It was a rocky area surrounded by trees and foliage. Even as they had ridden north and not towards the mountains, it still became a lot denser with stones and gravel as the mountains curved around the land towards the sea. Shania pointed out an area with a few rocks in the dirt, where they could sit. Her hawk circled in the sky seemingly minding its own business, even if it had followed them on their escape.

"Before you begin your questions, Prince Rayar, I must first apologise." Hinsani began as the other two sat down. His protector bowed his head sorrowfully as he spoke. "As your Royal Blade I have failed you. I should have been with you in the keep and not left you and your sister to Raimon. My honour is stained by such an act." Shania gave the prince a side glance with a puzzled expression. She did not seem to get all this highborn, honourable customs that he had lived by all his life.

"No, Sir Hinsani I must apologise. I have dragged you into this, whatever this is. You came and saved us, I will forever be thankful to have someone like you by my side." Rayar replied offering the man a warming smile. Hinsani dropped to his knee and bowed his head once more.

"And you always shall, Prince Rayar. You are my charge. It is my duty to protect you from any and all." His head rose to lock eyes with his prince. "If you would still have me as your protector, I will follow you. Yet, we must speak of these claims against you. I know you did not do it, I have known you since you were a baby. Why have you left the capital and where are you going?" That question had so many questions connected to it; Rayar did not know where to start. Well, the beginning seemed the sensible place.

"The attack at home... well, this may sound strange so I will explain what I can. It was mother, the Queen, who sent me from our home. After Raimon was killed by some giant of a man, Shania here rescued me and Nymin with... well... magic, druidae magic. I know it sounds crazy, but it is true. Then the Queen arrived with her maiden and she spoke to Shania as if she knew who she was. She told me I must go with her and find a man named Quale. From what Shania says, he lives in the mountains on the border between Mayhen and Hextheene. Mother said that those attackers came because of me and the pearl I always wear. There is something special about it, about... well... me. I know it sounds like riddles of a madman and perhaps I was mad myself to go along with it. Mother has never led me astray. I did not think that this was any different. So we are heading to find Quale but now if they think I am some sort of traitor to my family at home, what am I supposed to do?" Hinsani listened to him intently, still knelt in front of him with his brow low above his eyes. Shania sat there listening also, her expression not much different from his protector's.

"I see. The Queen wished it so. The Queen disappeared after the attack and was supposedly badly wounded and Princess Nymin was shut away in her quarters. The King told me of what happened to Raimon but nothing like this. The Princess had already whispered some things to her sisters before she was taken away, for her safety, or so I am told." Rayar felt his body begin to shake in fear and panic.

"Mother was hurt!?" He barked out almost jumping from his seat. Shania placed a calming hand on his shoulder.

"She was fine when we left her. She was with your sister, also, the way I came through the keep, all those attackers had been killed by your family's men," she said trying to reassure him but it did not really have the desired effect. Hinsani tried next.

"Hyar and I slaughtered most of them. The way Raimon took you is the way we had come. There were no more of those black armoured men that way. We made sure of it." He sounded quite confident in that statement but the prince already knew that was not true.

"But the two who killed Raimon, they were waiting for us!" Hinsani wrinkled his nose in annoyance.

"Impossible. We checked each room before we reached you." He seemed certain of it, even offended that he may have missed something. Shania sighed and slipped in her opinion.

"You were facing Controllers... mages, if you like. If they didn't want you to see them, they could have easily made it so you couldn't." Controllers? It was not a term he was familiar with but mages, he was. They were rumoured to be in the Order but other than that his knowledge of them was limited. If she spoke true, it would make sense, it wouldn't take a genius to figure out the safest exit once the Royal Blades had cleared it of their foes. If anything, it was obvious that they would have taken that route.

"I am not a noble, girl. I have seen the real world. I have seen war, I have seen death, and I have seen terrible things. I have never seen magic and I have been across half the world with nothing but a blade. The Order claims to be mages, they

155

trick rulers into taking them as advisors. Southrous, Brexxia, Breton, the Wise Isles, all Southern countries have the Order pulling the strings with their lies and illusions. Yet..." The dark haired man flashed a glance to his prince, a look of sadness briefly touching his expression yet gone within a second.

'Was that... emotion?' Rayar thought.

"... Yet, I trust Prince Rayar. If he says you are a druidae, you can use fire as a weapon and that he must go see this mystery man for answers, then I accept it all. I have seen much but I am not so ignorant to say I have seen all. I will not believe it however until I see it with my own eyes. I am a soldier, not a scholar." The pair shared a moment of agreement before the attention returned to the rather quiet prince.

"What do you want to do?" Hinsani asked. He was being oddly kind to him; he was used to the stony and stoic defender and never really saw him as a friend. For the first time, he got this feeling.

"Part of me wants to go home, to see my family, and end this journey now. I do not even know why I am still entertaining this... but at the same time, if this Quale has answers, if my mother still has faith in me doing the right thing, Above and Below, I have to keep going. We need to get to the bottom of who attacked our home and prove it was not me. If we go home now after all those men were killed, we would not stand a chance. I do not even know who to ask for help." Shania muttered to herself at his last comment and chipped in.

"The more people who know where you are, the bigger the danger you are in. The Queen trusted you to protect your family. You can't protect them from a cell in Heldon or any of these castles in this country. You can protect them if you help me and Quale stop these people from doing whatever it is they're trying to do. Those mages still have your pearl and they are going to use it for something terrible. Are you really the type of man to sit back and do nothing?" Her words rung harsh but true. What sort of man was he exactly? He had never been in a situation like this before. He would have imagined himself as a good man who would have done anything to help those who needed it. Rumeo had taught him that much. Now he was here, all he wanted was for this to never have happened. He again looked to Hinsani for some sort of verification.

"I am your Blade, Prince Rayar. My duty is to let none harm you or endanger you. Heldon is dangerous. I would be forced to fight to protect you until the end if they wished to arrest you. Your father is not in his right mind. Though I have spoken my piece, the next step you take is yours and I will only follow." Lives hung in his hands, not only his own. Both hands found their way to his face as he rubbed it in frustration.

'If I go home, Hinsani will fight for me. I cannot stop him but I will be able to speak to father and try and get some truth out of this mess. I would get to see my sisters, Ayla... Nymin, Nyer. I would be home. Though whatever mess is happening in this world, I will have no part in. If I carry on I get answers, I can help and save lives I hope, as well as find those who truly struck at my home and family. Then again we could be going to nothingness with no aim and this is all a mistake without end. Father, what would you do...?' He knew both their eyes were on him as he sat there with his face covered. So many decisions were resting on his shoulders; something he knew would come as he grew up but not this quickly. Both hands ran back over his hair as he stood, the choice had been made. He had no choice.

"We carry on. Father would do what is right. He would face those who have hurt his family. If he thinks that is me, then I will prove this wrong. I will find and face those who did this. It is my duty to serve my country and the Royal Family as much as any man of Mayhen. I am Prince Rayar Granlia, I am no coward." The doubt of this still hung heavy in his heart but he could not falter now. There was only forward, as Lanni had told him, stop looking backwards; always go forwards. Having Hinsani with him now made him all that more confident, if there was to be fighting in the coming days or weeks. Shania seemed pleased with this and Hinsani had returned to his unreadable demeanour.

157

"Then we've wasted enough time." The druidae returned to the horses and mounted her chosen steed. "Whatever their plan is, they won't wait around forever to commence it. Let's go see the old man in the mountain." The two men followed her lead and mounted their horses.

This is what I must do. No more wavering, no more second guessing. Forward, only forward.' Their destination once again was the Leon Mountains and whatever lay beyond.

* * *

Chapter XV
Commander of
the Shield
~Vesir~

"You can't be serious!?" Vesir said in disbelief as he drank with his men. The commander found himself in the favoured inn in the town of Meyer, The Sullen Crone. His usual style of braided hair was now let loose over his shoulders and he wore a casual light brown long sleeved shirt with small but obvious stains of ale spotted across it. As a man who was brother to the King, he did not keep up appearances; even his lower half was tattered and common in comparison to what they wore in Heldon. He always found it much more appealing to be in the company of regular soldiers, than those rather stuck up Nobles or stone figures of guardsmen in the capital. He was a man of basic needs and pleasures, well his wife always said so anyway. The inn he frequented was a large and master crafted building. He had helped design it after all. The Shield of Mayhen emblem hung above the bar with a roaring fire warming the interior. A large rug with symbols of lions circled the floor by the fire with two huge high backed chairs for those wishing a bit of quiet relaxation in the usual rowdy tavern. Throughout the rest of the inn, chairs and tables were aplenty with a couple of musicians playing their arts for coin in the corner, one with a lute, the other with a drum. Drunken soldiers danced awkwardly with their mistresses for the evening or their wives if they could convince them to come to this establishment. Vesir used to get his wife down here regularly but ever since his new child was born only a year ago, she had remained at home caring for him. They were not one for maids and servants to tend to them; they much preferred to be hands on when raising their children. Beside Vesir, on the table were a group of soldiers in their casual attire, all drinking merrily.

"No word of a lie, I had to wrestle that boar absolutely ruined on wine because my father was also too drunk to hunt, but gave me a hammer to bring back food. The bastard boar didn't even run, bloody charged me he did!" Wedyar roared out, one of his soldiers, a large man with a big belly and stumpy appearance. Beside him was Briyar, a gaunt, skinny and awkwardly tall man. He did not join the boisterous laughter like the rest of the soldier's did. Instead, the soldier snorted.

"Don't believe it for a second, Wedyar. You're always coming out with nonsense." The friends exchanged glares with rosy drunk cheeks, before their commander stepped in.

"Oi, Oi now boys. Let's play nice. If you get into a scrap I'll have to break it up and I don't want Wedyar sitting on me!" The chunky man shot a glance of shock while Briyar threw his head back in laughter, almost falling back from his chair.

"Hahaha! He's got a point you chubby bastard! How have you been serving on Shield all this time and still can't lose a shed of weight!?" the lean man teased. Wedyar shrugged and laughed out loud as well.

"'Cos the commander keeps bringin' me down here and fillin' me up with ale. I don't think he wants a handsome man like me stealin' his wife." Vesir spat his drink out as the jest came amid sip and almost toppled out of his chair in laughter.

"You cheeky bugger!" He retorted. Briyar now composed, took a long sip of his ale, almost finishing the jug before giving his mouth a wipe.

"Wife will be asking questions soon, should probably head home. Say, commander any word from Heldon lately? Can't remember the last time I heard any gossip from the capital."

His smaller friend seemed to pass him a strange look but Vesir thought nothing of it.

"Well, I can't say much but there's word of marriage, but hush hush. That was weeks ago however, other than that, haven't even had a messenger pigeon. Rumeo, ha, the King used to send one every other day with his latest list of the kitchen's servings, bless the man." The door to the inn opened and this time it was not another patron. The rest of the group began joking between each other as Zanmir came through the doorway, as if they turned their attention away from the son they knew to be rather pious. Vesir looked over to his son and offered with an overly enthusiastic greeting, a long wave and cheesy grin.

"Zanmir! Come join us, hear some ridiculous tales from the men!" His eldest sighed and adjusted his long coat that covered almost all his form.

"Not quite father. I have a message for you." He began. Vesir chuckled and tipped himself back in his chair.

"You came all the way to my second favourite place, beside your mother's bed, to say there is a message? No offence son, but normally you'd think that's a bit below you." Zanmir rolled his eyes at his father's somewhat drunken jest but moved passed it. He could not help but throw in the odd tease for his sons.

"Normally, yes. Yet this is different and of high importance. A rider from Heldon has come. She has requested to speak with you directly. A matter of life and death she claims." Vesir rubbed his furry chin and nodded as he tried to take it all in, it was not much to take in but the drink he had enjoyed made him a little bit slower than normal. Well, if it was a matter of life and death, he supposed, it was something that needed the commander's instant attention. The old Granlia pushed himself from the table and gave a salute to the soldiers who remained, to continue their night of drinking.

"Commander business. Carry on boys," he said with a large grin before turning to follow his son out of the inn. The soldiers gave him a cheer as he left before returning to their drunken antics.

"You should not encourage this kind of behaviour, father," his eldest advised as they strode back towards the keep on the Shield. Vesir shrugged his shoulders, he was a fun loving man and he could not help but enjoy himself when there was an opportunity.

"It's no harm. When you've been around as much as I have you'll learn. Sometimes it is better to be one of the men than someone they are forced to follow. While I would never wish it, these men would follow me to battle anywhere. I respect each one of them and trust them all with my life, and your life. All our lives, Zanmir. So lighten up a little, you've got a great future ahead of you son." His elbow found its way into his son's rib cage which caused the slender man to wince slightly and roll his eyes once more. This eye rolling thing looked like it was becoming a habit. Night had befallen the town of Meyer. It was a mellow place at night, apart from the odd drunken soldier stumbling through the streets and the patrols of those who had been unfortunate enough to get the night shift. Families ate within their houses lined up in rows, with each connected to the next. While it was not the most advanced or richest place to live and the houses were fairly basic in terms of space and diversity, they all made the most of it here. A city for soldiers and their families aimed to keep up the morale of the army stationed here. After living here so long he could not imagine returning home to Heldon, this place had become his true home. The smell of the brewery, the people and their livelihoods, the cooler air that filled his lungs, the feel of the countryside around him. Not once in the past twenty years had he felt the need to return to Heldon to live there. After a long walk with him teasing the eldest of the Granlia children, they made their way to the Shield Keep where his family lived. The keep itself was no more than a glorified house. There were a few defences in place which strengthened it against the elements, with one guard at the door. This particular guard's helmet covered his eyes and a spear rested on his shoulder as he sat slumped against the doorway. As they passed the guard, Vesir gave him a kick.

"I guess I've got the soldier for emptying the barracks latrines tomorrow, eh?" He mocked as the guard was startled awake and could only embarrassingly salute and accept his new duty.

"Sorry sir! Yes sir!" The half asleep soldier blurted out as he tried to scramble to his feet. Vesir smirked at the man and patted him on the shoulder.

"Next time will be a punishment and you know my favourite." The guard whimpered and in an instant became like a pillar. His back ridged and his spear held firmly as if everything around them was a potential threat. The commander could not help but let a laugh escape him as he left the man to his duty. He felt Zanmir would make an attempt at another quip about his leadership skills but he remained silent, most likely sick of always trying to convince his father to be more like an adult. Once inside, the main hall of the keep was small, like a dining room, and at a long table near the centre sat his wife with their baby, Lanmir, in her arms cradling the child to sleep. The aura was not as pleasant as the inn; a wall of tension slapped him in the face as he entered. Beside his wife stood Jonnas and sitting at the table was another woman he did not recognise. She was visually trembling in her seat with a cup of hot tea between her fingers. She looked shaken and rumpled as if she had ridden for days without even stopping to relieve herself.

"Vesir. You are not too drunk are you?" His wife asked. Every time he laid his eyes upon her, he fell in love all over again, or perhaps the drink was making him soppy, either way he smiled his warmest smile towards his loving wife. She was younger than him by ten summers, with long black hair, smooth as silk down to her waist with pale skin and large green eyes. Kaylen Granlia, to him, the most beautiful woman that had ever walked the earth. She was in her nightgown with a shawl over her shoulders to keep her warm in the cold of the

163

night. "This is something serious by the sounds of it," Kaylen added as she relocated her attention to him from their child.

"A little but nothing that'll make me act foolishly. In any case, a pleasure. I am Vesir Granlia, Commander of the Shield. What brings you to my little corner of the country, miss...?" He plopped himself down at his table with a clonk a bit less graceful than he had intended. The young woman at the table bowed her head respectfully; still shivering from what he assumed was the cold. Yet, with the large fire in the main hall, he felt as if he was beginning to roast.

"My Lord Vesir, I am Niyla, maid of Her Grace the Queen," she introduced herself. Vesir cocked a brow with a puzzled look on his face.

"Julian? Well this is an odd place to find yourself. You look like you've been on the march for days." His joke did not appease the room, only receiving a small head shake from his eldest and a bewildered expression from Jonnas.

"Yes My Lord. I rode here just after the attack in Heldon." The commander's usual humorous attitude shifted instantly.

"Wait, wait. Heldon was attacked?" He could see his second son grip the hilt of his sword that never seemed to leave his hip. Even the mention of a battle seemed to get that boy's blood pumping.

"You... were not told? I am sorry My Lord, I should not have assumed. Heldon Keep was attacked from the inside, many were killed but do not fear, all the Royal Family are... alive." Vesir nodded as he listened.

'Why am I hearing of this now? If it was attacked and she left just afterwards, it would have taken her days to get here from the capital if she rode without rest.' He pondered over reasons in his head, yet it was futile, nothing seemed to click in his mind.

"Her Grace the Queen asked me to come here during the fighting. She told me to find you and tell you something of great importance. I came as fast as I could and stopped for nothing." The commander pushed himself out of his seat and made his way to the woman's side to give her a reassuring squeeze on the shoulder as he lowered back down to her height.

"You've done well and my son will make sure you are tended to here with anything you need. Firstly, what does Julian need me to know that needed you to come and not a messenger pigeon?" The young girl seemed to swallow a lump in her throat from fear; her shaking was from fear, not the cold. He saw this now.

"She told me to tell you, 'You must return to the capital. Your brother needs your help, he is not Rumeo and harm will come to many if you do not help. Your family need you home.' She also said at the end to say, 'The roses in the garden still have not grown back.' I was not even allowed to write it down, My Lord. She would not let me." Vesir could not wipe away the frown from his features. His brother was in trouble? Surely news would spread if he was. Not to mention he had not sent his own brother a message about an attack. Something was amiss.

"You've done very well, Niyla." Vesir stood, now was the time for action and no more jokes.

"Jonnas see that Niyla here is tended to and given a good meal and a bath. I'm going to get my horse and a squad of men. Time to pay my good old brother a visit." Before he could leave the room, Zanmir put his hands up to block his path.

"Wait a moment father. You do not even know this woman, this could be falsehood. A trap to lure you from the keep? And to abandon your post here on such a whim. I know you are foolhardy, father, but you have a position you cannot just leave." He let a smile slip past his lips as he patted his son's hair.

"The roses in the garden still have not grown back. The message is real, a story I'll tell you one day perhaps. For now, my brother needs me, my family need me. I'm going and you're coming with me." His face dropped and even Jonnas could not withhold himself.

"Father! I should surely come with you. You may need my sword by your side. We do not know what we are walking into!" his broader son bellowed out from across the room.

"No, I want you to take my place until I return Jonnas. I'm leaving command of the Shield to you. Zanmir will go with me. If something is going on, I want his insight. If Heldon was attacked, I want the Shield organised and prepared in case the same happens here. Ensure men are stationed at the keep at all times and night patrols doubled. While I am away, the games and idleness are put on hold, they know the drill. The Shield will be on high alert." In times of possible war in the past, before his time as The Shields commander, high alert was a phrase for imminent attack. While nothing of note had really happened here for many, many years, he had made it his mission to make sure the soldiers under his command would be prepared for the high alert scenario. They had their fun, but they had their duty. Zanmir wrinkled his nose in dissatisfaction, but eventually nodded to his father's wish.

"Very well, you are my father and commander. I will do as you command. I will ready some men, supplies and horses for the journey come the break of dawn." With that the boy turned from the table and swept out of the keep like a shadow. With such a long coat, Vesir could barely see his legs move underneath; it was actually quite unsettling. His other son saluted and took the maid from the main hall to ensure she was cared for after the daring quest she had made to reach them, leaving the husband and wife alone with their newly born boy.

"Not being too brash are you?" Kaylen softly asked as she made sure Lanmir remained in slumber. Quietly so as not to wake the baby, Vesir sauntered over to his wife and wrapped an arm over her shoulder. Lanmir must have gotten his deep sleeping skills from his father; neither of the antics of his other sons had disturbed the young boy. While his face was buried into her long smooth hair he whispered.

"I'm always the brash one. If Julian is doing something so brash herself, then how can I not be?" She sighed while turning her face towards his.

166

"I just don't want you getting yourself in trouble without me there to save you, as I always do," she joked before planting a light kiss on his lips.

"Don't fret, I'll ride to Heldon, sort out the mess and be back in a week. Trust me, how can I stay away from you and this little future warrior, hm?" Her eyes followed his as they both gazed down to the beautiful gift. The fulfilling moment of being with his family always lightened his heart.

"Vesir..." Kaylen whispered.

"Yes, dear?"

"Your breath stinks of ale." The commander blinked and covered his mouth to catch a whiff of the breath. It did indeed reek. After planting a kiss on the top of his wife's head and chuckling to himself, Vesir slipped away. It was time to head back to the capital. The last time he had been there, Heldon was holding a tournament. This time, he felt, it would not be such a refreshing occasion.

As the sun broke free from its shackles, the men Zanmir had chosen were all readying their steeds and their equipment by the keep of the Shield's entrance. There were six men in total all armed with swords at their hips, kettle helmets upon their heads and leather and chainmail armour with the emblem of the shield upon their breast. Vesir emerged from his home with the same armour as his men, excluding the helmet and wore a long black cloak with a trimming of fur around the collar. This would be as noble as he wanted to look. His sword hung from his belt, a blade that had seen many battles and a bow across his back over the cloak. He liked to think he was an expert archer but so far he had never won any competitions. Behind him from the doorway, his wife followed with Lanmir in her arms and Jonnas a step behind.

"Jonnas," he began. "Don't get too comfortable in my position. I'll be back in no time." He said in jest as he gripped his son's shoulder. Jonnas nodded his head respectfully, to his father and commander.

"I will keep everything here as you leave it." He replied.

"I would hope so." He gave his son a firm pat on the shoulder and turned to his wife who offered him a light smile, though signs of uneasiness seeped through. He leaned forward and landed a kiss on her forehead.

"I love you, Kaylen. Look after the boys for me." She cupped his hairy chin with one slender hand.

"And make sure Zanmir looks after you." They both shared a laugh and finally he tore himself away from his family. His eldest son was already upon his horse in what appeared to be riding gear, a long cloak like his own and leather and cloth underneath. It was peculiar not to see him in his usual dark coats. As he mounted his own stallion, a beast of a horse he had named Angul, he turned back to his wife, one last time.

"Oh and be careful of Wedyar, he wants to steal you away and now might be his greatest opportunity." One last joke before he took his leave. His wife let out another laugh and shook her head.

"I shall try to control myself." With that the horses reined north and began their canter out of the town of Meyer and towards the capital. At this speed, it would take almost a week to reach their destination. That offered lots of time to pester his eldest son, giving Zanmir no escape from his playful goading.

*

~Nyer~

In the capital of Mayhen, the air was sour. More guardsmen had seemingly come out of the wood-work, but always kept their faces covered by their helmets. Patrols lingered in the courtyards throughout the day and now they found their way to the usual quaint and quiet gardens of the castle. Heldon barely felt like home to Nyer anymore. The respect she was once treated with had vanished with only her close friends showing her any sign that she was in fact still a princess. Her father had not entertained her since Hinsani had escaped from his cell and had men sent out after him to scour the countryside. Ever since the attack, things had been changing dramatically, for the worse. She stood on the ramparts peering over the city below the castle. They looked like ants down there, common ants blissfully unaware of the hardships she was contemplating. Beside her Titania stood on guard, with a hand causally upon the pommel of her sword, her long red hair blowing in the strong winds that had come from the west. The heat that had befallen the city had made way for a spell of cold winds from across the sea. Nyer had wrapped herself up warm with a thick dark blue cloak with masterful designs of patterns in silver along the trim. However Titania wore her usual attire with only a thin cloak hanging off her shoulders.

"What is on your mind, My Lady?" her protector asked. There were so many things meandering across her thoughts, she did not know which to burden her companion with.

'Father's madness, Rayar's suspected crimes, Hinsani somehow escaping, not being able to see mother and even Nymin being locked away in her chambers for this long.' It felt like they had all become prisoners in their own home. Finally she decided to reply.

"Have you heard anything from Sir Dedred?" The red haired woman nodded sombrely.

"I have. He still waits beside Princess Nymin's chamber, with the guards posted outside. He claims since his decision to remain, they have tripled the number of guards, up to twenty four now." This simply did not make any sense. Why would father place so many guardsmen outside Nymin's door and not allow her sworn Royal Blade to protect her. There was only one thing in her mind that could answer this, it was not to protect her but to keep her locked in. She herself was not allowed to see her; Ayla was also not allowed to see her. Just then the sound of a young woman's crying, filtered through the harsh winds. Coming down the battlements was her younger sister Ayla. No words had time to be traded between them before Ayla threw her arms around her older sister and buried her tearful cheeks into her chest.

169

"Father is horrible! I hate him!" She cried into the cloth. Nyer wrapped one arm around the girl and pulled her into a tight hug.

'I know he is...' She thought but withheld her actual feelings for the moment, to find out what had actually caused this sudden hatred.

"What has he done, Ayla?" The younger woman sniffed and raised her head to look upon her sister's face. Her eyes and nose were red from crying and her lips frozen from the cold. She had come bumbling out here without even putting on something warm to protect herself from the cold. Almost instinctively Nyer found herself pulling off her own cloak and attaching it to the distraught girl.

"He has cancelled the wedding with Prince Kerrin Hextor! He had his cronies tell me in the oratory during my prayers to the Above." Nyer cocked her brow at that.

"You were praying?" She asked with a stern but puzzled tone. Ayla nodded ever so slightly as if somewhat embarrassed.

"For Rayar... I know he is innocent. Whatever evidence they claim they have against him, it is a lie. He would never do anything like they say. Rayar is... he is... the most honest, loyal and trustworthy man I have ever known. And he is our brother." Nyer had to agree on some of those points, as much as he annoyed her with his lack of passion and commitment to anything, he was a loyal boy, loyal to his family and his country. He was an honest man with a good heart. She had not believed those claims either, from the second she had heard them, not to mention that when she had asked to see some of the evidence, she was denied.

'I am to rule one day and they do not even grace me with the opportunity to involve myself with these important matters. Never have I been so insulted.' Ayla pushed her face back into her sister's shoulder when tears began to reform in her eyes. She spoke but it was hard to understand as her words were muffled by the cloth.

"I just want everything to go back to normal. I want to see mother, I want Rayar back, I want my marriage to happen. It is not fair sister!" As selfish as she sounded, she spoke true. Everything returning to how it was before would certainly be the best outcome. It had only been a week since the attack and so much had changed. Rayar was out there somewhere, probably distraught, fleeing from his own people.

'Just come back you bloody idiot...' No, he could not come home. He would not be given a fair trial and nor would Hinsani. They were on their own. A burst of determination coursed through her veins as she gripped Ayla's shoulders and pushed her back yet remained gripped on to the girl.

"Listen to me, Ayla. I, you and Nymin must stick together no matter what. I promise you now, I will not let this go on. When the opportunity arises, I will take it and ensure our family is returned to normal. We must get to mother and we must get to Nymin. Trust in me and I will fix this. Do you understand?" The younger princess was clearly unfocused in her distress whilst listening to this brief speech, but she seemed nevertheless to take in some of the words.

"Okay Nyer... Whatever you want to do... I am with you." Her words were shaky, from the cold and her tears, but together they could figure this out. They would need help, yet who was left in this city that they could trust?

* * *

Chapter XVI
Brothers
~*Vesir*~

Vesir had forgotten just how tiring the ride was, between the Shield and Heldon was. The countryside between his station and the capital however, had been as pleasant as he remembered. There were only towns and villages between the two destinations, which had actually worked out for the better, allowing them to travel without pause due to delays by lords and ladies he had not seen for years, reeling him into their castles and reliving stories of the past twenty years. They had followed the Heldon River north, the river stretched across all of Mayhen through the capital. Seeing the common people at work filled him with pride and joy. The country of Mayhen was nothing like that pig sty that Hextheene had become. Some men, who had held the wall with him, had originally been Hextheene refugees and from what they had told him, the war with Southrous had caused much poverty in the capital as well as some of the neighbouring towns. Luckily for him he was not in Hextheene, he was in his own land and as usual it was uplifting to see the people faring well. They had slowed to a trot as they approached the village houses outside the outer wall of the city. The population had grown so vast in the capital that now homes were being built on the very outskirts, though these were usually owned by the gatherers by trade; huntsman, fishermen, farmers and the like, who would only travel into the city to sell their goods. Many of the people they passed had their attention stolen by the group. It had been a while since men of the Shield had graced the city with a visit, let alone the famous Vesir Granlia. He doubted though that any recognised who he actually was. Zanmir trotted up beside him. Despite his usual stern exterior, he clearly was in awe.

"I know I came here as a child, but I never remembered Heldon being this huge." He followed his son's eyes to the outer wall. In the distance in the centre of the city, a castle stood that almost pierced the heavens. It sat upon raised ground and could be seen for miles around with its glistening white stone glimmering in the sunlight.

"Ah, it's nice alright. The Shield has more character I think." He said with a small grin towards his son. Zanmir gave him a perplexed look before returning his attention to the road ahead. The dirt road led towards the outer wall's gate. Upon seeing their attire, the guards wasted no time in allowing them entry. If anyone was to recognise Vesir, it would be the stationed soldiers. He nodded to them all, and they saluted in return as he passed.

"These men here Zanmir, would be your perfect type of soldier. Quiet, professional and like stonework. Most of them barely move," the commander teased as they rode past and through the city. The interior of Heldon was bustling with business. People scurried around performing their trades; horses trotted by carrying travellers; guards patrolled the streets in tight formations. If there had been an attack on Heldon, no one down here was aware of it. So many people going about their daily struggles, he envied them. Many times he had wished to hide away with Kaylen and his children and become a fisherman by the coast, or a blacksmith. He would have to learn those trades first naturally. Unfortunately for him he was the King's brother and that ensured him a life of servitude to the country. He simply had to make the best of it. The group of men from the Shield rode through the lower city and made their way towards the castle in the centre, heading up the King's Way. The passage was a long spiralling road that carts and common people took, to visit the Royal Family. He could not help but notice however the lack of people taking this road, they seemed to be the only ones on it. Zanmir had suggested taking the East Road, bypassing the city, but the desire to witness the busy streets of Heldon was too enticing for nostalgia. Eventually after the climb, they reached the courtyard gate. This is where he felt his interest piqued. The gate itself had over two dozen guardsmen protecting it and Vesir could not even begin to count how many were positioned along the walls above them. They came to a halt but none approached them.

"Hello!" he began from upon his stallion. "I am Commander Vesir Granlia. I've come at the Queens request." His smile sat on his lips for some time but it slowly began to simmer to a blank expression. None of the guards made any sort of move in response to his welcome. Zanmir trotted up beside his father once more.

"I should be introducing you," he stated as a matter of fact before he continued forward, closer to the gateway. As he reached no more than ten metres from the gate, the guards suddenly shot into defensive formations with spears pointed towards his son and his horse. Zanmir fell silent, the shock made him obviously speechless. Within seconds, Vesir was beside his son instinctively and quickly dismounted to confront the horde of guardsmen. Anyone who pointed a weapon at his son truly did not know who they were dealing with. Not moments after he had dismounted, the men of the Shield with him cantered up to Zanmir and created a defensive circle around him, whilst also supporting their commander's flanks.

"Who is in command here? You brand a weapon at a member of the Royal Family." The tension in the air began to rise, as the guards remained silent. They only held their ground with spears arced for attack. Vesir could feel his usual joyous features grow burdensome with a frown, not a look he liked to express. His hand was now upon his sword's hilt as were all the soldiers of the Shield. This certainly was not the welcome he had expected. Just then the large gate began to rise, being pulled up from the other side. They all waited patiently, yet that patience could be broken within moments should the wrong move have been made. Finally he saw a face he recognised. Commander Brayton in full armour, plate and chain, strode from within the keep and motioned the men to lower their weapons. He had gotten much larger since he had last seen him, though only in width.

"Commander Vesir." He greeted the arrivals.

"Commander Brayton. A little hostile here, don't you think? What's the meaning of this?" Brayton nodded; a sigh followed as heavy as his plate armour.

"I apologise. Since the intruders struck, we have been fairly cautious of any who come to enter the castle."

"Overly cautious perhaps?" Vesir interjected. The fellow commander shrugged his shoulders.

"We do what we must. What brings you to the capital?" He asked, his eyes briefly flashed over the company that were in tow.

"Request by the Queen, Commander. She sent a messenger for me so I thought I would pop by. Not to mention, I missed my big brother so much, felt like we could do with a catch up." The commander's face turned sullen at the mention of the King, a sickly pale white pallor overtook him.

"I see... Well, I suppose you should come to the throne room. He is currently holding court there. Though I must warn you..." His tone quietened which caused Vesir to over dramatically lean in to listen with a hand over his ear. "He is... different... The King. I would never speak ill of His Grace and I am sworn to serve to my last breath. Simply... it is hard to explain. You will see for yourself but he is not the same as you may recall, Commander Vesir." Brayton motioned them all to follow. One of the soldiers Vesir brought with him tended to the horses with the stable boys, while the other five followed him and his son towards the keep.

"So the girl was right... I forget her name." Vesir whispered to his son. Zanmir nodded in agreement but decided to remain silent for the moment. Probably still shaken by the events that had just transpired at the gate. The courtyard was no different from the gate, being littered with guardsmen after guardsmen standing along the walls below the battlements and covering the doorway inside the keep itself. As they reached the door, Brayton turned towards them, this question clearly weighed heavy upon him.

"I must ask your men to remain outside. Your son of course can join you. All your weapons can be given to them, before entering the throne room." Well that was to be expected by greeting a King that was not your brother, but this man was his flesh and blood. They had grown up together side by side. Yet a weapon was just a weapon, there was no need to carry it inside. Without concern Vesir passed his sword and bow to one of his guards.

"Of course. Wouldn't want to make my big brother tremble now, eh?" he joked. It was not received as intended, only leading to a choleric expression on the face of this fellow ranked soldier. "Never mind..." He mumbled to himself as they continued to be taken as if by a lead. Before they entered the doorway, Vesir glanced over the walls. Upon the ramparts stood a girl, much older than he recalled, but he knew it was little Nyer, standing with the red haired girl that had been by her side since she was a pup. The young princess glared down at him, in that way only she could. In return he offered a smile and a motionless wave to greet her. Seemingly Vesir could not please anyone in this new world of Heldon, as the princess merely turned from his sight followed swiftly by her Royal Blade. The old commander clicked his tongue and turned to carry on to his meeting with his brother.

'Does no one smile in this place anyone? I didn't remember everyone here being so stuck up. Above and Below.' The throne room was full of people, Lords and Ladies from their castles in Mayhen, courtiers along the sides of the hall with a line of guards at every pillar. There was chattering between them as the King sat on his throne, inattentive to what was occurring around him. A cup clasped in his chunky fingers, his hair had grown longer and beard even bushier. His clothes even, were not the style Vesir remembered his brother preferring. He wore

176

his crown within his grey hair, yet he wore mostly black and was covered in a long fur cloak, bear fur by the looks of it, due to its taint. Black bear of Mayhen indeed it would seem. Beside the King on one side, were four empty seats for the Royal Children and one empty on his left for the Queen. Vesir strode towards his brother with a large smile on his face, half expecting the King to leap from his chair and give him a bear like hug. As he reached the steps to the throne, two guardsmen blocked his path with crossed spears.

"Halt. None may approach the King," one of them said with a stern voice, his face hidden by a closed face helmet. Vesir could not help but look at them with a puzzled expression before attempting to lightly push one of the spears aside.

"Settle down boys, I'm Vesir Granlia, his brother. I'm here to chat with Rumeo." This caught the attention of the large figure perched on the throne.

"You wish to speak with the King, you announce yourself properly and then His Grace will decide if you may speak," a man beside the King informed him. He was a crone of a man, bald head and snake like features. One notable trait he held was the lack of a right hand, with a hook instead in its place. That was definitely not a face he remembered. His eyes flicked to his older brother who did not interject or speak on his behalf, the man simply sat there watching him emotionlessly. Vesir took a deep breath to settle his irritation but before he could speak, his son did the deed for him.

"This is Commander Vesir Granlia of the Shield, Royal Blood of Granlia, and brother of the King of Mayhen." He could not help but pass his son a small impressed smile. Zanmir may not have been a warrior like himself and Jonnas but he was a man of worth.

"I know who he is," the King muttered from his throne. He swirled his water in his chalice and took a loud long sip. "Why are you here, Commander Vesir?" Rumeo bluntly asked.

"Can we remove these spears from our faces and perhaps go to the meeting hall for a catch up, brother?" he asked. Having a detailed and possibly delicate conversation in front of

177

all these people, did not seem the wisest idea. The little man spoke once more, much to Vesir's displeasure.

"The King does not take private meetings with any after the events that unfolded of late. Any words you wish to speak, you can address to the court as well." This man was really beginning to wind up the Granlia commander. Though years of dealing with all kinds of people, gave him the experience to keep himself composed and simply push through the idiots of the world.

"I see. Very well," he began. "*Your Grace*, I have come by invitation from the Queen concerning your welfare and state of mind. I had thought perhaps it was an over exaggeration but seeing all this, I think she was right. You aren't yourself, brother," he stated firmly. The crowd in the hall fell silent; his son stared at him with wide eyes. Brothers or not, he was the King, though King or not they were brothers and had always been close. Rumeo leaned forward in his throne, his face a picture of disgust.

"You come from your little wall in the corner of muck and piss and tell me that I am not myself. Then who am I, Commander Vesir?" The tension in the throne room was weighing down on all; he could hear gasps and whispering around him. Fearful whispers.

"You are supposed to be the King, you are supposed to be a husband and father, you are supposed to be my brother. Never has my brother treated family in such a way. Where is the Queen?" His voice was as dominating as the King's.

"Not that it is any of your concern, but she was wounded badly in the attack and rests to regain her health under close watch for her protection. Now, do you think it is wise to insult a King? I do not believe it prudent, for a commander stationed far away, to stroll into my home and make demands of one he is sworn to serve. Ignorance will get you killed." Vesir growled to his brother as two alpha wolves battled for superiority in the pack.

"If this is the King my brother is becoming, then I insult and will insult again, until your head is knocked back into place and you remember who you are." With that the King burst from his seat, causing the guards to move once again into their defensive stances. There were gasps of horror throughout the court, as people shuffled back in fear.

"You dare!? Brother or not, I am the King! I will not be spoken down to by some pathetic excuse for a man, who hides away because he is old and weak!" The rage was ablaze, so scorching he felt like the room could burst into flames at any moment. There was nothing to gain from his talk. He had only to converse with Rumeo for a few minutes to know that something was direly wrong with him and in Heldon.

"Then this old weak man will return to his corner of muck and piss. Clearly this city, no, nation has lost a good King." With that Vesir turned on his heel and strode towards the exit. The guards watched him cautiously, any reason he gave them to pierce him with those spears, they would have surely taken.

"Go back to your bloody grave you worm! If you ever set foot in Heldon again, I will have your head at my feet! Do you understand me!? Get out!" His voice boomed across the room, carried like a thunder storm. Vesir did not look back and stormed through the door without another word. The anger inside him had reached his limit and if this was the man his brother was now, anything else he could have said would surely have ended with his head on a spike.

Once outside the keep, he could still hear the yelling of the King from inside. The words cut like a dagger; as angry as he was those words caused him great pain. It was if Rumeo intentionally wished to rouse him to say something he would regret. The commander snatched his sword and bow from one of his men and attached them to his back and hip. They made their way through the courtyard and to the stables to attend to their horses.

"Father," Zanmir spoke. "Why did you antagonise the King? It was a foolish thing to do," he explained. Vesir did not need to hear that from his own son. That boy was as cold and logical as they came. Unlike his son, he was driven by emotion.

"Because son, my brother would not be angered by words. He would not threaten his brother. He would not refuse to meet a man whom was practically joined with him by the hip as children. Even if there was an attack here, he is not so closed minded as to assume all those close to him are threats and surround himself with people he doesn't even know. It is madness and I'm not letting this go so easily." The last words exclaimed caused his son to wince.

"What do you mean? If we stay here or return, you will be executed. Did you not hear his threat?" Vesir ruffled his son's hair, much to the boys annoyance, and continued.

"I heard him. Bloody right I heard him. Even if he thinks nothing of me, I love my brother and I will help him no matter what. I need to speak to Julian as soon as possible." With that another voice chimed in.

"I can help you with that, Uncle." It was a woman's voice, yet as stern as a veteran soldier's. There stood the princess, who had been observing him earlier, with her red headed Royal Blade at her side.

"Princess Nyer. You have grown, Above and Below, you've grown into a beautiful young woman. Were you eavesdropping on us?" he asked in a teasing tone. Nyer rolled her eyes, much like his son seemed to do, time and time again.

"You have witnessed it now, my father's madness. I have much to discuss with you, much to tell you of the past two weeks. I need your help, and I believe you need mine." She had a way with words this one, much more of a schemer than her mother and father. "There is an inn in the city, The Golden Crane. I want you and your men to meet me and Titania there after night falls and we can talk more. For now, you must disappear. Soon the guardsmen will have you escorted from the city." Without allowing an answer she turned from the stables and disappeared off into the courtyard. Something about that girl was very rigorous. He could admire that. He turned to his son.

"Son, what do you think of all this?" The young Granlia cupped his chin in thought as the events clearly ran through that analytical mind.

"The harm to the Queen could cause his anger to strengthen and the faces we have seen that we do not know, could be whispering in his ears telling him things that the King we knew, would never have considered before. All I can tell from what we have seen is that he is unstable, very unstable when confronted, as before you spoke he seemed relaxed and complacent. While I do not wish to involve us in any plotting, I know you will do whatever it takes to help him. So, if you wish to meet with cousin Nyer, then we must slip away now, appear as if we have left the city and return in the cover of the darkness to this inn." Vesir nodded to pretty much all Zanmir's words. That boy, even when shaken by these events, made sure to take in everything around him and give a truly considered response.

"Very well, let's take our leave. I don't want to upset your mother, by having my head sent back to the Shield. If that happened no one would be able to stop her." The group mounted their steeds once more and left the castle upon the hill, moving towards the outskirts of the town. The plan would be to return on foot during the night. No one knew this city as well as he did, he knew hundreds of ways in, without being detected.

* * *

Chapter XVII
Fallen Queen
~Vesir~

The evenings in Heldon were still as busy and bustling as during the day. People danced and drank at the local taverns; families ate their meals outside their homes by candle light. Night stores stayed open to sell their wares to those who had been working through the day like the soldiers and other shopkeepers. In the less reputable areas, ladies of the night practiced their trade, though they were hard to spot these days, as one travelled through the city. One thing Vesir had noticed was the lack of guardsmen in the streets. Sneaking back into the city had been considerably easier than he had imagined it would be. It would appear that the majority of the stationed garrisons in the city were now located in the castle itself. The Heldon army in its entirety had around ten thousand fighting men, yet they were spaced out between the castle, the city, the barracks and the surrounding countryside. The only Noble Lord who could come close to matching that number was the Pale Lord of Stoneside Keep, Tismiar Loysse. Yet the number of soldiers wasn't a concern for Vesir, each and every dark corner in Heldon to sneak through and hide in. From his brief visit to the castle it would appear a big chunk of them were placed in the castle and barracks whilst the city had been neglected.

"Is that it?" a Shield soldier asked from under his hood, as the eight men slipped through the streets under cover of darkness. They all wore dark, heavy cloaks and hoods and moved swiftly, though not in a bunched group, to their destination. There was no need to attract unwanted attention. Vesir nodded to the soldier who had accompanied him at the head of the convoy and turned to motion the rest further back, The Golden Crane had been found. The door was old and showed signs of rot. The sign barely hung on his hinges above the doorway, a worn and peeling painted golden crane. Not the sort of place he expected a princess to spend her time but having three sons he was not an expert in what young women did these days. The soldier beside him placed a hand on the sword at his hip, as he went to be first to enter the inn, to confirm it was safe. However, Vesir patted him on the shoulder and strode in defiantly. If it was a trap, so be it. They had come this far so they may as well take the bull by the horns and get on with it. Once inside, the smell was ominous, the odour stung his nostrils with putrid meat and stale drink. An old withered man stood behind the counter, serving a couple of other men their drinks but overall the density of people inside was slim. Upon seeing Vesir and his men enter, the old man squinted over in their direction trying to get a clear look at them.

"You them boys for the lady upstairs?" he asked in a suffering tone, his voice crackled like wood in a fire. Vesir looked between his men and nodded.

"We are." Well hopefully they were. As funny as it would have been to go upstairs, only to see a whore waiting up there, today was not to the day for humour. Though it would be a story he was sure his wife would find entertaining.

"She's waitin' upstairs lads, go right up." With that the group advanced through the inn and towards the staircase. To be on the safe side, he ordered two of the soldiers to remain at the base of the stairs.

"Stay here, keep an eye out. Though don't look obvious, get a drink or something." The two soldiers looked to each other, shrugged and made their way to the bar. Hopefully they heard him say get *a* drink, not as many drinks as they liked. Upstairs held a long corridor that reached across the length of the building. At the far end of it was a door with a particular guard one could never forget. The red headed warrior Titania stood with her arms crossed and eyes glaring down the hallway, as if anything that locked eye contact with her would instantly be turned to stone. Vesir led the remaining members of his group towards her and pulled down his hood to reveal his face.

"Royal Blade Titania, a pleasure. She inside?" he asked. She nodded in reply and outstretched one hand to push open the door. This Titania was certainly a quiet one. Inside sat Princess Nyer, crossed legged in a high back chair next to a fire place across the room. A book had her attention, though once Vesir and his men filled the room, she redirected it to them. That cold expression matched the Royal Blade's at the door.

"Uncle Vesir," she greeted him. He replied with a smile. The commander's men spread out absently around the room, so not to seem too intimidating.

"Little Nyer. Not the usual place I would expect to find a young princess. You come here often?" He asked with a slightly joking tone. She ignored the joke.

"No, not often. The barkeeper has been paid a substantial sum to offer his room to my need. I had Titania make contact with him last week, to ensure it is secure. He does not know who I am and he is paid enough so it remains that way." Her words were full of confidence and dominance, though not as strikingly aggressive as her father's had become.

"Money can only buy so much loyalty, respect buys the most." She sniffed at his retort.

"I use what I have at the moment, respect will come later. Your meeting with father was brief, no? What did you think of him?" She asked bluntly. Not a woman to mince words. Vesir took a seat next to her and opened his hands in the direction of the fire.

"I didn't need long with him to realise he is not himself. How did he turn out this way Nyer?" He felt his joking demeanour weaken and the feelings of sadness began to grow. He probably was unable to hide it in his voice and features, as she returned his look with one of melancholy.

"Ever since the attack in our home he has been like this. Ever since mother was hurt, we have not been allowed to see her. The attack was blamed on Rayar as if he betrayed the family and let the attackers in, which is obviously absurd and now he is out in the world somewhere being hounded by Heldoran soldiers. Nymin is locked away in her room. She spoke of the events that occurred before being taken away. I have not seen her since. The wedding plans between Ayla and Prince Kerrin Hextor have been dissolved, not that I thought it was a good idea in the first place. Now he surrounds himself with men and women who either we do know, or Lords and Ladies that have always strived for better positions but the father I remember, would not entertain such ambitions. War mongers. The father I remember would not lash out at those who hurt him like that. He would protect his family and strive forward for peace to improve the situation, not become part of the problem." It seemed a lot had happened in the past couple of weeks. No message had been sent to the shield to inform him of any of this; not until the maiden arrived at his door. Things had truly gone wrong in the capital.

"Rayar is on the run alone?" Vesir asked with a cocked brow.

"No, Hinsani was arrested due to his involvement with the prince and was to be tortured for information yet somehow he escaped. I can only assume he has gone after Rayar as well." Vesir chuckled to himself. "What is so funny?" the young princess asked somewhat annoyed at his little outburst.

"Funny? No, no. Not funny, it's just..." The smile refused to leave his lips. "With Rayar on the run, innocent or not if Hinsani is with him, then I'm sure he will be fine. I wouldn't want to try and capture him with that monster at his side." He noticed Nyer flick a glance to Titania as they seemed to speak without words before she returned her eyes to him.

"As you say," she mumbled. Zanmir, who had remained silent behind his father, finally spoke.

"If I did not know any better, all these actions, ruining possible alliances, tearing the Royal Family apart and being

185

associated with people whom may not have been in the best interests of the kingdom, is something an infiltrator would try to do, to weaken a country. Cripple from the inside, as it were." Nyer flashed her eyes to his son, they had the same kind of analytical mind he thought.

'I imagine these two would have been the greatest of friends if I had lived in Heldon, though by the looks of it, they aren't ones for having many friends. Bless them.'

"Yes I would agree. Yet a King would not do such a thing to his own kingdom, it would be suicide for his reign and possibly life. If King Braska Hextor figured that Mayhen was in such a way, no, if Southrous learnt of this, what would stop them continuing the war against Mayhen from hundreds of years ago. They have the largest military might in the Freeland and they disagree with our way of life more than Hextheene ever did. No, this country needs a strong ruler to regain its security and safety." Vesir's brow lowered into a tight frown as he narrowed his eyes at his niece.

"What are you suggesting? If you say regicide, then you and I may have a big falling out." Surprisingly a small scoffing laugh escaped her lips at his comment.

"Do not be ridiculous. I do not wish to steal the throne from my father. He is my father, as foolish as he was before and as wicked as he has become now. He is still my father. While I did not agree with him before, he was still a good and loved King and the realm was safe. That is the man we need again." He let out a sigh of relief. Perhaps it was unfair of him to imply she thought such a thing but considering what he saw his brother become and the dire straits the capital appeared to be in, who knew how desperate she was.

"Then what is it you have in mind? Knock the stupidity out of his head with a stick?" She shook her head at his obvious sarcastic comment.

"We need my mother, we need Queen Julian. We need to find her, speak to her and have her speak sense to him. I need you to slip into the castle and find her. You know the castle better than I, better than Titania and you were her childhood friend, you can find her and speak to her." It seemed like a reasonable plan, apart from the big hole about *him* stalking around the castle. If he was spotted there would be World Below to pay.

"I must ask, Rumeo will surely not take kindly to me poking about the castle, but you and your Royal Blade can walk around undisturbed. Why do you want me to do this and not have your lady friend here find her and bring her to you?" The princess pushed herself to her feet and wandered to the window with her hands clasped behind her back. Her words spun well like a spider's web, he had no love for that.

"Titania does not have the relationship you do with my mother and I am not about to climb walls and slip through shadows in my own castle. If I am caught doing something I should not and my movement is restricted, then I will not be able to help my father and save this city. Being here was a risk enough but I must also take risks if I am to ask others to do so as well. No, it must be you, it can only be you. You know this castle better than anyone bar my father and if anyone can slip unnoticed, it's Vesir Granlia. I know what you did in Hextheene during the war." Vesir gripped the arm rest of his chair tightly as his stomach sunk.

"How do you know this?" he growled through his teeth. Zanmir looked confused, looking between him and Nyer, obviously unsure about what was being spoken.

"The records Lanni Ni'Tella holds contain much, some things that should not be written down. This is not a threat to release this information, simply a statement that you and I both know you have the skills to complete this where Titania or I would fail." Those actions she spoke of occurred during war. He had a job to do and he was the best one for it. She couldn't understand, she wasn't there, nor did he have any reason to justify it to her. This girl was pushing memories to the front of his mind after being long buried into the shadows.

'It was war, we had to fight... I suppose she knows more than she lets on. Then she probably knows why I renounced my title of prince... and why I left to stay in the Shield. Damn her,

she's crafty and more dangerous than I would've first expected.' A woman many would underestimate in her reign in the future no doubt. For now, those worries far into the future were not a concern. What to do now though, was.

"Very well," he began as he rose from his seat. "I will go to the castle and seek out Julian. If anyone can speak sense to the bumbling oaf, it will be her." The dark eyed young woman turned back to him, her usual cold expression slightly softer, with an air of gratitude.

"Thank you. We will remain here and await your return. I suggest you move quickly. Under the cover of darkness would be preferable, yes?" she suggested as if feeding a baby. The commander smirked and turned towards the doorway.

"No problem. Zanmir stay here and look after the helpless princess, with the men. I won't be long." As Vesir strode past his son, he was stopped by a grip upon his shoulder. Much like he did to his sons', yet now found the roles reversed.

"Father, be careful." Zanmir advised. Vesir smiled warmly to his eldest son and returned the firm grip over the cloak.

"You too son." With that he slipped out of the doorway and through the inn, like a shadow in the darkness, a skill he had not used since the war, slipping in and out of keeps and homes to disrupt from the inside. A skill he had never truly wished to use again but to help his brother this day, he would make an exception.

This would not be a simple task, slipping past the hundreds and hundreds of soldiers within the keep, yet Vesir never said never. Anything was possible if intelligence was applied. Getting through the city was not much of a challenge due to the lack of guardsmen inside the city walls. However, there was a secret way into the keep through the outside stables of the castle itself. Below the castle walls upon the East Road to the keep, sat a stable which was rarely defended. The only ones he knew who were aware of it were himself, Rumeo and Julian. If Rumeo had remembered such an exit, he would likely have closed it up or perhaps placed watchmen to protect it. He

188

would soon find out. Wrapped in his long cloak with his hood covering his features, the commander silently stalked alongside the wall of the keep towards the small stable. Inside the horses were silent. One overweight stable boy sat on a chair with arms crossed and eyes closed, slumped against the wall, fast asleep. As if he moved in the wind itself, Vesir flew past the sleeping boy and reached the back of the stable in one of the horse's pens, which was luckily empty.

'No guards, fingers crossed.' He moved a few planks of wood that blocked a small door hidden in the very corner. Slowly he pulled the door open; he remembered the creak from many, many years ago. Each time he pulled on the wood it creaked. There was the sound of shuffling at his back and in a flash he turned his head with a hand on the hilt of his sword. The sleeping stable boy grunted and fidgeted in his sleep. Vesir sighed in relief.

"Above and Below," he muttered to himself before pulling the door open and shifting inside. No guards were present, which was a good sign. The passageway led all the way to the castle basement. It was not a long hike up a flight of stairs, yet it was dark and gloomy inside the narrow passage. Soon he found himself under the hundreds of guardsman patrolling the castle walls and hallways. The basement was littered with old furniture, books, barrels and various other objects covered in webs and dust.

'Those days of playing hide and seek down here. Father would look for hours and never find us. Look at me, an old coot reminiscing about times long gone,' he thought as he moved through the shadows of the basement without so much of an echo of his steps. If he remembered correctly, the basement had several exits. One to the kitchens, one that led to the stairs connected to the main hall and under the Advisor Study, Lanni Ni'Tella's and the last to the hallways near the front door of the keep. He had to admit there was a moment when he felt torn, after what Nyer had said that Lanni had many documents. Some he would prefer never saw the light of day yet if he let his own interests side track him, his selfishness could get him

caught. After another curse mumbled under his breath, he headed to the castle kitchens. At this time of night they should be deserted, giving him an open path up towards the royal chambers and beyond. From there, he stuck to the shadows moving from hallway to hallway, room to room until he reached the upper levels of the keep. Eventually passing through the corridors became too dangerous. Vesir darted like an arrow into one of the royal chambers, Rayar's in fact. It sat empty, naturally with the young prince somewhere out on the run. His eyes lingered in the room for a moment as he studied the boy's possessions and what had become of them. The room had been completely torn apart with the bed broken and turned over, all drawers opened and dashed on the floor, the curtains to his window ripped off. It was a complete mess. By the looks of it, they had destroyed everything in search of anything that could help them find where the prince had gone.

'This isn't you Rumeo...' The next part would be beyond risky. Slowly Vesir pulled himself out the window and latched onto the wall above it. The guards completely filled the royal chambers hallways giving no chance to slip past towards the King's chamber further up the keep. Like some sort of monkey from Brexxia, he clambered up the walls of the castle, up the stones and vines that coursed the height of the white towers. The wind was not too powerful which he thanked Above for but still it had been a good few years since he performed this tumbling trade. Vesir clung on for dear life as he climbed higher towards the window of the King's chambers. If the guardsmen below in the courtyard saw him now, he would be a sitting duck for archers. Not his first choice of cause of death, naturally. One rock came loose in his grip and toppled from the tower. He gritted his teeth as he held himself to the wall with one hand and one foot and watched as the white rock went tumbling to the floor. It landed in the bushes of the castle garden with only a light thump. Vesir once again found his breath, as the fear had stolen it from him.

'I'm getting too old for this.' Just above him was the room he had sought. With much strain yet as silent as a mouse, he

lifted himself up to the window sill and peered inside. Rumeo did not seem to be present though the form of a person lay in the bed, a small, fragile body. Finally inside the room the commander quietly wandered over to the bed-side.

"Julian..." he whispered. The Queen lay on the bed above the sheets, her body nothing but skin and bones, her skin pale and cold and her eyes closed. She looked like all the life had been drained from her. Carefully, Vesir placed a hand on her arm and gave her a very gentle shake. "Julian, it's me. Vesir," he whispered again. Slowly with what seemed to be a painful effort on her part, she forced her eyes open and gazed up towards him. Her mouth was dry, lips cracked and as pale as her skin. This was no battle wound she had sustained, there was something vile afoot here, some sort of illness.

"Vesir... you... came," she gasped, her voice sounded worse than she looked and that was certainly saying something. A comforting smile grew on his lips as he leaned in close to her and cupped their hands together.

"Of course I did, I always come running when my favourite marriage-sister calls," he said jokingly though seeped with concern. Julian attempted a smile but it only grew for a moment before her muscles were too weak to hold it.

"I am... your only... marriage-sister," she replied. "Vesir... listen... to me." He nodded slowly.

"Yes, Julian?" By the looks of her, it was painful to speak but whatever information she had for him, he needed to know.

"Rumeo... please... I beg you. Avenge my... husband. Your brother... Please..." He could not help but frown to this.

"Avenge him? What do you mean? What has happened to Rumeo?" This was getting stranger by the second. He had come back to Heldon to find his brother turning into some sort of ruler of cruelty, Nyer plotting against him or to save him, he was not sure which yet and now the Queen asking him to avenge the King.

"Avenge... my husband... stop Rumeo... protect... my children." The words ended there, her eyes closed once more, as the strength she had needed to whisper the last words, had caused too much strain. Vesir leaned down his ear to her mouth, she was breathing, she was alive. Though in this state there was no way he could get her out and back to Nyer. He had to tell his niece what had occurred. Hopefully she would understand this more than he did. Did she mean to protect the children from Rumeo? Rayar wherever he was in the world, would certainly be a challenge to protect, yet if Hinsani had found the prince then he could think of no better man to protect him. His fingers brushed over her straw like hair, it felt as dead as she looked, the sight was heartbreaking. Vesir considered himself a strong man as well as an emotional one, to hold back tears here was not an easy task.

"Don't worry Julian. I'll be back for you. I'll get to the bottom of this. I promise."

* * *

Chapter XVIII
Blood Bonds
~Nyer~

"Tell me about the Shield, cousin?" Nyer asked from her high back chair, with her legs crossed under her baby blue dress. Most of her attire was some sort of shade of blue; she felt this colour represented her most efficiently. Her slender fingers intertwined on her knee as her cool gaze focused on Zanmir. The boy had a somewhat calm and cool demeanour about him that she respected, his words were those of logic and calculation like her own and she sensed potential in him that she did not see in the other younger Granlia generation. "There must be fewer challenges there than in the capital I imagine. I read that there has not been an attack from the nation of Ghaul or the 'crazed men' as the scholars put it, for quite some time, many years in fact. What is it you do there?" she asked with a curious expression. While this was an attempt at idle small talk while they waited for her uncle to return, she was genuinely unsure of the purpose of the Shield in this day and age. Zanmir cleared his throat after taking a sip of water, perhaps a trifle uncomfortable by the questioning.

"I do not disagree. The Shield's previous purpose has become obsolete. Men stricken with madness do not try and clamber the walls after blood anymore. The nation of Ghaul is no longer a threat. Perhaps they all killed each other with the madness. The Red Mist is likely to be some sort of natural phenomenon created by the mountains to the west, near Hellsbane Castle. For the most part, it has become a place where soldiers who no longer have an active role in protecting the country, go to live out their days. The commander has made it significantly better since his arrival, I am told. Previously, it was a place with a barracks and a few squads of soldiers, now it holds one of the larger garrisons in Mayhen and has a profitable town." Nyer listened intently, nodding her head occasionally to show she was interested.

"I see. So Uncle Vesir has done some good work there. I had heard that as well. The town, Meyer was it, truly is a benefit to the kingdom yet the Shield itself seems like a burden no?" she interrogated. Zanmir sniffed at her words, seemingly they did not agree on everything.

"Burden? No, due to the commanders training and routines, he has crafted some of the best soldiers in the country. While I may not always agree with his methods, he does bring about results. Each soldier of the Shield is worth perhaps five or six of those in the rest of the kingdom." She could not help but let a mocking chuckle slip past her cold exterior.

"Truly... I will remember that." Her cousin now began his probing.

"And yourself? As you are next in line to rule Mayhen, you must have many responsibilities upon your shoulders?" Nyer felt as if she was not one to boast about her position and power, well former position and power. The last week had stolen many of her responsibilities like a tidal wave clearing a small town. All she did now was wander the castle and was unwelcome in all matters of the kingdom. She was given no time to answer as sounds of a ruckus could be heard from downstairs; men yelling and then several thumps, before a stampede of footsteps rattled the building coming up the stairs and towards the doorway. In a flash, Titania appeared by her princesses side, with her blade drawn and aimed towards the doorway. The soldiers of the Shield began to stumble back and draw their own swords, inches from their sheaths and move closer to Zanmir. The door suddenly burst open and over a dozen Heldoran guardsmen poured through with swords and spears at the ready. Some of the weapons were already stained with blood.

"What is the meaning of this!?" Nyer roared at the soldiers. "You point your swords at a Princess of Mayhen!" She knew she was in a precarious situation, so any hand she could play she would. From the crowd, a man with a bald head and crane like nose slithered into sight. She recognised him from the throne room as one of the new faces surrounding her father. He was draped in a long red cloak over his brown leather armour; she remembered normally seeing this man in black. If she did not recognise the face, there was one thing she would never forget, the hand replaced by a hook. This was the man going by the name of Sirus, a captain in the Heldoran guard.

"Dear oh dear. I apologise wholeheartedly My Lady. We received word that the good Princess of Mayhen, Nyer Granlia, had been apprehended by brigands from the Shield, so being the valiant men we are, we came storming to the rescue." His dark gaze flickered to the men of the Shield. "There they are now. Kill the soldiers, take the boy," he ordered. The Heldoran guardsman advanced towards the soldiers who drew their blades to protect their lives and the life of their commander's son. Nyer opened her mouth to speak but Zanmir was too quick for her.

"Wait!" he barked and stepped forward with his hands held up to show he is unarmed. "There is no more need for bloodshed. I assume you killed the men downstairs. No more need to die. I will tell the men to sheath their weapons and come with you peacefully. This was my doing, they were only following orders." The princess blinked in shock. He seemed like such a careful man, why would he throw himself in front of the wagon so recklessly.

"What are you doing?" she spoke with a harsh tone, ordering him to respond. Zanmir nervously looked over to her with a somewhat regretting expression.

"This is all a misunderstanding. If they fight here, then more lives will be lost pointlessly. If we go and explain ourselves, then the matter can be resolved. It was the commander he exiled from Heldon, not me or his men." Sirus stretched a toothy smirk and nodded.

"Indeed it was. You are in no danger but yes, you'll need to come with us. There's some explaining to do I think! My Lady Nyer Granlia, we *humbly* request you return with us. You can take the Shield men with you, add them to your little bodyguard group. I think having a fragile woman protect another fragile woman is a little embarrassing, hm?" he taunted. Titania tightened her grasp on her sword, never lowering it.

"You wish to test how fragile this *girl* this?" the red headed warrior retorted. Nyer knew her ability and her confidence were not inflated. She knew one thing for sure, that when she became Queen of this kingdom, no man like this snake would ever find their way into the court again.

"I would not presume I would have the skill needed to fight a child, let alone a woman, in my current state," he replied as he waved the hooked hand around like a wet fish. Nyer strode past her Royal Blade, with her head held high and expression as powerful as any sword.

"Come then. If you are escorting me back to the castle, then escort. I grow weary of this idle chit chat," she ordered. Even if these guardsmen had been led astray, as she approached, their swords quickly found their home at their sides and they stepped aside to give her room, even bowing their heads respectfully to the royalty. Titania was not far behind, followed by the soldiers of the Shield. If they had any sense, they would take their chances by sticking with her. Zanmir on the other hand was quickly bound by chains on his wrists, much to his dismay and dragged at the rear of the group. They needed to leave with haste as she knew she could not afford to lose Vesir this early in the game. If he arrived at this scene, it would have been the end of him. Her father was always a man of his word, an honest and good man of his word. Even though he had become a vile man, he still was one to keep his word.

The night was still young when they reached the keep. There were people still in the city streets, as they made their homeward journey. There would be a good few hours until the sun rose in the east over Hextheene. As expected, the castle was littered with so many guardsmen she lost count. Every time she looked, they seemed to be growing in number as if populating like rabbits. Nyer was escorted into the throne room through the main hall and the usual painting lay before her. Guardsmen lined the walls and shady courtiers were seemingly roused from their slumber and brought to the throne room, to witness some kind of event. Some were still in evening wear. Her father, the deplorable King, sat on his throne as awake as he always seemed to be, in his royal attire. He wore his crown upon his greying hair, and his new black cloth to symbolize the Black Bear of Mayhen. Next to him sat an exhausted Ayla, even she had been woken from her bed and brought to the throne room. Nyer could tell that under her light blue cloak she wore her nightgown, she could recognise it anywhere. The silly girl had a habit of chasing Rayar around at night wearing those revealing clothes thinking that no one noticed.

"Come, sit next to father," Rumeo ordered his eldest daughter. Without a word she moved to the chair closest to the King on his right hand side. Her eyes lingered over to the two empty chairs near her, Rayars obviously but still Nymin's was vacant.

'Not the time to occupy myself with these thoughts. I must focus on the next step. I must play these cards carefully. I cannot be caught out now.' The fact she was not in chains in front of the King and sat beside him was definitely a good sign, unless he had some other sick play up his sleeve. Either way patience was the tactic here.

"I hear you have been misbehaving Nyer," he muttered towards her, his glare as dark as a pitch black room. "But as you are my first daughter, I will let you off with only a warning. Any who betray me will end up as... well, you will see." A grin grew across his face. A smile so repulsive it almost made her forget the old warm smile that usually graced her father's lips. She remained silent, which he only found amusing. The King leant back in his chair and bellowed out across the throne room hall.

"Bring him in!" The attention of all was now on the doorway, the sounds of chains chimed throughout the room. Zanmir waddled as best he could with chains around his wrists and ankles, with guards marching beside him. That confidence he had in the inn had disappeared. She had not thought of it, no, forgotten what they seen downstairs in the Golden Crane. Blood and bodies everywhere but after seeing that, Zanmir's courage began to crumble. There were many whispers and murmurs in the court, from the tired men and women who had been gathered, but nothing she could make out. Once her cousin finally reached the last step towards the throne, he awkwardly bowed his head with respect.

"Your Grace, I humbly beg mercy. This has been a terrible mistake," he said, his tone shaky.

'I am sorry cousin. You will not be able to talk your way out. He will not listen...' The King rose from his throne and threw up his arms in a dramatic performance.

"What am I to make of this? I order the men of the Shield out of my city and yet we find one here, back in the city. Not only this, he plots, plots of treason like many around me. How should I as King, accept this? Another Granlia wishing my throne?" Zanmir dropped to his knees, his courage shattered even more.

"Your Grace! I have no ill thoughts or plans towards you. It was not me, Your Grace. I swear it." In his ramblings he looked to Nyer, their eyes locked. If he blabbed now, he could risk staining her name against the people. Would this man do it? Would he risk her plan to save his own skin? He would, of course he would; he does not know how much she has at stake, he does not understand how important it is. This boy does not understand. Their eyes continued to remain fixed on each other without a blink between them as she felt him reading her like a book.

"It was not you, was it!? Then pray tell, who was it? Vesir Granlia betrays me perhaps? Where is your father?" the King demanded. Finally, their trading of eyes broke as Zanmir turned away.

"I do not know," he muttered. This was not received well by the King.

"Speak up boy!" Rumeo roared down the stairs. Zanmir shuddered in fear, his fingers gripping his trousers so tightly, Nyer could have sworn she saw the cloth rip.

"I do not know, Your Grace. He is gone, left. I am no traitor! I am a Granlia and I demand to be treated rightfully to my position!"A burst of confidence poured over him as he roared back at the King. Both daughters looked to Rumeo, she half expected him to lose his mind with anger but much to her surprise, he stood there as calm as a mellowed tide.

"No, you are right. You are a Granlia and should be treated as such. You have my blood within you. You are my nephew, son of my brother. Very well, I will treat you as you should be treated." The King dropped back into his chair, speaking his next words with so much composure it made the sentence all that more terrifying.

"You will be executed by beheading in the morning for treason and for returning after exile. If your father comes and offers himself, you will be spared and sent back to the Shield, then he will take your place." Brayton, who had been standing on the sidelines tried to speak to the King, warning him of the dangers of killing not only a kinsman, but the son of Vesir but Rumeo waved him off without compassion. Zanmir's face went as white as snow, words unable to break free from his shock. The only words that escaped him were yelling for mercy as he was dragged off by the guardsmen towards the cells. That logical composed man had been completely broken, it was sickening to watch.

"Nyer," she heard her father mutter without passing her a glance. "Next time it will be you." With that he pushed himself from the throne and turned off to the meeting chambers behind the throne room, with Brayton close in tow as well as that vile man Sirus. A few others she did not recognise, followed from the crowd, like ghosts gliding across the floor.

"This is madness..." Ayla muttered from beside her. She turned to her younger sister and gripped her hand tightly.

199

"Do not fear. I promised you did I not? Stick together." As awful as this was, it was perfect. She was almost out of cards in this game and now she had been given the best hand she could think of. The execution of Zanmir was exactly what she needed to get the upper hand. The throne room was emptied soon after with Ayla returning to her chambers and Nyer taking Titania to the main hall. The pair strode along in silence as the princess processed the events that had just unfolded.

'If Zanmir is executed in the morning, Vesir will join me without hesitation. Not all the Lords and Ladies will support this. With this action I can gain the support I need to stop him. If Vesir comes and is killed in his place, then Zanmir returns to the Shield and gathers the men. Zanmir might not be the one to lead an army, but from what I have heard of Jonnas, he would storm the city in an instant if he heard Vesir was executed. Vesir must be delayed trying to get to the execution yet, arrive to ensure a commotion. Father, you fool, this one mistake will cost you more than you know.' For her it was a win-win situation, yet she needed to make sure when the opportunity arrived to make her move, she did not miss it. She would also need help, help she did not want but needed regardless. The long spiral staircase was, as ever, tedious as she remembered. Why did this old crone have to have her quarters in a tower like some kind of witch hiding away? Once at the doorway, Titania pushed it open and the pair entered the chambers. Lanni Ni'Tella sat by the window with a warm tea in her hands, but she seemed broken, depressed even.

"Miss Ni'Tella." The old advisor turned towards the doorway and took a sip of her tea.

"Princess Nyer... you never visit these days. The King allows you free roaming now?" she asked with a rasp in her voice.

"My movement has not been restricted yet, but soon I fear it will be. This may be my last chance, though I have not seen you in the keep for some time. I would say you were the one not allowed to wander the castle but I saw no guards at your door." Since Rayar had been deemed a traitor, Lanni had not been seen in the interior keep, gardens or courtyard. Part of her thought she had died of old age and no one had noticed. She privately didn't hope for this anymore however, she could think of no one better to aid her cause.

"I have no interest in being a part of this facade we are calling a Royal Family. Your father... the King, is not the King anymore. I have known that man since he was a child and the things he is saying, the things he is doing, is not Rumeo. No... I will wait up here and pray. That is all I can do." Nyer closed the distance between them cautiously. She never trusted this woman. As kind and gentle as she seemed, there was something about her she simply felt was out of place. It may have been purely that she had outlived so many people but whatever it was, she could not put her finger on it.

"There is something you can do. Something important, something that can help save us save the kingdom, Lanni. You and I have never seen eye to eye but this day, right now I need your help." Lanni frowned to her, her wrinkled features creasing like leather.

"You're asking me for help? Never thought I would live to see the day. Above and Below, I probably almost did not. Now what is it an old woman like me can do for you?" The princess joined her by the window with Titania moving outside to stand guard by the door. They would not be caught so predictably again.

"You have contacts. You know more people in the kingdom than any person alive can claim. Lord Tismiar Loysse sent a message that Rayar was in his keep and taken by Heldoran guards over a week ago. We know he escaped but we do not know where. That is not important at the moment. I need you to make contact with him, now. Not in the morning, send a messenger pigeon, now." Lanni blinked in surprise at her command and wrinkled her nose.

"Can you not do it yourself?" she asked ignorantly. Nyer sighed.

"No, any message I send will be intercepted. If I go down to the cages, you think they would let me send anything I wish?

No, you are the only one here who can still send messages undetected." Her eyes glanced over to Lanni's personal messenger pigeon, sitting idly in its cage. "If we are to save this kingdom, I need you by my side helping me. For the good of the kingdom Lanni Ni'Tella, will you help me?" The old woman appeared to be pondering over her offer, many clogs and wheels rotating in her head in thought, which Nyer could not help but imagine, were covered in spider webs from lack of use. Finally the elderly woman smiled softly towards the princess.

"I suppose I must, if I am to die, I would rather it be in my bed but helping save the King from himself is just as good. What will this message say exactly?" With Lanni on side, this could truly succeed. There was still a gamble; Tismiar Loysse. She would not have time to hear the reply once the message was sent. There was another message that needed sending, but that was not for Lanni. That was for her Royal Blade to deliver. Come morning, the true beginning of her plan would commence. Some would see it as her attempting to grab the throne from her father, but true men and women of Mayhen would see it as justice.

* * *

Chapter XIX
The Betrayed

~Nyer~

The sun had risen in a grey cloudy sky. Today was the day. Nyer had only been able to get a few hours sleep during the night, the anticipation and planning kept her awake through the most of it. The King wishing to have her cousin executed only hours upon dawn after sentencing him was a ploy to bring Vesir out from wherever he was in the city. They all knew he was still here; he would not leave and abandon his son in the hands of the tyrant that Rumeo had become. Many people of the court made their way to the stands that led from the courtyard and overlooked a section of the city. It was used primarily for public announcements as well as the act that was about to be performed; executions. The city would be filled by announcers calling the people of Heldon for the public execution to be held soon and many common people had already made their way to the lower area to watch. A row of stairs ran down from the platform towards the common area, which itself was covered in a line of guardsmen with their weapons poised. It would appear that Rumeo half expected Vesir to try and fight his way up to his son, if it came to it or perhaps the people would revolt at such an act. The latter would certainly be much more in her favour though if both Vesir and Zanmir died today, she would still have the second son, Jonnas, to fall back on. The Royal Family strode through the courtyard towards the doorway to watch the terrible act be played out. Nyer had ensured several people were at her side including Lanni and the Shield men, who had been granted to her ignorantly by Captain Sirus. Each person had his role to play. Their armour from the Shield had been replaced by the attire of Heldoran Guardsmen. Ayla walked just behind her. Both wore thick dresses with leather underneath, Nyer in dark blue and Ayla in a dark red shade. Even Lanni wore clothes that were sturdy; they would need them. Just before they reached the doorway, Nyer offered her younger sister a warm smile, as warm as her cold features would allow.

"Join me sister, we will sit by the side lines. I do not wish for you to be close to this act. It is an insult that we must attend at all, yet it is the will of the King." Ayla nodded sombrely as her gleeful and usually comforting presence was nothing but a shell of sadness.

"No." A deep voice sounded from behind them. King Rumeo came up upon the rear, with his entourage in tow and guards all around him. "My daughter Ayla will join me today. I want her by my side to see what justice is," he commanded. The girls traded looks of concern.

"Father, Your Grace, I think Princess Ayla would be more comfortable with me today, do you not agree?" Rumeo snorted followed by a deep chuckle.

"I do not agree. I truly, do not agree." With that, Sirus, the vile worm that he was, wandered over and held out his remaining hand, directing the middle daughter towards her father. Both princesses stared at each other, Ayla full of worry while she herself was boiling with anger. She tried to mouth 'Do not fear, it will be fine.' Yet her younger sister was directed away before she caught the movement of the lips.

'That bastard... bloody Above and Below. I will have to move as planned regardless, I cannot let this interfere.' The collection of people exited the courtyard and made their ways to their respective areas of the platform. Nyer and Lanni sat on the far right with the Shield Soldiers, dressed as guardsmen, standing around the pair. The crowd below were quiet; hundreds of whispers and mutters filled the air but nothing

anyone in the upper levels could hear. She turned her attention to the left, down from her stand towards the platform. On the other side of the execution block that had been set there in the morning, stood Rumeo and her sister, as well as dozens of guardsmen. There was no way she would be able to get to Ayla, or Ayla get to her at this rate. No, she had to focus on bigger things, more important things. As the crowd simmered down at the arrival of Commander Brayton who stood at the forefront, he addressed all those present.

"Good people of Heldon. Today we begin the bleeding of treason in our great city. There have been plots against the throne, against the Royal Family, against your true and honourable King. Last night a man who took part in these plots was arrested and sentenced to death. Today, you will witness this execution as an example to all those who would plot regicide." As he finished his small speech, chains rattled from the doorway and a bedraggled Zanmir was dragged out by two guardsmen. He looked bloody and bruised, beaten in his cell most likely throughout the night. Nyer could not help but show an expression of distaste towards such pointless actions. They were going to kill the man; there was no need to pointlessly torture him as well. Her cousin was pushed to his knees on the platform, looking over the people below, tired and confused.

'Chin up cousin. It will be over soon,' she thought to herself. Just then Titania arrived as silent as a mouse and bent over to whisper in her ear. Even after being friends since they were barely able to walk, the red headed woman could still sneak up on her without making a sound.

"This note was left in your study, My Lady," she whispered and placed a small note into her charges lap. Nyer stealthily took the note and unravelled it to peer inside.

'I have Nymin and I'm taking her out of danger.
Hyar'

The man actually did it. She had her doubts having Titania deliver that message to take her younger sister to safety. It was his duty after all. After the golden haired buffoon heard of all that was happening, considering he had been drinking wine outside the princess's room for so long, Titania said he was surprisingly onboard. That was one sister she no longer had to worry about remaining in his hellish castle. Hyar knew where he needed to escort Nymin, she *had* to place trust in his oath. The cold princess returned her attention to the crowd and Zanmir, there was a wretched show to watch after all. Her father had taken the centre stage and began to address his people in his loud, booming voice.

"My people, the people of Heldon, people of Mayhen! I, King Rumeo Granlia, have sentenced this man, Zanmir Granlia of the Shield to death for his crimes against the throne. I am the King. I am your leader and your protector. I will protect you all from the evil of treachery. Today, I will deliver the final blow myself." With a fluid motion, he turned to one of his courtiers who held a large scabbard with a huge great sword inserted inside. Smoothly he drew the blade free and held it in the air. "A King does not shy away from duties or what must be done. A true King, a true man, does what must be done himself!" The people cheered. They actually cheered at this. Were they all so ignorant they did not realise what was happening? No, of course they did not. They were sheep and the King was the shepherd.

"Vesir Granlia! If you are out there, your treason is far beyond that of any I know! Your son sits in your place! If you are out there, you coward, step forward and kneel at my feet and beg mercy! You will see your son live and you'll take his place!" At this the people did not cheer, in fact they all seemed very perplexed, looking between each other as if not understanding.

'Treason means death, father. Trading a life for another does not sound like justice, it sounds like vengeance for pretend crimes. Your sheep are scattering,' Nyer thought as she watched the scene. There was silence as the common folk looked for this supposed Vesir in the crowd, the guards remained motionless and prepared and the King gazed over the

city around him almost hopeful for his brother to make an appearance. They waited silently, and waited, and waited, minutes passed of silence. Nothing, not a whisper of the man, not a glimpse. Nothing. He had not come. Nyer trailed her fingers delicately across the arm rest of her chair; he would not make it in time. He would have been delayed. The announcers sent to yell it across the city all morning had been in the dozens. Knowledge of the execution certainly would have reached him. Her father let out a soft sigh and raised the huge sword above his nephews head.

"A shame. A true shame for you, boy. Any last words for your King?" Rumeo asked, poised to strike down with a mighty slash. Zanmir coughed while he struggled to keep upright on his knees, his words wavered with strain from his wounds.

"Last words? ... Doing this... you will cause... more grief to the people... than you could imagine. Not that... I, some... Lord's son from across... the country matters." Nyer frowned as he spoke, watching him intently. She admired his last burst of courage in such a situation, even more because he did not appear to be the most courageous man she had met. "... But the man I am... son of... will never forgive you... I love my father. He would... have been the greatest... King. He will... never stop until the debt is... paid." Her eyes narrowed at the King as she almost thought she could see his lips form the word 'Good' at her cousins last statement. The moment had finally come, there was no more waiting around for ghosts or miracles.

"Very well. I, King Rumeo Granlia, will now carry out the sentence." The people were dead silent watching the performance that could almost be a play meant to entertain them. Ayla covered her eyes with tears streaming down her cheeks, even Brayton showed signs of concern for the act before him. The huge great sword began its swing downwards to the boy's neck. Nyers attention was stolen by a manic scream from the crowd.

"STOP!" She knew the voice and the pain in the voice broke her ice heart.

*

~Vesir~

'Above and Below, what happened here?' Vesir thought as he returned to The Golden Crane. Two of his men lay sprawled on the ground, soaked in blood and the patrons who had been drinking by the bar had suffered the same fate. Their throats cut and their corpses collapsed on the counter. The owner of the establishment had been pinned to the wall with a sword run through his mouth. He hung their lifelessly. Vesir's sword instantly drew from the scabbard as he charged up the stairs towards the room where their meeting had taken place. From down the hallway, he could see the door wide open, cracked and damaged. The man sprinted down the length of the hallway and burst into the room ready to battle any who stood there.

"Zanmir!" He called out as he entered the room, yet it was empty. No bodies, no blood, no signs of conflict in the room. It was how he had left it just without anyone to greet him. It had taken longer to get back out of the castle than he had hoped; an hour or so longer, due to the sudden increase of activity and movement of the guardsmen defending its walls. It would be light soon and he now stood alone in the city, unaware of his sons' whereabouts, or where Nyer was or any of his men.

'Bloody Above and Below, could this get any worse?' Vesir thought as he turned back towards the stairs. He needed to come up with a plan to figure out what to do next. Finding Zanmir was paramount. He could guess what had happened; guardsmen must have come and taken him as well as the rest of them. If that meant they were now all back in the castle that would have been some kind of sick joke. As Vesir made it down the stairs, he stopped mid-step and locked eyes with a couple of men who had just entered the inn. Their eyes flicked to his unsheathed blade, the bodies and back to the commander. Vesir figured out immediately what had gone through their heads.

"No, no wait! This wasn't me!" he yelled out. Both men yelped in fear and fell over each other to clamber out of the doorway.

"Call the guards! Murder! Murder in the Golden Crane! Help!" one of them screamed as he ran down the road outside the inn. The other, who had completely toppled onto his face, tried his best to crawl away screaming 'get away' to the commander. Vesir burst out of the inn doing whatever he could to calm the situation.

"I didn't do this!" he snapped. As if his luck wasn't bad enough already, he saw the fleeing man with a squad of five guardsmen probably explaining to them what he had seen whilst shaking in terror. The commoner pointed down the path directly at Vesir and the guards followed his direction.

"Halt! In the name of the King, Halt!" The officer of the guards roared as they began their jog towards him; spears in hand and shields on their arms. He could not get caught now, not red handed like this, even if he had not been the one to do the deed. Vesir hesitated a moment, debating in his head whether to try and talk his way out of it, or run. The latter seemed like the better option as they closed in showing no signs of slowing down.

"Bloody...!" He blathered out before he turned on his heel and sprinted down the dark road away from the guards. Trust it would be him to fall into such a predicament at this very moment. It did not take long for him to lose the heavier armoured guards trying to apprehend him, after darting in and out of the alleys around the city. He had spent many years of his youth playing pranks and messing around in the city, much to the dismay of his father and mother and even his brother at the time. He never truly fitted in with royalty like the rest of his family. He had enjoyed the company of the common soldier over that of attending fancy balls, or engaging in courtly conversations and proper etiquette. Vesir spent the next couple of hours hiding in the shadows of the city. His face was not only known to the people of the castle which would have him arrested on sight, but now the guards in the city were on the hunt for him. The best thing to do was rest and wait until he was granted the best opportunity to make his move. He was not as young as he used to be and staying up all night would have certainly taken its toll. At least a few hours sleep would settle his nerves and give him some perspective when he awoke. Like a homeless man in the streets, Vesir found a dark and relatively warm corner in one of the many alley-ways; wrapped himself in his cloak and curled up looking like no more than a ball of cloth in the darkness.

The desperately needed sleep was brief. Light awoke him, beaming down the alley like a holy sign for him to come alive once more. The old commander stirred and mumbled to himself as he slowly realised the reality of where he was and what was going on.

"Great." He complained quietly as he pushed his body up the wall back to his feet. Both hands rubbed his face furiously, to help force his mind to follow the body to a more awake state. The sounds of yelling and chanting echoed down the alley, as if someone was announcing something in the streets. He carefully clambered to the exit of his *'bed'* for the night and peered around the corner. The streets were filled with people all heading in the same direction, talking about something that almost sounded like the word execution. This was soon confirmed by a large, chunky man who stood upon a wooden box with a scroll in chubby fingers, bellowing out announcements.

"Wake! Wake! Good people of Heldon! Today the King commands all make their way to the Stands for the public execution of the traitor Zanmir Granlia! Wake! Wake! Treason is punished by death and the King holds no bars on those who are traitors! Wake! Wake! Good people of Heldon! Today the King commands all make their way to the Stands of the public execution of the traitor Zanmir Granlia!" He felt sick, he felt furious, his heart sunk into his stomach and his muscles twisted in rage and fear. His mind was racing faster than he could think, blood churning and eyes watering. This could not be possible, Rumeo, his own brother was going to murder his son

210

in front of all in the city for the crime of treason. It was a lie, Zanmir was no traitor. If Rumeo thought any was a traitor, it would be him and he was using his son to grieve him. With no time to waste, the commander pulled up his hood and darted into the crowd, thoughts rushing through his panicking mind. The panic was sending him into a frenzy, unable to truly comprehend what he had heard.

'I can talk to him, talk him around. I can stop this, I will stop this. I won't let my son die. I will trade my life if I have to. Zanmir, hold on son your father is coming. I will not let you die!' Vesir became more and more aggravated as the people around him began to block his path, crowding in so tight they moved at a snail's pace. He tried in desperation to force through the throngs, though his disruptive actions led to a gloved hand grasping his shoulder.

"Sir, do not push now," a guardsman ordered him, as Vesir turned to see the face of the man whom had grabbed him, the face of the guardsman dropped. The luck he had was something no one deserved. It was the officer from the night just passed. "You! Come with me at once!" The guardsman roared as he reached for his sword. Vesir did not have time for this; he swiftly rammed his elbow into the man's face and slammed his foot down on the side of the guard's knee, a snap exploding from the contact. The display grabbed the attention of the other guards in the area who then rushed over with their swords drawn, ordering him to halt and drop his weapons. The commander growled in anger, his son needed him and these blind fools were in his way. He had no choice. They had given him no choice. Vesir drew his sword and clashed with the guards. Each one who approached him was no match for him, even when he was not fighting to kill. Guard after guard fell unconscious like sacks, with legs and arms broken, unable to detain the skilled fighter. This was precious time he did not have to spare, with his son's life hanging in the balance. The commoners around him had formed a circle to avoid being drawn into the conflict, some fled screaming, others watched in awe. His outburst luckily led to the people around keeping a

211

clear distance from him. Once the guards had been soundly dealt with, a clear path had been made by fleeing commoners, allowing him to sprint towards the execution stand.

'Zanmir, I'm coming.' He did not know what he would do when he arrived, he did not care at this moment. All he cared about was getting his son out alive; if he had to fight through a hundred men to do so, he would. If he had to fight the entire city alone he would, nothing mattered but the life of his son. The crowd ahead of him had reformed into a bundle of bodies, no longer making way for him as they were not privy to the actions he had performed further down the road. Vesir pushed. He pushed with all his might. He pushed so hard into the herd he thought his arms would snap like twigs from the pressure. As the road came to a turn and into an opening, he heard a voice bellowing across for all to hear.

"Very well. I, King Rumeo Granlia, will now carry out the sentence." A huge great sword in the distance dropped in a powerful strike towards Zanmir's neck. Whilst they were only specks in the distance, he knew who it was. The crowd around the stand were almost silent but for whispers between friends. He roared like a lion with the pain of a thousand cuts etched in his voice.

"STOP!" People turned to him to see the tears in his eyes. The great sword came full swing and the head of his eldest son dropped to the wooden floor, below the twitching body. He could see the King look over to him, squinting to confirm it was indeed his brother. It was Nyer who called out next, as she ordered his arrest. Four Heldoran guards by her side were the first into the pit of men and women around him, watching the spectacle. Fierce anger flushed over his very being and in a flash his bow was in his hand and an arrow in the other. The people around him screamed and ducked, giving him the view he needed. The arrow knocked and flew true towards its destination, the King. No one could react quickly enough as the arrow pierced Rumeo's shoulder causing him to stumble back and collapse onto the wooden stand. Like roaches, the guardsmen were around the King, giving no chance for a second arrow. The guardsmen pulled the King aside, shields and spears drawn making a wall to protect him and the daughter, Ayla. His bow was thrown to the side and the sword now replaced it as he started to charge through the many bodies around him, anger fuelled his actions, eyes seeing the red mist. Four guardsman were first to approach him and he swung like a madman to fight them off. One of them rushed him with no weapon drawn and wrapped his arms around him like a blanket while the others tried to grab the sword arm.

"Commander! It's us, commander!" The first guardsman yelled as he removed his helmet's faceguard. Vesir's swinging weakened, as he locked eyes with the man trying to restrain him. It was one of his men of the Shield, dressed in the armour of the Heldoran guard. "Please commander! We are sorry! We will avenge your son but now we must go! Please I beg you! We must go!" The words hit him but did not sink in, he was broken and distraught and full of wrath and despair.

Zanmir... Zanmir... son...' rang in his mind over and over, his little boy's name. Unable to get their words across, the four men of the Shield began to drag him through the crowd and away from the monstrous display. The rest of the guards could barely push through the now screaming and frantic crowd, to reach them. Tears filled his eyes; unimaginable pain filled his heart as he was dragged off into the city. The sight of the stand. The sight of his brother. The sight of the body of his son, disappearing into the distance.

*

~Rumeo~

Rumeo snarled as he pulled the arrow from his shoulder, a pool of blood formed at his feet. His eyes darted around through the hundred guardsmen who protected him from any further attempts on his life but Vesir was gone as quick as he had come. Then his attention was drawn to the right, towards princess Nyer only to find she had also disappeared. Her perch

213

was empty. Lanni was gone, Titania was gone. Brayton moved to his side and began ordering assistance while Ayla had fallen to the ground, holding her dress. Fear was the portrait across her features with guardsmen all around her.

"The King is wounded! Fetch the healers!" He could not hold back his smile, as much as he wanted, to keep in character. The smile grew and grew. She had fallen right into his hands and as a bonus she had left Ayla, there was no way he was going to let all the Royal Children leave after all.

'Too easy, ignorant girl thinking she is a paragon of justice, yet she is the bringer of war. Let this mayhem commence.'

* * *

Chapter XX
Commander-at-Arms
~Caskin~

Caskin had only been back in the Hexhold for a couple of days but he had not yet been given a chance to speak with the King. Baron Regnier Branberb had been visiting the Hexhold with his entourage. The business the Baron and the King had been discussing had taken up much of the King's time until now. Finally he had been summoned to an audience in the Chamber of Truth, the hall used as a meeting room by the Hextor family for generations. Before it was a meeting hall, it had been a place where the Kings and their courts put people on trial for crimes against the crown, hence the name Chamber of Truth. Braska's grandfather had kept the name but used it for another purpose, as he only desired truth to be spoken in his meetings with the Five Barons of Hextheene. Each Baron held a section of land in Hextheene, which they themselves governed and then oversaw specific duties for the realm. The Baron of house Branberb was in charge of the fertile lands nearest the capital's own designated land, which focused on agriculture and profit in the nation. Baron Branberb had no head for militaristic agendas but every army needed to eat. Not to mention that he was crippled last time Caskin remembered seeing him; a good man but useless in a battlefield and during times of war. It was soldiers he wanted, not politicians. Adorned in his grey armour with a new cleaned white tabard, after his previous one had been stained beyond recognition,

Caskin made his way towards the Chamber of Truth. His bastard sword hung at his hip as it always did, even in the presence of the King. He remembered a time where the shadowy advisor, Sli, mentioned him having a sword when graced with the presence of King Braska, to which he had no time to reply.

'A sword would not save him from me if he chose to use it against me.' The confidence and matter of fact statement of the King's words, still chimed in his head. The only King he would ever serve, until his dying breath, a man so powerful and feared, he truly showed what it meant to be a strong leader. The huge halls went from room to room, past the throne and through a doorway at the rear, not obvious at first glance. After passing through the empty throne room, he entered the meeting hall. Across a long narrow table at the head, sat Braska Hextor, the giant of a man, with a cup of water next to him. Braska Hextor had never allowed alcohol to pass his lips for as long as he had known him. Beside the King on one side sat Sli, on his other side, Baron Branberb who, unlike his King, sat drinking wine. A lot of wine. A half bottle of wine lay abused on the table and a cup touched his lips as Caskin entered.

"Your Grace. I have returned from my encampment as summoned. I am here to serve," Caskin said as he stood at the far side of the table. Braska did not appreciate bows from his knights, only salutes which he performed flawlessly.

"Commander-at-Arms Caskin Camaron, you made it here in good time. An uninterrupted journey?" the King asked with his stone face and cold eyes. Stern and dominant as always it seemed, he was glad nothing had changed in his tour in South Hextheene.

"Yes, Your Grace, the road was uneventful. I came at haste upon receiving your command, what is it you require of me?" Braska motioned him to take a seat further up the table, closer to where the trio already sat and continued to speak whilst Caskin selected a chair.

"The original order for you to return has become null and void. You were to safeguard the throne, during an event in

Mayhen, a wedding. I was to personally attend it, my son and their Princess Ayla Granlia. However a while ago I received a new message, one retracting the offer of marriage, an insult too, as it were." The King nodded to Sli who slipped the message to Caskin. It looked old and tattered as if many hands had accosted this parchment.

'King Braska Hextor II,

Being in any way joined to your kingdom would be an insult to all within Mayhen. I retract any offer of marriage with any of my kin from this time till the end of time. You fight your wars alone.

King Rumeo Granlia.' He could not help but crease his face upon reading the message. The insult was his towards Hextheene, a dire insult too. Did this man not know what fear he would feel when the Knights of Hextheene crashed down on him like a stampede of vengeance? He could feel his blood boiling with excitement at even the remote possibility of facing off with Mayhen once again. He was only a young boy during the first war, the moment when he took his first life.

"What do you make of this?" Braska asked him. Caskin passed the message back to the advisor and scratched his stubbly chin in thought.

"The marriage between Hextheene was not paramount but definitely advantageous and as much as I would like to show them the might of those who cross our nation, the fighting south grows in its violence. Southrous soldiers and brigands attack towns and villages and travellers from Hextheene daily and butcher them like dogs. Yet, I do not think this should go ignored and accepted," he replied. Sli sneered at him, his jagged teeth in plain sight.

"You ask a soldier, Your Grace, you get a soldier reply. More war. We have our hands full with Southrous raids and Mayhen is needed for a secure future. There is more to this than meets the eye. From my experience, such words are not the usual song from King Rumeo Granlia." Caskin cocked a brow at the elderly man.

"Roll over and show weakness? The Knights of Hextheene do not break or bow. We follow the King to war and destroy his enemies, nothing more and nothing less." The tension between him and the advisor climbed.

"The Knights do as they are told by the King, if he says bow you bow, if he says break, you break. Your job is to find those who use magic and apprehend them and now you consider yourself and your knight's heroes of war?" Before Caskin could throw his retort, Braska spoke in a firm and commanding tone, though barely raised his voice.

"Enough." They both fell silent and reclined into their seats. King Braska continued. "Both sides speak truth. This insult should not go unchallenged, yet we do not have the man-power to fight Southrous and Mayhen again, south Hextheene was littered with those savages the last time my father fought wars on both sides. It was only due to the understanding of King Rumeo Granlia's father, did that war end allowing Hextheene to focus on one front. I will not make the same mistake my father did," Braska commanded. A large taunting grin appeared on the face of Sli, much to Caskin's annoyance. "However, Baron Branberb here has been busy and has come with news. Most does not concern you, Commander-at-Arms Camaron. Some does." The King looked over to the Baron across the table from him and nodded for him to speak. He was a slender man with dark hair and blue eyes, gaunt in his features. Many said he was handsome in youth but age and his affliction had made him stressed and weary. Now he looked like a leathery old scabbard.

"Thank you, Your Grace. I recently had Baron Berethor in my home for our usual meet and games evening. He brings his children and wife and we discuss matters of politics and enjoy the evenings with feasts and the like." Braska tapped his finger on the table, the King's universal sign 'get to the point'. Regnier coughed into his hand and nervously nodded before continuing his story.

"Well you may or may not know that our Baron friend Harald Berethor keeps a close eye on events near the border of

Mayhen, spies and scouts and the like. Our friend seems to be under the impression that his scouts saw the Prince of Mayhen, Rayar Granlia and perhaps two companions riding into the northern mountains, the Leon Mountains, between our two countries. Well I thought this must be nonsense as a prince riding almost alone into such a horrible place is simply silly, until I mentioned it to Your Grace and the esteemed advisor here." The crippled baron motioned his hand to Sli who then took over the explanation.

"My spiders in the capital of Mayhen had spoken whispers and caught many flies. They claim that Prince Rayar Granlia is guilty of treason against the crown for assisting an attack into the royal keep and now is on the run, yet no one knows where he is. That is until Baron Regnier Branberb here enlightened us with a rumour. There are many rumours of the King's cruelty and rage all over the city and the call for the prince's head, all over his country." Caskin listened to their long winded explanation and briefly glanced to the King, and judging by his expression, was united with the same distaste of long explanations.

"What has this got to do with the Knights of Hextheene, Your Grace?" Caskin asked with a confused look upon his face.

"Commander-at-Arms Camaron, I am charging you with the apprehension of Prince Rayar Granlia. You will select a squad of Knights and take fifty men with you to Castle Harringmore near the Bridge to the northern wastelands. There you will follow the coast and intercept the prince and his companions. The man most likely with him is someone you will be very familiar with, the boy's Royal Blade." Caskin's eyes widened at this, he could feel the excitement grow within him, as he did his best to keep his professional composure.

"Hinsani Tannaroth," the King nodded at his correct assumption. His fingers gripped the pommel of his bastard sword; the desire to cross blades with such a famous swordsman once again, was undying. Now they were in their primes, to fight him again, after so many years, would truly prove who was greater. Braska continued to explain the commands.

"Baron Branberb here, will return to his land and ensure Baron Berethor has scouts constantly watching our side of the mountain range while Sli's spiders will watch the side of Mayhen. Once he emerges, he will be tracked. You will receive word of his movements and will intercept as swiftly as possible. If we cannot have Ayla Granlia, we will have something better. We shall marry Prince Rayar Granlia to my daughter Melyane. This will ensure that he ascends to the throne in due time. King Rumeo's rumoured actions will cause strife in his lands that we can use to our advantage. This must be spoken to none outside this room apart from the knights selected for your support, Commander-at-Arms." With that the King fell silent and awaited Caskin's response. He forced aside his excitement and rose from his seat to salute his King.

"I will do as commanded, Your Grace." With that the King dismissed him with a wave of his hands allowing the Commander-at-Arms to turn on his heel and swiftly exit the Chamber of Truth. Once outside, he began to make his way back towards his quarters, though a voice called out his name from behind. Sli had followed him from the meeting room, waddling in that elderly weak manner he had.

"Commander-at-Arms, a moment," he stopped and turned to the man he held no love for, yet due to his position, it forced respect.

"Yes?" he simply replied. The old man closed the distance between them and sniffed as if smelling something unpleasant.

"The King has trusted this task to you, and you alone. I agree with his choice this time. If we send those scouts to make an attempt of capture, there would be many lives lost with that man by the prince's side, this Hinsani Tannaroth. One slip up and the prince dies or another and he disappears with us unable to locate him. Once we have his scent, you must not fail. More than just lives of scouts lay on this. A plan to secure Hextheene's future relies on this. I am sure you will have the war you wish one day, but that is not this day." The words he spoke were true, as aggravating as he was. They were not after a bloodbath, they needed to abduct and then ensure this boy's allegiance to Hextheene. Caskin lowered down to the height of the advisor with a hand still comfortably on the pommel of his sword.

"I am a Knight of Hextheene, we do not fail." With that he turned and strode out of the throne room back towards the barracks. He could feel Sli's eyes burning into his spine, yet he continued forward without as much as a glance. As he left the castle and made his way across the large courtyard, he was surrounded by soldiers and knights going about their business. His long white cloak skimmed the mud at his feet, dirtying the trim. No matter how hard he tried, it was impossible to keep his white attire clean, yet it was the colour of his house and his position, so sadly, he would have to make do. Once he was out of Hexhold's inner courtyard, he found his way through the officer's barracks on the outside and towards his own personal quarters that had been held for him since he became Commander-at-Arms. His own true home was further south of Ganon; along the east coast, though he could not remember the last time he visited the lands and his family. His younger brother was doing a well enough job maintaining their small governed lands allowing him to focus on the only thing he truly cared for, war. Well, there was one more thing. As he pushed the door open to his quarters he found the young beauty known as Fifonia, sat upon an elegant light brown chair with a brush combing her long orange hair as she studied herself in a mirror upon a cabinet. A full length, almost see-through gown, covered her form and reached just above her ankles. She turned at the sound of the door opening and flashed him a seductive smile.

"My gallant knight returns. How was your meeting with the King?" she bluntly asked. Caskin shook his head and threw his gauntlets onto his bed after ripping them off.

"Interesting, our King has a mission for me of great importance. I will be riding west come morning, towards Harringmore Castle. After that who knows, I may be away for some time," he said as he approached the woman from behind and placed his hands on her shoulders. She laid her own hand on top of his and nuzzled his fingers with her cheek.

"I see, leaving again then. I suppose I shouldn't ask what you'll be doing when you ride west should I?" A small smile tickled his lips while his thumb rubbed her cheek in return to her affection.

"No, you shouldn't. You may stay in Hexhold for now. I will make sure you're not bothered by any soldier who wishes to try his luck." Fifonia leaned backwards to offer him a wide grin and replied, being as impertinent as ever.

"What if I want some soldier to try his luck?" she teased. Caskin returned the smile with a raised brow.

"Then they will understand what it is like to have a sword through their chest first hand. You are mine after all, I paid for you." His retort caused the whore to snigger and bat away his hand. She loved making him squirm and jealous, he knew it and could not even hold it against her.

"You must look after your property. You paid to rent me not own men Caskin," she teased again. The knight huffed like a child and turned to find a drink in his cabinet of many, many drinks.

"I suppose I will have to keep renting you then. Now I have much to plan and prepare for. I need a drink and silence while I select the knights I am to take with me," he commanded upon pouring his drink and lowering to his desk across the room. As second in command of the Knights of Hextheene, answering only to the King, he had records of each knight in their sect, hundreds of men, some far outside of Ganon and some prancing around Hexhold not even worth the title they held. Some gained their rank of Knight through valiant deeds, while others paid for the privilege. As much as he would have enjoyed taking those inexperienced boys on a mission that could end their lives, this mission was far too important for his own personal desires, to cleanse the Knights of the weak.

"The charge from the King must truly be of great importance, if you are considering your men this hard. Are you sure you do not wish to unburden it on me as well? I can surely help you while I am here. Otherwise I'll just sit here being bored," Fifonia complained as she gracefully flowed from the seat to beside her knight. Caskin replied without gazing up from his records.

"Asking too many questions can get you in serious trouble, whore. You are better off leaving these things to men and go back to what you are good at." The woman threw her head back in laughter and leaned on his shoulder, it seemed as if this woman was dead set on being distracting.

"You tell me everything Caskin, you always have. Let me help you. I have seen a lot more than you think. I know the Knights of Hextheene as well, seen many of them for years during my work. You think you are the only knight who has taken an interest in me?" With that she slipped onto his lap and wrapped her arms around his neck with a mischievous look upon her features. "Or we can go back to what I am good at instead?" The thought of others having their hands on her made his stomach lurch but he held back his discomfort; she would only tease him more. Whenever he was with this woman, his reason and wish for war always seemed to take a back foot. It was dangerous and he knew it. As dangerous as she was to him, he simply could not refuse her.

"If I tell you, you will be silent and not speak of other knights. I know my men and who should accompany me." She grinned at him and nodded enthusiastically. After a deep sigh, he revealed the plan the King had him in command of and she listened intently, before she rolled her shoulders with a shrug, as if finding no interest in it whatsoever. After hours of looking through the records of his men, he finally settled on his squad before retiring to his bed. That night he did not find much slumber, excitement boiled his blood for the coming bout with that man. He prayed to the Above that it was indeed him who was Prince Rayar's companion.

'Just you wait, Hinsani, our fight will be legendary. Songs will be sung about it, stories told. Just you wait,' though something else tickled the back of his mind. As he lay in his

bed, covered by the sheets, his attention shifted to Fifonia beside him in her deep sleep. Caskin watched her in silent slumber, her slender and curvy form under the sheets; even in sleep she was graceful. Why was she so interested in him and in what he had been commanded to do? No, it didn't matter. He refused to think about it, refused to care. She was his poison. Caskin loved being poisoned.

* * *

Chapter XXI
Knights of Hextheene
~Caskin~

It had been a dreamless sleep with the night passing in a blink of an eye. The soldier stirred from his slumber as drool dribbled down the side of his mouth in an uncouth fashion. His snoring was renown throughout the barracks when sleep took him. His large hand reached out across the bed to pet upon Fifonia while the other curled and rubbed the water marks from his cheek, but much to his surprise the ginger haired woman was nowhere to be found.

"Fifonia..." he mumbled sleepily as he gazed around the room, his cold blue eyes searching for the beauty, imagining her to be by the mirror being vain or gazing out of the window being contemplative yet she was nowhere to be found. Caskin sat up in his bed groaning loudly. He was half hoping she had prepared a mug of tea for his wakening after his trouble falling asleep, but it seemed he had drifted into quite the deep sleep eventually. It was not unknown for her to slip away for the day and slip back in the evenings; she was well known in Hexhold, long before he had set his sights on her. Now, her affiliation with him was something also well known, as much as he tried to keep it quiet. He was known for his battle prowess and as a fierce knight for the most part, but even he could not keep his little secrets hidden for long with the nosey men and women in Ganon and Hexhold. They would snoop about the place looking for any dirty mark they could, on anyone with status or position. Like a nest of vipers this place could be, even more so when the Barons came to the castle for their yearly visit and discussion of realm affairs. Then hundreds of people with their own agenda all came pouring into the same crevice, seeking out their own advancement. The light had penetrated his open window; it was time to begin the hunt. Once he had made his way through the barracks and into the training ground, he handed out the selected knights' documents to several aspiring squires. They shot off like bolts in various directions to locate the knights and bring them to the barracks. Caskin focused his attention on the men who had been granted to him by the King. There stood, lined on the grounds, fifty Hextheene soldiers, all dressed in leather over chainmail, swords at their hips and shields on their backs, standing rigid to attention. Upon inspection, they all seemed fairly veteran, not a man below twenty among them. King Braska was taking no risks in the careful touch of this mission, giving him some of the most experienced soldiers within the Hexhold garrison.

"Men of Hextheene!" Caskin snapped as he walked along the breadth of the line of soldiers. They all thrust their shoulders back and saluted together in harmony.

"Sir!" they bellowed out, almost in perfect unison. Caskin continued his stride, both hands clasped behind his back.

"You will ride with me, Commander-at-Arms Caskin Camaron. If you do not know me, you must know only this. I do not accept failure or cowardice. I will lead you to victory and you will be immortal. Understand!?" He roared out the last word which caused the soldiers to once again salute and roar back together.

"Yes Sir!" The blonde knight nodded and motioned to the Squad Leader at the end of the line.

"Have the men ready the horses and supplies, I will meet you at the west entrance in an hour; we move then." The squad leader, a chunky man with a dark brown moustache and goat beard, saluted his commander and began to ferry the men to their duties. An hour was an acceptable amount of time to get the knights updated. He was not waiting long in the barracks,

226

before the four knights he had selected joined him, each with their plate chain armour and the colours of their houses upon their banners. The first to arrive and his first choice, was a brute of a man in the colours of House Oathsworth, a minor family of southern Hextheene. He wore a gold and blue tabard over his armour with a gold crab on the chest. The only hair present was receding around the sides of his head and a beard that connected across his face, his name Sir Donnel Oathsworth. He had fought alongside this man many times and his war hammer that he always wielded was something to be feared. Strong, yet he could be unpredictable. The second knight to arrive, Sir Lancel Nash, a skinny man with shaven blonde hair, styled much like his own. This man had actually been Caskin's squire many, many years ago. His colours were blue and dark red with a broken wheel on the base of the tabard. The boy had started out as a farmer's son and had taken on the broken cart wheel as his emblem in respect to his father, or so Lancel had told him. The third to arrive was an older man with greying hair and a bushy beard covering most his face. A veteran knight named Sir Osmear Lorinstead. His house protected the border between Hextheene and Southrous. Brother of the current Baron, this man focused his life on the path of knighthood rather than politics; their emblem was the well known silver bull on a field of green. The last to arrive was Sir Donnel Jennin, a dark haired man with stubbly facial hair and tired eyes. In fact he had actually been out of luck with this man. Most the knights were already in the south or in their designated lands. Sir Jennin had been chosen simply because there were so few knights currently in Hexhold or the capital. All four knights stood around the room they had occupied, it was barely lit with only a few torches dotted around, in the depths of the barracks.

"Knights of Hextheene, I have a charge of upmost importance from the King. We are to ride to Harringmore Castle and from there, we will head further west and intercept a target to apprehend for the King. Prince Rayar Granlia of

Mayhen." The knights muttered between themselves, trading glances. Lancel Nash was first to speak.

"Commander-at-Arms, I must ask, what is the Prince of Mayhen doing in Hextheene?" the youngest of the group questioned. Caskin nodded to him before carrying on his explanation.

"He is not in Hextheene, yet. The prince is charged with treason in his home kingdom. So we are tasked with bringing him to Hexhold, willingly or not, and from there our charge ends. We find, we capture, and we deliver. If he is spotted returning to Mayhen then he is Baron Berethor's problem. He is likely fleeing his home though, so chances are he will be tracked into our territory. However it is believed he has a couple of companions, one being a particular man some of you may be familiar with. Hinsani Tannaroth, the Royal Blade." Oathsworth snorted and slammed his hand on a table in front of him.

"Hinsani!? I saw that man in the war when we were boys! I'd love to test myself against such a warrior, Haha!" Caskin sneered towards the large knight.

"The only one facing Hinsani shall be me." Whilst he desired the power of that brute of a knight, the man's love for violence even exceeded his own. No, it was not violence he loved, it was war. Donnel Oathsworth was a man of simple violence.

"Perhaps we should settle this now Caskin, and then the winner can face the Royal Blade and lead this expedition." The huge man pulled his warhammer from his side and rested the giant weapon on his shoulder. Caskin's hand instinctively landed on his bastard sword at his hip yet the increasingly tense situation was swiftly quelled by the eldest of the knights.

"Sir Oathsworth. The King has charged Caskin Camaron with command. We do as the King wills," Sir Osmear Lorinstead said quietly from his corner of the room. "Though, I'm curious to why you require a squad of knights and I counted fifty men give or take, to achieve this. Several well placed crossbow bolts could end the Royal Blade and a group of scouts could capture the young prince. Why are such numbers needed for this?" Sir Oathsworth had settled down after he listened to the wisdom of his elder knight. Caskin turned his attention to Sir Lorinstead with his reply.

"This is too important to be left in the hands of any but myself and you four, who I have selected as well as a squad of reliable soldiers. As commanded by Our Grace, Prince Rayar Granlia is not to be harmed and or lost from us. Simple soldiers without our leadership, could be unreliable or perhaps even worse, sell the prince back to Mayhen for a hefty reward. This is a risk we are not taking. We are Knights of Hextheene, the greatest sect of knights in the land. Now, ready your horses and meet me by the western gate out of the Hold as soon as possible. Long live the King." Caskin saluted all the knights in the room, who in return saluted back, one more begrudging than the others, before they exited the barracks to prepare with the rest of the soldiers assigned to the Commander-at-Arms.

'Four Knights, fifty soldiers. More than enough, no room for mistakes either.' Caskin could not help but smirk to himself as he stood alone in the barracks, the chance to battle Hinsani grew closer and closer. He would need to contain his excitement and appear professional for the men.

The party of knights and soldiers assembled at the western gate, equipped and supplied with a wagon in the centre of the convoy. Inside was a cell for the prince, should he refuse to act royally and misbehave. It was a precaution after all; he did not expect some young boy prince who was green to the world, to have the courage to refuse their escort or try to fight after his protector was killed. Any person who commits treason was a coward; he had no sympathy for this boy. The King's wishes were law and his command just. Caskin would do as commanded without fail. Caskin sat upon his mighty steed with the four knights in pairs behind him, followed by the soldiers on their own horses in pairs. They trotted forward in a double line out of the hold and towards the castle Harringmore to the west. The countryside outside the Hexhold was rather barren, the poor, sick and bed ridden begged on the side of the muddy roads for the knight's charity. They looked vile with boils on their faces, absent limbs and clothes so dirty they appeared as if they wore the muck from the streets.

'Useless. Falling about begging with nothing to give, give them a sword and throw them at Southrous. They send their bandits in our lands we should send them our poor,' he thought to himself as he ran a judging glance across the people around them. As he did so, he caught a glimpse of Sir Donnel Jennin, leaning down from his horse to pass a woman with her child a loaf of bread from their supplies. Rage shot over him as he roared back towards them causing the woman and child to scream. They stumbled and fell back into the mud; Jennin gasped and almost tumbled from his steed.

"Do not waste our supplies on these rats! That food is for fighting men!" he fired back to the knight. Sir Jennin bowed his head apologetically, visibly shaking.

"My apology, Commander-at-Arms Camaron. It shall not happen again," he mumbled in response. Weak. He had no time for weak knights by his side. This man was with them now, so he had to make the best of it. After sending him a dark glare which remained in his eyes for some time after, Caskin finally turned back to the head of the column and continued forward, giving Sir Jennin a moment to calm himself.

"Charity gets you nowhere. Every man, woman and child must serve for retribution. You should not reward those who are more pathetic than you. You should give them the chance to prove themselves instead," he preached to all, not directing it at any person in particular. There was no reply, though he assumed they received the message loud and clear. He was in command here. They would do as he commanded.

* * *

Chapter XXII
The Old Sage
~Rayar~

"Above and Below, this place is a nightmare!" Rayar yelped from the rear of the group. Just ahead of him, Hinsani pushed forward, showing signs of exhaustion in his heavy brow. If Hinsani was struggling, how was *he* supposed to survive this? At the head of the trio, Shania was showing no signs of tiredness or fatigue; though by what she had said earlier, she was well versed with this mountain range. They had only been in these mountains for a couple of days at this point. The horses had to be left behind at the base of the mountains and given freedom much to Hinsani's reluctance. There was no way for them to survive up here in the dangerous areas they had to navigate, it had been for the steeds own good. The mountains around them were massive and blocked all view of anything outside the valley; the tips were sharp and pointy like swords, thrusting out of the ground. The air was hard to breathe at such heights and with the temperature being so cold. Rayar had tightened his regal green coat as well as he could, underneath a stolen Heldoran guardsmen cloak. Even his Royal Blade wrapped himself tightly in his black cloak whilst Shania blended into the scenery with her cloak own keeping her form covered.

"Do you know where we are!?" the prince yelled out to the druidae at the head of the pack. She stopped in her stride and gazed around. There was a delayed response from her as she stood motionless, with only the harsh winds piercing the mountain side filling his ears before she finally replied.

"I think so." The golden haired boy could not help but blink in shock, his eyes wide and mouth numb from the wind.

"You think so?!" His blood boiled, which could assist in keeping him warm if he was lucky. Hinsani, on the other hand, moved to his charge and helped the prince catch up with Shania. The dark haired man's usual groomed appearance had become slightly more ragged with his beard larger and hair tucked backwards, no longer in its braid, while Rayar had not grown a single strand of facial hair in their travels. A late bloomer, Ayla used to call him.

"We cannot stay here another day or we will freeze to death. Girl, where are you taking us?" Hinsani commanded and gripped on Rayar's shoulder. The grip was tight and supporting. It was reassuring that he had a man like Hinsani always on his side. Shania sighed and looked back to them, her expression betraying her boredom with their complaints.

"We're close, I know it. Just a few more turns... this way." With that she shot off in a random direction, or at least he thought she chose it at random. The remaining pair looked to each other before accepting their fate and gave chase. They jogged at a careful pace so as not to risk slipping down on the many crevices, to certain doom. After all this, if he fell to his death, it would be a very embarrassing way to go. The druidae moved so quickly it was hard to keep up with her. He had pretty much given up on that task and focused on Hinsani's back, praying that he did not lose sight of her. As he turned the corner of a huge jagged rock, a wall of heat suddenly slapped him in the face. He gasped loudly at this unexpected change in temperature, quickly pulling open his cloak and undoing a few buttons on his coat's collar.

"What is this, a spring or something?" Rayar asked as his eyes danced around them. There was a large bare patch with nothing in it. No water, no snow, no greenery; just a flat surface, the size of the courtyard in Heldon. Shania stood there with her foot tapping the stone ground impatiently, while Hinsani looked as confused as he did. "Is this supposed to be it?" he asked another question. The druidae sighed and flashed her cold eyes back to him.

"You ask too many questions, just wait," she replied. His Royal Blade loosely rested a hand on the pommel of his sword as he stood next to the prince, waiting for something to happen. Anything to happen. It felt like a lifetime of waiting.

'... Has the cold made her go crazy...?' he thought as he awkwardly rocked on his feet back and forth. Finally her patience seemed to expire as she yelled out angrily.

"Open up Quale! You know it's us!" Rayar's eyes darted around once more to see who she was addressing, but they were the only ones present. Then something extraordinary occurred. It was as if a blanket that was also a mirror had been covering the scene before them. It was ripped free and revealed a sight he would have never imagined could be possible. A small house suddenly burst into view, a little stream ran beside it with a gentle current. The stone floor became grass and flowers, steam bellowed from a hot spring on the other side of the house. The entire scene was actually quite beautiful and quaint, if it had not been in the middle of Death Valley. A voice echoed around them, with no sign of where the voice came from.

"Come, come! Get inside! I can't leave this open for long boys and girls... or girl, just girl!" Shania looked back to the pair behind her. She knew they were completely in awe. Their shocked expressions must have been an amusing picture for her.

"Come on, let's go. Quale can't let *them* know where he is," she said and turned towards the house, now striding across grass in place of stone.

'Them?' Rayar wondered who she meant by 'them', yet he had many other questions that came first for this man of mystery. Rayar had been promised a waterfall of information would come from this gentleman. It was time to see if he could truly deliver. This time he took the lead and Hinsani followed

as they joined Shania through a small crooked door to the old house before them. As they passed through, he turned around to get one last glimpse of the area around them, only to see the blanket fall back over the landscape and swallow them inside. It looked like the reverse of what they had just witnessed, now with all the mountains around them becoming invisible. All he could see was clear open blue sky. He may not have understood how this all worked but he could understand what it meant. This old man kept himself hidden away in a closed-off world where no one could see in and he could not see out. Inside the house, Shania pulled off her cloak and chucked it over a small wooden chair in the middle of the room, pulled up against an old rotting table. Around the house in every corner, on every wall and inch of the floor, were documents, scrolls and books. At a glance, he could see words that made no sense to him and others that were simply peculiar.

'Secrets of Ghauls Fall, Illusions of the face, History of the Snow Hunters. Well I suppose if you keep yourself hidden away, you end up reading some strange things to pass the time, perhaps?' Rayar reached down to pick up one of the documents that read 'The Pearl' which appeared unfinished, when suddenly he was taken aback by the spouting of a voice he did not recognise.

"Wait! Don't touch! You'll put the letters out of order!" As the new arrival made his presence known, Hinsani appeared by Rayar's side, his legs spread and hand on the hilt of his blade.

"Identify yourself," his Royal Blade commanded. The prince turned to finally lay his eyes on the man he had heard so much about, someone who apparently had all the answers, the man of wisdom and knowledge. The image in his mind was immediately shattered. There stood a gangly old man, his grey hair full of grease and wildly out of control. His beard was shaven at some places on his face and bushy in others. He wore a long tattered cloak which had seemingly been stitched together dozens of times with several different colours of material attached to it. He held a tall brown staff to keep his balance. His shoes, for some reason, caught his eye, as the toe points curled upwards and back towards his shins. This man, if this was really Quale, looked a complete mess. Rayar hesitated before finally asking the fateful question.

"Are... Are you Quale?"

'Please do not be Quale.'

"Why yes! I am the one who I call Quale!" The old man replied.

"I was told... Quale was a man of wisdom, who could answer my questions," Rayar said softly, almost in a mumble.

"I can answer anything I know the answer to. If I don't know the answer to it, well I certainly can't answer it can I? You must be Rayar Granlia. My my..." Quale wrinkled his nose and hobbled over to the prince. Hinsani at first blocked his path, his stone hard face as unimpressed as he, himself, felt. After Rayar reassuringly patted Hinsani on his arm, the Royal Blade allowed the peculiar man through.

"Interesting, interesting, very interesting," the old sage said as he looked him up and down. Rayar was more than a head taller than this old man though the fact that his back was slightly hunched made it appear like he towered over him. "You look nothing like him," Quale said. The prince cocked a brow.

"Like who?" He questioned. The old man returned with a toothy grin and clonked him on the head with his staff lightly.

"Well, Rumeo of course, who else? Though truth be told I forget most people's faces these days. I don't even remember my own! I don't have any mirrors here. I mean I can make some if I wanted to, but why would I want to see my own face. We'd have eyes that could extend like a snails if people were supposed to see their own faces, don't you think?" Rayar's mouth hung open in disbelief. Shania slipped in.

"Quale settle down. You have a lot to explain. I'm going to bathe in the spring. Let me know when you're done." He could feel his cheeks flush red and burn up at the thought of Shania enjoying the warm waters of the spring and upon realising his face had turned red, prayed to the Above that no one noticed. Especially her. Luckily for him, she did not give the three men

235

another glance as she stepped outside and excused herself from any more of this nonsense. The old man threw his head back in laughter and in an instant; he suddenly appeared across the room with a pot of tea heating over a fire.

"Tea first. Can't have an important discussion without tea. Guests need to have tea," he muttered to himself. He could feel Hinsani lean closer to whisper into his ear.

"Prince Rayar, are you sure this is the right place to be? This man appears to have lost his mind. What logic could be clawed from the corners of that mind of his?" he asked in hushed tones. Rayar whispered in return.

"As... odd as he seems, I suppose we must give him a chance. Mother told me to speak with him. She would not do so without just cause." That answer seemed to satisfy the Royal Blade, at least for now, as he nodded and moved over to the nearest wall to find the perfect place to lean and brood. Quale motioned Rayar to take a seat and waddled over to join him with three cups of tea balanced in his hands. He slid one to the prince, placed one where he had decided to sit and held one out towards Hinsani whom raised his hand to decline.

"What sort of man dislikes tea? Madness! Madness I say!" With that he chucked the cup behind him and smashed it against the wall. The pair were not given time to be shocked, before the words continued to blabber from Quale's mouth.

"You've come a long way haven't you? Quite the journey from Heldon if I remember. If I don't remember then it could be a short journey. Regardless you've done well to get this far. I'd ask if Shania forced you but with that strapping young man beside you, I feel as if she convinced you by other means." Rayar tried to figure out which words were important in his ramble, as opposed to those that were just that, rambling, so as to know to what he should reply.

"She was not against forcing me yet it was my mother, Queen Julian Granlia, who told me I must come to you. This was to keep my family safe and find answers as to why we were attacked. She claimed they were after me and would be back if I remained." Like a flash, quicker than Rayar could react and faster than he expected a man of his age could move, Quale's fingers grabbed the chain around Rayar's neck where, the pearl used to be.

"They were not after you they were after the sphere, which they now have, though I think they moved too early and gave you too much time to react. Well it has been seventeen years since their last attempt, I suppose they got impatient." The golden haired boy awkwardly leaned backwards to free himself from the old man's grip and frowned a heavy frown.

"Who are *they*? And Shania said you're hiding from *them*, are these people the same?" Quale's skin turned pale and his face showed fear. He suddenly leapt from his seat and moved back across the room with a hand clasped around his face covering his eyes.

"No, no, no, no! It's too much! I can't, words never stop flowing, the souls fill up the stone, the noise is too loud, the fire burns too brightly. I need to think, I need to think!" Quale began spouting nonsensically as he fell against the wall at the far end of his small home. Rayar stood also and closed the distance between them.

"Quale, sir, I need answers. I have so many questions! Please think straight!" he pleaded. He could feel his patience wearing thin. After all this pain and mess they had been through, to reach some madman in a hut hidden away, who could not even give him a straight answer, must have been some kind of bad joke. He was stopped in his approach as the large hand of Hinsani gripped his wrist. They looked to each other as his Royal Blade offered his own wisdom.

"Let us step outside and allow him time to gather his thoughts," he said in a strong deep tone. Quale nodded manically and darted up a spiral staircase in his home.

"Yes, yes! Tomorrow, I read, tomorrow! I'm not home, come back tomorrow!" And with that the figured disappeared upstairs. They could hear the patter of his footsteps above them as he clearly was unable to remain still, but Rayar took the advice of his protector and the pair stepped outside into the greenery around them.

"We have a tough choice to make," Hinsani said firmly as he gazed absently around them, as if studying every inch of the landscape of illusions. "Can this man gather his thoughts and give you answers, or do we move on. Leave if we must, disappear." That idea annoyed him, he knew Hinsani deep down was only thinking of his duty. He wanted to protect Rayar against all, he did not care about being a hero or doing what was right for all. His duty was only to the safety of his prince.

"Couldn't get through to him?" the firm voice of Shania called out to them. Rayar leaned back to peer in the direction of the voice, to see the tanned woman chest deep in the spring water, her arms covering her breasts under the surface of the water with one leg propped up allowing a bare foot and calf to be exposed. The water was hard to see through. Even so, the bashfulness of the young prince took over and he embarrassingly stared for a moment before he redirected his attention, trying his best not to flick his gaze back to her. Beside him, Hinsani did not seem to care at all; the man simply crossed his arms and leant on the side of the house. Though he noticed the warrior did not look her way either. Perhaps Hinsani was secretly embarrassed too yet could hide it considerably better than he could? He doubted it.

'She is a cruel woman.'

"Above and Below..." Rayar muttered. "... but yes, I asked a question and he suddenly became erratic and started rambling on about some nonsense I did not understand. You assured me I would get answers and we would help each other. How am I supposed to get through to him?" Shania dunked her hair into the warm water and visibly relaxed without concern of the two men present. She probably saw Hinsani as a single minded old man who only cared about following him around and himself as a boy, too shy to worry about.

"I suggest getting some sleep tonight, out here in the garden and tomorrow, Rayar, you speak to him alone. Give him time to process what's been happening. The only company he has had for the past seventeen years is me and Jac. I told you, he's not the man he used to be, his mind is shattered after being here so long and the things that happened that led him to this point, and before you ask I don't know what happened, he doesn't speak of it." The druidae opened her eyes and stared at Rayar, who unfortunately for him, flicked his eyes back towards her at that very moment and was unable to look away. "You'll get what you want, I promise. Then we can decide what to do. Okay?" She was right. They had taken the time to come; they could wait one more day. He needed to be less childish, worrying about some almost naked woman near him. There was so much more to focus on.

"... I trust you Shania. Alright, we sleep tonight, a proper night sleep for once. Tomorrow I will speak with him and hopefully finally understand what exactly is going on, and what I must do." There was a brief exchange of smiles between them before Hinsani dragged the prince off, mumbling about being more respectful to women and began to set up an area on the other side of the house for them to sleep. Come tomorrow, finally, after all this travelling and danger and pain of leaving those he loved at home, things would start to become clear. Well, he hoped they would. Quale had not struck much confidence into him just yet.

* * *

Chapter XXIII
History of the Druidae
~Rayar~

Sleep was welcomed that night, as strange as it was to sleep under a mirrored blanket of illusion. At least that is what Rayar thought it was. The magic was hard to get his head around. During their resting outside, the blue sky that surrounded the little area of foliage and the tiny old house suddenly shifted into night. Stars bloomed all over the night sky and the moon hung low and close, a maddening illusion. This was magic. This man, Quale, was able to do things he would never have even dreamed of. Shania was powerful with her flames, but this was something else entirely. The power this man held was much more than he had anticipated. The thought of someone as unstable as him, with this kind of ability, was certainly nerve-wracking. Rayar lay in the grass under a sheet of soft bedding given to him by Shania. His green coat hung from a branch on the tree he had slept under and his sword leant up against it. Near to where he lay, Hinsani sat cross legged with his sheathed sword, Galad, on his lap. Somehow the man actually slept in such a manner. It was odd how he performed such a feat in that position but someone like him must never truly sleep, just meditate. His sharp emerald eyes scanned the clearing; perhaps we would be able to catch a glimpse of Shania enjoying the hot spring once more.

'Settle down, Rayar, not something a prince should think about.' Just then he heard mumbling from within the house.

Slowly the boy pushed himself to his feet and stumbled over to the doorway of Quale's run down home. How this place was still actually standing was in itself mind boggling. The door had been left ajar and inside Quale sat upon a chair with a cup of tea between his fingers, his tired dark eyes staring down at the table in front of him. Beside him Shania stood. He realised now why her accent sounded so peculiar. It was the same as Quales.

"How are you feeling this morning you old coot?" she asked as she topped up his tea. The old man nodded several times, it was clear he was straining to focus.

"Better, my dear, better. I think seeing so many faces made me a little jumpy. Don't you think?" he muttered in reply. Shania chuckled and punched the old man's shoulder. Rayar watched the exchange with interest. Unlike her usual stand-offish behaviour, she seemed warm with Quale.

"You'll be fine. You need to focus though. Rayar has lots of questions. Don't make our journey here be wasted. We need him." The young druidae girl moved across the room, back to the tiny kitchen where food also seemed to be cooking for breakfast. The smell was certainly rousing. He could feel his stomach rumble with anticipation.

"It is a shame. Rumeo did so well for so long. But, it was only a matter of time before the location of the sphere became apparent. Once I knew The Order was moving, I sadly had to send you. Normally I wouldn't have risked you Shania but I had no choice. If I went out, he'd know where I was straight away and he would have the rest of the Order to support him. Didn't think you'd go so far as to put yourself at such a risk though. I told you not to put yourself at risk didn't I? Do you like the boy?" he asked. Rayar had to hold himself back from gasping; he could feel his face flushing again. He heard Shania cough on her own tea at the old sage's remark and pass Quale a sharp blue-eyed gaze.

"I don't care for, nor have time for such pointless things," she snapped back. Rayar let out a sigh of relief; well he thought it was relief. In actual fact he felt a little bit frustrated. Just then his cover was sadly blown; perhaps Quale knew he was there all along. It was difficult to tell with this man.

"What do you think dear Rayar? Think she has a soft spot for you?" From behind the door, Shania's anger could be felt. The girl could control fire but her very presence incited a blaze. Slowly, ever so slowly the prince pushed open the door and gave the pair a small awkward wave. Shania sniffed angrily at him and stormed towards the doorway.

"Cowering behind doorways now Prince Rayar, such royalty." Before he was given the opportunity to throw forth a comeback, she barged past him and out into the clearing.

'Above and Below, women are impossible,' he thought as he strode towards the table and joined Quale by taking a seat.

"Sleep well, my boy? You look better. Better than I do at least, I look like a shrivelled shrimp these days," Quale jested as he finished off his tea. The young prince laughed as well, still somewhat in an awkward fashion. He had not come for small talk, unfortunately, and if this man had a stable mind he could probably learn years' worth of knowledge, but for now he had to grab all the information he could get, while he still spoke sense.

"Master Quale. What happened to make you so... well, you know, unsure of yourself?" Rayar worded as politely as possible. Getting some back story would like be helpful. The old man threw his head back in laughter and rattled his fingers on the table top.

"A long tale, long, long tale. Too long and if I told this long tale, we would have no time for the tale I need to tell you. In short, I did something I should not have and had someone close to me refuse to forgive me. Ever since then, I have been in hiding, waiting and watching." Quale seemed almost sombre as he revealed this. Rayar curved up one brow and leant forward.

"Waiting for what, may I ask?" A confused expression was plastered upon the golden haired boys face as he listened intently.

"Waiting to do some good in the world, as much as I can do, to make up for all the not so good things I have done.

242

Seventeen years ago was the last time I left my home, since then I have been here looking after Shania, teaching her, raising her, keeping her safe from those who would do people like us harm." Rayar nodded.

"Like the Knights of Hextheene? They hunt magic users do they not, witches and mages and such?" he asked. Many knew what atrocities the Knights had committed against those charged with witchcraft in Hextheene, not to mention by the people of the land who wished to appear loyal to the realm and crown. Quale's laugh was way too loud and maniacal and out of the blue, which almost caused Rayar to jump from his seat.

"Hahaha! Not quite my boy, not quite! While I would rather we were not in the hands of Knights, they are not who I hide from. Who I hide Shania from. You know of The Order don't you? Men and women with the power to control magic, the common name for them is mages, the name most use. They used to be called Controllers. In the south they probably still are. Mages is a term Hextheene came up with as Controllers sounded... well, too controlling! Hahaha!" He laughed at his own little jest. Rayar politely smiled back as he tried to take all the information in. It was time to get down to it, however.

"Master Quale," the prince began, "you spoke of the sphere, my pearl, which those who attacked Heldon came for. Shania said you need my help. My mother said you could tell me why I needed to leave home. They consider me a traitor back in Heldon, I cannot have come here for nothing but riddles. I need the truth and the why. Please, Master Quale." Rayar hoped he did not sound like he was pleading too much but after everything that had happened, Heldon, his father, his dream - he needed answers.

"I suppose I can tell you what I don't know first. The pearl you call it, you had it for so long, seventeen years I believe," Quale said absently. The prince frowned.

"Father, King Rumeo, told me it was an heirloom..." he did not continue. Not many knew he was not a true Granlia and he had no intention of adding to that short list. Instead he leaned back in his chair and crossed one leg over the other and

243

focused on listening rather than interrupting. Quale smiled his toothy smile and continued.

"I don't know exactly what it is. I know it is new. I have thousands of documents here of things that existed for centuries. That have been on the earth since the dawn of man. That pearl, the sphere, is something new. Very new but very important to many people. Your father asked for my help to find it many years ago. I looked and looked and looked and finally together, with your parents, we were able to find it. It was created at the time Shania's people were slaughtered. A random piece of jewellery amongst what I can imagine a royal families vast collection. Clever, very clever. That jolly man, I still vaguely remember his visit." Rayar could not help but let a small smile pass over his lips as Rumeo was mentioned, the great man he was and the great father he had been.

"I do miss home," he said softly, half to the old sage and half to himself.

"I can imagine. I miss home too! This old shack does its job, but home, that would be a sight. Anyway!" Quale seemed strained as he focused on his explanation. "Let me tell you a story, from years ago, a thousand years ago. You likely know the first part of it, everyone does. In the Firsts Age, the land was overrun by creatures and monsters beyond our imagination. They destroyed every town, city, castle, all history from the land. The survivors fled north and destroyed the pass between the north and south, which would be Oldome and the Freeland now. They hid in the snowy lands of what we now call Oldome until a miracle occurred. The First Coming of the Lord from the World Above came to our world to defeat the monsters of the World Below. He gathered every living person in the land and together he defeated the World Below and vanquished them to the depths to never rise again. By his side was his faithful friend, a young woman and warrior unmatched, whose name was Hextor. After that the people began to take back their former lands, and the kingdoms were soon formed. Sound familiar?" Quale asked while grinning. The prince nodded slowly as he listened. He recalled the tale, or at least something similar being told to him as a child. The First Coming and the creation of the world they knew. The final battle they had was at Hellsbane Castle in Mayhen, though it was not known as Mayhen then.

"I recall. Father told me, mother told me, people still speak of it as the legend of the beginning, yet many believe it myth." Quale chuckled and rattled his bony fingers on his cup of tea.

"Indeed, indeed. Myth or reality, there is a part of the story you were not told. No one is told unless they truly look into the old ages and the magic that comes with it. It's all very exciting!" He appeared giddy, almost unable to remain in his seat. This old man must have rarely had the chance to tell his stories to anyone with only Shania here and she did not seem like the type to put up with his ramblings. "The First Coming had two sons, and his power was split between them. The oldest son had the power to control the elements, fire, wind, earth, and water. He lived in the wilderness creating the greatest beauties of nature that the world had ever seen, after the monsters from below had devoured most the living land. The second son had the affinity for his father's magic and all the power that comes with it. The second child was known as The Second Coming. The text goes that The Second Coming grew so jealous of his older brother, for they both loved Lady Hextor, that he wished to win her love with a feat of power. He planned to release the monsters from below once again and defeat them to show her his power and have all her love showered over him. All very romantic and clichéd, I know. His power was so great he taught himself immortality and could not be killed. Once his brother and Lady Hextor learnt of his plan, they banded together and were able to defeat him, The Second Coming, and seal him away for all eternity. His name varies between texts, though The Second is the most used reference." Rayar listcned to the tale intently, nodding at certain points and knew he wore a puzzled expression. It was true, he had not heard this part of the tale before and as interesting as it was, he was not sure how it was particularly

245

relevant to him. He supposed he had to give Quale a chance. Getting to the point did not seem to be his forte.

"I see... Master Quale, what-" The prince was cut off with a raise of the old man's leathery hand as he continued to speak.

"The Order is an old group of Controllers, Mages, who have lurked in the shadows, seeking knowledge and observing how the world changed over many, many years. That was their purpose, to watch and document and learn. Though times change sadly, certain people are not happy to just watch anymore. Your pearl is something powerful, if it was not, members within the Order would have no interest in it. They are the ones who struck your home and tormented your family. The Order has an agenda, but I would be lying if I said they all had the same objective. Be it under the command of their Master or not, I don't know. I just observe. Now I know what they wished to achieve, those seventeen years ago. The druidae stayed in their grove, uninterested in the outside world, yet they were wiped out, slaughtered in their grove. Their natural magic that protected their home is gone. Only a druidae could find the grove when their power was strong. Someone betrayed them and allowed those members of the Order to slaughter them." Rayar's eyes widened.

"Shania... was in the grove when they were killed?" Quale nodded slowly and clucked his tongue in thought.

"I arrived after it all occurred and took her into my care. That pearl was created during this time. The power it holds was created. Members of the Order wish to unseal The Second Coming and begin another destruction of all mankind. The seal within the grove must be destroyed to release The Second Coming but it cannot be simply destroyed by anyone. As it was a druidae who sealed him many, many years ago, only a druidae can do the deed. That is why they had a druidae serving them, so long ago. She died, unfortunately for them, which left them at a dead end." Quale took a deep breath and fell back into his chair, exhausted from his long winded explanation. "Bloody Below, I think some more tea is needed after that! One for you!?" The old sage called out as he somehow seemed to appear by the fire in his home with more water boiling. He dropped a few leaves into the pot and turned to offer a wide grin at the prince. Rayar sat there, awe struck. The Second? Druidae slaughter? The Order Controllers attacking his family? As crazy as it all sounded, it started to make some sense in his head. The puzzle pieces were beginning to link. Yet how did they know he had the pearl? There was more to this, but he doubted Quale had the answers to it all.

"Mother told me to come to you to protect my family. I must ask, what are we to do now? Where do we go from here?" Quale slid a small cup of hot tea to the boy and slithered back into his chair.

"Well, well, well. You have options, you certainly do! I suggest staying here with Shania and never showing your face again. They want her alive to use her and you were their string that led to her after you escaped Heldon, no?" Rayar blinked in surprise. If the Order had been sticking their fingers into Heldon, those two attackers may have been part of this Order. They knew he was with the last druidae. They were not after him, they were after her.

'Above and Below... here was me thinking it was all about me... bloody selfish Rayar.' Quale took a loud sip of his newly brewed tea.

"Or of course, as you were with the pearl all your life, you should know where it is. Shania told me they had to use magic to pry it from your chain, meaning the pearl was enchanted to you, as part of you. Did you not wonder why you came this way? Did you not wonder why you kept travelling away from home? I wouldn't have! I would have found it crazy, stayed curled up in bed and waited for it all to blow over!" Quale joked. His expression must have been even more confused at this point of the conversation. Quale rolled his eyes and explained in a much simpler way. "You can feel where the sphere is. If you want to help your family, you can feel it, find it and protect it. A dangerous option, putting your life at risk..."

"And mine," a woman's voice sounded. This time it had been Shania doing the eavesdropping. Quale looked over and began to frantically shake his head.

"No, no, no, no! The heroic prince here can run off and risk his skin but you, no, no. It's too much of a risk if they catch you Shania." The druidae shook her head and stepped up beside Rayar, who was awkwardly perched on the chair with his tea between his hands feeling somewhat lost.

"You said it yourself, I call myself the Last Druidae, I can use their power... well, some of it. If Rayar is going to face the Order, then I'm going to help him. You think he can handle anything by himself, with his dim witted bodyguard? They need me, and I need them." Quale fell back into his chair with an overly dramatic sigh.

"Dear, dear, dear! You make everything much harder, you're so stubborn." Eventually the sage pulled himself up from his slump and sighed. "I suppose I can't stop you. I can't predict what they intend exactly, I simply know if you go after the sphere, you will need to fight. Your skill with fire is devastating. Truly, any Controller would be crazy to face you when fire is present. Yet, you need to make sure you can always access fire," Quale warned. Shania sighed as well and nodded.

"I know, I know, you've told me this a hundred times. I have my flint and my sword. I'll use the sparks like I trained to do!" Just then, Rayar could no longer take being left out of the loop, he stood and raised both hands to get their attention.

"Hold on a moment!" he snapped out. Both the sage and druidae looked over to him with perplexed expressions at his outburst. "This pearl could be anywhere! And I just need to feel where it is? That makes no sense!" Quale suddenly appeared in his face, eyes narrowed.

"Where do you want to go, don't think about your family, don't think about saving the land, don't think about fighting, don't think about Shania in a hot spring. Where do you want to go?" This was ridiculous. How was he supposed to do this? If Quale was right, he had been heading towards his pearl all this time. Was he supposed to just switch off his mind and trust his gut?

'Yet you focus too much on what has happened Rayar, not on what is to come. Serve your country, serve your family and lead as a prince. There will be a time when you will be looked to for leadership, as a leader of an army or a House, or even follow in Vesir's footsteps. Whatever course the current takes you, you must look to where you are going and not always from where you have come.' The words of his old friend, Lanni Ni'Tella infiltrated his mind. Focus on going forward. His eyes closed and his mind went dark. In the centre of the darkness a small blue light pulsated. Around the light, a forest grew, ash all around him, decomposing bodies lay in the burnt ground and in the centre, a giant tree, huge in stature, an evergreen monster. The light came from below the tree, under the ground, growing and growing. Suddenly Rayar shot open his eyes and gasped for air. He had fallen backwards and found himself being supported by his Royal Blade Hinsani and Shania by his side. Quale sat on the edge of his table with a menacing grin on his face.

"What did you see?" The old sage asked with a cocky look on his face. Rayar struggled to speak until air had returned to his lungs.

"I saw ... I saw a light, a blue light... in a forest... but it was destroyed, ash littered everything, bodies everywhere. There was a tree, a giant tree and it was still green... it was completely untouched by the devastation around it." Shania and Quale exchanged looks as they appeared to know of what he spoke. Shania mumbled quietly.

"The Druidae Grove..." The old man who had perched on the table, hopped off with a surprisingly elegant leap.

"It would appear so! Makes sense. That is where it started. I suppose that is where it was supposed to end. I imagine you were heading there already dear boy, through the mountains is the quickest way, along the coast and north to the land of Oldome. Fate would have it." Rayar thanked Hinsani for his support and returned to full height.

"It must be fate... So we are to head to the Druidae Grove, retrieve my pearl and then what?" It was a reasonable question. All that was occurring was not common knowledge. He was still considered to be a traitor at home, from what Hinsani had said and the attempt to capture him weighed on his mind. Even if they were able to stop these mages, part of the Order or not, it did not exactly help his own situation. He did, after all, want to return home when this was over. Quale stroked his oddly defined beard, in consideration of his question.

"Well my boy, you have to understand, it is these fiends who have put you in this situation. If you can defeat them, you can save your home. I know jolly Rumeo. He would not condemn you to treason, or any of his children. He would sooner die or give up the throne than ever see the Granlia's harmed. The only two options you have are, move forward and try and do some good, or hide here with me and let the world roll past you and observe. I will suggest the latter, once more," Quale offered. Rayar looked to Hinsani, the stone faced man at his back. That man would follow him whatever he chose and with him by his side, any soldier or warrior who crossed them would be making a grave error. Hinsani returned his look with a stern expression and offered only a simple nod of acceptance in his choice. He had missed most the conversation yet seemed to have figured out that his charge intended to go into danger. Then he looked to the druidae. Her expression was that of confidence and strength, she was a stubborn woman who had already set her mind on her direction. It was likely she would go without him if he decided to stay here with the crazy old fool.

'Risk my life for others, or hide. I stayed hidden in Heldon long enough... Even if I cannot clear my name, I can help Shania, and I can help my family even if they do not know it.'

"We get my pearl, we stop these bastards and then whatever road comes next, we take it. If these mages are harming my family and this will help stop them, then I must do it." Shania nodded to him in agreement though muttered under her breath.

"You have terrible language, anyone told you that?" She teased. A soft smile on her lips. He returned the smile, actually sucking in some of her confidence.

"Some. Master Hinsani, are you alright with this? It will be dangerous." He knew the answer already but he would not have been the man he was, if he did not at least give Hinsani the option to step down.

"Prince Rayar, you know my duty. I will protect you for as long as I draw breath. Last I saw Heldon, the King was not himself. If this old man speaks truth, then he is being manipulated by forces unknown to us. We stop their plan. We stop them. We can return things to how they are meant to be. You have my blade for life." Quale chuckled at the Royal Blades small speech. While Hinsani was not much of a talker, when he got into one of his preaches about duty, it did sometimes linger quite long.

"What a dramatic fellow!" the old sage teased towards the soldier, only to receive a cold glare in response. "So be it. The three of you will be doing something very dangerous, I will prepare some assistance don't you worry! While I wish I could join you, well, sort of wish, sort of do not wish! My enemies would know the moment I used any power outside my little pocket in the world, and put you all at risk. I will, however, help you plan the journey to be as safe as possible!" So it had come to this, a Prince of Mayhen, a Royal Blade and legendary swordsman and the Last Druidae were going to face off against mages. How did dancing balls, fine dinners and lying in the gardens of Heldon watching the world go by, lead to this?

*

"That is an amazing blade you have there," Quale said to Hinsani as they prepared to leave. After a hearty meal prepared by the sage and a show of him ransacking through his home to find them anything that could help, dusk was upon them, or so Quale said. Rayar still could not see through the blanket of illusions surrounding the clearing they were in. They had all been given new cloaks, thick brown cloth with fur trimming and inner lining as tough as leather. Nothing magic about those however, they were simply to keep them inconspicuous as well as to prepare them for the cold lands in Oldome in the North. The prince watched the exchange between the two older gentlemen as he waited for Shania by the door of the creaky house.

"My thanks. It is called Galad. It was passed down to me from my master, Miya, many years ago," the dark haired man replied. Quale rubbed his chin in thought and studied the pommel.

"Do you know who had that blade before him?" he interrogated. The Royal Blade placed a hand over the hilt to cover the majority of the sword.

"I do. His master." As usual Hinsani had grown somewhat defensive. Though the older man did not seem to mind, he only continued to stare at the blade in curiosity.

"Not many one sided swords around, these days. Northern Freeland is governed by long swords, Southrous use short swords, axes and even further south they use curved blades. Though not like this. Your Prince has a sword like it, hmmmm?" Quale questioned, flicking his eyes to Rayar. He did indeed have the same style sword as his trainer, however that was made for him by the master blacksmiths of Heldon; it was nowhere near as old and sentimental as Galad was for Hinsani.

"Indeed. Well then." With that the Royal Blade turned on his heel and ended the conversation. If he remembered correctly, that was probably the longest conversation the pair of them had since their first meeting. For someone like Quale, who did ramble continuously, he did not seem to direct too many words at Hinsani, who would likely only reject them. At that moment Shania returned from inside the house, wrapped tightly in her new cloak with a bag over her shoulder.

"I've got enough supplies and coin we stored away. We should have no issues passing through. Anything else we need to know?" she asked towards her long time friend. The old eccentric man waddled with his staff resting upon his shoulder.

"Well, only that I don't think this is the best idea for you," he said, through a toothy grin. Shania sighed and returned the smile.

"I know. I'll be fine. I'll be more on guard. If any Controller wished to try his luck with me, he'll end up as a roasting corpse," she boasted confidently.

'Wonderful, a pyromaniac,' Rayar thought but decided to keep it to himself. Quale's expression turned somewhat sterner as he gave his last bit of advice.

"Excellent Shania, excellent. I know of druidae power from my documents, fire was the rarest used but most powerful. Controllers feared the flames out in the open as it was a power of destruction, while druidae usually practiced in creation. Still, you must be careful. All three of you be careful. The Druidae Grove is no longer hidden by the old elements, yet it is still difficult to find. You must get to the land Oldome across the Hextheene Crossing. The bridge is guarded but since Hextheene has settlements on the other side of the bridge, it is open to traders and common folk passing by. You shouldn't have a problem crossing it. Once through there, you will need to pass through the Braska Border, the line between Hextheene and the land of the Snow Hunters. They were close allies of the druidae years ago, show them who you are Shania and they should help you. Well, this was many years ago, hopefully things haven't changed too much. Hmmm, maybe that would be risky... I'm sure you'll figure it out. Once you get your hands on the sphere, bring it here. While I can't go out to help you, if you get it to me I can ensure it is never found again." He grinned, his expressions changed so rapidly, it was impossible to truly understand what he was feeling or thinking.

"That was surprisingly helpful... and unhelpful at the same time," Rayar said, puzzled. Quale gave the boy's arm a slap with his bony hand and chuckled under his breath.

"This isn't my story anymore, it is yours. You take the road you think is best. I sadly can't affect much outside this little get away of mine, but, I can give you wisdom. It's helpful to you if you want it to be helpful." There was indeed wisdom hidden in the rambles, it just took a genius to decipher. Rayar thanked the old man and turned to leave Shania and Quale to their own goodbye and joined Hinsani at the edge of the illusion. The broader man gave him a side glance, his hand forever gripping Galad.

"The King that we remember would be proud of you. Your father would be proud." The words from the Royal Blade were uplifting yet still felt melancholic, knowing that the King they knew may no longer be *that* King. He longed to see Rumeo again and tell him everything that had happened, to see Julian, Nyer, Nymin and Ayla. Their well-being was always at the back of his mind.

'I wonder… if I keep telling myself I am doing it for them, will it make this journey easier?'

"I am doing this for them," He said quietly. Hinsani nodded in agreement just before Shania joined them at the edge of the clearing. Supplied and equipped they prepared to make their way down the mountain into the realm of Hextheene.

"I know this land well. I can lead us to the gate and the bridge to Oldome. We will need to move along the coast, through a couple of towns and into Northfreya, the city where the bridge's entrance sits. Other than that, it is roads and unkempt forests this far North," Hinsani stated. Rayar forgot that Hinsani had originally been born in Hextheene, though he had come to Mayhen at a very young age. He did not speak much on the matter though; simply that he was not a true man of Mayhen, only half on his father's side.

"Well it has been a pleasure! With any luck I'll be seeing you all again, very soon!" With a flourish of his staff, the blanket of blue sky around them suddenly lifted and revealed the cold, grey uninhabitable mountains. The sky was orange from the lowering sun and the winds howled through the valleys of the range. Rayar took a deep breath and pushed forward with Hinsani and Shania in tow. They would need to make it down the mountain side and into the land of

Hextheene. He hoped going down the mountains would prove considerably easier than the climb had been, Above willing.

* * *

Chapter XXIV
Hextheene
~Rayar~

The trek down the mountain pass was indeed easier than going up, though not by a huge margin. They traversed the small passageways through valleys and paths naturally created by the stone around them. Rayar could not believe he was actually about to set foot into the country known as Hextheene. The land of the Holy Blood Kings. He had imagined the roads all over the land paved and stoned, with colourful attire adorning its entire people. Singing in the streets, gold showered over all, as the legendary realm was a place for wonder and power. As they gained ground, closer to the base of the mountain range, the prince stopped in his tracks. The view over the nation loomed before them in all its glory.

"This is Hextheene?" he asked though mainly to himself rather than his two companions. A large forest lay where the base of the mountains touched soil below them. Small villages and roads were scattered in the far distance. It felt dark, gloomy and not at all what he expected. Whilst he could only see the landscape around him in the moonlight, it did not seem all that different from Mayhen. The same trees, the same towns, and the same normality he had seen in his brief travel north. Hinsani stepped up beside him, as they stood perched on a rock gazing over the scenery.

"There," he pointed off to the east. There was the shape of a castle in the far distance with lights from the torches filling in the night sky. It seemed tiny from where they stood. "That is Beregin Hold, home of Baron Berethor. He governs the lands from here to the Mayhen border. We'd do best to keep as close to the coast as possible," he advised. Rayar nodded in reply, squinting to see if he could see the hold any better at such a distance. A loud screech sounded above them as a hawk swooped in the skyline and darted down to the shoulder of Shania, who was further down the mountain ahead of the two men. Shania and the bird exchanged that creepy look that Rayar had seen, and then the hawk shot off into the air once more. Shania turned to the two men and motioned them to hurry.

"Men near the forest on the coast, could be nothing, could be something. Though Jac says they have been there for some time, waiting." He saw his Royal Blade cock a brow, he clearly had already forgotten about the hawk, or he had not explained it. This time he seemed to accept the idea without questioning it.

"Your hawk been out here long?" Hinsani asked. Shania shrugged her shoulders and continued forward.

"Jac has been scouring the lands around the Leon Mountains." That was all the explanation she gave them.

"Well," the prince began, "let us trust the bird and keep our wits about us, I suppose." With that he quickly but carefully descended after the druidae, with his protector not far behind. It took a good hour, perhaps more, to reach the base of the mountain. Clambering over rocks and crawling through uncomfortable spaces between the stones, was certainly an unpleasant experience. Much to Rayar's joy, they reached the base and were finally rewarded with grass below their feet. They did not have much time to rest before Hinsani insisted they continued forward. The trio strode along muddy dirt roads, not at all as he had imagined, with their hoods covering their faces and their new cloaks shielding most of their bodies. The heat in Mayhen had seemingly reached Hextheene, appearing quite damaging. The grass around them did not seem healthy and the trees showed no signs of blossoming. Back home the rain would fall at least once a week to support the plant life that surrounded the cities and castles, yet here it appeared as if the rain had not graced the greenery for months. Tiredness had set in, Rayar wanted to take a rest here, perhaps cook some food and not rush their advance but once again the Royal Blade insisted they do not stop.

"There is a town not far from here. If you wish to stop briefly, we can stop there. There should be an inn we can rest in, unless the town has gone under. The war with Southrous is draining the life from this country," he replied to Rayar's request for a short break.

"When was the last time you were in Hextheene?" the golden haired boy asked as they walked side by side down the muddy path. Shania had taken the head of the group, keeping out of any conversations.

"Many years ago, I left as a baby. I briefly returned during the war, still a boy." How could Rayar forget, Hinsani was a soldier, once upon a time, in the war with Hextheene. Younger than Rayar was now, Hinsani was out here fighting and killing for his country. A feeling of sadness swept over him and disappointment in himself. If *he* had been a soldier in those days, at the age Hinsani was, he would not have stood a chance.

"I respect you, Master Hinsani," Rayar said trying to focus ahead. He could see in the corner of his eye, the man turn to him slightly taken aback by his comment.

"I thought you found our lessons taxing and tedious," he replied. Rayar could not help but smile.

"Part of me did, I just thought I could never be as amazing with a blade as you. I was in a life or death situation twice in Heldon. One man I killed by accident and the other almost killed me, had it not been for Shania." Goosebumps still shivered across his skin, when he recalled that night and seeing Raimon die so brutally. A few seconds longer and he could have suffered the same fate.

"I am the only man I know, who has been taught Blade Dancing. I am passing these lessons on to you. One day, if you learn well, you will be as fierce as any warrior I have met." An actual compliment escaped his protector. Rayar could not think of a single time Hinsani had given him one before. To think the first would be for his sword work.

"We will need to continue our lessons when this is over then." the prince replied. Their talk had distracted them from their progress made through the dense forest. It was not long before stumps of trees replaced the fully grown ones. The path continued along the eastern road but the trees that surrounded them now, were all stumps from foraging. Lights ahead in the distance signalled life in the desolate wilderness they were passing through. It must have been the town that Hinsani had mentioned earlier.

"That it?" Shania asked from the head of the pack.

"That is," Hinsani replied as he quickened his stride to take over the lead. Rayar followed suit and caught up with the druidae girl who had been surprisingly quiet. Back when he first met her, he thought it would be unusual for her to say much at all. The more one spent time with someone new, the more you got to know them, even if they barely spoke. While that was common sense he was used to most people who were not part of the Granlia family, treating him the same, as a prince. In reality being a person of royalty he rarely was gifted the chance to speak with anyone. It had been surprisingly lonely at times in Heldon. As they closed the distance to the town, there seemed to be loud yelling and cheering from inside.

'This time of night, is there some sort of celebration?' he thought as they soon came to the entrance of the town. The sounds of chanting echoed through the town, coming from the town centre. It did not appear like an overly large place but there were many houses directly on the coast where it held a significantly large dock with dozens of fishing boats in the harbour. The ground was muddy and unkempt and the people had the same aesthetic as the town. Unruly.

"Should we see what is going on?" he asked, looking between his two companions. Hinsani did not seem too interested in whatever antics were occurring nearby, though he made a sensible point.

"If we are to stay in the inn here, it is wiser to know if there is something here we must avoid. A brief look, that is all." Shania nodded in agreement. It was not hard to find the centre of the commotion as a crowd of men and women holding torches ablaze, stormed past the group. They followed as inconspicuously as they could to the town centre. The voice of one man in particular, bellowed out over the crowd around them. On a stand stood a tall man in a blue tabard with chainmail sleeves and slacks. In one hand he held a torch and in the other, an unsheathed sword. Next to him a woman, as young as he was, if not younger, was tied to a post with logs at her ankles.

"What other evidence do you have against this woman being accused of the crime of witchcraft!?" the armoured man roared out to the peons below him. The cheers and screaming of the crowd roared back in return, as he searched around the group of people for someone to pick out.

"You!" he called out, his blade pointing to a woman in the crowd.

"She put a curse on my husband and stole his seed! She cursed him!" the woman screamed out. The young girl cried out to defend herself but her voice was drowned out by the cheering.

"Cursing men for your vile ways, witch! This must not go unpunished!" the armoured man snapped as he whipped the tip of his sword towards the girl's neck.

'What is this?' Rayar thought as he stood at the rear of the crowd. This was horrible. By the look of Shania's face, she too found this disgusting. Not just disgusting but infuriating.

"Do not do anything," Hinsani whispered to the pair, his expression as stone as ever. He looked over to his protector; he wanted to yell at him to do something to help her. He wanted to say anything. Yet what could he do? Could they save her? Shania here could, of course she could. The moment those

260

flames began she could do anything with them. It was quite possible she was already planning to do so.

"Witch Neeve Galeon! For your crimes of witchcraft. For dishonouring your family. For dishonouring your home and worst of all, for dishonouring your King, long live King Braska Hextor II. You shall be burnt at the stake. Witches do not get last words." Like something out of a nightmare, the announcer leaned down to the pyre and set the logs at the girl's feet alight. The cheering of the crowd exploded in madness, fanatic with excitement. Rayar glanced to Shania as her hand rose, but she was grabbed at the wrist by Hinsani. The pair exchanged glares so sharp he thought he had been sliced in two.

"You'd let her burn?" she snapped as quietly as possible.

"Yes," he replied in a whisper as calm as anything. Rayar frowned, he knew Hinsani was cold at times but surely this was colder than even he could be.

"We can help her, Master Hinsani," Rayar chimed in, his tone as dominant as he could muster.

"We could. Then announce our presence to all. We have to move quickly and quietly, not attract attention. If you are willing to kill everyone in this town, then we can do so. Are you, Prince Rayar?" He shot a glance at all the people in the crowd. Men, women and even children all cheering. What they were doing was evil. It was wrong, yet could they slaughter all these people? That was madness in itself. Shania on the other hand seemed unconvinced and tried to wrestle her arm free from the man, though his strength far surpassed her own.

"I can help her without them knowing it was us," she snarled at him. Hinsani nodded. He had not seen the extent of what she could do but Rayar assumed Hinsani had assumed she had power.

"If you could, then do it. What would they do to her after you freed her from the flames? Or used the flames against the people? I do not think we should take the risk." The words he spoke had wisdom in them but they did not make Rayar feel any better about the situation. He was slightly surprised the Royal Blade showed such insight, he always saw him as a

261

simple swordsman. The prince had underestimated the man. With that question left in the air, Hinsani released his grip from the girl. Shania stood there for a moment with her hand raised, her body shaking. Rayar had seen her angry before, but not like this. She said nothing else and simply turned away from the scene, the screaming of the girl beginning to fill the night sky. It was horrifying. They had no choice but to leave, there was nothing they could do. Rayar kept telling himself that.

'There was nothing we could do... it was too late. Nothing...'

Once they had found the inn Hinsani had mentioned, The Bulky Baron, there was a forlorn feeling between them. Hinsani had done most of the talking to acquire rooms for the group while Shania had kept her distance from them both. Once the rooms were purchased the druidae disappeared as quickly as her hawk flew, up the stairs. The inn was quiet, dead even, with the locals parading their victim around the roads, in the dead of night. Rayar desperately wanted to speak to Shania, say something that could possibly help. Say anything. He sat next to his protector in the downstairs hall both with a drink beside them, complimentary drink at that, for renting a room. The innkeeper claimed they rarely had people stop this way nowadays, ever since the war had drained so much income and trade from the town. Anyone who wished to stay was welcome.

"Master Hinsani," Rayar sucked up the courage to speak. "I did not know things could be like this outside Heldon. I know what you said made sense, intervening could put us at risk... yet..." His words fell short as he considered the end of the sentence.

"The King of Hextheene, Braska Hextor, not only has an ongoing mock war with Southrous, but he has a personal war with magic," the Royal Blade stated. He was aware of this. King Braska hated the idea of magic, but to think that the people could behave in such a way was something he had never considered. Whilst he had heard rumours of terrible acts, witnessing such acts in person was something he was not prepared for.

"Why?" he asked.

"From what I heard, his older brother was slain by magic. His brother was a more reasonable man, who wished to end the fighting and was next in line for the throne. He was killed before he could sit upon that throne, leaving Braska Hextor as the heir. Ever since then the Knights of Hextheene were formed to root out magic and slay any who use it. They have become nothing more than soldiers in the army these days, as actually finding those with magic is nothing but myth. The result is what we witnessed." The prince nodded as he listened and finally decided to take a long swig of the drink in front of him.

"Do not feel guilty," Hinsani added. Rayar coughed into his hand and passed the man a curious look.

"Why not? We did not do anything. A young girl was brutally murdered and we watched." It felt wrong, it still did and no amount of trying to justify it could fix what had happened. He portrayed himself as some sort of good person who wanted to help people but when it came down to it, he chose to ensure his own safety over that of a helpless girl.

"People die every day, some peacefully, some brutally. You cannot save them all, and you cannot save anyone else if you die doing something brash." Words of wisdom once again filled the air. He was not wrong and the choice had been made, whether it was the right or wrong choice, the die had been cast. Rayar took a deep breath and stood from his seat.

"I am going to speak to Shania," he announced. Hinsani watched him silently for a moment, his stone expression betraying nothing until finally he nodded and stood as well.

"I will be in our room. I will also be on watch." With that the soldier turned and strode up the stairs like a ghost on air, his long cloak gracefully trailing behind him. The prince followed him up the stairs and found his way to the door of Shania's room. He took another deep breath and rapped his knuckles on the wooden frame. There was no answer. He knocked again. Nothing.

'I guess I will have to take the risk,' he thought to himself as he slowly pushed the door open with his outstretched hand. The room was lit, though only barely, by a candle on an old table pressed up against a wall. The room was basic; a small bed on the other side, a tiny window the size of a person's head and a green tattered rug stretched out across the floor. On the end of the bed sat Shania, her cloak on the floor with her sword thrown on top and her boots tossed across the room. She sat there barefoot, slumped forward in her shirt and trousers with a small black and white rock between her fingers. The druidae did not look up to acknowledge him but continued to stare at the stone in her hand.

"What is that?" Rayar asked as he cautiously closed the distance between them after ensuring the door was closed upon his entry.

"You think you're the only one with trinkets from your family, though mine actually was. Yours was just a tool for someone else's bloody schemes," she replied rather harshly. The golden haired boy stopped in his tracks and cocked a brow. Normally this kind of comment would have hurt, but after what they had seen, words simply lost their sting.

"I am sorry, Shania." His apology was genuine though it felt like an excuse. She finally turned his way with a rage filled face and snapped.

"You want to save people and you gave up so easily! I thought better of you!" On this rare occasion, he felt anger bloom inside him as well.

"What about you!?" he growled back. "You could have done something! You did not need to rely on me! Hinsani cannot tell you what to do! You chose to give up as well!" With that she was on her feet, with a hand tightly on his collar as if she was about to direct her fist straight into his jaw.

"You don't know anything!" she roared in his face. Rayar grabbed her arm and the power struggle began. They locked eyes full of anger for some time before finally the druidae released her grip and wandered back to her bed, a deep breath slipping through her lips as she plopped herself down. "Is that it, an apology or do you want something else?" she asked absently. While the anger in her seemed to have diminished, the prince could still feel the fire ablaze.

"No, that is not it. We all made a choice and we need to live with it. The guilt I feel is gnawing at my insides, Shania, I will not let it happen again," he stated. She raised a brow in question.

"What do you mean?" Shania asked.

"What I mean is..."

'Here I go, being all ridiculous again,' Rayar thought as he knew the words would not stop flowing.

"I will never leave a person in need again. I swear this now. I am not like you, I did not know how dark the world was before I left Heldon, what people could be like. I have seen friends die, my sisters in despair, men try and kill us, been called a traitor by my family and now seen a woman die by burning alive. How can I claim to be any better until I have done something to change this? Well, I am not any better because I have done nothing. I will not let this happen again, this is not about me, this is about people, all people. I will make a difference," he preached. Shania seemed to stare at him for an overly long time, an uncomfortably long time after the words exploded from his lips. Finally, much to Rayar's relief she spoke.

"Don't make those just words, Rayar. Make it true." A small smile curved in the corner of her lips, though it did not appear to be a smile of joy only that she was accepting his word. The prince sat himself down beside her on the bed with a deep sigh.

"I must sound foolish. I had such a warped view of everything. How are we supposed to stop these Controllers with whatever scheme they have, when I can barely see what the world is truly like?" he asked, half to her and half to himself.

"Together." Rayar turned to face Shania to see her sharp eyes locked intensely onto him. "You, me and Hinsani. We do it together." Their eyes remained locked for some time. He could feel his heart pounding in his chest, his cheeks grew warm and eyes unable to look away. He could have sworn the same rosy colour flushed over her own face, as her eyes flicked between his and his lips, though it had to have been a trick of the dim lighting. Silence fell over the room as they stared deeply at each other, until finally she spoke once more. "Rayar..." she whispered.

"Shania..." he replied as he could feel the distance between them closing.

"I should get some sleep," she added. The prince swallowed and swiftly lifted himself from his sitting position, like a baby lamb taking its first steps. He could barely compose himself with his heart beating so heavily.

"Yes of course, I am sorry to have kept you up with my ramblings." A soft chuckle escaped Shania as she leant back on the bed and cocked a sultry brow towards him.

"I have grown to like those ramblings, sometimes. I don't mind if you keep me up sometimes, too." With that Rayar struggled to find his words as he began to back away towards the door.

"I see, then I shall be... sure to ramble at you... whenever I get the chance!" Her face seemed puzzled though not as puzzling as the words he was trying to find. The prince backed into the door with a bump and then embarrassingly grabbed the handle and stumbled around the wooden frame like a toddler walking for the first time. "Well, good sleep." At that the door shut, he was unable to look at her any longer upon realising how ridiculous he sounded. Once outside the room he took a long deep breath with a sigh and muttered to himself. "Good sleep? Above and Below, Rayar." The room Hinsani had got for them was only next door so it was a short walk to his own bed. Inside his own room, Hinsani had already found his bed for the night, sitting cross legged in the middle of the room with his blade laid out over his knees in that mediating fashion the Royal Blade always seemed to adopt when resting. As quietly as possible the prince attempted to sneak past to the bed across the room, their room as basic as Shania's had been. Mid-stride, the deep voice of his companion sounded.

"How did it go?" he asked with his eyes closed.

"Fine, went fine. No problems," Rayar replied apprehensively. For a brief moment he could have sworn he heard a chuckle come from the crossed legged soldier on his floor yet when he shot his narrowed eyes over to see if it was true, the stone expression was present as ever.

"Did you say something?" he questioned.

"Not a thing," Hinsani stated, without skipping a beat.

* * *

Chapter XXV
Those Who Follow
~Nyer~

Nyer could not believe the plan had actually succeeded. The only downside was the fact that she had no choice but to leave Ayla behind. There was no slipping out in the commotion if she had to rush over and grab her younger sister as well. Whilst she felt awful for leaving her behind to the mercy of their father, it was for the good of the cause. She could only pray to Above that her sister would be spared from harm for the choice she had made. The opportunity presented itself and she could not resist it. Not far in the distance stood the great castle in the mountains, Stoneside Keep. Their steeds had galloped from the city of Heldon all the way as quickly as they could. There was no time to rest or gather their thoughts. They could do that as much as they pleased once safely inside the walls of the keep. Titania, Lanni, Vesir and his men all, were able to slip out of the city and make for their escape. It had been tricky at first, though she had planned their escape the night before the execution at dawn. It was not extravagant, it had been simple. It was merely the timing that had to be perfect. Now with Vesir on her side, fully committed to bringing down her father, their cause grew that much more possible. Before long, they had arrived at the gates of the first huge wall around the keep and to greet them was the Lord and Lady of the keep itself, Tismiar and Seldine Loysse, with many, many armed men. Nyer slowed the party to a trot and approached the pair cautiously. She knew of this man and his honour. She had read the letter after the visit Rayar had made. This moment would be the moment that decided which way the river would flow.

"Lord Tismiar. Lady Seldine." The princess greeted them both with a light bob of her head. Titania was already beside her, hand upon the hilt of her sword. The lord stepped forward and bowed his head gracefully. He was a sickly looking man, tall, skinny and pale but he held command that was appropriate to his position.

"Your Grace. Princess Nyer, we have been waiting eagerly for your arrival to our home. I must first ask, before we continue. Is it true, was Zanmir Granlia executed at the hands of King Rumeo?" His eyes flickered from Nyer to Vesir, as did her own. Her uncle sat upon his horse, a broken man; his face sullen and pale. He had lost his son, she could not think of a worse fate for a father. Since the man was unable to answer in his current state, Nyer continued.

"It is true. We fled after the act was committed. The horrors my father, the King, is inflicting upon those close to him, is dire. Those acts are beginning to harm the people. This lack of honour and respect for our country is something I can no longer stand for. I loved my father, the man he was. I must stop the man he has become, for the good of the kingdom." Tismiar listened and briefly glanced at his wife, perhaps for agreement. She nodded to him in a sombre fashion.

"Then let us get you all inside, we have much to discuss." The lord motioned them to follow him into the keep and through the town inside the first wall. It was as frantic and full of havoc as she remembered. The common people ran around unchecked, attempting to sell goods to her, not knowing how important she was. The princess held up her nose and ignored their advancements as they moved through the small walled town. As they reached the inner circle of the actual keep, they dismounted their horses and left them to the stable boys to attend to and entered the hold.

"You must be weary after such a journey, you look simply exhausted. Perhaps you would desire a change of clothes? I shall also have the maidens prepare rooms for you all. I doubt they would be as beautiful as the ones in Heldon, but we will do what we can," Seldine offered as they entered the meeting room, which doubled as a dining room as well as a court room for people wishing to speak with the lord. It was indeed not as grand as Heldon, yet she did not come for grandeur, she had come for alliances and safety.

"Thank you. That would be most kind." Nyer replied as she smoothly strode across the room and took her place at the head of the small table, before Tismiar had a chance to take the seat. Lord or not, she was a princess of the country and would not sit anywhere but at the highest position. Titania took her protective stance at the princess's side with her hand never leaving the pommel of her sword, as if it was attached. Lanni Ni'Tella then took a seat whilst Vesir had parked himself in front of a nearby fireplace, staring into the flames in silence. The Shield men had remained outside to perhaps find some food and attend to their own matters. They had certainly been very helpful though at the end of the day, they were soldiers. She did not even remember their names nor care to ask for them. For now she would leave her uncle to brood, his mind would be in no acceptable state to discuss the current affairs. After Seldine gave her husband a quiet whisper, too quiet for her to capture, she left to make arrangements for their guests. Tismiar did not seem bothered that his seat was taken, without a second glance he took another seat nearby.

"I must offer my deepest regrets to you Commander Vesir, for your loss. I cannot begin to imagine the pain you must be feeling," he offered to the commander. Nyer watched the exchange curiously.

"No... You couldn't imagine," he mumbled. Well, fortunately it was a quick exchange. She did not want to appear callous but she had much more important matters for discussion.

"My Lord Loysse. We thank you for your hospitality yet as you said yourself, there is much to discuss," Nyer interjected. Tismiar nodded to her in reply.

"Of course, much. From your letter it sounded as things were truly horrific in the capital. From the letter I received concerning Rayar's supposed betrayal, I had come to the conclusion that something was irregular in Heldon. You have confirmed my suspicion. Tell me, Your Grace, you have come here knowing that I too share your fears for the future of Mayhen but I am curious to what your next move could be?" he explained as his pale face showed his curiosity. Lanni ran her long fingers over her chin.

"I do hope you are not the only lord in the land who feels the same as us or our cause we intend to lead would be without reason. Have you been in contact with any concerning this matter?" the old woman asked.

"Allies," Nyer said commandingly. "We need allies if we are to stand up to the King and make a change in this land. I am not one to desire bloodshed you must understand My Lord, but if we do nothing, there can only be more bloodshed." While she did not desire it, she knew it was inevitable. The only pieces she had on the board currently were the Shield and Stoneside keep. Rumeo had Heldon, though the rest of the pieces on the map were up for grabs as far as she was concerned.

"I feared my feelings were only for me and my wife. I was concerned if I made my thoughts known to the other lords, the King may have caught wind and then who knows what would have come next." Nyer narrowed her eyes at him as he spoke.

"So you were prepared to sit here and do nothing? That is why change is so hard to do. Many people feel the same yet they refuse to take a stand. I am telling you now, My Lord Loysse, today we are going to make a stand." The poor lord seemed somewhat out of his depths with her, he was not used to such commanding royalty in his presence. She doubted when Rayar was here, that he was as forward in his demands.

271

"I... yes, I was prepared to do nothing. I have served the King loyally for many, many years Your Grace. Yet I put my own loyalty into question when bandits dressed as soldiers came willing to kill the prince, when he was a guest in my home. I did not ever think a time would come, when I would disobey my King." The heaviness of his words was evident from the strain upon his features and in his voice. However it was the right decision, the decision that was best for the country.

"I too never thought I would betray Rumeo. I loved him as a King as I loved his father," Lanni said with the same pain in her voice. "Yet as Princess Nyer has stated, this man is no longer our King. I will not sit idly by and allow such terrible things to happen. In the little time I have left, I will help make a difference." Annoyingly, Nyer agreed with the old advisor.

"Do not see it as disobeying a King, or disobeying your oaths. You are serving your country and your future Queen. Everything we do is for the betterment of the country of Mayhen. I would never have thought in my lifetime I would go against my father. However, that day has come." She ran her cold eyes over to Vesir, who had not moved from his corner by the flames. "Uncle?" There was silence in the room as the attention rested on the commander of the Shield. He did not turn to them as he spoke.

"The Shield will fight. I shall go home and see my family," he muttered. Unfortunately she could not allow him to leave.

"No, uncle, I must disagree. I need you here," she commanded as respectfully as she could. That was the comment that got him to finally turn and face her. His glare made her briefly feel like a child once again, being scolded by a parent, but she quietly retrieved her composure.

"My son has been murdered!" he snapped. "I have to go to my wife and two surviving sons and tell them what has happened. I don't want some messenger pigeon to give them the news and have them worry even more. I have to see them!" He was very emotional. It was understandable considering the situation, but she needed the commander she had heard tales

272

about from Rumeo when she was young and not this broken father. Using all the logic she could, Nyer tried to find the right words to convince him of the best course of action.

"Uncle, please listen to me, father would know what you plan. He would expect you to return to the Shield and there would be countless scouts and guardsman looking for you. I cannot hope to stand against him if you are on the other side of the country, let alone if you became his prisoner. I do not understand exactly how you feel but I can respect it is hard and painful. Please, see sense. You are needed here." The fact that Vesir did not explode into more anger and storm out of the room was a good sign that he was contemplating her words carefully. Deep down, he must have known she was right; it was his emotions that were driving him to head home, not his tactical mind.

"We will ensure your family is informed by more than messenger pigeon," Lanni added. "No one knows King Rumeo like you. No one has the insight we need. No one here has won as many battles as you, should it come to battle. If you choose to leave now, it is only a matter of time before we fail. You, Vesir Granlia, are the lynch pin that holds the plan together." The commander was clearly debating both sides in his head. He was a good man, an honest man like her father used to be, but he was also a smart man.

"Very well, for now I'll remain. Lord Loysse, if you could please send your fastest and most competent rider to the Shield, to personally inform my family of the events in Heldon. I'll have a message prepared for them." The anger was seemingly being reined and his mind appeared to regain some sense. She needed that anger controlled and directed the right way. Towards the King.

"Of course Commander, anything you need you may just ask and receive. *Anything* you need." Vesir offered the lord his gratitude before requesting to go to his room to compose himself and prepare a message. The room remained silent until they were sure he was out of ear shot.

"A terrible thing, simply terrible," Lanni said with a shake of her head.

"Indeed it is." Nyer did not feel as strongly affected by the loss as the rest of them seemed to, she had more far reaching concerns on her mind. "Now is not the time to focus on losses, we should focus on what we can gain. My Lord Loysse, I wish for you to command messages to send to all lords and ladies of the realm, with every crime the King has committed, which Miss Ni'Tella here will document for you. The country needs to band together and see the horror cease. If they stand with the side of justice and honour, they must join us in our intent to save the kingdom. If they stand on the side of false power and abuse to Mayhen's people, they may decline us," Nyer preached. Tismiar cocked a brow and responded.

"A bold claim, Your Grace, do you think many lords in the kingdom will bend to this? Not all have seen the same things we have. Some may see this as an opportunity to rise in the good graces of the King. I am sad to say, not all the Noble Lords hold the honour that we do." The princess nodded in agreement, it was a shame but true.

"You are correct. If we do not make a stand and make our intentions known and public, then how can we expect others to join our cause? You have the largest garrison in the kingdom, Lord Loysse. Many will see that as a feat of power and perhaps success in itself. With the Shield led by Jonnas Granlia, my cousin, it would form a large army, should we need to use it," she explained. Lanni, as usual, had to throw in her two silvers.

"True, however the Shield is on the other side of the kingdom. Merging the two armies would be extremely difficult if all the Noble Lords between here and there do not take kindly to our intentions." Her words rang true though she was also mistaken in her assumptions.

"I do not intend to merge the armies. The men of the Shield have trained under Commander Vesir's guidance. If, and I say if, it comes to bloodshed and war within the kingdom, the Shield will need to be ready to move wherever we need them and to attack or defend anywhere we need separately. Zanmir told me the men of the Shield are worth five men in the capital. I hope he was correct." Tismiar shook his head at her, much to her dismay.

"True or not, amidst battle on the field, it's numbers that win wars. Though I shall, of course, do as you ask, Your Grace. I pray to the Above we are doing the right thing. I also must ask, your siblings, Princess Ayla and Princess Nymin, are they not with you?" Lanni looked over to her with a look of concern, they had expected Hyar to bring Nymin to Stoneside Keep, yet it would appear they had not arrived. The princess had been so caught up in her own agenda; she had not even begun to consider where her youngest sister may be. She had to be truthful however, if this relationship with the Loysse family was to flourish.

"Princess Ayla unfortunately could not escape Heldon and is currently in the hands of our father. To what end I do not know. The sooner we can help her, the better. Princess Nymin is under the protection of her Royal Blade Hyar Dedred, far out of reach from the capital." She may not have known exactly where she was, but last they knew Hyar was with her. That would have to be enough for the moment. Worrying about possible outcomes would assist no-one.

"I see. Then I pray for your sister also and thank Above, Princess Nymin is safe. All the Royal children separated, very saddening. If there is nothing else for the moment I will attend to the matters requested with Miss Ni'Tella as well as have my officers see to the defence of Stoneside Keep, should the worst case unfold and all talks fail." Nyer allowed Tismiar to be dismissed and take Lanni with him, leaving her alone in the room with Titania. Her protector had remained silent for the whole conversation. She knew not to overstep her bounds in a place of discussion between those of noble birth, though the princess had half expected her to speak now they were alone. The silence continued for longer than she was comfortable with.

"Nothing to say, Titania?" she finally asked, bored of the lack of enthusiasm from her Royal Blade. She directed her gaze

275

over her shoulder towards the red headed warrior, whilst leaning back in her abducted high seat.

"Hyar is not here," Titania simply stated. Nyer gave her a quizzical look.

"You are worried about Sir Hyar Dedred? Really?" she asked surprised. As much as those two clashed, the red headed woman as a child had looked up to Hyar and Hinsani. It was one of the reasons she trained so hard to reach the level of skill she had now. Unlike her brother's Royal Blade, Hyar was not an honourable and serious man; he was a jester, drinker, and jumped into bed with any that would take him, but aside from all those things, he was reliable and kept to his oaths.

"Worried? No. I simply do not know where he may have gone. You are not concerned about your sister?" her protector retorted.

"Of course I am worried," Nyer replied. "Though I cannot let such fears cloud my judgement. I am worried about Ayla, I am worried about Nymin, I am worried about mother and I am even worried about Rayar, wherever he is, but if I let these worries consume me, I will not focus on what must be done." She knew her tone was somewhat harsh but she needed to get her point across. Her friend could be secretly quite sentimental at times; however she did rein in that bad habit when it became a hindrance. On the other hand, she was a voice of reason on occasions, when Nyer found herself getting carried away.

"I apologise, I did not mean to offend you My Lady." The apology was not needed but continuing the discussion further was also pointless.

"It does not matter. With word sent to all the Noble Lords and Ladies of Mayhen, true just men and women will become clear among their ranks. Then, it will be the people we need to gather. Lord Loysse was right, soldiers win wars, but the people can make it easier depending on which side they support." In a graceful flow, Nyer stood from her seat and made her way towards the bed chambers for some well needed rest, her Royal Blade close behind her. The past few days had been taxing, very taxing. Now she had a chance to reflect, compose and await the word of her possible alliances.

'Hold on Ayla. As long as you can, whatever torment he puts you through, be strong.'

* * *

Chapter XXVI
The Forgotten Child
~Ayla~

This is what a broken heart felt like. This was what betrayal felt like. This is how it felt to be left behind. The castle was in an uproar, two of the princesses of Mayhen had disappeared during the horrific execution of her cousin and she had been left in the jaws of the beast, alone without a single friend. This was truly what surrendering felt like. Ayla sat in her bed chamber, her chair facing the window as she gazed out longingly. She absently brushed her long black hair over her shoulder to keep her hands occupied. Her expression was cold and worn from mental exhaustion. Even her regal attire was something more akin to Nyer, a long mauve dress with a silver flower pattern rising from the hem. It was not as elaborate as what she usually wore.

'You left me Nyer, like Nymin left me, like Rayar left me. Mother... I need you.' She was hurt, the pain curdled in her stomach alongside brewing anger in her being. How could she possibly forgive Nyer for this, her very own sister who had promised to look out for her, promised to stick together - had abandoned her here, alone. The sun hung low in the sky outside her window. She had watched the day and night cycle quietly by herself for the past couple of days, without any interaction with the outside world. Ever since her cousin was executed, she had been locked up in her room; the only people who visited her were those dropping off meals three times a day. They said

278

it was for her protection, yet all the guardsmen in Heldon seemed different, they were not the same men as before. They all seemed dead inside with no personalities, there was nothing to them. They were like husks. The only soldiers left in the castle who even resembled men anymore, were Commander Brayton and Captain Caidarian, though the captain had been sent on constant guard duty at the western gate after Hinsani had escaped the city. This was probably as punishment for being unable to prevent the Royal Blades escape. Her own Royal Blade had died almost a month ago now, but changing Royal Blades was such a rare occurrence she did not really know the process for it. She never really cared for the idea of a protector and Raimon was never one to really socialise, yet now she wished so badly for what Nyer and Titania had or even Nymin and Hyar. Anyone she could talk to, anyone who would sand by her side no matter what. The tears in her eyes began to well up as the feeling of solitude ate away at her spirit.

"Ayla," a deep voice sounded. The voice sent a chill up her spine and almost caused her to scream. She had been so lost in her thoughts; she had not paid any attention to someone opening the door. Her eyes fell upon the King, her father. Rumeo stood in the doorway, broad and commanding with his black fur attire and crown upon his grey hair. Hesitantly she spoke in her soft tone.

"Yes, father?" Her slender fingers gripped her dress at the knees as she awaited whatever cruel behaviour was about to befall her.

"I hear things have been tough on you lately. For that, I wish to offer my sincerest apologies." It could not be true. He had not spoken this way since the attack on their home and now he was apologising. The King made his way into the room, his eyes studying the bed chamber around them.

"Lovely room you have here. You must love the colour yellow," he stated. Perhaps her room was considerably one-sided with colouring but something about yellow, gold, blonde anything like that made her feel safe.

"You know I do... father," she replied still apprehensive. Rumeo chuckled, it was a dark chuckle, not like he used to. Nothing about him was how he used to be. It was as if her father had been replaced.

"Of course, I have come to take you somewhere. There is someone you need to see." As if expecting her to do as she was told, the King turned on his heel and made his way out of the bed chamber, not looking back to check if she had followed his command. Of course, she was no fool and within an instant she was on her feet and quickly behind him. They moved hastily through the castle hallways. It had always been a maze of a castle and but after living her whole life in Heldon, she knew every nook and cranny of the labyrinth. As nervous as she felt, as scary as the thought of going somewhere with her father was, she followed him. The way she was being led would have taken them to his bed chamber, a floor up from the royal children's. After a short walk in silence, they reached the doorway. Rumeo stopped in his tracks and finally addressed her once more.

"I warn you, it is not a pleasant sight. We are doing what we can, but she is very sick after the attack." It could not be, could it? Through that door, finally she would be able to see her once again. With a heavy sigh the King pushed open the door with one hand and there before them, lying in the King's bed, was her mother. She could not believe it. Without caring about carrying herself any longer, she suddenly exploded in tears and darted across the room. Ayla dropped down beside her mother and threw her arms around the Queens neck, giving her a desperate hug. She did not care if she was ill. She did not care how sickly she looked. This was her mother and after not seeing her for what felt like a lifetime, it had been like a nightmare.

"Mother! Mother it is me, Ayla! I have missed you so much, Above and Below I have missed you!" She cried into her mother's shoulder. There was no reply. Only the faint signs of breathing. Her father had not been exaggerating; she looked like a skeleton with thin skin over the bones. It was like she had aged a hundred years; her hair was like bristle and her skin white. It was horrible, so horrible she almost vomited from the sight of seeing the woman she loved more than anything in the world, in such a state.

"She has not woken since the attack. We have kept her safe here, though the healers can do nothing," Rumeo explained as he stood behind her. Ayla could not take her eyes off her mother's face as she gently stroked the Queens cheek with the back of her index finger.

"How did this happen?" she was able to ask while choking on tears.

"Magic," the King stated bluntly. This *did* get her attention. Ayla turned to face her father with a heavy frown.

"Magic? What do you mean magic?" She had heard bedtime stories of magic, she had heard of the Order who claimed to be magically inclined but were known as frauds. How could magic possibly have done this to her mother? Did magic even actually exist?

"I will not lie to you Ayla. The reason we know that Rayar was behind this was he had a companion. A woman who has control over magic. She did this to my wife, your mother. Rayar let the attackers in. I did not believe it at first, but magic is real. It exists and it is dangerous." This made no sense to her. Rayar had a friend who was a woman was a surprise in itself, but that was not nearly as important as the fact that his companion had done this to their mother. He would not do this, he could not. He was a good man.

"Rayar would not do this, you know him father. He is your son!" she tried to exclaim though tears still filled her eyes and throat.

"The boy has been plotting with Nyer for some time, my people tell me. Together they planned to take the throne. Brother and sister against their family. Sadly for them, their plans have failed. That is why I have been so ruthless in my rule, daughter. I knew Rayar was a traitor but I did not know which daughter had betrayed us. I am sorry for ever suspecting you." His large hand found itself onto her shoulder and gave it a tight reassuring squeeze. There was too much information; it did not make sense to her. They were family, how could they do this to her, to father, to mother and the people. The doubt that he was telling the truth still lingered in her mind yet after Nyer had abandoned her here; she no longer knew what to believe.

"This all... sounds insane, I do not understand how this all happened," she whimpered. Like a doting father, Rumeo took both her arms and lifted her back to her feet, holding her in place in front of his large form.

"Nor do I, Ayla. Nor do I. All I know is that now we must be careful, we must stick together. Nyer is in cahoots with my brother Vesir, Rayar is on the run and Nymin has been stolen from our home. You and I are the only Granlia's who are left, the only ones who can protect the people. I love all my children, but I cannot forgive them for this." She could not speak; the words did not find their way to her tongue. She could only bow her head in submission and accept the fate that had befallen her. "Do not worry, I will not ask much from you. I just need to know you will not betray me and your mother as well. I need to know this," he demanded, though, in a fatherly manner.

'What do I do... what do I do... Nyer.... Mother... Please Rayar. No, no, no you all did this.' The young girl clenched her eyes shut as if somehow that would return everything to how it was. Yet no matter how badly she wished for that to be true, things would never be the same. She had no choice.

"I would never betray our family father." With that he wrapped his arms around her and gave her a tight hug. It had been so long since she felt the warmth of his body around her, yet something seemed different. He felt different. Ayla was given no time to consider it before he released his grip and motioned her to follow once more.

"Come, let your mother rest. The healers will return soon to continue their work. There is someone else I would like you to meet." Someone else? As if all of this information was not enough to boggle her mind already, he had more to throw upon

282

her. Ayla quickly moved back to the side of her mother and wrapped her arms around her once more. She did not know when next she would be given the chance to see her. After using the sheets of the bed to wipe away the tears reforming in the corner of her eyes, the princess rose back to full height and took a deep breath. Needlessly to say the princess had no choice but to continue being led around like a dog on a lead. They made their way back through the castle, through the numerous hallways and finally into the courtroom. There were courtiers in the throne room attending their usual daily activities, activities that she never really took an interest in, as well as hordes of guardsmen now littering every corner of the castle. One other man was ever present, much to her distaste, the one armed captain Sirus. Whenever she looked at him, he reminded her of some sort of insect that preyed on the weak with his vile glare. Covered in brown leather with a hook for a hand crossed over his other arm, he had taken his place by the closest pillar to the throne itself, where he always seemed to be. Slightly hidden in the shadows but everyone knew he was watching. As the King made his arrival known, the court bowed to him in a courteous manner, every person except the guards bent at the waist.

"Rise," Rumeo commanded as he took up his seat upon the throne. "Stand next to me, Ayla." The young princess slowly stepped up next to her father. Her fingers dug into her dress as all eyes seemed to be resting on her.

"A while ago, during the attack, one of our Royal Blades was slain brutally. My daughter, Ayla Granlia, lost her protector. In these troubled times I cannot stand for such weakness. Those who shall protect the Granlia name must be strong. They must be unbent and unbroken. They must never fall in battle; they must never lose. Bring him forth!" The King addressed the audience. As he commanded the unknown to come forward, the large doors of the throne room flew open and a figure stood between them. Ayla's eyes widened at the man, he was a giant. The man approached the throne, his body was muscular, his beard covered his face and his clothes were entirely made of fur. At his hip sat a giant axe strapped to his thick leather belt. As this man reached the throne, he lowered to one knee with a fist pressed into the ground. His voice was gruff and strong, as deep as her father's if not deeper.

"Your Majesty. I've come to serve." Rumeo lifted his arms in the air for his performance.

"All here today, welcome the new member of the Royal Blades. The only one who serves the kingdom faithfully. Rise, Royal Blade and swear to protect your princess." The man could be mistaken for a bear at a quick glance, though as he stood, he towered above the people around him. A smirk on his lips sent a shiver down her spine.

"I, Shan Hannabel, swear to protect my charge, Princess Ayla Granlia, against any an' all that threaten 'er. I swear ta be at 'er side when beckoned and to give my life to defend 'er's. I swear to see ta their safety without guidance of the law of the realm and honourably carry out all duties they require of me. I swear to be honest and valiant in all ma duties as a Royal Blade." Claps echoed through the throne room as the oath was sworn. Rumeo glanced over to her and must have seen the shock and fearful look in her eyes, as his hand reached out and grasped her arm. Ayla shot her eyes to her father, startled, and blinked at his touch.

"Do not fear my daughter. He may seem rough but there is no man out there whom would try their luck with him. He will protect you against anything and everything. With Sir Shan by your side, you will be untouchable." His words were somehow reassuring even though fear coursed through her veins. The dark haired girl turned her attention back to the bear of a man as he now strode up the stairs towards her. Once the distance had been closed, he lowered to one knee, now being somewhat closer to her height.

"Times 'ave been 'ard on ya. I know. I 'eard. Nothin' ta fear now, princess. I'm your shield, ya can always rely on me. I promise." With that he returned to full height and made his way to the side of the thrones and crossed his arms. She did not know what to think, Nyer would say this man had been placed to watch her yet how could she trust what Nyer would think after she had been left? No, she had to stop relying on her sister; she was a princess of Mayhen. The only thing that could be done now was to look after herself. Ayla focused on grasping the strength she felt slipping from her body every passing second. Nyer, Shan, Rumeo, all of them could not be trusted.

"That is not the only order of business I have to announce, good people of Heldon" The crowd grew quiet from their conversations to once again focus their attention on the King upon the throne. Ayla now took a seat, though not her usual one. This time she took her youngest sister's seat furthest from the King. "As you all know, treason has been a poison in our land too common of late. My son, my daughter, my brother and his children. Now it has grown to a larger scale. My daughter, Nyer Granlia has joined with my treacherous brother in an evil plot to steal the throne. We cannot allow this to stand. As noble men and women of Heldon I tell you now, we will crush any who try and ruin this kingdom. I condemn and renounce Nyer Granlia. I condemn and renounce Vesir Granlia. I condemn and renounce any who stand with them. Let it be known this day, here and now. The Noble Lords of Mayhen will not stand for this. The armies of Mayhen will not stand for this. I, King Rumeo Granlia, will call for the armies of Mayhen to stand with the Royal Family and their King and destroy the usurpers!" The room erupted in cheers and clapping, the courtiers of the court showed their undying loyalty to their King. Ayla watched the scene play out, doing her best to control her emotions. Was there really to be bloodshed? Whatever Nyer was thinking, she would never go into open rebellion against the kingdom. That would be madness. With what army? No; words had to be used first. The light that shone from her father before, that she thought she saw, had already become so dim, it was impossible to see or feel it. This new Royal Blade, showing her that mother was alive to then exclaim a plot of war. This man, whoever he was, was taunting her and trying to torment her mind. The grin Rumeo passed her way as he returned to his seat only cemented her fear.

'Please... just go back to the way it was before. World Above, I beg you.' As much as she prayed in her heart and mind, she knew these prayers could not be answered. The wheel was rolling, the world was changing. She would need to learn to go forward with it or be dragged in the mud behind.

* * *

Chapter XXVII
Zanmir
~Jonnas~

Jonnas had never seen his mother in such a way before; to witness her in such pain was something he could never have imagined. His mother sat on the edge of her bed within her bed chamber, her face in her hands and tears pouring down her cheeks. The maid Niyla cradled the young child Lanmir, rocking him gently as he too sobbed uncontrollably. In his mother's intense distress, she was unable to attend to Lanmir. Next to her, an older gentleman stood draped in long dark blue robes. He was a balding man with a warm face, even in saddened times. The Duke was how he was known, yet his real name was Kannu. He was a priest for the World Above. He stood beside her with a hand upon her shoulder, attempting to console her in any way he could. The conversation was too quiet for Jonnas to hear from the doorway, yet as soft as his tone was, and gentle the words, they would not bring back his brother. Word had spread pretty quickly that a Granlia had been executed in the capital of Heldon. At first they had assumed it might have been Vesir, but soon it was revealed by a messenger from across the country it was actually Zanmir. Jonnas never truly got along with his older brother; the man had been insufferable, cold and always thought he was right but he loved him regardless. Zanmir was his brother. He loved his family more than anything in this world. The rider had a message that claimed Vesir was now in Stoneside Keep with

Princess Nyer and the Lord of the hold, planning to stand against the cruelty of the King. At least they knew father was alive and the message had definitely been from him. Jonnas continued to watch his mother's expression of desolation a moment longer, his heart broken into shards with his gloved hand wrapped around the hilt of his sword so tightly he thought his fingers would bleed through the leather.

'I will avenge you brother. I swear it. Father... I will not sit idly by.' The captain told himself as he finally tore his gaze from the depressing scene. No longer could he look upon the pain of his mother without his own tears breaking free. He was a man and he had to act like one. Father had placed him in command, now was not the time to be seen breaking into pieces. Draped in his long black cloak and covered in his leather armour, Jonnas strode out of the keep and towards the gathering hall. As he passed, soldier after soldier lowered their heads respectfully, removing their kettle helmets as they did. Word had spread around the entire Shield of Mayhen and the town of Meyer, of what had occurred. All knew the Granlia family here well; they did not sit up in their high castles and separate themselves from the common folk. They were just the same as everyone else, trying to live a good life. The gathering hall was a large building constructed for the purposes of meetings between all men and women of the Shield. Soon after news arrived that Zanmir had been slain unjustly, Jonnas sent out word that representatives of the soldiers and the people be selected, to attend a gathering to discuss the events that had unfolded. It was something father would do if he were here. The great hall was one of the largest buildings in the town. It was an oval structure and the interior was circular, to symbolise the equality of all who attend and wish to speak their piece. The noise inside was deafening as so many people who had gathered, debated amongst themselves around the large hall. Jonnas strode past them all, his gut still wrenching in pain yet he had to put on the face of command, he had to show he was not weak. He would be strong. Once in the centre of the hall, the voices began to die down to allow him to speak first.

"Firstly, thank you all for coming," the Granlia captain announced as he looked around the people. The usual cocky expression he wore had been replaced by one of stone, something people would relate more to Zanmir than himself. "You have all come for the same reason, to discuss what has happened in Heldon. To what has happened to my brother, Zanmir Granlia. All will be given time to speak if they so wish it. Yet I will begin. I loved my brother and as you all know, we did not always get along, but he was my blood. My father, your commander, is out there, most likely a broken man. We cannot rely on him to return home just yet. We cannot rely on him at this moment. While we all know Vesir would know what to do, we do not have that luxury right now." He addressed all in the crowd, doing his best to hold back his nerves for speaking to so many at once. He had never had to do such a thing before but he was the only one who could. A man from across the hall motioned that he wished to speak. He stepped forward; Jonnas stepped back and allowed him the stand. If he remembered correctly, he was a blacksmith, the best blacksmith in Meyer and he used to be a soldier in the Mayhen army.

'Heran Hyre, I think?' Jonnas thought as he tried to place name to face.

"Vesir's son speaks true! As people of the Shield, we must decide ourselves the next course of action. We all love Vesir and his family but if there is cause to believe there was treason, what right do we have to involve ourselves? Go against our King?" he put forward. There were many whispers and mutters throughout the hall as his words were considered. A woman spoke out, she was head of the tailors who worked tirelessly to craft the clothes they wore every day, Kalin Jayer.

"Commander Vesir built everything you hold dear here. Before him there was no town, no economy. Everything comes from that man and his hands. If our commander wishes to stand against the King, then I say we stand with him. All of us, soldiers and common people alike," she called out from her place in the hall. As she spoke, more than half of the hall roared out in cheers, or so he imagined it was more than half, due to the sheer volume. The people who stood in this hall were mainly townspeople, with trades and skills, rather than soldiers. The representative of the soldiers' of the Shield was him, and he already knew where he and his men stood. They would gladly follow whatever order Vesir gave them and if the order was to fight, they would fight. Then the shouting commenced, people yelled across the hall at each other with reasons to fight or the risks of doing so. Jonnas did his best to try and hear them all yet, as the meeting continued, the shouting intensified and soon it became impossible to follow the constant din.

"Good people listen! Quieten down and listen!" The captain tried to regain control though the arguments were so frantic, it was impossible to get the attention of anyone. His temper began to grow shorter as he tried desperately to get some order, when suddenly a loud horn bellowed throughout the hall. The stunned crowd, to his relief, soon settled in their squabbles and turned birth of the sound. At the entrance of the hall, two figures stood, one was the Priest of Above with a horn between his lips while the other was his mother. Her eyes were red and lids swollen from tears, her expression was one of weariness from the mental exhaustion she must have been suffering. Upon seeing the commander's wife enter the hall, every person fell respectfully silent. Jonnas frowned, unsure of her purpose here and quickly darted over to her.

"Mother, what are you doing here?" he asked with concern. After the news had been confirmed, of the loss of her son, he did not think she would leave the keep for days. Seeing her in tears again, would break him. His mother offered him a warm motherly smile and lightly caressed his cheek.

"I wish to speak also, if I may?" Jonnas swallowed nervously and nodded. Kaylen took the centre stage, silence still filling the room as none wished to disrespect the wife of the commander.

"Good people of the Shield," she began with surprising strength in her voice; even more powerful than his own. "I am a mother. I had three sons, the youngest just born, who still feeds upon my breast, Jonnas, your captain and leader in times of need when my husband is not present. My eldest, Zanmir, was the smartest person I had ever met. Smarter than me and smarter than my husband, he saw the world in a way I could never imagine to see it. He would read people like books and understood the tiny details most of us would miss. His future was bright. He would have made the country an even greater land to live in. Zanmir is dead. As a mother, I have lived to see my son die. Mothers of soldiers live to see their sons die. There is nothing more... painful... nothing more devastating in life I can imagine. All of us here, in the Shield, in Meyer, we are a family. We live our lives looking out for each other and never involve ourselves with the rest of Mayhen and they never involve themselves with us. Until now. Now, they have stolen someone from our family and wish to steal another, they wish to steal away the father of the Shield." As she spoke, she walked around the centre of the hall with her hands clasped together in front of her hips, her powerful gaze burning into anyone who looked her way.

"It is true, we all have a choice. We have a choice to stand by and watch my husband fight to avenge his son. We can see it that way, none of your business. There is another choice. We take a stand, now, and help your commander, the father of the Shield, put an end to tyranny and cruelty in our kingdom. The soldiers will fight when ordered to, each and every one of them is prepared to put their lives on the line for their commander yet the people of Meyer, all of you, we need you to be at their backs helping them, supporting them. Here we are not like other lands. We do not force people into submission. We give them a choice." Her speech ended and she became silent. She never broke however, his mother continued to stand tall and dominant in the centre of the gathering hall, without showing an ounce of weakness. Suddenly a man yelled from the side lines, somewhere within the crowd.

"We fight for Vesir Granlia! We refuse tyranny!" After this one chant echoed throughout the hall, another spoke.

"We fight for Vesir!"

"The people stand with the Granlia of the Shield!"

"We won't stand for tyranny!"

"Down with the King, for Zanmir!"

More and more voices began to erupt showing their support for their commander. Jonnas could no longer remain silent either and cheered out.

"For my brother!" As he yelled out, his mother passed him a glance and nodded with a soft smile. The smile betrayed her sadness. She could hide it from the people but never from him. He knew the difference between her smiles after years of witnessing them. The hall did not stop cheering until a chant began to overtake the random declarations of what each person stood for.

"For the Commander, Fight! For the Commander, Fight! For the Commander, Fight!" So it had begun. The people would stand behind them, yet that was only the beginning. It was now down to him to prepare the soldiers for battle. Many of them had not seen battle for some time, but they had all trained hard. It was how Vesir ran his ship. Train hard, work hard, do your duty and live a fun life under his command. It was not the most professional ship, but it sailed strong. As the crowd cheered, they began to exit the gathering hall and spread the word of the decision around the town. Jonnas made his way to his mother who was keeping her mask well in place.

"What now, mother?" he asked as the hall became increasingly silent. The pain was still present in her eyes, so looking too deeply into them was not an option. The pain he knew she held in her heart, was something Jonnas could hardly bare.

"We prepare any and all for what may come. The enemy are not blocked by a wall so defences will need to be crafted for the town. You know what to do Jonnas. Your father taught you everything he knew and what to do in all possible circumstance, even ones we would never expect. Like this one." The young man nodded at her words, she was right as always. Relying on her too much could make him look weak.

He would have to earn the leadership he was given, much like his father had. He was the captain, after all.

"Alright..." He started as he pondered the next move. "...Supplies will be needed, equipment for anyone who wants to fight. We will send the rider back with a message to father, informing him of what we intend to do. Then we wait for his next command. As much as I would love to march into Heldon and extract vengeance for Zanmir personally, I doubt that is an option. Father will have a plan. We will need to wait for what he wishes to do next." Kaylen offered a weakened smile, the strain still pulling her down.

"Just like Vesir. Sounds good, Jonnas. I will be here to help you. We will make them pay, all of those in Heldon who had a hand to play." Her statement took him back a bit as did the sudden glare in her eyes. Without saying another word, his mother swept through the gathering hall and towards the exit. Jonnas watched as she walked away.

'I have never seen mother like this before...'

The sun began to set on the hectic day. Upon the unity of the people, the soldiers of the Shield began to scamper around the wall and town like ants following their directive. The blacksmiths had their job of crafting as much steel as they could, the tailors and armourers would begin work tirelessly to ensure any who could take up arms would be protected. Word spread to the farmers nearby the town of Meyer and their livestock would be prepared for supplies. Jonnas leant on the battlement of the huge wooden wall, gazing off to the south, studying the red mist in the far distance. The wall had stood here since the country of Ghaul had been a threat; rumours of monsters on the other side had led many to believe it protected Mayhen from all sorts of creatures. In truth, it was something created by men to keep other men out. Now this possible war would be on their side of the wall, such irony was not lost on him. He had trained under his father, learnt everything he could learn, watched him so closely and listened to every tale he could recite. Vesir had prepared him to be a battle commander, a soldier and a good man. Somewhere across the country, his father was beginning his preparations for battle and they would meet side by side on the battlefield. Though he never imagined the first real battle he would take part in, would be against people of Mayhen. It was a sad thought but an unavoidable one.

"One of your soldiers said you would be here, captain, sir." A young voice spoke from beside him. He looked over to see the maid Niyla; she stood a couple of heads smaller than he did. She was a plain looking girl though there was sweetness to her. Her shoulder length hair had been trimmed into a bob after the mess the ride from the capital had caused it. She was adorned by a grey dress untypically practical with trousers underneath and leather boots upon her feet. She had endured much and now served his mother as her personal maid. This post was not as fine and elegant as serving in Heldon though from what they had learnt, perhaps it was not so elegant there either anymore.

"I am. What can I do for you, Niyla?" he asked as he turned to face her while still propping himself up on the wall. The young maid gulped as she seemed somewhat nervous.

"I just wanted to say, I think what you're doing is good. I mean... I hate violence, war, anything to do with it. If things could be settled with words, I would prefer it. It's just... well... I think I am rambling." Jonnas chuckled at her falling over her words. It was a compliment at least, even if it sounded rather accidental.

"I do what I must. I did not think I would be in such a situation as this ever in my life. I never thought father would not be around during something so dire, but here I am, in charge of all these soldiers, all these people and now I must do something no commander should want to do. Fight, and lose lives." He gazed off the wall once more for dramatic effect, showing the girl how intense he could be. He was not one to pass up the chance to impress a woman.

"I would not presume you enjoy fighting, captain. I did not mean to offend!" she blurted out, clearly concerned that her words were heavier than she thought they were. Jonnas could not help but laugh once again and place a hand lightly on her arm.

"You did not. Do not worry. You are sweet, I appreciate your words. I will make you a promise. If you look after my mother and my little brother, I will take you for a drink, I think getting to know you better could be quite the pleasure." The girl blushed red and struggled to find the words once again.

"I... I promise I will. I will look after them. No matter what happens." She smiled at him, an adorable little grin. He returned the smile with his usual lopsided smirk. Focusing on things like this helped distract him from what was happening. Anything to drag his mind away from his mother's pain, anything to drag his mind away from the looming battles ahead and anything to drag his mind away from Zanmir. Those thoughts hurt too much, a pain he could not bear.

"How is it you found yourself working for the Royal Family as a maid, I doubt they select anyone from the streets?" Anything to distract him.

"Well, I am from a Noble Lords family, the forth daughter of Noble Lord Tutor. My father offered me to serve the Queen to learn how to be a proper lady. I did not think I would end up here of all places." She sighed as she joined him leaning on the wall. "I wondered if by going to Heldon, I would be spotted by Prince Rayar, the handsome golden haired prince." Jonnas rolled his eyes. He heard women mention the prince from time to time, he did not care for it. From what he knew, he may have been 'handsome' but he was pretty dim witted and dull. His opinion of course was biased, another Granlia to compete with.

"Did the handsome prince not give you his attention?" Niyla bit her lip in thought before replying.

"We spoke once or twice, he mentioned seeing the world and helping people. Noble and adventurous yet... he always lay in the gardens simply wishing to do more, never doing it. I pitied him, he had everything he ever wanted as a prince, as royalty, but never did anything but watch the world go by." He did not know Rayar that well and if he was honest, he did not really wish to talk about him, but her words struck home. He had been at the Shield all his life, he had visited other places after all but the thought of staying here and dying here sent a shiver down his spine.

"Not the prince for you then?" he questioned with an arrogant smirk. Niyla let out a small laugh and shook her head.

"No, not for me. I wish for a man to be who he wants to be. To know who he is and where he wants to go in life. I am sorry. I am talking about pointless things when there are so much more important matters at stake. You shouldn't be concerning yourself with me and my silly fantasies." Little did she know that even though there were many things that were high on the list of priorities, speaking to her about such casual matters was surprisingly uplifting. If she could not marry a prince, perhaps she would settle on a captain, or stand in commander - whichever one sounded more appealing.

"I have enjoyed our talk, I hope for many more after this is all over with." A small soft hand appeared on his and gave it a squeeze.

"I hope so too. I am scared of what may happen, but you give me confidence, you give everyone confidence. You will be a great leader, captain." Jonnas hoped that was true. To be anything close to the greatness of his father would be a true achievement. He would just have to do his best, look after his people and ensure the rest of his family never suffered this kind of fate again.

"You can call me Jonnas."

"Thank you, Jonnas."

* * *

Chapter XXVIII
True Unity
~*Jonnas*~

"Come at me!" Jonnas roared out at the two soldiers of the Shield that stood before him. In his gloved hand, he held a training sword as did the two challengers in front of him. One stood as tall as he, with a gaunt face and slim body while the other was shorter and much larger, broad but also chunkier. Wedyar and Briyar were their names. Father had spent many nights in the Crone, drinking with many of the soldiers, but these two in particular always happened to be there to join in on the fun. Dressed in his leather armour, he twirled the training sword around fluidly and slid into a defensive stance. The pair looked to each other with doubtful expressions.

"You first, Wedyar," the taller one said as he motioned forward with his sword. The larger man sighed and tried his luck. He charged at the captain as quickly as his short legs could carry him. From above, his strike came with both hands on the hilt of the sword. With one hand on his own, the captain shifted to the side and clonked the swords together, before passing the soldier and whacking him on the back which sent him tumbling forward into the dirt.

"Way too slow." Jonnas taunted, as he looked down at the groaning soldier with a smirk comfortably upon his lips. Then the sound of footsteps caught his ears. Just within the nick of time, he turned his body to block a horizontal strike from the companion of the fallen soldier. Briyar was a better fighter than Wedyar, this much he knew, but he gave up too easily. After his first attack was blocked, the soldier leapt backwards and pointed the tip of his training sword towards him, to keep him back.

"Alright, alright, you win. I yield." Jonnas laughed and shook his head.

"No yielding today, soldier!" He charged and aimed to slam the sword directly into the stomach of the man. As quickly as he could, Briyar leapt to the side and skidded along the ground to avoid the swift attack. Jonnas followed like a cat with a mouse, striking and slashing, only to have Briyar barely avoid every attack. This chase was tiring out the soldier, as beads of sweat trickled down his face and his body appeared more and more exhausted.

"Wedyar, come on!" Briyar called out for help. Startled, Jonnas swiftly turned his eyes back to see the stocky soldier attempt another downward slice from behind. This time however, Briyar did not sit idly by. From the other side he struck vertically. As quickly as he could move, Jonnas dropped down to his knees to avoid the attacks with the pair accidently smashing each other with their training swords. The pair smacked each other on the head and both fell to the ground, stunned. With two loud thumps the duo lay on their backs gripping their heads and groaning. As the captain returned to full height, he gave the pair a mocking shake of his head.

"I have seen that tactic used on the commander. It did not work then, it will not work on me either," Jonnas teased as he turned to the crowd of soldiers watching the display. They all laughed and pointed at the pair on the ground until finally a few of them went over and helped them back to their feet.

"As amusing as it is, we need to ensure our swordplay is sharpened. Each of you pair up and begin sparring. Remember, there is no yielding if you get scared, Briyar," he teased once more. The lanky soldier grumbled and nodded in acceptance of his defeat.

"Yes, sir," they announced in unity. The soldiers, hundreds of them began to pair up in the training field beside the wall and began to spar. The ground had been covered in gravel and sand to make their duels more difficult and to give them footwork practice on unstable ground. They were rotating in their hundreds. Other soldiers were on patrol, guarding the wall or on their breaks. Approximately every hour or so the soldiers sparring left the training ground and took over the duties of the Shield, whilst another couple of hundred replaced them to begin their sparring sessions. It was a tiring system but it was practical for them. The training field could not hold many more than a couple of hundred men anyway. Jonnas watched the progress from the side, with his training blade resting on his shoulder.

'Not bad, not bad. We are still greatly outnumbered but their skill is a start, from there we can look into any strategies that would give us an advantage on the field. I am sure father, you would so the same thing, bloody probably doing it now.' Across the country Vesir was out there with his cousin, planning how to take on the capital and all the Noble Lords who would stand behind the throne. Jonnas would need to think like his father would, think of how he won battles when he was greatly outnumbered. Just then he looked over across the training field to see his mother, Kaylen, watching the sparring as well, with the priest Kannu by her side. The balding man as usual seemed other worldly. His hands tucked in his robe and his warming aura glistening around him like a warm fire in a dark night. Jonnas was not really a godly man, he never trusted fate or in the World Above to solve his problems. His problems were his own to solve, not some higher power that could fix everything with a flick of the wrist if they so chose. The captain made his way around the training field and joined his mother and the priest. She offered him a weak smile as he closed the distance, as did Kannu, though his welcome was considerably warmer.

"Above Blessings upon you Captain Jonnas Granlia," the priest said in his humble tone with a bow. Jonnas returned the greeting with a simple nod.

"What brings you both here? I did not think you were one to like the idea of fighting Kannu?" he said, as a slight jab, alongside genuine curiosity. The priest chuckled under his breath and rubbed his balding head.

"Indeed. Not my forte yet I have come with Lady Granlia here. We received a messenger pigeon from the capital." Kannu explained before allowing Kaylen to take over.

"Thank you, Kannu. Yes, I thought you needed to see it. Yet it had been some time since I saw you use a sword, dear. You move like Vesir does." Jonnas could not think of a greater compliment and could not help but smile. She passed him the scroll while her eyes remained forward on the sparring troops. The captain looked over it with a heavy frown weighing down his features. The parchment would be read aloud.

"'To all Noble Lords of Mayhen, treason brews in our kingdom. I call all Noble Lords to support the Royal Family against the traitors Nyer Granlia and Vesir Granlia. They have been renounced and wish to take the throne against the people. All banners are called to Heldon. King Rumeo Granlia of Mayhen.' Above and Below, but why did we get sent one of these? They should know we have no Noble Lord here nor are we likely to support anyone but Commander Vesir." His mother clenched her teeth in anger, leaving Kannu to explain.

"We assume it is a taunt to you, a gesture to provoke you or scare you. King Rumeo knows his brother well, knows what he will do and how he thinks. Though he does not know you, perhaps he thinks you will hide in the Shield afraid to engage, perhaps he intends to lure you and your men out to rush to the side of your father. We do not know, but we can assume. There is more, we received another message shortly before this one. It seems both King Rumeo and Princess Nyer are playing the same tactic." His mother then passed him the second message even though it had arrived first. He was curious as to why he had not been shown this yet, if it had arrived before the King's word, but questioning his mother right now might not have been the wisest move. This one was read aloud as well.

"'To all Free People of Mayhen. The King has betrayed his rule and his cruelty is unjustified. He abuses his power and murders on a whim. This is not the King of Mayhen, this is a tyrant. All honourable men and women must stand against this false King and stand with us in bringing his reign to an end. We stand as one at Stoneside Keep. We must end a rule of cruelty. Princess Nyer Granlia of Mayhen.' Well I would say it has more poetry to it. But she gave away her position to every Noble Lord in the kingdom, even to those who would not stand with her." Even though Jonnas did not consider himself an intellectual strategist, this simply seemed strange. Kaylen replied, though her anger appeared to be under control.

"Only a fool would siege Stoneside Keep with the vast numbers of men Noble Lord Tismiar Loysse has. You would need tens of thousands of men to take that keep. One hundred men could hold it and Lord Loysse has thousands under his command. King Rumeo would need almost every Noble Lord in the kingdom to send all their men to Stoneside, to have a chance to siege that castle." Nyer and Vesir were in a better position than they themselves were. They could put up their defences around the town as much as they liked, but if the entire Mayhen army marched on them; their wall would not protect them. Perhaps it would be better to move to Stoneside. It would take weeks however, perhaps months to move everyone there.

"Maybe we should go to father. We cannot do much from here," he stated yet he felt it sounded like a question to his mother. Kaylen pondered on it for a moment.

"Maybe. Vesir knows we support him no matter what, yet the King is unaware of what we plan to do. It would take time to prepare to move everyone across the entire country, and the fastest route would be right past the capital. May I propose something?" she asked. She was treating him more as a commander at this point. Perhaps she did not want to undermine his leadership. His mother knew Vesir better than anyone, naturally, yet at the end of the day, as he was in command, the final word was his.

"Of course," he replied curiously.

"Send scouts to the capital lands. We wait and watch. We are greatly outnumbered here. If the army of Mayhen does march on Stoneside Keep, we attack the capital. I think your father would consider this. If they do not, we may have time to move to Stoneside or meet with the army of Princess Nyer. For all we know, this could end without any bloodshed. Though... there is one more person's blood that must be spilled. The King's." The determination in her eyes sent a chill down his spine. While she spoke logically, with tactics in mind, her desire to end the King's life was also very apparent. It was not as if he did not agree, he wanted nothing more than to run his sword through the gut of the fat bastard, but they had to act carefully, the risk of them being marched on was terrifying possible. Kannu sighed from the sidelines.

"I do not condone bloodshed of any kind. I know it is hard, Lady Granlia, killing does not justify more killing." Kaylen clicked her tongue against her teeth giving the priest a side glance and eventually a respectful nod.

"I know, Kannu. I know," she replied with a heavy sigh slipping past her lips. Jonnas watched his mother closely feeling her pain, whilst the guilt formed in his stomach that *he* could hide his true feelings better than she could. He did not want her thinking that he did not care about Zanmir. Yet if his brother were here right now, as insufferable as he would be, the next steps would be clear as day. He would know exactly which course they should take and the safest way to do so.

"I think having scouts watch the capital is a good idea. It will allow time for them to contact us if anything changes but if we need to move, we can move quickly. If the capital was to move an army, they would only move with such force that it would allow us plenty of time to counter, with the right plan. Does that sound alright?" he asked his mother. The woman agreed and took both documents from him, before leaving him to the training of the soldiers with a quick farewell. Kannu offered him a humble bow and followed the Lady of the Shield back into the city towards the keep.

'I want the same thing mother, I would love to charge Heldon and avenge Zanmir. Yet now I have many more lives on my shoulders. I have to remain calm, remain sensible.' Forcing

302

the doubts from his mind, Jonnas returned his attention to the men as they sparred. All these lives were in his hands, being reckless was not an option.

*

~Timur~

The ground was unkempt and unruly, grass and foliage grew unchecked, overgrown. No one had been here for so many years it was impossible to control the land. In the far distance, the huge wall of the Shield stood, preventing any who wished entry from the southern side, though not one person had tried for so many years, they had forgotten the reason it even existed. Figures moved along the structure, they looked like dots, many dots. It was manned relatively well, enough to hold against a disorganised rabble, if such a group attempted to strike. A man stood at the edge of the red mist, draped in a dark red leather chest piece and a shawl around his shoulders. His collar coloured a lighter red. At his hip a long curved blade hung from his belt. The rest of his armour was golden, his gauntlets, his boots, and his belt even; all shone with a glimmer of gold. His eyes were sharp and red in tint as he watched the activities from the south of the famous Shield. Beside him, a woman sat upon a horse, though her image was disfigured by the red mist. The faint image of another steed without a rider, stood beside her.

"Warlord Timur, we should not stay out here too long," the woman advised from the red mist. The daring figure did not turn back to her; he focused his gaze ahead, studying every inch of the wall. His long raven black hair that hung loosely but smoothly down his spine, gently fluttered in the wind, his face was cleanly shaven. All men had their faces shaved in his culture, beards were for the poor. Even when on a conquest, there was no place for beards for people of such high position. Not to mention he did not want to look like one of the northern savages of Mayhen and Hextheene but most importantly, decree demanded it. The warlords sharp red gaze lingered a moment longer.

"Should we not? They have become so flaccid. They would not notice an army of one hundred thousand men at their wall, if they did not knock on the door first," he said being callous. His golden gloves rattled the pommel of his curved blade; this Shield was not as mighty or as formidable as they had been told. The witch, Ilena of the Order, had greatly overestimated the strength of the country of Mayhen. Yet he had to give credit where credit was due, it may have been a land of great power not a couple of months ago, now with all its civil unrest and armies supposedly being used for personal gain within the country, it would stand no chance if someone decided to strike now. Hextheene was a place of pitiful false Lords and a false God, but they had unity, they all followed the same goal. If a snake strikes at its prey when its back is turned, that snake lives to fight another day.

"True or not, you have many matters to attend to. This is a task for scouting parties, not you," the woman warned. Timur sighed and turned on his heel to retreat back into the red mist. Ever since they had come to this place, this desolate land that used to be thriving with life, the mist had affected them. The true effect was not known yet, apart from the tint of their eyes. His own, hers and the others had all grown a red colour around the pupil. It was peculiar to say the least, but nothing that had hindered him. If it was damaging to their body, they would soon find out, yet for the moment, God willed their presence in the red mist of former Ghaul. Who was he to argue? The Warlord pulled himself up onto his steed and turned the rein towards the South.

"Justice of the Lord will bring these savage heathens their just deserves." The two figures trotted deeper into the mist, far from the sight of the Shield.

* * *

304

Chapter XXIX
The Dragon
~Ayla~

Life had begun to take a strange turn in the court of Heldon. While the new faces became regular faces, the anger of her father did not seem nearly as apparent. It was as if now that her sister Nyer had left the capital, everything had become calmer. The guardsmen still covered the keep at every turn. There must have been a thousand of them just in the keep these days. The garden had a guardsman at every pillar, wall, gate, and fence. The hallways had a guard at least every five steps and the courtyard was always lined with squads up to three deep and twenty across. The walls were completely covered with men and the gate to the castle itself had a whole garrison placed there, with sleeping arrangements prepared for them. Ayla did not know exactly how the city below fared these days, if all the guardsmen were here, then one could only assume the city was suffering. Not only were there guards watching every movement of every person in the castle, but also the bear, Shan, seemed to be lurking in the shadows or stalking her wherever she went. He was not trying to hide or be aggressive with his actions, he was simply always present. Their relationship was not like Nyer's and Titania's and was never likely to be. She was not able to sit there and talk with him or have him in her room at night - not that she would ever dream of such a thing. They had barely traded two words since he took his oath and swore to be her shield and protect her. The beast of a man was simply always there.

'I do not know if I feel safer or more at risk...' Ayla thought as she sat in the gardens of the castle. While she had become used to being alone in the gardens, it still caused her sadness to look over to the wall where Rayar used to perch himself, watching the world pass by with that laid back attitude of his. She missed Nymin jumping on her to surprise her, which usually ended up with them getting into a childish scrap. A couple of months ago she was preparing to marry arguably, one of the most handsome men she had ever heard of, a prince of the Holy land Hextheene. She was playing in the flowers, teasing Rayar, laughing with her family. But now she was alone, in a garden that used to bustle with life, colour and plentiful scents. Sadly it no longer held such glory. The plants were dried up, all brown and grey from lack of water and nurturing. She knelt down to the ground and cupped one of the flowers between her fingers.

'I know how you feel...' she thought as the flower crumbled in her soft hands.

"Should a princess be playing in the dirt, My Lady?" a voice spoke behind her. She squealed and leapt to her feet in shock, quickly brushing the dirt from her silver dress. Ayla turned to the man who seemed to think it appropriate to sneak up on a princess. It was a face she did not recognise, a young man only a bit older than she. His eyes were a deep blue and his hair red like fire. He had a soft jaw and a lopsided smirk on his lips, but it was not an insulting smirk at all, it was charming. "I did not mean to startle you," he said with that smirk plastered in place. The young man bowed gracefully and opened up his arms in an overly dramatic manner, his attire dark black with a long cloak attached to his chest by a golden brooch. The princess felt as if she might gawk and muddle her words, after all he was rather handsome, however after a moment to compose herself, and a chance to consider how Nyer would act, she erected herself to a noble stature and replied.

"A princess does as she pleases. Who are you to address someone of my position?" Ayla said as confidently as she could. The young man laughed and bowed his head once again.

"My deepest apologies, my Lady, I am Noble Lord Arthus Pendmir, Lord of Riveroth and Riveroth castle." She had heard of this place, it was the closest keep to Heldon, just to the south-west of the city. If she remembered correctly, both the Lord and Lady died after a period of illness some years ago and their young son had taken the title, unmarried, and ruled since he was a child. This man was surely the son. Ayla forced a smile.

"I see. You have come at the King's command, then?" she asked sheepishly. Calling Rumeo her father to others was not only improper, but the desire to do so had long descended from her mind.

"Indeed I have. The King calls, his Noble Lords answer. It is the way it is. I received two messages though, the other from your sister. As noble as her cause may be in her mind, we are sworn to the King and the country. I imagine all the Noble Lords will be arriving within the next few weeks. I have found I am first to arrive." The red headed young man scratched the back of his head as he looked around the garden. "I thought the gardens of Heldon were supposed to be beautiful and serene. This is... not quite what I expected. Not to mention, there are more guardsmen in the castle than my entire garrison. Is it that dire here?" he questioned wearing a curious expression. The princess followed his gaze, struggling to maintain her own stone expression; she could feel it switching to one of sadness.

"It is not what it used to be, Lord Pendmir. Ever since the horrible acts that were committed here... things have not been the same." She could feel the pain welling up inside her. To save face, she turned away from him and back to the dying flower bed.

"I see. Well one can hope that such matters are addressed in the coming gathering at the King's command. Though while I am here I am your humble servant, anything you request of me, I shall deliver." Ayla knew it was the position he held that required him to say such a thing, though she could not help but feel her heart lift. The young woman took a deep breath and turned back to look upon the red headed lord.

"If I told you to take me away from this place, you would do it?" she asked. From the expression upon his features, he was stunned and somewhat taken aback by her suggestion.

"I... My Lady that is not... something..." The words stumbled out of his mouth like a calf attempting to take its first steps. She stared at him, with a heavy heart slipping past her sleeve, and studied his reaction. As Ayla expected, it was a formality and nothing more.

"Do not say things you do not mean, Lord Pendmir. Though, I was just testing you," the princess lied. In the corner of her eye, in the far distance of the garden, the brute Shan, her newly appointed sworn protector, was watching as he always did. Cross-armed and leaning against the keep wall, watching. Arthus sighed and rubbed his hand over his forehead, as he was clearly confused at the situation before him.

"Quite a request, my Lady. Though I must admit, my service is extended to all the Granlia Royal Family. Though as much as I would love to be a dashing hero and valiantly rescue a damsel in distress, I am not much for fighting. I fear I fall short in that area," the lord replied. Ayla thought this was partly in jest. A small smile slipped past her lips as she turned to walk along the garden, naturally motioning him to follow.

"I thought all Noble Lords were expected to be able to wield a blade efficiently, were you not trained in Riveroth Lord Pendmir?" she interrogated as the pair walked side by side through the formerly stunning garden. His long black cloak reached the grass beneath them at their feet; even the grass was not as green as it used to be. The brooch that clipped his cloak to his chest showed the emblem of Riveroth, a Golden Dragon.

'The Dragon that lives in the Golden Lake of Riveroth. Its spirit is passed down between Noble Lords for each generation. Charming as he is, he does not seem to have the fiery, strong spirit of any mythical dragon,' she thought as his character was scrutinised.

"Ah, I did not say I was not trained, I just do not like fighting at all. That is why I came here swiftly. I was hoping I would be able to perhaps advise the King against it. See a different path, perhaps one of words. I have never taken part in a war like many of the other Noble Lords. Their stories and the tales of the people under my rule inclined me to seek an alternative solution." The princess could not help but let laughter escape at his words. While she knew she was considered naive by many that statement was on a whole different spectrum of naivety.

"The way fa... the way the King is now, you would be lucky to even be given a private audience let alone convince him of anything other than his passion for revenge. A passion I never knew he had..." she teased.

"Never say never. Our history was not only built through war, it was built through words as well," he retorted. Unconvinced, she looked his way and gave a light shake of her head.

"You have not been in the capital until today. You do not know what I have witnessed these past months. How insanity has taken over where reason used to rule." As much as she disdained her sister for leaving her in the capital alone, trying to copy how she would speak and act, felt like the more intelligent course of action. Without her family and friends to protect and guide her, acting like the spoilt girl she was would get her nowhere.

"True, I have not. I can always try my best. That is what my father taught me. Even though you may fail, always try your best. Not as fancy as some of the lessons I bet you were taught, but we were not a particularly fancy family." The smirk on his lips had returned as he seemed to tease her back. Well, it seemed like teasing. Ayla stopped in her stride wearing a deep frown which was now focused on the lord.

"Are you mocking me, Lord Pendmir?" That composure was slowly slipping away again. The lord's hands rose defensively but she could tell he was struggling not to laugh.

, no, no. Not at all! I would never risk my own head to a princess. I do not think my handsome face would sit ⌐ on a spike. I prefer it comfortably on my shoulders, My ⌐ady." Ayla stared at him for a moment with a glare that could melt ice, until finally she rolled her eyes and sighed.

"Well, regardless. I wish you luck in your attempt to speak to the King with your idea of words over war. I am *sure* he will listen intently and take all words into consideration." Another lord in a sea of lords, who thought their idea, was the best idea. With all his looks and charm he was the same. Maybe he really wished to be different but after all that had happened, trusting anyone else could have dire consequences.

"Arthus, by the way. I do not mind if you call me Arthus," the lord slipped in. Ayla cocked her head to the side curiously.

"That would not be proper..." the princess replied. Arthus laughed as a hand ran through his red hair.

"I do not see why we must always be proper, My Lady. Though if I am to call you Ayla, I would likely only do it in private. I doubt many would take kindly to me being so familiar with you," he added. Ayla's cheeks quickly warmed, that smirk and those eyes staring into her. There was a boyish charm about this young man, even when she was attempting to push him away and force herself to think badly of him, there was still something there that almost made her revert into a young girl. She had fought it the whole conversation but whatever it was about this lord, it sent pleasant shivers across her skin and it was getting harder to fight.

"What makes you think I would ever see you in private, Lord Pendmir?" As much as she wanted to call him Arthus, she could not show her weakness. Not yet. Awkwardly Arthus scratched once more. The young lord appeared embarrassed by his forward behaviour, as he should.

"I did not mean to presume you would. Perhaps, I just hoped it." The princess could feel her cheeks blushing even more so. That was too far. To hide her face she turned on her heel and crossed her arms tightly under her breasts.

"Well, you may continue to hope as you wish, but that is all it is, hope, nothing more." Did that even make sense? she wondered.

"All a man can do is hope, My Lady. I did not mean to ruin your day in the garden. Next time we speak, I hope you will not hold this against me." After he spoke she could hear footsteps moving away from her. There was some internal debate flashing through her mind until finally the side of compassion was victorious and she turned back around.

"Wait!" Ayla called out, perhaps slightly too loudly as many guardsmen quickly looked over with concern. The princess covered her mouth as if that would redraw the yelp and shook her head to the guards hoping they would not think to come over. Luckily they did not. Nor did Arthus, the young lord stood motionless watching her with a crooked brow, waiting to see why he was commanded to halt.

"My Lady?" he asked politely.

"I do not mind if you call me Ayla... and... I do hope we speak again, privately is fine. If you do not leave soon, I mean, I am not asking you to stay... I am just... you are the first person in a while who talks... genuinely. Honestly." Now that definitely did not make sense. She could tell by his expression how amusing he found her little outburst, which agitated her even more.

"I understand, Ayla. I will ensure I remain here for as long as you wish it. I am at your service, am I not?" The lord offered a low bow and then turned back towards the doorway to the keep. Part of her did want him to stay in the garden with her; company was something she had missed. Someone nice to speak to, someone who cared about what she actually had to say. Nyer did not truly care about her words, she only saw her younger sister as a love struck child. Nymin was too immature, perhaps she saw Nymin the same way Nyer saw her. It was Rayar who always listened, always cared and always looked out for her. While Arthus and Rayar seemed worlds apart as people, they had something in common, they were good men. Well, she had argued with herself throughout their meeting, if

311

.s true or not. Perhaps sometimes going with her
.ts was the right course of action.

Thank you Arthus," she muttered to herself before she
.umped back onto the nearest stone-bench. For a brief time,
her worries and sadness had been lifted and once the cause of
that uplifting had disappeared, the feeling of doubt and pain
returned. Was it possible Arthus could talk her father around?
Maybe this all could end with words instead of war. A foolish
dream for a foolish girl.

'Mother... Please wake up,' passed through the young
princess's mind as she leaned forward on the bench and
covered her eyes as they grew increasingly tearful.

* * *

Chapter XXX
Honour Above All
~Rayar~

Leaving the terrible events in that town of fanatics was a good feeling. It was a pleasure to leave yet to his disgust, the road itself did not hold sights of any greater merit. Rayar never pulled down his hood, as it helped shield his eyes from the sights above them along the dirt road towards the bridge to the north and to Oldome. Shania had done the same, her hood keeping the majority of her face covered so her eyes needn't rise. Hinsani on the other hand, was unfazed by the atrocities committed here in Hextheene.

'This place... this realm is devoid of all sense,' the prince thought as he made the mistake of glancing upwards. Stands stood erect along the sides of the roads. Stand after stand with a body strung by the neck and swinging in the wind. Each had a sign over their chests to explain in brief their crime for being hung, for all to witness. Traitor. Witch. Thief. Murderer. This was civil justice, not the King's justice. The smell was horrifying and the images stayed within his mind, even when his emerald eyes refused to look upon such acts. Hinsani had explained to them both, once the first body was seen by the three friends, that due to the soldiers all off fighting or preparing to fight in the south, that the people here were barely ruled. The cities and castles were well maintained and cared for but the common men and women were forced to fend for themselves. Sometimes that fending led to unspeakable acts like those they witnessed. Rayar could not imagine a King accepting such lawlessness in their lands, a King should be for

the people, to protect them and support them. It was as if everyone in Hextheene had been forgotten and left to rot in the streets, as if they served no purpose to Braska Hextor's war on Southrous, and on magic. Shania kept close to his side, as they walked along the road.

"I wanted to ask before..." the druidae said hidden under her hood. The prince glanced to the side to give her as much of his attention as possible without making the mistake of catching a glimpse of the corpses around them. "... You never said anything to Quale about that dream you had. I wondered why?" she asked. It was a reasonable question.

"I did not think it was important. A nightmare is a nightmare. It was nothing compared to what I am seeing here, in this realm, and I am sure I am wide awake for this," Rayar replied. Shania did not seem convinced.

"Dreams aren't always dreams, you know. I've seen things in my dreams before. I saw the sphere around the neck of a golden haired boy. That turned out to be true, didn't it?" Rayar stopped mid stride in shock. She had seen him in a dream? And only just mentioned it? Above and Below, what was this woman trying to do to him?

"Why did you not say anything before?!" he gasped out. Hinsani, who had been leading the group stopped and turned to see what was causing the commotion behind him, though he did not seem surprised at the pair locking horns once again. Shania rolled her eyes at his childish reaction.

"Does it matter now? I just found it interesting is all. No need to get all emotional about it," the girl teased. Just the other day she had been almost in tears and in full rage in the inn room and now she was telling him not to get emotional. Rayar came to the conclusion at this very point in time, he would never understand women. They were impossible. "But you're right, it's probably not important. I get dreams like that occasionally due to what I am. You're just a regular man. A prince, yes, sounds lovely, but just a man." The insult was not particularly full of malice, more like an unintended jab at the fact he was indeed a man. Rayar could only shake his head and

314

dismiss the whole conversation and continue to walk alongside the druidae.

"Is there anything else about me you have kept to yourself?" he asked. Shania shrugged her shoulders.

"It's not all about you, Rayar." She continued to tease. Perhaps the fact they were walking under a line of corpses was inclining her to tease him, as a distraction. Whatever her aim, it was aggravating to say the least.

"I suppose it is all about you, then?" the prince attempted to give as good as he got but before she had a chance to reply, a loud screech echoed above them. It was Shania who reacted first upon hearing the screech and drew her sword in an instant. Hinsani, who had noticed her reaction, followed her lead and in fluid motion, Galad was released from its sheath. The Royal Blade stood in his Blade Dancing form, the Lion stalks, his dark eyes studying the trees around them. Rayar was not far behind to take his own blade into his hand, then pressed his back to Shania's own back, to cover her rear should she need it.

'What's going on? Did Jac see something?' he thought to himself while flicking his eyes around the tree lines. Something was indeed out there watching them and luckily the druidae's hawk had given them fair warning.

"I see them," Hinsani said as he began to stalk closer to Rayar and Shania, eyes directly focused on the trees ahead. Figures moved in the shadows of the leaves, revealing their position. Whoever was watching them realised their game was up.

"Ain't no element of surprise now, eh?" an unknown voice sounded from within the foliage. From its depths, five men revealed themselves. They were all dressed in orange leather and chain with swords at their hips, while two of them held crossbows with bolts ready to release. With the emblems of Hextheene upon their breast, they must have been soldiers. Three of them blocked the road ahead, with one crossbow, while the other two and the second crossbow blocked the retreat. Hinsani focused on the three while Shania turned her attention to the pair behind the group. Rayar felt a bit lost, not sure where to focus his attention. Knowing Hinsani, he would not need any assistance; even so he shifted his attention between the two ambushing parties. He prepared himself to leap to the druidae's side if she needed it. In the corner of his eye he could not help but notice a small stone in Shania's spare hand while the other gripped her sword.

"What is it you want?" Rayar asked towards the one who had spoken, assuming he was the leader of this little brigade. The soldier spat to the side and sniffed loudly as if his nose and throat were blocked.

"Sorry 'bout that. Bloody cold. Now, just put down your weapons. Ain't no need for anything silly." Both the soldiers wielding crossbows aimed towards Hinsani; it was him they feared most by the looks of it. Clearly they did not know what Shania was capable of.

"I think not," Hinsani stated firmly. There was a moment of silence as the situation grew more and more tense. The crossbowmen were locked on their targets and the rest of the soldiers looked like they were ready to pounce. They were cocky, clearly, they had the three travellers surrounded with projectiles and they outnumbered their quarry. Any person watching would place their bets on the Hextheene troops. That would be a poor bet. Finally the loudest of the soldiers sighed and drew his sword, followed by the remaining soldiers.

"Bring the golden haired brat, kill the other two!" He barked out his order. The battle commenced. For anyone else, those two bolts would have slain them instantly leaving Rayar to fend for himself. Hinsani's speed was too quick for one crossbowman and before he knew it, the Royal Blade was upon him. Hinsani struck his sword upwards, knocking the crossbow off its sight, sending the bolt whistling into the air. The soldier did not even have the chance to be shocked at the impressive feat, before the blade came home from its first strike and sliced down his stomach. On the other side of the group, Shania whipped the stone in her hand across her sword causing a spark to ignite. That was all she needed. The flames exploded from her sword and twirled around her wrist before encasing the other crossbowman in a blaze. He screamed in pain as he went up in flames and collapsed into the dirt, crying words that no person could understand or would ever to hear. The soldier who beside the flaming man fell back in fear, his sword dropped from his hands and he began crawling in retreat along the dirt road watching his friend swallowed by the flames. Shania did not need his help. He shot a look back to Hinsani, who was now engaging the two soldiers in a dance of swords. Rayar could not stand idly by. Even though the Royal Blade did not need his assistance, he assisted regardless. The prince propelled himself forwards and moved to his protector's side, catching one of the swords with his own.

"Bloody brat!" the soldier growled as their swords clashed, metal ringing on metal.

'Remember what Hinsani has taught me. Remember what Shania had told me. Do not give in to fear.' The Hextheene soldier thrust his sword towards the prince's gut, aiming to pierce his stomach. The strike reminded him of a much less skilled attack Hinsani had used on him back in Heldon, The Wolf Gnarls. He had no time to defend himself from the second strike the Royal Blade had used during that lesson. Swooping of the Hawk, Hinsani had shown him this attack as the counter towards the first. Rayar did his best to remember the lesson. He skidded to the side to narrowly avoid the piercing sword and then swung downwards twice. The first hit the soldier's sword; the force of the strike caused the soldier's grip to loosen, the long sword in his grasp being hindered. The second strike aimed for the hand guard and the hand itself. Due to the stunning first attack he had launched as a counter, the soldier could not regain his defence and the blade skidded up the length of the sword and sliced him across the hand. The soldier roared out in pain as he dropped his weapon and gripped his bleeding hand. It had worked. It had actually worked. He had disarmed his enemy as quickly as the fight had begun. He had been in such a focused state of mind, he had not had time to think, or feel or worry about the outcome. Swords were drawn, the fight commenced. The fight was over.

317

'We won...?' Rayar quickly glanced over to his two companions to see their progress. Shania had thrust her sword through the begging soldier's chest as he had pleaded for mercy while Hinsani had dispatched his last foe and now his eyes stared in awe at the druidae. It was the first time Hinsani had seen her use the power she claimed to wield. It was a surprise to see Hinsani in such a state of astonishment, his usual stone face shattered. Shania used the flames as if they were a part of her, fierce and vengeful.

"Above and Below..." the Royal Blade mumbled under his breath.

"All done?" Shania asked as she cleaned her sword on the leather of the fallen foe. As quickly as the fight had begun, it was over. Five men had attacked, and one remained alive; the man Rayar had decided to challenge in battle. The soldier knelt in the dirt road with blood pulsating from the wound on his sword hand. He growled in pain, and continued to moan and groan until he looked up and saw that he was the only one left. Then his demeanour changed dramatically.

"Please, I beg you. It was a mistake, I swear it. 'ave mercy!" the soldier pleaded. The prince blinked in surprise. This was something he did not think about at all, once the fight was won - what came next? His one edged blade still sat gripped tightly in his hand with the tip of the sword aimed at the soldier's throat. Could he do it? Finish off an unarmed man? No, he could not. He was not like them, he was not a killer. Hinsani appeared next to him with a knife in his hand now; Galad was safely home in its sheath. He pushed the knife up against the wounded soldier's throat.

"What was your purpose?" the raven haired man demanded. His expression cold and unforgiving, back to what Rayar was used to. Shania had joined them as well, the charred body still smoking on the road. Thoughts passed through his head he could never say to her; the way she killed that man was brutal. Awful. Those flames truly did reveal her rage.

"Wait, wait, wait!" the soldier gurgled as the cold metal touched his flesh. "We're just scouts, we were told to watch you! Just watch you!" he admitted. Shania cocked a brow.

"That was watching?" Shania asked sarcastically. The soldiers breath became more and more uncontrolled as the fear of what might be about to happen to him began to set in.

"I'm sorry! We thought we could... we made a mistake, I beg you. Don't kill me, please!" Hinsani pressed the knife even closer to his throat.

"Why did you attack? Answer now and have a quick death." Fearful eyes flashed between all three and finally rested on Rayar.

"We heard who he is, a prince of Mayhen. We thought... we thought we could capture him... give him to the King." The terrified man struggled to let those words out. He must have known full well that his actions would lead to his death at this point, though part of Rayar was still against this. It was not right. The soldier lost but lived; they could not kill an unarmed man who sat there begging. There was no honour in this. Hinsani frowned heavily, looking to his prince with concern.

"Your presence is known in Hextheene, we should disappear. Who knows how many more are out looking for you," the protector wisely suggested. "We cannot let this one talk either. Pray to The Above, nameless soldier. You will be there soon." Before the sharp blade could slice through flesh, Rayar placed a hand on Hinsani's shoulder.

"Stop," he simply commanded. The Royal Blade sighed; he must have known exactly what Rayar was thinking.

"If we let him live, the chance he will speak to others in the area is too high. It is a risk we cannot take." Hinsani had a good point, it was a risk but to Rayar keeping your honour was worth the risk.

"We are not about to kill a man who cannot fight back at all. I will not allow it. We will tie him up in the forest. By the time someone finds him, we will be long gone. It is the right thing to do," the prince ordered.

"Now is not the time to consider right and wrong, it is the time to focus on the best way to survive. I can assure you, this is not it," Hinsani insisted. As much sense as the swordsman made, it still weighed heavily on his heart. He refused to be as callous and merciless as those they had already seen, as the people who burnt the young girl or the people who had executed all these men and women they had seen along the road. They were from Mayhen, a place of honour and justice, not butchery.

"I understand your concern but I will not waver." Rayar stood strong and regal. The principles he had been taught back home now showed their colours. It was not a usual occurrence and something quite out of character, but he had made up his mind and would not be deterred from his decision. His protector had no choice but to obey and slowly pulled the knife away from the crying man's throat. Shania had been watching, arms crossed under her chest without saying much. She probably had the same concerns as Hinsani.

"Thank you, my lord, thank you. I promise I won't say anything, thank you!" Begrudgingly Hinsani dragged the man into the forest away from the remaining pair and saw to his binds. Rayar let out a sigh of relief that his command had been followed. Part of him expected Hinsani to kill the man regardless of what he said. While it may have been the wiser action, it was not the right action.

"You sure about that?" the druidae questioned. Her cockiness once again was shining through. The bodies hanging in the stands around them had been ignored. The adrenaline of the fight had forced him to forget yet once the event had settled; the reminder of the corpses swaying in the trees above them brought him back down to the stark reality.

"We are not like the people who did this." Rayar motioned to the corpses around them, his brow furrowed and tone direct. He would hold his ground on this decision. "The man was a fool but he lost, we are not about to kill someone who can barely stand from fear, let alone not wield a sword. We are better than that." Shania nodded slowly as she seemed to take in his words. He half expected her to fight him further on his decision however she was surprisingly quite accepting.

"I trust you. We will need to move quickly, no more hanging around in towns. We will get some horses in the city by the bridge and then move as quickly as possible. I don't want this coming back to bite us Rayar," she stated simply. The young woman offered him a smile and looked over to the returning swordsman. Hinsani stomped back to them through the tree line while dusting off his hands.

"He is bound. I did not have much for rope so I was forced to break one of his legs as I could only bind his hands with what he already had on him. Gagged as well, would not want him calling out once we have left." Hinsani was as resourceful as always. Well he stopped him from killing the man, breaking his leg to ensure they had a safer trip would have to slide for the moment. Hinsani gave him one last stony look and questioned if he was sure that this was the right course of action.

"It is. We will be in the wind before anyone can find him." Rayar cemented his decision. Without wasting any more time, the three travellers pushed forward at a quicker pace towards the nearby coastal city and the bridge. As they quickly strode down the long dirt road, Rayar glanced back down the path they had come, giving one last glance of respect to the bodies of the fallen attackers scattered on the road. Those men lay there, bloody and burnt and completely forgotten. Their deaths were by their own making and to see men die again and again, brought a feeling of numbness, as if he was less traumatised by it. Was he getting used to seeing people die in front of him? Something he did not wish to consider.

'It was the right thing... it had to have been. As bad, as awful as these people here can be, I refuse to be like them. I refuse it through to my very soul. It was the honourable thing to do.' Even as he thought this, repeated it in his head, the doubt of this possible mistake seeped through the cracks of his mind. If this was the right thing to do, how could it go wrong?

* * *

Chapter XXXI
A Man's Fear
~Rayar~

The dirt roads which were filled with bodies of those deemed unfit for this world, grew scarcer, as the looming noise and huge pillared flames of the City of Northfreya came closer. Huge spires held bowls on the tower tops with raging flames bellowing smoke filling the sky above them. The forest Rayar, Shania and Hinsani had passed through had thinned, revealing fields and farmland. There was a general aura of comfort and safety, rather than the cruelty of the forests they had escaped. Hinsani had mentioned the city Northfreya was clustered with the rich and privileged, so their lives were considerably more pleasant, whilst the villages on the outskirts were forgotten. The city itself was surrounded by high walls and a broad moat, similar to castles in Mayhen. They could see a great length of the structure protecting the city. Gates were located all along the walls with bridges over the water, allowing entrance to all. In fact there only seemed to be one guardsman at each gate, two now and again, perhaps if they were feeling lonely. Yet common people passed freely without interruption, through all the gates. They had taken the most northern road along the coast, down the desolate forest pathways. The roads leading to the city from the south, were strong well-kept paths with inns along the way, houses and many, many people. In fact, this place vaguely reminded Rayar of Heldon.

"The City of Northfreya," Hinsani said as they briefly paused to look upon the magnificent sight.

"It looks... actually grand," Rayar replied as he stared in surprise. The Royal Blade nodded to him in agreement.

"Indeed. It is known for its trade. Due to it being so far north in Hextheene, it receives most its trade from the fertile lands in Oldome. Not to mention the naval trade from the far east." Rayar cocked a brow. Far east? What was to the east?

"Do you mean there is land further east than Hextheene?" he asked as he scratched his golden hair. Shania sighed and ruffled his hair as she strode past him.

"For a prince with, what I imagine, a good education, you really do say some stupid things sometimes," she taunted. Hinsani followed the druidae, as he continued to explain.

"It is where the art of Blade Dancing originated. It is not like it is here. Islands, lots of small islands, all governed by different lords, or whatever they call their leaders out there. They do not involve themselves much with mainlanders, like us, only to trade occasionally." Rayar started to recall what his protector spoke of. He remembered the Master Librarian Vayers mentioning something about the Eastern Islands when he was young. Some were savage, some were mad, some were full of crude tradesmen and some had not even discovered how to sail yet. They had mainly traded with Southrous and Brexxia, far south but very occasionally, they did trade with Hextheene, never Mayhen though. They had always steered clear of Mayhen. Embarrassed, the prince followed after his two companions, deciding it was best to avoid asking silly questions in future.

The huge city of Northfreya made Rayar feel like a lost child. The buildings were gigantic, towering above him in their grandeur. The keep in Heldon was taller mind you, but that was one majestic building in the centre of the city, all these buildings were simply spinning his mind as he gazed upwards. Even Shania seemed rather in awe at the spectacle. It was a nice change from the corpses in the trees they had recently passed under. Noble men and women strode down the streets conversing whilst others were drinking fine wine on the streets outside various establishments. Even the guardsmen dotted around the paved roads appeared relaxed, not patrolling or standing guard, but sitting around tables while perched on wooden boxes playing dice. The stores that stretched along the lengthy roads were bustling with people and activity, people cheering on their goods to grab the attention of any who passed. Fish, meat, cloth, jewellery, pottery, trinkets, wine, ale, dresses, paintings - anything he could think of was being sold in the stalls they passed. Except one particular thing, weapons. Nowhere had he looked, could he see a blacksmith, or weapon smith or anyone peddling steel. Rayar wanted to ask about it, but out of fear of asking something he should again have known, he decided to remain silent. The white paved roads led them to a large town square, with a central fountain filled with clear water spraying out from the middle. Around it, a minstrel group played their various instruments, dressed in elaborate clothing; multi coloured cloaks and puffy garbs. Their flat hats sat upon their heads, with feathers attached flowing alongside each elegant fluid dance they performed. This city felt worlds apart from the landscape and villages of Hextheene. It felt like an entirely different kingdom.

"This place is outstanding," Rayar muttered under his breath as his green gaze did not know where to linger the longest.

"Northfreya, from what I know, is almost like its own realm within Hextheene. The trade here is so vast, it supplies Hexhold and the rest of the kingdom in the agreement it remains free of war or oppression," Hinsani said as he too seemed rather taken aback by the cheer and joy that filled the very air they breathed. "This part of the Hextheene realm is governed by the Merigold Family. Cannot say I know much about them at all." After the Royal Blade explained his very limited knowledge concerning this part of the world, he motioned towards an inn across the white paved centre of the city, The Broody Braska.

"Come, we will head there and plan out our next move, perhaps get a good meal too. I think you need it Rayar," Hinsani commented as he gave the prince a once over. Rayar cocked a brow towards him questioningly.

"You do look a bit pale," Shania added as she placed a hand on his forehead. He had not realised he looked unwell, in fact he felt absolutely fine. Perhaps he was simply tired from the walk across the north of Hextheene. A warm meal would certainly not be turned down.

"Fine folk of Northfreya, listen to my words!" a loud voice boomed from near the fountain. A large, round figure with what looked like numerous chins covering his neck, stood on a wooden box to announce to all present. In one of his chunky hands he held a long parchment that almost stretched the length of his entire body. "I bring to you, fine folk of Northfreya, the news of the day!" The companions looked between each other, as if to question if they should wait and listen.

"There could be something about Mayhen. It is worth taking a moment," Rayar stated as he turned and joined the crowd forming around the town announcer. Shania and Hinsani were close to behind him.

"More raids from the devilish Southrous bandits plague the southern border of Hextheene! Yet fear not! The gallant men of Hextheene continue to battle against those savage dogs and protect the people in peril! To the brave soldiers of Hextheene!" The large man cheered followed by the crowd cheering in unison. Rayar had not been prepared for the sudden cheer from the people around him and awkwardly cheered a tad too late; this caused several folk next to him to give the prince some puzzled glances. Rayar tried to chuckle off his embarrassment and pulled his hood slightly further over his face avoiding the odd looks. The announcer continued to preach.

"In other news! Our fine Lady Merigold has given birth to a beautiful baby boy! He has been named after his late father, Gerald Merigold! Born strong and beautiful, he will surely grow to be a hero of the people! To the health of the young

Gerald Merigold!" Again the cheers flowed from the crowd, this time Rayar was somewhat more prepared and cheered with them, he was just part of the crowd after all, not anyone special. After his outburst he turned back to Shania who had not been cheering, but staring at him with a blank expression.

"You're an idiot," the druidae whispered. Rayar blinked, confused, but he had no time to reply as the last announcement came.

"Lastly, this news is not as joyous! Trouble in Mayhen, the Black bear and his cubs do battle! The kingdom is on the brink of civil war! Who do the people side with, the King of the Bears or his righteous and ambitious cub!? Only time will tell!" The last announcement was not met with cheers; instead the people in the crowd began to mumble to each other. Whispers of what was occurring to the west filled the gathering; to them it was some other nation's mess they need not concern themselves with. To Rayar, it was his home in peril. The prince turned to his two companions.

"Civil war? What does he mean?" he asked. Shania shook her head and shrugged her shoulders, not being aware of anything that had happened there. It was not her home after all; he doubted she even cared about Kings and soldiers fighting. The druidae had her eyes on the larger picture after all.

"I can only imagine Princess Nyer is taking some sort of stand, if that is true information. If your father, the King, has become worse in his downward spiral, since I fled Heldon, then who knows how dire the situation in Mayhen has become." Hinsani may have said this in his matter of fact way, yet even he could not completely hide the concern in his eyes at the news. As stone as he could be, Mayhen was still the Royal Blade's home and the people there were still his people.

"This whole thing started with the attack in our home. The sooner we stop them, the sooner we can return home and hopefully put an end to it all," the golden haired prince said. They were close to the bridge now, they were close to the island of Oldome, and they were close to the Druidae Grove, of stories and songs. If they turned back now, everything they had travelled for would be for nought and any chance of making a difference quelled. They would have been forced to pick a side back home, he was sure of it. That was not an option for him, the only course he would accept would be stopping any more horrors befalling his people. The group slipped through the crowd and found their way to the inn Hinsani had suggested. Shania and Rayar found seats in the far corner of the inn's hall, whilst Hinsani spoke with the innkeeper about meals for the group. The inn was lavish, curtains every colour of a rainbow, draped from the ceiling. Banners hung across the walls in-between windows and the furniture was elaborately designed with patterns of animals, castles, people, nature, anything and everything, as if they told a story across their wooden structures.

"I'm surprised," Shania said as an off handed comment.

"What surprises you this time?" Rayar asked as he slumped in his chair.

"That you didn't say 'we must return to Mayhen at once, my family need me!'" Shania replied, as she mimicked his voice poorly, making it overly deep and dramatic in its execution. Well, he thought it was a poor imitation, though imitation was supposed to be the sincerest form of flattery.

"If I always try and run back home at any sign of danger, I have not grown at all. I can help my family, even if I am not with them." She offered him a smile and leaned across the table. As she closed the distance between them, he felt his cheeks warm.

"I'm impressed. The world isn't the most beautiful at times and you're pushing forward. I thought you would've broken ages ago. You've done well." Was that a compliment? It felt like a compliment as well as a cheap poke at his character. She had a habit of feeding with one hand and punishing with the other.

"Well, as long as you are impressed," Rayar joked. "And that impression was awful," he added. The druidae laughed softly into her hand.

"I thought it was spot on." Just then Hinsani joined them and passed each of them a hot meal. Chicken with boiled potatoes and bread. It was not the most amazing meal yet it would do. He half expected a place like this to have been overwhelmed with glorious types of food to offer their customers but then again they had sent Hinsani up to the counter, so it was more than likely he had selected the simplest thing.

"Eat up. We will not be staying long. We move after we have eaten." With that he began to munch loudly on his chicken. Hinsani had actually been a lot different from what the prince had expected. At Heldon he was like a statue, who trained him for battle and acted like nothing more than a puppet. Yet out here, the more they travelled together, the more his Royal Blade seemed human. Rayar passed a glance around them to ensure they were alone before more private matters were brokered on the table.

"So, the Bridge of Freedom. We can just walk across it? By the looks of it the guards here do not seem truly active and from what Quale said, people cross it every day. Should not be too difficult to just... walk over it," the prince put forward. Shania agreed.

"Quale hasn't left his home in a while, a long, long time but I think he's probably right. From how he described this city to me in the past, it seems pretty spot on. I never imagined it would be this harmonious." This is what Rayar had pictured the whole of Hextheene to be like, from what he had been told in his youth. The land of the Holy blood, wealth and pleasures. The war in the south did not even seem to worry these people here at all. He could only imagine what it was like on that southern border under constant threat of attack. He doubted it would be as flowery as Northfreya.

"I recommend we find horses first," Hinsani suggested. "We do not know how many soldiers or even common people are looking for you. Now, the only feature that gives you away is your golden hair. Keep your hood up to hide this trait and our risk of being noticed will lessen greatly." Rayar gave his hood a small tug absently to ensure it was still in place.

"Then it is settled. Eat, find horses, then cross the bridge. Where are we going to find horses? Did you bring enough Hex gold with you, Shania?" The druidae nodded and tapped the pouch on her hip. She had grabbed a pouch full, back in Quale's house. For all he knew that old fool could have stored thousands of pieces of gold over the years. The plan was set, within the next hour or two they would be crossing the Bridge of Freedom towards Oldome and from there - the Druidae Grove was within reach.

*

~Caskin~

"Sir! Sir!" a Hextheene soldier called out as he carried another of the same brand. The soldier supported his fellow man who winced in pain with every step. His leg had been badly broken and his hand bandaged from a severe cut across the length of it. The soldier had been severely beaten. It must have been quite the sight for two Hextheene soldiers to be stumbling through the city of Northfreya, in such a manner. Usually the soldiers, who passed through here, were either visiting or on official business with a captain or commander, much like himself. Caskin sat in the Hextheene Army Garrison, in the southern part of the city. It was fenced off from the rest of the city as Lady Merigold and her late husband were firmly against weapons, soldiers and war in general. The only reason the Great King Braska had let them have this meaningless way of life, was due to the fact they funded his own cause so significantly. The stay in Harringmore castle had been considerably friendlier for the knights and their men; here they were considered butchering barbarians and shunned to the darkest corner of the city.

"I'm hung over and someone is being very loud," Sir Oathsworth barked as he lay on a large couch beside a dying fire. They had drunk a fair amount of ale the night before; it had actually grown quite out of hand. While waiting for word from the scout squads tracking their targets, there was little to pass the time. Caskin waved Oathsworth aside and told him to silence himself. This was only retorted with a grumble. The man was too hung over to argue. The rest of the knights that he had selected were also present, all sitting around a table eating a very late breakfast.

"Report," Caskin demanded firmly. All attention was on the two exhausted soldiers. The wounded one, who had clearly been in either a terrible riding accident or soundly defeated in a fight, spoke first.

"Commander-at-Arms Caskin Camaron. I 'ave a report on the prince of Mayhen's movements." Caskin cocked a brow at him.

"Messages via direct pigeon, is the method of relaying information to avoid being seen. You come charging into the city? This better be good." His voice was deep, authoritative and unsympathetic. In the back of his mind he knew exactly where this was going to go.

"Sir, me and my squad attempted to apprehend the prince and his two companions but... bloody Above, they were skilled. I was defeated by a monster with a sword." Caskin pushed himself to his feet, a hand on the pommel of his bastard sword.

"Hinsani Tannaroth?" The soldier nodded frantically.

"Aye, Sir. I almost had him, but I was hit in the back by the prince, sneaky bastard." Caskin nodded and began to pace around the wounded soldier. He could feel his temper rising.

"Your squad did not help you in the fight?" one of the knights asked from his position in his seat. It was the elder Osmear Lorinstead. The soldier was becoming increasingly nervous as he flicked his eyes between the pacing Caskin, and the other knights.

"They were all killed Sir! I had this boy sir," the trembling soldier motioned to the young scout beside him. "I had him remain on the side to watch. They tied me up and left me for dead, if it weren't for this boy 'ere. We came as fast as we could. They're heading straight 'ere, straight to this city Sir!" The older knight nodded a few times and raised his hand to Caskin, signalling he had no further questions. The Commander-at-Arms retook the reins of conversation.

"How was your squad killed? Scouts usually if engaging an enemy, tend to ambush, no?" the blonde haired knight asked as he finally fixed his position in front of the wavering soldier.

"There were a witch, sir, a bloody real witch! The woman they're with, she looks like nothing. Just a girl. They all do those witches. She used fire, sir! Fire to burn my men, she burnt them all!" The room fell silent. Even Sir Oathsworth had removed the cold towel from his forehead and looked over in shock; the ox of the man was rarely surprised. Caskin's brow was heavy, heavier than his armour or his sword.

"A witch... used fire?" His blue eyes flicked over to the young boy, a soldier of course but a boy nonetheless. "Is this true?" The young boy choked on his own words and bowed his head in submission.

"Y-yes... sir. Fire sir. From her hands..." A witch, a real witch. Not these stupid peasants, burning girls they do not favour. They were claiming a witch was with the prince. This could not be true, could it? Perhaps they were all simply defeated in combat and in their embarrassment, they blamed it on magic. It was a tragic state of affairs.

"And you say they are here, in the city, now?" Caskin asked.

"Yes sir! They came in just before we did, after they left me for dead. My man here cut me free and we followed them to the city. We did what we did to serve the King, Sir. Long live King Braska Hextor II!" He saluted and winced in pain as he did so, for using his damaged hand, like a fool. Upon hearing they were in the city, Sir Oathsworth was on his feet, hungover or not, and grabbed his giant war-hammer which was propped up on the wall.

"If they are here, let's go!" The bull snapped. Caskin raised a hand towards him; they needed to wait a moment longer.

"Soldier, you do recall your orders, do you not?" the commander asked. The soldier flashed his eyes around in terror, looking for anyone to support him. The room was silent but for the racing beat of his heart and the cold glare from Caskin screaming a thousand words. "Well?"

"I do Sir, I do. To watch and report," he finally answered.

"To *watch*... and *report*." Mercilessly, Caskin drew a dagger from under his long white cloak and thrust it straight into the soldiers gut. The soldier gasped for air and clawed at the commander's chest plate, blood curdling from his newly acquired wound. "You failed in your objective and betrayed your King. I do not need traitors in my ranks. Now watch as you bleed out, worm." Caskin taunted the man in his final moments of life. The body dropped to his knees as he tried to hold the puncture in his stomach, but to no avail. He dropped lifelessly at the commander's feet. The room was still silent as they watched the man die, the veteran soldiers unfazed by the act of their commander, all bar one, the youth under the fallen scout's command. The boy watched in horror as he must have assumed the knife would find his stomach next.

"You watched, and you reported. You served your King. Now you will report to the King. Return to Ganon and Hexhold. Tell the King of what has occurred. Pray he gives you the same mercy I have. Before that, describe to the men who they are looking for. I do not want them to slip from our grasp now we have them within reach." With that Caskin tossed the knife to his former squire Sir Lancel Nash, whom awkwardly caught it trying not to lose a finger. The orders were given.

"Form the men up. If they are in the city we find them. We kill Hinsani Tannaroth and this supposed witch and take the prince to our King. Failure is not an option." The command echoed round the room as the knight's leapt to their feet as did the soldiers who had joined them for their late breakfast. Out of the corner of the room, the quietest of the knights spoke in his quivering tone.

"Uh... Commander-at-Arms. Sir Oathsworth is gone..." Donnel Jennin mumbled. Caskin frowned towards him then shot his eyes around the garrison hall.

'That sneaky... surprisingly sneaky for his size, bloody fool,' he thought. Sir Oathsworth wanted the prize of killing the famous swordsman, Hinsani, before anyone else had the chance to challenge him. He took one long deep breath and focused on their objective; dealing with Oathsworth could come later. To think he personally wanted that man in his squad, more than anyone else, for his fighting ability. He had already turned out to be a liability.

"Matters not. Knights, move out." The Hextheene force began their move into the city. Prince Rayar was here, Hinsani Tannaroth was here, and now supposedly a witch who could use fire, was here. The prize for such a capture would be substantial.

* * *

Chapter XXXII
The Hawk and the Bull
~Rayar~

Merchants filled the streets, shouting out to advertise their wares to the people passing by. Rayar actually found himself being drawn to some of the stands, peaked by their exotic attraction. One of the clothing stands in particular, had a long gold and black coat, it was mostly black though the sleeves, collar and trim all had golden embroidery, such craftsmanship glistened in his emerald eyes. While the clothes he had been gifted by Lord Tismiar Loysse were indeed fine, he had been in the same clothes for so long, the desire for something new was dwelling in the back of his mind. He was fully aware it was not dire and that there were much more important matters at stake, but the itch in the back of his head was there, and he simply wanted to scratch it. The downside of growing up in royalty, it seemed.

"Keep up!" Shania called back to him as they moved at a brisk pace, through the wide and bustling white paved streets. The crowds were so dense; it was difficult to even see where his two companions were going. He occasionally caught a glimpse of Shania's cloak or the scabbard of Hinsani's sword through the crowd.

'Above and Below, why are they rushing? It is not like we need to sneak over the bridge.' Rayar thought to himself as he did his best to keep up with the pair ahead. The herd of people

began to thin out a little, though not enough to allow him to avoid bumping straight into someone.

"Watch it!" a loud voice roared out as Rayar was knocked right to the floor with a loud thump. The prince groaned and rubbed his lower back in pain.

"I apologise," the prince mumbled as his emerald eyes ran up the form. The man he had collided with was huge, built like a bull. He wore thick armour with a large war-hammer in his hand. It was actually quite the surprise to see someone so heavily armoured and aggressive in this harmonious city. As he looked up from his position on the ground, the pair briefly locked eyes. He could feel strands of his golden hair sliding down his forehead from under his hood and quickly pushed them back into hiding. The man had not been gifted with such locks at least not at this stage of his life, as his receding hair betrayed his age.

The large man simply grumbled at him and carried forward on his war path through the crowd of people. Rayar watched the armoured man's departure until Shania appeared in front of him.

"You're an idiot," she stated, once again, before helping him back to his feet.

"You are getting into the habit of saying that," he replied. The druidae threw a laugh his way and turned to continue on in pursuit of the impatient Hinsani.

"You keep doing things that cause me to say it, sadly." After a few moments the pair caught up with the Royal Blade and they continued on towards the Bridge of Freedom. Rayar passed one last look over his shoulder and the sight caused a sinking feeling to swell in his stomach. The balding man encased in armour was no longer charging through the crowd, he had stopped in his tracks and was looking their way. The distance between them was so great he could not truly see the features on the face of the man, yet he could picture a toothy grin plastered on his face. For his own sanity he focused on the path ahead, wishing he had never turned his head. His companions continued forward, the crowd of people becoming

336

less of a group and more of a stream as they were clearly travellers between Hextheene going across the bridge of Oldome. They were certainly heading in the right direction.

"Cannot be far now," Hinsani said from the head of the pack. The glamorous buildings around them had lost their height and colour, with dozens of dark alley-ways at every turn. The nobility of the town centre seemed to have faded away and the sights became more akin to what he had seen on their travels in Hextheene. Beggars were curled up in the streets, the paved road was turning into a rotting brown dirt track and the number of soldiers grew fewer. They had clearly wandered into poorer side of the city. Every city, town and keep had them. Merchants and traders, or even just travellers, still followed the road ignoring the beggars that pleaded on the sides of the streets for a coin or two. Perhaps the closer you got to the actual bridge, the more the poverty festered.

'It is a sad sight, but beggars are everywhere you go... even in Heldon,' Rayar thought to himself as he cast his eyes from homeless man to homeless man. He also could not help but notice the majority of them, if not all, were men. Their advance was halted with a skid, as a squad of Hextheene soldiers stood beside the path, checking all who passed. Possibly seven or eight armoured men stood before them. Too many to fight whilst being so crowded by common people, who were at risk of being injured should Shania choose to use her peculiar power. One of the soldiers in particular appeared to notice them and mumbled something to his fellows. They all traded looks between themselves, while Rayar, Shania and Hinsani did the same.

"Walk on, do not act suspicious," Hinsani commanded as he continued to walk at a much slower pace. All three of them did their best to become ghosts within the crowd marching towards the Bridge of Freedom. One of the Hextheene soldiers kept his eyes on them as they passed; he appeared unsure if he should stop them or not. Rayar was ready at any moment to break into a sprint, should they need to flee. Yet there was no need for concern. The three passed the soldiers without

337

disruption. Although *one* in particular seemed interested in them, the rest had paid no heed.

"We should pick up the pace," Hinsani advised, as he took the lead once more. It was possible the soldiers were looking for them; it was also possible they were just following routines and patrols, checking those who were intending to pass over the bridge. These were the first soldiers they had seen who had taken any notice of the people in the city and their activities. The soldiers they had seen earlier in the wealthier part of the city, appeared as laid back as the city's common people. The Royal Blade had explained that from speaking with the innkeeper, he had learnt of a stable near the bridge itself, with cheaper horses for purchasing. Though their breed was not as fine and their pace not as brisk, these horses would be hardy enough to get them across the bridge and further into Oldome. None of them knew, not even Hinsani, what would welcome them on the other side. Shania had only heard stories from Quale and had shared a few in their travelling here, but nothing that would have prepared them for what the land was like.

Once again the distance between the prince and the others began to grow, as the roads narrowed and the streets were filled with wagons of merchants passing through the city.

'Above and Below, slow down!' the prince thought to himself. It was not that he was so slow he could not keep up with them; Hinsani's graceful step allowed him to dart around people without them even realising he was there, whilst Shania was so much smaller, she could slip through gaps in the crowds where he would have struggled to fit. Suddenly his path was cut off. A large wagon pulled in front of his swift jog and blocked the way that his two companions had proceeded on.

"Of course," Rayar muttered to himself as he moved to go around the wagon. Just as he turned the corner, he was faced with more Hextheene soldiers, as they had been following the wagon. They traded glances; five of them in fact, traded glances with him. He was taller than all of them, though they were considerably broader, older and looked stronger.

338

"In a rush, boy?" one of them asked as he stepped back to allow Rayar to pass them. The prince swallowed, grateful they had given way to him, yet there was still a tingle on the back of his neck. Hinsani and Shania had carried on, likely not aware he had fallen behind.

"Th-thank you." The prince bowed his head respectfully. He had to simply do the smart thing, just carry on walking without giving them a second look. Just as Rayar took his first step, a hand whipped across his hood and knocked the cloth down to his shoulders, revealing his messy golden hair. His fringe hung loosely over one of his eyes. After all this travelling around, it had grown since he left Heldon, and was now much harder to maintain. His green eyes flickered over to the guards. They stared at him, wide eyed in surprise as the prince did the same to them. They stood there for a moment staring at each other before finally one the soldiers barked at him.

"I knew it! It's him! Grab him!" As if he was covered in a slippery substance the prince narrowly avoided being tackled and grabbed by the soldiers, his cloak being torn from his shoulders in the process.

"Don't let him get away!" another soldier yelled.

'Bloody, bloody, bloody, bloody!' rolled through his mind as he turned heel and fled. The young prince sprinted as quickly as his long legs would carry him down the streets of Northfreya, no longer caring about being inconspicuous. He was barging into people, pushing them out of the way when he could not slip around them, of course apologising to them as he did. Rayar glanced over his shoulder to see if he had created some distance between him and the soldiers of Hextheene.

"Above and Below!" he yelped out as they were just behind him, all five of them charging like crazed wild dogs chasing their lonely meal. The adrenaline pulsed through his veins, his heart pounding against his chest. He had no one to rely on now, it was just him. He had to run, and keep running. How in the Above's name did they know it was him? Was his hair colour really that rare? Or did they have some other information?

Whatever it was, they had their sights on him, a deer in the sights of a crossbow and they were not about to let him slip away easily. The prince turned down an alley-way, barely avoiding skidding over in his haste. Down his chosen escape route, barrels of fish and other meats were lined up along the wall to his right. As quickly as he could, he tipped over one of the barrels of fish behind him, letting the slippery meat slide all over the paved floor. He did not wait to see its effect as he turned the corner, almost toppling over in his awkward run. From the other side of the alley, he could hear several loud clashes, curses and thumps. With any luck, some of the Hextheene soldiers had not paid attention to their footing and taken a heavy dive into the white stoned floor. Of the five soldiers, three appeared at the exit he had just escaped from and continued their chase. Their game of cat and mouse led to a long flight of stairs with stalls along the length of it on both sides. The steps were not steep; they were oddly flat with only one step every three or four paces but slowly it led down and back towards the town centre. The pathway stretched for what felt like to the horizon. The people filled the street struggling to move as they were conducting their browsing of wares. Rayar decided that running into the crowd, might only cause him to become stuck within the bodies and be unable to escape. So instead he shot across the width of the pathway and slammed into the adjacent wall before running down the narrow gap between the wall and the back of the trading stalls. One of the soldiers followed him directly while the other two stuck to the main staircase, they simply rammed people out of the way. Every time he passed from one stall to another he looked to his left to see the two soldiers following his every move.

"Give up boy! Stop!" a voice rang out from behind him. The third soldier was struggling to keep up, due to the size of the gap. The armour seemingly hampered his movements which eventually became his undoing. The unfortunate soldier lost his footing and tripped into one of the stands. He fell straight through the wooden structure and was swallowed by dresses and other garbs, followed finally by the wooden stand itself on top of his sprawled out body.

'Two left.' The last two soldiers were still barging through the crowd; their eyes darted between him, behind the stalls and the path ahead of them.

'Three, two, one!' With all his strength the prince suddenly halted in his sprint and gripped a stall of pottery wares to help him come to a sudden stop. The soldiers continued further down the pathway into the large collection of people not quite realising Rayar had stopped running. The golden haired boy panted like a dog as he tried to catch his breath. There was no time to sit around cheering at his deception, it would only take a few more seconds for them to realise their mistake and double back. Rayar found the entrance to the nearest alley on the right side of the long staircase and glided down as stealthily as he could. Once he was confident he had created enough distance between the large market area and himself, he fell against a wall behind him, his aching legs felt like jelly, unable to support his tattered form. Rayar gasped for air like a fish out of water, with his heart pounding against the surface of his chest. He had lost Hinsani and Shania, he had lost his cloak and now he was hiding in a dark alleyway in an unknown city, alone.

"Just walk across the bridge..."Rayar groaned in annoyance. That would be his point of contact, the only place he could think to find his two companions, at the entrance of the Bridge of Freedom. Hopefully by now they had realised that he was no longer behind them and knowing Hinsani, he would be charging around the city streets looking for him. The princes hand was shaking, his legs too were shaking. Was it fear that coursed through him? It was an unpleasant feeling to say the least. The sooner he found his two companions the better. Sneaking through the city was not as hard as he had first thought it would be. There were not many Hextheene soldiers around though occasionally he spotted a pair or a few clearly searching for something, most likely him. The goal was to reach the bridge; fingers were crossed that the other two would

341

be waiting for him. If they were indeed scouting out the city looking for him, it would become even more difficult when they were both on the move. However staying still and waiting was not an option either. There was just as much of a chance those soldiers would find him as Hinsani and Shania. After a few well-placed turns and avoidance of large areas, Rayar eventually found himself in front of a large gateway. It was propped up with two tall white pillars, with flames crackling at their points. The huge wooden gate was pried open, with a red star painted in the centre. This must have been the gate that led to the bridge. Traders were passing through on horseback and with wagons, some on foot, going each way. They were all involved in their own conversations; none passed a second glance his way. Rayar leaned to the side and peered through the gate. He could see it, the bridge, a giant structure which had been built to lead the people across from Oldome to the mainland, a thousand years ago. It was larger than the gateway, the width perhaps of three of the streets he had passed down on the way here and they were wide enough themselves to allow wagons and stalls to be set up on either side. There were towers along the length of the giant construction of history, tall with white stones supporting them. Ribbons had been tied all across the bridge's supports, thousands of ribbons of different colours. Some with messages, some with sigils on them, some simply plain. Thousands upon thousands of them.

'It is beautiful...' the prince thought as he cautiously took his first steps towards the opening of the bridge. As he reached the sturdy stone structure, he peeked over the side. The sea was calm, the water flowing elegantly against the lower supports which were also pure white stone. In the distance on both sides of the bridge, large galleys bobbed on the surface of the ocean; Hextheene Warships. The cries of gulls filled the sky and the bells of fishing boats chimed as they littered the western side of the Hextheene waters. The dock on the northern side of Northfreya was massive in its size. Acres of wooden platforms bustled with life and energy. There were large ships flying flags he had never seen before, they looked nothing like those

342

of Hextheene. Long and slender, thin paddles grew from the hull and tall grey sails looked like blades whipping in the sea wind. Perhaps they were the trading ships from the Eastern Isles? They had seen the sea from afar when travelling near the coast even from Mayhen, yet he had never been this close before. It was awe inspiring.

"Stunning isn't it?" a deep, gruff voice sounded from beside him. Rayar shifted his body around in shock that someone had approached him. His heart sank to his ankles. A huge bull of a man covered in armour and wielding a large warhammer stood beside him. He had been so engrossed in the view; he had not even noticed the heavy footsteps of the balding man close in on him. The large man offered him a toothy grin and leaned on the secure wall that ran across both sides of the lengthy bridge.

"Took a gamble you would come this way, looks like my gamble paid off. Just you though? I didn't come here just for you, Prince Rayar Granlia," the armoured man taunted. Rayar wrinkled his nose and joined him leaning on the wall.

"You know who I am? Who else did you come for then?" His heart was racing once again, however he did his best to appear as calm as possible. All he wanted to do was run. Run as far as possible. Something told him he would not get very far.

"Your guard, Hinsani Tannaroth. Many men like me want to fight him, kill him. Only reason I came along. Unfortunately I have to settle for you at the moment, can't even kill ya." The words he spoke were provocative. Rayar was being underestimated, a boy of royalty with no stomach for fighting. That is what he felt others thought of him, that is partly what he thought of himself. "Doesn't mean I can't beat you around a bit, stop you from running. Sure it'll lure him out." With that the large man pushed himself off the wall and reached out to grab the prince. Using his superior agility the young golden haired prince also pushed off the wall and launched away further down the bridge. As he regained his balance, one hand gripped the hilt of the sword at his hip.

"I will not go with you," Rayar stated firmly. Deep breaths. Focus. Relax. Remember your lessons. Remember what Shania said. He was not weak. He refused to believe he was weak. The large man threw his head back in laughter and rested his warhammer over his shoulder.

"I had too much to drink last night, I'm tired. Don't be a fool. I can't promise I can hold back and not kill ya, if you try and fight me." The arrogance and smugness on the face of this man reminded him of someone he had fought very long ago, during the attack in Heldon. He had been called Shan, the one who had taken the pearl and slain Raimon. Yet, this armoured knight did not feel as murderous, or as threatening. No one he had met since that man had sent the same shivers down his spine and twist in his stomach.

"I do not intend to die today Sir, and I do not intend to go with you either." Rayar retorted. This caused another burst of laughter to explode across the bridge. People had started to catch wind of what was about to happen. They no longer passed over the bridge but stopped to watch, muttering amongst themselves. It was almost like they had formed a barrier around the two. There was no slipping away now.

"Do you know who I am? I'm Sir Donnel Oathsworth, a Knight of Hextheene. No idea? That's a shame." The man, who called himself Sir Oathsworth snorted, seemingly annoyed. "Here I thought mothers and fathers of Mayhen told stories of me to little boys and girls to scare them at night. Well, you're about to see the nightmare, little prince." The knight gripped the warhammer in both hands and held the giant weapon in front of his stomach. Rayar slowly drew his one edged sword and slipped into the basic Lion Stalks stance. This was actually happening. There was no Hinsani to charge in and carve up the foe to protect him; there was no Shania to use her fire to save him. There was only his sword, only him. Like a charging bull, the huge knight roared his battle cry and thrust his entire body towards Rayar. As quickly as the more agile fighter could, he leapt to the side and rolled along the floor, narrowly avoiding being rammed by the beast of a man. He never even had the chance to push himself back to his feet before the knight was above him, with his hammer above his head.

"RAGH!" The knight brought down the massive hammer. Rayar kicked his feet off the wall beside them and skidded along the ground, avoiding the powerful strike. The hammer crashed into the ground and cracked the white stone upon impact. People around began to either push back to watch at a safer distance or flee from the sight of the battle. The longer the fight took, the higher the chance of more Hextheene soldiers appearing. Rayar found himself back on his feet. His mind could not drift to the possible arrival of soldiers; his mind could not drift to Hinsani coming out of nowhere. It could only focus on the brute. He was strong, very strong. However, the strength came at a price of speed. Rayar was quick. This knight also underestimated him greatly; he did not even see Rayar as a fighter, not even a slight threat. Even if the prince could calculate some way of winning this bout, the looming bull of a man still sent a shadowy shiver of fear plunging into his heart.

"Like a bloody fox, ain't you?" the knight said within his laughter as he began to close the distance once more. The huge warhammer came from the right, a powerful, dominating strike.

'I cannot block it. Avoid it.' Rayar squatted down as low as he could and the hammer passed over him, he could feel the sheer pressure of the attack, as the wind roared over him. Above and Below, one hit and he was dead. If that hammer struck him just once, it would be all over. Yet using his speed to an advantage, once the hammer passed over his head, he spread out his legs for support and thrust the one edge blade towards the knights arm, to perhaps disarm him. Sir Oathsworth even looked surprised at the counter attack and with his large armoured hand; he battered the sword to the side barely avoiding a piercing blow to his armpit. It was close, very close. Oathsworth very quickly created distance between them, as he seemed to re-evaluate the situation.

"*Almost* got lucky there," the knight taunted and charged once more. His attacks were strong though Rayar was quicker. He could follow the movements, use the training he had been given by Hinsani to foresee the next move of his foe. Focus his mind and not give into the fear that had halted him once before. He did not speak, it would be a distraction. He did not joke and taunt like his foe, that would also be a distraction. Blade Dancing was a world of silence and reflection, of calm and reaction. The more the knight swung, the more tired he became. Sweat began to form on his forehead and cheeks, his breath became heavy. Rayar too had grown exhausted from the prolonged dancing around his enemy. They would have to end this soon.

"He taught you, didn't he? I knew it!" Sir Oathsworth growled. "No wonder you have those sort of tricks up your sleeve." The bull had grown increasingly angered by his failure to kill him instantly. The fact the fight had lasted this long, was no more than a miracle for Rayar, and a disaster for the knight. With one more charging roar, the huge knight stampeded towards the prince, twirling the war hammer above his head, it was an overhead strike. The hammer's movements were a distraction, he could see it.

'Remember Rayar, remember. Disarm... The Heron Pries.' The distance had been closed. The mighty knight was upon him. This was his one moment. Rayar took a deep breath and focused his mind; the next three movements would have to be fluid and precise. The hammer came from above; Oathsworth hands gripped the long handle with a fair distance between them. Rayar slightly slipped to the side, only slightly, and the edge of his blade whipped across Oathsworth's hand closest to him, knocking it off the handle. In that brief moment, Rayar turned and twirled his sword, so his hands gripped it in a reverse stance, the blade facing backwards. With all his strength Rayar pushed down on the pommel of the blade. The blade pierced through the giant's throat, the brief moment of the knight's hand being disconnecting from the hammer, caused him to stumble forwards. Rayar stood facing away from his enemy; he could feel the metal of the sword through the flesh of the knight behind him. It was a horrible feeling. The prince did not want to turn and see, yet it was not over yet.

Smoothly he pulled free the blade and blood splattered on the ground beside him, followed by the large form of Sir Oathsworth. The crash to the white stone floor was loud, the sound of metal slamming into stone echoed across the bridge. He had won. He had actually won.

'How did... I... actually... beat him?' the prince pondered before he collapsed forward himself, partly from exhaustion and partly from shock. He turned to see the corpse spread out face first upon the stone, motionless, blood pooling around the knights face.

'I did this...' He had killed before, in a panic. This time, his mind was clear, he followed his teachings and performed a Blade Dance hoping it would end the life of a man. The feeling of dread pummelled down on him, like a tidal wave.

'It was him or me... I had no choice. This is how it is supposed to be. If I cannot fight to kill, how can I be expected to fight those members of the Order?' The crowd around him had begun to scatter away. Something other than the bloody fight had spooked them. From across the bridge, on the side of Northfreya, soldiers had been brought due to the commotion. Rayar was barely able to stand; he was too tired for this to continue. The young man ran his gaze over those who began to approach him. Soldiers. Many, many soldiers, knights as well by the look of their attire, full armour and colourful tabards. At the head of this group, a tall man stood in dark grey armour, a white tabard and cloak covering his shoulders. He had light blonde hair which was carefully shaven at the sides and short on the top.

"You defeated Sir Oathsworth," the leader of the Hextheene squad stated, it was not a question. "I am impressed," he added. Rayar frowned. One of his men had just been slain and he was impressed. The prince could not find any words. He could only scramble to his feet, sword in hand. His glare was as sharp as any blade, a cornered wolf. The soldiers equipped with swords, shields and some with crossbows were all prepared for battle, bolts aimed his way, swords and shields closing the distance on the bridge entrance. The leader of the knights did not seem as cautious. He stood there arrogantly with a hand resting casually on the hilt of a large sword at his hip, a bastard sword in fact. "It is over, there is nowhere to run. Lay down your sword and come with me. No harm will come to you, Prince Rayar Granlia." Everyone around here knew who he was; hiding had not gone so well. Regardless, he could not give in. There was another roaring sound around them; it filled the air with smoke and fire. The flames from the towers of the gate screamed out and coursed around the pillars holding them. The soldiers yelled in shock, some stumbling off their feet, some jumped behind walls to hide. The blonde haired knight turned towards the cascading fire behind them, his mouth hitting the floor. Though he did not run or hide, he watched in complete awe. The flames spiralled around the towers and finally connected at the base before aggressively exploding over the soldiers of Hextheene. Now they all dropped, each one of them fell to the ground and covered their heads in sheer horror of what was happening. Rayar could only watch in confusion but relief, he knew exactly what was coming.

"Rayar!" a woman's voice called out. Three horses came galloping through the gate. Hinsani, Shania and a horse being led by the former, charged through the cowering soldiers, the fire dispersing around them as they moved swiftly. Once they reached the prince, Hinsani helped him up onto the vacant horse.

"We've been looking for you. Word spread of a battle on the bridge so we came as quickly as we could," Shania explained from the back of her steed. Hinsani passed his gaze to the fallen knight and then back to him. His expression was stone cold, not a shred of emotion could be seen.

"...Well done," he quietly praised. Their reunion was short lived. The soldiers had begun to realise what was happening and nervously started to return to their feet. All were nervous but one, the white garbed knight. He leapt to his feet now that the fire had drifted into smoke, grabbed a crossbow from one of his troop and shoved the soldier back to the floor.

"Halt!" he screamed towards them. Not all the fire had disappeared. A small flame was all the druidae needed. She raised her hands towards the entrance of the bridge and the flame hovering in her palm expanded into a maelstrom of fire and completely engulfed the bridge on the Northfreya city side. The blonde knight fell backwards and out of sight, all they could see were flames. The heat was so intense, people screamed and fled in panic. It was mayhem. Hinsani reined his horse and called to Rayar to follow closely, before he whipped the steed into a gallop, north, across the bridge towards Oldome. Shania was close behind, leaving the entrance to the bridge covered in flames.

* * *

Chapter XXXIII
A True Witch
~Caskin~

The roaring flames danced over the entrance of the bridge, uncontrolled, burning the white stone black. People of Northfreya scattered and ran, some to find safety while others rushed to collect water to put the blaze out. Caskin sat on the ground, he had been blown over by the sheer force of the flames being propelled towards him and had yet to return to his feet. The knight merely stared wide eyed at the flames before him. Smoke filled the sky, yelling filled his ears, fear and excitement filled his mind. His heart had not pumped this vigorously in so long, this feeling he had almost forgotten. A voice tried to reach him, yet he ignored it. Sir Osmear Lorinstead shook the armoured knight whilst he gripped the shoulder of the man, but to no avail. Caskin could not be reached. He could vaguely hear the older knight beside him, ordering the soldiers to assist in putting out the flames and to ensure the safety of the local people.

"Make sure the area is safe, that is the priority!" Sir Lorinstead ordered. The soldiers rushed to help in putting out the flames, before they became too fierce and risked burning the bridge to a cinder. That was unlikely; the bridge had stood for a thousand years, it was not about to crumble after a bit of fire tickled the surface. Caskin raised a finger and traced it over his cheek. The smoke and flames left a coating of black soot. His white tabard had been singed at the sides.

'A true witch. A witch that can play with fire like a toy. Use it like it is a part of her. It was supposedly to only be a myth, a legend. Magic was not real. Yet I saw it. Real magic.' Still in a state of shock Caskin slowly pushed himself to his feet and wandered towards the blooming fire. Osmear tried to warn him to keep his distance but the older knight was ignored. The Commander-at-Arms pulled off a gauntlet and threw it aside before he held up his hand to the flames. Hot. Really hot. The heat was terrifying. He was terrified. Yet the only thing that had terrified him in the past was pure war. Being knee deep in bodies, surrounded by rivers of blood with only your sword to see you through. That feeling had terrified him. Whenever Caskin became terrified, another feeling washed over him and took control, excitement. Now he could become the man to bring the very first witch to the feet of his King, Braska Hextor, and be remembered for another thousand years. He wanted to fight Hinsani to the death; he wanted and was ordered to capture the boy prince. It would be a pleasure to bring down that woman, to fight someone with that kind of power. There was not a more difficult challenge in his mind was more important to overcome.

"Commander-at-Arms Camaron." Finally the voices began to reach him once more as his mind returned to the world they were in. Sir Lancel Nash, the young knight who had attempted to emulate him, stood beside him and saluted.

"We are attempting to put out the flames. Then we will be able to pursue. Shall I have the men ready horses?" Caskin stared at him, still not completely focused, and nodded.

"Yes... horses. Prepare them." They could not wait too long. The fire was out of control and risked stretching to the docks. Though if he was honest, he did not care about the docks, he did not care about Northfreya at all. It could burn to the ground for all he cared. All he cared about was going after them. Their scent was caught, they were within his grasp and the stakes had suddenly become so much greater. On their side of the bridge, the body of Sir Oathsworth lay sprawled out face down on the stone. Blood had now circled around the body and the fire had even turned his cloak and tabard to a crisp. Beside the corpse, Sir Osmear knelt and attempted to turn him over onto his front, though the man was so large and heavy it would take more than one man to move him.

"I am surprised. He wished to defeat the swordsman Hinsani Tannaroth yet could not defeat a boy prince. The price of rushing ahead and not being in top form, his arrogance got him killed," Osmear stated as he shook his head in disappointment.

"It... it makes sense the Prince of Mayhen was trained by his protector after all. It looks like we are chasing three dangerous individuals. Much more dangerous than we thought they would be," Sir Donnel Jennin, whom was usually quite quiet, muttered from the rear of the group. Caskin snorted at him.

"If you let fear take your heart, you will be as useless as the lump Sir Oathsworth here." Sir Jennin swallowed and turned his head to the ground. That man was not prepared for this kind of expedition, yet now with one knight fallen he could not afford to leave another behind. The commander had finally returned fully to the world of reality, no longer lost in the shock of what had occurred. Anger fuelled his excitement.

"Hurry up! Put this bloody fire out!" Caskin commanded to the soldiers as well as the people of Northfreya who were scurrying about with buckets of water. A bell began to ring on the dock, signalling to the rest of the city of the danger at the bridge. Soon the small garrison of Northfreya soldiers would arrive and begin attending to the area and would likely get in their way. They did not have time for this, the longer they sat here waiting for the raging blaze to be removed from their path, the further the prince and his companions escaped. The four remaining knights watched as their men rushed around the bridge slowly getting the fire under control. They were able to manage the flames, but had yet to be successful quelling its wrath. From behind them, a huge crowd had formed in the gateway that led to the bridge.

"Here we go, perfect..." Sir Osmear muttered under his breath as he rubbed his grey beard. Caskin turned to see a group of fancily dressed soldiers, all in multi-coloured attire and armour, wielding tall halberds, marching towards them. They moved in two separate lines on either side of a large stand, being carried by several servant men. It would have appeared that the nosey sultry Lady of Northfreya had decided to poke her nose where it was not welcomed. The blonde haired knight sighed under his breath and rattled his fingers on the pommel of his bastard sword. Lady Merigold, the Lady of Northfreya was a beautiful, curvy woman with long blonde voluptuous hair, curled down each shoulder, and down her spine. She was the most beautiful woman he had ever seen, the most beautiful woman in Hextheene as far as he knew. However she was gluttonous, greedy and untrustworthy. Caskin had always believed the death of her late husband to be a peaceful relief for the former Baron Merigold; he no longer had to deal with this unpredictable woman. Lady Merigold sat in her carried stand, pillows wrapped around her, her clothes utterly too revealing and perhaps even transparent in places. This woman knew how beautiful she was and she enjoyed others knowing it too. The Lady had her servants carry the stand towards the knights and set it down in front of them. Her large green eyes ran over the huge blaze that covered the bridge. She was perched in a large throne-like chair, being carried around like some kind of Queen. She was no Queen, as much as she wished it and pretended it was true. She was a Lady who pushed the boundaries of her station. Caskin had no love for her. The stunning creature turned her attention to the knights, mainly the commander, and flashed a coy smile, while she leaned on the arm rest of her chair, using her hand to prop up her cheek.

"My, oh my, what are you doing to my city, Commander-at-Arms Camaron? I let you in here with a force and this happens?" Lady Merigold teased, clearly not too concerned even though she pretended to be.

"It is under control, My Lady. You need not concern yourself with it. Once the fire is cleared, we will be on our way." As pretentious as Caskin found this woman to be, at the end of the day she was a Lady of Hextheene, she had the respect of the King and she had position. Treating her with at least a little respect was expected, even if they were both aware of how little he thought of her, and how little Lady Merigold cared. Appearances needed to be kept.

"I concern myself because it is my city. To hear violence has been occurring in my city, which has no place for violence, needs my direct attention. The people of Northfreya look to me for guidance, now that my husband has passed. I am not the type of Lady to sit in my keep, inattentive to the matters of the people," she preached. Caskin could feel the vomit curdle in his stomach at every word that slipped past those soft lips. The Lady offered him a seductive gaze, taunting him.

"Word must have spread quickly for you to come all this way from your keep. The fire has been raging less than an hour," Sir Osmear commented from the side lines. Although not wanting to get between Caskin and Lady Merigold if something tickled his mind, he needed to voice it. The commander agreed however and cocked a brow to the Lady.

"Quite, good knight, quite. I was already nearby, attending a party as you can see from my gown. I do not strut around the city in such clothes, as much as many would prefer I did. Regardless, the people need to see me present. I will direct the controlling of the blaze from here on in. Please, Commander-at-Arms Camaron, pick up a bucket and get to work." The vein in the side of Caskin's forehead pumped with anger. There was no time for this woman and her games yet there was also no arguing to be had however, that would only slow their advance and allow Rayar and his party more time. The curvy and beautiful Lady leant back in her chair; one leg crossed over the other and rested her arms under her bulging chest. "Well, we have a fire to put out. Let's get to it." Caskin grumbled and pushed aside one of the common folk, taking their large bucket and began to assist in putting out the flames. All the knights followed suit joining the people and the Hextheene soldiers in their task. She would get hers one day; he would make sure of it. Another person on his list.

It took quite some time for the fire to finally be put out. Many people created a chain passing bucket from person to person and dowsing the flames until they had been suffocated. Luckily the blaze had been considerably close to the docks allowing quick work for attending to the flame. Once the fire had been quashed, the soldiers gathered their horses and all began to mount up. Lady Merigold watched bemused at the sight, the fair maiden had not lifted a finger to assist, only lifted a finger to point and delegate.

"You continue on your quest from the King, now?" she asked from her perch. Caskin pulled himself up onto to the closest horse.

"We do. I would say it has been a pleasure, My Lady but I am no liar." Politeness had been far stretched already, there was only so much Caskin could take when dealing with people like her. They were a plague on the realm. They sucked the life out of the people around them for their own greed and grandeur. Selfish, they had no wider picture of the realm and what it needed. King Braska Hextor did, he saw it all. He saw how their actions now would better the future of Hextheene. That is why he followed him so loyally; his strength gave strength to the land. That is why this place, Northfreya was a city of pacifists, dancers and dandies. They did not know what true horror was, what true war was.

"And your companion, I hope you do not intend to leave that body there. It is unsightly," Lady Merigold said, her voice was condescending to say the least. Caskin had not stopped to think about Sir Oathsworth corpse still sprawled out in the now black stone floor.

"Have him sent to his family home, Oathsworth - the least you can do after we personally stopped the flames burning your city to the ground, no?" Lady Merigold rolled her eyes at him and slumped in her grand chair.

355

"Oh very well, I will take care of it for you, since you are indeed my favourite knight, Sir Caskin Camaron. Perhaps next time you come to Northfreya, you will pay me visit in the manor. It has grown obscenely dull of late," she requested. Sir Lancel Nash almost choked on the very air he breathed. The young knight had not once had the courage to even look the way of the beautiful woman; his face had never been so red. Caskin however, did not have time for her games here or ever. Not to mention, Fifonia. The knight reined his horse and turned it towards the bridge.

"A humble knight like me has nothing to discuss with a Lady of your position." With that he whipped the reins and his steed charged over the bridge. The remaining knights and soldiers were close behind. The prince and his companions had been given over an hour head start. They had fewer men to move and knew where they wanted to go, he imagined. They had the advantage but it would not save them. Caskin was close on their trail and nothing in the world would set him off course now. He would have Hinsani dead by his hands, he would have the witch in chains and he would have Prince Rayar delivered to the King as charged to do so. That was his goal, Above and Below he would achieve it.

*

~Quale~

"Oh Shania, you are a silly girl." Quale had perched himself on a nearby rooftop in Northfreya. The old sage had draped himself in his multi coloured cloak, patched together with novice stitching. Northfreya was just as he remembered it, so many years ago. It was a shame he would not have the time to enjoy all the pleasures and excitement the city had to offer this day. It had been painful not being able to intervene with the bout, he watched as Rayar fought bravely, he watched as Shania wielded her fire recklessly and watched as the knights charged after them.

'I'm sorry I couldn't help you, I'm sorry I couldn't tell you anything. It is for your own safety," passed through Quale's mind as he slowly pushed himself to his feet and intended to hastily follow the two groups north. Using his power was dangerous, very dangerous. If *'they'* knew he was on the move, they would find him quicker than he could pass wind, and he could not allow Shania and her friends to rely on him either. He could do what he always did, and observe until the moment struck where he could do some good. The magical power keeping his presence hidden from those with the same power as his, as well as the sight of those without such power was draining, very draining. While he was not invisible to the naked eye, his presence was hard to detect as if a ghost lingering just beyond the unknown. It kept him lurking behind Shania, further than he would have liked. The brief moments of respite where he got to see her were always a joyful moment in his heart, but they were always too fleeting.

"Well, no point prancing around here!" Quale mumbled to himself as he slapped on his straw hat and turned to climb down from the rooftop. He would continue to watch them and wait until they needed him the most. Once they were in the Druidae Grove, his former friend of the Order would play his hand. Their game of chess was ever lasting; pieces were passed around the board. Quale had no intention of losing his Queen and King just yet; Shania and Rayar were paramount in not only defeating his old friend, but humiliating him, embarrassing him and ultimately destroying him. This was no longer a battle of good against evil for them both, it was who was smarter, who was stronger, who was better. Rayar would be the final card to truly enjoying a sweet, obnoxious victory over *that* man. His old friend.

* * *

357

Chapter XXXIV
Next Steps
~Nyer~

"Your move," Lanni muttered behind her bony fingers. Nyer had been stuck in Stoneside Keep for quite a while now. It had become taxing simply waiting for replies. They had slowly been ferried in, messenger pigeon after messenger pigeon, with the majority of the replies being somewhat not in her favour. Most of the Noble Lords had declared for their King, she should have suspected as much. The honour of all these Lords and Ladies would certainly be put into question, when all this was over. Even with Lord Loysse's considerable military strength in the country, they would still be outnumbered if it came to all out civil war. For the moment she would sharpen her mind. Playing chess, the famous game crafted by the Kings of old with Lanni Ni'Tella, would give her time to contemplate and reflect on their next steps. Although they had played several games together in their time cooped up in Stoneside, Nyer had yet to best the older woman. Once again they sat in the meeting hall of the keep, dusk falling onto the land and the wind turning rough. She could hear the whistling of the storm brewing through the open windows. Currently she had only moved one pawn one space forward; Lanni had retaliated with a pawn on the far side of the board, nothing of a threat to her advancement. Nyer moved another pawn forward, next to her central lead attack.

"There. Yours," she replied. The advisor swiftly moved her piece, the rook advanced on the far flank behind the lowly pawn.

"I hear your plea for assistance is going unanswered against the crown. What did the message say? Appealing to their honour and sense of justice was it?" she asked. Nyer wrinkled her nose in annoyance.

"Indeed. The only castle to claim side with us is Castle Crewyn to the south of here. Perhaps it is due to their close proximity to Stoneside or the friendship they have with Noble Lord Loysse. I doubted upon reading the reply that it was anything to do with my claims for justice. These Lords and Ladies do not know what side they are joining, it is ludicrous," Nyer explained. The reply from her foe began with a shake of her head.

"You are right. They do not know. How would they know? All the Noble Lords are sworn to the crown, to ride when called upon and to protect the nation when it is in peril. The many Noble Lords stretched across Mayhen, likely only see you as an impatient daughter, grasping for the throne." Those words sent a ripple over Nyer's flesh but she did her best to control her growing anger.

"You utter those words casually? Do you think there is any truth in that assumption?" the princess asked. Her pawns continued to advance in the centre, she had taken a few of Lanni's though had lost her defence of the eastern flank of the board. She would need to send a priest to intercept.

"Obviously I do not, Princess Nyer, or I would not be here now. You need to remember that the people of Mayhen, the Noble Lords of Mayhen - do not know what you know. I have said it before. You need to appeal to more than simply honour and justice. Some would think it dishonourable to go against the King regardless of his behaviour. He is the King. Good King or bad King, he is still the King." The eastern attack was briefly halted yet the removal of her priest allowed the knights to come forth across the board unhindered. This blasted woman was as sly in words as she was at this game.

"You speak many issues, but not many solutions Miss Ni'Tella," she retorted. It was all well and good to throw issues into the plans they had created, yet without any way to fix these problems, it became nothing but complaining. This was not the sort of advisor she desired, she needed one who could reaffirm her ambitions and find the fastest path to achieving said ambitions.

"If I am completely honest, you are too direct, you charge head in without taking into account your plays from the side." Lanni motioned her hands to the game in front of them. Nyer's attack came from the centre, hoping to checkmate the king as quickly as possible. The flanking from Lanni had disrupted her advancement and caused her to fan out, thus the main point of the attack had become vulnerable. "You expect to go at things alone. You are the head of the pack and you lead at the head. While that is a good leadership quality to have when you are in the mix of everything, you do not have an eye on the bigger picture. You do not see what is happening around you. Honour and justice are important, indeed, yet have you looked into the welfare of the rural lands, the farmers? How are they faring? How are the minor villages and towns? You claimed you would get the people on your side yet you have done nothing to employ such an important task. You relied on your first plan, have the Noble Lords join you and simply take the throne without bloodshed. It is not only the Noble Lords that have influence, the people do." Nyer listened, frustrated that the old crones words spoke true. While she considered herself an intelligent woman and expected many others thought the same, she was not a military master mind and she did not know the hearts of the people. Above and Below, she clearly did not know the hearts of the Noble Lords, clearly. Lord Loysse had joined them since he had witnessed first-hand the mistreatment of Rayar. Luckily he did, if he had not taken a role on her side, then this entire endeavour would have been for naught.

"So what are you suggesting, I go out there and speak to the common people?" Nyer asked sarcastically. The older woman chuckled and shook her head once more.

"I once told Rumeo, if the people love you, they will follow you. Show yourself as a good person, as simple as that. This country is not like Hextheene or Southrous, the people here wish peace, they have different values. Show yourself a good woman to all, support them. Surely if King Rumeo is planning for war, he will begin collecting supplies from the nation. We have supplies here for years. Show the people their well-being comes first." Nyer had not actually considered this. In fact she had considered stripping the supplies first, not allowing her father a chance to do so. They had not heard much from the capital since they had left. All she knew was that her father had denounced her and that the Noble Lords had all been called to court to uphold their oaths. This news meant a few things, the most prominent being a possible organisation of soldiers. With her scouts out in the field, she would soon learn if armies were beginning to form.

"So instead of planning to feed my soldiers should we go to war with my father, I should feed the people instead? Tactically that sounds foolish, I am sure my uncle would agree, as would Lord Loysse." Lanni chuckled once more. Their game progressed steadily. Nyer had been forced from her eastern side of the board and now stretched out into the western but found very few openings. Her mind screamed at her to strike at the heart of the enemy lines, yet if she did so, Lanni would unleash her queen and wreak havoc. Perhaps it was best to play the patient game and wait for the advisor to make a mistake.

"Tactically, yes. That would be disadvantageous to your soldiers. Yet there are more options. I have a personal question for you, if you do not mind me asking?" Nyer cocked a brow towards her adversary. Was this a possible ploy to loosen her game or did she truly have something of note to question?

"...Fine. What is it?" she reluctantly inquired.

"Princess Ayla was betrothed to Prince Kerrin Hextor, and there was a possible conversation of Prince Rayar to Princess Melayne Hextor. So for some reason, out of nowhere your father was aching for an alliance with Hextheene, with Braska Hextor. When your father broached the subject with him, he did not explain why, simply that times were changing and he could think of no better ally than Braska Hextor. I have no love for *that* King and the things he has done but I ramble. My question, why have you not married or been betrothed? You are the elder daughter and heir to the throne yet no word of marriage has passed your name." Nyer tapped her finger on the table between them. If she had indeed intended to shake her up, then the plan was successful. It was a touchy subject to say the least, something she had many discussions with her father over. Many arguments was a better phrase to use.

"I have no interest in a man stealing my ambitions from me, taking a role higher than my own. They are weak," she explained though this was only partly true.

"Men can be weak," Lanni started as she moved another piece on the board, piercing the princesses back line. "Men can be cruel, men can be foolish, men can be cowardly. Men can also be brave, they can be righteous, they can be strong. Everyone can be anything, regardless of who they are. I am surprised your father did not tell you who to marry instead of allowing the option. When I was young, you were married off without any say. My husband was twenty springs older than me, minor noble soldier. He became a commander and died. I did not know him when we met, I did not love him. I suppose we never truly loved each other. Sad, really." There was only so much Nyer could take before she rolled her eyes at the older woman.

"True or not, I have my reasons and now I am still unmarried. As things stand there are few Noble Lords in Mayhen eligible currently, and their sons would not hold enough sway." Lanni grinned and leaned forward in her chair, her bony fingers linked together and propped up her chin.

"Well, the Noble Lord of Riveroth, Arthus Pendmir, is it?" Lanni jokingly offered. The princess scoffed.

"The red headed boy? Too young and he has an illness his children will inherit. I would not want my family dying young." The elderly advisor nodded slowly, her smile slipping from sight.

"Joking aside, there may be a solution that will support us in our current position, allow you to support the people and gain supplies from elsewhere," she explained. Nyer leaned back in her chair and crossed her legs. There was a tickle in the back of her mind, she had an inkling of what Lanni was about to suggest. There were few options she had not already considered herself, she did not charge into this so recklessly without weighing her options, even if she had been slightly hasty in her approach.

"Go on," Nyer offered with an unimpressed look upon her face.

"We could look into the possibility of gaining support from King Braska Hextor. He has an unmarried son, you are unmarried. While it would give us superior military strength, it also solidifies your position as royalty, even after being denounced. If King Braska Hextor decides to support you, instead of King Rumeo, then perhaps the power will shift in your favour," Lanni explained. Her words, once more, spoke truth and logic. While attempting to convince Hextheene to support her claim would certainly increase their chances of success, there were several holes in the plan.

"I see. There is no guarantee King Hextor would side with an inferior military force or a member of the royalty of Mayhen that has been denounced. He may even assist my father to once again push his desire to marry Prince Kerrin and my sister," she retorted in an attempt to poke as many holes into the plot as possible. The thought of marrying that prancing boy was unpleasant enough as it was, let alone having men from Hextheene intrude on her life. Lanni nodded to her claims, but did not give up so easily.

"I have no love for King Braska Hextor, he is a vile man bent on war. Yet what would be better for him than to have his son marry the eldest daughter of Mayhen. Once you ascended to the throne, whether it is after this affair now or in the future, he would have a son as King and full support. I cannot claim to know the relationship between the Hextor families but perhaps this would be a better deal for him than the previous one." The

363

older woman seemed confident in her words; there was no hesitation in what she said. It was possible the crafty woman had been considering this for some time, waiting for the right opportunity to speak her mind. Nyer rattled the tips of her fingers, frustration beginning to claim her.

"I think not. Any victory we had would be Hextheene's victory. If you believe I should focus on the people, how do you think they will react when foreign soldiers march through their lands? For an advisor whom preaches wisdom, your ploy here lacks the foresight to see all and any outcomes," Nyer taunted. The princess would not be outdone so easily in an exchange of words. They had continued to play their game during their discussion, though Nyer had not been focusing as much as Lanni had and now found her side of the board almost empty. Her central attack had been crushed, and now she was fleeing with her king and pawns while the enemy surrounded her. Once again she had been out-played by the old crone.

"I lack foresight? Perhaps in my old age I do. Though, in this I do not think so. I think it is you who thinks that the straight road is always the quickest. When there are obstacles, it is sometimes wiser to go around them instead of trying to smash through. Checkmate." Her king was completely surrounded; there was no escape for that piece now. In a fit of frustration Nyer slapped her own king piece over and crossed her arms tightly under her chest.

"You continue to mock me even in my defeat. To your idea, the answer is no. I will not marry Prince Kerrin. We will be successful with justice on our side. The people will see that is so. I accept your advice to support the people should they need it. The chances of them rising up will increase and we will gain an advantage in the land," Nyer commanded. Lanni could not help but let out a small sigh at her decision. It was as if this woman forgot who she was speaking to. They may not have been in Heldon but she was still a princess, a future Queen. When this was all over with she would see Lanni educated on the fact. Slowly the older woman pushed herself out of the chair and reached for a cane leaning on the table side.

"Very well, I will speak to Lord Loysse and prepare arrangements for the possibility. I implore you to consider my suggestion with Hextheene. They may not even respond yet there is no harm in asking. Silence when you need help will never find you the help you need." Everything the woman said sounded as if she wanted it to be remembered for a hundred years, it was infuriating.

"The harm is my pride and possible support from the Noble Lords. If they heard I requested help from Hextheene, a deal with King Braska Hextor, they would never rally to the righteous cause." Nyer's voice started to harden. Her tone became darker and more dominant. Though even as she attempted to push the advisor into the dirt, she only smiled in return, a warm smile that was meant to taunt her, of course.

"My dear, the Noble Lords are not rallying with or without Hextheene's support." With that the princess slammed her hand onto the table which sent the pieces of their chess game tumbling all over the table top.

"Get out." She did not yell, her voice was flat and dangerous. Without another word, only a courteous bow, Lanni slowly made for the exit with the assistance of her cane. The condition of that woman had been getting worse; she had been able to ride to Stoneside and now she was struggling to walk.

'Just die you old hag...' Nyer thought to herself. It was not how she truly felt. Lanni was a voice of reason, even if she spat at that reason when it angered her. Without her by their side, their future would become even more uncertain. Nyer poured herself a glass of wine and leaned back in her chair, the silence was refreshing.

* * *

Chapter XXXV
People of Mayhen
~Vesir~

The fields and hills of Mayhen were as spectacular as always. For the most, part there were vast green fields, sloping hills that covered the land and dirt roads connecting villages and cities throughout the country. The blazing sun which had hung low over the land for the past few months had begun to become covered by thick sheets of cloud in the blue sky. The winds from the far unknown west, had plummeted over the kingdom and rain clouds travelled eastward with it. The rain season would come soon, which would be long and tedious. It would however bring new life to the land after the heat had caused so much damage and the weather would make certain a plan tinkering within the mind of Vesir plausible. Any armies moving in such conditions would certainly be slowed down by the excessive rainfall; the land around Stoneside Keep would become extensively muddy and difficult to pass. The long Heldon River would rise, as it did every year that the rain plummeted down from the World Above, though many safeguards over the years had been constructed to avoid any loss of property or life. These protections were in place long before Vesir had been born into the world. The commander sat upon his horse as he gazed westward towards the distant forming rain clouds. They were only minor at the moment, but he knew the tremendous storms always followed.

"Are you alright, sir?" A soldier beside him asked, a man from the Shield. The group of soldiers had stuck close to Vesir ever since they had made it out of Heldon; they were even becoming similar to a personal guard. He could give them some fancy name like Shieldguard one day, but to say that out loud would have probably sounded quite ridiculous.

"I'm fine, soldier. Just thinking," he replied absently. Vesir had found it difficult to connect with anyone after losing Zanmir. However, he was a commander at the end of the day and as badly, as desperately as he wanted revenge on his brother, for the death of his son, he had to continue to be strong for his men and for Nyer's cause. He had not considered her cause an honourable one, not even a righteous one. Reading the minds of people was sadly not in his skill set, yet whenever the girl spoke, whatever she planned - it never seemed to be a just strive to victory. It felt more like she had seen an opportunity to rise quicker and she would take it. Was she a liar? No, he did not think so. She was just blinded by her own beliefs and now she thought this charade was true. Vesir had promised his men, he had promised himself to her cause. For the moment after what he had witnessed, she was the lesser of two evils. Once he had ensured the safety of his family and dealt with Rumeo himself, then retiring far away from all this was the smartest solution.

"Sir," another soldier trotted up beside him with a map over the horse's mane; it was an awkward way to hold a map. "Where to next? The areas near Stoneside are clear. Do you wish to go further west?" the soldier asked. Vesir had volunteered to scout the surrounding landscape to ensure no Heldoran soldiers were setting up camps nearby, nor other scouts were doing the same as he. As much as he would have preferred to settle this matter civilly, man on man with Rumeo, the possibility died with his son. The more time that passed, the more he felt as if the final outcome would be mass bloodshed. The only time anything had happened like this in the history of Mayhen, was many, many grandfathers ago. Two brothers separating the land in war for the throne. Vesir did not want the throne; he never wanted to sit upon it. He had been content serving at the Shield where nothing happened and time floated by without strife or fear. Nothing good lasts forever, it seemed.

"Alright, yes. We will ride to the farmland a good few miles east of Heldon. I want to see if livestock and supplies are being shipped to the capital. If they are, it'll give us a good indication of things to come," Vesir casually ordered. It sounded flippant yet those men close to him knew what an order sounded like from the famous Vesir Granlia. The small group of riders headed east across the wide grasslands of Mayhen. Vesir had never been much of a skilled rider. In his brother's prime, Rumeo had been a fantastic rider and jouster in tournaments and had ridden into battle whilst Vesir had either been with the archers or infantry. Neither had adopted the ideology of remaining behind the lines, they had both been leaders on the front much to their father's displeasure. Father had found Vesir's' other skills even less desirable, though he had sworn to never use such skill again to kill. The past was the past.

'Wouldn't even be thinking about it if my niece hadn't used it to get me into this. Above and bloody Below.' Such thoughts would only hinder him, so they were violently shoved aside as he focused on their objective. The only other thought that tickled his mind, was his family and how easily it would be to ride there now. A week or two and he would be home with those he loved. Yet he knew Nyer had been right. They would have expected such a thing and Heldon guards bent on taking him in, would be littered around the land between the Shield and the rest of the kingdom. After a short ride, no more than an hour or two, they came across an old farm. It was in the furthest outskirts of farmland from the capital, land barely visited by those from Heldon. The group set out to scout the landscape and livestock. The hot season had not been particularly kind to the crops yet with rain soon to arrive, it would revitalise the fields. The livestock itself seemed like slim pickings, the cattle fields were practically empty. Their investigation did not last long however before cries for help interrupted their discreet scanning of the farm from afar. Vesir

368

ran his gaze from atop his horse, looking for signs of a struggle, and then he caught it in the far distance. It was hard to tell exactly what had occurred yet by the looks of it, someone was laying in the dirt of one of the pens, probably meant for chickens, while another two figures stood around the fallen person.

"We shouldn't get involved, sir. It could give us away," one of the soldiers advised as he followed his commander's line of sight. Vesir shrugged his shoulders and whipped his horse forwards into a gallop.

"Never leave someone in need, I always say." With that, his steed took him galloping down the hillside they had been loitering on, towards the fallen person. Upon arriving, it was not what he expected. An old stocky man with sparse grey hair and tattered peasant clothing, lay in the dirt groaning, with his hands holding his leg. Beside him a young girl and a young boy, children no older than nine springs, were doing their very best to help the man up, yet his weight made such a task impossible. Without a moment of hesitation, Vesir dismounted his horse and dashed over to the side of the fallen man.

"What happened here?" he asked, flicking his eyes between the two children while doing his best to appear as welcoming as possible, not wanting to scare them. The boy, the younger of the two, moved back behind the girl, who Vesir assumed was his sister. "Don't be afraid, I'm here to help." The girl looked between him and the man in pain, before she spoke.

"Our grandfather, he's hurt. We can't get him inside," she said defeated. Vesir nodded while he offered a small smile and placed a hand on their grandfather's shoulder.

"Hello sir, attacked by something or just a nasty fall?" the commander asked. Just then the rest of the soldiers, who had joined him on his scouting mission, had caught up. A couple of them dismounted to offer their assistance, whilst the other two kept a stern watch around them.

"Attacked?" the fallen man groaned. He spoke through his moans of pain with a thick common accent. "No, no. Just a bad knee, it gave in. Bloody hurts I'll tell you that!" Vesir looked over towards a small house not far from where they were located, their home he guessed.

"Alright sir, me and my men are going to help you up and get you into that house, are you fine with that?" The elderly man seemed to look over the new arrivals for a moment, by his expression something clicked in his mind seeing several soldiers appear at his farm. Vesir hoped he would not resist their help; the people of Mayhen must have known by now, the divide of royalty in the kingdom. After a few seconds of contemplation, he nodded and together they helped him back to his feet and continued towards the run down home of the farmer. With Vesir on one side, and a soldier on the other, they carried the farmer as carefully as they could. It was not an easy task, his size made it particularly difficult even with two men sharing the burden. After a short walk that actually felt like an eternity, they pushed open the door and helped the old man inside, finally finding a seat in a small dining area and set him down upon it. The house was basic as expected, old chairs, old table, dusty windows and cobwebs all over the corners of the ceiling. It was as if no one had cleaned the house in years. By the looks of it, this old man lived here with the two grandchildren, yet there was no wife to help him or any farm hands to help with the work.

"Just you three here?" Vesir asked, aiming to confirm his suspicion. The old farmer nodded.

"Aye, just us. Do me a favour please, on the cabinet above the cooking pot, there are some herbs in a jar. Couldn't grab them for me could you?" the old man requested through groans of pain. Vesir nodded and began to rummage about looking for said herbs. The two soldiers who had joined them inside the house stood there awkwardly, not really sure what to do next. The two children now stood beside their grandfather, the young boy gripped his hand seeing his grandfather in obvious pain while the girl began to put together a drink, taking the herb from Vesir and stuffing it into a mixing bowl. After the leaves were crushed and stirred in, she passed the pot to her grandfather who took a long well needed swig of the ill looking substance. A few moments of silence passed before the farmer leant back in the chair and let out a long sigh.

"What was that, I've never seen it before?" Vesir asked with a cocked brow. One herb seemed to suck all the pain from the farmers face. Was it some sort of miracle cure? Whatever it was, it worked quickly.

"Ah, this? My wife made it years ago. She taught the recipe to my daughter and then to her daughter. Once it's inside you, it dulls pain. Never heard of it? Oh Above and Below, I'm sorry! Thank you for your help, Sir. I'm Sternmir Morah." The old farmer raised his hand to shake the commanders which he gladly did.

"Quite the herb, it didn't look local to me. Where was it from?" he asked. Sternmir coughed into his hand after the shake, luckily not before, and patted his chest vigorously.

"Far, far east my friend. Wife got some from some traders years ago, we've been growing it ever since." Vesir made a mental note of this. It was strange to come across a regular farmer in Mayhen, with such a plant growing in his land. For there to be something that *he* had never heard of or seen, was quite curious. It was not only those in high positions with their secrets. "Please, take a seat. Got a drink for your men as a way of thanks. Damn knees been playing up for years, that herb is the only thing that quells it. Gorphina it's called, I think. I can't remember exactly, been so long since I called it by name." The old farmer chuckled and patted his large stomach. He then motioned to the young boy to fetch the soldier's drinks. Vesir took a seat beside Sternmir and accepted the gift with a nod and a ruffle of the boy's hair.

"Must be difficult here by yourself, no farm hands to help you? I can't help but notice your livestock is low as well. Sickness?" the commander asked as he took a sip of his drink, which tasted sweet and smooth, surprisingly not ale. The soldiers he had brought, also took their drinks and moved outside to join the other two, leaving Vesir to converse with the farmer. They had no reason to linger, they had seen that.

Perhaps they were trying to urge him to leave as well, though Vesir had another objective in mind. Information.

"Aye it is. No one works this far out but me and mine. Ever since my wife passed, it's been me and the children here, Kaylen and Tissir." The farmer passed an affectionate look to the two children who were watching the conversation from the side lines, somewhat nervously. It must have been the fact that he was covered in weapons that made them uncomfortable.

"My wife is named Kaylen also, a good name." He flashed a smile to the young girl, who bashfully looked to the floor.

"Aye, strong name. What brings a group of fine soldiers out to these parts so far from Heldon?" As Sternmir asked the question he flicked his eyes over Vesir's attire. The commander's cloth was akin to the Shield's yet he had changed into Stoneside armour with only hints of the Shield remaining. "Or wherever you're from, lad," the farmers tone sounded more concerned than before. Word was out that there was a clash between the King and the princess; it was not so far-fetched that even in these parts, this man knew the outline of what was happening in the kingdom.

"Just a soldier of Mayhen sir, nothing to worry yourself with. Scouting the area and just happened upon your farm. I don't want to intrude though. We can leave, if you wish?" Vesir politely offered. Last thing he wanted to do was cause any distress for the children quietly watching their conversation.

"No... no, it's fine. You helped me out. I wouldn't be the man I was, if I didn't invite you for a drink. I would pay you yet... things are not as easy as they were. You asked before about my livestock. Taken to the capital. I've heard hundreds of farms being... well, I don't want to say robbed, but they had their crops, stock and anything useful to Heldon, taken within the last couple of weeks." Sternmir's words supported his belief that the capital was rallying soldiers.

"Do you know why?" he asked. Sternmir shook his head and shrugged his shoulders.

"I have my guesses, not my place to pry. I just work on my farm and look after the children. I don't care for wars anymore, be it with invaders or royalty squabbling over nonsense," the farmer replied. It was a good way to put it, to others it would seem like squabbling. Yet if Zanmir had not been caught up in that squabbling, he would not be here now. It was his fault his son died, it was up to him to do whatever he could to make things right. That was what he told himself anyway; there was no true way to put it right. For now he would change the subject.

"If I may ask, where are their parents? I can imagine it being difficult with all that on your shoulders. I had three sons myself. They were a handful, let alone if I was handling it without my wife to walk me through everything. I mean everything." Vesir chuckled, as did the farmer before his expression turned somewhat more sombre.

"Aye, aye, I had a son too, these younglings father. Soldier he was, never wanted to be a farmer like his old man. Had dreams of greatness, following the footsteps of the famous Hinsani Tannaroth. Regular soldier in the ranks, proving to be a great swordsman, heroic even and becoming a Royal Blade. Such big dreams for such a simple minded boy." Vesir made sure that his expression reflected his interest as Sternmir explained the details of his son.

"Did he fall?" the commander asked. It was a straight forward question though he wore a face of empathy.

"Aye he did," Sternmir replied. He did not seem offended by the question, most likely due to the fact he had come to terms with it long ago. Somehow this was reassuring to Vesir, that he was not the only one who had lost someone important to them. He knew many people had, of course, yet to talk to someone face to face about the loss was surprisingly calming, even therapeutic.

"I'm sure he fell bravely. As did my son." Sternmir glanced to the children still watching and motioned them to leave with a flick of his wrist and bob of his head. The children awkwardly sauntered off out of the dining room and shut a door leading to a bedroom behind them.

"A rock killed my son. A bandit in the Northlands of Mayhen beat him to death with a rock, after they tried to protect a woman being... taken. That area is riddled with lawlessness I hear, north-west of Heldon by the coast, and they only had a few men to look over it. My son was one of them. He died not long after he passed being a recruit, to a man... with a rock." The elderly man clucked his tongue on his teeth in thought. Vesir was unsure what to say next. That was something hard to hear let alone live through. To think if Jonnas or Lanmir were to die in such a way, at such a young age, it would break his heart more than it had already been shattered.

"I'm sorry to hear that," he was able to squeeze out. His words felt hollow, simply saying sorry to something tragic that you had no involvement in. At this moment, he felt weak.

"Don't trouble yourself over it. It was a long, long time ago. I make the most of what I have, and that is two young grandchildren who need me more than anything. So again, thank you for helping me. It means a lot." Vesir forced a smile before the sounds of his men calling out to him, caught his attention.

"Sorry, excuse me." The commander bobbed his head respectfully to the farmer and darted out of the door. Once outside, he saw his men standing off with four guardsmen, Heldoran guardsman. They all seemed fairly shocked to see men of the Shield in a farm this far into the mainland of the kingdom, so shocked their hands gripped the hilts of their swords, as did his own men.

"Sir, Heldoran guards," one of the soldiers said, eyes intently focused on the potential enemies. The same glares were directed back at them. The tension in the standoff could be sliced with a blade like butter.

"You're... you're from... Stoneside! What are you doing here?!" one of the guardsmen called out. She was a woman, in fact, a rarity in the military force even in these days. Her long brown hair had been tied into a braid which ran down her back;

she was tall, as tall as he was. Quite the scary sight in fact, it reminded him of that Royal Blade of Nyer's, Titania.

"Just passing through. Though, unfortunately we were spotted by you. Not a good thing for us, not a good thing for you," Vesir replied. As much as he wished there were alternatives to violence, with the growing tension in the air, it felt as if this was where the path would take them next.

"Wait... you're Vesir Granlia!" the woman barked out as she almost ripped her sword from its sheath. "Vesir Granlia... you must come... with us. You're a wanted man." She demanded. He let out a small sigh and placed his own hand, finally, on the pommel of his sword.

"Stand down, leave. This won't go your way," he pleaded with them. There was only one life he truly wanted to take, as much as he wished it was not true, the rage that continuously burned in his soul could not be extinguished simply with time. Suddenly the young girl, Kaylen, burst through the doorway and sprinted over to the woman guardsman and pushed her back, followed by the young boy, Tissir. The cries of the farmer Sternmir could be heard behind them as he screamed for them to come back. The old man came bumbling out of the house, using a thick stick as a walking cane, putting most of his weight on the object.

"Children get back here now! And you, all of you! This is not a place for violence. Enough!" he roared out. The woman guardsman blinked in surprised and released her hand from her sword, followed by her squad of guardsman.

"I'm... I'm sorry Sternmir. It's just... you have... him here!" Her speech was stuttered; the sentences struggled to form completely, but it was easy enough to understand. Sternmir pulled himself through the crowd of Shield soldiers and Vesir, and then fell to a knee to wrap his arms around the grandchildren.

"I don't care who *'he'* is, or why you're at each other's necks. This is not the place for such thing. These men helped me, you will cease. Do I make myself clear!?" the farmer roared out again. His voice carried like a waterfall. While the

375

men of the Shield appeared confused by the scene unfolding in front of them, the Heldoran guards simply bowed to the man's will and accepted defeat.

"I ... understand... Sternmir. We just... came to... purchase more milk... and be on our way..." The old farmer grumbled and pushed himself to his feet, with the assistance of one of the Heldoran guardsman before sending Kaylen to fetch their milk. Vesir watched with a confused expression plastered on his face. Guards coming all this way to buy milk? That simply made no sense. Unless his milk was the finest in the kingdom, even then it was a strange request. The transaction between the two parties was completed by a guardsman handing Sternmir a bag of coins and the milk being passed over to the guardsman. With that, they focused their attention back upon the men of the Shield.

"I do...not know why... you are here... yet if... Master Sternmir says you ... helped him... then we won't arrest you... today." She spoke with her stutter though her tone was sincere. She did not seem to be pleased with allowing them to go unhindered yet somehow this farmer held power over them. She looked over to Sternmir, bowed her head respectfully and claimed they would return in a few days for more trade before they turned to leave. The old farmer let out a deep breath and returned his gaze back to Vesir.

"I think now is the time to go. Thank you for the help, but after that, it's safer for all of us if you leave." It was a reasonable request, but his curiosity of the event that had just unfolded, stayed uneasily.

"Those guardsmen come here often to buy... milk?" the commander asked. Sternmir wrinkled his nose as he struggled to keep standing even with his make shift walking stick.

"They come, her in particular, to check in on us. It's complicated but you could say she owes these children a debt, a big debt. That is her way of... making sure they don't go hungry. I wouldn't accept charity after all. It doesn't matter to you, my friend. Again, I thank you for your help. It doesn't matter to me who you are. You're simply a soldier after all."

Vesir swallowed his pride and nodded to the man in agreement. Something told him that this farmer had an inkling of who he was from the beginning of their meeting. Regardless he did not want to cause unnecessary issues for a good man like this, their conversation had been pleasant for what it was, yet there was no need for them to remain here any longer. With a courteous bow, followed by a salute, the commander turned from the farmer and back to his horse. He briefly looked over his shoulder once back upon his mount and flashed a forced smile to the two children, whose gaze only returned fear.

'Can't win them all over with that dazzling smile of yours, Vesir, I suppose,' he thought to himself. The small party of soldiers trotted off the farm.

"That was close, sir," one of the soldiers said absently as they took their leave. "Back to the keep?" he asked. Vesir shook his head; their objective had not been completed just yet.

"Not quite. We're following those guardsmen. They did not look particularly travel worn and Sternmir's farm isn't close to Heldon at all. It's made me curious," the commander explained. The soldiers let out a sigh in union but of course, they agreed to their command. The group turned westward after moving out of sight over the hilly landscape, to follow the small group of guardsmen, to see what they could see.

* * *

Chapter XXXVI
The Seed of Rebellion
~Vesir~

"So it has come to this," Vesir muttered under his breath. They had left the horses by a nearby abandoned cottage. It had not seen any attention in countless years yet still just about held its structure. He and his men had continued forward on foot tracking the small squad of guardsmen that had visited Sternmir's farm. They squatted by a collection of fallen logs that had clearly be recently cut down and stacked in piles, the landscape itself had been considerably altered by the introduction of soldiers. Many soldiers in fact, perhaps a thousand of them, had grouped together. Vesir could not be sure of the numbers from where they had perched themselves for their sightseeing. In the far, far distance was Heldon. The outline of the city and the heaven piercing keep could be spotted on the horizon, a good half a day ride. However, where they were investigating, there were rows of tents and Mayhen soldiers going about their daily business. Each group of tents had a banner protruding from the ground, to signify which Noble Lord those soldiers served in the kingdom. It was not the full army of Mayhen, not even close. It was more like a settlement of a hundred men, each from every Noble Lord in Mayhen. The Dragon of Riveroth, the Flame of the Forks, the Sword of Dormer, The Three headed horse of Maymir. Every Noble Lord and minor Lord in the kingdom he could imagine had a banner stationed in the huge encampment. All but three, at least three that he saw were absent, The Shield, Stoneside and Castle Crewyn. Nyer's attempts to lure the Noble Lords to her side, with the preaching of justice and honour, clearly had not been as successful as she would have liked, not that Vesir had expected any different. The notion of honour was a dying tradition in the lands, the notion of wealth was something all men and women could or wanted to relate to.

"They're quite far from the capital, Sir. Why are they stationed here and not in the city outskirts?" a man of the Shield questioned as he peaked over the log. Vesir pushed the man back down below with a hand on top of the soldier's kettle helmet.

"I don't know. If true civil war had broken out, leaving a garrison of men this far from a defensible position wouldn't be wise at all. No, there is something else to this. They must know our scouts would venture this far and come across this encampment. Which means, Rumeo does not intend to hide it at all. If anything, he wanted us to see it." The soldiers looked between themselves with puzzled expressions and then back to their commander, their faces no less puzzled.

"Why, sir?" Vesir pinched his bottom lip in thought as he turned back from his spying and slumped down the side of the fallen logs.

'Why... why, why, why,' these tactics did not match Rumeo at all. Perhaps someone in his council was advising him against what he was normally inclined to do. Giving away your intentions and positioning was a rookie error in the art of warfare. They had both been taught by the same man in their youth. They both knew this. Then the question of why had become a very good question. Nyer and Lanni had hoped he would have had a good insight into the mind of Rumeo, and his strategy of warfare, but this behaviour was completely out of character. With a pondering mind, the commander pulled his lip in and out repeatedly, pondering their motives. His soldiers stared at him, even more confused than before.

"Still with us, sir?" a soldier questioned as he scratched his nose.

"I am I am. I'm here, just thinking. The only thing I can think of is that it is possible Rumeo wants us to prepare. He wants to provoke us into forming an army and preparing for battle, giving him the excuse to raise the banners of the Noble Lords, fully. If any regular scout came across this, he would report it and we might have seen it as the beginning of the Mayhen armies forming. Possibly, of course, not certainly." Vesir peered over the logs once again. Soldiers strolled the site, some of them on guard duty, others drinking around fires. They did not seem at all prepared for a fight; they appeared relaxed as if not even on duty. Most of them at least. The commander could not imagine why they would be dispatched so far from the capital, but he had his suspicions, so there would need to be the base of his judgement from here on in.

"We need to return to Stoneside and let Nyer and Lord Loysse know first. Hopefully she doesn't jump the crossbow and react recklessly. Miss Lanni will keep her in check, no doubt." The group of Shield men turned from the direction of the encampment and began to furtively make their way towards their horses, not far from where they were positioned. The spark of rebellion had been ignited. The path to civil war had become dangerously close and narrow with very few turnings off the awful destination. With someone as cruel as who Rumeo had become, leading one side and someone as zealous as Nyer leading the other, Vesir had slowly begun to accept the inevitable outcome. War.

*

~Ayla~

The court of Heldon had not been this packed since Rumeo's' birthday months before. Guests from all over the kingdom had brought themselves to the capital to discuss and plan the next steps in the situation with princess Nyer. Colourful attire graced the hall with a magnitude of beauty, from long flowing cloaks to extravagant gowns to headdresses with flowing feathers. The fashion of all parts of Mayhen had been thrown together to create a sea of wonder to the eyes. Noble Lords had come all this way from their castles and cities and minor lords, from their homes and towns they governed. All had been invited to the city of Heldon by the King and all had a right to speak. While it was a formality for them to speak their piece, the way the King was now, made it very apparent that no matter what the cost to reputation, he would have his way and only his way. Along each side of the throne room, Noble Lords and Ladies stood with a few courtiers of their own, personal guards and the like. Each had a banner hung from the balconies above them, to show where they were from and where they needed to stand. King Rumeo was where one could usually find him these days, on his throne, though the chairs for his Queen and his children had recently been removed. There was only one throne atop those stairs and it was for the one true King. No one who had not been given previous permission by the King himself was even allowed to step upon those stairs and above the court. The only people Ayla had seen who had been given permission to do so, were the vile one handed man Captain Sirus and the other, a figure always draped in a dark blue cloak and hood, always hiding in the shadows who always kept their silence. She did not know this figure; whoever they were they maintained a low profile, both in presence and views. Commander Brayton had been moved down to the base of the staircase alongside a line of guardsmen around the stairs, allowing none to pass. Ayla had not been told whether she would have been allowed to climb those stairs and had not wished to try. Surely she would not have been stopped if she tried. The fear of the embarrassment of being turned away, even if she was a princess, was ever present, as was the fear of even standing next to this man, her father. Ayla stood in the corner surrounded by minor nobles who frequented the throne room daily. Her new Royal Blade Shan was in the shadows behind her, ever watchful. Ayla's gentle gaze ran over the contents of the room, so many faces she did not recognise standing below banners she did. Master

Vayers had taught her much about the Noble Lords in the land, who were their heads and where their castles stood. Though for the most part, they did not visit Heldon unless called upon and in the peaceful times she had been brought up in, there were few situations that called upon a gathering of Noble Lords and Ladies. There was one face that stood out across the hall from her, the red headed young Lord Arthus Pendmir. Since their recent meeting in the garden she had not been granted another opportunity to speak with him but the fact they were all gathered here now, suggested his attempt to reason with her father had failed.

"You know why you have all been gathered here this day, Noble Lords and Ladies, lords of the land, people of my court. There has grown a threat to our great kingdom in the form of one of my daughters, the rebellious Nyer Granlia. While it pains me to say it, my daughter has begun to take up arms against me and my remaining family. She has locked herself away in Stoneside Keep with the traitorous Tismiar Loysse and my villainous brother Vesir Granlia," Rumeo roared out over the crowd. His voice carried the weight of a country on his shoulders with no hesitation in his claims against his family. Even when he spoke of the suffering it caused, there was no evidence of pain in his voice, only statement of fact. The nobles who had gathered muttered to themselves, whispering concerns and anger towards the claim. Ayla flashed her eyes to Arthus to see his reaction. The young lord stood there with his arms crossed and expression puzzled.

'What are you thinking about, Arthus?' she wondered as her gaze lingered too long. The young lord looked back at her and offered a light and reassuring smile, which she quickly ignored and shot her attention back to her father. The princess could feel her cheeks warm with embarrassment; her face tingled with what felt like a timid fire. A Noble Lady spoke from the back of the hall; all were free to speak here after all. It was the Lady of Maymir to the east, if Ayla remembered the banner correctly.

"Lord Loysse has the largest single force in the kingdom, as passive as that man is. If we were to bring our armies together, we would certainly outnumber his force, yet there would be a great loss of life, Your Grace," the elderly Lady suggested. Another Lord standing close to her, Jarem Yormiya, she stood then said his piece. He was an older gentleman, with a stocky build and a bushy moustache covering his upper lip, Noble Lord of the Forks to the south.

"Large force or not, have we tried to negotiate with him? Let him know the folly of siding with a denounced daughter. Nyer Granlia no longer holds any claims, only those she preaches herself. If we were to have Lord Loysse simply turn her over, we could end this situation before it spirals out of control?" A good and fair question. Surely that was best for the kingdom yet something told her deep down, her father had no desire for a peaceful resolution. The loud clattering of superior people began to shake the hall once more, people arguing and complaining, trying to come up with solutions. While these meetings were good for coming to a consensus, she had been told many years ago by her father, that for half the time it was just a bunch of old people arguing about nothing. After a moment of sucking up her courage, she returned a quick glance towards Arthus, who still stood in silence with his arms crossed. An older gentleman, perhaps the young lord's advisor, whispered into his ear. He was a leathery skinned grandfatherly man with a hunch back but warm face. The only response Ayla could see was Arthus occasionally nod to the words whispered in his ear. Rumeo raised his hand into the air to force silence upon those present.

"All attempts to speak have been returned with refusal. Tismiar Loysse has sided with the usurper and that is a fact we must accept. We have placed all of those men you were instructed to bring with you, on the far outskirts of the Heldon farmland border. I want to show those traitors that we are a united kingdom against all threats, be it from outside or within. A plot to dethrone me and kill my wife has been brought to light and those with my blood are the culprits, as you are all already aware. An attempt on the life of a King is an attempt on the life of all his people. My youngest daughter was snatched from her chambers and is being tracked as we speak. My son betrayed the Royal Family and threatened the very foundation of this city. There is only one course left open to put an end to this rebellion against the crown." The room was silent as the King spoke. The lords and ladies stared intently at their ruler as they hung to every word he spoke. For Ayla, this was a nightmare. The more her father spoke, the further from her memories he dwindled. He even looked different. How could this man still be the loving father they once all shared? Not just the Granlias, he was a loving father to the entire kingdom. She gripped her dresses between her fingers and took a deep breath to compose her growing anxiety. She knew exactly what was coming next. "We must form the Mayhen army, march on Stoneside and show, not just the traitors, but the rest of the known land that Mayhen does not take insults lightly. I will not be seen as weak to Hextheene, Southrous, Brexxia, Breton and all the other countries in the Freeland. If we cannot deal with threats in our own borders, how are we expected to deal with them from other countries?" With that the room exploded into obnoxious chatter. Nobles arguing amongst themselves, even shouting exploded from parts of the room. For the most part, it sounded as if the majority of the hall had agreed with the statement from the King. This plan would mean the end of Nyer, her sister, the girl who had guided her, taught her and loved her. She wanted to scream and charge up to the throne, to knock some sense back into Rumeo. Yet fear kept her in check, fear she would follow the same path as her older sister or even worse, Zanmir. Nyer may have left her here, but she loved her dearly and the thought of her possible death was mind numbing.

"Are you alright?" a voice sounded from beside her. She looked over to see the red headed lord standing next to her. He had left his allocated position in the hall and casually made his way over. Ayla's cheeks were damp from quiet tears, there was no use hiding it.

"I am fine, Lord Pendmir," she replied. She could not exactly call him Arthus when surrounded by people and give them the wrong impression.

"I know it is difficult. It is your sister being discussed here. We will find a solution, I promise," he said in a soft tone with a warm smile on his lips. Why was this man taking such an interest in her well-being? Even in this situation he was being kind.

"What can we possibly do? Father will have his way and the army will be formed and then... then war..." To think war after such a long period of peace was brewing and even worse it was with her own flesh and blood. Ayla had attempted to force herself to be strong, yet the wall around her had been crumbling ever since she put it up.

"My Lords, My Ladies," Rumeo spoke again, the room settled down from their din. "I hereby call all Noble Lords and Ladies to form their armies at the point designated by my advisors. Generals will be selected from among you and you will be informed of such. For the moment a feast will be prepared for all present as an offer of gratitude for your loyalty to Mayhen and the Royal Family." The hall turned into a ring of applause for the King and his generosity. Most clapped at least, though Arthus had not joined into the celebration and nor had she. Clapping for the call of death to her sister was something for which she could never raise joy. Ayla could take no more of this farce and turned on her heel towards the exit. Arthus called after her yet she ignored it, she was sick of Noble Lords, soldiers, Kings and royalty. She was sick of all of it. The garden of Heldon, even in its decay, was the only place she could breathe in this castle anymore. The only place she could still feel the presence of her beloved family.

* * *

Chapter XXXVII
Braska's Border
~Rayar~

Rayar and his companions were lucky enough to escape being caught at the bridge; still it was too close for comfort. To think their journey could have been brought to an end by those they had not even intended to face off with. The prince had hoped he would have regained most of his strength by now, after the challenging bout against the bull of a knight yet unfortunately for him, riding a galloping horse had its own stress on his body. The feeling was similar to when they had been travelling from Heldon to Stoneside and the mountain pass. He was absolutely exhausted. Hinsani on the other hand appeared like an unstoppable force that did not waver or grow tired, no matter what situation they were in. Shania too was tenacious and stubborn enough to push herself forward through any obstacle. He felt like the loose link in their chain. It was no secret to him, and probably even the pair of them, that he was the weakest of the three. The only reason he had been able to keep up with the two of them so far, was sheer determination to achieve what they had set out to accomplish. It was imperative they stopped the members of the Order plotting against his family and planning great evil deeds against the Freeland. If Rayar was honest with himself, he had not even begun to consider how he would fare against those who could use the magical powers he had seen back on that fateful night in the capital; he did not even understand how it worked. There were a lot of secrets to this power. One day he hoped he would be able to understand the hidden truths of that world.

"How are you feeling?" Shania asked him. Their hard gallop had slowed to a canter once they had left the long bridge behind them. Rayar were unsure how long those raging flames Shania had left in their wake, would hold off the Knights of Hextheene but the distance they had created already should have given them enough time to gather their thoughts and consider their next move.

"A little worse for wear, but I shall live," Rayar replied with a deep sigh following his statement. Hinsani slowed his horse allowing the pair to catch up to him. As usual, he held the head of the party.

"I am proud of you Prince Rayar. That man you fought was no push over. It is a shame I did not witness the fight, though I would have intervened if I had," Hinsani said. It was a strange feeling to be praised on killing someone, death was not one of his fortes as it was his Royal Blade's. The raven haired warrior had killed so many, he had lost count. Perhaps that was why he could be so cold and shield himself from any feelings of guilt. Rayar certainly had not learned that skill. Even if that knight had planned on capturing him or even killing him, there was still an unpleasant weight on his shoulders for the act he had committed.

"I did what I had to do, I suppose. I hope I will not have to be in such a situation again anytime soon," the prince said in a nervous tone escaping past his lips. The Royal Blade simply nodded back to him and retook the lead of the group. There was nothing more to say on the matter, the fight began, the fight ended, Rayar won.

"With what Quale has told me about the Snow Hunters in Oldome, they will help us if we can find them. I don't know much about them, apart from that they live in villages dotted all over the northern lands and that they rarely venture past the makeshift border set up by the King of Hextheene. Jac won't be able to help us find any villages either, while he is helpful, he's still just a southern bird, he won't fly this far north," the druidae girl explained. Having Jac's eyes certainly would have been useful in this situation but it appeared that they would have to make do without him. Ahead of them to the north, huge snow covered mountains pierced the skies. The only snow Rayar had ever seen before had been on the tips of the Death Valley peaks near Quale's home. Up to this point there had only been a light layer of snow on the road below their horse's hooves but now there were sheets of ice christening the blades of grass, stretching from the coast by the bridge all the way to the mountain range to the north. In the distance to the west, a mile long wooden fence stood, perhaps the height of two men, with gateways dotted along its length. This could only be the Braska Border. Most of the villages and towns that Hextheene had colonised on Oldome, lay to the east nearer the warmer coastline. No trace of Hextheene had been established past that long fence, from what he had learnt many years ago, back home.

"We will need to pass through the border and find these Snow Hunters then?" Rayar asked as he ran his emerald gaze along the wooden fence. The road they were on split in two. One path led to the border while the other turned east. Any traders or travellers who had not witnessed their antics on the bridge, continued to ride east or south back to Northfreya. No-one was heading towards the land of the Snow Hunters. This was something to keep mindful of.

"From what I know, which is not much, it is simply Hextheene wants to establish border of control between the two lands. I do not believe there is any official conflict between the two. If we are lucky and they do not get many people trying to pass the border, the guard numbers should be low." Hinsani had a point. Even though Hextheene and Southrous were not officially announced to be at war, the two countries had skirmished for so long, everyone knew of the conflict. Rayar had heard nothing of Oldome; while he was not always the sharpest or knowledgeable about current affairs, he was not completely ignorant.

"We should keep moving anyway. I don't want those bastards catching up with us. Controlling that much fire takes a toll on me, I can't do it forever," Shania mumbled in frustration as she cast an unamused glance back in the direction they had ridden.

"Agreed, let us get to the border and see what it looks like up close. We cannot do much waiting here," Rayar added. The trio reined their horses towards the west and made their way towards the wooden wall. Unlike Mayhen which had a landscape of hills and Hextheene that had many forests stretching across its land, Oldome was a flat land. The sheet of ice made it difficult for the horses to move at their fastest pace, even without slopes on the ground beneath them. The frozen grass was sharp and stiff, cracking under every step of a hoof. As they gained ground to the border the temperature suddenly became colder. It would not be long before they were trudging through thick snow. The issue now was how to get a good look at the entrance to the Snow Hunters territory, without being spotted by any Hextheene soldiers who may have been keeping guard. However there was nowhere to hide, no rocks or trees to peer out from, simply a flat icy plain. Rayar also had lost his cloak in Northfreya, torn off by soldiers, which did not assist him in managing the cold. He could feel himself visibly shaking atop his horse while once again the Royal Blade seemed completely unaffected by the same cold. He knew Hinsani had gone through much to make him so indestructible, but it could be somewhat annoying at times. Nothing seemed to stop this man, not swords, weather or even emotions. Not that Rayar would complain having such a capable warrior by his side, no matter what the situation; it was simply envy that he felt.

"Wait," Hinsani spoke back to the pair as he halted his horse. Rayar trotted up beside him and followed his gaze. Ahead, was a narrow opening in the fence they had set their sights on and beside it, a small hut had been built. Most likely the home of the soldiers stationed there. It made him wonder how often the guards changed, if they had their own little home beside the border. To think someone could be stuck here for days, or even weeks, protecting something that no one cared about. Then again, some would argue the same for the Shield in Mayhen. It had become nothing more than a glorious retreat for old or inactive guardsmen.

'I think Hyar told me that. I bet he wished he had been stationed there.' It definitely sounded like something the golden haired Royal Blade Hyar, would have mentioned. This place however, lacked the appeal of the Shield. Beside the hut two soldiers sat around a dancing fire. They appeared to be enjoying their dinner completely oblivious to the approaching party.

"I can kill them quickly without a problem," Hinsani stated as a hand found its way to the pommel of Galad. Rayar was quick to interject.

"We do not need to kill them," he commanded. The Royal Blade stared at him, once again with a look of concern.

"Didn't you learn your lesson from before?" Shania asked. The prince turned to her with a curved brow in question, unsure of what she meant. "Think it was a coincidence they cut you off in Northfreya, I bet the scout you let live let them know we were on our way. If we leave them alive, it's possible they'll let the knights know which way we are going as well. To be honest I think we'd be doing them a favour." The last part was obviously a joke, or Rayar at least hoped so. Once again a dilemma where it was two against one brewed. He had gotten his way last time and it was indeed quite possible that his decision had put them in a greater danger. However the prince had been pondering a plan.

"I said we do not need to kill them, I did not say we need to let them know who we are. If we cause a ruckus, other soldiers might show up, not to mention we do not want to be followed beyond the border. If we are going through, we have to go through without them even noticing us." Shania was now the one wearing the confused expression.

"What do you have in mind?" Hinsani asked. Rayar flashed them both a small smile and motioned them to follow. They trotted further along the length of the fence, close enough to keep it in sight as well as move around the part of the hut that shielded them from the eyes of the two soldiers engrossed in eating. There was not much cover for them to hide behind but at the distance and angle they stood, they could just about conceal their presence.

"So, here is my suggestion. I run over there and ask for help, something like my father or mother is in trouble, something along those lines. I lead them away, and then you two slip through the gateway without being noticed. Fingers crossed, they follow me away from the gate," Rayar explained as he flicked his eyes between the Royal Blade and druidae enthusiastically. Shania and Hinsani exchanged looks before their barrage of questions flowed.

"How will you get through the gate afterwards?" Shania asked with a cocked brow.

"It would be easier to just knock them unconscious if you do not wish to kill them," Hinsani added soon after. Rayar ran a hand over his golden hair as he pondered how to rein these two in.

"I will lead them to my horse, jump on and ride past them through the gate. They do not seem to have steeds so I can easily outrun them. They will not have seen you two going through the gate and therefore will not be able to pass on the information to anyone chasing us that three individuals crossed the border. Knocking them out, Master Hinsani, would also draw attention." His two companions once again, traded confused glances.

"This actually is not that complicated or well thought out you know Rayar. You're just telling them to follow you and then you run away. Also, why are you the one putting yourself at risk, why is it not Hinsani or I...?" Shania did not seem too impressed with his ploy, nor did Hinsani for that matter, as he pinched the bridge of his nose and shook his head.

"What if they do not follow you? What if they just grab you before you get on the horse? Shania and I will already be through the gate and unable to help you," the Royal Blade voiced his concerns. Indeed, these were risks, but a good and honourable man like himself had to take risks from time to time.

"Listen! It is a good plan!" Rayar snapped as the frustration of their lack of cooperation began to prick his temper. "I do not think Master Hinsani, no offence, is one to act like someone in trouble, let us be honest, and Shania, I simply do not think this is a job for a girl. Trust me, it is the only way to get us all through, without getting caught or seen. Are you going to do it, or not?" The prince made two fatal flaws in his explanation and he had realised them from the moment they slipped past his lips.

"I could act..." Hinsani mumbled to himself, but he was overwhelmed by the sudden burst of anger from Shania.

"You think you can do it and I can't because I'm a woman?!" The druidae trotted closer to the prince and repeatedly jabbed her index finger into his chest. Rayar did his best to hide the prodding pain but it was surprisingly difficult. She became terrifying to him when she became this annoyed; rivalling even the knight he had recently crossed blades with. "I have been through a lot more than you and I'm sure I can handle myself better than you can. Don't get ahead of yourself just because you have a-" She was suddenly cut off by Hinsani as he briskly hushed the pair of them.

"Enough, someone is coming." They had been so caught up in their escalating argument; they had failed to notice a man upon his own horse following the beaten path towards the gateway. He was pulling a cart along behind him full of various goods, clothes and supplies while he was wrapped up tighter than a newborn babe. Upon his head, a straw hat covered the majority of his face not allowing his features to be seen under the shadow of the trim, though they noticed that the swaddled man looked their way and dipped his head in a welcome. Rayar raised his hand in return much to the annoyance of Shania who pinched the bridge of her nose in disbelief of his casual behaviour.

"Evening," the traveller said. The group awkwardly replied with their own 'evenings'. With that, the man trotted on and towards the gate through the border. The trio trotted behind a bit closer to watch as the man approached the guards. This would be a good chance to see what sort of reaction someone would receive when trying to pass out of Hextheene's controlled lands and into mainland Oldome.

'Maybe you need papers, or perhaps they will check his cart. Maybe we should get a cart...' Rayar rattled endless thoughts through his mind as they watched with rising interest. The moment of truth arrived; the traveller reached the gateway but showed no signs of slowing his horse at all. In fact he simply trotted along at the same speed. The two soldiers continued to eat and drink their supper without even looking up from the fire. The traveller tipped his hat towards them and spoke the welcoming 'evening' once more to which the soldiers replied whilst their gaze remained down on their dinner. The traveller passed through the gateway completely unhindered. The trio stared forwards with blank expressions plastered over their faces.

"Is that it?" Shania mumbled as she looked over to the two men. Rayar blinked in surprise, they barely acknowledged the presence of the traveller at all. Could they simply just walk through? He did not have time to pitch the question to the rest of the group before Shania had grown impatient and began her own approach upon the gateway. Rayar and Hinsani were quick to follow. They kept their speed slow, Hinsani never let a hand leave the hilt of his sword while Shania seemed confident enough to simply take the lead. As she reached the long fence she kept her eyes ahead.

"Evening," she said without a care in the world. Rayar bit his lip in suspense as his emerald eyes locked on the two soldiers.

"Evenin'," one of them said before he took a swig from his mug. Shania continued forward and was through the gateway with no problems whatsoever. Next Rayar was upon them, in his head he ran the word evening over and over and over like it

393

was some sort of magical password that you needed to say correctly or be turned away for all eternity. Once he was within ear shot, the young prince awkwardly croaked out.

"Mo-eve.... evening." He could imagine Hinsani covering his face in his hand in disappointment behind him, yet refused to turn and make such an act reality within his mind. One of the soldiers chuckled as he stuffed his face with some steaming pie.

"Ha, evenin'." Yet still the eyes did not leave the fire. It was clear; they did not give a damn who passed out of these gates. At least he was able to give them a brief moment of amusement in his inability to speak normally. Once he and Hinsani were through the gate as well, Shania awaited their arrival on the other side. They continued further down a makeshift path which seemed to be the chosen route of any who would follow in this wasteland. They stopped once they were at a safe distance from the border.

"You're an idiot," Shania said before cracking up and throwing her head back in laughter. Even his Royal Blade beside him couldn't help but let a snigger of amusement escape his stone lips. Rayar frowned, flashing his eyes between the pair of them.

"We are through, so let us just forget about it and move on." Shania wiped her eyes as she shook her head at his slip up. His lack of vocal ability was the least of their concerns now. The snow here was heavy and thick on the ground; the road was hard to follow. Constant flakes of snow gently tumbled from the World Above. Night would catch up with them soon; dusk was just around the corner. They would need to locate a Snow Hunter village as quickly as possible. Unfortunately too, the traveller with the cart, who Rayar had hoped to follow, was no longer in sight.

"If we do not hurry and find somewhere soon, we could freeze to death out here," the prince advised. The increasing cold felt like it was even hardening his long green jacket. In any case, staying out in the open would be a very unwise course of action.

"If we need fire I can take care of that," Shania added to reassure the prince. She offered him a warm smile that alone would be enough to warm his blood. Forcing her to spark a flame from her blade after what she did in Northfreya simply felt selfish. "Though I think we'll leave the talking to the Snow Hunters to me and Hinsani, hm?" she added to tease him. Rayar could not help but wrinkle his nose. Now when she taunted him, there was underlying warmth, whereas before, she appeared genuinely aggressive. It felt different now.

"Let us waste no more time," Hinsani said in his deep tone. The companions followed the partially hidden pat as best they could, into the snowy wasteland. There had to be a village nearby, right?

* * *

Chapter XXXVIII
Oldome

~Rayar~

The snowy wasteland stretched as far as the eye could see. The gentle trickle of the snow from above, patted the surface of the ground making it hard to see any tracks that may have been left in the white covered grassland. Hinsani had been charitable enough to give Rayar his cloak; the Royal Blade did not seem as effected by the cold as he did. He made put up a fight though, so as not to appear selfish. Shania had wrapped herself up as tightly as she could, while a flame danced around her palm. It was an unimpressive flame in comparison to what she had shown she was capable of in the past. That was not to say the ability to even showcase such a feat wasn't still amazing in the prince's eyes. He doubted he would ever get used to seeing such magical things being performed. Not long ago, the idea of magic and druidae was simply a myth and within the space of a couple of months, he was surrounded by it. Not only that, they were on a quest to stop people with those kinds of powers as they put those he cared for at risk. It was a bit late to start second guessing this decision, their choice had been made and they needed to stick to it.

"Are you faring alright there, Shania?" Rayar asked as they trotted along, side by side. The druidae passed him a sharp glance and nodded in reply.

"Just a bit of cold, I'll be fine. Hinsani is the one we should ask, he barely has anything on as it is." The pair looked ahead to the man of iron, leading the group. With his cloak now in the hands of Rayar, all he wore was his trademark Royal Blade leather garb with the single shoulder pad. He had taken the head to see if he could spot any tracks in the snow that could lead them to a nearby village or perhaps find the traveller with the wagon, yet so far nothing had caught his attention.

"Think I should give his cloak back?" Rayar pondered aloud, partly to Shania and partly to himself. Shania snorted a laugh at him and stretched a devilish grin.

"Are you serious? He can handle it. You'd be turned to ice in seconds not to mention the complaining we'd have to put up with," she teased. Rayar could not help but crack a small smile in return. It had become one of her favourite pass times, teasing him. At first he had found it rather frustrating and allowing himself to be annoyed was exactly what she wanted. Instead letting her throw whatever she had at him, created a pleasant distraction. A bit of humour was what they needed in these kinds of situations; who knew how difficult the path ahead would be. A burst of freezing wind pierced his body which caused a shiver to run over his skin. As he looked over to Shania, her flame was blown out and she too shivered from the cold.

"Maybe I should give this cloak to you as well?" Rayar taunted in an attempt to get his own back. The druidae girl sniffed at him while she rubbed the skin under her reddening nose.

"Don't get cocky." The sudden breeze had even caused Hinsani to shiver. The Royal Blade was putting on a brave face that was for sure, but slowly he could tell the temperature was beginning to effect the warrior was well. They needed to find a village fast, or some cover at least. Anything to keep them alive. There was a major risk of freezing to death in this wasteland which they had not properly considered. As deadly as the landscape was, it was still beautiful. The sun still hung high in the sky; however the freezing wind and falling snow negated the heat from its rays. A long range of mountains that pierced the clouds, stretched as far as the eye could see to their left. They trotted, he believed, towards the north of the land. Hinsani had a knack for knowing directions, while he himself always seemed to get lost. He was gradually losing the feelings in his fingers; his toes too were becoming numb. The cold seemed to be getting worse and worse the deeper they ventured into Oldome.

"We cannot stay out here much longer," Rayar mumbled through a shivering voice. Hinsani nodded in agreement and turned around to face them. His beard had frosted over and his face was coloured a sickly blue.

"Agreed," he grunted back. The man looked as if he had been frozen to his horse; the horses too, were beginning to seriously struggle. Just then, as if the World Above answered their prayers, or in actual fact, the World Below cursed them, a spear flew from behind a mound of snow and pierced the ground in front of Hinsani. As if the cold no longer mattered to the Royal Blade, his hand gripped the hilt of his blade, as did Rayar's whilst Shania reached for her cinder block.

"Don't move a muscle!" a voice echoed out, the voice of a woman carried on the heavy winds. In the snow around them, figures began to appear from their hidden positions. Over a dozen men and women draped in heavy fur clothes, all wielding spears and bows, emerged and surrounded the party.

'Snow hunters?' Rayar thought to himself as his emerald eyes flickered from figure to figure encircling them. A pair from the group approached them from the flank with their spears poised ready to strike at any given moment. The trio grouped together, as close as they could, their horses reacting nervously to the sudden ambush.

"Who goes there!?" Hinsani called out as he inched his blade from its scabbard. The two figures near them pulled down their large leather and fur hoods. One was a young woman with dark skin and piercing brown eyes, who was naturally attractive, Rayar thought. Quite a strange opinion to suddenly have in such a situation, but women seemed to have that effect on him. Her dark hair was short and unkempt and she wore an expression of curiosity, not aggression. Whilst her gaze only briefly shifted over Hinsani and Shania, for the most part, it rested on him. Beside her stood a young man, who looked strikingly similar to the woman. He stood shorter than his female companion but was much more stocky and broad.

"That's our question to you," the woman draped in leather and fur retorted, barely taking her eyes off him. "Don't see many mainlanders come through this way, usually just the same old folk. Got to stay vigilant of new faces, can't trust mainlanders," she stated. The young man beside her grumbled and stumbled forwards. He eyed up Hinsani, who in return cast his dark cold glare.

"Something you want to say, old man?" The young man was trying to antagonise him, little did he know who he was talking to. The Royal Blade reined his horse closer to the man covered in fur.

"Words are for those who cannot act," he stated as harshly. Shania rolled her eyes and finally interjected to try and disperse any hostilities.

"I apologise for my friend. He's stubborn. We mean no harm to anyone. We were looking for somewhere to find some warmth, food possibly. We're looking for Snow Hunters," she explained. The pair dressed in fur looked at each other and burst into laughter, much to the dismay and confusion of Rayar and his companions. The prince scratched the top of his head, unsure of what they had found so entertaining.

"I am sorry but what is it that is so funny?" he asked. The young woman turned to Rayar and grabbed the rein of his steed.

"Snow Hunters? That's a pretty basic name you've given us. Mainlanders call us by that do they?" she asked. Rayar wrinkled his nose.

"Mainlanders is not much better, either." This only caused the woman to laugh even harder. After a few more moments of laughter, she shook her head and motioned them to follow.

"Our village isn't far. If you're looking for ... Snow Hunters, you've found some. Well, got found by some at least. I'll make sure you won't freeze, this time," she said in a sultry manner. Rayar heard a cough from behind him as Shania almost choked on the very air she was breathing. The prince glanced back to see a heavy brow and a glare that could burn through his clothes.

'Why am I getting glared at!?' he thought as he peeled away his eyes and pretended not to have noticed the world ending glare of the druidae. The group, who had claimed to be Snow Hunters, circled the three horses and led them through the snow. There was not much talking between the two groups. The pair, who had now removed their hoods, took the lead for the entire short journey. Rayar could feel the searing eyes of Shania in his spine. The walk did not take long; it was strange to watch as this group of hunters knew exactly where they were going while to him everything looked the same. They trekked over a few snow mounds and around some large oddly shaped boulders that looked hand crafted with patterns covering the surfaces covered in snow. He eventually found himself confronted with a large village. The houses were like tents, yet seemed structured and fixed in place with wooden supports keeping them upright. The supports were huge logs as thick as a stone pillar. It was also surprisingly bustling for such a remote area of the land. A river ran through the centre of the village where a small dock had been built and tiny boats were lined up along the bank. Children ran through the paths between the tents, chasing each other with sticks and planks of wood used as shields, claiming they were knights in battle. Skins hung on stands along the side of what appeared to be a small market area. The cold and powerful wind had all but disappeared. Rayar quickly figured out that the crafted boulders they had passed, shielded the village from the elements around them; the same boulders encircled the village as far as he could see. As the trio were led through the town pathway, the people of the village stopped in their day to day business to watch them curiously, whispering to each other. It all felt a little bit

awkward, though the brief flash of a cheeky smile from the Snow Hunter ahead of him, settled his nerves. They stopped at a large open tent, occupied by giant fur coated horses. Most likely used as a stable, but the beasts inside were like nothing he had seen before.

"You can leave your horses in here, I'm sure you'll want to meet the Kra'Urn... well, what would you say? Chief? Leader? The person in charge basically," the stocky young man said as he motioned into the vast tent.

"Yes, if that isn't a problem," Shania slipped in before Rayar had a chance to reply. The group dismounted their steeds and were taken towards another large tent, across the way from the makeshift stables. The tents themselves shaped like domes were covered in patches of fur and animal skins and were painted a variety of colours with symbols he had never seen before. Rayar wondered were in fact letters, yet the language from unknown to him. He did not know much about the Snow Hunters, nor did Hinsani as it happened and even Shania had little knowledge of their ways and customs. So far, apart from the sudden ambush, they had been fairly friendly and much more welcoming than he had expected from the occasional rumours he had heard. Once outside the largest tent in the village, the young man motioned them inside with his spear.

"Go on then, he's probably just filling his face with food. He usually does." The young woman entered first followed by Rayar and his friends. The rest of the Snow Hunters, who had escorted them to the village, had already dispersed with their game, presumably their hunt of the day. Once inside, Rayar felt a wall of heat collide with his face. The tent was completely open with a raging fire in the centre. The smoke gently drifted up through the tent and exit a small hole in the ceiling. The decor of the tent was astonishing, something close to what he had in Heldon. Paintings propped up against wooden supports, chairs, tables and even a giant curtained bed at the far end. On the other side of the fire from where they entered, sat a very large man. His skin was darker than his own pale flesh and he was rotund, huge in fact. He didn't appear tall but he was

401

stocky and round, larger than Rumeo that was for sure. He sat topless with drawings all over his arms, chest and stomach and he seemed somewhat older than Hinsani, but perhaps younger than his own father. This man had a warm look to him as he munched joyously upon a boned leg of an animal, perhaps elk. As they entered, the large man threw up his arms.

"Pola, Seran! Welcome back from your hunt! Ho, ho, ho! You brought some visitors too. Didn't even give me time to properly prepare myself," the big man joked. He motioned for Rayar, Shania and Hinsani to sit by the fire next to him. The trio had remained somewhat speechless since entering the tent, stunned by the overwhelming sight. "Sit, sit! Who have I got here then?" he asked enthusiastically. As soon as Rayar took a seat, the girl the chief named Pola suddenly plopped herself down beside him, almost knocking Shania out the way. She offered the young prince a sly grin to which he could only swallow nervously. The druidae allowed a quiet grumble to pass through her lips before sitting herself down on the other side of Pola. Hinsani stood with his arms crossed; his eyes scanned the room slowly for any potential threats. Being welcomed so easily was probably setting off an alarm bell in his head. He was always very cautious, after all.

"Greetings, I am Rayar Granlia of Mayhen. This here is Shania Tear and Hinsani Tannaroth." Rayar introduced all three of them but decided to leave out the introduction, that he was a prince. He decided also to allow Shania to reveal she was a druidae in her own time if that was her intention. She already seemed angry enough as it was with him and he had yet to figure out why. The large chief patted his bare stomach and chuckled with a heavy tone.

"I see! Well welcome to Mahaai. I'm Tecamah of the Mahaai and these are my children, Pola of the Mahaai and Seran of the Mahaai." He briefly glanced over to his son who, like Hinsani, had not taken a seat and instead was picking at some of the miniature feast the chief had been enjoying. "Where did you find our new friends?" Seran glanced up with his mouth full with food and gave a muffled reply.

"Our hunting ground, just walking about lost." Seran continued to pick the food apart that was still left on the long mat beside the fireplace. Rayar watched in awe, they were so friendly and relaxed. It made a pleasant change from their recent experiences in Hextheene and not at all what he had expected. The chief returned his attention to Rayar and Shania while Hinsani finally took a seat. He must have finally been satisfied that this was not some sort of trap. As paranoid as one might assume the Royal Blade was, his suspicious nature and perseverance kept them alive. Rayar on the other hand, was rather naïve and much less aware of danger. Deep down he knew it this, even if it would have been more practical to train a more watchful eye.

"Well, my friends - eat and drink. Tell me of the tale that led three mainlanders to be wandering aimlessly in the great white plain?" Tecamah leaned forward; his intense focus on them caused Rayar to stiffen in his seat. Shania looked over to him as they mentally debated who would speak. Shania decided it would be her.

"We're travelling to stop something terrible happening and stop people who want to do those terrible things. You may or may not know of the Order. Members in their group attacked my... friend here." She motioned to Rayar, "and stole something precious. We believe what was stolen is in the former druidae grove and we need to get there to get it back. But, we don't know the way. We came to Oldome in the hope that someone in your land would help us find the path to the grove?" The moment she mentioned the druidae grove, all three of the Snow Hunters froze and traded glances. Seran had been half way through filling his mouth as he suddenly turned rigid and stared at Shania.

"The Druidae Grove? You want to go to that forbidden place?" Pola asked the druidae girl.

"We must go. It is not a matter of want. It is a matter of need," Rayar interjected to support his friend. The young woman of the Mahaai looked over to him and offered a smirk.

403

"Sounds important, *and* dangerous." Once again he heard a groan from Shania.

"I see, I see. My daughter is correct, it is forbidden to step into the grove I'm afraid. The druidae were slain many years ago and we were unable to help them. For that it is forbidden to enter those lands," the chief, Tecamah, explained. Shania raised her hand towards the flames; Rayar knew exactly what was about to happen. The fire in the centre of the tent began to grow and twist and dance. It took on the shape of a large tree, being manipulated in ways a fire could not naturally perform. The people of the Mahaai leaned back in shock and surprise as the flames seemed to have a will of their own.

"Not all the druidae were slain," Shania added. The chief laughed out loud, which was as surprising as the flames becoming alive, and rested his attention on the young druidae woman.

"Well by the Frost God, I never thought I'd see the day a druidae still lives and breathes! This is wondrous news indeed! Druidae should be able to return home whenever they please, but you still need our help to find it?" Rayar had become an observer to this conversation at this point; it was a feeling of being out of his depth.

"I did not live in the grove. I don't know where it is unfortunately. That is why we need your help to find it. Quale said Snow Hunters would help us if we asked them, if they knew who I was. You know who I am now, will you help us?" Shania spoke with a sense of urgency and dominance. She was not one to beat around the bush when there was something she wanted. It was something Rayar admired about her. Tecamah appeared to consider her proposal for a time, rubbing his chin in thought as he looked between the three companions. By the looks of his struggling expression, it was not an easy decision to make.

"Very well, the Mahaai will help you. I know the Quale you mentioned. My children here will guide you, they can only lead you to the grove, but they can't enter it. Tomorrow though, the weather is taking a turn for the worse. I sense tomorrow will be easier for travel. It would be fine for us, of course, but for you three, perhaps too harsh. We will also see about getting you some warmer clothes. I'm surprised this one, the quiet one here, could stand it in just those flimsy garments! Haha!" The chief motioned to Hinsani who had remained silent for the entire conversation. That moment pressured him to make a bit more of an effort, they were guests after all.

"My body is trained to withstand any and all obstacles," he stated simply. Tecamah chuckled at the reply.

"He's a stiff one isn't he?" Both Rayar and Shania responded in union with a nod. With that the chief pushed himself to his feet and motioned to Shania to join him.

"Come, my dear. Tell me about Quale and how he fares. I have not seen that man in over twenty years. He used to visit Oldome all the time, but then simply vanished." Shania passed the prince one more glare before she rose to her feet and strolled over to join the chief for their conversation across the tent. Seran, whom had finally eaten his fill, turned towards the exit.

"Suppose I will see about getting you some warmer clothes and somewhere to sleep for the night," the Snow Hunter said as he strolled towards the doorway flap. The young man raised a brow at to which she simply smirked in his direction and waved him away. Rayar however, for the latter point of the exchange, had been sitting there awkwardly, not sure what input he could have made to benefit the conversation. The dark skinned girl leaned closer to him and placed a hand on his thigh, her piercing eyes locked into his own.

"I like your hair, never seen anything like it before. It's so colourful," she said, her free hand slipped a slender finger into the strands and began to play furtively with his locks.

"Oh... thank you," Rayar squeezed out. He could feel his cheeks flushing a deep red; women were always acting so strangely with him.

"Don't see many mainlanders here, they're usually old men transporting goods, selling and buying. Someone coming here on some dangerous quest, it's like a tale of old. It'll be fun

405

showing you the way," she added with her face dangerously close to his.

"I appreciate the assistance." Whenever he found himself in these kinds of situations, which in truth was very rare, he became very rigid and overly formal. Like a stone pillar he sat there, unable to move a muscle.

"Cold got to you? Did say I'd make sure you're warmed up." There was another sensation. A burning feeling in the side of his face. His emerald eyes travelled across the tent to find Tecamah and Shania talking quietly, though her sword sharp eyes were on him. Shania's glare was as hot as the fire she controlled and she was currently charring him to a cinder. Just then he was saved, as Hinsani placed a hand on his shoulder and lifted him to his feet.

"Perhaps another time. We have something to discuss, Rayar." As if the World Above had answered his prayers for salvation, Hinsani dragged the bewildered young man out of the tent and into the fresh air. Finally the prince could breath, the stiffness of his body subsiding.

"Master H-Hinsani, something to discuss?" he asked, unsure of what was on the Royal Blades mind.

"Not really. I did not want the druidae girl to burn the tent to the ground and take me with you." Was that a joke? Had Hinsani actually made a jest at his expense? Shania was rubbing off on him.

"I did not do anything, did I?" Rayar pleaded. He was an innocent man. He had simply sat there and had a conversation, even if his side of the conversation had been pretty lacking in substance.

"I will protect you from any danger and serve at your side until my dying breath. Yet, Prince Rayar, I do not think I can help you when it comes to women." With that the Royal Blade turned on his heel and began to investigate the village as he strolled down the paths between tents. Rayar was quick to follow.

'Help me with women? I do not understand! They are all mad as far as I am concerned.'

*

~Caskin~

Caskin sat upon his steed eyeing up the surrounding snow covered land beyond the border. The two guards of the gate, who had allowed multiple people to pass through unopposed, swung from the nearby window of their assigned hut. Rope wrapped around their necks as their limp bodies swayed from side to side, briefly bumping into each other in the increasing wind. Disobeying an order was treason, and neglecting an order was similarly so. The moment they did not take their position seriously, those two soldiers would find the noose. The blonde haired knight eyed the far landscape; there was no way to tell which way the witch, prince and famous warrior had gone, or if they had even passed through the gate. The tracks Sir Osmear was clever enough to have noticed, had led to the border. The two guardsmen had admitted to allowing people to pass without checking who they were. That was enough to fuel his motivation and belief that they were still possibly on the right trail. Sir Donnel Jennin trotted up beside the Commander-at-Arms, following his hopeful gaze. It was harder to see in the distance with the darkness of the night slowly approaching - the sun setting, allowing the last rays of orange glow to fill the sky,

"What do we do now? How can we tell which way they went?" the knight nervously asked. Caskin restrained the desire to strike the knight down from his steed. Something about that man's inability to show any pride or strength, struck deep within him.

"That is what I am thinking, 'Sir' Jennin, I am attempting to figure it out," his tone betrayed his distaste as he spelt out the words with a stark tongue. The men were not dressed for this kind of environment. Their metal armour and chainmail was not coated in fur or leather to withstand the cold. Trekking through such heavy snow without a direct destination could lead to the unneeded death of his men. Would he have to end the search here? King Braska would never stand for such failure. They had them by the tips of their fingers and they let them go. Such a miserable failure would never go unpunished. Sir Osmear soon joined the pair upon the back of his horse.

"The men are seeing to rations. Sir Nash is overseeing it while we come up with a plan. Got anything yet, Commander?" the elderly knight asked as he rubbed his moustache. Caskin shook his head in reply.

"Tracks would be even more difficult to follow and the thought of being ambushed by those savage Snow Hunters makes me uneasy. We may not have hostilities, but it is not the most loving relationship. However, the boy's golden hair is not hard to miss if we spot him in this forsaken place." Caskin ran a gloved hand over his short blonde hair as he continued to ponder any idea that sprung into his mind. Most, unfortunately, were a waste of time.

"I can help you." The three knights turned at the sound of a croaky old voice. There stood an old man wrapped in a long multi-coloured patchwork cloak, it appeared homemade and tattered, with a variety of colours spanning its length. His hair was messy and grey under a straw hat. He gripped a long staff as a walking stick in one hand and a sword was tucked away in his belt. It was small and well-hidden but not hidden well enough for the keen eye of the Commander-at-Arms.

"And who are you old timer?" Caskin asked as his fingers caressed the pommel of his bastard sword. After what they witnessed in Northfreya, they could never be too careful.

"Just a tradesman, my lord. I saw I think who you're talkin' about. A golden haired boy had two others with him, a girl and a strange lookin' man. I know where they're going, I overheard them." The three knights traded glances before Caskin snapped at the older gentleman.

"Well, where!?" A large grin grew across the face of the old man.

"The Druidae Grove," Caskin's eyes widened. Such a place was purely myth, stories the people of Oldome gabbled on about, but had never actually seen. Was this man mad, trying to get a rise out of them? He was picking a bad time to try and be a jester.

"The Druidae Grove does not exist, are you speaking falsely?" Osmear wisely asked before Caskin had a chance to lose his temper. The old knight must have noticed how impatient he had become since Northfreya.

"I speak true. Whether exists or not ain't an issue, it's where they want to go. I've been round these lands for donkey's years my friends. I know the way, I can lead you." The Commander-at-Arms grimaced at the thought of some peasant being the saviour of their expedition, if he did indeed speak true, but what other choice did they have.

"What is in it for you, old timer?" Caskin asked as he weighed the man up. The figure in the straw hat rolled his shoulders in a shrug.

"I'm a loyal man of Hextheene my lords. Been seein' some shady people goin' that way, want to do my part." This was a gamble. If this was a mad man, they could be led into the middle of the snowy wasteland and simply die from the cold. If he was telling the truth, then it was possible he would not return to Hexhold empty handed. Osmear looked to him and offered a reassuring grandfatherly smile, his moustache twitching above his lips, from shivering.

"Commander, it is your call." They may never have a chance like this again. There was only one option to take.

"Show us the way, old timer." The die had been cast. The outcome had yet to be decided.

* * *

Chapter XXXIX
Path to the Grove
~Rayar~

The room Rayar had been granted was surprisingly quite pleasant. It was a basic tent with a small fire in the centre, much like the tent the chief had occupied. The fire ablaze in his abode was considerably less impressive than that of Tecamah. It did however keep the tent warm in the cold land, which he counted as a blessing. The weather in Mayhen was either scalding hot with periods of draught or with heavy rains for one whole season. It was never truly cold. Not like this anyway. The first time ever he had walked in snow, had been an uplifting experience yet now all he wanted to do was return to a place of warmth, to walk along the grass without frozen blades below his feet. To think he had come all this way and still found a longing for home. Yet, when he was out in the wilderness with Shania in the Mayhen countryside, he had never felt so at home. It was an odd feeling. He felt at peace in the forests; it had been strangely calming. Hooked up on one of the nearby posts that supported the tent, Seran had placed clothes for their travel through the snowy wasteland; a large fur and leather coat, tanned in colour and rather simple. It was not something he had worn before but for the climate and landscape they were travelling, it made a lot more sense than his usual attire. While he was admiring the garments, the flap to the tent slipped open and in the doorway stood Shania eyeing him with that sharp glare she had grown so fond of using on him. Rayar sighed and held up his hands defensively.

"What now? Come to pick a fight with me?" he asked with a rather unneeded confrontational tone. The druidae sighed at him and shook her head apologetically.

"No, Rayar. I shouldn't have been acting that way towards you but you're still an idiot." The prince raised his eyebrows at her as she wandered into his assigned tent and peered around inquisitively. "I'm surprised. I didn't expect them to been so... sophisticated I suppose. They may live in tents in the snowy wasteland but it is as if they have the same... the same..." She pondered for a moment as if the word had escaped her.

"Customs as us?" Rayar suggested. Shania laughed softly under her breath and found a spot to sit down next to the gentle flickering fire. The chairs were not like the ones at home, they were so low. To sit upon them a person had to cross their legs as if they were meditating like Hinsani.

"Something like that, like you anyway. The way I lived was nothing like the way you did Rayar. Fancy castles and gardens with servants and guards protecting you all day and night. I lived in the mountains, hidden away with a crazy old man who half the time spoke in riddles." The prince lowered himself down next to the druidae, into his awkward cross legged position. Being somewhat taller than an average man, it made his long legs look peculiar. Rayar could not help but notice a pattern with Shania's behaviour, in regards to himself at least. She could be cold but then sometimes joke around with him in public yet when it was just the pair of them; she had begun to open up more and seemed more natural. Not that he tended to pry, but she had lived an interesting life.

"Had you always been stuck in the mountains, I mean after Quale saved you from the grove?" She shook her head.

"No, I was able to leave and travel around as long as Quale used his little illusion to hide me from our enemies. I wasn't as restricted as you might have been, if that is what you mean?" she explained. He had never really understood what she and the old man had meant about hiding their presence. Quale was

411

certainly a man of mystery with many stories and talents. Rayar felt as if the old sage had not been completely open in everything he had told them.

"Before you came along, I had never left the capital. I had seen the city a few times but mostly I remained in the keep. Spent most of my days lying in the garden watching the clouds drift by. I talked a lot about seeing the world and making a difference yet... I suppose I was pretty lazy. A comfortable lifestyle can lead to such an unfavourable trait." He thought his explanation sounded somewhat silly as the words actually left his lips, but that was who he was, laid back with no problems or responsibilities. Even issues of the kingdom were not his concern, Rumeo had seen that he was cared for at all times and was prepared for his future. Nothing like this, of course. He had never been prepared for anything like this.

"In a way I guess that was kind of nice? Have no troubles, to be the son of a King. Quale used to tell me about royalty. He taught me that they were all fighting over something that never belonged to them, it belonged to nature. The land, the people, the kingdoms, it was nature which owned everything and the druidae kept that nature safe. That was until they were all killed. He couldn't teach me anything about using my power. I had to learn that all on my own, using his notes of druidae." The prince leaned back in his chair and listened to her tale. This had been the most she had opened up since they had met.

"It was nice. However I envied those with more freedom. I can imagine that old coot having notes on everything. His house was like a mangled library." Rayar chuckled to himself at his small joke, though it was only rewarded a slight smile from the druidae.

"As crazy as he seems and as odd as our relationship was, he was the closest thing I had to a father. He protected me, looked out for me, taught me and cared for me. He may not look the type to have raised a child. In truth, he wasn't that bad at first. Over time, the more research he did, the more his mind decayed. He claimed it started long ago, something happened which he could never recover from. He never told me what it

412

was." Her eyes seemed to sadden as she reminisced about her past. Rayar realised there was one thing in particular they could relate on.

"Well, I too know what it is like in a way. King Rumeo is not my real father, nor is Queen Julian my real mother. They adopted me as a baby after my home, in Highhall, was burnt to the ground. My father was a man named Randal Vienne. Sadly I never knew who my mother was. She died not long after I was born; I was told and was not a Noble Lady. Yet Rumeo and Julian were amazing parents, I could not have asked for more." Shania blinked at him in surprise. While his heritage was indeed a secret, there were quite a few in the capital who knew he was not a true Granlia.

"Oh really? You hold yourself like a fancy prince; I thought it was in your blood. I suppose you're just posing as a nobleman then?" she said jokingly as she nudged him in the ribs with her elbow. Rayar laughed softly in reply and rubbed his superficial wound.

"You think I am fancy then do you?" he replied. A boyish grin stretched across his lips, "well, I think yo-" his words were suddenly cut off as her hands clasped his cheeks and her lips pressed against his. All the blood in his body exploded into his pale cheeks at the sudden kiss planted on him. He sat there with his hands hung loosely at his side unsure of what exactly was happening. While his eyes were wide open, the emerald green glistening with shock, hers were closed. Shania's lips felt soft and supple, not like anything he had felt before. They remained in place for a while longer before finally Rayar drew the courage from his inner being and wrapped his arms around the druidae girl.

'Women are crazy,' he thought as he finally closed his eyes and embraced Shania.

Morning bloomed over the snowy landscape. Rayar was adorned with his gifted fur attire as were Shania and Hinsani. Their horses were to be left in the stables for their return as Tecamah had recommended going by foot. The horses would struggle too much in the cold and would be unable to pass into the grove. Apparently they would be going through mountains once more. Rayar could think of nothing he would want less than to climb through rocky mountains again but with their journey fast coming to an end, they needed to get through the last few remaining obstacles. Pola and Seran had also prepared themselves to travel, with large sacks strapped over their backs containing supplies and their spears in their hands. The two Snow Hunters were briefly talking to their father across the village, while the companions prepared their own packs with supplies for the journey, generously given by the village folk. Rayar could not help but pass a small bashful glance towards Shania who in return offered him a small soft smile. Typically, at that moment Hinsani loomed over him, the shadowy figure eyeing him intently.

"Everything alright, Prince Rayar?" he asked in that deep tone of his. The prince swallowed and nodded rather vigorously.

"Of course, everything is good, great. Why would it not be? Something happened? What did you hear?" Hinsani continued to stare down towards the young prince as he was packing his sack.

"You seem on edge," the Royal Blade pried. Rayar chuckled nervously in reply.

"I am fine, do not worry about me! Ready as I will ever be." He briefly glanced to Shania during his embarrassing laugh, to which she responded with a pinch of the bridge of her nose and a small shaking of the head.

"Good, Shania come here too. I have something to say," Hinsani commanded. The druidae rolled her eyes, she never seemed to like being ordered around by the warrior but she responded this time regardless. Was Hinsani actually about to give a speech?

"Listen to me closely," he began. "You have your reasons for being here, for coming this far. I follow Prince Rayar of course, but I understand his plight. We are about to step into the belly of the beast. If Prince Rayar's vision is correct and the

414

pearl is in the grove, it is likely being protected by those of the Order. Magic is still a mystery to me. I will do what I can should battle erupt. Take heed of this, we are going against people we do not know, nor know their true motives, regardless of what Quale has told us. We act carefully and we work together. Shania, with your power I cannot think of much that can stop you. Rayar and I will have your back when this battle begins. Rayar, why are you here?" Rayar blinked as the attention was focused on him but he quickly conjured up his resolve.

"To protect my family, to help clear my name in Mayhen and... and to do some good in this world." He hoped that sounded convincing enough. The same question was pitched to Shania across from him.

"You know why, I'm here to finally get revenge on those bastards for what they did and like Rayar, stop them from bringing back the Second Coming." Hinsani nodded to them both, a hand found each of their shoulders.

"Remember that. Remember what drives you forward; what gives you motivation and clarity. We are in deep, facing forces that I never knew were truly a threat. We only have each other going forward, understand?" Rayar nodded together with Shania. It was true, the three of them embarked on this journey when everything behind them was going mad. Mayhen going into ruin, even civil war. Yet if he could stop it from where he was, he would do so, even if they did not know it was him who helped them. There was no one standing up for the people of this world anymore. This calling, he would take and serve it as well as he could. He may not have had the skill of Hinsani or the power of Shania but nothing would stop him doing what he had to do to ensure the safety of everyone he cared for as well as the safety of the people in the Freeland. Pola and Seran soon joined them as they prepared to take their leave of the Mahaai village.

"You folks ready?" Pola asked passing a smirk towards Rayar as she did. The prince flashed a smile in return and turned towards the exit from where they entered the village.

"Lead the way." With that the siblings took the head of the group and made their way from the village. The other inhabitants of the village still gave them strange glances and stared as they took their leave, just as when they entered. Children ran around playing games, fighting each other with long sticks, though in a playful manner. It was quaint here, calming and friendly, something he would actually miss. He wished he could have spent more time with the Mahaai. He had thought the same thing about Northfreya and that turned into a complete debacle. Perhaps at the moment it was wise not to remain anywhere for too long. The group of five left the village and set out into the snowy wasteland. It was not long before Seran had taken the lead, as he seemed like the more sensible of the siblings, from what Rayar could gather. Neither of them seemed particularly mature, perhaps only sixteen seasons old each, if he had to guess. Pola had retreated from the head of the group and firmly settled herself by the side of the prince. Shania walked behind the pair though her anger from the other day did not seem as apparent, in fact she did not seem too concerned at all. Hinsani held position of the rear guard. It was a strange change to have him watching the rear, as he had become known in their little group for wanting to lead.

"So, what exactly is the terrible thing you are stopping in the Druidae Grove?" the Snow Hunter asked as she strolled close to his side. Rayar glanced back to Shania to see if she would oppose the question yet a shrug was the only response he was returned. The fact that these people used to be allies of the druidae, should surely mean they did not need to hide such details.

"A group named the Order. Members of it with an evil agenda have stolen something precious of mine which supposedly holds great power. We are going to take it back and stop these mages," he loosely explained. By her expression, he would have guessed his explanation was slightly confusing. In her defence, he had not been that particular with the details.

"I see. The Kra'Urn, uh... the chief, my father, he has told me some things about mages, Controllers aren't they? They can manipulate energy, people's souls he says." Well Rayar had not heard their power be worded that way, which made the entire situation they were walking into, even more terrifying.

"What do you mean manipulate the soul?" he asked dubiously, in the hope of some clarification.

"Hard to explain, only people who can do it can explain it I think. All father could really explain was the use of energy, imagination. I don't really know myself. Yet if you're going to fight people like that, you'll need more than just swords." She almost sounded smug when she spoke; in fact she was indeed very smug. Shania found an opportunity to slip into the conversation.

"Well we have more than just swords, we have me," the druidae stated proudly. Pola glanced back to her, her smirk plastered across her lips.

"I saw; a druidae who can control fire! I was told that was rare too! You'll be fine. These two are in real trouble." Before Rayar had a chance to defend himself or Hinsani, the brother of the mouthy girl called back.

"Stop teasing them, Pola." The young woman chuckled and nodded.

"I apologise, I'm sure they'll be fine." Neither of the pair of Snow Hunters seemed too concerned really, even with the knowledge that the group were heading into certain peril. Since it was forbidden land, Tecamah had made it clear they could only take them to the edge of the grove and that his children would not go inside.

"Why did you laugh when we called you Snow Hunters?" Rayar asked, to change the subject. Pola glanced over to him, offering that signature smirk.

"We just found it funny. We hunt in the snow, so Snow Hunters. Here in Oldome we are called The True Born, or perhaps Firsts. Either one is usually fine," she exclaimed. Both names were particularly odd to the prince; he imagined there was something more to it.

"I must ask, why is that?" he inquired.

"The First Coming was born here and led the people south, a thousand years ago, to retake the mainland from the monsters. Our people stayed here and held the homeland. That is the story we were told, anyway. I was also told that Oldome basically means old home and also that Oldome used to be a sunny and green land until a few hundred years ago. Again, just stories we are told when we are young." Rayar listened intently. It was actually quite enthralling to hear about places such as these. He had heard little of Oldome back in Heldon apart from that it was a frozen wasteland and always had been but even he knew the First Coming had led the charge to save humanity from the north, many, many years ago.

"And you call us mainlanders, our land is the Freeland. Should we not be Freelanders?" The golden haired boy asked. Pola laughed at his attempt to be witty.

"Maybe, but mainlanders' works fine with me and the rest of us." Shania soon moved up alongside the pair, beside Rayar, leaving Hinsani alone at the back of the group. Once she joined them, the conversation changed to basic, simple questions like *'What is the mainland like?'* or *'do you live in a castle?'* anything to pass the time, it seemed. She was a sweet girl, if a bit cocky in her attitude. It was hard to have an opinion of her brother Seran; he only really focused on guiding the party and not so much their company. The walk did not continue for long, as before they knew it, they had reached the mountain-side. Before them a steep and piercing natural rock formation that reached higher into the clouds than Rayar could see.

"Alright, we need to pass through the mountain range. There is a hidden pathway somewhere around here." The prince ran his eyes over the stone, curious as to how Seran knew that this was the location, until his emerald gaze rested upon a pattern in the rock. A large symbol had been carved into the stone. A circle around a star with five different points poking from various sides. Shania strode up to the engraving with a look of awe etched into her face. Her gloved fingers traced the carving inquisitively.

"Wind, Earth, Water, Fire... and one more... I don't know this one," Shania mumbled. Rayar realised what the symbols represented. The four points of the star pointed to engravings, a flame, a droplet, four lines and a tree. At the very top however was an odd symbol that did not seem to resemble any sort of element he could imagine. It was a face, or perhaps a mask, with one eye carved in and the other not. It had a mouth with two dots for nostrils.

"People?" Hinsani suggested as he caught up with the others.

"The druidae couldn't control people," Shania quickly threw back in rebuttal. Seran had been running his own hands along the length of the stone while Pola traced the other side.

"Found it!" the female snow hunter called out. She pushed her back into a rock that protruded from the mountain face and slowly the stone where the symbol had been located began to rise. Shania, who had been inspecting it, suddenly jumped back in surprise as the rock formed an archway and opened up into a long dark tunnel. A steady flow of air coursed through the length of the chasm and at the very far end, almost too small to see, a speck of light.

"Above and Below..." Rayar gasped, his mouth gaped open in sheer awe. It was like a drawbridge gate, built into the stone which worked with a single push of a lever instead of needing several men to turn a wheel. Hinsani also seemed somewhat surprised by the sight.

"Not seen that before," the Royal Blade mumbled under his breath. The two Snow Hunters returned to their companions and bowed their heads.

"This is as far as we can go. We can wait here to help you escape if you like? Only because father said we should, if you asked us to. I don't really want to sit in the snow and wait for you," Seran stated in a not so charitable manner. Pola flashed a cheeky grin. Her opinion differed from her brothers.

"I don't mind waiting for you," Pola admitted. Shania looked over to her two male friends to address them.

"I think we can handle it alone?" she half asked, half told. Rayar and Hinsani had no chance to say anything before Seran grabbed his sister by the fur collar and began to pull her away.

"If you say so," Seran shrugged in reply. That boy certainly had no desire to be here, it would not have been fair to force them to stay. Pola on the other hand, was not so keen to abandon them.

"Father suggested it because it is the right thing to do, Seran. You can go back if you want. I'm waiting here for them to get out. They might need us." She knocked her brothers grip from her clothing and plopped herself against the steep mountainside. She may have been slightly intrusive and even rude, but Rayar could not help but feel respect towards her, as well as concern. If they were really going against people with such power they could not conceive, then he did not want to feel responsible for their safety.

"No, Pola... of the Mahaai. As honoured as I am, as we are, that you wish to stay for us, I could not forgive myself or ever face your father, should something happen to you as well. Trust in us, we have it under control," Rayar preached. One of the few times he actually felt like an adult. The young woman smiled at him, not a smirk this time, before she made her way over and planted a kiss on his cheek.

"Don't die in an embarrassing way," she said coyly. The two Snow Hunters wished them luck and began on their return journey back to the Mahaai village. The trio peered down the long, dark tunnel to what they had been told, was the Druidae Grove. There was no turning back now. Shania stepped up beside the young prince and wiped the side of his cheek playfully.

"You heard her, don't die embarrassingly." Rayar rolled his eyes at her jest.

"Same to you," they shared a brief exchange of feeble smiles, he knew his was out of concern for her and suspected hers was the same for him. Hinsani took the lead once more, hand wrapped tightly around the hilt of Galad at his hip.

"The time for games is over. We must all be on our best form. Agreed?" There was nothing more to do than continue on into the darkness and hope the other side was their destination. What lay on the other side would likely be their biggest challenge yet. They had come this far together. They would see it through together.

* * *

Chapter XL
History of Hextor
~Braska~

The King of Hextheene always felt out of place in these halls. In the eastern wing of Hexhold, a long hall had stood for generations of Hextor Kings. To commemorate their service to the realm and their place in history, busts had been carved from precious marble found on one of the far East islands, shipped to Northfreya and then to Ganon. It was a difficult material to get one's hands on these days and cost a hefty sum. Despite this, it was used to sculpt the busts of all the Hextor Kings throughout the known history. Braska had never felt welcome here, he was never meant to be the King of this great country. He was simply the second best after the death of his brother at the hands of unknown mages during the battles with Southrous, an event which still haunted him even to this day. Yet even in his ascension, in the line of succession, he would always do his best to show that he could rule just as well as his brother would have. The blood of a Hextor was that of holy origin, precious and rare. No meek human could merely wield such blood and ascend to the throne; they must have proved their worth. Braska felt that he would never have the luxury of complacency. He would always be expected to prove himself again and again. That also extended to his son, Kerrin. The young boy was nothing like him. He was small, fragile, feminine – the opposite of his father. Each man had his strengths and weakness it was true, yet a Hextor was expected to have only strengths. The King strode down the long narrow hall with his son close behind him, as they gazed upon the busts of the Hextor Kings. Torches graced the room along each side and above each bust. They did not create much light for the hall itself, the light allowed each bust to be surrounded by a glorious glow, focusing attention on each one, as if they projected the World Above themselves.

"Why are we here, Your Grace?" his son asked as he followed close behind. Kerrin, as usual, was draped in his overly flowery attire. His light blonde hair hung over one shoulder, tied into a tail and his clothes glistened with silver emblems. A long patterned puffy sleeved shirt covered his upper body. This he paired with black leather slacks, which were overly tight, respectively, for a man, almost like tights. Braska, wearing his simple grey armour, did his best to ignore the clothes which he would consider more acceptable upon a woman. Battle was forever in his mind, forever on his body. Snakes slithered in the darkest corners, be it in the battlefield or in the bed. No one was truly prepared for a strike from a venomous creature.

"To learn, boy," he replied. Braska could hear a small groan from behind him but ignored it for now. As disappointing as his son was turning out to be, there were many he could blame, none being himself of course. The boy's mother, his own wife, was too soft and he relied too much on his assistant, the boy from the far south. Kerrin needed to become tougher and quickly. He would not be around forever. The first stop along their walk found them in front of a stone faced almost bald figure, with strong features that resembled Braska, yet older and slimmer.

"Edwaran Hextor II. 301 AS to 378 AS, the Child King that became the Wither King. Do you know why he stood out from the rest?" Braska asked his son, though never looked the boy's way. He could only focus upon the bust in front of him. The honour it was to have the name and blood of these God like figures, was something for which he would never truly be able to show enough gratitude.

"He lived a long time, Your Grace," Kerrin absently replied. The King let a small frustrated cough escape his throat.

"The longest reigning King in the history of Hextheene, a time of peace triumphed under this great man. He sat upon the throne as a pup and stayed upon it until he could barely walk. He was the youngest of seven, the others all stillborn. The only child who survived," Braska explained. He then turned and continued down the hall with his son following close behind. Once again they stopped, facing a bust on the other side of the hall. The figure was proud, strong jawed, with a stern expression. To be honest, all the marble sculptures were of the former Kings' best qualities. Since the marble only began trading between countries in the years after two hundred and fifty, the sculptures before then were crafted upon descriptions in literature.

"Braska Hextor I, 420 AS to 455 AS. What do you think made him a good King?" Braska asked. His son shuffled on the spot, clearly unsure of the answer.

"Perhaps because he was called Braska, Your Grace," Kerrin replied. He was not sure if his son was purposely being ridiculous and ignorant, in an attempt to get under his skin or had really become this foolish. Either way the King would not allow himself to be riled by mere words of an insubordinate child.

"His crusade south conquered half of the Freeland and brought technology from all over the world to Hextheene, improving our armour, weapons, castles, economy, even skills with trades to improve the livelihood of the people. He was murdered however, for his accomplishments by those in his court. His brother..." Braska looked across the room to another marble bust. This one was sullen, gaunt and much less impressive than the previous Braska who had sat upon the throne. "... Severan Hextor. Reigned from 455 AS to 488 AS. He claimed he could see the future, the end of mankind itself. Claimed that what he did to his brother was to secure the lives of everyone in the known world. He was a madman who used the weak minds of others to do his bidding. The World Beneath

424

will swallow us all... Indeed." With that he turned from the busts of the brothers and moved further up the hallway. Kerrin was close behind, clearly growing bored with the history lesson. The boy had no eye for the past and its lessons, only the vanity of his own desires. That was the thing he hated the most about his son. Eventually they stopped.

"Your Grandfather... my father, loyally and honourably sat upon the throne for twenty five springs, 725 AS to 750 AS. Led the war against Mayhen when I was just a boy, seventeen springs old I believe. The current King Rumeo was a boy then also. Your grandfather was murdered in his bed with his wife not long after the war was over." Braska felt his eyes focus on this particular bust longer. The likeness was uncanny, his father Nathun Hextor IV, a true and great King, Slain in his sleep like some sort of livestock for slaughter. The giant of a man forced his mind away from those times, as he felt himself growing weary of the recollection.

"And then, you," Kerrin added. Finally Braska turned to his son, his brow heavy and his strong jaw clenched tightly. The urge to strike his hand across the boy's face grew, due to his disrespect, though this was not the place for such acts. This was a place of reflection and respect.

"Yes, then me. 750 AS to now, 776 AS, so far. With no intention of this year being the last year. There is too much for you to learn, before I can hand over the throne to you, boy," he stated harshly. Braska did not fear death; he feared the legacy of the Hextor family being left in the hands of this incapable boy. His daughter Melayne should have been born first, and born a boy, she knew what it meant to rule.

"As you say father. I thank you greatly for this lesson of our ancestors but I must ask, why are we here? Surely there are more important matters that need your attention, as King. This is a job for scholars, not us." Kerrin scoffed arrogantly. The giant man turned to his son and began to loom over the much smaller Hextor. Kerrin tried to hide his fear but his cowering became ever transparent.

"One day, it will be you who rules. You will be King and your word will be law. So tell me, Prince Kerrin Hextor, what sort of King will you be?" he demanded. He ensured to speak forcefully and dominantly. A King was allowed to feel fear from his father. He had learnt this way and his son would do the same. The young prince swallowed to clear his throat and tentatively replied.

"An honest King, I will be an honest King." Braska nodded a few times as he analysed his son's reactions and choice of words. An honest King was a weak King.

"Leader's cannot always be honest with all. Often it is down to them to make the hard decisions. Honesty is not a trait a King requires above all, honesty is something a King needs from others; from his advisors, courtiers, commanders. Honesty and loyalty. You need to strike fear into your subjects so that the prospect of no longer being honest is too terrifying for them to even consider." Fear was the motivator. Fear was the whip and the hand you fed your people from. Fear drove the world forward, forced it to be better. People, who were in fear, were inspired to become better, to avoid that fear in the future. That is what he thought anyway, some would have disagreed with him. Those who disagreed certainly did not know what true fear was.

"Fear... Your Grace..." Before the conversation could continue, the sounds of footsteps echoed through the quiet hall. The elderly man Sli wandered towards them after passing through two large grey doors. Once he stood before the pair, Sli bowed his head respectfully.

"I would drop to a knee, Your Grace, but my back is playing up again," the advisor admitted. Braska simply waved off the nonsense.

"What do you need, Sli?" he asked as he gazed down towards the snake like man, one hand on the pommel of his sword, though only casually, whilst the other rubbed his chin.

"News from Mayhen, Your Grace, from a particular Miss Lanni Ni'Tella. She sent a messenger pigeon that arrived less than an hour ago. Shall I read it to you?" Sli asked unnecessarily. The King nodded and motioned for his son to pay attention. The boy had become distracted whilst adjusting the buttons of his brightly coloured shirt. His vanity was sickening. "Great King Braska Hextor II," Sli began. "I am sure you would be aware by now of the lunacy that befalls Mayhen. I humbly request a discussion between the people of Free Mayhen and Hextheene. Yours sincerely, Lanni Ni'Tella. From Stoneside Keep Your Grace, signed by the Advisor of Heldon, Lanni Ni'Tella." What struck him first was the fact that it had not been signed by the eldest daughter of Rumeo, who had apparently been the culprit of all the indiscretions of Mayhen. That left two options, either this Lanni Ni'Tella was acting without consent or Princess Nyer was not interested enough in opening a discussion with him. Either way, it was insulting to assume that he had anything to say to that pretender. Yet something in his mind nibbled at him, something that could be of great value.

"What is the current situation with Commander-at-Arms Camaron's agenda?" he asked, shifting the subject and not giving too much away, due to the loitering ears of his son nearby. Sli grumbled and scratched his pointy nose with his long bony finger.

"Not much news, last we heard he was heading to Northfreya. Other than that, there has been no communication Your Grace." Braska nodded. A good tactician did not only have one direction he could follow, he had multiple choices. The more routes open, the greater the chance of victory, should one path be closed before the destination was reached. Not only that, a test for someone who greatly needed to be tested.

"Son," Kerrin looked up as his father called him, with a look of confusion on his face. It was rare to call him anything other than boy.

"Yes, Your Grace?" he nervously replied. Braska turned to the diminutive man beside him and cast him a heavy glare, showing the weight of the Hexhold itself within his dark eyes.

"I have something in mind you must perform. You will take note, so listen closely, yes?" The young prince awkwardly nodded, clearly unsure of where this was going. "You will ride to Stoneside Keep in Mayhen and there you will speak with Princess Nyer Granlia, the daughter of King Rumeo Granlia. You will speak with my authority on the matter of her petty squabble with her father. In return for our support in her disagreement with King Rumeo, the Realm of Hextheene will require various considerations. They will be written up for you, you will memorize them so you do not look the fool as you speak to them. Do you understand?" The order was set. In response all Braska received from the prince was a wide eyed expression of shock and horror.

"..Y-your Grace... I do not think sending me, your-" Kerrin attempted to plead his way out of this situation. It may not have been the safest assignment, but a man who is to rule, must learn to take risks.

"Enough. Do not argue with me. You have a week to attend to your errands here and then you will ride for Stoneside Keep. Take your 'friend' with you, if you must and of course you will be accompanied by a banner of soldiers. You are a Hextor, act like one." Braska could feel the anger brewing in his chest at his son's resistance to a command. Sometimes he wished he had gotten a son more like Caskin, loyal and fearless, who would follow his word to the death. Unfortunately he had a son who preferred to prance around with other men in the gardens rather than attend to his duties as a prince. His son stood there a moment longer in silence, eyes flickering between Braska and Sli, until finally he grit his teeth and stormed out of the Hall of Kings, as quick as his legs could carry him. Once Kerrin was safely out of the room and far from ear shot, Braska felt the slithering from his advisor streamline to his side.

"Your Grace, I must protest. We do not know how the people of Mayhen in Stoneside Keep will react to a visit of Royalty of Hextheene. Think of him as you will, but he is still your son and heir to the throne. This is a great, great risk." Sli was not incorrect. His words always held high esteem in Braska's eyes, yet this time he was over cautious.

"Indeed, it is dangerous. Though I will not have my son take my throne as a weakling. He thinks he can outsmart me. He is a child and such an expedition will make him a man." Sli wrinkled his nose. They both knew what he spoke of. His son was not strong and brave, he was becoming a snake. His ploys to play the same game as that rowdy princess in Mayhen would not go unchecked in Hextheene; they were not as flowery and weak as their neighbour.

"My spider only spun webs of his intentions, not that he had any sort of plan in place, Your Grace. All children of royalty dream of taking their fathers place, it is natural," Sli mumbled.

"I did not," Braska quickly interjected to which the advisor could only bow his head in acceptance of his mistake.

"Yes, of course Your Grace. You are the exception, I suppose. In any case, it is an interesting play you have in mind I think. I assume you wish to support Nyer to strengthen your grip of Mayhen?" his advisor asked. Braska offered the man a dark glare before he strode past him and made his way towards the exit of the hall.

"Do not assume anything, prepare a scribe and have him sent to the Hall of Truth where I will await them to speak my demands. Mayhen is a country of peace loving fools, they are not my enemy. My enemy are those who wish to crush our way of life because they do not agree with it. I will do whatever it takes to ensure that does not happen." With that, Braska left his advisor in the hall to attend to the duties assigned to him. Princess Nyer, from all the rumours he had heard and the reports of his scout as well as the reports of Sli's spies, was greatly outnumbered in her support. The girl would have few options left to her if she wished to live out the end of this fall. He did not want to be the saviour of Mayhen, he did not want to involve himself in the civil war of another country, however if ending that war and choosing to instate a leader that suited him more, or had a debt to him and supported the agenda against the growing threats of the south, then that is what he would do.

'King Braska Hextor, the King remembered for bringing the north together and finally ending the savage ways of the southern countries and crushing the Order to its knees. That will be my legacy.'

* * *

Chapter XLI
Birth of War
~*Nyer*~

Vesir had brought some sour news back to Stoneside. Nyer was unsure exactly how to take it, with anger or consideration or even precaution. It was not completely unexpected, her father would have brought the Noble Lords together at some point sooner or later, to address the threat that she posed. It was in fact a compliment. Rumeo must have feared what she could do so greatly that he called an emergency gathering of all the people of power within Mayhen. At least those who had refused her call. Lord Loysse and Lord Leodri of Castle Crewyn had shown their honour by ensuring their loyalty to justice. Although Lord Leodri had yet to make arrangements to join them at Stoneside or even visit the keep, there was still time. Nyer would force herself to have faith in him that he would not switch sides, given the predicament they were currently in.

"Only about a thousand you say?" Nyer asked her uncle. She stood within the meeting hall of Stoneside Keep; it had become a regular place for her of these days. She rarely ventured out into the small city beyond the second wall or even strolled along the ramparts like she used to in Heldon. Most of her time was focused on plotting with the wily Lanni Ni'Tella. The elderly advisor was also present at the meeting. She sat by the table in the centre of the room with an expression of doubt on her features. It was unlikely she had reservations about

Vesir's words, more likely doubt in managing their situation. Lord Loysse and his wife Seldine were also present. His wife had adorned herself in a long green dress with red seams and flowery silver patterns, perhaps trying to appear regal, since a princess was within her home. Tismiar wore his usual cloak that covered the left side of his body and clipped together with a silver strap. The more she had seen Tismiar in casual garments, such as shirts and basic slacks, the less noble he appeared to her. It was refreshing to see him once again making an effort to appear appropriate. Titania leant on the wall beside the doorway with her arms crossed under her breasts and eyes closed. Her Royal Blade was unlikely to involve herself in these sorts of meetings, not until it was over and she would speak her piece when it was just the two of them. The last in the room, was Vesir. He appeared somewhat informally dressed with the stains of travel about his person. The meeting had been called rather hastily upon his return to the keep.

"Aye, about one thousand. Though not just Heldoran men, soldiers from all over the kingdom. Every banner I can think of in Mayhen had been raised. It's obviously not an invading force, but we couldn't figure out why it was so far from Heldon. I had my theories but for now we can't be sure, or do anything rash," her uncle advised. The rage her uncle had been carrying seemed to be under control. Previously he wanted to charge into the capital and deal with her father himself. Now, he was preaching caution.

"Stoneside Keep is a strong fortress, it can withstand siege of months, maybe even years. King Rumeo knows the strengths of this keep. I doubt he would launch a siege," Tismiar added from his side of the room. Like Lanni he was currently using a cane to keep himself standing, his gout had gotten the better of him today. She was surrounded by allies who could barely keep on their feet or would question her every move. If there was any doubt lingering in her mind on the course they were taking, this would be the moment it became apparent. Regardless of this she had to push forward, giving in now would only allow tyranny to succeed.

"He would," Nyer said as she turned from those gathered. She clasped her hands behind her back, her gaze drifted through the small window across the room. "As long as I stand, I am a threat to his rule. If he allows me to openly stand against him unchecked, other nations would see that as a weakness. A weakness he cannot afford to accept." Seldine grimaced at the notion.

"King Rumeo does not think like that. He does not care about what others think." Little did she know how different her King had become.

"I thought as much. I used to think that, yet now I am forced to think there is an ulterior agenda. My father is no longer the man we knew, the reasons are hazy and his new road of thought is questionable. What I do know is that he has not once sent word. Not once as my father requested a truce or attempted to settle the matter. From the first moment I left and declared my intentions, he has been on the war path calling all Noble Houses to his side. No, there is no more room for talking. He does not wish for words, he only wishes for war. If that is the case, then even if I am the one acting against him, he will come to us." The room fell silent for a moment as those gathered looked between each other, taking in the words of the princess. It was the hard truth. The lives of those Rumeo once cared for, were meaningless to him now.

"You really think Rumeo has become that twisted that he would march thousands of men to their death?" Tismiar asked as he looked from Nyer, to Lanni and to Vesir with a face of concern. The Pale Lord had grown even paler. Vesir spoke first.

"... I hate to say it, but I do. He killed my son in cold blood on false charges without a trial. He did that... to antagonise me. Something has happened, something terrible in his mind that's making him do the things he does but that doesn't mean he can be excused for what he's done. He may be my brother but that doesn't excuse him..." Lanni gently patted Vesir's arm to comfort the commander, to which he offered her a weak smile.

"So, we must prepare for war?" Seldine asked after being somewhat meek in the corner of the room by her husband. She was an old fashioned woman who relied on her husband too readily. Nyer felt alone, even with all these people round her it was only herself she could truly rely on.

"We must. To gather Mayhen's armies would take time, a long time which also gives us the time to act as well. We will not sit here and wait patiently for my father to walk to the front door and give it a knock. No, we must begin our actions now." Nyer began her speech but the interruption of Lanni halted her vocal advance.

"And what is it you propose we do, Princess Nyer? Heavily outnumbered, we may be, yet you must speak to those who are going to fight for your cause. These men in these walls fight for Tismiar, no offence My Lord, and the men in Crewyn fight for Lord Leodri. These men must believe they are fighting for a greater good, for you. Show them you are a cause worth fighting for." Once again the wise words of the advisor were angering in their truth. Nyer wrinkled her nose in frustration as the rest of the room agreed with Lanni's proposal. She was not one for mixing with commoners; they should do their duty without question and should not need to be won over. However, as it stood, the morale to fight for a greater cause would certainly be beneficial.

"Very well, Lord Loysse, if you could arrange for me to make an announcement to the people of Stoneside, I will speak with them as their leader and true Queen. While Lanni, I need you to look into spreading word throughout the country, not just to those in position but also those without such status, the... common people if you will." Lanni offered her a smile though Nyer only saw it as her being smug that her previous advice had resonated in her decision making. Now was not the time for petty squabbles within her *own* camp. There was much that needed to be done.

"I can do that, Princess Nyer." Lord Loysse bowed his head respectfully.

"And I can also see to such things. Have town criers in lands near us spread word of King Rumeo's cruelty and the just acts of the Princess Nyer. A good call to the cause I think. However, we should talk about what we spoke of before. Have you reconsidered?" the old woman asked.

"Hm, what's this?" Vesir asked, as he looked between the two women. Nyer shot her a glare of daggers. This was not the place to bring such a topic to the table.

"Something of no importance to the current matter," the princess quickly argued, her glare still focused on the smug older woman. Lanni rolled her shoulders in a shrug; she would not let this go so easily.

"I spoke to the Princess not long ago, about possible support from Hextheene. We have an unmarried heir to the throne and we are in a situation where we need more allies than we can currently accumulate. I simply suggested speaking with them." The room fell into soft whispers between the Lord and Lady and a deep frown plastered on the features of her uncle.

"If you wish to play this game in front of the rest of my council, then we will play it truthfully." Nyer shifted her attention to the rest of those present within the meeting hall. "Miss Ni'Tella suggests I inquire about marriage within the Hextheene royalty, Prince Kerrin Hextor to be precise, in a bid to gain foreign support. I informed her that this course of action would be most disadvantageous to our cause, as many would see any support from Hextheene as an invasion." Nyer crossed her arms under her breasts after she put the advisor back in her place. That old woman still attempted to push the boundaries of her position. She may have been an advisor to her father once upon a time, but those days were over.

"For once I agree with my niece. I'm not onboard looking for aid from Hextheene. King Braska Hextor is not a man you want by your side. He will find a way to use you to his advantage. Not to mention I've met the man, he's a bit of a bastard," Vesir commented with a slip of humour. Nyer scoffed at the understatement. While she had never met this King Braska, from the rumours she had heard, there was not a shred of decency in the soul of that man.

"I must humbly disagree with you, Commander Vesir," Lord Loysse interjected. "If we look at the situation logically, I have around ten thousand men at my disposal. The combined armies of Mayhen without my support, the support of Castle Crewyn and the Shield could range between forty thousand to fifty thousand men. If King Rumeo is truly on a rampage to end this before it begins, he will throw everything he has at us without any mercy. Even if Hextheene agreed to support us, they would not need to march on our soil. The very knowledge that a country with a well known powerful military might, stands behind us, would be enough to stall any advance. This would give us some extra time to come up with a more suitable strategy," Tismiar spoke realistically. This gamble was still being based on the assumption that King Braska would even consider giving them aid.

"There is one more option," Vesir added. He sat on the table next to Lanni and clasped his fingers together. "We still have my forces in the Shield. If you believe Rumeo will march on us here and risk the capital as a show of strength, then the chances are Heldon itself will not have a sufficient force to hold it from an attack." The room all focused their attention on the commander. Nyer could sense where this conversation was going and secretly she liked the sound of it.

"Go on," she requested. Vesir clucked his tongue against his teeth as his eyes studied those around him, Nyer hung on his words.

"We lure the army to Stoneside. Even with a superior force he won't be able to take the keep easily. When his army is moving on us, the men and women of the Shield move north and take the capital. That leaves the army of Mayhen trapped between us. Still, in an open field battle we remain at a disadvantage. There are many pieces of this puzzle, and we don't want any army wiped out, be it ours or his, they are still good men of Mayhen. We need to find a way to have the kingdom learn of what he has become. Taking Heldon could be a start." It was a risky move her uncle proposed. There were a lot of ifs, buts and maybes. It relied on the fact that Heldon would not be particularly well defended and also that the men of the Shield would be able to move freely without being locked down in their land. If it was her, she would expect such a ploy and ensure the Shield would have no time to march or have the line protected. Her father had men to spare, to still siege them as well as block any advance from the south. Yet part of her liked this plan. There was no better way to unveil the deeds of the King, than to take his home with him inside it, but if not, there was still a chance they would panic at the loss of Heldon and hastily retreat. Wars had been won in the past with poor decisions made by larger forces, allowing the smaller army to succeed.

"Quite a tactic, Commander Vesir," Lanni exclaimed as she wiggled her eyebrows at the man. "Though you are capable of more, are you not? You have been surveying the land and scouting the areas around Stoneside and Heldon no? I do not wish to imply your strategy has no merit because surprisingly I think it could work. Do you have something concerning the actual Mayhen army if the Shield succeeded? You are the most experienced battle commander in this room and perhaps even Mayhen," she asked him with a narrowed gaze. The old woman was a realist; her game was facts and logic, not fantasy. The commander was quick in rebuttal.

"Of course, sounds like you're underestimating me Lanni. I might have something if we have both Stoneside and Heldon under our control." The advisor nodded slowly even though the details were not offered. It was clear there was trust in the Granlia.

"We can discuss war strategy should the time come. Yet for now we all know what we must do," Nyer began her speech. It was time to lay down their objectives so all were on the same page. She would not allow any dissension under her command. "Our cause is to free Mayhen from tyranny. Some would say we have acted too quickly, too recklessly but I do not see it that way. It is only a matter of time before my father shows his new colours to all and puts our great kingdom in jeopardy. I would not be the woman I am, if I sat idly by and allowed such acts to befall us and our people. This is not a game to put me on the throne in his place. It is to bring to light the evil that has been birthed in our home and ensure that Mayhen returns to the greatness it once was. My uncle is right, showing Mayhen what Rumeo has become should be our priority, it is simply a question of how. Spreading word from us, can only achieve so much." Those gathered nodded in agreement with her words. Never did she think she would be standing in such a position that would change the course of her country so drastically. Never did she think she would be crossing swords with her father. She loved that man. Even with all his flaws she still loved him. There had to be something or someone who had answers to this madness, an explanation for why this had all happened. It was a matter of finding evidence to resolve this matter before too many lives were lost. It was still a strange position to be in. The reality of the situation they were in truly hit her; Mayhen was in civil war.

The meeting ended with those present quickly dispersing to attend their specific duties. Lord Loysse was to prepare a stage for her to speak to the people of East Mayhen while Vesir had a secret message sent to the Shield to inform his son of their plan. Lanni would see to having her message passed through the villages and towns, a message of peace and protection to all those under Nyer, as well as revealing the crimes and evil of her father. It was still strange to picture the word evil and her father in the same sentence, yet it was the reality they now lived in.

"My Lady," Titania said. The pair of them had retired to the princess's bed chambers. Nyer had stripped to her nightwear, a long loose gown that stretched down to her ankles and hung loosely from her shoulders. She strode across her room in barefoot, her toes feeling the pleasant texture of the fur rugs that covered the chamber's floor. Her long dark hair had been

438

released from its braid and flowed elegantly down her spine. She was not a woman who cared much for the beauty of herself, or cared whether the masses considered her beautiful. Though, she was not so naive to ignore the benefits of being seen as such. Her Royal Blade had also dressed down for the evening, with her leather armour replaced with a cloth of black hue to contrast with her ginger red hair.

"What is it, Titania?" Nyer asked as she perched herself on the edge of her bed and crossed her legs while twirling a glass of wine between her fingers. These moments were for reflection and relaxation. The weight of the kingdom sat heavy upon her shoulders each day. If she did not take the time to set down such a weight on occasions, her back would surely break in two.

"Have you considered where Rayar or Nymin are currently?" the Royal Blade asked. Her friend also had a drink between her fingers however she was not much for drinking wine, instead she sipped natural cup of water. Titania leaned on the wall by a window, a long thin slit in the stonework christened with velvet red drapes on either side, whilst facing her princess.

"How do you mean?" Nyer questioned.

"I do not interrupt your meetings, it is not my place. In public I am your protector and nothing more. This allows me to see everything, and hear everything without a biased mind..." the woman explained, her expression was one of concern.

"It is why you are such a beneficial Royal Blade, Titania. Not all have your mind set." Hyar was the man who jumped to her mind, the man was a drunken fool and was out there somewhere with Nymin. To be honest, she was not sure who she felt sorrier for in that combination.

"All your siblings are separated. Princess Ayla is stuck in Heldon, Above knows what she is going through. Princess Nymin is somewhere with Hyar and Prince Rayar is on the run for a charge that would have him executed if he ever showed his face back in Heldon. My point is, you wish for something to reveal to all what your father has become. It is possible King

439

Rumeo did not want Princess Nymin or Prince Rayar to speak, because they know something?" Titania made a good point.

"I have been focusing so vigilantly on addressing father myself I have not stopped to think what advantage I could gain by finding Rayar and Nymin." Nyer stated. Her Royal Blade nodded in return. "In truth, we do not even know if they live. The hunt for them by the guardsmen of Heldon or even us could be a wild goose chase." Nyer took a long sip of wine before running her slender fingers through her soft hair.

"It was simply a suggestion." The red headed warrior pushed herself from the wall and turned towards the exit.

"Stay in here tonight. I do not wish to be alone," Nyer requested. Her tone was soft, a rarity in her case. Her protector knew why. As much as she tried to hide her fears behind her cold exterior, it was still etched deep into her skin like poison. Titania stopped and nodded in acceptance, before wandering over and perching herself on the edge of the bed. The torches in the chambers remained ablaze along the walls and the candles on the bedside tables continued to burn as Nyer set aside her cup of wine and wriggled herself into her bed. Princess or not, keeping up the appearance of such a hard woman was tiring, very tiring. Her closest friend was the only one who truly understood her and would stand by her. People would not see it, yet without Titania, she would have broken a long time ago.

"Goodnight..." Nyer mumbled before burying her cheek into the pillow. The warrior at the end of her bed lay down beside her, sword propped up against the bedside table that housed the bright candle keeping the room aglow.

* * *

Chapter XLII
Granlia
~Ayla~

Night had fallen upon the city of Heldon; the talk of war was on the tongue of everyone. That evening the Nobles had a celebration and the topic was of course, war. Ayla did not care for it, she never had. War was something evil in her mind, she had never lived through such things but all the history lessons from Master Vayers and the teachings from her father when he was still the man she loved, informed her of one thing. War only bred more war. Now her family were on the brink of all out civil war. This was complete nonsense.

'What have I been doing? Sitting here, complaining. I was no help to Nyer, no help to Nymin, no help to Rayar. I have been useless ever since this all began,' Ayla thought to herself as she sat in her bed chambers. The keep had become exceedingly rowdy of late with many of the Noble Lords and Ladies being present in the castle. Many of them feasted and pranced around the hallways, talking about their wealth and their achievements, or discussing who was going to lead in the coming battles and bragging about how big their army was. It had been some time since all the nobles had come to Heldon and now they would waste their time attempting to outdo each other's position. Very few spoke to her, which she had found surprising. The only noble who had given her any attention, more than a perfunctory bow, had been Arthus. Last time she had spoken to him, she had abandoned him in the throne room

during the meeting of the nobles. He deserved it, he was being foolish. Why should she waste her time with someone who was all talk and no action?

'But that is what I am... all talk, as I sit here, moping around.' Ayla sat on the floor of her chambers, propped up against the end of the bed. She wore her nightgown, a laced light blue dress that lay over her form. The princess had her moment of reflection stolen by a sudden thump from outside, followed by the chattering and laughing of a group of people. The nobles were up late drinking once more and stumbled around the keep without a care in the world. She had been taught that Mayhen was a respectable and proper kingdom, not some coven to litter with drunkards. For them, they were celebrating a new unity of Mayhen whilst she could only feel despair towards it. The voices drifted off down the hall, away from her room, finally leaving her in the midst of silence.

'I cannot sit here and be useless any longer;' Ayla forced herself to her feet and made her way towards the door. As quietly and carefully as she could, she slowly pried the door open and peered through. There was nothing, a dark hallway with torches pitched along each side of the corridor. With her courage fuelled, she poked her head slightly further through the doorway. Ayla held back a gasp as she saw the newly appointed Royal Blade on a chair across from her bed chambers. The huge beast of a man sat there 'on guard'', yet was sound asleep with an almost empty bottle of rum abandoned on the ground at his feet. The man was out cold. It was amusing to see such a small intake of drink could disable a man of such size.

'This is my chance,' the princess thought, then sneaked through the gap in the doorway and carefully closed the door behind her. Shan did not react. The hairy man snored loudly and was completely knocked out. Quiet as a mouse, the young woman tip-toed past the hulking warrior, refusing to take a single breath. She did not want to risk anything that could possibly stir him from his slumber. She did not catch her breath

again until she was safely down the hallway, far from the giant and safe from being caught.

"Above and Below," she gasped while drawing in her breath. It was time to move. There was one person left she could trust whole heartedly; Julian, her mother. Her father had shown her a while ago that she was still in the royal bed chambers. Ayla had not been granted the opportunity to visit her since. The inner castle guards were sparse, many of them had been moved out to the garrisons in preparation for their long march to Stoneside. Not to mention, with Nyer and Nymin no longer in Heldon, the sheer volume of guards within the hallways had lessened. Rumeo had seen Nyer as a threat, that much was clear but herself, she was not threat to the King. Or so he blatantly assumed. This could be her one chance to see Julian alone, and she would take it. With celebration after celebration, feast after feast that she was not a part of, her lack of presence would go unnoticed. Ayla knew these halls well. She knew where the shadows and blind spots were along corridors from when she used to hide whilst following Rayar for his late night sword lessons. Only once had she gathered the courage to ask him if she could watch one of the training sessions. He must have thought she was so arrogant and selfish but in truth, speaking to him was difficult. Rayar had always been so laid back and carefree, she wanted to be just like him. He was an idol of sorts to her. She had always concerned herself with petty issues.

'What am I thinking, I am selfish.' The soul searching would have to wait for another time. She no longer had the luxury of being selfish. Her family were divided and as far as she was aware, she was the only one watching from the side-lines. It did not take long until Ayla found herself upon her parent's bed chambers. The princess had noticed her father rarely visited his own chambers these days, every evening he would retreat to the meeting hall with several advisors and that vile man Captain Sirus, yet she rarely saw him walking the hallways of the upper keep levels. It was as if that man no longer had the need to sleep. The door was in front of her, the

large patterned door to the room of her mother. This moment would be a gamble. If she opened it and Rumeo was in there, it was already over. Ayla took one long deep breath, her heart pounding, body shaking, skin breaking into a sweat and pushed the large door ajar. There was no sound from inside, pure silence. She pushed a little bit more, still nothing.

'Just do it, Ayla,' she told herself and finally pushed the door fully open. The room was silent. Her mother was there, lying on the bed as if she had not moved since the last time she had seen her. Furtively Ayla slipped into the room and pushed the door closed behind her, then she rushed over to Julian's side. Her mother had become worse, if that was even possible. Her skin was a grey-white, her hair had practically shed itself from her scalp and her muscles had wasted away. The once beautiful and serene Queen of Mayhen appeared no more than a husk of her former self. While it was shocking to see that ghostly form, appearances did no matter, she was her mother. That was *all* that mattered.

"Mother..." the young woman whispered as she knelt beside the bed. There was a small stir under the sheets as Julian reacted to her voice. As if the skin of her eye lids had been plastered shut, the Queen cracked them open to look upon her daughter. Her eyes were grey and aged, almost vacant.

"...Ayla..." the broken woman croaked out. It was a husky voice, nothing like Ayla remembered and it clearly caused her pain to speak. Tears formed in the eyes of the princess as she buried her face into the pillow.

"Mother, why has this happened to you!?" Ayla cried. She could not stop the tears. She came here to be strong and help, yet seeing her mother in such a way sent a blade through her heart.

"Ayla... I am... sorry," Julian said weakly. The girl shook her head violently and pulled back to lock eyes with the Queen. Ayla could feel the pain in her mother eyes, tears upon her cheeks. It destroyed her.

"Do not be sorry mother, just tell me how to help you? So much has happened! I need to tell you everything." All the events in the past couple of months ran through her mind. What did she need to start with? So many things all piled into her thoughts at once it was difficult to know what took priority. Before she could begin to unveil everything, she felt a leathery hand rest against her cheek. She blinked in surprise and stared down to her mother.

"It is... too late... for... me... run and... leave... Heldon," too late for her? Leave Heldon? Did she already know of what was happening? Ayla could not be sure but leaving her mother was not something she could do. Nyer may have been able to leave them here to their terrible fates but she would never do such a thing. There was one thing she needed to know however, one important thing that was paramount.

"Mother, what has happened to father?" The tears in Julian's eyes began to stream down her cheeks. The question struck deep. Seeing her mother cry caused her to follow suit and soon tears completely drenched the skin upon her face.

"He... he's gone." Gone? What did she mean by gone? There was no time to pry further as suddenly she heard voices outside looming closer and the door being pushed open. As quick as a rabbit escaping a hound, the young princess slipped under the bed and covered her mouth with her hands.

"I will report to them as soon as I can, tell them to wait. It is not easy keeping up appearances." The voice was her fathers. Ayla watched through a small gap between the floor and the bed sheets as two large boots sauntered across the room towards the bed. The door was closed by someone else, another pair of boots with a long cloak down to the figure's ankles.

"You do not want to be the odd one out do you? All the others have made progress, the crusade will begin soon. There must be no defiance or resistance against it. After that, only Hextheene will remain," a male voice explained. It was a voice she did not recognise. Whoever it was, they stayed by the door, while her father now stood just in front of her beside the bed and next to Julian. Rumeo replied, his tone spewing sarcasm.

"I know, I know. We all have our part to play. We all must do this for the greater good nonsense. I have been told a hundred times. Oh, look. The woman is awake again." Ayla swallowed, fear drenched her.

"Why do you keep her alive?" the male voice asked from across the room.

"Am I not allowed my fun?" Rumeo replied. There was an ominous dark glow in the room, though Ayla could not see what was happening. "There we go." The man across the room let out a small sigh.

"And your guest in the dungeon is still alive?" Another question was posed towards her father. A loud obnoxious cackle filled the bed chambers before Rumeo replied.

"Who knows who cares? Last I saw him he was snacking on rats to survive. A lot slimmer now though, did him some good I'd say." A feeling of confrontation sparked.

"This is not about fun and games, you fool. More than your amusement rides on this. We put up with your sick games because you serve a purpose but I assure you, we get no pleasure in them. She is dead anyway when the crusade commences. Now stop wasting time, grab what you need, we have a meeting to attend." With that her father chuckled and strode across the room towards a cabinet. She could hear him fumbling about before exclaiming that he had found whatever it was he had been looking for, before they made their way towards the door.

"It has been fun here you know. It will be a shame to leave." After that last statement, the pair left the bed chambers. Ayla could briefly hear them continue to talk outside the room, though the words were too quiet for her to hear through the walls.

'Above and Below... what was that? What were they saying?' Once she was satisfied they were truly gone, Ayla scrambled back out from under the bed and turned to her mother.

"Mother," it was a terrified whisper. As she looked upon Julian once again, the older woman was asleep; there was no response to her voice. Calling out to Julian and shaking her frail form did nothing to wake her. However, she was

446

breathing. She was still alive, if only barely. She could hardly control her own breathing, panicked breaths pumped in and out of her lungs. Her father had done something strange to her, almost as if he was using magic. Yet the way he spoke, the way he acted was nothing like she ever had seen, neither before nor since the changes in him. In some sickening way he was almost comical. Not full of love like he used to be or full of hate like he was now. It felt like it was nothing but a game to him. What did this all mean? If she had been found, if they knew she had witnessed what had just occurred whatever that was, she had no doubt she would have joined Julian in that broken state.

'I need help, someone, anyone. Brayton? Caidarian? Arthus? Someone here must be able to help me.' Ayla had to find someone she could talk to, someone she could trust and tell them what she had seen and heard. Would they even believe it? Brayton was so loyal no matter what position the King put him in, he would follow it blindly. Caidarian was just a captain and had been sent to the outskirts of the city. The only person she could tell would be Arthus. Could she truly trust him? He was a Noble Lord sworn to the King. His words had been flowery and his demeanour had been welcoming, but when it came to something as dire as this, would he be able to do anything? There was hope. If she abandoned that hope then this risk would have been for nothing. The man in the cells, the crusade, and the power Rumeo used. She needed answers to it all. First thing was first; she needed to get back to her chambers. Ayla turned to her mother one last time and brushed her hand across her cheek.

"Do not worry mother, I will not sit here idle any longer. I will think of something." They were brave words, though they were easy to say when she knew no one could hear her say them.

* * *

Chapter XLIII
Secrets of the Grove
~Rayar~

So this was the grove in all it grand wonder and splendour. Once the three companions had finally passed through what felt like a never ending tunnel right through the core of the mountain range, they reached a heavily wooded area. There was no snow; the sky was an alluring clear blue as if within its own world, shut off from the outside. Hundreds of trees filled their line of sight, all green and lush. It was beautiful, the nature was awe inspiring. Rayar had felt a sudden flow of calmness fill his body as he stepped onto the soft grass between the tall trees. Part of him wanted to simply lie down and relax, even end the journey right here and spend their days in this natural wonderland. Shania seemed to feel the same, the frustration she appeared to carry with her, floated off into the clear air and shimmered into a state of nothingness. Flowers blossomed around the tree trunks; the wind softly shifted the branches. Only Hinsani seemed to have kept up his guard, his sharp eyes focused intensively forward. Once he realised his two friends had slowed in their pace and had become almost docile, he spoke up.

"What are you doing?" His tone was as commanding as always. "We cannot play around here. Stay prepared for anything." Rayar was shaken back to reality by his words. Something about this place caused his mind to wander, his muscles to loosen and mind to relax. Never had he felt such a feeling in his life.

"Sorry, Master Hinsani. It is just... strange here," the prince replied as he picked up the pace to keep up with the Royal Blade's wide strides. Shania too shook her head and caught up with the pair.

"Something strange, do you hear it?" Hinsani insisted. His gaze traced the branches in the tree tops.

"What is it?" Shania asked. Her hand instinctively gripped the cinder block she carried with her at all times.

"No animals. I hear no birds, insects, anything. Just us and the wind," he had a point, it was deafly quiet. Apart from the odd shuffling of the leaves above them, there were no other natural sounds to be heard that Rayar would have expected in a forest. Well, in his limited experience of course. He had only really spent time in two woodland areas, below the Leon Mountains in Mayhen and in Hextheene. The Heldon garden could've been considered a forest due to its vast size and magnitude of plant life. He recalled hearing the songs of various animals within its trees and foliage back home. However, this was not the time to be so easily distracted.

"Come, let us push forward. I saw a particular tree in that vision at Quale's. The pearl was with it." The group shifted carefully through the tree line. If there were any members of the Order here, they did not want to be seen just yet. The advantage of surprise needed to be in their favour. After a brief calculated stalk through the woods, they soon found themselves furtively entering a clearing. It was in stark contrast to the surrounding grove, remains of fallen trees littered the ground, scorched earth still teased the dirt, and even pieces of what looked like human skeletons lay scattered all around. Clearly something terrible had happened here. From the tales Shania and Quale had told, he had a rough idea of what that was. In the very centre of the clearing, a giant tree stood. It was massive in comparison to anything Rayar had ever seen before. The branches stretched out into the forest around them, the trunk was perhaps the width of a castle tower. It was simply massive in all sense of the word. A natural masterpiece of an evergreen tree seemingly completely untouched by whatever horrors had occurred here long ago.

"So this is where it all started, hm?" Shania asked, mainly to herself. She wandered past the other two and inspected the devastation of the Druidae Grove. Rayar could only imagine the sheer horror that must have befallen these people those many years ago.

"Are you alright, Shania?" the prince nervously asked as he followed her footing, doing his best to avoid standing on any remains of what he could only assume, were the fallen druidae of old.

"I will be, when we come face to face with the bastards who did this. They will realise their mistake letting one of my people live. They should have killed us all." Rayar could feel the anger coursing from her. He understood how she felt, if he had come face to face with the ruins of Highhall Castle and seen the remains of all those who had been in his family, he would have felt the same. Any precious beauty the Druidae Grove once held was gone, extinguished by the devastation left behind in the wake of its attackers. The atmosphere had turned sullen, the mood sour.

"Where now, Prince Rayar?" Hinsani asked as he knelt absentmindedly investigating some of the remains.

"I am... I am not sure. In the vision I think the pearl was under the evergreen tree. It was glowing and I could feel the presence it emitted." It was hard to know where to look but something in his heart told him they were in the right place. Just then Shania whistled to the pair and motioned them closer to the Evergreen tree. Near the base of the trunk sat an opening which led to a long flight of stairs leading down, deep below the clearing, where they stood. Roots hung in a tangle above the staircase, the smell of the earth filled Rayar's nostrils. They would, unfortunately, need to investigate. Rayar had been relieved that they had not needed to climb over any more mountains to get to where they were now, yet apparently tunnels were the new obstacle.

"If your vision showed the pearl below us, I bet it is down this way," Shania exclaimed as she peered inside. Torches were definitely present down below, keeping the underground chasm alight.

"We will not be able to retreat easily once we enter. Stick together, watch each other's backs. If we come across a foe, we surround them and fight them as a group. That is to you Shania, do not rush in alone." Hinsani had taken the role of leader and advisor. They would have been foolish not to listen to him. Shania responded with a barely audible *'yes sir'* whilst grumbling. The trio descended down the steps, deep under the earth into the world beneath. The cave was surprisingly well lit with torches embedded into the walls. The earth was being supported by wooden pillars and stands to stop crumbly walls collapsing. Around them was another surprising sight, documents spread all over dozens of tables. They appeared old and dusty, as if they had not been attended to for many years. Rayar approached a table and lifted one of the documents at random.

"The Illusionist - how to conjure soulous illusions... like magic?" he asked as he glanced back to the others. They too, had begun to investigate various documents along the tables. There did seem to be an order to them all, it reminded him of a more organised version of Quale's home. Shania lifted up a couple of documents and peered over the dusty contents.

"Druidae element control... theories to their power. Druidae blood sample research..." She had stumbled upon the druidae section much to her disgust. Hinsani also, following the others example, lifted a document and spoke the title out loud.

"Red Mist theory and research, it seems they were researching the red mist by the Shield." Rayar had always been curious to what that mist really was. It had been rumoured to be so many different things, he had lost count.

"What does it say?" the prince asked as he approached his protector.

"Created by the Second Coming, theory notes - first attempt at releasing the World Below. Threat high, must be supervised.

There are numerous more documents on the red mist. This whole table is full of it." Hinsani frowned heavily and began sorting through the documents cautiously. This wealth of information had even claimed Hinsani's attention, briefly relaxing his constant vigilance.

"The Vienne Family?" Shania mumbled, the sudden mention of his true heritage pricked the prince's ears and he turned towards the druidae. He had told her of his real father's name not long ago. Hinsani was not privy to that information however and he quickly stepped over to her side and motioned her to be silent.

"We have not got time to look through all this, but perhaps some of it could be useful to proving the Order has agents within wishing to do the world harm. Above and Below, there may be something on the attack of Heldon somewhere in here." There was suddenly a booming noise from further inside the cave. A huge door across the tunnel caught their attention. There was a sensation, a feeling emitting from behind that door. Rayar could not explain it, yet he could feel it.

'The pearl... it is through there, I know it,' he thought to himself as his emerald eyes rested on the metal door. The prince swiftly took the document titled 'The Vienne Family' from Shania and stuffed it into his fur coat before approaching the doorway. Hinsani was quick to his side with a hand grasped tightly around the hilt of his sword.

"On your guard," he commanded as they finally reached the impressive metal structure. Shania had become impatient, before the men had a chance to carefully push the door open, she slipped past them and thrust the metal from their path. The other side held an even larger chamber, wide and round with light shimmering down from a gap in the ceiling. Bottles of strange liquids, tombs embedded into the walls, more tables of documents littered the chamber to the brim. At the very far end of the underground chamber, a tall slender figure stood. His cold eyes slowly rested on the three intruders. Beside him, finally, the pearl sat on an old, rusted metal stand. A pulsating

452

light omitting from the pearl, appeared to dim as the attention of the long coated man drifted from it and fixated on Rayar.

"I suspected you would arrive sooner or later," the pale man uttered. Rayar recognised him from Heldon, as one of the pair to set all this in motion when his home was attacked in the dead of night. He was draped in the same long dark green coat that the prince recalled, which reached down to his knees and a collar that covered the majority of his neck and the lower half of his face. A silver brooch sat clipped on his chest, but with the distance between them, he could not see what symbol it held. The name of the man pounded in Rayar's head over and over, forever etched in his mind. He would not forget those names easily; Vasca and Shan. This man could only be the one named Vasca. The same dead look in his eyes was still apparent, as was the calm and collected aura he projected. The pearl beside him felt slightly different, something about it felt peculiar. The usual glistening blue light that it had always shone with had grown dull and darker. "I finished in time though," Vasca mumbled to himself as he glanced over to the pearl, eyeing it longingly.

"That is mine and I have come to take it back," Rayar growled towards the agent of the Order and at the same time, drew his one sided sword. As he did, Hinsani had Galad in his grasp and Shania had already drawn her own, with her small block in her other hand.

"Yours? I think not. This belongs to the Master," the mage calmly replied from across the underground chamber.

"What is your plan? The release of this 'Second'?" Hinsani inquired as he began to prepare his charge. Rayar knew that stance, *The Sparrow Springs,* but the distance between them and Vasca was quite great. It would take time even in that dance, to close the gap. Shania on the other hand showed no desire to speak, the anger in her eyes spoke more than any words could. Vasca tilted his head to the side curiously at the Royal Blades question.

"Why would I reveal anything to you?" That was enough for Shania. She did not have the patience to learn anything

453

more, not that this man had any intention of telling them anything. She struck the cinder across her sword and the moment a spark ignited from the metal, she caught it with her power and twirled it into a whirlwind of fire. Rayar followed the lead of Hinsani, who at that moment darted around the side of the underground chamber towards their foe. The prince took the other side in an attempt to pincer him in. With two warriors charging on both sides, a pillar of fire from the centre, and a wall blocking the back of the mage, he was pinned on every side. Yet they still knew little about magic and of what controllers were truly capable. Vasca raised his slender pale hand in front of his body towards the incoming fire and from his fingertips a large bloom of darkness flowed freely and formed what appeared to be some sort of wall, which blocked the incoming volley of flames. His other hand shot towards Rayar as he charged around from the left side. The prince was unable to react in time and unavoidably was rammed by a flying table pried from the ground. The wooden object smashed into him and sent him tumbling down the stairs he had just climbed, like a sack of potatoes. He thought he heard Shania call out his name yet the sheer shock on the impact stunned him too effectively for him to be sure of what he heard. The prince finally regained his composure as he sat slumped against the wall of the cavern to see Hinsani almost upon the mage. In retaliation to this attack, Vasca released the wall that had dispersed the flames and in his hand now, a long black smoking sword expanded into existence and shifted around to deflect the oncoming strike from Hinsani. Their blades collided and the Royal Blade began his onslaught. Flurry after flurry of dance after dance. By the looks of it, from the side-lines, the mage had quickly realised his sword play was not up to par with that of the master swordsman.

"Hinsani, watch out!" Rayar called out as he scrambled to his feet. It was too late, Vasca twitched his spare hand and a long dark spear of smoking energy exploded from his palm and slammed into the stomach of the Royal Blade. It was not a piercing weapon however and the force lifted Hinsani from his feet and pushed him back across the chamber, thrusting him into the opposite wall from the prince. The golden haired boy began his advance once again; he could feel his blood boiling in anger though his skin shivered in fear.

'This kind of power is unimaginable, how can he just make anything appear like that?' They had charged in, sword first, without even considering the capabilities of this mage. During Rayar's second charge, Shania had not been standing idle. As her pillar of flames had not been successful, she now launched fire like arrows towards the mage. The two swordsmen should have been a successful distraction, for Shania to find some sort of opening to end this bout as quickly as possible. It had been a wise tactic even if it put them at risk, up close with this monster of a man, yet if they were not willing to take risks, how could they succeed? Vasca was pinned down using his power to block each arrow of fire, creating a dark smoking shield each time the flames almost caught his person. Rayar took this opportunity to slide in and do his best, to land that killing blow. From the mages flank, he shot forward and brought down his sword from a vertical strike in an attempt to cleave the man in two. Yet just before his blade made contact, Vasca's form changed into a smoke like substance. Rayar's sword passed right through the smoky form of his enemy.

"Fools, you came here unprepared," the pale man simply stated. He did not even pass the prince a glance but instead flowed like a gust of wind through the air towards Shania with a hand outstretched towards her face.

"Shania, I am coming!" Rayar roared out.

"Come to me druidae!" Vasca gurgled in his smoke like form. It was as if a shadow had a mind of its own. The metal of his sword could not stop it, the flames briefly dispersed his form yet they did not stop his advance. Rayar did his best to give chase and leapt from the top of the stairs they had been fighting upon, yet the dark smoke moved too quickly for him to close any distance. In seconds Vasca was upon Shania, who stared wide eyed in shock. As he reached out to grab her throat, she suddenly screamed out in rage and the flames she had been

455

twirling around her wrists like rings, erupted in a huge blaze around her entire body, singeing her fur clothes at the edges. The sudden uproar of fire caused Vasca to bellow out in pain as his body began to ignite. There were clearly limits to this monsters magical ability. The shadowy form backed away, thrashing about. While he had not been completely turned to ash as Rayar would have hoped, the fire clearly had affected him. Whatever this form was, it did not make Vasca untouchable. Yet his blade was useless, what was he supposed to do to help?

"Druidae are nothing to us. We slaughtered you all once, you thi-" Before any more taunts could escape the mages lips, a long one sided blade slid through his stomach and out the other side. Blood spurted from the wound and trickled to the stone floor. Vasca's shadow form faded and again he returned to that of a human. Behind him Hinsani stood, Galad thrust through the mage's stomach. Blood also trickled down the forehead and smeared over the lips and chin of Hinsani, the brunt of the strike he took had done some damage.

"How did you... I... cannot be touched by a mere man," Vasca groaned in pain as the metal filled his insides. Hinsani pulled the sword free without dignifying him with a response and the lifeless corpse of the pale mage collapsed to the floor in a heap. Rayar stared at the body for a few moments unsure of what to think or feel. Had they just won? It had been so intense and sudden. They had been tossed around like twigs yet they had bested this complete monster.

"Above and Below... we lived," the prince blurted out as he dropped onto a step behind him, doing what he could to catch his breath. Shania soon joined them from the entrance to the chamber, her leather and fur had been singed, as had her hair, however she did not appear too harmed by her own flames. That power she held had been truly terrifying but these mages, if they were all as unpredictable and powerful as Vasca, they were truly in deep water. Shania wrapped her arms around the young prince, after inspecting him for injuries, embracing him for quite a considerable length of time.

"You idiot," she muttered under her breath. The feel of her touch around him was calming; it was as if his bumps and bruises were no longer stinging over his body. Her very touch was enough to bring the exhausted prince back to life.

"Time for that later, grab your pearl and we will get moving. Now," Hinsani commanded. He had been the worst wounded by the fight. Shania and he had been lucky enough to escape with minor injuries while the Royal Blade had taken the brunt of the attacks. There was still something strange about the entire situation. When he himself had attempted to cut through Vasca in that shadowy smoke form, it had failed, whilst Hinsani had been able to strike home. It was something to consider later, perhaps something to speak with Quale about when they escaped this place and returned to him. For now they had one last objective. Rayar was released by the druidae girl and darted up the long flight of stairs towards his pearl. There it sat, after so long. It did not matter to him what others claimed it to be, for him it was a reminder of those he had lost when he was no older than a spring. It was his and therefore it belonged with him. The prince snatched up the pearl into his gloved hand. It felt right to have it once again, in his grasp, its weight, the smooth touch. This pearl was a part of the Prince of Granlia.

"Let us make haste out of here."

* * *

Chapter XLIV
The Truth of the Order
~Rayar~

"We must get it back to Quale. He will know what to do next," Shania explained as they sprinted towards the exit of the tunnel. The fight had been brutal. Shania must have been exhausted afterwards. Rayar had done what he could to help but for the most part he had felt somewhat useless. Regardless, his pearl was back in his grasp and the resistance had been minimal, in the form of numbers at least.

"With the knights on our tail as well, how are we supposed to make it back?" Rayar asked both Shania and Hinsani. It was a reasonable question. They had been so absorbed with making it north, that they had not considered returning south.

"The Snow Hunters; there is a chance they will help us sail back. I'm not much of a sailor though," the druidae replied. Hinsani scowled as he took the rear of the group.

"Not keen on the water myself. I suppose if we have no choice," the Royal Blade added. Whatever their plan would be, they needed to get out as quickly as they could. Shania had proved just how skilled and powerful she was, but if they had to fight again, with others like Vasca, they would certainly be in trouble. Rayar had not truly anticipated just how dangerous magic could be. They had come here together to defeat the Order's agents who had led this scheme, however the only other member Rayar was aware of, was the brute Shan. Where was he? Could he be out there, still lurking about in the grove? The trio burst out of the tunnel near the Evergreen tree with the intention of continuing their sprint to the mountain exit to the west yet once the sunlight hit their eyes, so did the sight of over a hundred men. Dread filled the air, they had been cornered.

'Above and Below... is this a trap?' Rayar's heart sunk into his stomach as he stared wide eyed at the scene before them.

"I am surprised. I did not expect Quale to send his druidae girl with a few regular beings and not come himself. In fact I had hoped I would be seeing him again today, after so long. However it appears you have the sphere in your possession, excellent. Quale taught me many years ago the best way to defeat your foes is to let them think they have won." A strange man dressed in a long grey coat stood at the head of a few similarly garbed figures. They all had their hoods covering their faces, half a dozen figures draped in shadowy clothes hiding their features. The man who stood at the head of the pack however, had revealed his face to them. The man was aged with long silver hair that curled down the length of his back, yet was smooth and well groomed. A goatee as silver as his hair, covered the bottom of his face and his hands were clasped behind his back in an authoritarian stance. The emblem of the Order, as Rayar assumed it was, a silver brooch of a heron, clipped his long grey cloak to his shoulders. Rayar and his companions had halted mid-stride from the depths near the Evergreen tree. Behind the robed figures stood more soldiers than he could count, dressed in dark amour. It was the same uniform as those who had attacked Heldon, on that fateful night. In an instant, Hinsani drew his blade and moved defensively in front of Rayar. He and Shania were moments behind the Royal Blade, weapons in hand and prepared to face a force they had no hope of defeating.

"Who are you!?" Rayar snapped as he gripped his sword in one hand while the other held his pearl. The elderly man in front of them spoke with an accent he could not identify; it was similar to Quale's and Shania's.

"No need to hide anymore, I suppose. I am Isham Dertilderon, Master of the Order. Welcome to the former Druidae Grove and now a place of research for the Order," Isham announced to them all. The soldiers around them all appeared ready to strike at a nod or a whisper from the silver haired man. The moment they did, there would be no hope. Rayar was desperately searching his mind for a plan, and prayed the others were doing the same. Shania on the other hand was losing her mind to anger; her fingers gripped her sword so tightly, he thought her hilt would snap. In her other hand, the tinder she used to create a spark, was ready to strike.

"You set up an ambush. You knew we would be here?" Hinsani asked, calm as ever even in their current predicament. Isham seemed to ponder this for a moment as he chose his next words carefully.

"Knew? Predicted you could say. I knew it would come to this eventually. No, you misunderstand. You, Royal Blade, and the Prince are irrelevant. We have no need or use for either of you. It is the druidae girl we desire. Well, and Quale, yet without him here, I suppose we are delayed for the moment. You see, this druidae girl is paramount in finally releasing the Second, only she can break the druidae seal that holds him. The second of the three keys, that is," the Master of the Order explained. Rayar did not fully understand, as it was he who knew how to find the pearl, Quale had said himself, it was he Rayar, who felt its presence and could locate it. It did not make sense.

"Then how did you know!?" the prince barked out nervously. Their situation was dire. He could feel the hostility from all those around him. He could feel their desire to kill them. He could feel it all. Isham let out a sigh and shook his head.

"A boy like you, unbeknownst to the world that we live in, the true power of those who remain in the shadows and await their time of glory. You would never understand. This game of chess, between Quale and I, has far outstretched your existence and will continue to do so when your existence ends. He played his piece this day, and that piece is about to be taken. From there, it is checkmate." Shania's temper roared. She had heard enough. The spark danced off her sword and the flames exploded at once, in an almighty burst. The young druidae girl raised her hand towards the members of the Order, yet to no avail. In unison the robed figures raised their own hands; energy in the forms of spiralling lights circled their arms and formed into a spear point which shot forward, faster than any arrow he could have imagined. The point pierced the druidae's head and caused her to slump to her knees, the fire dispersing into nothingness.

"Shania!" Rayar yelled as he dashed to her side and caught her mid-fall. In a panic, the prince lowered Shania's head back, awkwardly checking for injuries. There were none, no wound, no blood, no burn. Nothing. Rayar could feel his heart pounding against his chest, the fear of what was to come filling his very being. Fear would keep him strong, he would not give in to it, and he would use it to fight on.

"She belongs to me, now. Take the sphere," Isham ordered simply. Before Rayar knew what was happening, he felt a sharp pain in his abdomen. It hurt, a lot; it made the rest of his body feel numb and cold. His emerald eyes drifted down to the point where the pain had begun. A sword had pierced his stomach, Shania's sword, with her hand around the hilt. Had this truly happened? Had Shania really stabbed him? She stared at him, her eyes blank and devoid of life, as if she had become some sort of puppet with no free will. As he fell back, the sword slipped from his stomach and was dropped to the ground. Shania used her now free hand to snatch the pearl from his fingers. He could not focus, his body trembled, the wound hurt, it bled. Hinsani was soon beside him with his arms supporting his weakening body.

"Rayar!" Hinsani called out, it sounded so far away, even though his protector knelt just beside him. "Hold on, Rayar, hold on." The usually composed man seemed to begin to panic. Rayar imagined Hinsani desperately trying to think of a way to survive, to escape, to win. The prince felt this need fading; there was no way to escape this. It was over.

"Good girl. Now, you have work to do. It is a shame. The last druidae, who helped us years ago, was considerably more enthusiastic. To resort to this kind of soulous always leaves a sour taste in my mouth." Shania slowly, in a zombie-like state, wandered away from her two companions. Rayar could do nothing but lay pierced on the ground, unable to move and unable to think clearly.

'Shania... come back... fight it...'

"Destroy the seal," the grey haired Controller ordered, while another robed figure wielded a torch in their hand. Without a shred of hesitation, the pearl began to vibrate in her grasp. Power, far beyond anything she had before, now surged through her whole being and the land around her. The flames from the torch spiralled in a beautiful and graceful dance then catapulted towards the huge evergreen tree towering above Rayar and Hinsani. The searing heat from the flames briefly gave the prince a feeling of life once again, his cold flesh masked by the blaze. The huge tree was resistant at first, the fire only danced on the branches, being unable to engulf the huge wooden creation. It couldn't hold forever, unfortunately. Soon the entire tree was covered in the burning blaze from Shania's acquired power. "Wait... something is wrong..." the man who had named himself Isham, muttered to himself. Once the flames had begun to turn the gigantic tree into a charred husk of its former glory, Shania once again fell into a lifeless state, appearing to be unable to move or think for herself. Suddenly, as if the Above answered, the ground began to shake uncontrollably, causing them all to stumble where they stood, even the master of the Order was unprepared for the violent tremor in the earth.

"It... it is him!" Isham barked out. In front of the tree, a huge face appeared in the sky, the wrinkly eccentric face of Quale grew into focus, the size of a building. The toothy grin of the crazed man filled their sights. Such a feat was impossible; the floating image of the sage's head was simply unfathomable.

"Dear, oh dear, oh dear! My dear Isham, my dear cronies of the Order. You have all come together after so long, you did not think I would miss out on the reunion did you?" the large face bellowed across the grove. Many of the Order members' footmen stumbled backwards in confusion and uncertainty. Even some of the robed figures were ill prepared for such a sight and were clearly stunned. Isham, however, was not so easily fazed. Rayar could only watch helplessly from his position on the ground. He was not part of this scene anymore. Had he been used?

"Quale, I thought it madness you would send them alone. So you have come, after so long. It must be a horrible feeling to once again be in the ruins of your past, no?" Isham taunted. The image of Quale's gigantic face only chuckled in return.

"It took all my power to hide myself, but I do not think I need to hide myself any longer. Did you think I'd allow you to sim-" Quale's words were suddenly cut off, as a pillar of energy burst from Isham's palm and blasted through the floating image of Quale. It vanished into mist.

"If you wish to speak, show yourself. Your illusions will not save you here," the silver haired mage commanded. There was silence. A painful, long silence as Isham shot his eyes around the clearing, appearing more and more on edge. Rayar felt his life slipping away but he had to know what would happen, he had to know if Shania would be okay. Without warning, a gust of wind shrieked through the grove, followed by a spiralling cloud of red mist. All were blinded, yet it only lasted a fraction of a moment. Within that moment, the mist disappeared into the hordes of trees around the clearing and beside Shania, Quale stood with a straw hat covering his straggly hair and a hand on the druidae's shoulder. Isham's eyes were wide, face pale. The elderly Master was clearly lost for words. It was not just the arrival of the old sage that sent all those present into shock, the evergreen tree stood strong, proud and unharmed, as if the flames had never touched it. Whatever

463

trick Quale had orchestrated, the wool had been pulled over the eyes of all in the clearing.

"Quale... why are... you here?" Rayar asked weakly. The old sage stretched his toothy smirk as he pulled off a straw hat that covered most of his features and tossed it to the floor.

"I'm sorry, this is the stage of my battle my dear boy. I couldn't let them know I was coming. I couldn't let anyone know I was coming. You think I would let my dear Shania be here without me? No, no, no. That is a nasty wound, I must say. Your role is not yet finished, not yet Rayar." At that moment, the old sage whisked his hand, pain rippled through Rayar's mind as the flesh from the wound began to sew together. He could hardly focus, but he could feel strings piercing around the wound. It was painful, too painful. "I can't have you dying just yet, dear boy. You are my special surprise." Hinsani growled like a rabid dog towards Quale and began to pull the prince back against the tree. Rayar watched the old sage's back, helpless and useless. He could only watch.

"The seal… the evergreen, what did you do, Quale?" Isham snapped towards his rival. The old sage threw his head back in laughter whilst he gently released his grip from Shania's shoulder.

"You know me, Master Isham, illusions are my specialty. It was easy. With my dear Shania being engrossed in so much power, it was not hard to deflect your attention elsewhere. What was it you said, my old friend? Let your enemies think they've won?" Quale teased. The Master of the Order took a deep breath and looked to be regaining composure; even Rayar knew losing one's temper with Quale would be pointless.

"Of course, I should have suspected as much. Your arrogance precedes you. You think your soulous imagination exceeds mine, you think because of this you can outwit me?" The prince struggled to understand their conversation. Soulous imagination? Illusions? What were they talking about? Somehow the Evergreen tree above him had been spared of harm, yet he could have sworn he felt the flames of Shania's fire upon his skin. Then he saw it, the ploy. Rayar, with the little strength he had, turned his body to see the earth in the clearing beside him. The earth was drenched in weak flames, though the ground was newly scorched to a crisp.

'Illusions, was he able to use magic on all of us?' The power Vasca had crafted felt insignificant to the power Quale handled. Mages were capable of something like this?

"Ho, ho! Don't feel bad Isham! I've always been better. Not to mention, the red mist runs deeper than you think, hmm?" Quale taunted, again. The eccentric attitude of the old sage simmered, the battle was soon to commence.

"You are powerful, Quale. Even you are outmatched here. I have the druidae, I have you outnumbered. If you thought we would be battling alone, just you and I, you are mistaken. You moved your pieces, you moved them poorly," Isham pronounced as he raised his arms signalling to all the men and women he had around him. His pawns in their game, it was true, Rayar could see that much. Quale was just an old fool, how could he hope to make any difference.

"Expect the unexpected, Isham. Didn't I teach you that?" The silvered haired mage frowned. What trick did Quale have up his sleeve, now?

"Attack! Bring me the witch and kill the others!" From the tree line, the blonde knight from Northfreya, burst through with his soldiers and charged at the entire group. Isham thrust his hand towards them and ordered his own soldiers, who had been circling Rayar and his companions, to engage, passing the old sage a murderous look as he did. The soldiers of Hextheene fired a volley of crossbow bolts into the clearing, striking down numerous black armoured Order soldiers as well as a couple of robed figures behind Isham, before closing the distance for close combat. The all out brawl had commenced. Hinsani , he thought, had left his side to join the fighting; he could no longer feel the presence of his friend beside him. He could barely feel anything. The sounds of fighting, screaming, metal upon metal rang in his ears. They were becoming dimmer and dimmer, with each passing second. Was this it? Was this

465

dying? He was not ready. He did not want to die yet; he had so much he had to do.

'Ayla... Hinsani... father... mother... Shania...'

'Move...'·
'You must stand...'

Light glistened in the shadow. The pearl hovered in a world of darkness. It was so close, just within reach. Rayar's mind screeched for him to reach for it, to touch it. He had to take the pearl. It was there, in front of him, to be grasped. Life surged through Rayar's body, as if light itself coursed through his veins. The endless void he had begun to plummet into closed. A hand reached down from the Above, outstretched and begging for him to snatch it before it was too late. He would not squander his second chance. The golden haired prince thrust up his hand and reached for salvation.

"Stand Rayar! Your life doesn't end yet!" Quale's strained voice echoed from the beyond. Rayar's emeralds eyes pried open. The draining of his soul had ceased, new life filled him. This was not the end. His strength began to return, yet the sights before him were not of life, only of death. Fighting. So much fighting. So much pain. So much sadness. Was this how the world was supposed to be? People killing each other for their own ambitions. Who could he trust? No one. Rayar could only trust in himself. His eyes slowly opened, once again to the Druidae Grove. Fighting surrounded him. Hextheene soldiers were crossing swords with those soldiers of the Order. Hinsani danced like a bolt of lightning between both sides, killing any that came close to the his dying body, slumped against the Evergreen tree. Quale, the old fool seemed to be facing off with the men in robes and the silver haired leader. It was impossible to tell what they were doing exactly; it was like a tug of war with energy pulsating between them. Quale was holding them back even with so many foes, yet could he last much longer against such odds? To think that old man was so powerful after all. Then there was Shania, she stood in the middle of the clearing, lifeless and slumped forward, like a propped up corpse. Rayar could not tell if she was alive, he needed to know she was. He needed her more than he knew. With life growing in the prince's veins, Rayar pushed himself back to his feet and began to lumber over towards the vacant Shania. Hinsani's voice roared at him to stay down but he ignored it. Men fell about around him, fighting with sword and shield, tooth and nail but he ignored it. His tired and broken gaze focused only on Shania. She was all he cared about.

'I am coming... Shania...' Blood covered the lower half of his body, yet a voice urged him on. The stitching Quale seemed to have performed kept his wound closed tight.

"Rayar! Take the pearl, save your friends!" Quale roared through the strain of dancing with the mages. Rayar closed the distance between Shania and himself. Just then the blonde knight charged towards him from across the clearing, yelling words he could not understand. The only words he could hear were the ones ringing in his head over and over. Hinsani, his true protector, intercepted the knight. They clashed like two monsters of war, sword dancing on sword. Rayar could not focus on this; Shania was just a few steps away. Two more steps. One more step.

"Shania...." Rayar croaked. The druidae girl did not respond. She stood there with nothing in her eyes, no life; her mind had been snuffed out. She was nothing but a husk.

'Take the pearl,' Rayar reached out and took the pearl from her limp hand. There was no resistance. Whatever power had been used on her with those Controllers now occupied with Quale, they seemed too distracted to use her for whatever devilish means they desired.

'Save your friends,' Rayar gripped the pearl tightly in his hand. It felt different from before, it felt heavier.

"Feel the earth, Rayar! You are the earth!" Quale called back to him, the pressure of the magic between him and Isham tearing the wind like a storm. Rayar did not understand the words the sage spoke. They made no sense, they were commands he could not follow. The golden haired prince focused the borrowed life filling his form, into the pearl, and then it happened. He felt it, the power of the sphere.

"Enough!" Rayar roared out in pain as the earth around him began to become distorted. The earth tore abreast the ground and shot out in the forms of cones and pillars. The entire landscape was evolving to his will. In the corner of his eye he noticed Quale and the Controllers cease their exchange and stare at him in a state of shock. Not only them, but all the people present in the Druidae Grove, stopped their fighting and stared at him. Wide eyes, mouths dropped open, fear and awe and shock. Why? Why were they all looking at him like that? Rayar raised his arms; the earth around him arose with them. It was time to follow through with his promise. Trees spiralled into weapons and began crushing everyone around him. The earth erupted and swallowed soldiers of both Hextheene and the Order. The Order did this to him, they did this to Shania. It was their fault. Rayar aimed his palm towards the surviving robed men and roared out once more. His voice carried like a giant, the earth below him extended forth and launched from the ground, slamming into them. Isham put up a defence, as best he could, a barrier of energy attempting to force back the onslaught of wood and earth but it was overwhelmed. The ground covered most of them, the trees crashed into them like battering rams without mercy. Vines wrapped around soldiers' ankles, pulling them to the ground and choking them, if they had escaped the crushing power.

'Vengeance of the earth... end them all.' There was no discrimination from the earth and its power. Everyone was a target. In the complete mayhem of the earth spiralling around him, the ground crushed soldiers as if it had a mind of its own, like monsters grabbing and swallowing them. He had lost sight of his friends, Shania, Hinsani and Quale. Had they been swallowed as well? It did not matter. Rayar could only destroy those who threatened him. All of them.

"Rayar..." a soft voice spoke from beneath him. He had not realised until now that he had been propped up in the air above everybody else like some sort of religious symbol. Held up by nothing but a cone of spiralling wind at his ankles. Shania gazed up at him, still broken yet with life once again in her eyes.

'Shania... is alive...' She was alive. If this continued she would be killed along with everyone else. He had to stop, but he did not know how. The power grew and grew; it grew so immense, he thought his body would be torn apart.

"Run Shania!!" Rayar screamed, but it was no use. The spiralling wind around him exploded into a maelstrom of carnage. He lost sight of the druidae girl in the hurricane that now completely surrounded him. The huge storm formed in the sky above, lightning struck the ground, rain poured down as hard as arrows. Lightening thrust from the World Above over and over, striking every tree within the grove, including the Evergreen tree with every blade of natural magical power at his disposal. Hit after hit, the trees burst into flames. The Evergreen resisted as best it could but it simply could not stand against the overwhelming power at Rayar's hand, yet not in his control. The Evergreen burst into flames and began to crumble, trembling under the weight of the rage of the pearl. Rayar was lost within the spiral of his own power, the power the pearl was giving him. The penetrating spears of rain could not put out the fire of the evergreen tree behind him, the continual blaze raged unaffected by the change in the weather. Though he did not care about the tree, he did not care about the Order or the Hextheene soldiers. He cared about Shania and Hinsani; he cared about his beloved family. The fear of his lack of control began to penetrate him to his very core.

'What... am I... doing... stop... I have to stop...' There was no one. No one he could turn to, no one who could help him. He was alone and he was unable to stop the destruction being caused by his own hand. Rayar could feel his arms being pulled from their sockets, his legs felt like they would be torn from his body, his mind felt like it was melting. At this moment, he wished he had simply died, been dead and had never been given more time by Quale, more time to bring this horror upon others. Then he would never have experienced this pain. A

figure appeared in the storm. The figure pulled itself through the unstoppable hurricane and armour piercing rain, and every step a strenuous effort, as if pulling a dozen bulls by rope.

"Hinsani..." the prince muttered. His Royal Blade, the man who would never leave his side, was clawing his way towards him. The pain in the face of the man was horrific.

'Just stop... run away... leave me!' Rayar cried within his mind. Hinsani would not stop, he would never have stopped. His clothes were being torn apart from the sheer blade like streaks of wind; the pressure on his body was causing blood to trickle from his nostrils, his ears. But the man would not stop his march towards the prince. Once the Royal Blade was finally below him, the man reached out and grabbed his ankle. The moment he felt his body being pulled, everything went black once more. All thought escaped his mind, drifting into a deep sleep.

"Shania!" Rayar called out. There was no Druidae Grove when his eyes finally opened. No Shania, no Hinsani, no Quale, none of the people who had attacked them. None of the people he knew around him. He was alone, or so he thought. The image was eerily familiar. The colours around him never stayed the same shade, the hall walls rotated and fluttered like paper while the stone paved ground he stood on, rippled like water yet felt as stable as steel.

"You again," a voice echoed through the fluctuating hall. Rayar turned abruptly to see a figure sitting in a tall throne. The figure's hands gripped the arm rests as if he would be pulled into the abyss if he even released a finger. The black robed figure from his nightmare so long ago, had returned. Those golden eyes of dread peering deep into the very fabric of his being, his pale white skin giving him the appearance of a ghost. "And you can talk?" Rayar took a deep breath and patted down his own form. He was not floating like before; he was not flowing like water anymore. The wound in his stomach was there, the bleeding had stopped, and the flesh had sewn itself together. Had it been Quale's doing back when he was on the brink of death?

"Where are we?" He asked. This time in this nightmare Rayar was considerably calmer.

"My prison. It has been that way longer than I can remember. Yet to see you here again, well, in such short time frames, is certainly interesting for me. It does get tedious here," the dark robed figure explained as he leant back in his throne.

"And... who are you?" Rayar asked again. This must be death. The World Below perhaps? This was certainly not what he imagined the World Above to be, from all the sermons and speeches priests had given about its glory. It felt too dark and trapping to be a land of bliss.

"Me? Well, I am a forgotten relic. What brings you back here?" the figure asked bluntly. Rayar was not sure how to answer. He thought he was already dead.

"I think so... I do not understand..." this made no sense. This must have been his dying nightmare. To think he would not see the ones he loved before the last moment, that he would just see this. It was some kind of sick joke to say the least.

"Do you want to live?" The figured bluntly asked again. Rayar blinked in shock.

"... I do... I have so much I need to do, so many friends and family who need me. I cannot die yet!" Rayar was desperate.

"Why do they need you? What can you do?" the robed man retorted with a tilt of his head. The prince choked on his words. What could he do? What use was he? This entire journey he had travelled with Hinsani and Shania, he had felt like a burden. If he died here, what difference would it make? No, he couldn't think like that. He was not useless. He refused to be useless. He swore he would help people. He swore he would make a difference.

"I... I can... make a difference!" Rayar snapped back in reply. He would not have his soul destroyed as his body was, by some vision trapped in a throne.

"Can you? By the looks of it, you won't be going back. No, you aren't going anywhere." The figure smirked, his eyes glared with a deadly piercing gold that stunned Rayar's body into submission. "I hope you enjoy the abyss as much as I do, sweet boy." With those last words, he felt his body being sucked into the blackness like a rough current. Everything went pitch black.

*

~Hinsani~

Hinsani repeated the prince's name several times, yet there was no response. He was breathing, at least he was alive. The strength had been sapped from the Royal Blade; he could barely lift his sword.

'This kind of power. Rayar, all along you were...' Hinsani pushed his thoughts aside. It was not the time to be concerning himself with what Rayar was. There were considerably more pressing matters now. They both lay sprawled on the ground of the decimated clearing in the Druidae Grove. The earth had risen and dropped, distorted and manic like something out of a dream. The trees were bent and twisted in ways a tree could never grow, crushing men against the ground or against other trees. No battlefield he had ever seen before had been this merciless, people killed so brutally beyond all imagination. The dust cloud that had been created by the sheer force of the spiralling wind had begun to settle, allowing Hinsani to see the carnage in all its terrible glory. The huge Evergreen tree that had pierced the heavens had become a burning shell of its former self. Most the soldiers had been slaughtered on all sides, many dead and a few clearly out cold. The blonde knight, Caskin Camaron, lay flat in the dirt nearby. He was still alive; their fight had been brief but threatening. He had not had a fight like that in some time. Shania too laid unconscious, blood trickling from her forehead. Quale, the sage who had been watching them all this time but had hidden his presence, was nowhere to be seen. Perhaps crushed beneath the rising earth or perhaps he had fled. The old man was not trustworthy therefore

not his concern. Those Controllers from the Order were crushed. Their mangled corpses lay below mounds of earth. Vines had bent their limbs out of shape, twisted and foul. All but one. The survivor was kneeling; his breath heavy and wounds covered his body. The man who had announced his name as Isham, their leader, still breathed and had remained conscious. They were the only two who still stood, though not literally. Hinsani pushed himself to his feet and pulled Galad up to his chest, holding the blade with one hand. His other arm had been badly hurt in the storm. The man named Isham looked over to them both.

"That boy... is a druidae... to think there was another all along," Isham groaned out. Hinsani frowned heavily. A druidae? How was that possible? No, it was possible. Rayar had been that baby boy from long ago. "That power... I must destroy him now... before it is too late," Isham growled as he tried to rise to feet as well, yet his wounds forced him back to his knees.

"Druidae or not, he is my charge," there was no choice. He did not know what kind of strength this Controller had left, what he could do even in that state. There was a chance to rush him, kill him even, yet if he died in the process, the Knights of Hextheene could get their hands on Rayar as well. After what they witnessed, he would meet a gruesome fate. There was only one option for them both. His honour demanded he follow it through. "And you will never reach him again," Hinsani finished. The Royal Blade sheathed his sword and pulled Rayar up over his shoulder. It was painful to carry him in his state, he could barely stand himself. Duty forced him on; duty forced him to complete his task. Hinsani would never break his oath.

"What... what are you doing!?" Isham snarled. The surviving soldiers began to stir awake. All the men of the Order had been slain, and only a handful of Hextheene soldiers remained alive. Hinsani was in no state to fight. "He must be destroyed! You do not understand!" Isham continued to call out to Hinsani as he limped away from the battlefield. The prince lay limp over his shoulder. Shania and Quale would be left behind, though truth be told, he could no longer trust them. Ensuring Rayar's survival was all that mattered. While he continued to drag his weakened body through the dirt, the shouting of the Controller followed him until it suddenly went silent. They had one option left to them, disappear.

* * *

Chapter XLV
The World Below
~Isham~

Isham sat in his office covered in bandages under his long grey coat. It had been some time since the battle in the Druidae Grove, perhaps a week. He had lost track of time. Quale had slipped through his fingers. The Druidae had slipped through his fingers. Damn that Rayar, the Prince of the Earth had also slipped through. To think that boy had the power of a druidae, and not just any druidae. The sphere had granted him supreme power, something that could not be allowed to get into the boy's hands again. With that kind of power, not even he could challenge Rayar. A cup of wine twirled in circles between his fingers as he pondered their next move. A voice spoke from beside him, a voice that that had become all too familiar over the past few years. It had always been a cool, floating voice that drifted into his ears like a soothing melody.

"What a turn of events, Master Isham." A tall man draped in vibrant red attire, covered in jewellery and with long flowing white hair, leant against the wall in his office, dancing a coin between his fingers.

"Indeed it was. Have you come to insult or something more desirable?" Isham asked the red clothed man. The man in red chuckled under his breath and turned to face the wounded Controller.

"I never insult. I just point out the facts, Master Isham. Your plan worked. Perhaps not the way you would have liked but the seal to The Seconds prison is destroyed. You seem as if you are upset it did not unravel the way you wanted it to," the man in red teased. Isham sighed and took a long swig of his wine; it was smooth and sweet upon his tongue.

"History will remember me as the Third Coming. The one who crushed darkness back into the World Below. How the World Below rises again is up for interpretation. Just because there was a second druidae, does not hinder my advance," Isham fought back with his own facts. Long had this been planned, many years had passed before this new opportunity arrived.

"You tried this many years ago, eighteen years was it now? Failed then. You did not have a rein on your druidae and she, what? Killed herself did she not? Now you do not even have a druidae to play with, there are two out of your reach. Your cast is one short, Master Isham," the elder Controller rolled his eyes at the pestering of the critic.

"I do not need a druidae as a piece. The only thing that still stands in my way is Quale. The key to the Second's lock is in his possession, the last chain that keeps that madman trapped in his abyss. The next move is his but I will strike the final blow soon. Quale's arrogance and desire to utterly destroy me led to his failure to protect the Evergreen. The fool underestimated one of his own pieces, and destroyed the seal himself. His mind is a dangerous one, unpredictable, but it is also his weakness. Not to mention his need to humiliate me, to ruin me before he kills me. This Rayar was a gift and curse to that old fool," Isham stated simply and went to drink from his wine once more before he realised it was already empty. That key, wherever Quale had hidden it, would be the final resolution to this battle between them for so many years. Knowing his old companion, he would have hidden it far, far away and without draining the mind of Quale, chances are they would never be able to locate it. Yet, where there was a will, there was a way.

"You need to kill the boy, Prince Rayar Granlia. You have to destroy him," the man in red commanded. Isham snorted at him.

"You are telling me what I must do? I am the Master of the Order." The only man, who could anger him more than this jester, was Quale.

"He must die for your own good. What happens when he learns how powerful he really is, and comes to stop you. Or even worse, takes your role in history and becomes legend while you are left on the side, irrelevant and forgotten. People believe soulous is a long forgotten myth, they do not know how close you are to finally reaching the knowledge of the old ways, when soulous shaped the world you live in. You shape this world Master Isham, you have the crusade beginning in the north, and the south under the thumb of your Order and you are only one old man away from bringing true horror upon the world." What annoyed Isham the most was the fact that his visitor was correct. He did not understand how this simple prince, someone who was not even worth a mention, had such power. Rumeo, it had to have been Rumeo. Rumeo and Quale. Those two, who thwarted him once before, now were attempting to do so again with the King of lard's son. It was an insult that could not be ignored. The man in red was right, Rayar needed to die for the good of the world they lived in, for the good of his own future and his legacy.

"Yes, he must die..." He finally gave in. The man in red clapped his hands together excitedly.

"Lovely! The stage is set. The heroic Master Isham Dertilderon stands in the jaws of the beast, ready to strike home. The dastardly Quale plots against him, the mysterious druidae boy, the valiant warrior who protects them, the cruel King of Hextheene. So many acts I cannot wait to witness, a tale truly as old as time." Just then a knock on the door forced Isham back into reality. The office was dark, lit only by a single candle on the huge oak table that he worked behind daily. The room was cold, so very cold. Slowly the huge door to his office creaked open and a woman stood in the doorway.

"Master Isham," she greeted him with a respectful bow. "The Order's Elders are gathered for the meeting... who were you talking to?" Isham looked across his room where the man

477

in red had been twiddling his thumbs and rambling on about tales and other nonsensical things. The room was silent, he was alone.

"No one."

The Hall of Knowledge, also known as the Order's meeting place, was a large, circular structure with lanterns scattered around the walls. In the centre of the hall was a large ring table; in the centre of that ring sat a rusty black chair. No one had been forced in that seat for many, many years. Isham though, did not let such thoughts distract his attention from the ongoing meeting. Even as Master of the Order, he sat in the same style of chair as his cohorts; Controllers known as the Elders of the Order were placed around the large ring table. Most of them had drinks and documents spread out in front of them, some organised and some preferring a mess of nonsense to refer to.

"So we are gathered finally. Much has occurred of late, no time for idle chat I think." A man spoke opposite Isham on the ring table. He was an elderly man; most here were in their later years, with a pipe between his fingers and short grey hair. Gorman, the only Controller in the Order Isham was weary of; he was not so easy to pull the wool over as the others. Suspicion was in his blood. Regardless, there was a meeting to attend to.

"Well," Isham began to speak and turned to Irena sitting nearest to himself. "Elder Irena, as your agenda is the most significant at the moment, would you enlighten the rest of us." The old woman bowed her head respectfully and began to sift through her documents.

"Of course, the crusade is currently underway. Reports from Ler'Del inform us that Mayhen is in no position to counter any sort of invasion at the moment due to internal affairs. He has yet to be more precise on the matter of his involvement yet as I am sure you have all heard the rumours, the royalty of Mayhen are currently in the motions of a civil war. The King of Southrous and the Council of the South have been given their directives, as well as to ensure as few civilian casualties as possible, yet when it comes to war that is difficult to oversee," Irena explained, her eyes flicking between the documents and the numerous other Controller Elders present.

"I see. We will see relief is sent to all those affected by the 'crusade' once the monarchy is replaced by a more agreeable form of government. Any other news from Southrous, Elder Irena?" The old woman shook her head slowly in reply, at first.

"The new King, Raiva, he follows in his father's footsteps and he's countered by the council at every turn. He will not be a problem in maintaining order. Aside from that, the current affairs and economy continues as expected." With that, her report came to a close. Isham turned to his other side, towards a younger man, the youngest in the hall in fact.

"Elder En'oso, please update us on the vessel that can withstand the storm to the west being built in Breton?" The young man was about to speak before the Elder, Gorman, interjected.

"I have something of urgency to bring up." Isham cocked his brow in surprise at the rude interruption; well he threw on a mask of surprise at least. He had suspected such things from Gorman.

"It is not like you to be so abrupt, Elder Gorman. Though, if it is of urgency then by all means, do as you please," Isham explained with a wave of his hand, showing his dissatisfaction with the manner of how the meeting was being held. Gorman tapped his pipe with his finger and tipped some ash onto the table beside his pile of documents.

"Well, my friends. I have some dire news. Many of our own have died in the former druidae grove." Whispers and gasps ran through the hall. As Gorman spoke to all in the hall, his heavy gaze rested solely on the Master of the Order. Isham returned the glare, his brow twitching as he held back his anger.

'Arrogant fool, he plans to corner me.'

"The list of the dead is here, but for time's sake, ninety eight soldiers, five fledgling Controllers and Agent Vasca have all passed to the next world." Not only did Gorman know that something had occurred in the north, he knew the exact deaths, though it was not like he could hide such a fact. In reality he was going to reveal it himself but it seemed this oaf of a man beat him to the punchline. Yet it had been Quale they were facing, and after using the fledgling's power to control the druidae, there was no way they would have had enough power to fight Quale, let alone that prince. Prince Rayar had not been in his equation.

"This is dire news. Do you know what occurred?" Irena asked as she stroked her chin. Gorman inhaled on his pipe and nodded slowly.

"We know the criminal Quale was present, we were able to track traces of his soulous power to Oldome but we have yet to investigate in person." The whispers and gasps increased in volume as the name Quale was mentioned. Isham tapped his finger on the surface of the ring table, his scowl weighing down his features.

"Oldome is out of your jurisdiction Elder Gorman. I must question why you have been interfering with matters that do not come to your desk." The room fell silent as the pair of men stared at each other in condemnation.

"Indeed, I was out of line and I will accept my punishment. For the moment, I have more questions. Questions about why Quale would return to the former Druidae Grove, the place of one of his crimes? Why Agent Vasca and these men and women were in the Druidae Grove? Also, why were you there, Master Isham?" All eyes were now on him after Gorman preached his arrogance. There was silence. Silence for longer period than Isham was comfortable. He was no fool, however, and had prepared for such an event. In reality, if he had been completely successful and defeated Quale there and then, reached into his mind and found the location of the last key to the Second Comings Seal, he would not have to deal with these dull relics of Controllers anymore, yet a good tactician plans for numerous eventualities. The worst part of this revelation was the fact Gorman was most likely tracking his power as well as Quale's. This slight would be ignored for the moment; this man would get what was coming to him eventually.

"Research. I have been trying to locate Quale for some time as you all know. We learnt he had been frequently seen in Oldome. The former Druidae Grove was a good place to start when investigating any activity by this deplorable criminal." It was time to reveal a little more to these ignorant children. "We learnt of a sphere that holds much power, and we were experimenting on its origins and power. Vasca lead the research team, however Quale struck us when we were unprepared and used this sphere to destroy... the Evergreen tree. He has a druidae girl with him, using her for his foul means. We were unable to stop him. I was intending to speak of this today and have a full report written for all concerning the events, but it seems the Elder Gorman believes he is above the Master of the Order." This should satisfy their thirst for a time. There was no way for them to know what really happened, it was impossible. Isham would not let his plan be hindered when he was closer than ever. If anything, Gorman had brought his plan further along, it was his intention from the beginning to leak Quale's fabricated agenda.

"Quale wishes to bring back the Second Coming? We must find him at once and put an end to this scheme. It would destroy all the order we have created thus far," Irena declared with a worried look upon her face. Gorman seemed less convinced by the explanation yet at the moment he had no evidence against Isham; it would remain that way.

"I see. We will investigate the grove regardless, and I agree, Quale must be stopped, and the druidae girl must be saved from his grasp. She may be the last of her kind. She is an endangered race and must be put under Order protection," Gorman agreed.

'Yes, she is the last one of her kind. The boy Rayar, I will see dead before you even learn of him. Now the evergreen is destroyed, the girl can die along with him.' This had played into his hands well, though caution would still be a top priority. With Vasca dead, his soldiers dead, the only ones left under his

481

direct command were Shan and Ler'Del and a few Controller trainees. Still, victory was within reach.

'Quale, now the full power of the Order will be coming after you. Once I have you, you will reveal the last key. You will watch as I prove once and for all, I was superior all along. It was me, always me.'

* * *

End Part One

Glossary

Above and Below*:* A commonly used curse in the Freeland. It was born from the religious belief in the World Above for those who follow the faith and the World Below for those who commit terrible sin.

Anguss, Quale*:* An old sage hidden from the world. He is an eccentric man and holds a grudge against the Order, leading to his complicated plots.

Baron: Title given to the Heads of the houses governing over land in Hextheene.

Bergin Hold*:* A castle close to the Leon Mountains in the north-west of Hextheene. Home of House Berethor.

Blade Dancing*:* A forgotten and ancient form of using a sword, passed from master to disciple for many years. The only known man who can use such forms is Hinsani Tannaroth who is currently training Prince Rayar Granlia. The forms are said to be from the Far East on one of the many, many islands that litter the eastern sea. All forms are named with an animal and an action, e.g. The Lion Stalks.

Bran, Raimon*:* The newest recruit to the Royal Blades and native Mayhen man. He is a plain man but very skilled with an arming sword.

Braska's Border: A makeshift wooden wall between the Hextheene territory and the Oldome territory in the most northern continent. King Braska Hextor wished to expand influence in the north but found that the resources worth gathering were only found on the most eastern side of Oldome, leading to the creation of the border wall.

Breton: A southern nation directly south of Mayhen over the Free Sea. Breton is known to trade with Mayhen, other than that it has little interaction with the northern kingdoms.

Brexxia: The most southern kingdom on the mainland, the Wise Isles consisting of islands in the sea. This kingdom has the most connection to the Order as the Order has almost entirely taken over the government. A very peaceful nation, all men are expected to wear veils when in public and women are expected to have their heads shaved upon reaching womanhood.

Bridge of Freedom: The famous indestructible bridge that was said to have been built by the First Coming to connect Oldome to the Freeland a thousand years ago and lead the people against the monsters of the World Below when they conquered the Freeland.

Briyar: A gaunt and lanky soldier stationed in the garrison at the Shield of Mayhen.

Camaron, Caskin: Commander-at-Arms of the realm of Hextheene. He is a broad, blonde haired knight who loyally serves his King without hesitation. He loves war and battle, being the only time he truly feels alive, with the exception of being in the arms of the whore, Fifonia.

Castle Crewyn: Southern Mayhen castle next to the border between Mayhen and Hextheene and home for many, many years to the Noble family Leodri.

Castle Harringmore: Northern Hextheene castle near the city of Northfreya, formerly the home of the Merigold family who moved their home to Northfreya due to the rising profit of trade passing through the city.

Commander-at-Arms: One of the highest military positions within the Hextheene army used more as a figure head leader than for actual tacticians, currently held by Caskin Camaron.

Controllers: The name of those who can control magic. They serve within the largest register of the famous Order. This name is not as used as the name spoken by the common folk, Mages. King Braska Hextor pushed the name Mages, instead of Controllers, due to his hate for users of magic. They have been around in the world since the Age of Gods yet their numbers have dwindled over time. Many seek knowledge and wisdom within the Order without ever interacting with the outside world. Many Controllers are simple scholars hidden away in the Orders' Keep, which is also hidden from the world.

Death Valley: The mountain range between Mayhen and Hextheene. It has stood as a natural defence for both sides as the mountains are so dangerous to traverse it is impossible to move vast numbers of men through it. It is also the home of the crazed sage, Quale Anguss, though this is known by very few. Its true name is, the Leon Mountains.

Dedred, Hyar: A golden haired drunk and skilled warrior. He serves within the Royal Blades and one of the few men documented to have golden hair, the others being Rayar Granlia and the Vienne family.

Dertilderon, Isham: Master of the Order, serves as a chairman for the Orders' democratic meetings and decisions.

Druidae: Until recently the druidae lived in solitude in the grove in Oldome yet seventeen years ago they were slaughtered by unknowns. Shania Tear is the last known druidae. Yet their existence to most of the population is considered myth and stories.

Druidae Grove: The home of the druidae in the frozen wastes of Oldome. However the grove has its own weather and ecosystem and is unaffected by the cold weather on the northern continent.

Evergreen Tree: The largest tree in the world hidden within the Druidae Grove. It is suspected to be the key to keeping The Second Coming sealed away.

Eye of the Lost: A mountainous range deep in the western point of Mayhen. Rumoured to be where the monsters from the World Below were forced back into their own realm.

Fifonia: A red headed and beautiful woman who works for lonely men. She is currently in the employ of Caskin Camaron.

First Druidae: The eldest son of the First Coming. He, alongside the first Hextor, defeated and sealed away the Second Coming, his younger brother.

Freeland: The name of the mainland which holds the majority of the kingdoms; Mayhen, Hextheene, Ghaul, Breton, Brexxia, The Lost Desert and the Wise Isles. It was named the Freeland after the First Coming led the people of the earth to victory against the monsters from the World Below. The Freeland stands between the World Above and the World Below.

Galad: A one sided sword with a long wooden grip and unrivalled sharpness that is passed down between masters of Blade Dancing. Hinsani Tannaroth is the current holder of this blade.

Gallina, Brayton: Long time friend and servant of King Rumeo, a trusted commander who has seen many years of peace. This has caused him to put on large amounts of weight. He has a bushy beard and strong look about him, though he is beginning to bald.

Ganon: Capital city of Hextheene. The city is overpopulated and rife with poverty and crime.

Ghaul: An ancient kingdom neighbouring Mayhen on its southern border. The people of this land all went mad and ravenous and attacked each other as well as Mayhen. A wall, the Shield, was put in place to keep the madmen at bay. For hundreds of years there has been no movement in Ghaul apart from the increasing Red Mist covering all the land.

Gods Age: The Gods Age was a thousand years ago when people were pushed to the brink of extinction and forced to live in the wilderness of Oldome. The story goes The First Coming descended from the World Above and rallied all the survivors from the monstrous purge. Together they launched a war upon the monsters and retook the land, now known as Freeland, and forced the monsters back into the World Below. The Age ended at the birth of the First Druidae and his younger brother, the Second Coming, just over two hundred years later.

Gorman: An Elder of the Order.

Granlia, Ayla: Second daughter of King Rumeo and Queen Julian. She is a beautiful and serene princess with dark hair and loving eyes.

Granlia, Jonnas: Second son of Commander Vesir and Lady Kaylen. Strong and well built, a man who follows his morals and fights for what is right and for glory.

Granlia, Julian: Queen of Mayhen and wife to King Rumeo. She is younger than her husband but loves him unconditionally, as she does her love her children. Born to a minor Noble family in Heldon her father was able to convince Rumeo's father that is was a beneficial marriage many years ago.

Granlia, Kaylen: Wife to the Commander of the Shield, Vesir. She is younger than him, as is custom in Mayen. She is a naturally beautiful woman with dark hair who is also a skilled fighter.

Granlia, Lanmir: Baby son of Vesir Granlia and Kaylen Granlia.

Granlia, Nyer: Eldest daughter of King Rumeo and Queen Julian. She is a stern and cold woman who thinks logically and precisely. She is the heir to the throne of Mayhen.

Granlia, Nymin: Youngest daughter of King Rumeo and Queen Julian. She is childish and plays pranks on any she can.

Granlia, Rayar: Adopted son of King Rumeo and Queen Julian. He is known for his golden hair and being the only son in the royal family. His true name is Rayar Vienne.

Granlia, Rumeo: King of Mayhen and father of four. A joyous and peace loving King who in the past did whatever he had to do to secure the safety of the world.

Granlia, Vesir: Former prince of Mayhen and now Commander of the Shield as well as brother to the current King, Rumeo. A skilled warrior and brilliant tactician with a past shrouded in darkness and despair.

Granlia, Wiliam: King Rumeo's father and former King of Mayhen.

Granlia, Zanmir: Eldest son to Vesir Granlia. A brilliant and intellectual mind he wishes to learn the secrets of the world and help create a better one.

Hannabel, Shan: An agent of the Order. He is a brutish and dangerous man who only knows the path of violence.

Heldon: Capital of the Kingdom of Mayhen. It was formed after the Age of Despair once the Second Coming had been sealed away. The original capital had been Hellsbane. The city is large in size with a huge wall surrounding the inner city and the Heldon Keep. The keep in the centre is formed from white stone, many people debate on if the city was crafted by magic or builders. The tower in the centre of the keep is so tall it appears like a sword piercing the heavens and considered one of the most stunning cities in the Freeland.

Heldoran: The commonly used phrase by people of Mayhen for people who live in Heldon.

Hellsbane Castle: Said to have been the last stage of battle in the war between The First Coming and the monsters from the World Below. Surrounded by steep and razor sharp mountains and defends against the mythical Eye of the Lost.

Hextheene: One of the oldest kingdoms in known history and with one of the strongest military in the Freeland. The people of Hextheene are under the impression they are descendants of the true invaders from Oldome and everyone else was born after they retook the Freeland. The ruler of Hextheene must always be of the Hextor bloodline, containing the Holy Blood from the very first Hextor who fought alongside The First Coming. This kingdom has seen more war and strife than any other country in the Freeland. The current ruler is King Braska Hextor II.

Hexhold: The impenetrable castle where the royal family of Hextor reside alongside the highest Knights of Hextheene and those loyal to the court. It is broad, huge and dark in contrast with the keep in Heldon. It is near the city of Ganon, the capital of Hextheene.

Hextor, Aya: Queen of Hextheene and wife to Braska Hextor. She rarely ventures from her chambers; many believe it is due to illness.

Hextor, Braska: King of Hextheene. Braska is a giant of a man without a sense of humour or time for anything other than the forwarding of his own goals. He detests magic more than anything and strives to wipe any trace of it from the known world.

Hextor, Kerrin: Prince of Hextheene and son to Braska Hextor. Unlike his father he is short, slim and beautiful for a man. He has a twin sister, Melayne.

Hextor, Melayne: Princess of Hextheene and daughter to Braska Hextor. She is calculating and realistic, someone whose qualities Braska wishes his son carried. She has a twin brother, Kerrin.

Hextor, Nathun*:* King Braska Hextor II's father and former King of Hextheene. He was murdered in his sleep after the war with Mayhen alongside his wife.

Highhall Castle*:* A ruined castle in the north of Mayhen which burnt down in the largest fire ever recorded. It was the home for the Noble Family Vienne.

Irena*:* The Order representative in Southrous.

Jac*:* The wild hawk that from time to time assists Shania Tear.

Jennin, Donnel: Knight of Hextheene. He is a skinny and unimpressive man with little confidence.

Kannu*:* High Priest in the Shield who preaches the word of the World Above. He is a fatherly man with only kind words to say to everyone.

Kinsani, Caidarian*:* Captain in the Heldoran guard.

Knights of Hextheene*:* A sect of knights created by Braska Hextor to hunt and kill anyone related to magic. They tend to serve in the military more so than their original reason for creation.

Kra'Urn*:* The name of a chief or leader within a Snow Hunter Tribe.

Lady Merigold*:* The stunning and voluptuous ruler of Northfreya after her husband passed. Desired by many and uses her sexuality to manipulate favours from those in high positions with weak minds.

Leon Mountains*:* The official name of Death Valley.

Ler'Del: Member of the Order sent to treat with the King of Mayhen. He is a large and hairy, chestnut haired man.

Lorinstead, Osmear: A knight of Hextheene. While considered old and right for retirement he still continues to prove his worth to the realm of Hextheene.

Loysse, Seldine: Noble Lady of Stoneside Keep and wife to Tismiar Loysse.

Loysse, Tismiar: Noble Lord of Stoneside Keep and husband to Seldine Loysse.

Mahaai: The tribe of Snow Hunters in Oldome who have a village located in a valley to provide shelter from the elements. A friendly and respectful tribe who have lived in the snow wastes since the Age of Gods.

Mahaai, Pola of the: Young daughter of the Kra'Urn in the Mahaai Tribe. She is a fun loving and easy going girl.

Mahaai, Seran of the: Young son of the Kra'Urn in the Mahaai. He is a serious and no nonsense boy.

Mahaai, Tecamah of the: The current Kra'Urn of the Mahaai. He is a large and boisterous man with a love for all those living and for enjoying one's time on the earth. He is covered in engravings of the history of the Mahaai on his flesh.

Mainlanders: Phrase used for all those who live in the Freeland by Snow Hunters in Oldome.

Mangel, Timur: Warlord of Southrous and leader of the Crusading army. He is an honourable and gallant man with a drive for justice and fairness.

Master Vayers: Head librarian in Heldon.

Mayhen: A kingdom with a rich history of war and progression for hundreds of years. It has had a constant strife, much like Hextheene, with the south of the Freeland due to conflicting religious beliefs. Allegedly it was the last kingdom formed in the Freeland as it was the location of the last battle of The First Coming against the monsters from the World Below. In Mayhen women are seen as equal with rights and position i.e. an older princess can ascend to the throne before a younger son. The current ruler is King Rumeo Granlia.

Merigold, Gerald: Infant son of Lady Merigold of Northfreya.

Meyer: A town located just north of the Shield of Mayhen, built with the directions of Vesir Granlia to house numerous soldiers and their families who serve on the Shield.

Morah, Kaylen: A young girl living on a farm on the furthest outskirts of Heldon land.

Morah, Sternmir: An old man living on a farm on the furthest outskirts of Heldon land.

Morah, Tissir: A young boy living on a farm on the furthest outskirts of Heldon land.

Moran, Sli: Advisor to King Braska Hextor. Many compare him to a snake who claims to use spiders to listen to webs being spun all over the world. Whether he has spies or actual spiders is still open to debate.

Nash, Lancel: Knight of Hextheene and former squire to Caskin. To appear more like the Commander-at-Arms Lancel has copied his hair style and attempted to wield a bastard sword in the past, but found it too difficult.

Ni'Tella, Lanni*:* Advisor to King Rumeo Granlia and previously an advisor to his father, the former King. She is an elderly woman with a struggling memory but a strong sense of justice.

Niyla*:* The loyal but newly appointed maid to Queen Julian. She is not exactly beautiful but she has a loving aura about her.

Noble Lord/Lady*:* The major families' heads in Mayhen are referred to as either Noble Lord or Noble Lady.

Northfreya*:* The advanced city in northern Hextheene. It almost acts as an independent nation in itself; Hextheene allows this due to the large profit from trade that is made in the city. The rulers of Northfreya must continually support the crown with coin to keep its independence. The ruler of Northfreya is currently Lady Merigold after the passing of her husband. Passing through this city is the only way to reach the land of Oldome without a ship.

Oathsworth, Donnel*:* A Knight of Hextheene. He is famous for being able to wield a giant war hammer due to his massive size. He is a strong built balding man with a dark sense of humour.

Oldome*:* Land of the Snow Hunters as north as any man can travel covered in snow and ice. The only place not touched by snow is the Druidae Grove yet that is a forbidden land. The people of Oldome believe they are the descendants of those who protected the Home land, or Old Home, when The First Coming left to retake the Freeland. They believe they must remain in the north to protect the passage to the World Above. While they never involve themselves in any wars to the south they are still regarded as a dangerous people and are rarely ever seen south.

Pendmir, Arthus: Noble Lord of the castle and city of Riveroth located east of the capital. A young and handsome noble with a terrible illness that will drastically shorten his lifespan as it did his parents. A man who believes that violence can always be avoided if only words were used more often.

Red Mist: A strange mist that has covered the majority of the Kingdom of Ghaul. None truly know what it is or its purpose however any who venture within the mist are never seen again.

Rengecko, Zachary: Personal assistant and advisor to Prince Kerrin Hextor. He is a skilled swordsman preferring the use of a rapier.

Riveroth: Home to the Pendmir Noble Family. A city and castle that is located beside the largest lake in Mayhen which is connected to The Golden River that passes from the north of Mayhen to the south of Mayhen through The Fork into the Sealed Sea. The current Noble Lord is Arthus Pendmir.

Rivers, Payton: Captain and torturer for the Hextheene army.

Royal Blade: Four men or women are selected to serve as the Royal Guards for the Granlia family, they are known as Royal Blades. King Rumeo created this group of soldiers seventeen years ago and handpicked men and women to protect his children, having them swear an oath that relieved them of following his commands before those of his children. This would allow the Royal Blades to protect the royal children against absolutely anything or anyone. The current Royal Blades are Hinsani Tannaroth to Rayar Granlia, Hyar Dedred to Nymin Granlia, Titania to Nyer Granlia and Raimon Bran to Ayla Granlia. The newest recruit is Raimon after the previous Royal Blade died from old age a year previous.

Shield of Mayhen*:* A large wooden and stone wall that borders the Kingdom of Ghaul. It is a garrison of soldiers of Mayhen who protect the rest of the country from the south however since there has been no threat from the south for so long the Shield has become a place of retirement or for those who wish to serve under the famous commander, Vesir Granlia.

Sirus*:* Captain of the Heldoran Guard. He is a slimy and arrogant man who only appeared in the city recently.

Snow Hunters*:* Name given to the natives of Oldome by those living in the Freeland.

Soulous*:* Term used by the Order in place of magic. The magic is the word spoken by those who do not truly understand the power behind the Controllers craft.

Southrous*:* Southern nation bordering Hextheene. This kingdom has been in a cold war with Hextheene for many years without either side sending a large military force to invade since the end of the war between Mayhen and Hextheene. However each side supposedly is sending bandits, brigands and criminals into each other's lands to disrupt the populace and abstract information. The people of Southrous believe in The Great Lord as their God, a God of War who wishes to bring peace to the world but first must bring despair. The current rulers are King Raiva Tempestade and the Body of Distribution. (Southrous is ruled by one King and a council of chairmen.)

Stoneside Keep*:* A strong and secure castle located within the side of the Death Valley mountain range. It is home to the Noble Loysse family. The current rulers are Lord Tismiar Loysse and Lady Seldine Loysse.

Summerfall*:* Small village north-east of Heldon.

Tannaroth, Hinsani: Royal Blade for the Prince Rayar Granlia. Hinsani is a famous swordsman known throughout the Freeland and the last known user of the Blade Dancing sword techniques.

Tear, Shania: A brown haired and peculiar woman who has a hawk that she can converse with. She is the last druidae in the world and also the only one to be known to have used her powers to manipulate fire.

The First Coming: The title of the hero of the Age of Gods who led the people of the world to victory against the monsters of the World Below. He is said to be the incarnation of the World Above saving mankind from the horrors of the World Below.

The Second Coming: The title of the youngest son of The First Coming. He is said to have been malicious and pure evil wishing to bring destruction to the Freeland and all other lands in the known world. He was supposedly stopped by his older brother, the First Druidae and the first Lady Hextor.

The Lost Desert: A wide open wasteland between Southrous, Breton and Brexxia. It is inhabited by various clans and dangerous warring tribes. Trade routes between the three nations are set up on carefully protected roads between the borders. Many trade routes have been set up via sea to avoid the dangerous waste however the sea far south of Breton and the Wise Isle is treacherous as well. It is the single largest land mass in the Freeland with the sparsest population.

The Order: An organisation with the agenda of complete order in the Freeland, and then the world. Controllers are the prime members of the Order however people without magical ability may also join as foot soldiers. They claim no allegiance to any kingdom however they have political control of almost all, except Hextheene and Mayhen. Their current Master of the Order is Isham Dertilderon, though the Master does not have full control as the council of Elders resides over territories and objectives; research, military, trade, naval, etc.

The Pearl: A small sphere given to Rayar as a baby by his adopted father, King Rumeo Granlia. He believes it to be a memento of his family, the Vienne family who all died in the Fire of Highhall castle. However, its origins are unknown to most with only a small handful knowing what it truly is and how important it is.

The Third Coming: A prophecy - The First Coming brought salvation. The Second Coming brought despair. The Third Coming will bring an end to all.

The Wise Isles: A collection of islands off the coast of the Freeland inhabited by the Wisemen. They are a collection of people who live by fishing and trading between their settlements. It is ruled by numerous elected officials on each island who discuss matters of state every year on the largest island, Icelanedon'Kal or Gather as it is known to the rest of the Freeland, which is the most southern island within the collection of the Wise Isles. The people are rumoured to be refugees from the far west hundreds of years ago but any record of such is sealed away by the Wisemen.

Titania: The red headed Royal Blade to Nyer Granlia. She is a skilled warrior and composed woman who has stood beside Nyer since they were young.

True Born: The name the Snow Hunters refer to themselves as. They believe they are descendants of the original people who protected Oldome while the rest of the population followed The First Coming South to retake the Freeland.

Vasca: An agent of the Order. He is a pale man with a monotone voice and dark presence. He is also a powerful Controller.

Vienne, Randal: True father of Rayar Granlia and formerly Noble Lord of Highhall. He died many years ago.

Wedyar: A chubby soldier with an upbeat view on life stationed at the Shield of Mayhen.

World Above: The prominent religion in the north of the Freeland and Breton, many believe this is where the First Coming came from to save humanity from the monster crisis one thousand years ago. The World Above is the God who watches from above and protects those who are righteous and just.

World Below: Unlike the World Above, the World Below is where evil resides. It is famous for being legend of the home of the monsters that once conquered all of the Freeland. The Second Coming attempted to release the World Below once again after the death of his father, the First Coming, but was unsuccessful.

Printed in Poland
by Amazon Fulfillment
Poland Sp. z o.o., Wrocław

Legends of
CRICKET

RALPH**DELLOR** and STEPHEN**LAMB**

Legends of
CRICKET

This revised edition first published in the UK in 2007

© Green Umbrella Publishing 2007

Printed and bound in China

ISBN: 978-1-905828-32-6

CONTENTS

Legends of
CRICKET

WASIM**AKRAM**

It was fortunate for Pakistan that when their great all-rounder, Imran Khan, retired after the 1992 World Cup, the pretender to the mantle had already served a full apprenticeship before taking his place in the team that won the trophy. Three tournaments later, when Wasim Akram himself called it a day, he had established his own exalted status among cricket's elite. He was a cricket lover's dream and seemed, at his peak, to be capable of anything.

Wasim was a one-off. As a bowler, he generated real pace off a brisk run-up with a whippy left arm, but it was his mastery of late swing that could leave the best batsmen dumbfounded. Allan Lamb became a crucial wicket in that 1992 final when Wasim eluded the bat with a searing delivery that swung sharply from leg to clip the off stump. Arguably the best left-arm seamer ever, Wasim was also one of the original exponents of modern-day reverse swing. With another, Waqar Younis, he formed one of the great bowling duos of all time, and certainly the most devastating in Pakistan's history.

Wasim's strong forearms and supple wrists also served him well at the crease, where his powerful strokeplay, particularly when driving straight, could turn a match on its head. Although he never matched the achievements of his mentor Imran with the willow, a Test average of less than 23 does him scant justice. In one-day cricket bowlers knew of the dangers he posed, whatever the state of the game on his arrival. And crowds the world over watched, breath held, prepared to expect the unexpected.

Wasim made his first-class debut aged 18, taking seven for 50 in 1984/85 for the BCCP's Patron's XI against the New Zealand tourists. It emboldened the selectors to pick him for the tour of New Zealand that followed, and they were not disappointed. In his second Test at Dunedin he took five wickets in each innings, and his potency was confirmed when he first toured England in 1987. He took 16 Test wickets at 29, and along with Imran was a constant thorn in the batting side as Pakistan won the five-match rubber 1-0.

Although he found wickets costlier in the return series back home, Wasim confirmed his pedigree in Australia in 1989/90, striking 11 times at Melbourne and six more at Adelaide, where he rescued Pakistan with his maiden Test century, adding 191 with Imran. In the drawn home series against the great West Indies in 1990/91 he took 21 scalps in just three games, including four in five balls at Lahore. Lamb's wicket in the 1992 World Cup (followed next ball by that of Chris Lewis)

Born: Lahore, Punjab, 3rd June 1966

Test Debut: New Zealand v Pakistan, Auckland 1985, 125 Tests, 2,898 runs at 22.64, 414 wickets at 23.62

Best batting: 257 v Zimbabwe, Sheikhupura 1996

Best bowling: 7/119 v New Zealand, Wellington 1994

Legends of **CRICKET**

inevitably tarnished his sparkling reputation. In 2000 he was one of six players censured and fined for not fully co-operating with a Pakistan Cricket Board investigation into the scandal.

Inevitably as the years passed, the demands of the international schedule took their toll and occasionally blunted Wasim's edge. In the course of his 356 one-day internationals he succumbed to injury several times, and his eyesight was affected by diabetes. He nonetheless managed to play at the highest level for almost two decades, and became the first to take 400 wickets in both Tests and one-day internationals. He passed the 500 mark in the latter format during the 2003 World Cup, his fifth and final tournament which marked the end of an era. Pakistan fared badly and Wasim was one of eight players dropped. He announced his retirement shortly afterwards.

was one of 18, with an economy rate of less than four an over. On the ensuing tour of England Wasim took 82 in all, including 21 in the Test series, which Pakistan again won. In 1993 he succeeded Javed Miandad as Pakistan captain.

Wasim took no less than four international hat-tricks. The first two, all clean bowled, came in one-day internationals in Sharjah in 1989 and 1990, against the West Indies and Australia. The Test brace was achieved against Sri Lanka in successive matches in 1999. His best Test score came in 1996, a brutal, unbeaten 257 that included 12 sixes, beating Wally Hammond's Test record of ten. Earlier that year Wasim had led Pakistan to a hat-trick of series wins in England, but he was in decline by the ensuing home series between the two, missing the famous Karachi defeat in 2000 through injury and making little impact on his fourth and final England tour, the drawn two-match series the following year.

Wasim gave sterling and lengthy service to Lancashire, following an explosive start in 1988 in which he scored his maiden first-class century on his second appearance, and made 98 off 78 balls against Surrey at Southport, following that with five for 15, including a hat-trick. In the later stages of his career, match-fixing allegations

SYDNEY**BARNES**

It is never easy to compare players of one generation with those of another. In most cases it is simply enough to say they were the best of their time. That is undoubtedly true with Sydney Barnes, for to a man batsmen who faced him said they had never encountered a more searching examination of their skills. Such was his mastery of the art that it is entirely justifiable to claim that he was the greatest bowler who ever lived.

Consider the evidence for that challenging statement. In all types of cricket he took 6,229 wickets at 8.33 each. For a variety of reasons he played in only 27 Test matches, yet he took 189 wickets at 16.43 apiece. All his caps came against Australia and South Africa – the leading batting sides of the time – while only ten of his Tests were played at home. Against Australia alone, he took 106 wickets at 21.58. In 133 first-class matches, he took 719 wickets at no more than 17.09 apiece.

The question has to be asked why he played so little first-class and Test cricket if he was such a force in the game. The answer is simple. He had an obstinate streak and was never an easy character with whom to deal. He played when he felt like it, and most of his long career – he was still bowling when over 60 – was spent playing in the leagues and for Staffordshire, where he was comfortable and could command a larger income than playing county cricket.

So what type of bowler was he? He could move it through the air both ways, and late at that. He could bowl both varieties of cutter and spin it both ways. Quite simply, he was the most complete bowler the game has seen and he was equally adept in whatever style he adopted to suit the prevailing conditions. When asked why he did not bowl a googly, he replied: "I didn't need one."

He had an easy, rhythmical approach to the wicket, transferring the ball from left to right hand just before going into an upright action with a high arm. He was blessed with large hands and developed a vice-like strength in his long, sinuous fingers. In fact, he claimed that he did not swing the ball in a conventional manner when the shine went, as it did early in his day with no manicured outfields and not even a new ball to be taken in mid-innings until 1907. Instead, he could impart such spin on the ball, even when bowling at pace, that it would swerve in the air.

It was the game's good fortune that Barnes ever played the limited amount of first-class cricket he did. It was even more fortuitous that he appeared in

Born: Smethwick, Staffordshire, 19th April 1873

Died: Chadsmoor, Staffordshire, 26th December 1967

Test Debut: Australia v England, Sydney 1901, 27 Tests, 189 wickets at 16.43

Best Bowling: 9/103 v South Africa, Johannesburg 1913

Legends of **CRICKET**

1911/12 to take 34 wickets in five Tests. He did not prosper at home against Australia in the 1912 triangular series, but he did against South Africa with 34 wickets, at 8.29, in three Tests. He bettered that on the mat in South Africa in 1913/14, when he was virtually unplayable. Four Tests produced 49 wickets costing 10.93 each, including 17 for 109 in the second Test in Johannesburg – the best match haul for any bowler until Laker worked his magic at Old Trafford in 1956.

Barnes was 40 years of age at the time and while that was the end of his Test career, he appeared in a handful of first-class matches thereafter and was still playing league cricket into his sixties. In all, he took 3,741 wickets at a cost, if that is the right word, of 6.83 in the leagues, while his final season of 1934, when he was 61, saw his wickets come at under 11 apiece. However greatness is measured, Barnes can be counted amongst the greatest of them all.

LEFT
Sydney Barnes (front row left) with the England team that toured Australia in 1911/12.

BELOW
Sydney Barnes of Warwickshire, Lancashire, Staffordshire and England, 1910.

Test cricket at all, although there were a host of batsmen who would have disagreed with that statement.

He made his first-class debut in 1894, appearing in four matches for Warwickshire. He then went into the leagues in Lancashire where he began his phenomenal success.

Lancashire invited him to play in two matches in 1899, and two more in 1901 when he began to take serious wickets. Even so, he had only 13 victims to his name when, while appearing for his club, Burnley, play was halted as a telegram was delivered to Barnes. It was from Archie MacLaren who had experienced the difficulties of facing the great bowler in the Old Trafford nets. With total disregard for convention, it was an invitation to tour Australia the following winter.

Barnes began his Test career with a five-wicket return, and claimed another victim in the second innings before claiming 13 more in the second Test. He limped out of the next encounter with a knee injury, the result of too much bowling. Back home the following summer, he was given just one Test against Australia, before disappearing from Test cricket until 1907. By than he had disappeared from first-class county cricket as well. He had fallen out with Lancashire in 1903 and from 1904 he plied his trade with Staffordshire for 30 years.

On the 1907/08 Australian tour he took 24 wickets. He played against Australia in three Tests at home in 1909 (17 wickets) before returning Down Under in

RICHIE**BENAUD**

There are a number of disciplines of the game in which Richie Benaud could be described as a legend. As a leg-spinning all-rounder he set new standards, as a captain he was reckoned to be one of the shrewdest of them all, while as a commentator he was peerless. He simply oozed cricket knowledge from every pore without ever being overbearing.

It says something for the modern, television age that whatever his achievements as a player, it was as a commentator that he was best known. He was not one of those players who made his way straight off the field thinking the media owed him a living. Benaud had trained as a journalist before reaching the heights as a player, and so found it relatively easy to combine a thorough understanding of the game with an ability to express himself.

Whether he was employed to deliver his thoughts in print or on the air, he always maintained the highest professional standards. He spent many years commuting between Australia and England to follow the sun as a television commentator. It was said that he never once forgot where he was by, for example, talking about "sundries" in England nor giving the score as " 284 for seven" when in Australia. Much imitated but never emulated, his commentaries remained fresh, keen and totally relevant right up to the moment when he completed his final stint in the UK at the end of the 2005 Ashes series.

Benaud came from a cricketing family. His brother, John, also played for Australia, while the boys' father was a good enough grade cricketer in Sydney to have once taken all 20 wickets in a match. Even so, Richie appreciated that pedigree counted for nothing unless inherent gifts were nurtured. He made himself into a top cricketer by dint of hours of practice, absorbing knowledge and then applying it with a finely-tuned cricketing brain.

He was 18 when he made his debut for New South Wales, and he made his first appearance in a Test at the age of 21 in the final match of the 1951/52 series against the West Indies in Sydney. He missed the first Test against South Africa the following season, but appeared in the remaining matches as a prelude to his first tour of England in 1953.

It was in South Africa in 1957/58 that Benaud came to the fore as a world-class all-rounder with 106 wickets (30 of them in the five Tests) and 817 runs with four hundreds. It was an opportune time to rise through the ranks, for when Ian Craig's illness forced him to miss

Born: Penrith, New South Wales, 6th October 1930

Test Debut: Australia v West Indies, Sydney 1952, 63 Tests, 2,201 runs at 24.45, 248 wickets at 27.03

Best Batting: 122 v South Africa, Johannesburg 1957

Best Bowling: 7/72 v India, Madras 1956

RICHIE**BENAUD**

After the success against England, Benaud took the Australian side on victorious tours of Pakistan and India, and set the tone with Frank Worrell for the series against the West Indies in 1960/61 which included the tied Test in Brisbane before Australia's series win. He again retained the Ashes when England went to Australia in 1962/63.

As those results would suggest, he was an inspiring captain who brought the best out of his players as individuals and as a team. He was thoughtful and innovative, while all the time displaying a tough, competitive streak. Able to turn the game himself with an outstanding spell of bowling, a forceful innings, a blinding gully catch or an intelligent piece of captaincy, Benaud had a great array of weapons in his armoury and the intelligence to use them effectively. A genuine legendary cricketer.

the next series, at home to England, Benaud was elevated to the captaincy. Australia regained the Ashes and he remained in the post until 1963.

Benaud was never at his best in England. He made three tours but, not a great spinner of the ball and relying more on bounce to get his wickets, he found that English pitches were not of the type he would want to roll up and carry around with him. Nonetheless, it was at Old Trafford in 1961 that he made history with a remarkable spell of bowling.

England were cruising towards a comfortable victory in the fourth Test. 150 for one chasing 256 suggested that the hosts were set for a two-one lead in the series. Despite severe pain in his bowling shoulder, Benaud took the ball himself and bowled round the wicket into the rough caused mainly by the extensive follow-through of Fred Trueman. Had the English batsmen not been chasing the result, they might simply have padded Benaud away. As it was, they saw this as an opportunity to finish the match with a flourish.

150 for one became 163 for five as Benaud dismissed Ted Dexter, Brian Close, Peter May and Raman Subba Row in five overs. He then accounted for John Murray and David Allen to finish with six for 70 from 32 overs as England were bowled out for 201. In doing so, he made the Ashes safe for Australia once again.

ALLAN**BORDER**

Born: Cremorne, Sydney, New South Wales, 27th July 1955

Test Debut: Australia v England, Melbourne 1978,
156 Tests, 11,174 runs, average 50.56

Best Batting: 205 v New Zealand, Adelaide 1987

When Kim Hughes resigned from the Test captaincy at a tearful press conference in 1984, Australian cricket was at a low ebb. Still suffering from Packer defections, the team was unable to match the powerful sides from around the world that were preying on its obvious weaknesses. Hughes had been a fine stroke maker but was not necessarily a strong, uncompromising leader. Border offered everything that Hughes lacked.

He was more of a pugnacious left-handed batsman than a player to excite the aesthetic senses (John Woodcock wrote that he had "not so much a style as a modus operandi"), but he could chisel out innings of significant magnitude. He was a scrapper, as tough as teak, and no battle was ever lost while Border was involved. From a trough of despair, he dragged, coerced and when necessary bullied Australian cricket into a position from which his players could become undisputed world champions. By the time he had finished with it, the national side was playing in his image.

Border's monumental success did not just happen. He learned his trade playing grade cricket in Sydney and league cricket in Lancashire. He never stinted when it came to practice. When he travelled to play for Essex in 1986, he arrived in Chelmsford after the long and tiring flight from Australia, took his wife and young family to the house that had been secured for them, before going to the County Ground for a net.

He made his debut for New South Wales in 1977 against Tasmania, in a match where he made more of an impression with his left-arm spin than as a batsman.

Nought, batting at number seven, and eight not out did not hint at what was to come. But he did feature in a winning side on his debut, just as he would for Australia.

His Test debut came in the Boxing Day match against Mike Brearley's England in 1978. Border managed 29 in the first innings and was run out for nought in the second, but it was Australia's only win in the series. In the next Test, in Sydney, he scored 60 and 45, undefeated in both innings, to ensure that while a succession of players came and went during the years of World Series Cricket, the name of AR Border would appear again and again on Australian scorecards.

His maiden Test century came later in the year against Pakistan, and by the time he had shown all his grit and fortitude on a tour of India, he was established as Australia's number three. The West Indian pace battery found a weakness outside his off stump, but he recorded the first of his eight Test centuries against England and rounded off a busy and successful

BELOW
Allan Border celebrates in Christchurch, New Zealand, after going to the top of the all-time Test run-scoring list in 1993.

ALLAN**BORDER**

season with magnificent innings of 150 not out and 153 against Pakistan in Lahore. It was the first time anyone had scored 150 in both innings of a Test.

Border went over the border in domestic terms at the end of the 1979/80 season, leaving New South Wales for the very good reason that his new wife, Jane, came from Queensland. Eventually he played in the state's first Sheffield Shield winning side but following the move, his form was uncertain more or less right through to the 1981 tour of England. He finished that series on the losing side, but not before he had made two hundreds in the final two matches, despite a broken finger, and closed with an average of 59.22.

There were further fluctuations in form before Border reached new heights to put himself in pole position when a new captain was urgently required. It was often said that he was at his best when faced with adversity, and that was certainly the case when he took over the national team. He had just become captain of Queensland, so he had no great experience of the job. It is fair to say that there were not vast expectations.

It took him time to mould the side, and as he became more comfortable in his role, so the team improved. There was no sudden transformation, and Australia received something of a trouncing in 1985 in England, but he was outstanding with eight first-class centuries on the tour. It was the same story in the series that followed, but the tide was beginning to turn. Border masterminded the World Cup triumph of 1987 and

LEFT
Border secures the one-day series against India in 1984.

FAR LEFT
Border finds he can play English bowling with one hand.

BELOW
Border with the World Cup, Calcutta 1987.

went on to regain the Ashes and retain them twice. Only the West Indies proved immune from the Border effect, and he failed to defeat them in 1992/93 when the opposition got home by one run in Adelaide.

He retired from international cricket in 1994 after yet another successful series in South Africa. At the time, he was the leading run-scorer in Test cricket, he held the record for Test catches, he had played in more Tests, more consecutive Tests and had more Tests as captain than anyone else. No wonder the Australian Player of the Year is now honoured with the Allan Border Medal.

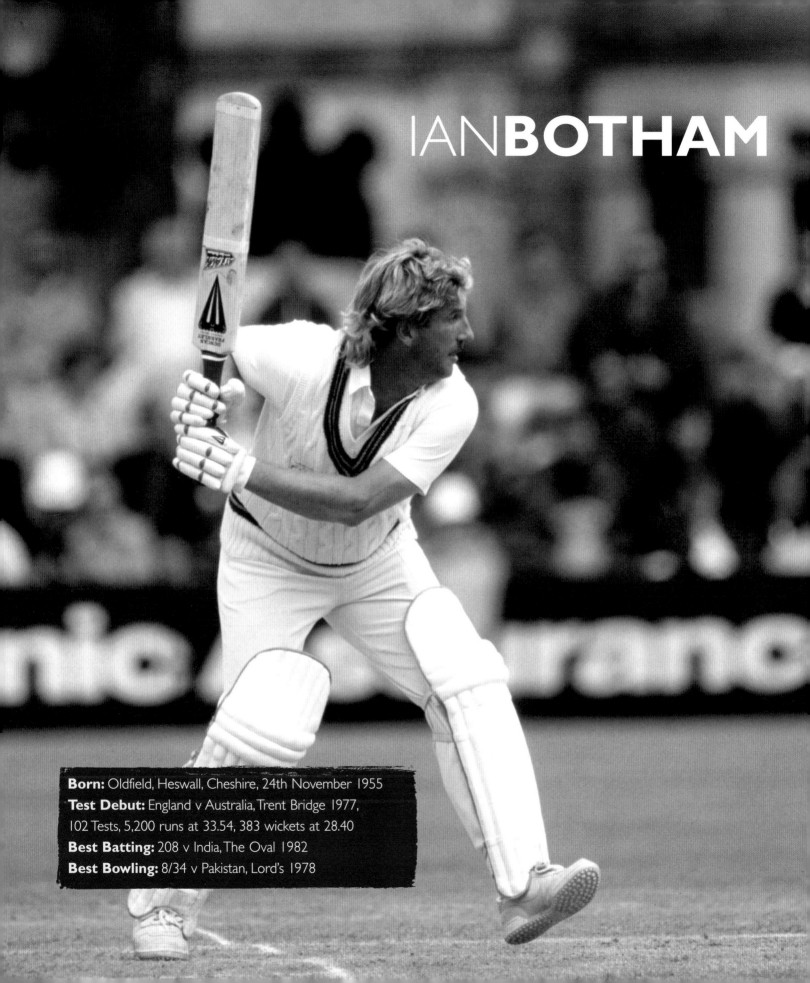

IAN**BOTHAM**

Born: Oldfield, Heswall, Cheshire, 24th November 1955
Test Debut: England v Australia, Trent Bridge 1977,
102 Tests, 5,200 runs at 33.54, 383 wickets at 28.40
Best Batting: 208 v India, The Oval 1982
Best Bowling: 8/34 v Pakistan, Lord's 1978

The word "legendary" can be over-used in sport, but surely no England cricketer in living memory deserves the epithet more than Ian Terence Botham. In three Ashes Tests in 1981, immediately after resigning the captaincy of a struggling team in poor personal form, he thrilled an entire nation with his all-round bravado. If his name will forever be associated with his unbeaten 149 at Headingley, he played an innings at Old Trafford that was arguably even greater. In between he charged in like a bull to demolish Australia's batting at Edgbaston, and repeatedly, as throughout his career, took catches that sometimes appeared well out of his reach. Not until England's Ashes triumph in 2005 was cricket again so compelling a spectacle.

Botham announced himself at international level in 1977 at the age of just 21, with the wicket of Australian great Greg Chappell. If there was an element of good fortune (Chappell dragged the ball on to his stumps) there was nothing fluky about the performances that followed over the next five years. Instinctively and effervescently, Botham became England's match-winner. At Christchurch the following winter he scored a century before taking eight wickets in the match. At Lord's in 1978 he repeated the feat, taking eight for 34 in Pakistan's second innings with his brisk out-swing, the best Test figures of his career. Surely it couldn't get better than this? It did. In Bombay less than two years later, in the Golden Jubilee Test, he scored 114 in between six for 58 and seven for 48. India were nonplussed.

Whether it was right to give Botham the England

captaincy on the back of such mesmerising all-round brilliance remains debatable. It was asking a lot of a 24-year-old, against a West Indies side on the threshold of world dominance, and with the home series (which West Indies won 1-0) followed by a return rubber in the Caribbean the following spring. Although Botham continued to pick up wickets, his batting fell away and he failed to reach 50 after his first Test as captain. Appointed on a match-by-match basis at the start of the 1981 Ashes series, he completed a pair at Lord's after England had gone 1-0 down, resigning before the selectors revealed that they had decided to replace him anyway.

The way was paved for the return of his mentor. Mike Brearley famously offered him the chance to sit out the Headingley Test, laying down a gauntlet which he must have guessed a man of Botham's ebullient character would be sure to take up. Heroic performances followed which turned the rubber on its head, and England ultimately won it 3-1. Botham's 102-ball

BELOW
A triumphant return to Test cricket for England all-rounder Ian Botham, as he dismisses New Zealand's Jeff Crowe to become the highest wicket taker in Test history with 356 victims.

IAN**BOTHAM**

innings of 118 at Old Trafford prompted The Times to ask whether it was the greatest ever. In his own account of the series, 'Phoenix from the Ashes', Brearley wrote that as the Australians clapped Botham out after his dismissal, "their looks expressed a rare Antipodean awe at the prowess of an Englishman."

Botham would probably have featured in this book had he not set foot on a cricket field again. In the event his Test career lasted more than a decade longer, much to the short-term chagrin of India's bowlers, who were pummelled for three hundreds and five 50s in the home and away series of the following year, including 142 at Kanpur and a Test-best 208 at the Oval. And although he could hardly be blamed for failing to repeat his Ashes exploits Down Under in 1982/3, who else but Botham could have saved the day when Australia were on the verge of stealing a sensational victory at Melbourne? With help from a butter-fingered Chris Tavare and a cool-headed Geoff Miller, Botham ended a 70-run last wicket partnership between Allan Border and Jeff Thomson to see England home – just – by three runs.

As the years went by the compelling moments became fewer, although as his bowling declined, Botham remained a fearsome striker of the cricket ball for England, Somerset (whom he helped to one-day glory before an acrimonious split in the mid

LEFT
Botham in action against Pakistan at Lord's in 1978.

FAR LEFT
The classical side-on action of Ian Botham in his pomp.

BELOW
Botham relaxes after his 149 not out in the third Ashes Test of 1981.

1980s), Worcestershire and finally Durham. Although he never reached the milestone he must have coveted more than most, a century against the great West Indies, he did manage a dramatic return after a Test ban for allegedly smoking cannabis. He dismissed Bruce Edgar with his first ball, and after two overs he had overtaken Dennis Lillee's world record of 355 Test wickets. "Who writes your scripts?" demanded Graham Gooch. If the cricketing arena is indeed a stage, Botham played his part both on and off it to the outer limits of mortal reach.

Legends of **CRICKET**

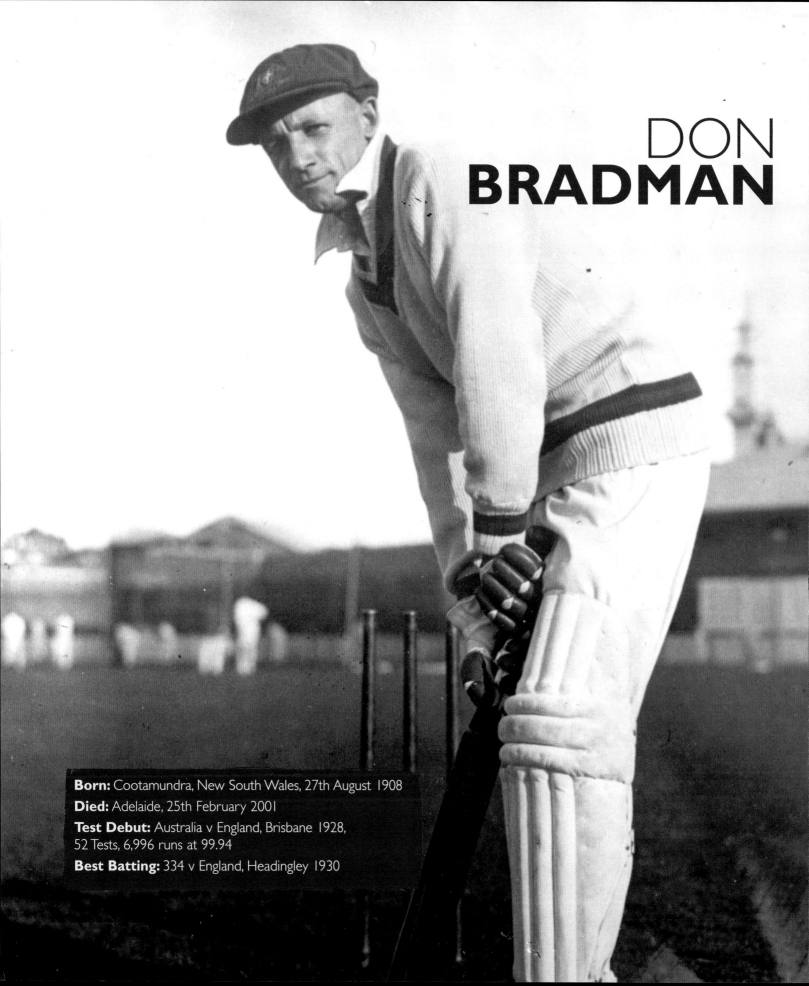

DON
BRADMAN

Born: Cootamundra, New South Wales, 27th August 1908

Died: Adelaide, 25th February 2001

Test Debut: Australia v England, Brisbane 1928,
52 Tests, 6,996 runs at 99.94

Best Batting: 334 v England, Headingley 1930

Don Bradman began his Test career at the Exhibition Ground in Brisbane against England in 1928, with scores of 18 and one. He ended it with a much-publicised duck at the Oval in 1948 against the same opposition. In between these two matches, he had the most spectacular career any cricketer – indeed any sportsman – could ever imagine.

Figures can, and do, sometimes lie, but the statistics associated with Bradman say virtually all there is to say about the greatest batsman of them all. It is generally reckoned that to have enjoyed a substantial Test career, a batsman needs to have averaged 40. To nudge the average past 50 puts him in the top bracket, while to top 60 is extraordinary. Bradman's Test average was 99.94.

It is an oft-told story how he arrived at the Oval for his final Test needing a simple boundary to take him into retirement with an average in excess of 100. With England bowled out for 52 and Australia already having reached 117 when the first wicket fell, it was always likely that it would be his last innings. He was given a standing ovation all the way to the middle, where the England captain, Norman Yardley, called for three cheers. Leg-spinner Eric Hollies was the bowler; Bradman played the first ball but missed the second – a googly – and was bowled.

The shock that engulfed the Oval could be felt around the world, but cricket is a game more capable than most of bringing a humbling mortality even to the greatest player, and Bradman could certainly claim that category for himself. Throughout a first-class career that extended from 1927 to 1949, he averaged a century every three visits to the wicket. His first-class average was 95.14,

his top score was 452 not out – a record at the time – while his highest Test innings also established a new benchmark.

With phenomenal statistics like these, it is easy to overlook the quality of the play while marvelling at the magnitude of the achievement. Bradman's was not necessarily an eye-catching style. He did not blast the ball with great power, and he did not lash it to all parts in the air. In 80 Test innings he hit only six sixes. He played the ball along the ground, relying on timing and placement. It was once said that he had a stroke for every ball, which is why he could score so freely. It was also said that he did not appear to be scoring, although a glance at the board would reveal that he already had 30 to his name when it seemed that he had only just arrived at the wicket.

Bradman was once tested to see if his eyesight was better than anyone else's; it was not. He merely had an outstanding ability to judge the flight of a cricket ball and the most nimble footwork to ensure that he

BELOW
Don Bradman acknowledges another double-century.

DON**BRADMAN**

was correctly balanced and positioned to execute his chosen stroke. It is often said that the great players do the simple things better than others. The Bradman formula for success appears simple, but he applied it more diligently than anyone before or since.

Always gifted at sport, he might well have excelled at tennis, golf, athletics or anything else that took his fancy. It was cricket's good fortune to attract his attention. It is the stuff of folklore that he threw a golf ball against a water tank and played the rebound with a cricket stump when a youngster at home in Bowral, some 80 miles from Sydney.

He was 17 when he scored a triple hundred for Bowral and attracted the attention of those higher up the cricketing echelons. He was soon playing grade cricket in Sydney, making a hundred on his first-class

Legends of **CRICKET**

the same position with the Australian side for the 1936/37 tour by England, and retained the post until he retired. His captaincy reflected his batting in that he won four series and drew one – the 1938 rubber in England. In all, he captained Australia in 24 Tests, losing the first two but only one more, while winning 15.

After retirement, he was equally sagacious as an administrator and selector, while the honours flowed as befitted such a colossus of the game. He was knighted in 1949, and in 1979 was appointed Commander of the Order of Australia. He received a host of additional acclamations as the best Australian sportsman ever, and even as the most influential Australian. It is hard to argue that he was not.

LEFT
More runs for The Don.

FAR LEFT
Bradman returns to the pavilion past admiring fans.

BELOW
Bradman with a much-loved bat in 1930.

debut for New South Wales, and from there he made his way into the Australian side. After his ordinary start, he was dropped for the second Test but recalled for the third when he scored 79 and 112. He was never dropped again.

He did particularly well against England. At Headingley in 1930, he ended the first day on 309 before going on to the then record score of 334 on the second. In all, he scored 974 runs in that series at an average of 139.14. England became so obsessed with stopping Bradman that the infamous Bodyline strategy was devised to negate him. To a certain degree, it did. In 1932/33 he averaged a mere 56.57!

He had moved from New South Wales to South Australia for the 1935/36 season, taking up the captaincy as soon as he arrived. He was elevated to

GREG**CHAPPELL**

Anyone requiring a technical role model for batting could hardly have done better than watch Greg Chappell. Tall and slim, with the upright gait and bearing of a swordsman, he cut attacks the world over to ribbons. Added to his faultless technique was a steely desire to win. He was a successful captain (and, after retirement, coach), a fine close fielder who missed virtually nothing, and a handy medium pace bowler. Had he not joined Kerry Packer's World Series Cricket when in his prime, or occasionally made himself unavailable for selection, his glittering career figures would be even more magnificent.

The grandson of former Australian captain Victor Richardson, Gregory Stephen Chappell soon established himself in the South Australia side and broadened his experience with a couple of seasons at Somerset. His Test debut came against Ray Illingworth's Ashes-winning England tourists in 1970/71, when at the age of 22 he scored the first of his 24 Test hundreds. Although it was to be his only century of the series, there was no doubt about his class, or his future as Australia looked to avenge their defeat in England. In the meantime Chappell took toll of a quality Rest of the World attack in the unofficial series of 1971/72, with 115 not out at Sydney, 197 not out at Melbourne, and 85 at Adelaide.

With his elder brother Ian now installed as captain, Chappell was an automatic selection in the 1972 squad to tour England. Although Australia failed to regain the Ashes (the series was drawn two-all) he made two vital contributions. Australia's victory at Lord's in "Massie's Match" – the swing bowler Bob Massie took 16 wickets on Test debut – would not have been possible without Chappell's technically perfect 131. His next hundred was no less influential, coming at the Oval to set up Australia's win. It featured in the first-ever double century partnership involving brothers, as Ian too made a century.

Consistent performances followed back home against Pakistan and on Chappell's first visit to the Caribbean, while at Wellington in 1974 New Zealand were punished especially severely. Chappell followed what was to be his best Test score, 247 not out, with 133, while Ian also scored two centuries to establish another fraternal record. In the 1974/75 series, his best against England, Chappell did more than any other batsman to help Australia regain the Ashes, with 608 runs at 55.27. He also caught superbly at slip, no sinecure given the pace being generated by Lillee and

> **Born:** Unley, Adelaide, 7th August 1948
> **Test Debut:** Australia v England, Perth 1970, 87 Tests, 7,110 runs at 53.86
> **Best batting:** 247 v New Zealand, Wellington 1974

He cruised past Sir Donald Bradman's Australian record Test aggregate in his last innings, making 182, and also passed Colin Cowdrey's record of catches, finishing with 122.

Chappell was a good enough one-day player to finish with a batting average above 40, and led Australia to victory in the triangular series against India and New Zealand in 1980/81. However that series is best remembered for what was perhaps the one aberration of his career. With New Zealand needing six to win from the last ball of the third match of the best-of-five finals, he told his younger brother Trevor to bowl an underarm grubber. The batsman, Brian McKechnie, flung his bat away in disgust and a fair amount of international mud slinging ensued. It was an unbefitting moment in the career of a player who should be remembered primarily as one of the greatest batsmen in cricket's history.

LEFT
In his customary position in the slips, Chappell leaps in the air to take a brilliant catch.

BELOW
Chappell cuts a short ball from Bob Willis during England's 1982/83 Ashes tour.

Thomson. Although he went off the boil in England the following summer, his muse returned in his first series as captain, bringing him 702 runs at 117 as the West Indies were beaten 5-1.

After further success at home to Pakistan, Chappell led Australia on the Packer-ridden tour of England in 1977. Although he made 112 in the second Test at Old Trafford, both the game and ultimately the Ashes were won by England. Due to World Series Cricket it was to be Chappell's last Test series for two years, although he resumed the captaincy (and normal batting service) against the West Indies and England in 1979/80. His second Test double century came against Pakistan at Faisalabad, and a third against India, crucial to Australia's cause, came at the SCG the following season. Chappell then decided against touring England for the 1981 Ashes series.

Recharged for the 1981/82 season, he scored his fourth and final double century against Pakistan and again dominated the New Zealand attack, although he struggled in between against the West Indies. The following year he achieved his ultimate ambition of leading Australia to an Ashes victory, scoring hundreds in the two games Australia won. Chappell's farewell series, against Pakistan in 1983/4, proved a fitting finale.

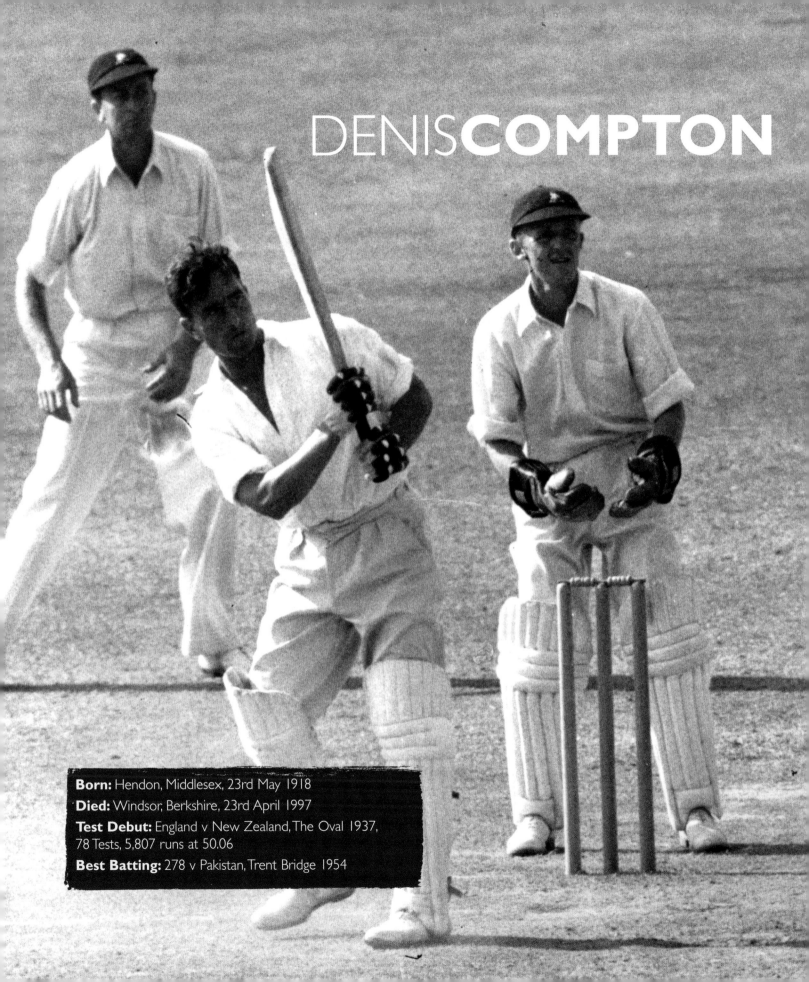

DENIS**COMPTON**

Born: Hendon, Middlesex, 23rd May 1918

Died: Windsor, Berkshire, 23rd April 1997

Test Debut: England v New Zealand, The Oval 1937,
78 Tests, 5,807 runs at 50.06

Best Batting: 278 v Pakistan, Trent Bridge 1954

One of the finest of many vintage (and some no doubt apocryphal) stories about Denis Compton was told by the legendary cricket commentator Brian Johnston. It concerned a party at Lord's for Compton's 50th birthday. As the champagne corks popped in the Middlesex office, the telephone rang. "It's for you, Denis," he was told. He went to take the call, and returned looking a bit glum. "Who was it?" he was asked. "It was my mother. She says I'm only 49."

True or not, it characterises the endearing vagueness of the cricketer who did more than anyone to revive English spirits after the Second World War. If it was feasible to be more than the complete batsman, Denis Charles Scott Compton managed it by sheer audacity. His sweep, often played brazenly late, was his trademark, although he possessed a sublime cover drive and was an accomplished stroke player all around the wicket. Like Viv Richards a generation later, he was sure footed enough to keep the bowler guessing, moving around his crease in all manner of directions. The result was untutored artistry on an exalted level that had to be seen to be believed.

Cricket was in Compton's blood; his father and brother were both keen participants, and Denis was in his father's team by the age of 12. At 18 he got his first game for Middlesex, and although he started at number 11, by the end of the 1936 season he had passed a thousand runs. And he couldn't just bat; he was a naturally athletic fielder when concentrating (he took 425 first-class catches), and his unorthodox left-arm spin was to reap 622 first-class wickets, 25 of them in Tests. He was also a fine footballer, playing in a cup final for

Arsenal, and wartime internationals for England. But for the war, he might well have won a full cap.

Although he made his Test debut in 1937 – with 65 against New Zealand – Compton's great years came in the wake of the war. In 1947 he scored 3,816 runs, including 18 centuries, two of them in the same Test against Australia at the start of the year. Back home he decimated South Africa with 65, 163, 208, 115, 6, 30, 53 and 113. But even such sensational statistics cannot convey the show-man-like flair with which the runs were scored, enrapturing the cricket-starved crowds who flocked to watch. Two more big hundreds followed in the 1948 Ashes series, and the following winter he took just three hours to score 300 at Benoni in South Africa.

Shortly afterwards an old football injury to his knee resurfaced, reducing Compton's mobility. It did not prevent a prolific series against New Zealand in 1950, but he failed to reach 50 on the ensuing Ashes tour. However he savoured the most magical of moments in 1953 when, with his "Middlesex Twin" Bill Edrich

BELOW
Runs for Denis Compton through the gully.

DENIS**COMPTON**

at the other end, he hit the winning runs to ensure England's Ashes triumph. Runs flowed in the Caribbean that winter and in 1954 he amassed his best Test score of 278 against Pakistan. Compton himself regarded the 53 he made on a damp wicket at the Oval later in that series as one of his best innings.

By his standards he was again below par in Australia, but South Africa suffered sorely at his hands again in 1955. In November of that year his right kneecap was surgically removed (it now resides in the Lord's museum) but he was able to play his final Test against

Legends of **CRICKET**

LEFT

A young Compton in action for Middlesex in 1938.

FAR LEFT

Compton the pin-up, but before the Brylcreem had been applied, 1948.

the Old Enemy the following summer, scoring 94 and 35 not out. After the winter tour of South Africa, Compton bowed out of Test cricket.

By then he had an agent, Bagenal Harvey, who not only did the deal that identified his client as the "Brylcreem Boy" but also brought a semblance of organisation to Compton's life. Poor timekeeping had always been a consequence of his vagueness; heaven knows how he would have managed current rules on punctuality. Another trait was his erratic calling and running between the wickets. As Trevor Bailey once asserted: "A call from

Denis was merely the basis for negotiation." He even contrived to run his brother Leslie out in his benefit match.

Compton lived life to the full after retirement. He was awarded a CBE, wrote and broadcast about cricket, and turned out for the Lord's Taverners. When he died, paradoxically as spring was ushering in a new cricket season, there were more applications to attend his memorial service at Westminster Abbey than for any in 30 years. If Len Hutton was the peerless batsman of his age, no one played more enchantingly, or was more widely loved, than Denis Compton.

COLIN**COWDREY**

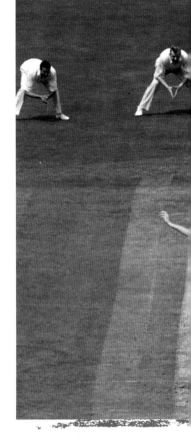

Colin Cowdrey featured prominently in English cricket for over half a century. The son of an enthusiastic cricketer, he was given the initials MCC and was a schoolboy prodigy. He made 102 out of 191 in only his third Test, became the first man to play in over 100 Tests, was knighted and then became the first English cricketer to be ennobled. He toured Australia a record six times, and scored over 43,000 runs in first-class cricket as an elegant right-handed batsmen and one of the safest slip fielders in the game.

Cowdrey's father was a tea planter; hence one of England's premier batsmen was born in India. He was educated in England, securing a place in the Tonbridge XI as soon as he arrived, as much on the promise of his leg-break bowling as his batting. He fulfilled that promise with eight wickets and innings of 75 and 44 against Clifton at Lord's when he was only 13.

Four years later he was playing for Kent, becoming the youngest player to be capped, and at 18 scored a century for the Gentlemen against the Players, captained by Len Hutton, at Scarborough. He then went up to Oxford where he scored nearly 2,000 runs in 1953. While 1954 was not as productive, Cowdrey was nevertheless selected to go on the 1954/55 Ashes tour, led by Hutton.

Despite the sad loss of his father three weeks after leaving Tilbury, Cowdrey scored a promising 40 in the first Test and a valuable 54 in the second. He then totally justified his selection with a hundred in Melbourne. He recorded another 21 for his country and totalled 107 in all first-class cricket, although it was not until 1957 in Cape Town that he reached three figures again. But after a spell of seven innings following that match with only one fifty, his Test place was in jeopardy.

Then he went out at Edgbaston to face a West Indian attack including the mystery spinner, Sonny Ramadhin, who had taken seven wickets in the first innings. At 113 for three, England were in trouble, still 175 runs behind. Cowdrey joined his captain, Peter May, and the pair proceeded to add 411 for the fourth wicket. It was then the third highest partnership in the history of Test cricket, and remains the best for England, and for the fourth wicket anywhere. Cowdrey's share was 154; he followed it with 152 in the next Test at Lord's to secure his place.

Cowdrey took over the captaincy for the first time in 1959, doing the job for two matches until May returned for the tour of the Caribbean in 1960. May's health was

Born: Bangalore, 24th December 1932
Died: Littlehampton, Sussex,
4th December 2000
Test Debut: Australia v England, Brisbane
1954, 114 Tests, 7,624 runs at 44.06
Best batting: 182 v Pakistan, The Oval 1962

Legends of **CRICKET**

whom he turned and said, "I don't believe we've met; I'm Colin Cowdrey." Thomson was a bit taken aback, while Cowdrey made 22, and opening in the second innings, 41. The sixth Test of that tour was his last, but he led Kent to a win against the Australians at Canterbury in 1975 with an innings of 151. He retired at the end of that season, although he returned for one match in 1976 – the year before his son Chris played his first game for the county. Another son, Graham, continued with Kent until 1998.

Colin Cowdrey's involvement with cricket did not finish when he stopped playing. He became president of MCC and was chairman of the International Cricket Council. He was responsible for the Spirit of Cricket initiative and his name lives on at Lord's with the presentation of the annual Cowdrey Lecture. It lives on in the record books as well, and in the hearts of those that saw his delightful play.

not good, however, and by the fourth Test in Georgetown, Cowdrey was back in charge for a run of nine matches until May resumed the job against Australia during the Ashes series of 1961. When May finally retired before the 1962 series against Pakistan, Ted Dexter was preferred, but Cowdrey stepped in for the third Test that summer. When Dexter returned for the Oval, Cowdrey compiled his highest Test score of 182 while sharing a second wicket partnership of 248 with the skipper.

His record as captain was good. 27 matches brought eight wins and 15 draws, but whenever it came to leading the side to Australia, someone else got the nod. Dexter in 1962/63, M.J.K. Smith in 1965/66 and then Ray Illingworth in 1970/71. It seemed that Cowdrey had played his last Test in 1971 but he continued with Kent, recording his 100th century and in 1974 scoring a thousand runs. That was hardly enough for him to be at the head of the queue for another Ashes tour, but when injuries and Lillee and Thomson rampaged through the England ranks, Cowdrey, aged nearly 42, was the man called from the depths of an English winter to the heat of battle in Perth.

During his innings Cowdrey found himself walking towards the drinks trolley alongside Jeff Thomson, to

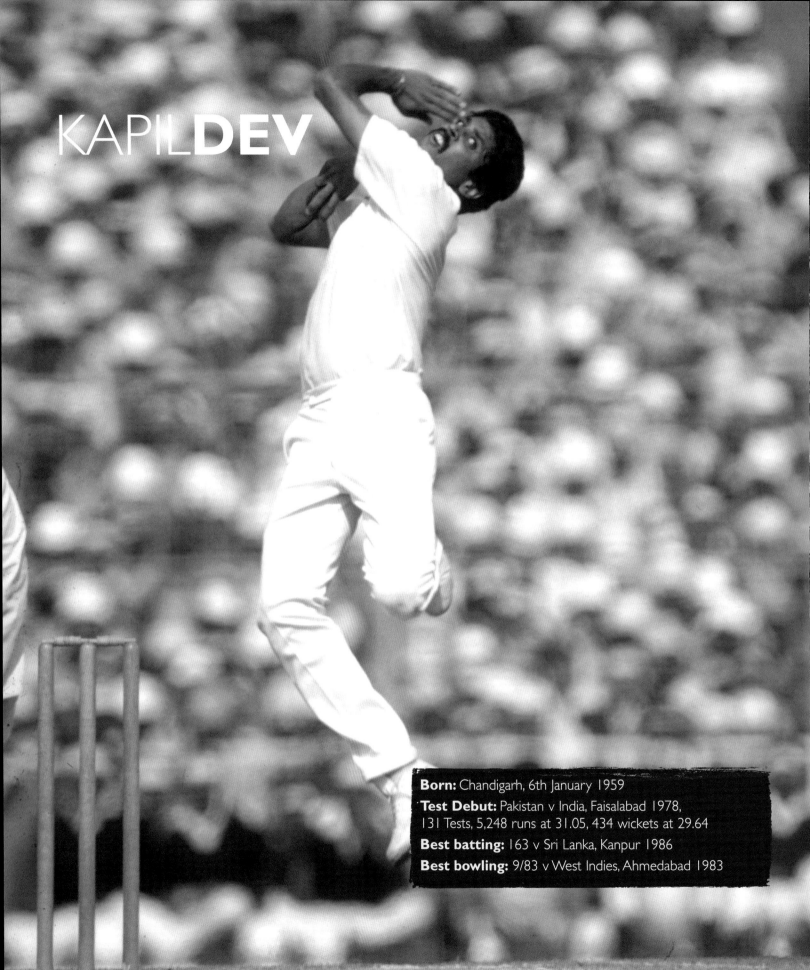

KAPIL**DEV**

Born: Chandigarh, 6th January 1959

Test Debut: Pakistan v India, Faisalabad 1978,
131 Tests, 5,248 runs at 31.05, 434 wickets at 29.64

Best batting: 163 v Sri Lanka, Kanpur 1986

Best bowling: 9/83 v West Indies, Ahmedabad 1983

A wonderfully effervescent all-rounder, Kapil Dev was as important to India in the 1980s as Ian Botham, Imran Khan and Richard Hadlee were to their respective countries over the same era. India's World Cup win against the mighty West Indies (and all the odds) in 1983 was achieved under Kapil's captaincy. He was the best fast bowler to play for India, and overtook Hadlee in his penultimate Test in 1994 to become the game's leading wicket-taker. He was also a strong, uninhibited striker of the ball, and a fielder of athletic prowess. His iconic status in India, though threatened by match-fixing claims in 2000, was confirmed in 2002 when he was named as India's cricketer of the 20th century.

It did not take Kapil long to reach the top. He made his Ranji Trophy debut for Haryana against Punjab in 1975/76, taking six for 39 in the first innings. Consistent performances over the next three seasons resulted in a Test debut, at just 19, against Pakistan at Faisalabad in October 1978. Although he struggled for wickets, he did better in the ensuing six-Test rubber against the West Indies, confirming his all-round potential with 17 wickets and 329 runs. At Delhi he made an unbeaten 126 – his maiden Test century – at better than a run a ball.

In England in 1979 Kapil impressed more with ball than bat, taking all the wickets at Edgbaston before the hosts declared on 633 for five. He impressed back home against both Australia and Pakistan, and in his 25th Test became the youngest-ever player to reach 1,000 runs and 100 wickets. He averaged over 50 in six Tests against England in 1981/82, and his batting in the return series the

following summer provided a magnificent spectacle. At Lord's he hit 89 off just 55 balls, as well as taking eight wickets, and scores of 41, 65 and 97 in his other innings posed the question whether Botham really was the greatest contemporary all-rounder.

It was 1983, though, that was truly Kapil Dev's annus mirabilis in England. After a stuttering start to India's World Cup campaign, they were in danger of humiliation by Zimbabwe when Kapil arrived at the crease in Tunbridge Wells, with the scoreboard reading nine for four. Although this became 17 for five and then 78 for seven, the Kentish crowd were to witness one of the most astounding innings ever played in one-day internationals. As Sunil Gavaskar, already dismissed for a duck, wrote afterwards: "He launched a counter-attack the like of which one had never seen before." After a circumspect start Kapil hit out at will, making 175 not out, off just 138 balls, with six sixes and 16 fours.

The innings kept India's path to the final open, but when they reached it few expected them to match

Kapil Dev bowls for India against England in 1982. Ian Botham is the non-striker.

the West Indies who, despite an earlier defeat by India, remained odds-on favourites to complete a hat-trick of tournament wins. Kapil took a critically important catch to dismiss the threatening Viv Richards as West Indies, set just 184 to win in 60 overs, subsided for a paltry 140 to the gentle medium pace of Madan Lal and Mohinder Amarnath. So it was Kapil Dev, not Clive Lloyd, who raised the trophy in triumph at the end of an extraordinary day at Lord's.

The West Indies were not slow to take revenge in either form of the game, and Kapil lost the Indian captaincy in consequence. The job returned to Gavaskar, with whom Kapil did not always see eye to eye. But after a comparatively quiet series against England in 1984/85 he was back in charge for the 1986 tour, as India won at Lord's for the first time and ensured a series win at Headingley.

His fourth and final tour was in 1990, when he contributed in his inimitable style to the great Test at Lord's, after Graham Gooch had scored 333. An enchanting century from Mohammad Azharuddin formed the backbone of India's riposte, but Kapil nonetheless found himself in the company of Narendra Hirwani, a genuine number 11, with 24 still needed to avoid following on. Four balls later, thanks to

four clean strikes from Kapil off the unfortunate Eddie Hemmings, the runs were on the board.

The contribution was typical of the delightful exuberance with which Kapil Dev played his cricket. In his remaining four years at the top he passed 5,000 runs and 400 wickets in Tests, a sensational achievement in his or any other era. His pursuit of Hadlee's bowling record was relentless, but the tank was plainly almost empty by the time he passed it. He retired just one match after doing so, ending a 16-year international career in a game he adorned with dazzling, uncomplicated chutzpah.

ALLAN
DONALD

Born: Bloemfontein, Orange Free State, 20th October 1966

Test Debut: West Indies v South Africa, Bridgetown 1992, 72 Tests, 330 wickets at 22.25

Best bowling: 8/71 v Zimbabwe, Harare 1995

The final session of play at Trent Bridge on 26th July 1998 was as spellbinding as only Test cricket can be. England, one-nil down in the series, needed 247 to draw level with one to play. Although they had lost Mark Butcher early, Mike Atherton and Nasser Hussain were going well and optimism in the English camp was high. Then Atherton got a ball from Allan Donald, South Africa's and arguably the world's premier fast bowler, that appeared to brush his glove on the way through to wicket-keeper Mark Boucher. The appeal from the entire South African team was turned down by umpire Steve Dunne.

The consequent reduction of Donald to not particularly mute fury produced one of the most hostile and venomous spells of fast bowling ever seen. Bouncers were propelled with regularity at speeds of around 90 miles per hour. Words were uttered, by both Donald and Boucher, for the accomplished lip reader to savour. Amid the tension, Boucher contrived to drop an edge from Hussain off Donald, an error which, could we but know it at the time, let England off the hook. The bowler's expression at this point was bordering on the apoplectic. Boucher himself had little alternative but to heed the batsmen's advice to shut up and get on with the game.

It was, as they say, pure theatre, albeit rather more entertaining in the stands or on the sofa than if you happened to be either batsman, or indeed the next one in. Despite Donald's efforts, England reached the close intact and went on to win both the match and the series. Both Donald and Atherton, whose steely resolve can never have been more rigorously examined,

regard that gladiatorial contest as a highlight of their respective careers.

Allan Donald is probably the most influential cricketer to play for South Africa since their re-admission to international cricket in 1992. His first Test was also South Africa's first after isolation, although by then he had already shown his mettle with Orange Free State, for whom he first played in 1985, and Warwickshire, whom he helped win the County Championship title in 1991 and served with distinction for a decade. He had also played in an unofficial Test for South Africa against Kim Hughes's rebel Australian team.

A superb natural athlete, Donald reduced a youthful run-up of 23 paces to 15, preceding a high, powerful and perfectly balanced delivery. His length was generally full, giving him a good proportion of lbw victims, and he could move the ball away as well as slant it in.

It is a measure of his quality that he would have challenged for a place even in the great West Indies side of the time, which included bowlers of the

BELOW
Allan Donald celebrates bowling Mike Atherton, 1999.

calibre of Curtly Ambrose and Courtney Walsh.

Four Tests into his career, Donald was the catalyst for South Africa's first Test win of the new era, over India at Port Elizabeth in December 1992. He took 12 for 139, including seven wickets in the second innings, becoming established, to the surprise of no one, as the spearhead of his country's attack. He announced himself in England with a five-wicket haul in his first Test there, at Lord's in 1994, and took 19 English wickets in the 1995/96 series back in South Africa, which his team won 1-0. Effective against any team in the world, including Australia, Donald could hardly be blamed for his team's defeat in that 1998 series in England; he took 14 wickets in the two games lost at Trent Bridge and the Oval.

Nor was he slow to clean Atherton up at his next opportunity, in Johannesburg in 1999. After England were put in, he bowled Atherton in the first over of the match. Donald took 11 in all to put the hosts one up, and his twentieth five-wicket haul in the first innings at Cape Town where they took an unassailable lead. The following year he became the first South African to take 300 Test wickets, passing the milestone against New Zealand on his home ground at Bloemfontein.

By this time, over-bowled and ageing, even a physique as strong as Donald's was beginning to creak. In the 2001/02 series against Australia he broke down on day one, and announced his retirement from Test

Legends of **CRICKET**

cricket shortly afterwards. Although he continued to play one-day cricket until the 2003 World Cup, there were signs before South Africa's unfortunate exit at Durban that it was a tournament too far. By then he had taken 684 one-day wickets, including 272 in internationals, after starting with a five-wicket haul against India. His value to his country had been matchless in both forms of the game, as it continued to be when his coaching services were secured by South Africa soon after his retirement.

ANDREW
FLINTOFF

Born: Preston, Lancashire, 6th December 1977

Test Debut: England v South Africa, Trent Bridge 1998, 67 Tests by April 2007, 3381 runs at 32.5, 197 wickets at 32.02

Best batting: 167 v West Indies, Edgbaston 2004

Best bowling: 5/58 v West Indies, Bridgetown 2004

There was a strict criterion for inclusion in this book as a cricket legend. Players had to have already achieved greatness. In the case of Andrew Flintoff, we have a legend in the making. He does not yet hold records or, apart from in the physical sense, tower head and shoulders above others in the game, but there is an aura about him that transcends the normal to elevate him into a special category of cricketer.

He went through a lot early in his career, which perhaps shaped the character that appears on the field today, for not all of it made for an easy ride to the top. There are some players who impress at an early age merely because of physical maturity in advance of their years. The young Flintoff impressed not only for his size but also for his precocious talent. A fast bowler and big-hitting batsman, he had to shelve his bowling aspirations while his body became strong enough to cope with the enormous strains that were placed upon it.

He emerged through the Lancashire youth teams and attracted the attention of age group selectors. However, by the time he was captaining the England Under-19s, it appeared that he might gain top honours as a batsman alone because of back injuries that threatened his future as a bowler.

The path to the top was not smooth. After his Under-19 appearances, he progressed to the England A team for a tour to Kenya and Sri Lanka in early 1998. He did well enough to be propelled into the Test side that summer, at a time when youngsters were not necessarily made welcome in the England dressing room. He showed promise against South Africa in his first Test

but in the second, recorded a pair and took no wickets in either innings. England won both matches but Flintoff was dropped.

Back in the ranks with England A, he toured Zimbabwe and South Africa where, after some initial problems, he came of age. He sowed doubts on that tour by getting himself out when set, the result of poor shot selection. Twice in a match against a ZCU President's XI in Kwekwe he holed out at long on and long off. It appeared that he might never learn the lessons that were so obvious. However, later in the tour in Johannesburg, he played a dominant innings against a Gauteng XI that showed his full potential.

He went to South Africa again the following winter with the full England side, and to Sharjah to make his one-day international debut, but struggled to find his best form. He was overweight and apparently lacking in motivation as a persistent back injury restricted his bowling and mobility. Back home, he played a one-day international against Zimbabwe at Old Trafford

BELOW
Andrew Flintoff deserves his celebrations after playing such a crucial role in England's successful Ashes campaign of 2005..

ANDREW**FLINTOFF**

where he did not bowl, but was named man of the match for an innings of 42 not out. He accepted the award with the words: "Not bad for a fat lad." Flintoff appeared about to be consigned to the scrap heap of unfulfilled potential that has littered English cricket over the years when he took himself in hand, spent time with the Academy and emerged the stronger for it.

He was called up for the tour of India and New Zealand in the winter of 2001/02 and, after a torrid time against the Indian spinners, made an impact in the one-day internationals and showed increasing maturity in New Zealand with his maiden Test hundred. He established himself in the Test team in 2003 with an outstanding series against South Africa, scoring 423 runs at 52.87, although his bowling average was even higher. He was labelled as an unlucky bowler, but at least he was bowling again.

Having missed out on the 2002/03 Ashes series due to a hernia operation from which he failed to recover,

was dubbed an MBE, and won just about every sports personality of the year award going, not to mention the Wisden award for Leading Cricketer of the World in 2005. He deserved it, because here was a character who would always rely on his cricketing ability to maintain his celebrity status.

This he showed in abundance when he toured India at the start of 2006. Already the key player in the England team as major batsman, strike bowler, stock bowler and reliable slip fielder, he took on the additional burden of the captaincy when the need arose. He was a natural leader, showing that while he can be relied upon to serve his country in every capacity for the foreseeable future, he will remain Big Freddie from Lancashire however great the pressures of fame become.

LEFT
Four runs out of 102 during Flintoff's brilliant innings against Australia at Trent Bridge in 2005.

FAR LEFT
Flintoff in one-day international action against Bangladesh at Trent Bridge in 2005.

BELOW
Flintoff in action for the Rest of the World XI in Australia in 2005.

despite travelling to Australia, he was keen to show his mettle in what he regarded as the true cricketing test. He did not disappoint in England's triumph of 2005. For many, it was Flintoff's triumph. 24 wickets in the series at 27.29 and 402 runs at 40.20 propelled him to national and international stardom.

It was his ebullient character that shone through during the Ashes series and made him so admired. The England and Wales Cricket Board wanted heroes with whom the young could identify and here they had a ready-made candidate. His cheery personality, folksy wit and imposing physical presence meant that Freddie's was the name on everyone's lips. Even when he "over-celebrated" after the final Oval Test, his behaviour was restrained enough to attract sympathy for his hangover rather than criticism for getting it in the first place.

He was selected for the Rest of the World team to play Australia in both Test and one-day internationals, like the rest of the Ashes-winners he

ANDY**FLOWER**

If Andy Flower had merely played out his career in Test matches and one-day internationals, he would have ranked as the greatest cricketer his country has produced. The statistics guarantee that status. However, he was elevated from being a mere player by the fashion in which he ended his international career.

During the World Cup competition of 2003 in southern Africa, he staged a personal demonstration against the Mugabe regime. Along with fast bowler Henry Olonga, he went out to play wearing a black armband "to mourn the death of democracy in Zimbabwe". It was a courageous statement of his beliefs, but it also marked the end of his international career in a dictatorship that did not take too tolerant a view of opposition in any form, let alone such a public display of contempt.

Flower had played an extraordinary part in his country's emergence as a Test-playing nation. His own Test debut was Zimbabwe's as well. When he appeared in his 63rd and last Test against Pakistan in Bulawayo in 2002, Zimbabwe had played only two more. It was a similar story with one-day internationals. Flower missed only five from the time he marked his debut in the 1992 World Cup in New Zealand with 115 not out, until he bowed out against Sri Lanka in the 2003 World Cup in South Africa. The only reason he missed the matches he did was a broken thumb sustained while helping Zimbabwe to a rare Test win, against India in Harare in 2001. The injury did not stop him from going in down the order at a time of crisis to hit the winning runs.

His was an exemplary record, for he also kept wicket in all but a handful of those matches and was captain in 20 Tests and 52 one-day internationals, when he usually opened the batting as well. With so much responsibility in a weak side by international standards, it was a remarkable achievement. He became so consistent as a batsman that he reached number one in the world rankings, while enabling Zimbabwe to become dangerous opposition for any side in the world in limited overs cricket. Even Flower could not make them a force in Test cricket.

He did, however, lead his country to their first Test win when beating Pakistan by the little matter of an innings and 64 runs at Harare in 1995. It was Zimbabwe's eleventh outing and Flower was to the fore. He scored 156 and shared a stand of 269 with brother Grant to take Ian and Greg Chappell off the top of the list for fraternal partnerships in Test cricket. It was certainly not the only time he featured in the records list.

Born: Cape Town, 28th April 1968

Test Debut: Zimbabwe v India, Harare 1992, 63 Tests, 4794 Test runs at 51.54

Best batting: 232 v India, Nagpur 2000, 160 Test dismissals (151 caught, 9 stumped)

Legends of **CRICKET**

temperament as a cricketer. Only three months earlier he had been stripped of the captaincy, for a second time, following a tour of England. Lesser individuals might have lost the will to give their all; Flower became more determined to maximise his efforts in his chosen art.

It was typical that he made a positive response to the situation. He did the same when his international career ended with such an incredibly courageous and selfless gesture. He returned to England, where he had played much of his early cricket in the leagues, to join Essex with outstanding success. In four seasons from 2003 to 2006, his first-class averages in county cricket stood at 47.84, 43.11, 71.00 and 73.14, with a thousand runs in each of those campaigns in addition to all the runs he made in limited overs cricket. It is the mark of a truly outstanding cricketer.

LEFT
Flower about to sweep another boundary for Essex in the 2006 C&G Trophy.

BELOW
Flower celebrating a dismissal, Zimbabwe v New Zealand, Bulawayo, 2000.

Returning three months after sustaining his thumb injury to play against South Africa in the first Test in Harare, he marked his comeback by keeping wicket for five minutes short of 10 hours without conceding a bye, before scoring 142 in the first innings and 199 not out in the second. He did not manage to avoid the innings defeat, but he did become the first wicket-keeper to make hundreds in both innings of a Test. That helped him become the first wicket-keeper/batsman to achieve top place in the world rankings, and earned him the title of International Cricketer of the Year.

Flower's highest score of 232 not out against India in Nagpur in 2000 was the best by a wicket-keeper in Test history. His scores in that two-match series were 183 not out, 70 and 55 before the double hundred to give him a series average of 270. With a couple of fifties either side of that sequence and yet another in his next innings against Bangladesh, he joined the great West Indian Everton Weekes as the only man to have scored at least a half-century in seven consecutive Test innings.

There were two significant features about this run. It showed that he had mastered the art of batting against the highest standard of spin in favourable conditions, to add to his ability to counter pace bowling. It also revealed his admirable character as a man and

SUNIL
GAVASKAR

Born: Bombay, Maharashtra, 10th July 1949

Test Debut: West Indies v India, Port of Spain 1971, 125 Tests, 10,122 Test runs at 51.12

Best Batting: 236 v West Indies, Madras 1983

It would be very easy to explain Sunil Manohar Gavaskar's inclusion in a list of legends merely by listing statistical achievements that are virtually unparalleled in modern cricket. They are all there and must be mentioned, but to confine an appreciation of the man to mere figures would fail to portray the true measure of his greatness.

In Indian society, Gavaskar is often referred to as a demi-god. It is even debatable whether the prefix "demi" is necessary. Suffice to say that this friendly, cheerful, likeable man deserves all the plaudits that come his way. To retain all those adjectives under the intense public scrutiny and intrusive interest that he endures in his native India is a remarkable achievement.

It is a revelation to see how he is treated in his homeland. Try travelling to an airport with him in the same car. Get out and collect your luggage from the boot before making your way to the fast-track boarding channel. Whisked through, you are first on the plane – you think. But no; when you board you will find Gavaskar already in his seat, as if he de-materialised in the car and re-materialised on the aircraft. It is an extraordinary performance.

Gavaskar's status arises from his genius as a batsman. He might be short in stature at under five feet, five inches, but he was a batting giant. His nimble footwork enabled him to manufacture the length of the ball. He seldom hooked, but played more or less every other stroke in the book with technical perfection that was a wonder to behold. Not the first, nor the last to be labelled the "Little Master", he was indeed a master of batting.

He had appeared in only six first-class matches, with three centuries to his credit, when he was selected for the Indian tour to the West Indies in 1970/71. He was 17 at the time. He missed the first Test in Jamaica through injury, but marked his debut with 65 and 67 not out in the second Test, India's first-ever win against the West Indies.

He did not look back. In the remainder of the series he scored 116, 64 not out, 1,117 not out, 124 and 220. 774 runs, dismissed only three times and boasting a Test average of 154.80.

So he continued, using his immense powers of concentration and technique clinically to dismantle all the great bowling attacks arrayed against him. He practiced diligently. He was not renowned as a fast run-scorer, particularly after batting through 60 overs for 36 not out in the first World Cup match at Lord's in 1975, when he thought England's total of 334 was too great to chase. However, he would end any net session by practicing straight sixes, to the delight of the locals on his home grounds.

BELOW
Sunil Gavaskar sweeps towards his century against Australia in 1979.

SUNIL**GAVASKAR**

His ability to score quickly manifested itself at the Oval in 1979. India were set 483 to beat England in 498 minutes; Gavaskar responded with an innings of 221 that took India to within nine runs of an unlikely victory. The match was drawn, but Gavaskar had played a majestic innings of immense charm and character.

At various stages of his career he held the record for the most Test runs and the most Test centuries. When he equalled Sir Donald Bradman's record of 29 Test centuries, he was the first to point out that he had taken 95 matches to do so while Bradman set the mark in

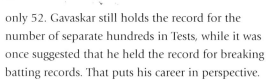

batting partner to leave the field with him. Had he done so, India would not have levelled the series.

That was not typical Gavaskar. He made friends and runs wherever he went, including one season for Somerset in the County Championship and in all the Test countries around the world. Furthermore, he achieved his records while opening the batting against some of the great fast bowlers of the age. Few easy runs were to be had, but then Gavaskar did not need easy runs. When talent and application come together in one such neat package, there was an inevitability about the result.

LEFT
Gavaskar playing for Somerset against Kent in the Benson and Hedges Cup, 1980.

FAR LEFT
Gavaskar in action against England at Edgbaston in 1979.

BELOW
India have won the first Asia Cup in Sharjah and the proud captain displays the trophy, 1984.

only 52. Gavaskar still holds the record for the number of separate hundreds in Tests, while it was once suggested that he held the record for breaking batting records. That puts his career in perspective.

Apart from the World Cup debacle in 1975 at Lord's, the only other time he acted below the highest standard of dignity was at Melbourne in 1981. On one of several occasions he was called upon to lead his country, he was emerging from a bad spell when he was given out lbw to Dennis Lillee. Such was his disgust that he ordered his

ADAM
GILCHRIST

Born: Bellingen, New South Wales, 14th November 1971

Test Debut: Australia v Pakistan, Brisbane 1999,
90 Tests by April 2007, 5,353 runs at 48.66,
381 dismissals

Best batting: 204 v South Africa, Johannesburg 2002

A modern-day England wicket-keeper said of Adam Gilchrist: "He's put the cat among the pigeons, and put us 'keepers under a lot of pressure." When Gilchrist preys on an attack, fielders need the agility of cats to contain him. Nothing could better illustrate the colossal impact made by the New South Welshman on cricket in general and the role of the wicket-keeper/batsman in particular, which he has taken to an unprecedented level simply by the pace at which he scores his copious runs. Kept out of the Australian Test team until he was nearly 28 by the consistency of his record-breaking predecessor Ian Healy, Adam Craig Gilchrist has since played as if there is no time to be lost.

"Just hit the ball" is the batting gospel from which he has been unswerving since making his debut (as a specialist) for his home state in 1992/93. Determined to win a regular place as a wicket-keeper/batsman, he moved to Western Australia after just two seasons, quickly displacing the former international Tim Zoehrer. His one-day international debut followed in 1996 and less than a year later the position, amid some controversy, had become his own. Upon Healy's retirement in 1999 Gilchrist gave immediate notice of his unique batting credentials, scoring 81 from just 88 balls on Test debut at The Gabba against Pakistan.

To confirm the explosion of a meteor upon the Test firmament, Gilchrist shattered a Pakistan attack including Wasim Akram, Waqar Younis and Shoaib Akhtar with an unbeaten 149 in the next game at Hobart, again at almost a run a ball. Facing defeat when he walked out to bat, Australia instead

snatched a sensational win that also secured them the series. As Steve Waugh's men marched towards the status of immortals, primarily through their ability to win consistently by the pace at which they scored their runs, Gilchrist was already the team's heartbeat.

As a wicket-keeper, he may not quite possess the acrobatic agility of Alan Knott, Healy or another great Australian, Rod Marsh, but Gilchrist is nonetheless infectiously enthusiastic, robustly athletic and almost entirely reliable. He is forthright in his encouragement of individual bowlers, and offers welcome advice to his skipper from a viewpoint that is invariably valuable. Australia's vice-captain for much of his career, he has stepped up on several occasions, most famously when Australia won in India in 2004 for the first time in 35 years, avenging their defeat in the classic encounter of 2001.

But it is his batting that transfigures Gilchrist from a mere great to a living legend. He possesses that priceless ability to change a match in a session. Scrupulously fair (he once walked when given not out in a World Cup

BELOW
Adam Gilchrist – a fixture behind the stumps for Australia.

ADAM**GILCHRIST**

semi-final), he appears merciless when he is annihilating an attack. Witness his 152 (from 143 balls) against England at Edgbaston in 2001, or his Test-best unbeaten 204 (from 213) against South Africa in Johannesburg the following year, which set up victory for the tourists by the little matter of an innings and 360 runs. Or his 162 (from 146) against New Zealand at Wellington in 2005, which paved the way for another victory. What a performer to have coming in at number seven!

He can be vulnerable to deliveries bowled from round the wicket and angling away from him, an

Gilchrist's influence on one-day internationals has been no less seismic. Initially going in at number seven, he was soon promoted to open, enabling him to exercise his unique brand of aggression with the fielding restrictions in place. He scores at a rate of around 94 per hundred balls, a statistic enough on its own to assure him of a place in the putative best ever one-day World XI. No one in the modern era, with the possible exception of Viv Richards, can have instilled such trepidation in the heart of a bowler – or such expectations beyond the boundary – as Adam Gilchrist on his way to the crease. No wonder his teammate Justin Langer described him as a freak.

LEFT
Gilchrist at his best at Brisbane in 1999.

FAR LEFT
Another one-day hundred for Gilchrist, this time against Sri Lanka at Sydney in 1999.

BELOW
Australia top the cricketing world – it's official. Gilchrist shows off the trophy in 2002.

Achilles' heel primarily exposed by Andrew Flintoff (and some brilliant close catching) in the great Ashes contest of 2005. Gilchrist failed to reach a half-century in the series, an almost unimaginable rarity. This dip in form was by no means the least significant factor in Australia's surrender of the famous little urn that they had held, metaphorically at least, for 16 years. But he was back into his stride later in the year, falling just six short of a century in the one-off Test against an ICC World XI, and with 86 against South Africa at the SCG.

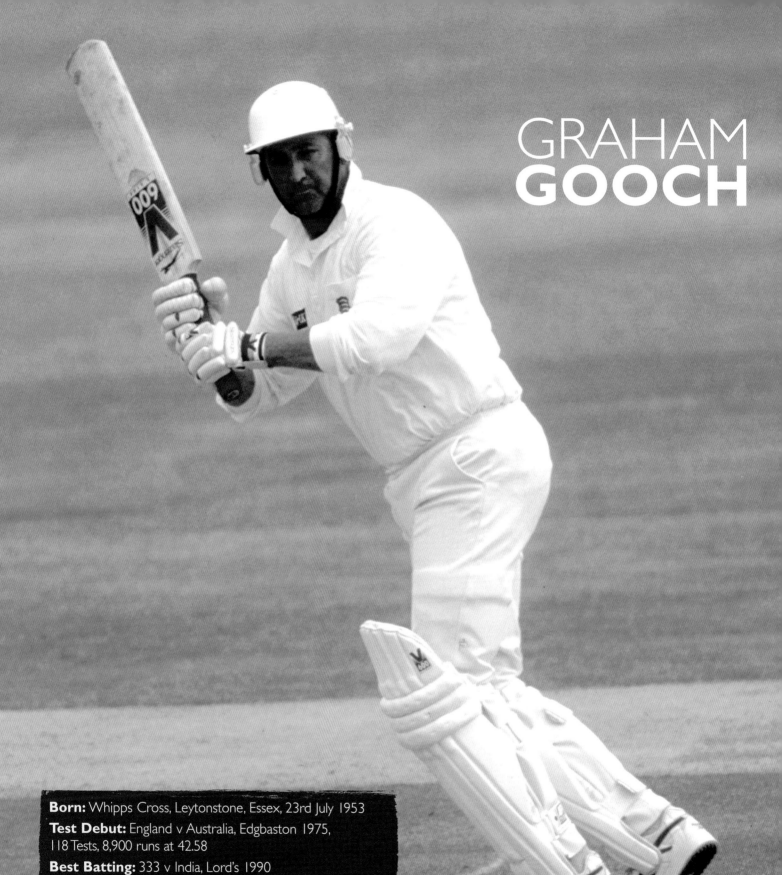

GRAHAM
GOOCH

Born: Whipps Cross, Leytonstone, Essex, 23rd July 1953

Test Debut: England v Australia, Edgbaston 1975, 118 Tests, 8,900 runs at 42.58

Best Batting: 333 v India, Lord's 1990

You can just imagine the type of aura that will surround Graham Gooch in the years to come. "That Goochie; he used to say when he was going out to get a hundred – and did!" Perhaps that is going a little too far, because he did not forecast each of the 128 first-class hundreds that he compiled over a long career that saw him score more runs in top-class cricket than anyone else in the history of the game.

He thought he had scored his hundredth hundred on a South African Breweries 'rebel' tour in 1982. Despite the fact that the opposition contained bowlers of the quality of Mike Procter, Garth le Roux, Clive Rice and Vincent van der Bijl, the International Cricket Council had deemed that the match was not to be accorded first-class status. Gooch shrugged off the disappointment and is reported to have said in that rather high-pitched voice that belied his physical presence: "I'll just have to go out and get 100 against Cambridge University at Fenner's when I get home." It goes without saying that he did just that.

Graham Alan Gooch was marked out as something rather special as soon as he made his way into the Essex side and, at just 21, he was propelled into the Test team. In retrospect it was possibly a little too soon, but England wanted new, young blood to take the attack to the Australians in 1975 and that was exactly the way Gooch batted.

He used a massive bat that he wielded with a purpose, but the likes of Dennis Lillee, Jeff Thompson and Max Walker were a little too much for him and he got a pair on debut at Edgbaston. He did slightly better at Lord's, with 6 and 31, but that was to be the end of his England

involvement until 1978, when he had re-invented himself as an opening rather than middle-order batsman, and marked his return to the Test side with an innings of 54 against Pakistan. He established himself in the team, took 91 not out off a decent New Zealand attack and reached 99 against Australia in Melbourne in 1980 before being run out. It was not until his 36th Test innings that he finally recorded a hundred, against the all-conquering West Indians.

By now he had tightened his technique with obvious benefits, but at the time when he should have been at his peak as a Test batsman, not to say a murderous one-day player, he went on the rebel tour to South Africa. He was lost to international cricket until the series against Australia in 1985. The highlight of his return came in the sixth Test at the Oval, where he savaged the Australian attack. He scored 196 while putting on 351 with David Gower for the second wicket.

His first foray into international captaincy was in somewhat bizarre circumstances. He was successful

BELOW
Graham Gooch during his first Test century against Australia at the Oval in 1985, where he made 196.

GRAHAM**GOOCH**

as Essex captain, guiding them to the County Championship in his first year in charge when he was at the top of his game. When Mike Gatting lost the captaincy following his spat with Shakoor Rana and an alleged dalliance with a barmaid, both John Emburey and Chris Cowdrey were tried, before the selectors eventually turned to Gooch as a stopgap.

Gower resumed the captaincy when the Australians next visited, in 1989, and Gooch was suffering a dip in form. His somewhat idiosyncratic upright stance had started to let him down as he fell across his stumps to be lbw on numerous occasions, to Terry Alderman in particular. But Gooch was back in charge for the tour to the Caribbean the next winter, and stayed in post for another 32 Tests.

Legends of **CRICKET**

when immersed in England matters, and in one season scored at least one fifty in every match he played for the county between international commitments.

He continued with Essex after retiring from international cricket in 1995, before admitting that "the tank was empty" at the age of 44. After all those runs, even a fitness fanatic who ran marathons was entitled to put his feet up. He performed some coaching duties, served time as a selector and now, as well as playing a role with Essex, surprises people who knew him merely as a rather dour and straight-faced individual. He is a media pundit and makes humourous appearances on the after-dinner circuit, remembering his scores on his Test debut in a splendidly self-deprecating way. "They stare back at me every time I sign my surname."

In 1990 at Lord's, he played a gargantuan innings against India. At a time when the highest individual innings in Test cricket was Sobers' 365 against Pakistan, Gooch reached 333 on only the second afternoon before fatigue got the better of him and he was bowled. Not as great in terms of runs, his 154 against the West Indies at Headingley the following summer was a match-winning effort that might well rate as his finest performance in Test cricket.

With limited resources, his tenure was not marked by spectacular success in terms of results, winning ten and drawing 12, but he instilled a strict fitness regime in the England team to set the standards in years to come. He had always maintained strong links with his beloved Essex even

DAVID**GOWER**

Born: Tunbridge Wells, Kent, 1st April 1957

Test Debut: England v Pakistan, Edgbaston 1978,
117 Tests, 8,231 runs at 44.25

Best batting: 215 v Australia, Edgbaston 1985

Every so often, cricket is graced by someone who, intentionally or not, transforms the game into an exalted form of art. Dennis Lillee managed it with the flowing menace of his approach to the wicket. Derek Randall and Jonty Rhodes achieved it in the field, and Alan Knott behind the stumps. In the 1980s there was surely no stroke in the world more sublime to witness than the cover drive of David Gower. Several of his contemporaries – like Allan Border and Javed Miandad – had superior records, but there was no doubt who was the greatest pleasure to watch.

In his autobiography, Gower mentions two pairs of words that he found particularly irritating. The first, "caught Dujon" signalled the depressing number of times he edged a ball from a member of the lethal West Indies pace attack to a man behind the stumps. The second, "laid back" was widely and ignorantly applied to him in consequence of his batting style, which was fluid enough to seem almost effortless. He was a prince of left-handers, a breed of batsmen whose strokes, played to deliveries angled across the body, can seem all the more sublime when they succeed, or ridiculous when they fail.

Gower was on the fast track from the moment he made the XI at King's School, Canterbury aged 14. Leicestershire, to the club's astonishment, were allowed by Kent to offer him terms, and he first played at Grace Road in 1975. Three years later he was at Edgbaston, pulling his first ball in Test cricket (a tempting one from Pakistan's Liaqat Ali) to the boundary. He made 58, and posted his maiden Test century against New Zealand

at the Oval that same summer. Instantly recognisable with his curly blond hair and athletic prowess in the field, Gower already looked a class apart.

He was fortunate to embark on his Test career against some mediocre attacks. Sarfraz Nawaz and Richard Hadlee were the only real threats in 1978; in Australia Gower batted against a team shorn of its best bowlers by Kerry Packer. He made another century in Perth, but was dismissed four times between 30 and 49, prompting the charge, levelled at others before and since, that he was dismissed too often when set. But set he remained back at Edgbaston – a propitious ground for him – in 1979, as he made exactly 200 to expose the decline of India's once daunting spin attack.

Gower found life harder against a full-strength Australia in 1979/80, although he made 98 before running out of partners in the Sydney defeat. He was dropped after the first home Test against West Indies, but showed his mettle in the Caribbean, with an unbeaten 154 against Marshall, Holding, Croft and

Garner. After a series of Ashes dismissals in the twenties in 1981 he was left out again, but he showed more consistency on the sub-continent, and in Australia in 1982/83 he was England's outstanding batsman, with 441 runs. Appointed captain in Pakistan when Bob Willis fell ill, Gower responded with 152 and 173 not out, almost rescuing the rubber.

He was England's captain for two successive 5-0 defeats by the West Indies, but the period in between brought his apotheosis. He led England to victory in India, despite indifferent personal form, and rectified the latter in the glorious, Ashes-winning summer of 1985. He scored 166, a Test-best 215 (again at Edgbaston), and 157 at the Oval, where he shared a spectacular partnership of 351 with Graham Gooch. 732 runs at 81.33 was a record aggregate for an England captain. Gower batted better than any England player in the Caribbean as well, but another blackwash and defeat by India in the first 1986 Test lost him the captaincy.

He was to feature in three further Ashes series, contributing effectively to their retention in 1986/87 and resuming the captaincy in 1989. Although he made a battling hundred at Lord's, England were beaten 4-0 and Gower was not only sacked, but omitted from the squad to tour the Caribbean. Restored in 1990 he made a match-saving 157 against India, but despite further success Down Under he was increasingly at odds with his captain, Gooch, and manager Mickey Stewart, daring to "buzz" the ground in a Tiger Moth during a tour

match. He became England's highest run scorer the following summer (Gooch later overtook him) but to widespread outrage, he was omitted from the 1992/93 squad to tour India.

The continued lack of international recognition prompted Gower to retire after the 1993 season, embarking on a highly successful commentary career. To many supporters his departure seemed premature, the sense of loss exacerbated by the pleasure, occasionally all too fleeting, that he had given them. But like human nature, batsmanship is not without frailty, and after all, cricket was most fortunate that Gower came along at all.

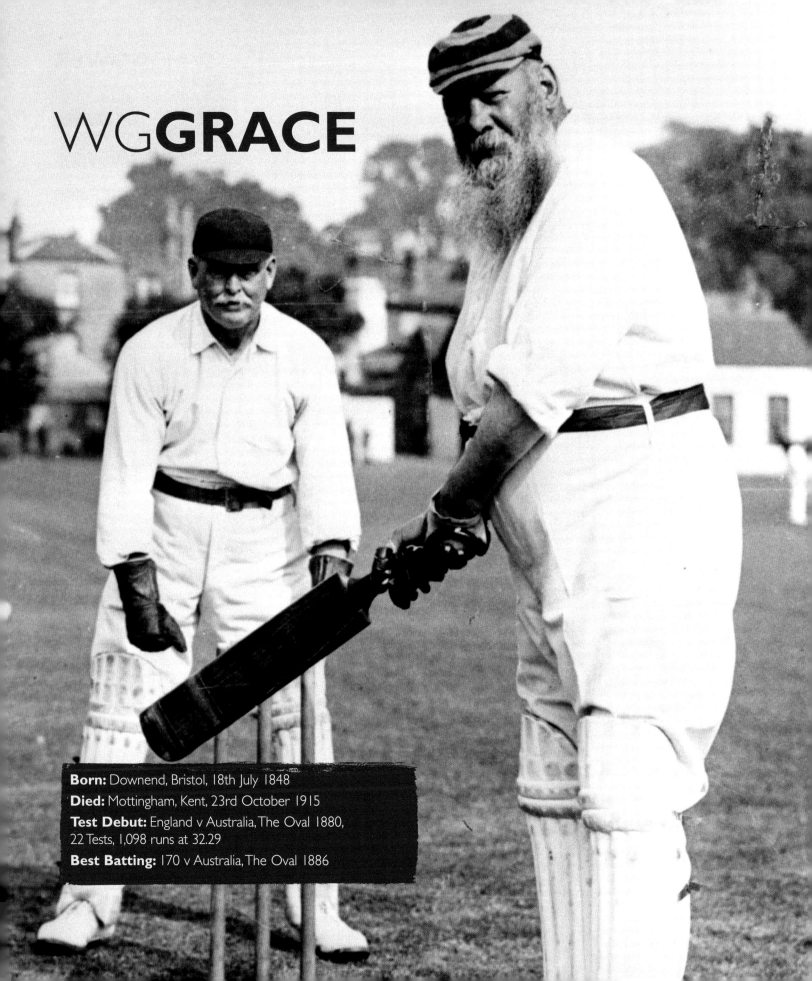

WG**GRACE**

Born: Downend, Bristol, 18th July 1848

Died: Mottingham, Kent, 23rd October 1915

Test Debut: England v Australia, The Oval 1880,
22 Tests, 1,098 runs at 32.29

Best Batting: 170 v Australia, The Oval 1886

Difficult though it is reliably to portray a legend barely seen in action by anyone alive, WG's statistical record, combined with his immortal status as cricket's special ancestor, makes an irrefutable case for inclusion. From the moment when, at the age of just 18, he scored an unbeaten 224 for England against Surrey at the Oval (in a match he left briefly to win a quarter-mile hurdles championship at Crystal Palace), he was the dominant figure in English cricket for four decades. In an age of uncovered and capricious pitches, the "Champion" scored over 54,000 first-class runs at an average a shade under 40. His round-arm bowling accounted for more than 2,800 wickets and he held over 870 catches. His burly figure was probably the most familiar of his day, and his bushy beard remains the most recognisable in cricket's history.

The fourth of five brothers, William Gilbert Grace was coached from an early age in the garden of the family home near Bristol, and was already making a formidable impression as a teenager. At just 17 he took 13 wickets for the Gentlemen v Players of the South; over 41 years he was to make over 6,000 runs for the Gentlemen, including 15 hundreds. His two greatest seasons came in 1871 and 1876. In the first, he reached the astounding total of 2,739 runs, with ten centuries and an average of 78. Although he fell marginally short of that aggregate in 1876, he hit the purplest of patches between the 11th and 18th August.

Three prolific innings mark that period, the first triple century in first-class cricket – 344 for MCC against Kent – followed by 177 for

Gloucestershire against Nottinghamshire at Clifton. His subsequent unbeaten 318 against Yorkshire on a Cheltenham belter stood as a county record for 128 years, until the New Zealander Craig Spearman broke it in 2004. As he went in, in the high-pitched, squeaky voice that so contrasted with his physical presence, Grace warned: "You'll have to get me out today. I shan't get myself out." By stumps Yorkshire's attack was in tatters. In just eight days WG had amassed 839 runs at the none-too-shabby average of 419.5. To round things off neatly in September, he made 400 not out in an exhibition match against a Grimsby XXII, all fielding, to celebrate the birth of his son.

Although Grace's Test career spanned 20 seasons, he made only one Test tour of Australia and appeared in just 22 games in all, 13 of them as captain. He began imposingly, with 152 in his maiden Test innings at the Oval in 1880 (the first Test hundred for England). Two of WG's brothers also played in that match, EM, whose nickname of "The Coroner" derived from his

profession – he once had a corpse put on ice until he could attend to it after close of play – and GF, Fred, who tragically died of pneumonia two weeks later. WG himself outshone his maiden innings six years later with 170, also at the Oval. He reached the age of 51 before retiring from Tests in 1899, saying: "The ground was getting too far away."

Genius though he was, Grace undoubtedly stretched the rules of the game. Clean bowled early in a minor match, he replaced the bails and batted on, saying that the crowd had come to watch him and not the bowler.

LEFT
WG Grace (2nd left) with Australian cricketer William L Murdoch at the Crystal Palace Cricket ground.

FAR LEFT
WG Grace – the thinking bowler.

When given out on another occasion he remonstrated: "Shan't have it, can't have it, won't have it!" "But you'll have to have it!" was the riposte, and back to the pavilion he had to go. For an amateur he was also unashamedly mercenary, charging a fee of £1,500 from the organisers of his first tour of Australia in 1873/4, and regularly collecting testimonials.

Perhaps Grace's most astonishing season came in 1895, when the "Old Man" – he was 47 – managed 2,346 runs, including his hundredth hundred when he made 288 against Somerset. After playing his final first-class match for the Gentlemen of England in 1908, Grace died a year after the outbreak of the Great War. His reputation is measured by this extract of the obituary written for The Times by Sir Arthur Conan Doyle. "To those who knew him he was more than a great cricketer. He had many of the characteristics of a great man. There was a masterful personality and a large direct simplicity and frankness which, combined with his huge frame, swarthy features, bushy beard and somewhat lumbering carriage, made an impression which could never be forgotten."

RICHARD**HADLEE**

Born: Christchurch, New Zealand, 3rd July 1951

Test Debut: New Zealand v Pakistan, Wellington 1973, 86 Tests, 431 wickets at 22.29

Best Bowling: 9/52 v Australia, Brisbane 1985

Richard John Hadlee had cricketing pedigree. His father, Walter, had his career interrupted by the Second World War, but became captain of a weak Test side in the 1940s. He had two brothers, Dayle and Barry, who both represented New Zealand on the cricket field, and even his ex-wife, Karen, represented New Zealand Women on one occasion. Richard, however, was not only head and shoulders above his family members, but also above most cricketers of his type.

Quick bowlers, it is said, hunt best in pairs, but Hadlee was virtually a lone ranger throughout his long and distinguished career. Not especially quick in his pomp, but with quite immaculate control and all the arts and crafts in the trade, he became one of the most consistent and successful fast-medium bowlers that cricket has seen.

His abilities as a batsman should not be underestimated either, although he was considered vulnerable against raw pace. Who is not? Below international cricket he could be considered an all-rounder. In Test cricket he averaged 27.16 with two hundreds and 15 fifties. In all first-class cricket his average rose to 31.71 with 14 hundreds and 59 fifties. His highest score was 210 not out, for Nottinghamshire against Middlesex at Lord's in 1984, when the Middlesex attack consisted of Wayne Daniel, Norman Cowans, Neil Williams, John Emburey and Phil Edmonds.

1984 was one of Hadlee's most influential years for his adopted county. By then he had helped them to their first Championship title for 52 years in 1981, an achievement

to be repeated in 1987. In 1984, in 24 Championship matches, he took 117 wickets and scored 1,179 runs, becoming the first player to complete the double in an English season since 1967. Hadlee was revered by the people of Nottinghamshire, hardly surprising when you consider that his worst bowling average in ten seasons at Trent Bridge was 17.

He made his debut for his home province of Canterbury, where his two brothers were already playing, in 1971/72. With a long run and long hair, he was the epitome of the wild fast bowler. He was wild, too, sacrificing the accuracy that was to become his trademark for pace, not necessarily with outstanding results.

He played three first-class matches in his debut season, and in 1972/73 he appeared in six matches but trebled his wicket-taking to finish with 30 at 18.33. He also made his Test debut against Pakistan and was selected for the tour of England that followed.

Again, he played in just the first Test of the series, but by the time New Zealand visited Australia in

BELOW
Enthusiasm unrestrained – even in Sir Richard Hadlee's last Test for New Zealand against England at Edgbaston in 1990.

RICHARD**HADLEE**

1973/74 Hadlee was established as his country's leading new-ball bowler. His figures did not always reflect the fact, but when he got it right, he was a real handful. It was a deeply analytical mind, so focused on his bowling, that led to dramatic improvements in his game.

Hadlee always had a classical, side-on high action, but it was not yet the reliable, repeating model that was to give such consistency and allow him to achieve such accuracy and command of the ball. He realised that if he continued to run a long way and bowl at top pace the whole time, his career would not be long enough to reach the goals he set himself. The answer? Cut down his run, reduce pace and master control.

The results were spectacular. On any surface giving a modicum of help he could be unplayable. Few batsmen could get on top of him, while the pressure his accuracy created was always likely to produce wickets. It was quite a feat to change his mindset in this way. Patience did not come naturally to the young tearaway, and to develop an approach that relied on his powers of concentration outlasting those of the batsmen required great application.

His attributes were revealed to their full potential in Brisbane in 1985. Hadlee took nine for 52 in the first innings; the irony was that Vaughan Brown's only Test wicket robbed him of all ten. After scoring 54, he took six for 71 in the second innings. He might not have been able to reproduce such figures at will, but he took five or more wickets in an innings on no less than 36 occasions in Test cricket.

Milestones came and went. Hadlee became the leading Test wicket-taker in 1988, went past the then magical 400 mark in 79 matches, and by the time he retired in 1990, already knighted, he had amassed 431. He did not play first-class cricket after bowing out of the Test arena, but he still turned out for his old school's veterans side in presidents grade cricket in Christchurch, appearing on public park pitches. Casual passers-by must have blinked to see a legend in action; batsmen could never afford to do likewise.

LEFT
It's a record. Hadlee acknowledges the crowd after becoming the highest Test wicket-taker.

FAR LEFT
Richard Hadlee in action against Middlesex on the first day of their three day match at Lord's, 1978.

WES**HALL**

Had Wes Hall maintained his original guise in cricket, a generation of batsmen the world over might have been spared from much pain and torment. He kept wicket for his club side in Barbados, but one day the regular opening bowler did not turn up. Hall left the gloves behind, opened the bowling and took six wickets. On such little quirks of fate can cricket history turn, for Hall became the prototype upon which the next wave of West Indian fast bowlers was modelled. With his new-ball partner, Charlie Griffith, he spread terror through the ranks of even the best batsmen. They would have seen the irony in the fact that, in their youth, Hall had kept to Griffith's off-breaks.

Hall came in off a long, athletic, graceful run that gathered in menace and hostility as he approached the wicket. His tall, muscular frame then turned classically sideways-on as he leapt into the action that gave such lethal speed allied to relentless accuracy. But that was not originally the case when he toured England in 1957, having played in a single first-class match, in which he failed to take a wicket, before the tour began. He then had a couple of indifferent seasons back home, before breaking through on the 1958/59 tour to India and Pakistan.

Hall took his first five-wicket haul in the opening match against Baroda, and bowled well enough in the next two to be included in the side for the first Test in Bombay when he took the first three Indian wickets to fall. 46 wickets in eight Tests at under 18 each launched his career in earnest. Back in the Caribbean in 1960, the batsmen who had been so unimpressed when the raw bowler had been exposed to English conditions in 1957, had to reassess. After a few early warnings they arrived in Kingston for the third Test where Hall took seven for 69 in 31.2 fast and furious overs. For the fifth Test he was joined by Griffith as his new-ball partner, and one of the most destructive partnerships in Test history was formed.

Griffith did not take part in the series in Australia that began with the tied Test in Brisbane, but Hall featured prominently in the denouement of the match. He dragged his tired body to bowl the last over with Australia needing six runs to win with three wickets in hand. Hall took one wicket, dropped a catch, there were two run outs and Australia scored five of the runs they

Born: St Michael, 12th September 1937

Test Debut: India v West Indies, Bombay 1958, 48 Tests, 192 wickets, average 26.38

Best Test bowling: 7/69 v England, Kingston 1960

youth after 1963. His performances, while still considerable, never reached that peak again. He took 18 wickets on the 1966 tour of England and was still a force, but the same could not be said in the twilight of his career as his earlier exertions took their toll and he retired, along with Griffith, at the end of the 1968/69 tour to Australia and New Zealand.

An immensely likeable man, when not 22 yards away with a ball in his hand, Hall has enjoyed a varied career in cricket and outside since his retirement. At different times he has been minister for sport and tourism in the Barbados government, has managed the West Indies team on tour and has been president of the West Indies board. He even became an ordained minister. When he was in his pomp, rampaging in with shirttails flying and a crucifix swinging round his neck, it was the batsman who felt in need of divine intervention.

LEFT
Australia's Norman O'Neill evading a Hall bouncer, 1960.

BELOW
Hall demonstrates his classical, sideways-on action in the nets.

needed. His nine wickets in the match were very important, as was the rapid fifty he struck in the first innings.

Hall was now an attacking force propelling the West Indies towards success. They had lost the final Test in Australia to surrender an epic series, but trounced India at home 5-0 with Hall taking 27 wickets at 15.74. By 1963 Hall had Griffith back with him, and they put England's powerful batting to the sword. Griffith took 32 at 16.21 each, Hall 16 at double the cost, but this was a fast bowling partnership in the truest sense of the word; if one did not get you, the other would.

In the second Test at Lord's, Hall bowled unchanged throughout the last day as England closed in on a target of 234 to level the series. His 40 overs produced four for 93 as the hosts finished six runs short of their target with only one wicket in hand. That last wicket saw Colin Cowdrey back in the middle with his arm in plaster having had it broken by Hall earlier in the innings.

Whether that mammoth spell at Lord's took too much out of him or whether it was merely the passage of time, Hall was unable to recapture the fire of his

WALTER**HAMMOND**

Born: Buckland, Dover, Kent, 19th June 1903
Died: Kloof, Natal, South Africa, 1st July 1965
Test Debut: South Africa v England, Johannesburg 1927,
85 Tests, 7,249 runs at 58.45, 83 wickets at 37.8
Best Batting: 336 v New Zealand, Auckland 1933

It is a remarkable coincidence that two of the greatest cricketers in the game's history played for Gloucestershire. For W.G. Grace this was entirely logical, given his birth in Bristol. Walter Reginald Hammond, however, was born in Kent and taken to Hong Kong and then Malta in childhood before his parents returned to England, but not to Kent, when he was 11. He was sent to board at Cirencester Grammar School, whence he gravitated to Gloucestershire. For cricket lovers in and around the county, it must have been the most felicitous accident imaginable.

Kent's vain efforts to secure Hammond's return there resulted in him being forced, at the age of 18, to serve a two-year qualification. It was an unfortunate delay in the development of a player who, to paraphrase Shakespeare, was to bestride the cricket world like a colossus. Tall and strong, he batted with poise and grace, particularly against spin, while in the slips he made even the most difficult catches seem almost effortless. A resourceful bowler, particularly with the new ball, he might have been one of the game's greatest all-rounders but for a customary reluctance to turn his arm over.

Hammond's first tour was with the MCC to the West Indies in 1925/26, where he scored an unbeaten 238 in the first of three unofficial "Tests". He also contracted a near-fatal disease from which he took months to recover. But in 1927 he emphasised that recovery was complete with 1,000 runs in May, and took such toll of a strong Lancashire attack at Old Trafford that he reached 187 in just three hours. His Test debut came the same year in South Africa and included a half century as well as, ironically, his best Test bowling figures of five for 36.

Such success paled by comparison, however, with Hammond's first tour of Australia the following winter. 251 in the second Test at Sydney, 200 in the third at Melbourne and in the fourth, at Adelaide, he followed an unbeaten 119 with 177. He made 905 runs in the rubber, still an England record. On his next tour Down Under in 1932/33, he followed two hundreds in the Bodyline series with 227 and 336 not out in New Zealand, breaking Don Bradman's record individual Test score of 334, made at Headingley less than three years earlier.

Curiously, such riches amassed overseas were rarely achieved in Tests at home, although Hammond hit a purple patch against India in 1936, with 167 and 217 in successive Tests. His innings of 240 against Australia at Lord's in 1938 was more memorable still. With England reduced to 31 for three by the young fast bowler Ernie McCormick, Hammond's response – he was now

BELOW
Wally Hammond, captain of England, gets the ultimate accolade – his own autograph bat.

England's captain – was contained in a ferocious volley of his trademark offside strokes. He hit 32 boundaries in a chanceless display that brought him a standing ovation when he was dismissed six hours later. There was another prolific tour of South Africa before the intervention of war.

It says much for Hammond's pedigree that he was able to resume cricket afterwards. He led England in the victory "Tests" against Australia in 1945 and the next year, at the age of 43, scored 1,783 first-class runs (topping the averages at 84.9). But the heady days could not be relived at international level. Just two half centuries came in his remaining eight Tests, one in his

LEFT
Walter Hammond
(5th from left) with the
1928 England team.

FAR LEFT
Hammond on the
attack for England in
Australia in 1946/47.

final innings in New Zealand at the end of the ill-starred tour of 1946/47. By this time Hammond was suffering from fibrositis and had problems in his personal life. England were roundly beaten in Australia and on his return home, he announced his retirement.

His life after cricket was not easy. After moving with his second wife, Sybil, to her native South Africa, he embarked on two unsuccessful business ventures and was seriously injured in a road accident. His death from a heart attack in 1965 left his family in financial disarray, and with distressing bathos, his cricketing trophies were returned to England to be sold at auction.

The buyers, as David Foot wrote in the Guardian, "paid, in an inexplicable way, to purge their guilt – as cricket lovers – at the thought that the auction should have been held at all."

In first-class cricket, Hammond scored 50,493 runs with 167 centuries, took 732 wickets and held 819 catches. But as Sir Neville Cardus wrote, statistics only tell so much. "You might as well count the notes of Beethoven, or measure the Elgin Marbles." R.C. Robertson-Glasgow summed up the man who habitually sported a blue handkerchief while batting thus: "He enriched the game with a grace, simplicity and nobility that may never be seen again."

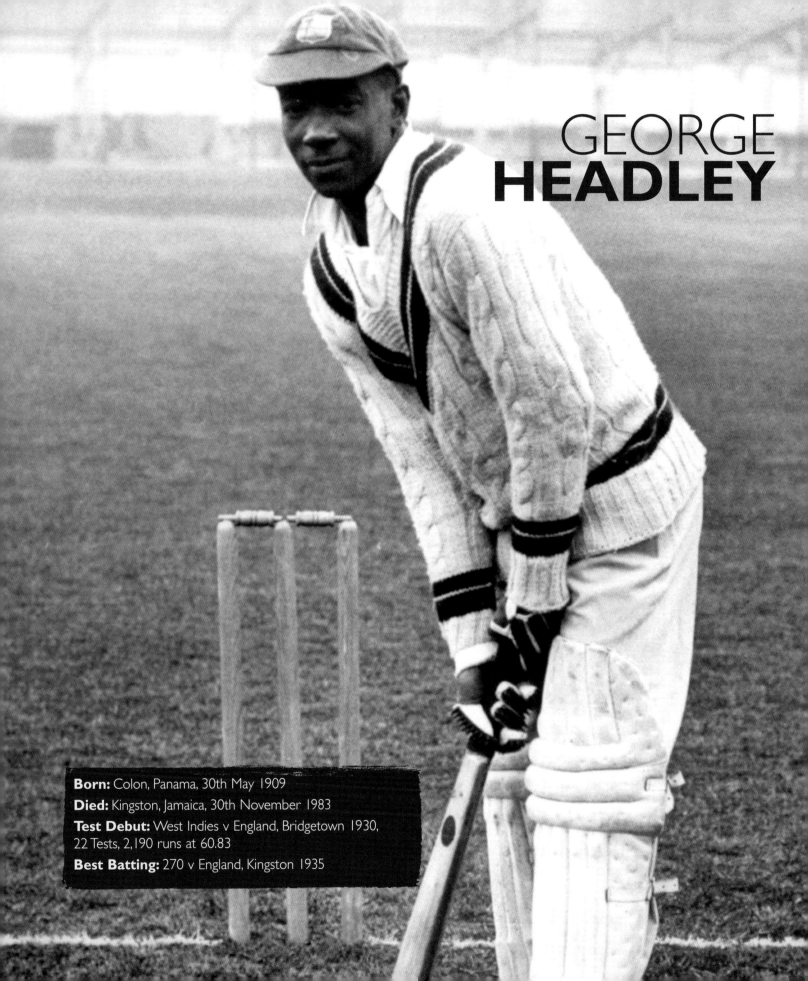

GEORGE
HEADLEY

Born: Colon, Panama, 30th May 1909

Died: Kingston, Jamaica, 30th November 1983

Test Debut: West Indies v England, Bridgetown 1930,
22 Tests, 2,190 runs at 60.83

Best Batting: 270 v England, Kingston 1935

There was a time when some respected judges described George Headley as the "Black Bradman". Supporters in the Caribbean countered by describing the great Sir Donald as the "White Headley". From a totally different and more colourful background than his Australian counterpart, Headley nonetheless came as close as anyone to matching Bradman's remarkable statistical feats.

Headley did not have as many opportunities as Bradman to play at the highest level, for the West Indies at the time were granted fewer matches by the established Test powers. His span of 24 years from first Test to last allowed him only 22 games, while Bradman played 52 in his 20-year career. For ten years before the Second World War, Headley never missed a Test for the West Indies. After the war, he played in only two further Tests because of a chronic back condition. At the start of his career, it was the vagaries of West Indian cricket politics that kept him out of the side.

It was purely by chance that George Alphonso Headley began an unparalleled dynasty of Test cricketers. His son, Ronald George Alphonso, appeared twice for the West Indies. He played most of his cricket in England for Worcestershire, and was called into the touring team of 1973. Grandson Dean Warren Headley played 15 Tests for England between 1997 and 1999 before he was forced into early retirement by a persistent back injury – just like grandad all those years earlier.

It is not often that the United States features prominently in cricket history, but the Headley story owes everything to the fact that the US immigration department were tardy in issuing a visa to allow George entry to study dentistry. Born in Panama, he went to his mother's native island of Jamaica when he was ten and soon showed a rare talent for the game. At 18 he was due to take up his studies, but the lack of a visa meant that he stayed to appear for Jamaica in two matches, against a team of touring English cricketers under the captaincy of the Hon. Lionel Tennyson.

Headley announced himself with an innings of 211 which was described by Wisden as "containing many strokes and with only one chance." To show it was no fluke, he followed it up with 71. Dentistry and the USA would have to wait, even though for some unfathomable reason he was not selected for the first West Indian Test team that toured England in 1928.

The West Indies lost all three of the matches in that series by an innings. What made the difference a year or so later when England became the West Indies' first Test opponents in the Caribbean? Headley. On his debut he scored 21 in the first innings and 176 in the

BELOW
George Headley of the West Indies.

second. He failed in the second Test in Port of Spain which the West Indies lost, but played a significant role in Georgetown in the next match with innings of 114 and 112 as the West Indies recorded their first Test victory. He was no less influential in securing the draw in the fourth Test in Kingston, where he scored 223 in the second innings. Headley finished his first Test series with an average of 87.88.

He found life a little more difficult on the tour of Australia that followed, but he still reached centuries in Brisbane and Sydney. English crowds saw him for the first time in 1933, and those at Old Trafford for the second Test appreciated what all the fuss was about

LEFT
Headley batting against
England in a Test Match
at Old Trafford, 1939.

FAR LEFT
George Headley hits
out during a game in
Kingston – Surrey,
not Jamaica.

when he played a superb innings of 169 not out. When
England toured the Caribbean again in 1934/35, it was
not until the final Test in Kingston that he really made
the bowlers pay. That was when he compiled his highest
Test score of 270 not out to clinch the West Indies' first
series win.

Headley had the distinction of a hundred in each
innings at Lord's in 1939 although, perversely, that was
the Test that the West Indies lost on that tour. After the
War, he was honoured to be named as the first black
captain of the West Indies. It was after the first innings
that his back became too painful for him to continue, so
he batted at 11 in the second innings. He played one

Test in India in 1948 before injury struck again, but was
recalled at the age of 44 to take on England in 1954. He
did not contribute greatly to a West Indian triumph by
140 runs, and bowed out of the game.

Headley had achieved so much during his glittering
career. It has been said that the West Indian tradition of
great batsmen was founded on his outstanding
performances. His success was all the greater because, at
the time, he was carrying West Indian cricket on his
shoulders, hence his nickname of "Atlas". But he
discharged his responsibilities without ever giving a hint
of being burdened, and he did so with the greatest style
and grace.

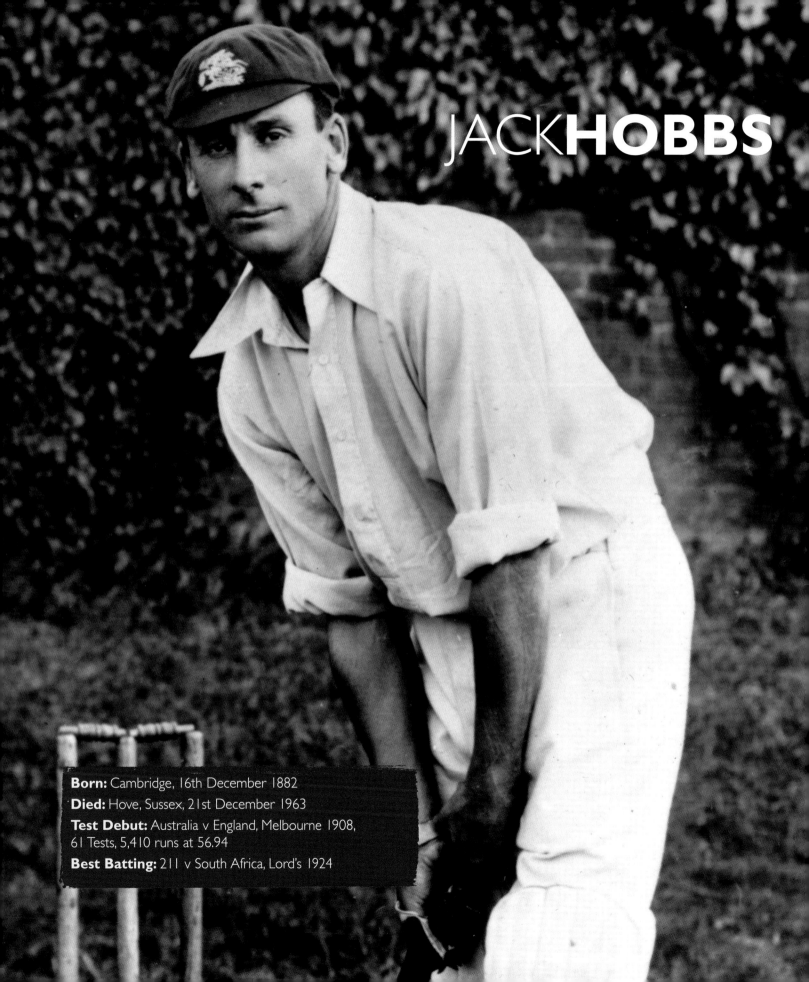

JACK**HOBBS**

Born: Cambridge, 16th December 1882

Died: Hove, Sussex, 21st December 1963

Test Debut: Australia v England, Melbourne 1908, 61 Tests, 5,410 runs at 56.94

Best Batting: 211 v South Africa, Lord's 1924

When John Berry Hobbs was the first professional cricketer to be knighted in 1953 and thus became Sir Jack Hobbs, there was not a voice raised in criticism of the honour even though the amateur/professional divide was still very much in evidence. Hobbs' supremacy as a batsman had earned him another title much earlier in his career – "The Master" – and while he might have been every inch a professional, it was his demeanour as a gentleman that endeared him to all.

The man who rose to the very top of the game had humble beginnings. The eldest son in a large family, his father was the groundsman and umpire at Jesus College, Cambridge. In fact, it was for the Choir of Jesus College that Hobbs first batted, having practiced with college servants using a cricket stump and tennis ball, with a net post as a wicket on a hard tennis court. He did not receive any formal coaching, but his natural eye/hand co-ordination and ability to learn by watching his peers enabled him to become peerless.

In his first-class career with Surrey and England he scored 61,237 runs with 197 centuries. He would undoubtedly have made more but for the intrusion of the Great War. He was 36 when cricket resumed after the conflict, yet 132 of his hundreds were still to be recorded. Hobbs himself did not pay much attention to records and statistics. He was known to give his wicket away once he had reached three figures to give others a chance, unless it was important to the team for him to stay there. And he did not rate his post-war runs as highly as those scored earlier, because "they were nearly all made off the back foot."

He arrived at the Oval only after Essex had spurned the opportunity to look at the young man playing on their doorstep. Given a trial by Surrey, he made an immediate impression, but had to serve a two-year qualifying period. Some of that time he spent playing as a professional for Cambridgeshire before making his first-class debut for Surrey on Easter Monday, 1905 against a Gentlemen of England XI captained by W.G. Grace. Hobbs scored 18 and a rapid 88, leading the Doctor to observe: "He's going to be a good'un."

His second match was, ironically, against Essex when he made 155 on his Championship debut and was promptly presented with his county cap. After three seasons of county cricket he stepped up a level on the 1907/08 tour to Australia, marking his debut with an innings of 83 in the second Test in Melbourne.

It might have been thought that such a talent would soon be recording Test centuries by the score. Yet it was not until his 23rd innings that Hobbs

BELOW
Jack Hobbs in action in 1926.

reached three figures for the first time. It came on the mat in South Africa, when he concluded a series in which he averaged 67.37 (more than double any other English batsman) with an innings of 187 in Cape Town.

Hobbs had such good footwork that he could cope as well with the South African leg-spin and googly bowlers on viciously turning matting wickets as he could with seamers on green wickets in England, the fastest bowlers of the day on quick pitches in Australia, or all types of bowler on rain-affected pitches anywhere in the world. He was the master batsman. Nor was it just a case of stroking the ball to the boundary. Such was his

control that if heavy scoring was not possible, he could hit the ball directly to a fielder, but slowly enough to take an easy single.

As a fielder himself, Hobbs became one of the best cover points the game has seen. On the tour of Australia in 1911/12, he was reckoned to have run out no fewer than 15 batsmen with his own hand. In his early days he had ability with the ball, his medium-pace bowling taking 108 first-class wickets at a shade over 25 apiece. But it was as a batsman that he set record after record. More runs than anyone else, more centuries, more times scoring over 2,000 runs in a season, and he shared in 166 partnerships of 100 or more.

Hobbs was the bridge between what was termed the golden age of batting and the modern era. His career was the thread that bound the fabric of the English game together during that period. His debut was made against W.G. Grace, while his final first-class match, at the age of 51, saw him captaining the Players against the Gentlemen with the likes of Wally Hammond and Les Ames in his side. He recorded his final hundred that season, for Surrey at a freezing Old Trafford against Lancashire and followed it up with 51 not out in the second innings. He stroked the ball about with ease while most other batsmen found the conditions most testing. It summed up Hobbs' career; he began by playing for Jesus and ended batting like God.

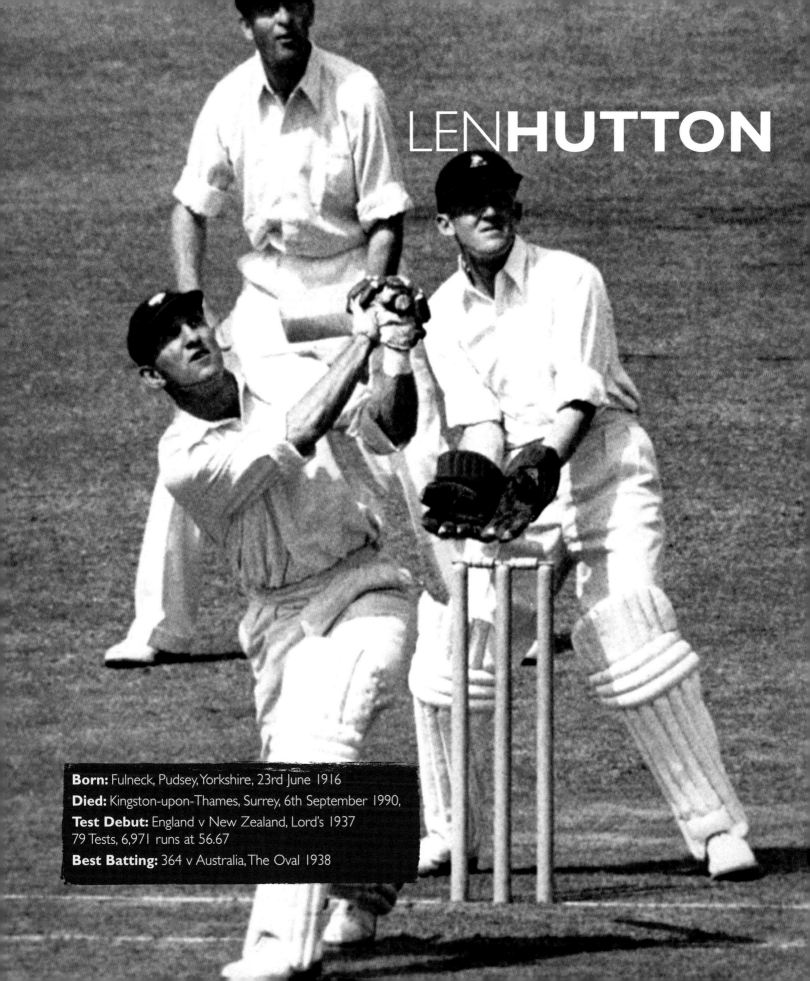

LEN**HUTTON**

Born: Fulneck, Pudsey, Yorkshire, 23rd June 1916
Died: Kingston-upon-Thames, Surrey, 6th September 1990,
Test Debut: England v New Zealand, Lord's 1937
79 Tests, 6,971 runs at 56.67
Best Batting: 364 v Australia, The Oval 1938

Not all Sir Leonard Hutton's greatest achievements are easy to put into present day context. He was the first professional regularly to captain England, and to be elected to the MCC while still playing, he set a world record for the highest individual Test innings that stood for a generation, and was knighted following retirement. The easiest, for sure, is the record most coveted by batsmen, since surpassed by two others in this book. Another, Jack Hobbs, was the only previous cricketer to be knighted, and that honourable list now extends well into double figures. The point is that in his time, Hutton was peerless.

He was playing first-class cricket as a teenager. In 1934, his first season, he scored 196 against Worcestershire before showing early signs of skill in adverse batting conditions, making 67 in four hours at Scarborough. The floodgates opened in 1937, the year in which Hutton made his debut for England, against New Zealand at Lord's. Although he avoided a pair only by the narrowest of margins, his class was apparent in the next game at Old Trafford, where he scored his first Test century. To add to his batting, he was a good close fielder and capable of taking useful wickets with leg-spin.

Already he was marked out as a batsman of considerable style and varied strokeplay, capable of tailoring his approach to any given situation. He also possessed huge powers of concentration, never displayed to better effect than the following summer when England went into the final Ashes Test needing a win to square the series. Hutton's 364, which broke Wally Hammond's individual Test record of 336 not out, took more than 13 hours and 847

balls, and by the time he was dismissed the total was 770. Hammond eventually declared on 903 for seven and Australia, with neither Don Bradman nor Jack Fingleton fit to bat, lost by an innings and 579 runs.

Two more big hundreds followed against the West Indies the next season before, with the cricket world apparently at Hutton's feet, the Second World War deprived him of six of his best years. It also left a physical scar, as he required three bone grafts on his left arm after an accident in a gym during commando training. The arm was left weaker and around two inches shorter than the other. Nonetheless, by the time Test cricket resumed, he was ready to feature in a steady England revival.

Hutton excelled in Australia in 1946/7, which caused general bemusement when he was dropped after two Tests (he made 77 in the first) of the 1948 series against Bradman's "Invincibles". Recalled for the fourth, he highlighted the selectors' folly with innings of 81, 57, 30 and 64. His best season in England followed; in

1949 he scored 3,429 first-class runs at an average of 68, again dipping the bread at the Oval with 206 against New Zealand. Another double followed there against Ramadhin and Valentine the following year, and England's somewhat insipid batting rested almost entirely on Hutton's shoulders (average 88.83) as they were beaten 4-1 Down Under.

But several of Hutton's finest hours were still to come. First appointed captain for the 1952 series against India (despite never having led Yorkshire, as the county maintained the amateur captain tradition) he led England to their Coronation Year Ashes triumph the following summer, in which he was by a distance the

LEFT
Len Hutton is congratulated on breaking Don Bradman's record during the 1938 Oval Test. Hutton went on to score 364.

FAR LEFT
Len Hutton strides out at the Oval to open the batting for England against Australia with Bill Edrich in 1938.

best batsman on either side. For pure artistry, the 145 he made at Lord's in that series was regarded as one of the finest innings he ever played. After a disastrous start in the Caribbean the following winter, it was Hutton who revived England, with 169 and 205 in the third and fifth Tests to square the rubber.

Despite occasional bouts of ill health, he still had another tour in him, to Australia in 1954/5. Although his batting energy had dwindled, Hutton's one half century of the series – 80 in the fourth Test at Adelaide – paved the way for a 3-1 lead, and ensured that the efforts of three youngsters – Peter May, Colin Cowdrey and above all Frank Tyson – did not go to waste.

England retained the Ashes, and Hutton ended his career against Australia with nearly 2,500 runs and an average 54.46. When he retired a year later he had captained England 23 times – then a record – without losing a rubber.

In retirement, Hutton pursued a successful business career and did a stint as an England selector, as well as writing regularly about the game he had adorned. He fathered a Yorkshire and England player in Richard, whose son Ben continued the family tradition, not with Yorkshire but Middlesex, where he was to be captain. Few names in English cricket bear the hallmark of such pedigree.

IMRAN**KAHN**

Born: Lahore, Punjab, 25th November 1952

Test Debut: England v Pakistan, Edgbaston 1971, 88 Tests, 3,807 runs at 37.69, 362 wickets at 22.81

Best Batting: 136 v Australia, Adelaide 1990

Best Bowlng: 8/58 v Sri Lanka, Lahore 1982

A wonderfully lithe fast bowler and consistently improving batsman, Imran Khan was undoubtedly the greatest all-round cricketer to play for Pakistan. Add his natural fielding brilliance, particularly in the deep, outstanding captaincy and film-star looks, and you could perhaps term him the real McCoy. The climax of his career – the World Cup victory for his young Pakistan team in 1992 – was the stuff of legends, worthy reward for a distinguished period of leadership in which he managed to instil collective pride in a talented, but too often volatile and disparate unit.

Imran had impeccable cricketing pedigree and connections. Two other Pakistan captains – Majid Khan and Javed Burki – were cousins. He won three blues at Oxford University, one as captain, by which time he had already made his Test debut aged just 18. After two undistinguished tours of England, he broke through as a bowler in Sydney in 1977, taking six wickets in each innings as Greg Chappell's Australians were beaten by eight wickets. His performances on that tour contributed greatly to Pakistan gaining their first Test win on Australian soil, and ensured a one-all draw in the series.

A move from Worcestershire to Sussex followed, along with two winters playing for Kerry Packer's World Series Cricket, as Imran's batting improved from useful to influential. His first Test century came on his home ground of the Gaddafi Stadium in Lahore, rescuing Pakistan against a West Indies attack including Sylvester Clarke, Colin Croft, Malcolm Marshall and Joel Garner. It was an early sign that the great fast bowler

could take it as well as dish it out. The following year he excelled in both disciplines in Australia although Pakistan lost the series, before achieving his best Test figures of 8/58 against Sri Lanka back in Lahore.

Imran led Pakistan for the first time on the tour of England in 1982. Although it was a personal triumph (212 runs and 21 wickets in three Tests) Pakistan narrowly lost an engaging rubber 2-1. No such reversals followed in the ensuing home series against Australia and India, in which Pakistan – and Imran – carried all before them. They won both 3-0 and in the third Test against India at Faisalabad, Imran achieved the astonishing feat of taking 11 wickets in the match for the second successive time, adding a first innings 117 for good measure.

None of the four great all-rounders of his era, apart perhaps from Sir Richard Hadlee, improved as much as Imran during the last decade of his career. In 51 Tests he averaged a stunning 50 with the bat and 19 with the ball, despite being unable to bowl for nearly three

BELOW
Khan bowls Pakistan to victory in the Lord's Test of 1985.

years due to a stress fracture of the shin. Perhaps he was inspired by the captaincy; in his 48 Tests leading Pakistan the batting average rose to 52. Highlights included 21 wickets in Pakistan's victorious series in England in 1987 (and 118 in the final Test at the Oval) and, more significantly, 23 wickets in the Caribbean the following winter as Pakistan came within a whisker of beating the all-powerful West Indies.

Imran described Pakistan's victory in the fifth World Cup in Australia in 1992 as "the most thrilling and satisfying cricket moment of my life". In the floodlit final at the MCG, they beat England by 22 runs after

memory of his mother, Shaukat Burki, who had died of the disease seven years earlier. Even though some of the most ardent England supporters were amongst those hoping he might manage one final tour the following summer, there could hardly have been a more appropriate moment to retire from the game he had graced so comprehensively over two decades.

Involvement with politics in Pakistan followed, as well as a high-profile, though ultimately unsuccessful, marriage to Jemima Goldsmith, heiress to a famous Anglo-French financier. But the shining, abiding memory of Imran Khan will surely be for his prowess on the cricket field where, Sir Garfield Sobers apart, he was one of the greatest all-rounders ever seen.

LEFT
Imran takes the final English wicket to win the World Cup for Pakistan in Melbourne in 1992.

FAR LEFT
Another victim for Imran.

BELOW
The captain shows off the spoils of the World Cup final success in 1992.

Imran, in his 40th year and with a troublesome right shoulder, had urged his team to imitate the action of the cornered tiger. Knowing that all four previous finals had been won by the side batting first, Imran chose to do so upon winning the toss, and his innings of 72, batting at number three, was the highest and most influential of the match. England's reply never gathered momentum, and it was Imran himself who sealed Pakistan's triumph with his final ball in international cricket.

Imran dedicated the victory to the cause of the cancer hospital he had founded in Lahore in

ALAN**KNOTT**

When he retired from first-class cricket in 1985, Alan Knott was hailed by Mike Brearley, his latter-day England captain, as a genius. Brearley was referring not only to Knott's wicket-keeping, an art in which he was peerless in his time and arguably ever since, but also to his batting, which was both audacious and increasingly unorthodox. Never more dangerous than in a crisis, he rescued numerous England innings with verve and bravado, at times batting, as John Woodcock put it, "with the effrontery of a bandit".

Alan Philip Eric Knott was heir to a glittering Kent tradition. Les Ames and Godfrey Evans had sparkled for England before him; Paul Downton (after moving to Middlesex) and Geraint Jones were to graduate later. By 1967, aged just 21, Knott was taking seven catches on his England debut. Evidence of his versatility with the bat came on his first tour, to the Caribbean, when he made 73 in four hours at Georgetown to help his captain and Kent team-mate, Colin Cowdrey, secure the famous draw that enabled England to win the series. Knott used his feet superbly against spin, a trait that would be apparent in later years against India.

As a 'keeper, his finest period standing up came early while he established his legendary partnership for Kent and England with Derek Underwood. It was off "Deadly" that Knott took his greatest Test catch (pictured left), from a slower ball edged by India's Dilip Sardesai and held, one-handed at full stretch, at the Oval in 1971. Standing back, as was often his preference, he was stupendous. His judgement on whether and when to go for the ball was unerring; time and again he dived in front of slip to take a catch of breathtaking brilliance. The bowlers, including Geoff Arnold who provided him with more victims than any other, stood and applauded.

Nevertheless, it was fitting that it was off Underwood that Knott stumped Lawrence Rowe of the West Indies in 1976, again at the Oval, to break Evans' world record for Test dismissals. There were more dazzling moments to follow, including a diving, leg side catch to dismiss his great Australian rival Rod Marsh in Ian Botham's first Test in 1977. And amongst those watching the reflex, one-handed effort off Tony Greig that dismissed Rick McCosker that same summer was a strip of a lad from Stroud in Gloucestershire. Jack Russell decided then and there to learn and master the same art.

As a batsman, Knott's favoured strokes were the cut and the sweep, which he played on length, not line, although he could belt the ball over midwicket (to Jeff

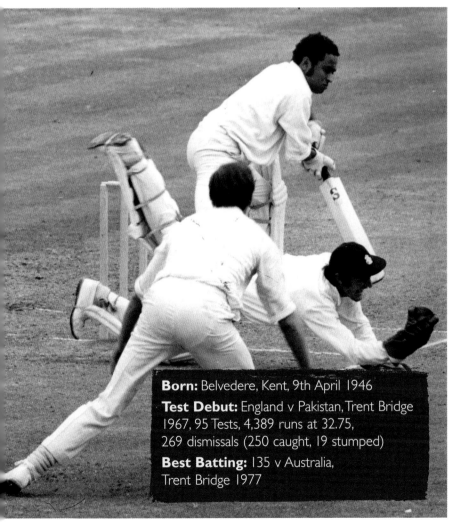

Born: Belvedere, Kent, 9th April 1946

Test Debut: England v Pakistan, Trent Bridge 1967, 95 Tests, 4,389 runs at 32.75, 269 dismissals (250 caught, 19 stumped)

Best Batting: 135 v Australia, Trent Bridge 1977

Legends of **CRICKET**

which caused irritation to some but were simply a means of keeping a naturally stiff body supple. He was chary of drafts, keeping his collar up and sleeves down on the field and donning numerous sweaters off it, even in India. He was fastidious about what he ate and meticulous in his match preparation. All of this was born of utter professionalism.

A devoted family man, Knott did a spell as England's wicket-keeping coach in retirement, but emigrated to Cyprus after the job was no longer deemed full-time. Since then he has been largely absent from the game he so invigorated. But to a generation of cricket lovers who grew up watching his feline grace behind the stumps and wonderful ability to improvise in front of them, the memories are imperishable.

LEFT
A typical Knott shot and four runs for Kent against Somerset in the B&H Cup.

BELOW
Alan Knott, Kent and England.

Thomson's consternation, Knott once hit him for an enormous six there) and he possessed a cultivated, if rarely employed cover drive. Three innings stand out. At Edgbaston in 1971, England were 127 for five in reply to Pakistan's 608. "He really is going berserk," observed commentator Peter West as Knott blazed a two-hour century. At Adelaide in 1975 he made an unbeaten 106 against Lillee and Thomson at their fiercest, adapting to the challenge by repeatedly upper-cutting the ball over the slips.

But his best Test innings came at Trent Bridge against Australia in 1977. He arrived at 82 for five to join Geoff Boycott, who had just run out the local hero Derek Randall. By the time he was out for 135 (Boycott also made a century), Knott had transformed a losing position into a winning one. By then he had joined World Series Cricket, allowing his rival Bob Taylor to flourish for England. But Knott was recalled, largely at Brearley's behest, in 1981 when he followed a scintillating half-century at Old Trafford with a match-saving one in his final Test at the Oval.

Knott was a cricketer of foibles. In the early part of his career he touched the bails at the start of an innings, not out of superstition, he claimed, but to make sure they were properly in place. He had a routine of bending and stretching exercises between deliveries,

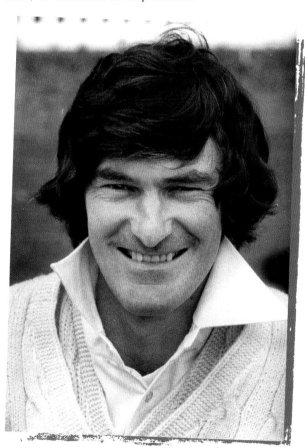

ANIL**KUMBLE**

Anil Kumble made his Test debut in England in 1990, but it was not until he went to southern Africa in 1992/93 that he established himself in the Indian team. The next series was against England at home, so the newly appointed England coach, Keith Fletcher, flew to South Africa to cast an eye over the opposition. He reported that he had not seen the new boy, Kumble, really turn a single ball away from the bat.

Kumble might not have had a big leg-break, but the usually shrewd Fletcher missed a vital point as the nominal leg-spinner took 18 wickets in that four-match series against South Africa. To ensure that Fletcher's

Born: Bangalore, 17th October 1970
Test Debut: England v India, Old Trafford 1990, 110 Tests and 264 ODIs by September 2006, 533 Test wickets, average 28.75
Best Test bowling: 10/74 v Pakistan, Delhi, 1999

words came back to haunt him, Kumble took 21 wickets in four Tests against England at all of 19.80 each. The point was that in India he was known as a top-spinner, for that is what his action tends to produce, rather than the classical leg-break of a Shane Warne or an Abdul Qadir. A tall man of six feet two inches, Kumble uses his height and rapid delivery to employ that ever-faithful friend of the spinner – bounce.

He became the first Indian spinner, and second bowler after Kapil Dev, to take 300 Test wickets, and he did it against England in December 2001 in his home city of Bangalore. In October 2004 he took his 400th Test scalp, again in Bangalore, but this time against Australia, and in March 2006 he went past 500 against England at Mohali. It was in his 105th Test, so he had reached the milestone quicker than anyone bar Muttiah Muralitharan. Kumble does not lure the batsman down the pitch with clever flight and he does not turn the ball prodigiously either way. Instead, he employs his strong action and immaculately straight arm to deliver at an unlikely pace for a spinner.

In 1995, already highly regarded as an international bowler, he accepted the challenge of a season in county cricket with Northamptonshire. He became the first spin

Legends of **CRICKET**

LEFT
Anil Kumble bowls
to Sri Lankan captain
Marvan Atapattu
in an Asia Cup
match, 2004.

BELOW
Kumble takes a catch
for India, 2004.

more than Laker's ten for 53, he only took 26.3 overs to Laker's 51.2.

With his lack of sharp turn, it was once suggested that Kumble could not be effective outside the sub-continent. That myth was exploded when he went to Australia in 2003/04. He took 24 wickets in three Tests, including eight for 141 from 46.5 overs in the first innings in Sydney with another four in the second innings. In the Caribbean in 2006, he snared another 23 victims in four Tests. He is a match-winner anywhere.

Unsurprisingly for a bowler of his type, Kumble has proved effective in one-day cricket as well. Over 300 wickets added to the 500-plus in Tests make him one of the most potent bowlers international cricket has seen. Yet he remains the quiet, studious man that set out on his first-class career back in 1989/90 with Karnataka. Fame and success have not changed him, so that when he played for his third English county, Surrey, in 2006 (he also appeared for Leicestershire), he was as unassuming as ever. And still one of the best bowlers in the world.

bowler to take 100 wickets in a first-class season since 1983 (John Emburey), and the first leg-spinner to do so since 1971 (Intikhab Alam). 41 of his 105 wickets were either bowled or leg before and there was not a single stumping, illustrating the reluctance or inability, or both, of batsmen to use their feet to him. Very few of the scarce boundaries off him came in front of square, while he only conceded 2.3 runs an over throughout the campaign. Furthermore, he was always courteous, fitted in with the camaraderie and banter of the dressing room and unfailingly helped players right down the age range. He was the model overseas professional.

Beyond that standard awe and admiration in which all international cricketers are held in India, Kumble did not have to put up with the intrusive attention reserved for the likes of a Sunil Gavaskar or Sachin Tendulkar. It is the batsmen who become demi-gods. But at the Feroz Shah Kotla Stadium in Delhi in February 1999 he achieved an arguably even greater feat than either of those compatriots to secure his place in any list of cricketing legends. In Pakistan's second innings he took all ten wickets, becoming only the second man in history to do so. Jim Laker did it in 1956, and while Kumble was a little more expensive, costing 21 runs

JIM**LAKER**

After Jim Laker had taken 19 Australian wickets in the 1956 Old Trafford Test, his spinning partner Tony Lock was asked if he felt bad about taking the one wicket that prevented Laker from claiming all 20 in the match. Lock is reported to have replied that Laker had taken 19 to prevent him getting all 20 himself.

It is highly unlikely that anyone will ever do better in a Test, which is enough in itself to give Laker his place in cricket's Pantheon. To take all ten wickets in a Test innings is an outstanding feat in itself; only Anil Kumble has matched that. But to achieve such an analysis in the second innings after taking nine wickets in the first is simply the stuff of legends.

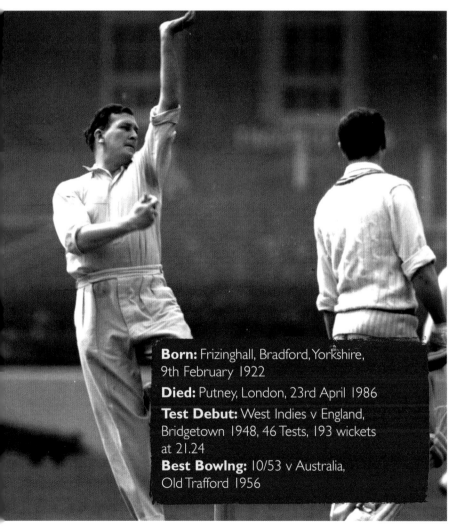

Born: Frizinghall, Bradford, Yorkshire, 9th February 1922
Died: Putney, London, 23rd April 1986
Test Debut: West Indies v England, Bridgetown 1948, 46 Tests, 193 wickets at 21.24
Best Bowlng: 10/53 v Australia, Old Trafford 1956

James Charles Laker was 24 when he made his first-class debut for Surrey in 1946. Playing against a formidable Combined Services side, he made an immediate impression with three wickets in each innings with his crafted, highly-spun off-breaks. Later in the season he took his first wicket in an inter-county match at Kingston-upon-Thames, when the unfortunate Rodney Exton of Hampshire was caught between the knees of Alf Gover in the gully as the fielder was pulling his sweater over his head. Laker was not to require such good fortune to take his other 1,943 first-class wickets.

1956 was a vintage year for Laker. He played against the Australians on no fewer than seven occasions, taking the little matter of 63 wickets at a mere ten runs apiece. 46 came in the Tests. Playing for Surrey against the tourists at the Oval before his 19 for 90 match analysis at Old Trafford, he took 10 for 88 in the first innings.

After his early matches for Surrey, he was taken on to the Oval staff in 1947 and the following winter he made his England debut in Barbados. It was quite an entry into Test cricket with seven for 103 from 37 overs. Despite that performance, and returning the remarkable figures of 14-12-2-8 in the 1950 Test trial in his home town of Bradford, he was not at first a regular in the England team.

Legends of **CRICKET**

Ted Dexter played one Test with Laker and remembers fielding at short leg. When a new batsman came in, he did not receive the fast dart that off-spinners so often deliver in the modern game. Instead, as Dexter crouched down, a perfectly flighted delivery came audibly fizzing through the air while the poor batsman tried to make up his mind whether to go forward or back as his eyes went ever further up to follow the trajectory of the ball. It represented a thorough mastery of the finger spinner's art.

That match in Melbourne in 1959 was Laker's last for England. He left Surrey that year, wrote a book which caused much offence among the authorities, but was persuaded by former England colleague Trevor Bailey to play three more seasons of county cricket with Essex. They were successful years, despite the propensity for green, seamer-friendly wickets in his new county. On one occasion at Romford, Bailey asked Laker to go out before the toss to give his assessment of the pitch. Laker wandered out towards the middle and came back some time later. "What do you think of it?" Bailey asked him on his return to the pavilion. "Couldn't find it," was the reply, delivered with the laconic wit that marked his television commentaries in the years following retirement from the game.

LEFT
A study in poise as Laker goes round the wicket.

BELOW
Another perfect 10 for Laker, playing for Surrey against the Australians in 1956.

1950 was his best summer with 166 wickets as Surrey made the County Championship their own property with eight titles in nine seasons. Perhaps that first success in the sequence owed more than a little to the fact that Laker played in only one Test that summer. He was in and out of the England team until his annus mirabilis of 1956, when weight of wickets at the highest level demanded his inclusion in the national side.

Laker had the ideal temperament for a spin bowler. Calm and unruffled, he bowled with the type of action that made you wonder why anyone should attempt to bowl off-breaks any other way. He rarely got excited, and even when he took those 19 Australian wickets at Old Trafford with the ball turning sharply off a rain-affected pitch, each success was acknowledged by a shy smile and a hitch of the trousers. Even when he took his tenth wicket in the second innings, there was no hysterical mobbing and hugging. A simple handshake from colleagues, a look on his face that said he had done a good job, and off he strolled towards the pavilion.

On a pitch like that offering help, Laker's great accuracy came to the fore. It meant that he kept pressure on the batsmen the whole time, while close catchers had the confidence to go really close in the days before helmets and the rest of the fielders' armour.

BRIAN**LARA**

Born: Cantaro, Santa Cruz, 2nd May 1969

Test Debut: Pakistan v West Indies, Lahore 1990, 128 Tests by November 2006, 11,505 runs at 52.05

Best batting: v England, Antigua 2004

Amongst all of cricket's myriad statistics, a unique distinction is held by Brian Lara. He is the only man to reclaim the world individual Test batting record. Add to that his current status as Test cricket's leading run scorer, and you already have a fair measure of the man's achievement. It is the more telling given the era in which he played, as the West Indies slipped from the great heights they reached in the 1980s. How Lara may have wished, since the turn of the Millennium, for a bowling attack of the quality once commanded by Clive Lloyd. In three spells as West Indies captain, he has had a far trickier furrow to plough.

It was more than three years before shooting to international stardom that Brian Charles Lara made his Test debut in 1990, in a West Indies batting line-up still headed by Greenidge and Haynes. Opportunities were limited until 1992/93 when Lara showed the first evidence of his huge appetite for runs, with 277 at the SCG against Allan Border's Australia. Just five feet five inches tall and left-handed, with a high backlift and a crouch like that of a panther poised to pounce, he was clearly offering something sensational to batsmanship, even by Caribbean standards.

It was back home that Lara confirmed his class the following season, and in doing so drove a suffering England attack to despair. He improved on 83 in the first Test with 167 in the second, but it was in the final match at Antigua that he first etched his name on the list of cricketing immortals. Watched by Sir Garfield Sobers, Lara made 375, ten runs more than the legendary all-rounder's world Test record,

set against Pakistan in Jamaica 36 years earlier. The moment when the two players marked the passing of a mantle with a celebratory hug was one of the most moving in recent cricket history.

It carried scarcely less significance when, just seven weeks later, Lara recorded the highest-ever score in first-class cricket, an unbeaten 501 for Warwickshire against Durham at Edgbaston. But his exalted status, particularly in the modern media age, had not come without constraints. And having broken two such records, where else was he to go? He could not maintain such stupendous standards when Australia toured the Caribbean in 1995, although he again feasted on England's bowling in the drawn rubber that summer. He struggled for most of the ensuing series against Australia, but contributed effectively against India back in the Caribbean. By the time England next visited in 1997/98, he had succeeded Courtney Walsh as captain.

West Indies won that series 3-1, but of more significance to them – and to Lara himself – was

BELOW
Brian Lara's West Indian colleagues welcome him back to the pavilion after his record Test innings of 375 against England in Antigua in 1994.

BRIAN**LARA**

the visit of Steve Waugh's dominant Australians in 1998/99. Lara took their bowlers on almost single handed to score 213, 153 not out and 100 in successive Tests. West Indies drew the rubber two-all; without Lara, they would most likely have been pulverised.

But the pressure of leading a team in decline soon told, and he had handed over to Jimmy Adams by the time West Indies were beaten in England in 2000 for the first time since 1969, and lost 5-0 in Australia the

Legends of **CRICKET**

Lara has served West Indies well in one-day internationals, helping them to the World Cup semi-finals in 1996, and leading them, against the odds, to the ICC Champions Trophy in 2004. But when the time comes for him to retire, it is for his Test exploits that he will be venerated. Such has been the pressure that at times he has railed against it. He once claimed that cricket was ruining his life, and later threatened to resign as captain if his team did not play better. But when he passed Allan Border's record of 11,174 Test runs late in 2005, the Australian was amongst the first to pay tribute. "I have had the pleasure of seeing him play a lot of cricket," Border said, "and there is no doubt he is a genuine genius."

LEFT
Lara listens to chin music; on the receiving end against Australia.

FAR LEFT
Another match, another record. This time it is the first-class batting record as Lara reaches 501 not out against Durham in 1994.

BELOW
Lara poses in front of the Edgabston scoreboard displaying his 501 not out.

following winter. Big hundreds continued to flow, but all too often in a losing cause. Nonetheless Lara was persuaded to undertake a second spell in charge, and after his Test record was beaten by Australia's Matthew Hayden in 2003, he astounded the cricket world by reclaiming it, again in Antigua against England, at the end of a lean series the following year. His undefeated 400 ensured that the West Indies avoided a series whitewash.

DENNIS**LILLEE**

Born: Subiaco, Perth, 18th July 1949

Test Debut: Australia v England, Adelaide 1971, 70 Tests, 355 wickets at 23.92

Best Bowling: 7/83 v West Indies, Melbourne 1981

Many claim, with total conviction and no little justification, that Dennis Lillee was the best fast bowler ever. To measure up to such a standard, it would have been necessary to possess all the attributes; Lillee did. At the outset of his career he was the fastest bowler around. When his pace was used more sparingly, following his back injury, he still employed the bouncer and yorker, but had added swing and cut, both ways, and a change of pace.

You had only to see Lillee run in to realise that you were watching a special bowler. It was a purposeful run, full of menace. Leaning forward, he took long strides but maintained perfect balance. His characteristic drooping moustache bristled, the luxuriant dark hair (in his early days!) flopped up and down, a medallion glinted in the sun, while his voluminous shirt billowed in the wind.

The action itself was an incomparable piece of living, moving art. On reaching the delivery stride, he took off in a leap that would get him airborne long enough to turn perfectly sideways while his left arm shot skywards and his front leg pointed at the batsman to give him a lean-back that had him like a coiled spring. Then the trigger was pulled. All the built-up energy was released towards the stumps, or any batsman who happened to intervene. He finished with his head in a perfect position to survey the damage he so often wreaked.

His appeal, which he frequently practiced, involved turning his back on the batsman to implore the umpire with both arms aloft, but all the time continuing his momentum towards the striker's end. Should the batsman be given not out,

Lillee was by then close enough to impart some well-chosen words to his intended victim, usually to the effect that the inevitable had been delayed. He would then turn and make his way back towards his mark, perhaps glancing at the umpire as he passed, and flicking perspiration from his forehead with a single finger. It was pure theatre.

Dennis Keith Lillee made his first-class debut in 1969 for Western Australia against Queensland in Brisbane, recording the first of what was to become a legendary line in the scorebook: c Marsh b Lillee. It would appear a record 95 times on Test scorecards. He took 32 wickets that season, and the following year represented his state side against the English tourists, but was not included in the Australian team that played the first Test at the WACA a few days later. He had to wait until the circus reached Adelaide before he pulled on his baggy green for the first time. It was also the first time that the Lillee and Thomson partnership appeared in the bowling analysis, but this was Alan

BELOW
Like every other facet of his action, Lillee's follow-through was perfect.

Thomson, not Jeff. Without the man who would become half of the most feared opening pair in Test cricket, Lillee still made an impression with figures of five for 84 on his first outing.

When Australia played a four-match series against the Rest of the World the following season, Lillee announced himself as the complete fast bowler with 23 wickets, including 8 for 29 in a devastating display in Perth, when he bowled out a World XI side that had Sobers batting at seven for 59.

He was lost to World Series Cricket for a time, yet when he came back, he was just as effective, even if he had lost some of his youthful pace and, increasingly, his hair. It was during this phase of his career that he recorded his best Test figures, and in doing so passed Lance Gibbs' record for the most Test wickets – 309. When he retired in 1984, his tally stood at 355.

Lillee was not immune from serious criticism and, perhaps, poor judgement. There was a great furore when he tried to use an aluminium bat against England, and even more controversy when he aimed a kick at Javed Miandad. He was admonished for putting a bet on England (at 500-1) to win the Headingley Test of 1981, yet nobody could accuse him of not trying. He always did.

LEFT
Lillee in a philosophical discussion with England captain Mike Brearley in 1979 over the legality of the infamous aluminium bat. Lillee lost his case.

FAR LEFT
Fast bowler Lillee in action, 1975.

BELOW
Lillee poses for the camera wearing a World Series Cricket T-shirt in Sydney Australia, 1978.

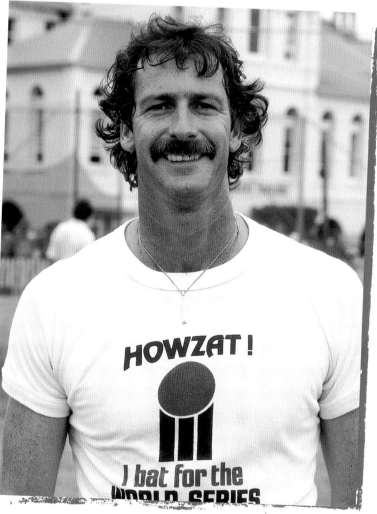

In England in 1972 he took 31 wickets, but in the Caribbean the following February, he played in just one Test before being diagnosed with four stress fractures in his lower back. He spent six weeks in plaster and underwent months of rehabilitation before he was ready to appear in the Test arena again, against the English touring team of 1974/75. England considered it impossible that he could be back to his best, but in partnership with the real Thomson, he destroyed them.

RAY**LINDWALL**

Ray Lindwall's greatness as a complete fast bowler lies not only in the achievements of his own career. He was the one who restored fast bowling's good name after it was besmirched by the Bodyline controversy, and he was the one who handed the mantle on to the next generation.

He had a wicked bouncer, but delivered it sparingly. Not like the young Alan Davidson, whom he once saw bowl at an opposing tail-ender. Lindwall said that Davidson, with that ball, had admitted that the number eight was a better batsman than he was a bowler. He suggested that he might like to visit the nets to learn to bowl properly, and Lindwall took him along to deliver a lesson.

In early life, Raymond Russell Lindwall played in the streets around his native Sydney. He was said to favour the street along which Bill O'Reilly walked home, just in the hope that he might catch the great leg-spinner's eye. It was duly caught and Lindwall eventually played for O'Reilly's club, St. George, where the great man helped the youngster with his game, using the then novel medium of photography as a coaching aid.

Lindwall was a stickler for practice and developing his game. He had seen Harold Larwood bowl on the infamous 1932/33 tour, and while he found it difficult to accept a Pommie as a hero, he did learn something of how to bowl with a similar physique. While serving with the Australian army in the Pacific during the Second World War, he was physically debilitated by illness yet still marked out his run between palm trees to retain his bowling rhythm.

Home from the war, he was one of seven Australians who made their debuts in the one-off Test in Wellington against New Zealand in 1946. Another debutant was Keith Miller, with whom Lindwall was to form such a dynamic new ball partnership in the years to come, while one of the four returning to Test cricket was none other than Bill O'Reilly.

Lindwall had a quiet match as New Zealand were swept away, despite the honour of taking the first wicket on the resumption of Test cricket, but he did enough to secure a place in the side to meet England in 1946/47. The first Test in Brisbane saw Lindwall and Miller open the bowling for Australia for the first time. Lindwall had figures of nought for 23 from 12 overs in the first innings, while Miller stole the headlines with seven for 60 from 22.

Lindwall was the quiet, unassuming master of his craft, while Miller was always liable to steal the headlines with a spectacular display. Lindwall did not mind that in the slightest. He was happy to blend in

Born: Mascot, Sydney, New South Wales, 3rd October 1921

Died: Greenslopes, Brisbane, Queensland, 23rd June 1996

Test Debut: New Zealand v Australia, Wellington 1946, 61 Tests, 228 wickets at 23.03

Best Bowling: 7/38 v India, Adelaide 1948

Perhaps the most significant thing about Lindwall was his metronomic accuracy. Not many bowlers of his pace have possessed his immaculate control. Early in his career, he realised that relying on catches would not necessarily give him a good return. It was a lesson well learned, because a remarkably high percentage of his wickets were bowled. On the tour of England in 1948, exactly half his 86 wickets fell in that fashion.

He saved some of his best performances for matches against England. At the Oval in 1948, he finished with figures of six for 20 as England were bowled out for 52. But the figures against any opponent reflected the relentless consistency of Lindwall's bowling.

LEFT
Ray Lindwall smashes to the boundary for Australia.

BELOW
The scorer of two Test centuries did not look best pleased with this dismissal.

with the background while his partner enjoyed the limelight. He also knew that he had the respect of his fellows and that the pressure he applied could bring rewards at either end.

Lindwall missed the second meeting in Sydney, where Fred Freer took the new ball in his only Test, but was back for the third in Melbourne where he scored the first of his two Test hundreds. He was to be a fixture in the Australian side for the next decade as Lindwall and Miller became one of the legendary fast bowling pairings.

Under six feet tall, with a bowling arm that never reached a classical height, he was nonetheless the complete fast bowler. He was not quite as quick as some of the other greats of his type, but he was operating under the old back foot no ball law, so by the time he had glided along on his toe end, he was a bit short of the statutory 22 yards. For the batsman, it was like someone bowling at around 90 miles an hour.

Lindwall was primarily an outswing bowler, but added the inswinger for variation. Both deliveries moved as much as anyone has ever achieved at his pace. His bouncer, from his low arm, would skid onto the batsman at a disconcerting height rather than ballooning over his head. Add to that the yorker and a change of pace, all after a liquid run that made him look as though he was gliding in on casters, and you can understand why he was acknowledged as the master of his art.

CLIVE**LLOYD**

Clive Lloyd is a giant of a man in every sense. Six foot five with stooped shoulders, a large moustache and thick glasses (his eyes were damaged when he was 12 as he attempted to break up a fight at school), he was a crucial ingredient in the rise of West Indian cricket. He was a hard-hitting batsman and one of the most successful captains in history. An almost ponderous, lazy gait belied the speed and power at his command and the astute tactical brain that led the West Indies to the top of world cricket for two decades.

Lloyd made his first-class debut as a left-hand middle-order batsman in British Guiana in 1963-64, and played for Haslingden in the Lancashire League in 1967. He joined Lancashire in 1968, having already made his Test debut, against India at Bombay in 1966.

Born: Georgetown, 31st August 1944
Test Debut: India v West Indies, Bombay 1966, 110 Tests and 87 ODIs, 7,515 Test runs at 46.67
Highest Test score: 242 v India, Bombay 1975

He scored 82 and 78 not out, putting on 102 runs with Garry Sobers to win the match on a pitch helping the spinners. His first home Test brought his first Test century, 118 against England in Trinidad that helped stave off defeat. Another followed in the fourth Test of that series to confirm he was at home at the highest level. Touring Australia in 1968/69 he hit another Test century at Brisbane.

Lloyd was one of those players really taken to heart by his adopted English county. He scored 1,600 runs for Lancashire at 47 in 1971. Often raising his game for the big occasion, he struck 126 against Warwickshire at Lord's to help Lancashire to the Gillette Cup in 1972, while he hit a wonderful century in the first-ever World Cup final in 1975 to take the West Indies to victory. At his best Lloyd was a flamboyant destroyer of bowling. His heavy bat, powerful shoulders and full swing of the arms could turn the course of any game. In 1976 he scored 201 not out in just 120 minutes for Lancashire against Glamorgan - equalling the record for the fastest ever first-class double hundred.

Lloyd's first tour as captain in 1974/75 marked a dramatic improvement in his batting after a run of low scores. 163 in the first Test at Bangalore (his century came in just 85 balls) was followed by a Test-best unbeaten 242 in Bombay to set up a series-deciding win for the West Indies. The unsuccessful tour of Australia in 1975/76 proved to be a major turning point in West Indian cricket, however, as Lloyd decided to adopt the

Legends of **CRICKET**

England in 1984 as the West Indies completed a famous five-nil "blackwash", and 50.85 against Australia in 1984/85, helping to secure a 3-1 triumph.

Lloyd's overall record as captain was remarkable, including a run of 26 Tests without defeat, and 11 successive wins. He also became the first West Indian to win 100 Test caps. Having been a schoolboy athletics champion, the "Big Cat" became a brilliant cover fielder before knee problems forced a move to the slips, where he pouched many of his 90 Test catches. He was also a useful right-arm medium-pacer, taking 114 first-class wickets with ten in Tests.

Lloyd remained involved in cricket after his retirement. He has coached and commentated on the game, as well as managing the West Indies at a time when they needed his presence. He has also been an ICC match referee - a position he occupies with great presence and no little humour to earn the respect and confidence of the players. They know he understands the game as well as anyone and holds it in the highest regard.

intimidatory tactics of the Australians and stack his team with fast bowlers.

Some may say his job as captain was fairly straightforward, with the likes of Roberts, Marshall, Garner and Holding at his command. Add batsmen of the calibre of Greenidge, Haynes and Richards, and he certainly had some handy players to call upon. But he instilled his talented side with the professionalism and determination to win consistently, and when the conditions suited the opposition. There was controversy too. Slow over-rates and intimidation of batsmen with short-pitched bowling were both characteristics of his reign.

During the Packer crisis, Lloyd resigned after disagreeing with the selectors on the eve of a Test against Australia (1977/78), but he returned to lead his team to the 1979 World Cup. On the subsequent tour of Australia he underwent surgery on his knee that improved his mobility and effectiveness. Centuries at Adelaide and Old Trafford followed, and back in the West Indies he found the most consistent form of his career; he averaged 76 against England and a phenomenal 172.5 in domestic cricket.

Although age slightly decreased Lloyd's belligerence at the crease, he remained a key player in the middle order. In Adelaide in 1981 he played the crucial innings to secure the West Indies a win to draw a series that had seemed destined to be won by Australia. Normal service was resumed with home and away victories against India and Australia. On his final tours he averaged 67 in

MALCOLM**MARSHALL**

When a fast bowler causes batsmen misery and pain, it is difficult to understand how they can like him. Respect him, yes; admire him, without doubt, but to regard him with genuine affection means that he must be a special person. Malcolm Denzil Marshall was accorded that standing, for he was not only one of the game's great fast bowlers but also a thoroughly likeable individual.

When he died at the tragically early age of 41, the universal outpouring of grief was a mark of the esteem in which he was held by colleague and opponent alike. He had a warm personality and a cheerful disposition, yet he also possessed all the weapons that one fast bowler could possibly desire. Ask leading batsmen of his time whom they rated as the best they faced, and with few exceptions they will plump for Marshall.

He was just a little bit different from both his contemporaries and predecessors in the West Indian pace battery that ruled world cricket for a decade. While Joel Garner measured six feet eight inches and the likes of Michael Holding and Colin Croft easily topped six feet, Marshall was no more than five feet eleven. But if he lacked inches, he was blessed with a phenomenally fast arm and, furthermore, dispelled any notion that fast bowlers merely ran in and hurled it down as fast as possible. He was a thinking bowler who happened to be very quick.

His father was killed in a motor accident when he was a baby, so it was his grandfather who taught him the rudiments of the game. His cricketing education advanced as, like most Bajans of his age, he played cricket for hour after hour on the beach, in the road or in clearings in the sugar cane. He was originally a batsman, but as he progressed into club cricket he developed as a bowler before making his debut for Barbados against Jamaica in February 1978. He took six for 77 and, incredible though it may appear, was selected to go to India with the West Indies on the strength of that single first-class match. Caribbean cricket had been decimated by defections to World Series Cricket, and there were few other candidates with such credentials.

Marshall's fifth first-class match was his Test debut, when he came on first change and took one for 53 from 18 overs. Both his economy and strike rates were to improve dramatically in the years ahead; by the end of his career he had conceded only 2.68 runs per over and taken a wicket every 46.76 balls. And these statistics vary little across all types of cricket – first-class, one-day internationals and domestic limited overs matches. Whenever he crossed the boundary rope, he tried his utmost. He also retained enough of his early batting promise to score ten Test fifties and seven first-class hundreds.

After his meteoric elevation, it took time for him to fulfil his potential. But he had already shown enough

Born: Bridgetown, Barbados, 18th April 1958

Died: Bridgetown, Barbados, 4th November 1999

Test Debut: India v West Indies, Bangalore 1978, 81 Tests, 376 wickets at 20.94

Best Bowling: 7/22 v England, Old Trafford 1988

Larry Gomes approaching a century, Marshall came in with his left arm encased in plaster. He batted long enough for Gomes to reach the milestone, and hit a one-handed four of his own, before taking seven for 53. He missed the fourth Test but was back at the Oval to achieve another five-wicket return, before confirming he was right at the top of his trade with a succession of successful series.

Marshall played on for Hampshire for two years after his retirement from international cricket, and spent some time with Natal where he was inevitably revered. Shortly after becoming coach of the West Indies, he was diagnosed with cancer of the colon. He married his long-time girlfriend Connie just weeks before his death stunned his many friends across the cricketing world.

LEFT
The ramrod straight bowling arm about to deliver.

BELOW
Marshall at the start of his run – a sight feared by all batsmen.

for Hampshire to take him on as the successor to another great West Indian fast bowler, Andy Roberts. Marshall's unstinting efforts meant that he was quickly accepted as more than just another hired gun: he became very much part of the family. Not only did he put much in, but he learned from the experience of playing county cricket, completing the education that had been denied him when he was thrust into the international arena so early.

When the Packer players returned, Marshall was used primarily as cover for Roberts, Holding, Croft and Garner. But as they grew older and Marshall improved, he eventually commanded a regular place in the side. In 1982 he took 134 wickets for Hampshire, and when the West Indies entertained India in 1983, Marshall staked his claim to be a first-choice bowler with 21 wickets in the series.

From then on, the sight of his somewhat frenetic run and explosive, if front-on, action became a feature of West Indian cricket. His stock ball was the outswinger, while he was never shy of dropping it short to produce a nasty, skidding bouncer. He developed an inswinger delivered with a scarcely noticeable change of action, and found a devastating leg-cutter.

As an example of his commitment, he broke his thumb while fielding on the first day of the 1984 Headingley Test. Yet when the ninth wicket fell with

PETER**MAY**

The best English batsman of his generation, he was also the epitome of the English gentleman as would be expected of a product of Charterhouse and Cambridge. It therefore comes as something of a surprise that those who played under or against him rate Peter Barker Howard May as one of the hardest captains they encountered. He led his country a record 41 times, winning 21 and losing ten at a time when the incidence of draws in Test cricket was rather higher than it is today. Those statistics demonstrate a very positive approach to the game.

From his earliest days it was clear that he was destined for a great future. May was a schoolboy prodigy at Charterhouse and the star of the Combined Services team for which he made his first-class debut while serving in the Royal Navy. He went up to Cambridge in 1950 and in a strong batting side, it took him time to settle. However, an innings of 227 not out against Hampshire showed that he was maintaining his steep trajectory to the top. He made his Surrey debut in the same season and by 1951 had been chosen for the fourth Test against South Africa at Headingley, marking his debut with an innings of 138.

He played throughout the following summer's series against India, but just twice in the victorious Ashes campaign of 1953. The Australians paid May the compliment of targeting him in the tour match against Surrey. It was not until the final Test at the Oval, with solid innings of 39 and 37, that he could be said to have regained parity. Nevertheless, he was chosen to tour the Caribbean in 1954, when another Test century made him a fixture in the side. While Frank Tyson took the plaudits for his explosive bowling in Australia in 1954/55, May's runs were vital in giving Tyson totals at which to bowl. Len Hutton's side retained the Ashes and May was the natural successor when Hutton retired through illness.

The captaincy can be a burden for some batsmen, while others are inspired. May fell into the latter category with two hundreds, a 97, an 89 not out and an 83 to average 72.75 in his inaugural season as captain against South Africa. In England's Ashes defence of 1956, his style of batting was an inspiration. Tall and upright, he could play strokes all round the wicket, while the quality of his on-driving became as much a trademark as Wally Hammond's cover drive had been.

May captained Surrey between 1957 and 1962, with his first two seasons in charge including the last of the celebrated seven consecutive county championships. 1957 was also the year of his highest Test and first-class

Born: Reading, Berkshire, 31st December 1929

Died: Liphook, Hampshire, 27th December 1994

Test Debut: England v South Africa, Headingley 1951, 66 Tests, 4,537 runs at 46.77

Best batting: 285 v West Indies, Edgbaston 1957

May had not completely recovered his health, and faced the prospect of an arduous winter tour to India and Pakistan and, as an amateur, the increased demands of his insurance business and family. He decided to retire from Test cricket, although he had a successful season for Surrey in 1962 and played three matches in 1963, finishing, disappointingly, with one and nought against Northamptonshire in his last first-class match.

He took up administrative roles, culminating in his stint as chairman of selectors from 1982, having served on the panel from 1965 to 1968. With England's fortunes, and apparent selection policy, at a low when he retired in 1988, it was an unfortunate way for May to bow out of cricket. Just as his career finished early at 33, so did his life, just four days before his 65th birthday.

score, 285 not out against the West Indies. His stand of 411 for the fourth wicket with Colin Cowdrey is still a record in Test cricket for that wicket and the best partnership for England.

That began a run of ten unbeaten Tests for May's England, with only three draws. It came to an unceremonious end in Brisbane at the start of the 1958/59 series, for which England had been firm favourites. Injuries to key players and a resurgent Australia under Richie Benaud's captaincy left England defeated, although May averaged over 40 with the bat.

He maintained his form in New Zealand, and in the first Test against the West Indies in 1959 he again reached three figures. It was the last time he would do so for England. May was forced home by illness from the West Indies tour of 1959/60 and missed the whole of the 1960 series against South Africa, and the first Test against Australia in 1961. He returned for the second, not as captain, but resumed the leadership for the third to help England back to level terms. Benaud stole the fourth Test from England's grasp despite an innings of 95 from May, before the fifth Test petered out as a draw. He scored 71 and 33 in that match, but it was his last for England.

GLENN
MCGRATH

Born: Dubbo, New South Wales, 9th February 1970

Test Debut: Australia v New Zealand, Perth 1993,
119 Tests and 225 ODIs, 542 Test wickets, average 21.55

Best Test bowling: 8/24 v Pakistan, Perth, 2004

It was at Lord's in 2005 that Glenn McGrath took his 500th Test wicket and immediately donned a pair of special boots with that magical figure embroidered on them in gold thread. He was not wearing those boots in a warm-up before the Edgbaston Test two weeks later when he trod on a stray ball in the outfield and turned his ankle so badly that he missed the match. Australia won at Lord's but lost in Birmingham. Such is McGrath's importance to his country as one of the best fast-medium bowlers it has produced that many observers believed the moment he trod on that ball cost Australia the Ashes.

McGrath comes from farming country some 200 miles north-west of Sydney. Tall and lean, he did not play much cricket in his youth, but by the age of 15 it was clear that he had serious ability, and he began to take the game seriously. By 17 he was starting to get representative games and making an impression on, among others, Doug Walters. The Australian Test batsman persuaded McGrath to move to Sydney to play for the Sutherland club where he learned much but had to take menial jobs and live in a caravan to survive.

He was improving throughout the four years he spent playing grade cricket, and in January 1993 he made his debut for New South Wales against Tasmania in Sydney, striking five times in the first innings. He was yet to indulge in the practice of holding the ball aloft when he took five wickets, much as a batsman raises his bat on completion of a hundred. For McGrath,

the ball is just as much the tool of the trade as is the bat to a batsman.

McGrath went on taking wickets with such regularity that in November 1993 he was proudly wearing the baggy green cap of Australia, in Perth against New Zealand as a last-minute replacement for Merv Hughes. There was little in his first performance at that level to suggest that he was going to develop into one of the very best of his type. He had not yet learned to hit the seam relentlessly on a good length, on or around off-stump. Never of express pace, yet with the ability to get bounce from an admirably high action, his consistency has since become a byword in the game.

That is the reliable package around which Australian attacks have been built since the retirement of one of the few comparable quick bowlers in modern times, Dennis Lillee, one of the major influences in McGrath's career. With Shane Warne also providing wickets at an unprecedented rate, the reasons for Australia's modern success are not difficult to find. Nor is it hard to

BELOW
McGrath in full flow.

GLENN**MCGRATH**

gauge the effect of taking a component like McGrath out of the attack.

His first five-wicket haul in Tests did not come until the 19th innings in which he bowled, but then they came at regular intervals as his strike rate, like his average and economy rate, gradually reached thoroughly impressive proportions. Nonetheless, in his first Ashes Test at Brisbane in 1994 he failed to take a wicket, even that of Michael Atherton who was to become one of his rabbits. He did not appear again until the fifth Test when he took six wickets. English batsmen have fallen to him so regularly since that a quarter of his Test wickets have been English, in only a fifth of his matches.

McGrath's first Test in England was in 1997, when he took two for 149 in Australia's defeat at Edgbaston. In the rain-ruined second Test at Lord's he took eight for 38 in the first innings to gain his first of three consecutive man-of-the-match awards in his three Tests on the ground. His ability to exploit the Lord's slope was uncanny, and he has arguably outshone any bowler of his type in his mastery of the unique conditions there.

Legends of **CRICKET**

That was not his best return, though; he took eight for 24 against Pakistan in Perth in 2004, inspiring Australia to yet another massive victory.

Batsmen the world over have been unable to halt McGrath's march to 100 Tests and to 500 Test wickets, to say nothing of 300 in one-day internationals. But he has been hindered by a serious ankle injury that cost him a year's international cricket in 2003/04, and the illness of his wife, Jane, with cancer.

He decided to take another break in his career to attend to her needs. The fact that he did shows the caring, sensitive side to his nature that is not in evidence the moment he steps over the boundary line, becoming the fiercest of opponents.

KEITH**MILLER**

Keith Miller would have been a legend even if he had never played cricket. He was the sort of man who would have excelled in whatever pursuit he had chosen and the game was fortunate to benefit from his sumptuous gifts. Named, fittingly, after two Australian aviation pioneers, Keith and Ross Smith, he was born and raised in the somewhat staid city of Melbourne, beginning his cricket career with Victoria. It was only after the Second World War that he moved to Sydney and New South Wales, where he could freely express his natural talents.

During the war he had enlisted in the RAAF, flying Beaufighters and then Mosquito fighter-bombers on raids over Germany. Perhaps that experience shaped his perspective on life and cricket. Once, when asked about the pressures associated with the modern game, he replied: "Pressure is a Messerschmitt up your arse. Playing cricket is not." A classical music enthusiast, he diverted on his way back from a raid to fly over Bonn – Beethoven's birthplace. Or so the story goes; it is often difficult to separate substance from myth when dealing with legends.

What is certain is that before the war he was regarded mainly as a batsman; by the time he returned from the conflict he was one of the most potent all-rounders the game has seen. It was at the end of the war that he emerged as a figure who was likely to dominate world cricket. "Flight Sergeant Miller" and then "Pilot Officer Miller" was receiving very good reviews for his performances with the Australian Services and Dominions teams that played in England before demobilisation.

His Test debut was delayed by the war, but once he could concentrate on cricket in peacetime rather than grabbing games between flying missions, his form demanded his inclusion in Australian teams, even if his cavalier lifestyle did not always endear him to the selectors. For example, after he had featured prominently in the success of Bradman's 1948 "Invincibles", he was left out of the original party to tour South Africa, although injury did open up a place for him.

It had been rumoured that he never got on with Sir Donald Bradman, because Miller's inherent joie de vivre clashed with The Don's very pragmatic approach to cricket and life. They were totally different, but it did not mean they were sworn enemies. Speaking at Miller's memorial service in 2004, Bradman's son, John, said, "My father told me that he never had a more loyal supporter than Keith Miller. People speak of contrasts, but the similarities go deeper."

Bradman could not resist the opportunity to score runs; Miller could be disinterested if they did not have

Born: Sunshine, Melbourne, Victoria, 28th November 1919

Died: Mornington Peninsula, Melbourne, Victoria, 11th October 2004

Test Debut: New Zealand v Australia, Wellington 1946, 55 Tests, 2,958 runs at 36.97, 170 wickets at 22.97

Best Batting: 147 v West Indies, Jamaica 1955

Best Bowling: 7/60 v England, Brisbane 1946

LEFT
Miller mayhem.
Entertaining, even
when out for a duck,
caught Trueman
bowled Laker at the
Oval in 1953.

BELOW
Keith Miller in the nets.

set the field by telling his fielders to "scatter". Or when they took the field with 12 men. Miller looked round and addressed the other 11 with the words: "One of you had better bugger off."

Despite such apparent levity, he led his state side to three consecutive Sheffield Shield titles. Miller was an inspirational character that players would always follow. He was a fine batsman and an outstanding bowler – one of those genuine all-rounders whose career figures will never convey the élan of the player.

His social life was as hectic as every facet of his existence. It was once written: "Women wanted to be with him, while men wanted to be him." There were rumours of a romantic involvement with Princess Margaret (that he neither confirmed nor denied) but they summed him up as a person. At total ease in the company of princes or paupers. They all loved him.

to be worked for. At Southend in 1948, the Australians rattled up 721 all out – in a day. Bradman top-scored with 187 while Miller was bowled first ball by Trevor Bailey. Bradman, at the non-striker's end, was heard to mutter, "He'll learn." There was some conjecture that Miller wanted no part in such an easy contest and simply lifted his bat out of the way of a straight one, or that he had an assignment back in the team hotel that was altogether more enticing than thrashing a few runs off an already dispirited county attack.

Not for him a life of denial. It is said that he was known to get out of a taxi shortly before the start of play, still resplendent in his dinner jacket from the previous evening's festivities. That was what opposition batsman feared, for when fragile or hung-over, Miller was at his most lethal. A few yards of run, the arm would sweep over in a high arc, and the ball would arrive quicker than anything else. Or he might come in off his full run and bowl a perfect googly as quickly as it is possible to bowl one.

Whether it was a match-winning spell of explosive fast bowling or a barnstorming innings, Miller was sure to enthral the crowd at some stage in the match. He would have made an excellent captain of his country, but somehow the selectors could never quite bring themselves to make the appointment. Stories abound of his time in charge of New South Wales. Like the time he

HANIF**MOHAMMAD**

If becoming a legend in the game of cricket were merely a case of taking more wickets or scoring more runs than others, compiling a list of those attaining such a status would be a relatively easy exercise. Hanif Mohammad did score a lot of runs and, despite the many more Test matches played nowadays, he still holds on to the ninth position in Pakistan's list of run scorers. His legacy, however, is that of a pioneer, and with all the added burden that places on a player, he still delivered.

Hanif's family came from India but settled in Pakistan at a time when there was much fluidity of population in that part of the world. He was the eldest of a cricketing family that became a dynasty. Four of his

brothers played Test cricket for Pakistan. Three of them (Hanif, Sadiq, and Mushtaq) appeared in one match together to become only the third family to achieve such a distinction, the others being the Graces and the Hearnes. Of the other members, Wazir appeared in 20 Tests with the fifth, Raees, never making that level but good enough to be 12th man for Pakistan in a Test.

Of no great physical stature, measuring just five feet six inches, Hanif soon earned the soubriquet of the "Little Master" after making his debut in first-class cricket at the age of 16. He played in Pakistan's first Test match just over a year later, marking his debut with a fifty. It was a revealing tour for Pakistan, because with Hanif's four centuries they knew that they had a class act to open the innings, whatever their other shortcomings as a new Test nation.

His strength was an immaculate defence, but he was not averse to hitting the ball in the air when pressed to do so. England's Brian Statham rarely bowled bouncers to anyone, but frustrated by Hanif's cast iron defence, he did bowl him a couple in one match; both were hooked for six. That was unusual, for much of his time in the middle was spent providing the foundation upon which the rest of his side batted. At Lord's in 1954 he scored 59 but took over five hours to do so.

Another example of his immense powers of concentration and tenacity, to say nothing of his run-scoring ability, came in Bridgetown, Barbados in 1958 against the West Indies. Pakistan were forced to follow on and in the second innings Hanif batted for over 16 hours to save the match and score 337 himself. Timed at 970 minutes (or over 16 hours), it was the longest innings ever played in first-class cricket. At the time it was also the second highest individual Test score behind Len Hutton's 364 against Australia at the Oval 20 years earlier. In the next Test in Jamaica, Garry Sobers recorded his 365 not out.

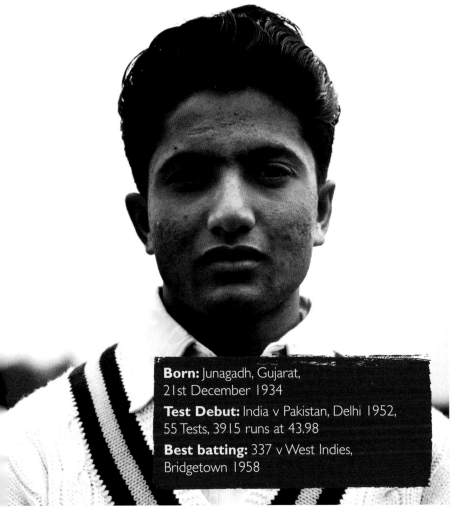

Born: Junagadh, Gujarat, 21st December 1934

Test Debut: India v Pakistan, Delhi 1952, 55 Tests, 3915 runs at 43.98

Best batting: 337 v West Indies, Bridgetown 1958

Legends of **CRICKET**

Until Brian Lara scored 501 not out for Warwickshire against Durham in 1994, Hanif held the record for the highest individual innings in first-class cricket. Playing for Karachi against Bahawalpur in 1959, he spent a mere ten and a half hours at the crease in hitting 499. He knew his brother Wazir, the Karachi captain, wanted to declare overnight and he was run out off the last ball of the day when going for his 500th run. He was probably not as quick as he had been at the start of his innings!

When the West Indies went to Pakistan in 1958/59, Hanif took his fourth Test century off them in the first Test, but then injured his knee and was forced to miss the rest of the series. That innings was his 41st in Tests, and as well as his hundreds, including the 337, he had seven half centuries. When he came back to Test cricket the following season, he took another two fifties and an undefeated hundred off the Australians in four matches.

The 101 not out was in a total of 194 for eight declared, with the next highest score 26. At Dacca in 1962 he took a hundred in both innings off the English attack, wearing the bowlers down by occupying the crease for nearly 15 hours as he did so.

Hanif became captain of Pakistan in 1964, holding the post for 11 matches from which his side took two wins and seven draws. He began his tenure against Australia in Karachi in 1964 and took the side Down Under later in the year, scoring 104 and 93. He also kept wicket as the regular 'keeper, Abdul Kadir, injured himself batting in the first innings of the match, despite the fact that he only faced three balls. So Hanif went on setting the standards for other Pakistani cricketers to aspire to and emulate. Others took up the baton that he had fashioned, and the debt owed to him by Pakistani cricket cannot be evaluated.

MUTTIAH**MURALITHARAN**

With a bent arm and a flexible wrist, **Muttiah Muralitharan** is undoubtedly one of cricket's freaks, and the most controversial player of the modern era. He is a prodigious spinner of the ball in every conceivable direction, and never ceases to attack batsmen despite the lengthy spells required of him as Sri Lanka's most potent weapon. In truth, the team has depended on his bowling like no other in international cricket, a fact that has further fuelled the fierce and probably interminable debate about the legality of his action.

The nature of that action can be traced back to his emergence into the world. The son of a Tamil biscuit manufacturer, Murali was born, as his three younger brothers would be, with a bent right arm. By the time he was 13 his potential was apparent to a school cricket coach, who persuaded him to turn from medium pace to off spin. The advice could hardly have been more significant; after taking 127 wickets in a year at school, Murali graduated to the Sri Lanka A team before making his Test debut, aged 20, against Australia, dismissing Tom Moody and Mark Waugh with successive deliveries.

But by the time Muralitharan took five wickets in Sri Lanka's first-ever defeat of England in Colombo seven months later, murmurings had begun. At first impression he looked like a chucker, and after his action was publicly questioned by New Zealand's Martin Crowe, it was soon challenged at a more significant level. In the Boxing Day Test at Melbourne in 1995, he was called by umpire Darrell Hair – seven times – for throwing. Ten days later another umpire, Ross Emerson, emulated Hair in a one-day international. Murali was distraught, but after contemplating retirement decided to fight it out.

His action was examined, from 27 different angles, but under laboratory conditions, not in match play, and medical evidence was supplied about his bent arm. The ICC eventually concurred with the Sri Lankan view that the impression of throwing was an optical illusion. Murali was not called again until 1999 – Emerson was again the umpire – after which he was again cleared, but he was reported by ICC match referee Chris Broad in 2004 after introducing his doosra, a ball that spins in the opposite direction from his stock off-spinner. Further hi-tech tests revealed that Murali was not the only bowler to bend his arm during delivery, ensuring that such controversy was unlikely to die down in the longer term.

Born: Kandy, 17th April 1972

Test Debut: Sri Lanka v Australia, Colombo 1992, 674 Test wickets by February 2007, average 21.73 and 432, ODI wickets average 23.07

Best bowling: 9/51 v Zimbabwe, Kandy 2002

numerous are the possibilities, confusion is an entirely feasible cause of downfall.

Murali played a key role in Sri Lanka's 1996 World Cup triumph before decimating England, with 16 wickets at the Oval in 1998. But he is rarely more potent than on a Galle dustbowl. He spun England to defeat there in 2001 (although Sri Lanka eventually lost the rubber), and all but repeated the outcome in 2003, when he was a key factor in Sri Lanka's eventual series win. Although he could not prevent a 2-0 win in England in 2002, he took eight for 70 in the second innings at Trent Bridge in 2006 to ensure the tourists a share in the spoils.

When he finally retires, Sri Lanka will miss him sorely. No doubt some will continue to question his right to be in the record books at all. But no one will be more relieved than those who have had to bat against him at international or any other level, and who have been tantalised, mesmerised, all the world over by his Machiavellian wiles.

In the face of such setbacks, he has nonetheless emblazoned his name on the record books. In 2004 he passed Courtney Walsh's record of 519 scalps to become Test cricket's leading wicket taker. He has since been overhauled by Shane Warne, his senior by two and a half years, but Murali remains hard on Warne's heels. He has maintained a record of six wickets per Test, and in 2006 he became the first bowler ever to take 1,000 wickets in all international cricket. He has taken five wickets in a Test innings a stunning 57 times, 20 more than Warne. On 18 occasions, Murali has taken ten wickets in a Test.

In achieving such stunning results, he has become one of the most recognisable cricketers in the world. The bulging eyes, the springy approach and the whippy delivery combine to create a wonderful sense of theatre when he is bowling. For the batsman, though, it is a nightmare. Will it be the stock off-spinner, or the top-spinner, and if it is the latter, which version? Will it be the one that goes straight on, or will it spin away off the edge to the waiting wicket-keeper or slip? Or will it rush on to the batsman out of the side of his hand? So

VIVIAN**RICHARDS**

Born: St. John's, Antigua, 17th March 1952

Test Debut: India v West Indies, Bangalore 1974, 121 Tests, 8540 runs at 50.23

Best Batting: 291 v England, The Oval 1976

"Funny how Viv tends to get becalmed in the 170s."
The words of Eric Hill, then an ever-present in the
Taunton press box, as Vivian Richards was taking a
comparative breather on the way to the highest
score of his first-class career, 322 against
Warwickshire, off just 258 deliveries, on an
unforgettable, sunlit June day in 1985. His 50
boundaries included eight sixes, one of them drilled
so hard and flat in the direction of the same press
box that some of the occupants dived for cover.

Few who saw Richards in his prime would disagree
that he was the most awesome batsman of his day;
indeed his great friend and contemporary Ian Botham
adjured that there has never been a better player. Hawk-
eyed, with feline reflexes and a powerful physique,
Richards' mere emergence from the pavilion was enough
to send the crowd into a ferment of expectation. He
never wore a helmet, and his swagger, head tilted
slightly skywards, contributed further to his intimidatory
demeanour as he approached the crease. The twirl of the
bat, the slap on the top of
its handle, as if he was
coaxing ketchup from a
bottle; the unhurried look
around the field, the
adjustment of his cap; all
contributed to the aura,
often further enhanced by
the disappearance of his first
delivery to the boundary.

Although he made an
unbeaten 192 in his second
Test at Delhi, Isaac Vivian
Alexander Richards came of
international age in the
1975/76 series against Greg
Chappell's Australians.
Promoted to open in the last
two Tests as Clive Lloyd
desperately sought to counter
the barrage of Lillee and
Thomson, he responded with
scores of 30, 101, 50 and 98.

By then he had already caught the eye in the field, with
three run-outs in the inaugural World Cup final at Lord's
in 1975 which contributed enormously to the West
Indies' win. He was also under contract to Somerset, a
team he helped to one-day glory later in the decade, but
which he was ultimately to leave amid much acrimony.

1976 was the year in which Richards, at the age of
just 24, set a record that has so far survived even the
current proliferation of international cricket. He scored
1,710 runs in the calendar year, at an average of 90 and
with seven hundreds, culminating in his 291 on a
parched Oval at the end of an unusually arid English
summer. Not for the first time or the last, England's
bowlers were at a loss as to how to attack him. Further
success followed against Pakistan in the Caribbean
before he joined Kerry Packer's World Series Cricket.

Lord's, described by Richards as the Mecca of cricket,
almost invariably brought out the best in him. After his
fielding exploits in 1975, he played a match-winning
innings of 138 in the 1979 World Cup final which

was followed by an unbelievable running catch at deep midwicket to dismiss Botham. He took the form back into the Test arena with a magical series in Australia before returning to Lord's the following year to make 145. Throughout he showed the wonderfully agile footwork, hand-to-eye co-ordination and ability to improvise which had by now become his hallmark.

Nowhere was this better illustrated than at Old Trafford in 1984, when Richards played what still ranks arguably as the finest one-day international innings. West Indies were apparently without a prayer at 102 for seven but Richards, aided first by Eldine Baptiste and then by Michael Holding, bludgeoned a scintillating,

unbeaten 189 off 170 balls. To illustrate the problems faced by England's attack, Neil Foster bowled one delivery of full length just outside the leg stump, only to see Richards take two steps towards square leg before driving it straight for six.

By the time he succeeded Clive Lloyd as Test captain the following year, the West Indies dominated world cricket. Their four-man pace attack was capable of destroying any batting line-up, while Richards remained the star batsman. England were often on the receiving end; in a one-day international at Port of Spain in 1985, he hit a breathtaking 82 off just 39 balls, and six weeks later he played a Test innings on his home ground of St.

John's, Antigua, that dazzled even by limited-overs standards. Time and again the arena looked too small for him as seven sixes were deposited into various different stands. Mobbed by his own people on reaching his hundred, his joy was palpable and unalloyed.

Richards retired from Test cricket in 1991, having scored a half-century in all five matches of his final series in England. Borne off the field by his teammates after ensuring they could not lose the rubber in the previous match at Edgbaston, he was saluted by the England team as he walked off for the last time at the Oval. He was later knighted for his services to cricket; no one, in his time or since, can have batted with such majesty.

GARRY**SOBERS**

Born: St Michael, Barbados, 28th July 1936

Test Debut: West Indies v England, Kingston 1954, 93 Tests, 8,032 runs at 57.78, 235 wickets at 34.03

Best Batting: 365 v Pakistan, Kingston 1958

Best Bowling: 6/73 v Australia, Brisbane 1968

Her Majesty Queen Elizabeth II reigns over Barbados, but the undeniable king of the island is Garry Sobers. To this day he can walk into a restaurant and other diners will rise to applaud him to his table. His fame is the result of being one of the most versatile cricketers ever seen in the game.

Versatility can sometimes be a cloak to hide deficiencies in the basic elements of cricket. That was not the case with Garfield St. Aubern Sobers, who excelled in all departments. It was Trevor Bailey, knowing a thing or two about the job as one of England's finest, who defined an all-rounder as someone who could command his place in the side as either a batsman or a bowler. Sobers transcended that simple definition. He could most certainly have walked into any team as a batsman alone, but he was also a top-class bowler in three styles, and he possessed a rare ability as a fielder. He was the complete all-rounder by Bailey's or anybody else's definition.

Sobers was born with an extra finger on each hand; they were amputated when he was very young. His father, a seaman, lost his life in the Second World War, so Sobers' boyhood was spent in humble surroundings. He was an all-round sportsman as well as a cricketer, playing football, golf and basketball for Barbados, but it was at cricket that he was to reach the pinnacle.

After the traditional Bajan upbringing of playing the game anywhere and any time it could be played, Sobers graduated to the Barbados side, making his first-class debut aged 16 as an orthodox left-arm spinner. That was in 1953 against the Indian touring team, when he made

seven not out batting at number nine, but more notably took seven wickets in the match, four bowled and three lbw. He bowled straight, even at such a tender age.

The following year he made his Test debut, against an England side in which Bailey was instrumental in his team's success. Sobers took four wickets and again batted usefully at number nine. He was not to stay there, for a number of promising performances propelled him up the order as his batting blossomed. It flowered fully in 1958, when he played against Pakistan in Jamaica. He not only recorded his first Test century, but also went on to break Len Hutton's record for an individual innings when he made 365 not out.

When Frank Worrell gave up the captaincy of the West Indies after the 1963 tour to England, Sobers was appointed and showed the flair he brought to his batting. He tended to be adventurous, believing that he had the ability to rectify any situation. It did not always work out that way. In 1968 he enlivened a match heading for a draw with a bold declaration that set

GARRY**SOBERS**

England 215 to win. There was much displeasure throughout the Caribbean when the West Indies lost by seven wickets, and criticism was not deflected by Sobers' heroic efforts to square the series in the final match. There were still mutterings of discontent despite his innings of 152 and 95 not out, along with 68 overs that produced six wickets. England hung on to their last wicket to secure the draw and the series.

Sobers' outstanding personal form against England attracted offers from county clubs and in 1968, he accepted the captaincy of Nottinghamshire. In his first season, he wrote yet another chapter in the record books by hitting six sixes in an over, bowled by the unfortunate

Legends of **CRICKET**

Everything about Sobers' cricket was both individual and exhilarating. Even the way he walked, with long strides and a certain give in the knee, was imitated by schoolboys everywhere. But it was the fluidity of his batting, with a high backlift and an extravagant follow-through, which made him special. And his extraordinary ability with the ball; it was not unknown for him to bowl in his three differing styles in one session of play. And his fielding, either patrolling the covers with feline grace or lurking at short leg where some of his catches appeared to be the product of a conjurer's trick. When the Queen visited Barbados in 1975, she took the opportunity to dub Sobers "Sir Garfield" on his own territory.

LEFT
Sobers catches Brian Luckhurst of England in the slips at Lord's in 1973.

FAR LEFT
Sobers resplendent in his West Indies blazer at the Oval.

BELOW
Sobers with the trophy after leading the Rest of the World side to victory over England in 1970.

Malcolm Nash of Glamorgan. He also appeared for South Australia where his influence was just as great. He was the only man to do the double of 1,000 runs and 50 wickets in a Sheffield Shield season, and he did it twice.

Perhaps Sobers' greatest innings came in Melbourne in 1972 when he was captaining a Rest of the World XI against an Australian attack spearheaded by Dennis Lillee at his most lethal. Sobers played majestically to reach 254 in the second innings (he was out for a duck in the first) to win a nod of approval from none other than Sir Donald Bradman. He described it as the finest innings he had ever seen.

FREDERICK**SPOFFORTH**

Although Frederick Robert "The Demon" Spofforth may best be remembered for the part he played in the first Ashes Test at the Oval in 1882 – he took 14 for 90 in the match, still the second-best haul in Australian Test history – his reputation preceded him. Australia's first great fast bowler had made his mark in England four years earlier on the other side of the River Thames. At Lord's on his first tour of England, he took six for four, including a hat-trick, against a strong MCC side led by WG Grace. He then took five for 16 in the second innings as the hosts were routed in less than a day.

Spofforth first played for New South Wales in 1874, and would have featured in the first-ever Test against

England three years later but for a point of principle. He refused to play after his team-mate, the wicket-keeper Billy Murdoch, was overlooked by the selectors. It was only when they relented, including Murdoch in the following match, that Spofforth agreed to make his Test debut. He was to take 94 wickets in just 18 games at an average of less than 19.

Over six feet tall and with a wiry frame, Spofforth took his fitness seriously, training at his brother-in-law's farm. His consequent stamina enabled him to bowl plenty of overs, which he did at fast medium pace, off a run-up of just ten yards that culminated in a great leap at the point of release. Like so many of his successors, his raw speed gradually became subordinate to accuracy, aided by variations in pace, lethal cutters on helpful pitches, and an annihilating yorker. As an assiduous student of batsmen's weaknesses he was ahead of his time, and the high proportion of wickets taken clean bowled is testament to his accuracy. In 1881 he took all 20 in this way after riding 400 miles to play in a minor match in Australia.

Although he only managed four wickets on his debut at Melbourne in 1877, Spofforth's impact on the next Test at the MCG a year later was shattering. In reducing England to 26 for seven he dismissed Vernon Royle, Francis MacKinnon and Tom Emmett to complete the first-ever Test hat-trick. Although the tourists recovered to reach 113, Spofforth got amongst them again in the second innings, finishing the match – which Australia won by ten wickets - with 13 for 110.

He bettered this haul in the immortal Oval Test of 1882, which was to become known as the first Ashes contest. His critical spell came in the second innings, after England had been set just 85 to win. With the hosts seemingly coasting at 51 for two, Spofforth was switched from the Vauxhall to the Pavilion end, where

Born: Sydney, New South Wales, 9th September 1853

Died: Long Ditton, Surrey, 4th June 1926

Test Debut: Australia v England, Melbourne 1877, 18 Tests, 94 wickets at 18.41

Best bowling: 7/44 v England, The Oval 1882

Legends of **CRICKET**

LEFT

Frederick Spofforth (1st left, back row) pictured with the first Australian team to play cricket in England, 1878.

he embarked on a spell of unparalleled devilry. In 11 overs he conceded just 12 runs and took five wickets, leaving England just eight runs short of victory. With full justification, he was carried back into the pavilion by his joyous team-mates.

By that time, Spofforth's figures in all cricket for 1878 and 1880 already took the breath away. In 1878 he took 763 wickets, 391 of them in England, and in 1880, 714 (326 in England). The cost? Just six runs per wicket. His tally on the 1882 tour was 188 at 12, and two years later 218, again at 12, including an Oval hat-trick against the South. In 1886, despite an injury to his bowling hand, he still headed the Test averages with 14 wickets at 18.5. He remained consistently effective at home, with 18 wickets in the 1882/83 series, including 11 in the

match at Sydney, and 19 victims in 1884/85 at a shade over 16.

Business interests took Spofforth to England, where he was to be a director of the Star Tea Company, and his last Test was in 1887. But he played with distinction for Derbyshire from 1889 to 1891, and also for Hampstead, for whom he took 200 wickets in 1894. His status in the pantheon of Australian cricketers is measured by his inclusion amongst the first ten members of his country's Cricket Hall of Fame in 1996. Look back down the years, from McGrath to Lillee, Lindwall to Gregory and MacDonald, and back further still to Charlie Turner and J. J. Ferris, who played in Spofforth's final Test; they may all have drawn inspiration from one of the giants of fast bowling history.

SACHIN**TENDULKAR**

It is a fair assumption that by the end of his career Sachin Tendulkar, after being one of the youngest players to make his Test debut, will have scored more Test runs than anyone else. If accomplished, such status will owe less to logic than to the utter dedication, physical and mental, that India's ultimate superstar has vested in his cricket since before he was a teenager. A scarcely less notable achievement is that he has remained unspoilt by his almost god-like fame or considerable fortune in this media-dominated age.

By the age of ten, Sachin Ramesh Tendulkar was batting on the bumpy lanes of Bandra near his home with a bat not dissimilar to him in stature. At 12, he was scoring a hundred for his school in the Harris Shield. The following year he made nine centuries (including two doubles) to reach 2,336 runs in total. He came under the tutelage of coach Ramakant Achrekar, who used to put a rupee on top of Tendulkar's stumps, saying: "Anyone who gets him out will take this coin. If no one gets him out, Sachin is going to take it." Although he lost a couple, Tendulkar still keeps 13 of the rupees.

He was practicing for a couple of hours every morning and evening, and playing a match in between. For barely a handful of cricketers can the maxim "practice makes perfect" have been as applicable. He flirted with bowling fast, but although he later became a useful bowler of varied disciplines, particularly in one-day cricket, he ultimately heeded the advice to make batting his forte. The results were increasingly stellar. In 1987/8, along the way to 3,000 runs, he established a world-record partnership of 664 with his school friend Vinod Kambli, which placed him firmly in the national consciousness.

Despite Achrekar's fear that he was being pushed too quickly, Tendulkar made his first-class debut for Bombay the following season aged 15, and his century in that game must have allayed the concerns. Nor was there any evidence that the predominantly bottom-hand grip, attributable to his use of heavy bats in earlier youth, was inconveniencing him. His broadening mental strength, acquired from a depth of preparation that belied his youth, was also a key factor. He averaged a shade below 55 in 11 innings, and his rise to the game's highest level was plainly going to be completed sooner rather than later.

His Test debut could hardly have come against more hostile opposition, or a more threatening attack. For Pakistan Imran Khan and Wasim Akram were joined by

Born: Bombay, Maharashtra, 12th April 1973
Test Debut: Pakistan v India, Karachi 1989, 132 Tests by November 2006, 10,469 runs at 55.39
Best batting: 248 v Bangladesh, Dhaka 2004

Legends of **CRICKET**

SACHIN**TENDULKAR**

put him on top of the list above his old mentor, Sunil Gavaskar.

Although Tendulkar's experience as India's captain was less productive, he played some of his best cricket – particularly in one-day internationals – after returning to the ranks. In 1998 he scored nearly 2,000 one-day runs, helping India reach nine finals. He remained ever eager to bowl his handy medium-pacers, which have taken well over 100 wickets. Add to that his reliable fielding and instinctive ability to read the game, and you have a peerless player of cricket in both its forms. For Tendulkar himself, a private man despite being India's most public figure, it is deserved reward for giving all he has to the game that is his life.

Waqar Younis, also on debut, and the leg-spin wizard Abdul Qadir. Tendulkar made 15 (one short of his tender age) amid a barrage of short-pitched deliveries, one of which hit him on the head. He reached a half-century in the next Test at Sialkot, during which he responded to Wasim Akram's sledging by asking him why a bowler of his class should find it necessary. His maiden Test century against England the following year saved India's bacon at Old Trafford; he was still only 17.

It is impossible to do justice here to the glory that has followed since. 148 not out against Australia at the SCG, ensuring a harsh introduction to Test cricket for Shane Warne, and 118 at Perth in the same series. 122 against England on an uneven Edgbaston wicket in 1996 showed the strength of his technique, before he rattled off 169, again in a losing cause, in Cape Town the same year. He has been a constant thorn in Australia's side, never more so than when he made 126 to help set up the famous 2-1 win over Steve Waugh's team at Madras in 2001. Back at the SCG three years later, he made an unbeaten 241 to ensure that there was no fairy-tale ending to Waugh's Test career. After missing six months with an elbow injury in 2005, he returned after surgery with a century against Sri Lanka, his 35th hundred to

FRED**TRUEMAN**

Born: Stainton, Yorkshire, 6th February 1931

Died: Keighley, Yorkshire, July 1st, 2006

Test Debut: England v India, Headingley 1952, 67 Tests, 307 wickets at 21.57

Best Bowling: 8/31 v India, Old Trafford 1952

To predict in August 1964, when Frederick Sewards Trueman became the first bowler to take 300 Test wickets, that he would drop to 19th on the overall list in little more than two decades, would have tempted ridicule. The fact reflects not on his achievement but on how much more international cricket has been played since his time. When Colin Cowdrey held the slip catch at the Oval, just above his right knee, to dismiss the Australian Neil Hawke, Trueman was saluted not only by the victim (who was the first to shake his hand), but also by his teammates and a grateful nation.

It was the culmination of a Test career that lacked nothing in spirit, controversy or humour. Five feet, ten inches tall, he had a frame tailor-made for fast bowling, with great strength in his shoulders, arms, back and legs, developed during his days in the mining industry as well as in junior cricket. With a classical action, a menacing scowl and unruly hair, "Fiery Fred" helped reduce India to 0/4 on his Test debut at his home ground of Headingley in 1952, ending the series with 29 wickets. A spell in National Service and brushes with authority on the West Indies tour of 1953/4 restricted his appearances over the next three years, after which he was consistency itself, with a deadly, late out-swinger the foremost weapon in his extensive armoury.

By 1957, when he took 22 wickets against the West Indies, Trueman was developing his legendary partnership with Brian Statham, the accurate Lancastrian who raced him to the 250-wicket mark in Tests. And on a far happier trip to the Caribbean in 1959/60 under the captaincy of Peter May, Trueman again impressed with 21 scalps. By this time he had developed into a useful tail-end batsman, particularly strong on the leg-side and good enough eventually to score three first-class centuries. He was also a specialist leg slip, although the ability to throw with either arm enabled him to field virtually anywhere the situation demanded.

Like many others before and since Trueman, who had begun his Test career as a bowler of raw pace, learned guile as his speed diminished. Against Australia at Headingley in 1961, he took five wickets in 24 balls with his off-cutters without conceding a run as Australia were skittled for 120 in their second innings.

He had match figures of 11 for 88 and the old enemy was beaten by eight wickets. At Old Trafford the following year he did almost as well with nine in the match as Pakistan were cast aside by a similar margin. By the time he retired, Trueman had taken 2,304 first-class wickets, an astonishing achievement for a bowler of his type.

BELOW
Trueman and Cowdrey share congratulations after the bowler's 300th Test wicket.

FRED**TRUEMAN**

In his comments about some players and officials, Trueman was capable of withering bluntness. In his most recent autobiography he described Freddie Brown, his manager on the 1958/59 tour of Australia, as "a snob, bad-mannered, ignorant and a bigot." In an earlier one he wrote of one of his captains at Yorkshire, Vic Wilson: "He didn't smoke or drink. That's fair enough. But he used to stand there sipping orange juice, which I thought was a diabolical shame for a man standing six foot three inches!"

Trueman's aptitude for anecdotes was to reach a wider audience during a lengthy spell with Test Match

LEFT
Fred Trueman takes his
300th Test wicket as
Neil Hawke of
Australia is caught by
Colin Cowdrey
at slip at the Oval
in 1964.

FAR LEFT
Trueman as an expert
summariser for Test
Match Special in 1997.

Special, where he drew productively on his excellent memory, especially during breaks for rain. But he could be over-critical of his fast bowling successors, notably at Old Trafford during the legendary 1981 Ashes series. After a two-over opening onslaught on Bob Willis by Australia's Graeme Wood, Trueman said he would be ashamed to draw his pay if he bowled like that in a Test. Willis took three wickets in his next six balls, unwittingly casting the curse of the commentator on his illustrious predecessor.

Notwithstanding such reversals, Trueman's career on and off the field has produced some legendary yarns. When Fred Rumsey, undoubtedly an inferior bowler, had the temerity to bowl him a bouncer, Trueman is alleged to have advanced ominously down the wicket to utter: "Does't tha' want to die, Rumsey?"

In retirement, watching footage of the West Indies dispatching him to the boundary five times off consecutive balls, he said: "Isn't it funny how black and white makes you look so much slower?" Some of the stories he simply disclaimed. "I hear things about m'self that I'd never have dreamed in 100 years, and I don't reckon to be short on imagination."

VICTOR**TRUMPER**

When Victor Trumper died in 1915 at the age of only 37 after suffering from a kidney disease, Australian cricket lost the most accomplished batsman it had produced, or would produce, until the emergence of Don Bradman. But while Bradman's acclaim was based on the quantity of runs he scored, Trumper's arose from the way he scored them. Poise, fluency and timing were what made him stand apart, along with his uncanny ability to make big scores when conditions appeared almost impossible for lesser batsmen.

Trumper made his debut for New South Wales in 1895 against South Australia in Adelaide. He was run out for 11 in the first innings and, batting at number nine in the second, made nought. His other match that season produced six and five not out – not the sort of season to make anyone take much notice. It was not until 1897/98 that he reappeared for New South Wales, with slightly more success, but it was in 1898/99 his rare talent came to the fore.

He played a full season of first-class cricket that year and recorded his first century in style, thrashing the Tasmanian attack for 292 not out in some four and a half hours, hitting 39 fours. New South Wales rattled up the little matter of 839 at nearly five an over against what was obviously a sub-standard attack, but Frank Iredale was the only other batsman to reach three figures. Trumper had announced himself in spectacular fashion.

His success that season led to his inclusion in the Australian party to tour England in 1899 as an extra player at the request of the captain, Joe Darling, and on reduced financial terms. He might have taken a while to make his mark in first-class cricket, but he was immediately at home in the Test arena. In only his second match, at Lord's, he scored 135 not out in 195 minutes with 20 fours. In a tour match at Hove, he destroyed the Sussex attack with 300 not out in 380 minutes.

Trumper had a range of strokes to suit every occasion. He could play with an orthodoxy that showed just how good his technique was; but his genius enabled him to improvise when the situation demanded. Pitches in those days were often treacherous, especially when the weather intervened to produce the "sticky dogs" of legend. Trumper was unfazed, despite the fact that his colleagues could hardly lay bat on ball. He simply dug deep into his repertoire of impudent strokes, almost as if the challenge brought the very best out of him.

The 1902 tour of England coincided with a particularly wet summer. Bowlers held the ascendancy over all – except for Trumper. He scored 2,570 runs at an average of 49.49, nearly a thousand more than any of his colleagues. In the second Test at Old Trafford, he opened and scored 104 in five minutes short of two hours. Australia won by a mere three runs.

Despite his 185 not out against England in Sydney in the first Test of the 1903/04 series, England won. In the next match in Melbourne, the pitch was hardly

Born: Darlinghurst, Sydney, 2nd November 1877
Died: Darlinghurst, Sydney, 28th June 1915
Test Debut: England v Australia, Trent Bridge 1899, 48 Tests, 3163 runs at 39.04
Best batting: 214 v South Africa, Adelaide 1911

Legends of **CRICKET**

His average in that rubber was 63.77, but in the home series against South Africa in 1910/11 he was even more dominant. He averaged 94.42 including an innings of 242 not out in Adelaide. He faced only 247 balls and hit 26 boundaries in a display of batting that exuded pure class, taking his reputation to new heights. He had one more Test century to come, against England at Sydney in 1911/12 but, sadly, it was to be his last series. His final Test innings was a fifty, while his last in first-class cricket was 81 in 1914 when Australia visited New Zealand. He averaged nearly 70 on that tour, with a top score of 293 at number nine against Canterbury in Christchurch. His 200 took all of 131 minutes.

At least Trumper's career ended on a high, for his fatal illness had begun to take hold by 1914. Many fine men and several good cricketers had died by 1915 as the Great War was fought in Europe. For all the bloodshed there, when Victor Trumper died it was his name that was emblazoned across newspaper placards throughout Australia. Such was his charm as a batsman, his genius lived on in the minds of all who had watched him play.

LEFT
Victor Trumper at the wicket, 1905.

BELOW
Trumper pictured in 1920.

suitable for play. However, Trumper scored a brilliant 74 out of 122 in the first innings and top-scored with 35 out of 111 in the second. Australia still lost. 113 and 59 went a long way towards their victory in the third Test in Adelaide, as did an innings of 88 in the fifth back in Melbourne, but when Trumper failed in the fourth Test, so did Australia.

CLYDE**WALCOTT**

Of the "Three Ws", Clyde Leopold Walcott was narrowly the youngest (they were born in the space of 18 months), but could undoubtedly claim the strongest all-round credentials. A dominant figure in every respect when batting – he was six foot two and had the physique to match – he was also the regular West Indies wicket-keeper early in his Test career. He later perched at slip, where precious little escaped his enormous reach. He was also a good enough change bowler to pick up 11 Test wickets with his brisk medium pace. After his playing days he served with distinction as an administrator, including a stint as Chairman of the International Cricket Council.

Walcott's first game for his native Barbados came at the age of just 16, when he was still at Harrison College. Four years later he featured in a monumental stand of 574 for the fourth wicket with his schoolmate, Frank Worrell, for Barbados against Trinidad at Port of Spain. Walcott himself finished on a career-best, unbeaten 314. But although he opened the batting on his Test debut against England (which was also Everton Weekes' first Test), his wicket-keeping was the initial cause of his retention in the side. It was the following season, in India, that his batting blossomed, and in 1950 he was part of the team that savoured the West Indies' first win on English soil.

Although possessed of a crouching stance, Walcott stood straight to drive powerfully between mid on and cover. His powerful forearms and wrist strength enabled him to pull and cut with great ferocity, and in 1950 he reached three figures no less than seven times in England, finishing the tour with 1,674 runs at an average close to 56. No innings was more important than the unbeaten 168 he made at Lord's, adding 211 for the sixth wicket with Gerry Gomez, then a West Indies record. Walcott also kept wicket to 231 overs of spin from Sonny Ramadhin and Alf Valentine, who bowled West Indies to their first win in England by 326 runs.

Hindered by back trouble, Walcott endured a lean spell with the bat in Australia in 1951/52, where he was not the only batsman to struggle against the pace of Lindwall and Miller. Only Worrell reached a century on that tour, as the West Indies were beaten 4-1. But Walcott bounced back in the Caribbean the following season, with two centuries against India.

It was against England in 1954 and Australia in 1955 that he reaped an almost unimaginable run harvest. At Bridgetown against England he made his highest Test score of 220, plus hundreds in two other Tests to finish the series just two short of 700 runs at an average of

Born: Barbados, 17th January 1926
Died: Barbados, 26th August 2006
Test Debut: West Indies v England, Barbados 1948, 44 Tests, 3,798 runs at 56.68
Best batting: 220 v England, Barbados 1954

LEFT
Clyde Walcott caught
by Tony Lock off Jim
Laker at Edgbaston
in 1957.

87.25. But he bettered the aggregate against Australia, with a then West Indies record 827 runs (82.7) including five centuries in three Tests, against an attack including Lindwall, Miller and Benaud, adding 242 for the third wicket with Weekes at Port of Spain. This Herculean contribution gains greater lustre still when set in the context of a 3-0 defeat.

Although he started well in England in 1957, Walcott suffered an injury while making 90 in the first Test at Edgbaston. He did not pass 50 again in the series, but had the pleasure of watching from the other end the following year as Garry Sobers reached the then Test record score of 365 not out against Pakistan at Kingston. After presenting a disheartening spectacle for the bowlers on his arrival at the crease at 602 for three, Walcott joined the run fest with an unbeaten 88. His final Test hundred came at Georgetown in the same series,

although he managed a half century in his valedictory Test, against England at Port of Spain in 1960.

Walcott's links with cricket after retirement were legion. He served as a selector, managed several touring teams in the 1970s and was president of the West Indies Cricket Board, as well as commentating and coaching. In 1993 he succeeded Sir Colin Cowdrey as ICC chairman, and he was himself knighted shortly afterwards. Despite such achievements he once modestly pointed out: "I can never do more for cricket than cricket has done for me."

When Walcott died in 2006, the great West Indies off spinner Lance Gibbs paid tribute: "He completely destroyed the myth that great cricketers can't be great administrators." After the funeral at Cave Hill, Barbados, Walcott was buried close to his great compatriot Frank Worrell, on a site overlooking a cricket ground named in their honour.

SHANE
WARNE

Born: Ferntree Gully, Victoria, 13th September 1969

Test Debut: Australia v India, Sydney 1992, 140 Tests to November 2006, 685 wickets at 25.25

Best bowling: 8/71 v England, Brisbane 1994

When Shane Warne broke Dennis Lillee's record of 85 Test wickets in a calendar year in 2005, the great fast bowler was there to watch. "There isn't a bit of sadness there for me in passing on the record to the greatest bowler we have seen," Lillee said. It was the crowning moment of a glittering year for the blond Victorian spin king with a penchant for jewellery. Amongst the haul was the mere matter of 40 wickets in the Ashes series, a five-match record, including his 600th in Tests; he is the first bowler to reach the milestone.

Not only has Warne been established as a legend for most of his career, he is widely considered to be the greatest spin bowler ever to set foot on a cricket field. And what a dramatist! From the moment he is handed the ball the effect can be mesmeric. Witness his ambling, unruffled approach to the wicket, the moment of release so often followed by a passionate appeal, and the affronted, prolonged look of injured, angelic innocence should the umpire inexplicably lack the discernment to raise a digit. So strong is Warne's will, you sense that no situation, however unpromising, is necessarily irretrievable.

His story includes enough twists and turns to make Shakespeare dizzy, and not just in the arena itself. What made him special, when he first made his mark, was his novelty. Pace, as purveyed by the all-powerful West Indies, had dominated cricket for more than a decade and Pakistan's Abdul Qadir, a notable exponent of leg spin, had not played Test cricket since 1990. Just when it seemed that the art was in danger of emulating the dodo, Warne rekindled it with a vengeance and a freshness that was utterly spellbinding. And

his entry into Test cricket's longest-running drama could simply never have been scripted.

Mike Gatting must be fed up with being asked about it. After all, he has had moments of more acute discomfort, like when he had to fly home from the Caribbean leaving a small piece of his nose embedded in a ball propelled by Malcolm Marshall. But the "Ball of the Century" was justly so dubbed in 1993. It was Warne's first in Ashes cricket, and while no leggie can expect to pitch it perfectly first up, this one landed outside leg, span in apparent defiance of geometric law and hit the off stump. England's best player of spin was aghast, while the tone was set for a series and a career.

It is just as well for cricket that Warne was not a few inches taller. He wanted to be an Australian Rules footballer. During a brief spell with the Australian Cricket Academy he met the former Australia leg-spinner Terry Jenner, who was to give him invaluable advice throughout his career. Selection for his home state

BELOW
Shane Warne – never shy of asking the umpire for decisions. He got 40 positive replies in the Ashes series of 2005.

SHANE**WARNE**

was followed by his Test debut against India in 1992, by which time he was giving the ball a real rip. The Gatting delivery was followed by a career-best eight for 71 against England at Brisbane, and a hat-trick in the next Test of the 1994/95 series, as wickets tumbled to Warne no matter who was batting or where on earth he was bowling.

Drama includes shade as well as light. Numerous stories about Warne's private life culminated in the

Legends of **CRICKET**

sharpened his appetite; he scalped 26 Sri Lankan batsmen in three Tests on his return.

After helping Australia win the 1999 World Cup – he was Man of the Match in the semi-final and final – Warne was denied a last tournament by the ban, imposed after he had already announced his retirement from one-day internationals. The decision was influenced by two major shoulder injuries, and the desire to play Test cricket for as long as possible. So batsmen continue to be caught in his web of intrigue, and bowlers are still piqued by a batsman who has scored more Test runs than anyone without reaching three figures. A strange record that, but then nothing about Shane Warne is run-of-the-mill.

LEFT
Shane Warne celebrates his 700th Test Wicket, 2006.

FAR LEFT
Warne in classical batting pose.

BELOW
Warne joins captain Steve Waugh with the World Cup in 1999.

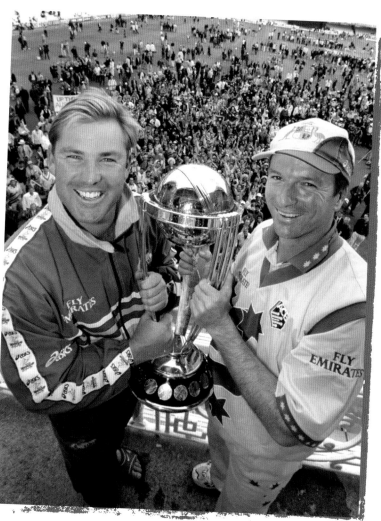

break-up of his marriage in 2005. He was fined Aus$8,000 in 1995 for accepting money from a bookmaker after talking to him about pitches and weather. To this day, he insists he did nothing wrong. He was offered, and refused, money to under-perform in a Test by Pakistan's Salim Malik. And a year-long ban from cricket resulted when Warne, after taking a slimming pill offered to him by his mother, tested positive for diuretics. Plainly it

STEVE
WAUGH

Born: Sydney, New South Wales, 2nd June 1965

Test Debut: Australia v India, Melbourne 1985, 168 Tests
10,927 Test runs at 51.06

Best batting: 200 v West Indies, Jamaica 1995

The fact that Steve Waugh has played more Test matches than anyone else might not, on its own, have made him a legend. What is more significant is the tenacity he showed after tasting Ashes defeat and losing his Test place to his twin brother Mark early in his career. He battled back, as did Australia, and both progressed from mediocrity to greatness. At the time he led them they were the best team in the world in both forms of the game; indeed some might argue that they were the strongest team ever to set foot on a cricket field.

By the time Waugh first played in an Ashes Test he had been in the Australian side for a year without making great waves. In the 1986/87 rubber he made three half centuries but failed to reach three figures as Mike Gatting's England retained the Ashes with a 2-1 win. It was a salutary experience for the 21-year-old, who had still not made a century in 26 Tests by the time he first toured England in 1989. To the chagrin of the hosts' attack, the floodgates opened. Waugh made 177 not out as Australia went one up at Headingley, and 152, again unbeaten, as they made it 2-0 at Lord's. In fact, Waugh made 393 runs before being dismissed by Angus Fraser for 43 in the third Test at Edgbaston.

Australia won that rubber 4-0, commencing a 16-year period of Ashes dominance in which Waugh was almost – but not quite – an ever-present. After going without a half century in the first three Tests of the 1990/91 rubber he was dropped, a justifiable decision which would have far-reaching implications for the way in which Waugh played. Determined not to repeat the experience, he

adopted a more cautious batting style while retaining the ability to punish anything loose which remained a trademark throughout his career.

His absence from the Test team was short-lived, and after his recall against the West Indies the same season he was on the plane to England in 1993. At Headingley he again gorged himself in Bradmanesque style, with an unbeaten 157 as Australia progressed towards a repeat of their winning margin four years earlier. But having established such dominance over England – later achieved to a similar degree against South Africa – Waugh's career reached its apotheosis in the Caribbean in 1994/95.

At that point, the West Indies had not been beaten in a Test series for 15 years, and the final Test in Jamaica began with the teams locked at one-all. After the hosts posted 265, Waugh shared a 231-run partnership with twin Mark which took Australia past 500 and set up an innings win which was surely as seismic as world cricket can have seen. Waugh himself made 200, his one

BELOW
Steve Waugh and Nasser Hussain at the fateful toss before the first Ashes Test in Brisbane, 2002.

Test double century, although he fell just one run short at Barbados in the great series four years later in which Brian Lara's heroics achieved a two-all draw.

By then Waugh had nailed England again, with a brace of centuries at Old Trafford to snuff out their early hopes in 1997. And no one can have signed off against the Old Enemy with such aplomb; 157, pretty much on one leg following an injury earlier in the 2001 Ashes, on his final Test appearance in England at the Oval, and 102 on his home ground at Sydney, the century reached with a trademark cover drive off the last ball of the day. It was at the SCG that Waugh bowed out of Test cricket a year later, his dismissal for 80 featuring two other legends, Sachin Tendulkar and Anil Kumble.

Waugh led Australia to 15 of their record-breaking 16 successive Test victories, but his influence on one-day cricket was no less immense. At the age of 22 he was a member of Australia's 1987 World Cup winning team, bowling a crucial penultimate over as, with England needing 19 to win the final, he conceded just two runs to put the task in the last over beyond them. In 1999 he lifted the trophy himself at Lord's, after the wonderful, tied semi-final against South Africa at Edgbaston when he was

dropped by Herschelle Gibbs, to whom he reportedly made the succinct remark: "You've just dropped the World Cup, mate."

Waugh was unceremoniously ditched from the one-day side after Australia fared poorly in the VB series in 2001/02. He never ceased in his efforts to win a recall for the 2003 World Cup, even resuming bowling, which he had shelved due to back trouble. But perhaps to the relief of many of his opponents, the recall never came. The "Iceman" may not have been the most spectacular batsman of his era, but his wicket was as highly prized as any.

EVERTON**WEEKES**

When Everton Weekes was batting, entertainment was a certainty. The middle of the "Three Ws" in age, he was probably the best batsman, and on his day the most remorseless pursuer of runs since Don Bradman. His instinct was always to attack, while he possessed another Bradmanesque quality in that he had the appetite, on reaching three figures, to go on. The consequence was a Test average just shy of 60, higher even than his great compatriots Frank Worrell, Clyde Walcott and Garfield Sobers.

As befits batsmen of compact build, Weekes was a powerful cutter and puller, although he rarely hit the ball in the air. He was also exceptionally quick on his feet, driving strongly off both front and back foot on either side of the wicket. Defence was often a last resort, and he hit the ball extremely hard. In the field he was consistently superb, whether close to the wicket or anywhere else. His preferred position was cover point, but was also top class in the slips when the spin twins, Ramadhin and Valentine, were in the attack.

Like many West Indian youngsters, Everton de Courcy Weekes took naturally to cricket and was playing in the Barbados Cricket League when only 12. His talent became more widely apparent during the war years, when he served with the Barbados battalion of the Caribbean Regiment. He was just 18 when he first played for Barbados, and his Test debut came during England's tour of the Caribbean in 1947/48. Although he made starts in each of the first three Tests, there was no immediate sign of his insatiable appetite for runs.

He was dropped for the fourth Test in Jamaica in favour of George Headley, but then reinstated when Headley was unable to play. Weekes justified his selection, despite the hostility of the Kingston crowd who would have preferred to watch their local hero John Holt. Weekes scored 141 to book his place on the tour of India, where he made consecutive scores of 128, 194, 162 and 101 before being controversially run out just ten short of a sixth successive Test century.

Nevertheless, his achievement in reaching five successive Test hundreds remains unsurpassed, indeed unparalleled, to this day. And even under a system of selection notorious for political and social considerations amongst the disparate group of islands that supplied the West Indies players, he had made his Test place secure.

Although Weekes was not as prolific in the Tests in England in the wet summer of 1950, he still made 338 runs in the series, and racked up 2,310 runs on the tour, including double centuries against Surrey, Nottinghamshire, Hampshire and Leicestershire and a triple against Cambridge University. He went through a comparatively lean trot on the 1951/52 tour of the

Born: Barbados, 26th February 1925
Test Debut: West Indies v England, Barbados 1948, 48 Tests, 4,455 Test runs at 58.61
Best batting: 207 v India, Trinidad 1953

Legends of **CRICKET**

LEFT
Everton Weekes
batting against
England.

Antipodes, but again gorged himself on India's bowling back home the following season. He found the England attack scarcely less succulent fare in 1953/54, reaching a double century in the fourth Test at Port of Spain. The 338 he added with Worrell remains a third-wicket record against England.

The feast continued when the Australians toured the Caribbean, finding Weekes a far tougher proposition there than they had done at home. His performances in New Zealand in 1955/56 were simply awesome. He reached three figures in each of his first five innings, averaged over 100 on the tour and made successive centuries in three of the four Tests, ending the series with 418 runs at 83.6. But his form in England in 1957 may well have been affected by the sinus trouble from which he was suffering at the time. He made a gutsy but unavailing 90 on a lively wicket in the second Test at Lord's after being hit painfully on the hand, in a match the West Indies lost by an innings.

Weekes bounced straight back in the Caribbean, with 197 at Bridgetown in the first Test against Pakistan. But this transpired to be his last Test century; troubled by a thigh injury for which he had an unsuccessful operation, he retired after the end of that series at the comparatively early age of 33. But he continued to play first-class cricket until the 1963/64 season, captaining Barbados, for whom he kept scoring plenty of runs.

Weekes also ploughed an immensely successful furrow in English League cricket, and went on Commonwealth tours to Africa and elsewhere. His endearing charm made him a popular figure wherever he went. He coached and commentated in Barbados, and was the ICC match referee for the series between India and Sri Lanka in 1994. Away from cricket he played a canny hand of bridge at international level. After being successively awarded the MBE and CBE, he became the last of the Three Ws to be knighted in 1995.

FRANK**WORRELL**

Frank Mortimer Maglinne Worrell was the sort of cricketer and man who appealed to everyone. For confirmation, consider that the streets of Melbourne were lined in 1961 as his West Indian team left Australia to a ticker-tape farewell. It was an altogether more sombre gathering, but just as heartfelt, when his body was borne home to Barbados after his tragically early death from leukaemia in 1967. That after he had done something unthinkable in those times by moving to Jamaica earlier in his career.

Worrell made a lasting impact in England as well. Westminster Abbey was thronged for the first memorial service to be held for a cricketer there, while the congregation consisted of not only his English and Bajan friends, but also representatives of all West Indian communities in Britain. His great legacy to Caribbean cricket was that he brought all islands together to play as a single entity, and this at a time when a trend towards political independence could have driven them further apart on the cricket field.

Worrell received little or no actual coaching, but developed into a technically correct batsman. So much so that he claimed he could not hit across the line, even when he should have done. Yet it was as a left-arm spinner that he came to prominence in Barbados, making his first-class debut at the age of 18. The first hint that he had the makings of an outstanding batsman came the following season, in 1943, when he was promoted to nightwatchman and carried his bat for 64. By the end of that same season he was opening the innings.

It was not long before he was comfortably established in his batting role, while he developed into a fast-medium bowler rather than a spinner. He combined with John Goddard in 1943/44 to add an unbroken 502 against Trinidad, with Worrell himself making 308. In 1946/47, the Trinidadian bowlers were put to the sword once more as Worrell and Clyde Walcott put on 574 – again undefeated.

It was only a matter of time before he made his Test debut. It came against England in Port of Spain in 1948. The legendary 'Three Ws' of Worrell, Walcott and Weekes, all from Barbados, appeared together on a Test scorecard for the first time, with Worrell coming within three runs of a century in the first innings. He put that failing right in the next Test in Georgetown when he scored 131 not out.

He went to England to play in league cricket in Lancashire, and although he did not tour India with the West Indies in 1948/49, he did go with a Commonwealth XI in 1949/50, when he gave the first indications of his captaincy skills as well as dominating with the bat. By his first tour of England in 1950 he was an experienced international cricketer, and underlined

Born: Bank Hall, St Michael, Barbados, 1st August 1924

Died: Mona, Kingston, Jamaica, 13th March 1967

Test Debut: West Indies v England, Port of Spain 1948, 51 Tests, 3,860 runs at 49.48, 69 wickets at 38.72

Best Batting: 261 v England, Trent Bridge 1950

Legends of **CRICKET**

He imposed himself with the coolest of heads when the series started with the tied Test in Brisbane. All that separated the two sides by the time they got to Melbourne for the fifth Test was two tail-end Australian wickets. The West Indies lost, but had won enormous regard and revitalised what had been a flagging interest in the game in Australia. Ever since, West Indies and Australia have competed for the Frank Worrell Trophy.

With the likes of Garry Sobers, Rohan Kanhai, Lance Gibbs, Wes Hall and Charlie Griffith in the side for his final tour of England in 1963, Worrell had at his command a unit that was worthy of a 3-1 series victory to establish the West Indies as a power in world cricket.

Worrell had studied in Manchester and, following retirement at the end of that 1963 tour, he took up the post of Warden of the University College of the West Indies in Jamaica, and became a senator in the Jamaican Parliament. Knighted in 1964, he seemed destined to play a major role in Caribbean affairs, if not on an even grander stage, before his sudden and most untimely death at the age of 42.

LEFT
Runs for Worrell against England in 1957 at Trent Bridge.

BELOW
Frank Worrell in 1963.

the fact with his highest Test score. His 261 at Trent Bridge was a masterclass when it came to placement.

Success followed success, and not only with the bat. He took six for 38 against Australia in Adelaide in 1951 and at Headingley in 1957 he took seven English wickets for 70. It was his batting, however, that elevated him to the Pantheon as, in combination with Walcott and Weekes, he gave the West Indian middle order a formidable potential.

Yet even that was not Worrell's greatest contribution to Caribbean cricket. George Headley had one match as the first black captain of the West Indies, but it was to Worrell that the honour of destroying the stigma fell. He was by no means a universally acclaimed choice to take the side to Australia for the 1960/61 tour, but by the end of it he was acknowledged as an outstanding and much-admired leader.

For the first time, a West Indian team became just that. No longer a collection of Bajans, Jamaicans, Trinidadians or whatever; island loyalties were set aside for the common good. Worrell instilled a strong code of discipline that gave the team self-respect and gained the respect of others.

WAQAR**YOUNIS**

Born: Vehari, Punjab, 16th November 1971
Test Debut: Pakistan v India, Karachi 1989, 87 Tests, 373 wickets at 23.56
Best bowling: 7/76 v New Zealand, Faisalabad 1990

It says much for the pedigree of Waqar Younis that he lent his name to a new cricket verb in the 1990s. His yorker, delivered at great pace and homing in on the batsman's toes, was as lethal a weapon as any to be seen in the game over that decade. If it did not hit the stumps as intended, it was liable to inflict a great deal of pain. And should the batsman be unfortunate enough to see the umpire's finger raised in the aftermath of such a crushing blow, he would leave the arena in the pain and ignominy of having been doubly "Waqared".

Not that the yorker, a standard weapon in the armoury of any accomplished fast bowler, was the weapon for which Waqar will primarily be remembered. Above all, he became a peerless purveyor of reverse swing at a time when it was a novelty. His partnership with Wasim Akram, though not without friction, was wonderfully complementary. Akram's left arm, which generated deliveries capable of swinging in almost every direction imaginable, was the unpredictable foil to Waqar's right. If an opponent managed to see off the new ball, beware; Wasim and Waqar would invariably make the old one behave like a rattlesnake with deadly reverse swing.

Waqar, particularly in the early days, was a wonderful sight, provided you weren't watching from 22 yards with a bat in your hand. Like Lillee in his pomp, he surged towards the crease at a menacing speed over a substantial distance. Rather than emulating the West Indies "chin music" of the 1980s he bowled full of length, swinging the ball at such a pace that reaction from the batsman was often fatally late. But his action placed such strain on his physique that he was injury prone, particularly amid the welter of international cricket that had become the norm by his time. And that was in addition to three county stints, with Surrey, Glamorgan and Warwickshire.

But for the injuries, particularly early in his career, Waqar might well have taken 500 Test wickets. His Test debut came in 1989 against India in Karachi, a year after a convalescent Imran Khan spotted him on television as he played in a domestic match. He took four for 80 in the first innings, including the wicket of another teenaged debutant, Sachin Tendulkar. Although Waqar made little impression on the ensuing tour of Australia, he was lethal in home series against New Zealand, the West Indies and Sri Lanka. The Kiwi captain, Martin Crowe, was persuaded to attach a grille to his helmet, averring that he had never faced pace and swing of such quality.

A vertebral stress fracture deprived Waqar of a place in Pakistan's World Cup winning team in 1992, but

BELOW
Waqar Younis bowls Justin Langer in the third Pakistan-Australia Test of 2002.

on his first tour of England he was a key architect of their 2-1 victory. Seven wickets at Lord's helped the tourists go one up, and his five for 52 in the second innings at the Oval (including four of the top five) paved the way for a series-clinching win. In the ensuing years no one could tame him; not even Mark Taylor's strong Australian side that lost 1-0 in Pakistan in 1994. England again had no answer to him in 1996, losing the three-match rubber 2-0 as he took 16 wickets.

Suspicions about whether or not Waqar's reverse swing was achieved naturally came to a head in 2000, when he and Azhar Mahmood were both fined by match referee John Reid for altering the condition of the ball during a one-day international against South Africa in Colombo. Television pictures had shown Waqar scratching at the surface of the ball and he was also suspended for one match, the first cricketer ever to be punished in such a way by the ICC, although it was not the first time such actions had been detected.

Injury restricted Waqar to just one Test appearance on England's 2000 visit to Pakistan, the famous encounter at Karachi where the tourists won in the gloom to take the series. But he led his country on his last tour of England the following

LEFT
Waqar Younis takes
the wicket of Nasser
Hussain, 2003.

FAR LEFT
Waqar Younis coaching
in the nets, 2006.

year, in which they came back from an innings defeat at Lord's to square the two-match series at Old Trafford.

He retained the captaincy through to the 2003 World Cup, by which time he had already played his last Test. The tournament itself was not a success for Pakistan – they beat only Namibia and the Netherlands – and a year later Waqar announced his retirement from international cricket. But the value of his bowling skills and experience was too great for him to be left out in the cold; in 2006 he was appointed Pakistan's bowling coach.

thewisden cricketer

Every month **The Wisden Cricketer** brings you the complete overview of the cricketing world. From Test match reports to village championships, from Andrew Flintoff's game plan to tips for improving your technique, and from eyewitness reports of historic encounters to debates about the game's future, the magazine is essential reading for all cricket lovers.

- Great savings on the cover price
- Free delivery to your door each month
- Free twice-yearly fixtures wallchart
- The best prices on cricketing tours
- Great competitions to win tickets and other fantastic prizes

For details of latest subscription offers, call

0870 220 6538

quoting reference LCB07

THE PICTURES IN THIS BOOK WERE PROVIDED COURTESY OF THE FOLLOWING:

GETTY**IMAGES**
101 Bayham Street, London NW1 0AG

EMPICS
www.empics.com

Concept and Art Direction:
VANESSA **and** KEVIN**GARDNER**

Creative and Artwork: KEVIN**GARDNER**

Image research: ELLIE**CHARLESTON**

PUBLISHED BY GREEN UMBRELLA PUBLISHING

Publishers:
JULES**GAMMOND and** VANESSA**GARDNER**

Written by: RALPH**DELLOR and** STEPHEN**LAMB**